THE PSADAN EVOLUTION
# DIAMOND JUSTICE

## KINDEL DANIELS

Story By: Kindel Daniels
and Tom Potter

iUniverse, Inc.
Bloomington

# Diamond Justice
# The Psadan Evolution

*Copyright © 2010 by Kindel Daniels*

*All rights reserved. No part of this book may be used or reproduced by any means, graphic, electronic, or mechanical, including photocopying, recording, taping or by any information storage retrieval system without the written permission of the publisher except in the case of brief quotations embodied in critical articles and reviews.*

*This is a work of fiction. All of the characters, names, incidents, organizations, and dialogue in this novel are either the products of the author's imagination or are used fictitiously.*

*Cover Art By: Gregory Woronchak*

*iUniverse books may be ordered through booksellers or by contacting:*

*iUniverse*
*1663 Liberty Drive*
*Bloomington, IN 47403*
*www.iuniverse.com*
*1-800-Authors (1-800-288-4677)*

*Because of the dynamic nature of the Internet, any Web addresses or links contained in this book may have changed since publication and may no longer be valid. The views expressed in this work are solely those of the author and do not necessarily reflect the views of the publisher, and the publisher hereby disclaims any responsibility for them.*

*ISBN: 978-1-4502-7462-3 (sc)*
*ISBN: 978-1-4502-7464-7 (dj)*
*ISBN: 978-1-4502-7463-0 (ebook)*

*Printed in the United States of America*

*iUniverse rev. date: 12/06/2010*

*In Memory of:*
*Robert Kevin Clark*
*Thank you for the adventures you opened my mind to.*

*"As many more individuals of each species are born than can possibly survive; and as, consequently, there is a frequently recurring struggle for existence, it follows that any being, if it vary however slightly in any manner profitable to itself, under the complex and sometimes varying conditions of life, will have a better chance of surviving, and thus be naturally selected. From the strong principle of inheritance, any selected variety will tend to propagate its new and modified form."*

—Charles Darwin
On The Origin of Species By Means of Natural Selection
1859



*Little did Darwin know when he wrote this that a new form of life was evolving that would forever change human existence; the meta-human. No other evolutionary step has had as profound effect on the evolution of man.*

—Samuel J. Diamond
2006

# Why I wrote this book

When I started this project, it excited me beyond words. It only took a few minutes for that elation to turn to fear, and that fear into despair. The sheer volume of work and commitment it presented was overwhelming, and a little bit scary. That was over twelve years ago and I never stopped to ask myself why write a book. It was simply something I wanted to do. It was so long ago and I was just a little younger and a bit more naive of the process. (*To me, old age is always fifteen years older than I am.* Bernard Baruch, "Newsmakers," *Newsweek*, 29 August 1955)

If I asked myself why I wrote this book today, I would have to give two answers.

The first would be that I like a good story. I've read many books over the years and seen many movies. Some were good, others bad, and some I never finished; but I was inspired by all of them. During these experiences, I often asked myself what would I have done different or what would have made it a better story. (To qualify as a great story, my answer had to be nothing.) Well, this book was an opportunity to do just that. It was an opportunity to do it my way. This does not mean that I didn't listen to input from others, especially Tom. The story has greatly changed over the years due to this input and it is a much better story for it. I am grateful beyond words to those that contributed. Criticism makes us better people when it is delivered with grace and we are humbled by seeking it.

My second reason for writing this book is to leave my mark on this world. All of us only have a limited time here. Life is far too short for many of us and we leave it having accomplished little. This book is simply one of the many tasks on my *bucket list*. It is one way for me to say I lived.

Find your spot and make your mark. Before you say: I can't do that, or I don't have any talent; just know I'm still telling myself that with this project finished. We may not all have talent, but we do all have skills that we can build upon. If you feel you don't have the talent, take the time to develop the skills you need to accomplish your desires. And who knows, you may discover the talent is actually there. Ralph Waldo Emerson said; *A true talent delights the possessor first.* ("The Scholar", *Lectures and Biographical Sketches,* 1883)

Last of all, even though this book is about "superheroes" it is not intended for little Tommy. Please review it before you let your children read it to ensure it meets your standards. It has adult situations and adult language. I considered using grammatical symbols (as often found in comic books) or using mock or fake words to represent the curses. In the end, I decided that the symbols and the mock words didn't change the underlining meaning. We are responsible for what we say, how we say it, and what we mean. The words contained in this book are meant to express frustration on the part of the fictional character saying them and is not directed at any individual or particular group of people. Please take them that way and I apologize if you are offended.

# Acknowledgments

It is only by the grace of God that I got this project completed. Thank you God for your grace and any spark of talent you blessed me with that has allowed me to accomplish this goal for my life.

Thank you Michelle, Jeremy, and Garion. I have not been the best husband or the best father over the years but I am grateful to have you all in my life. Thank you for tolerating my nerdy behavior and for never complaining when faced with embarrassment with your friends by my comic book collection or my *Starfleet* uniform. (Just kidding, I do not own a *Starfleet* uniform. Honest, I don't.)

Thank you Mom and Dad. You have tolerated me longer than anyone else. I am who I am because you both took the time to be parents.

Thank you, Kevin. You are largely to blame for this whole project. During our time in the Air Force, we spent many hours discussing comic books, sci-fi movies, computer games, and Dungeons and Dragons. Thank you for your inspiration. This book is dedicated to your memory.

Thank you Tom for helping me develop the plot to this book and for working to break it at every turn. More importantly, thank you for your input into the main character. If not for you, I would never have gotten it finished. Thank you for all the work you put into it; but just so you know, your efforts have condemned you. Our next project will be even bigger so get out your pen and paper so we can get started.

Thanks to Troy, Michael, and Brandon. Thank you for the time you have put into editing. You have helped me find pieces that were missing, pieces that needed further development, and pieces that simply didn't work. As I am sure you know by now, editing my grammar and spelling is quite a job. You are not the extent of my editors but you had to suffer through every draft of the book. Michael, special thanks to you for the insight you gave on specific characters. Your ideas are unique. As for the rest of you, thank you.

Thank you PG, Gopher, Novakane, Dawn-star, Cruiser, Ardwyck,

Jenscot, Radaco, Owen, HandieWmn, Lydda, and the rest of the COH crew (you know who you are). As of this writing, I have never met most of you in person but you have given me endless hours of entertainment and inspiration. Thank you for showing interest in the project and for asking me about it from time to time. It kept me going. If ever you are in my area, please look me up. I have a signed copy for you.

Thank you to anyone else I should have mentioned above by name but have failed to do so. I humbly ask for your forgiveness and thank you for your support.

God Bless.
Kindel Daniels

# CHAPTER 1
## SCENES OF THE PAST

With the last remnants of the life-stealing storm fading with the retreating night, the young male penguin didn't consider life or death as he moved away from the warmth of the waddle to wander up a small rise. The light of the dim sun was just enough for him to scan the tundra for his mate. Beneath him, his newborn chick struggled for freedom, but he kept it tucked safely away to protect it from the cold morning air.

The pale sun was already sinking on the short Antarctic day when the male finally saw movement. Within moments the air around him filled with a symphony of voices as the male penguins celebrated the return of the females to the clan.

*Kaboom!*

A flash rippled across the sky. It outshone the setting sun in its brilliant display. Thunder echoed behind it causing the icy tundra to shudder and groan.

Startled from their songs, the colony worked as one creature with a thousand eyes to scan the darkening terrain for the source of the disturbance, fear gripped them. It was a deep fear that started in their guts, swelling up to permeate every part of their small bodies. It was a fear without an obvious source, and one they would never shake. Not a single member of the clan broke the silence. There was no wind and the air around them grew thin. Small bits of snow and ice drifted upward from the ground to float in the air around the flightless birds. Energy prickled their skin as the air crackled to life around them. The effect was subtle at first, then became oppressive. The colony fought the urge to flee.

Dark clouds sprang to life above them. Like an enormous school of fish, they swirled first in one direction and then in another. Within moments violent strokes of lightning tore at the ice and sent booms echoing across the land. The center of the clouds sank into a deep vortex. The wind howled and the land descended into darkness as the last rays of the pale sun were blotted out. A moment later a glow filled the center of the vortex. It quickly grew in brightness to replace the defeated sun.

The horror was too much for the colony. Panic filled the air in a cacophony of fright and they fled. Dozens of startled and dazed chicks littered the ground.

In one great burst, the center of the monstrous cloud flared like a dying star; and a spear of light thrust down toward the icy tundra below.

*Ka-Boom!*

*Rruummmble!*

The impact of the spear of light sent icy chunks flying in all directions. The light bored a hole deep into the groaning ice shelf.

*Whoosh!*

A ring of energy exploded outward from the bottom of the shaft. The wave of death raced across the frozen land, sucking the breath from everything it touched. Fueled by each death, it spread from victim to victim. The wave passed completely over the colony of birds and across the tundra for several miles before collapsing back into the spear of light. Not a single member of the colony survived its touch.

Suddenly, the clouds scattered and the shaft of energy disappeared. A single ball of light remained suspended above the frozen land. Leaving the bodies of the penguins to mark its arrival, the ball descended slowly into the ice.

\* \*

John had never been this deep in the forest before. Like everyone else, he was forbidden to be out of sight of the colony. Between the natives and the wild animals, it was just too dangerous. *I have no choice*, he reminded himself, *the colony needs food*. They would all die without it.

The colony leaders had set out across the ocean for help nearly three months ago because the drought had not let up. Desperate, the women and children depended on him and the few other men remaining to provide food. Most of the grown men were vagabonds, likely dodging a prison sentence, and did not have the skills needed to support the colony. Others, like him, were barely men. Other than him, none of them had the necessary skills.

John's sister had argued that he was still a boy and too young to be a man. She was jealous. Being older, she tried to take responsibility for him and his two younger sisters, but John would not accept it. Determined to do what had to be done, he claimed the family's only musket. Despite his young age, he knew it was up to him to protect and feed them. The responsibility excited him.

The forest was thicker than any John had hunted in before, but the drought had left it with little life. A shudder passed through him as the closeness reminded him of the long journey across the ocean. John loved his freedom. He loved to run, explore, and encounter new challenges. The drudgery of the boats and the lack of freedom while on-board had frightened him. He had slept, ate, worked, and played with no freedom or privacy. Upon the colonists' arrival in the new world, John had craved freedom so badly that he dove off the ship and swam to shore before the rowboat was launched. He feared he would never want the touch of another person again for as long as he lived, except maybe for Alis.

John allowed himself a smile at the thought of Alis. She was considered a grown woman even before they had set out from England, and yet she fancied him despite their age difference. Hoping to claim her as their bride once they reached the New World, many of the colony's single men had eyed Alis during the journey. Alis had so far dodged several marriage proposals. John was determined to have her in his life.

*Flutter! Flutter! Flutter!*

A bird jolted John out of his reverie. He threw up his musket but held the shot. The bird was already out of range. Relaxing, he lowered the muzzle and cursed himself for getting distracted. The bird was not much, but anything was better than nothing. He was going to have nothing at the end of the day if he didn't concentrate; there would be plenty of time for Alis once they were relaxing around the cooking fire. Renewing his determination, he pushed deeper into the forest.

Over the next several minutes the smells of the cooking fires and the sounds of playing children faded behind him. With sharp limbs, the trees clawed at him as he fought his way through their gnarled branches. The tree limbs broke easily and the leaves beneath his feet created a constant babel of crunching and crackling. John knew he would not see any game with the constant noise. If he was anything, he was a good hunter. As a young lad he took easily to it and was often successful when others weren't. Only his distraction over Alis had caused him to miss the bird.

Nearly two hours later, John found what he was looking for and sat down on a large tree root to rest. Before him was a dry creek bed. It was a good spot to sit and wait, because even dry it would draw animals to it. The sounds of the colony had long faded away, the thin canopy overhead offered shade, and best of all, there were signs of recent deer activity in the area. John laid his musket on the ground, chewed on a piece of tough bread, and studied the area around him. Silence settled in around him.

Slowly time passed and noonday approached. By now his sister would have found the note he left her and she would be worried. The assurances that he would not be home until dark would not alleviate her fears, but he had at least tried. John checked his supplies and relaxed again. It knew his wait could still be several hours.

*Snap!*

The snapping twig was like a thunderclap to John. His heart began to beat like a drum pounded by one of the local natives and his breath came in short gasps. He feared the thumping in his chest would drive the creature away.

Chastising himself, he forced his breathing under control. Like any good hunter he needed to remain calm. Any approaching animals would sense his unchecked emotions. As his breathing took on a steady rhythm, he raised his weapon to his shoulder and studied the forest for signs of movement.

A gentle breeze began to blow through the clearing. John bit his tongue to keep from cursing.

*Snap!*

A second twig told John he was upwind of whatever was approaching. Patently, he scanned the forest. A cloud cast the area in shadow and distant thunder broke the silence. *Rain?* It hadn't rained in weeks.

A small deer stepped into the clearing. John raised his musket, pointing it at the game. As he took aim, uneasiness crept into him. His skin tingled like it had been rubbed against a pair of wool socks. Looking down the barrel of his musket, he could see the hairs along the back of his arm stand up. His eyes focused on them and his mind screamed that something was wrong. Something was coming...he needed to flee.

Paralyzed, John's gaze shifted to a single drop of sweat dangling from his hair. For a moment it filled his vision. Then it fell, landing on the back of the musket.

John watched the sweat slide down the side of the barrel. Stop. Shudder. Then slide back up. It clung to the barrel, pointing into the sky like a raindrop on the verge of falling from a leaf, only this drop wanted to fall up. Something terrifying was coming. It gripped John's heart, threatening to squeeze the life from it.

For a moment, the bead of sweat clung to the musket, then as he watched, it fell upward. He followed it with his eyes until it disappeared into the canopy overhead.

Dark clouds dominated the sky. They were blacker than any clouds John had seen before. He felt like he was looking into the bowels of the earth. The clouds began to swirl in anger, and John knew that he was the cause of that anger. His fear overwhelmed him. The clouds were alive.

John bolted from the clearing, his musket and gear left abandoned. As he ran, the trees came to life and clawed at his exposed flesh. He ignored the pain and sought only to flee the fear.

Behind him, the deer fell dead in the creek bed.

The clouds blackened further, sucking at his soul, weakening him. Stumbling, his foot caught a tree root and he crashed into a tree. Blood flowed from a gash in his forehead while stars danced across his vision. Pulling himself up, he fought past his dizziness and pushed himself forward even harder than before.

John tasted blood, but it wasn't from his forehead. It flowed from his nose, soaking the front of his shirt.

John ran on and for the first time in his life, he knew real fear. He didn't know if he was running away or toward the source, it seemed to be all around him now. The only thought his mind could cling to was; *he didn't want to die alone in the forest.* He would become a part of the evil, such an intricate deep part that he would be a finger of Hell itself. Somehow he had to find a spark of light to shield him from that fate.

*Kaboom!*

Overhead the clouds twisted and swirled as they threw bolts of purple lightning. Evil spread through the forest screaming at John through the strong wind. Several times he caught a glimpse of the evil, but fear kept him from looking into its eyes.

John ran as rivers of sweat and blood ran down his face stinging his eyes. The trees were living obstacles, but he would not allow them to stop him. He lost all sense of time. Fear pushed him onward.

Bursting from the forest, he flung himself across the beach and into the ocean. Salt water washed over him as he fell headlong into the surf. Even as the water stung the many cuts along his arms and torso, the spray formed a barrier between him and the evil. Only when his lungs were ready to burst did John emerge from the safety of the water. Immediately the oppressive fear returned.

*Eeeiiiiaaa!*

John spun toward the scream. Panic pushed his fear aside. The evil had not only come for him, it had come for the other colonists as well.

Visions of the black clouds choking the life from his sisters filled him with anger. Spurred for the first time by something other than fear, John rose from the water like a vengeful spirit and charged toward the village. Fear still grabbed at him, but now John was propelled by a need even greater than the need to protect his own life.

His chest felt as if it was going to explode and his heart pounded in his temples as John run up the beach into the face of evil. Exhaustion became his enemy as his lungs burned and his muscles ached. Cuts and bruises stung him with every step. Determination pushed him forward and kept the exhaustion from overwhelming him.

John rounded a bend and entered the inlet where the colony resided. Smoke from the cooking fires rose skyward only to be grabbed by clouds and twisted before being swallowed by a dark vortex dominating their center.

Expecting chaos to greet him as he entered the wooden gates, John found only the howling wind as it thrashed and tore at the shelters and scattered loose items around the campsite. The cooking fires were smoldering, tables were overturned, items were strewn everywhere, but there was no sign of the evil or any of the villagers.

John's eyes fell on his family's home. He started toward it when movement caught his eye. As he turned, Alis burst from a battered cabin.

*Fwssh!*

Something flashed behind her. The look on her face changed from terror to pain. John barely had time to react. Desperately, he managed to catch the bundle Alis was carrying as she collided with him and they tumbled to the sand.

Recovering quickly John rolled over to Alis.

She stared up at him with tears forming in her eyes, "Run John, ru..."

John's mind screamed with panic as he struggled to understand what was happening.

A gurgle pulled his attention away from Alis. Wrapped in the bundle she had been carrying was a baby. It began to cry. Looking back at Alis, his heart sank. She stared blankly up at the evil above them. Despair gripped John.

John rolled over onto his back and stared up at the evil clouds. His vision blurred as dizziness swept over him and he felt like he was tumbling toward them. His limbs were dead and the clouds mocked his earlier escape. They were an extension of Hell, reaching into the world to claim his soul. John lost all remaining hope. He didn't register the light that flared beside him or the tall figure it illuminated. All he saw were the clouds. They filled his vision, they filled his mind, and they filled his world. When the light flared a second time it left him tumbling into darkness.

\* \*

John had no idea how long he slept. It seemed like forever and also like he hadn't slept at all. Shapes, sounds, light, and darkness all struggled for dominance in his vision and in his mind. Nausea sat on the edge of his stomach, and his head pounded with ferocious thunder causing him to wince every time it echoed through his skull. He couldn't help but wonder if this was what it felt like to be dead.

Eventually light began to dominate. He didn't know how long it took, if it was real, or if it was just a trick of the mind, because there was also the darkness. It was just beyond the light, but also part of the light. The light moved and breathed as if it were alive, while the darkness was silent and still like death. The darkness seemed to retreat beyond the light, no longer pulling at him, while the light dominated to the point of being painful.

His light wasn't the only light. Others surrounded him. Darkness separated them and singled each one out. Suspended inside each light was a shape. Some were smaller, others were larger. One held a shape so small it was difficult to see. The shapes moved as well. Some quicker, others like him, slow and sluggish. Each time he tried to view one, it was different; larger than before, smaller than before, or not there at all. No matter how hard he tried, he couldn't make them out as they came and went.

There were the other shapes, too. These moved through the darkness as if they were a part of it. They were the only things that kept him from wishing the darkness back. As they moved around him he couldn't help but remember the storm and its evil. Somehow he knew these shapes were the source of that evil. One was tall and had a large trunk like a tree. It was skeletally thin and it flowed before the lights as if they were the most important things in the world, but also like they were insignificant. The other shape wasn't a shape at all. It streaked past him and no mater how hard John tried to view it, it always eluded him.

Only once did John get a good look at something outside his light. He didn't remember it appearing, but suddenly it was there. It was so close that it blocked everything else out. Desperate for anything, John pushed himself forward to get a closer look. It reflected his light into his eyes and he was forced to shut them against the pain. When he opened them again, it was his face he was looking at. It was distorted, smooth and curved all at once, but it was his face. It shifted colors from normal to red and then to green before appearing normal again. Then it was gone, as if it had never been there.

Over time, all the other lights disappeared and then reappeared and then disappeared again. Finally they were replaced one by one by the darkness. At some point only John and a few others remained. He tried to count them but couldn't remember what came after five. No matter how hard he tried, he could not count anymore, nor could he remember who he was, or anything else. Only the lights, the darkness and the shapes existed. One thought seemed to escape the void, and that was Alis. He didn't know who or what Alis was but the thought remained in his mind along with the shapes and the light.

John soon found the remaining lights circled a globe of light. The trees with the large trunks and thin branches stood around the globe, and the shapes that weren't shapes circled them all. The trees in the center grew old and the shapes that circled them became real. Time had no meaning to him. He had no idea how long this went on but he would remember how it ended. It wouldn't end for centuries, but he would remember it. For many years after he would hope it wouldn't end as it ended then. The pain was the most excruciating he had ever experienced, or would ever experience, until it all ended again.

# CHAPTER 2
# FLIGHT TO FREEDOM

Lightning flared around the plane as the storm tossed it about like a child's toy. Without warning or the ability to resist, a toy is forced in the direction of a child's imagination. Its fight is against imagined winds that no ordinary man can survive. The terror of the pilot is imagined and not his own. Ultimately his fate is not his own.

*Kaboom!*

Wolff felt like that toy and a child with a violent imagination drove the storm he was battling. He fought hard against the plane's course but it was not his to control. The pain in his side was a constant reminder that he might not survive.

Unlike the toy, his survival did not depend on someone else. It was up to him and that was how he liked it. If Wolff could not find land before the plane was torn apart, he would use the life raft. If the life raft was pulled under by the waves, he would swim. He would do whatever it took to survive. His fate was his own. Recent events had proven that.

Too many questions remained. Anytime there were questions, he sought answers. It was simply a part of his nature. Even though the temptation to analyze the night's events was strong, the need to focus on the storm was stronger. There would be time to deal with the betrayal later. He had known it was inevitable and had planned for it long ago. First he would survive the storm, then he would investigate it.

"One issue at a time," Wolff told himself as he turned his mind to the present. Reaching forward, he tapped the compass but only grunted when it spun wildly.

The storm made flying over the ocean risky; people, however, were looking for him and they knew where to look. Initially, flying low seemed the best option and the ocean offered the best opportunity to slip away. Now the waves forced him higher than he liked, and left him to battle the storm.

His course paralleled the coast with a northeasterly direction and would bring him ashore near Eureka, California. The storm made holding that course difficult, and forced additional fuel consumption; but counting the reserves he still had over two hours remaining. If he had calculated correctly, and he always did, he would have plenty despite the storm.

Focusing his mind on the present instead of the past wasn't hard. Years of training had taught him to do that. Focusing his mind past his injuries was more difficult. His blood loss was substantial and getting worse with each passing minute. Even with his training, it was getting difficult to concentrate. His limbs were growing cold, his vision blurry.

\* \*

*Kaboom!*

The lightning caused the plane to wrench violently to the right. The stick jerked free of his hand and startled Wolff to consciousness. He was cold, confused, and sweating so badly water dripped from his nose.

Unsure what had happened, he struggled through his confusion and slowly concluded that he had passed out. Despite that realization, Wolff found it difficult to do anything about it. The instrument panel's flashing lights only served to distract him. The plane's wheel dodged his slowed hand every time he tried to grab it. The steep descent of the plane caused him nausea. His hands were shaking, and his breath came in short gasps.

Determination flickered like a candle in Wolff's mind. It was weak and small, but Wolff recognized it, and responded to it. He needed a focus. He needed something stronger than the numbness.

Instinct took over, propelling Wolff into a fight against the confusion. Desperately he slapped himself several times. The brief pain helped, but it was fleeting; he didn't have the strength to hit himself hard enough to cause lingering pain. He closed his eyes and tried to meditate; but the plane's constant jerking fueled his nausea causing him to vomit. Reaching forward, he tried to grab the wheel, but it jerked free of his feeble grip. He slumped deeper into his seat with each passing minute.

Out of options, Wolff dropped his left hand to his side. He pressed it gently against the life-threatening wound. Through the confusion, he could feel the pain the slight pressure caused. Long ago it had subsided to a dull throb. Now he planned to reawaken it. Wolff squeezed with all the strength he could muster.

His muscles clinched as pain shattered the gathering darkness. His jaw was forced open in a scream that fought for dominance over the storm's thunder.

Blood squirted through his fingers, smearing across the instrument panel. Still Wolff held on. When he was able to fight through the pain enough to see the instruments before him, he relaxed his grip.

Collapsing in his seat, Wolff took in deep gulps of air. Pain, as a focus, was a trick he learned in some distant jungle whose name he had long ago forgotten. Many soldiers had permanent scars on their forearms, cutting long slow lines to force themselves to stay awake on guard duty or through several days of combat. When staying awake was the only way to stay alive, pain was easy to embrace.

Using his moment of clarity, Wolff reached forward and gripped the elusive wheel with both hands to begin a battle of wills against the storm. It fought hard, using flashes of lightning to blind him. Several tense moments later, Wolff's determination proved more powerful and the plane leveled off. Outside, lightning revealed the ocean below him still gnashed after its elusive prey with white crested fangs.

Unfortunately the plane was in bad shape. It was losing speed and no matter how steep he angled it upward, it struggled for altitude. If a light was meant to be a warning it was flashing. Systems were shorting out all over, and the wheel was tight and slow to respond. The compass was dark, the altimeter was obscured by blood, and the fuel gauge had a crack running across its screen. The right engine made a high-pitched whine that was getting louder and louder. Its surface was scarred where lightning had seared the paint off.

Wolff attempted to wipe the blood from the altimeter but succeeded only in smearing it further. He considered trying his shirtsleeve, but decided there was just too much blood. Giving up on it, he turned his attention to the fuel gauge. The crack made it impossible to read and the sparks beneath it indicated it would soon be dark anyway.

With no land in sight, Wolff made a calculated decision and turned east. Increasing the throttle, he pushed the engines to their limit. The plane's descent slowed, but the right engine whined louder. Fortunately, the new course brought the plane in line with the storm and for the first time in hours, it stopped rocking.

Not being a religious man, Wolff didn't bother to pray. There were things in this world that couldn't be explained rationally but Wolff never stopped to consider them. He relied on himself, not miracles or angels.

The shaking in Wolff's hands continued to increase, forcing him to grip the wheel tighter to steady them. It wasn't from pain and no amount of concentration or meditation would fix it. His strength was failing him. Wiping blood from his palm onto his pants, he gripped the wheel even tighter and gritted his teeth in determination. The plane plowed forward through the rain and wind.

*Kaboom!*

A lightning flash suddenly revealed a large rocky formation directly in his path. Wolff jerked the wheel to the left. The damaged engine protested loudly. The plane was rocked as it was brought back into conflict with the storm. It took several tense moments to get the plane under control again.

The turn proved too much for the weak engine. Power levels fell off swiftly and it slowed. Within moments it would stop all together and the sole remaining engine wouldn't be enough to keep the plane aloft in the storm.

Eyes stinging, Wolff leaned forward and peered out the window. The object was nowhere in sight. Only a couple of possibilities existed and Wolff allowed a little hope to creep in.

Calculating carefully, he pulled on the wheel and began a steady turn. As before, the wind fought the course change. The weak engine made the battle more difficult than ever. As soon as he could, he leveled the plane and began to search the storm tossed waves for further signs of land.

His search was short. A flash of lightning revealed a rocky cliff with a strange rock formation jutting up from the ocean, resembling a waving arm. Someone else may have taken it as an omen, but Wolff quickly dismissed it. As he had suspected, there was an island to the left of the arm. He turned south toward it.

The storm continued to fight Wolff by refusing to give up light to search by. All that he could see was rain splattering against the windshield. He considered lowering the plane for a better view, but feared the darkness hid additional rocks.

Hope began to fade, but something red flared in the darkness off to his right. It was too low to be lightning, yet bright enough to attract his attention. It could have been a trick of his mind but he angled the plane downward for a closer look anyway.

At first the area was dark. He couldn't see the flare or any land. Then he spotted the flare again. This time it was immediately followed by a streak of light that sped toward the plane. It was moving at incredible speeds and blinking in and out as it moved. It was unlike any landing beacon Wolff had ever seen before.

Admitting defeat, the storm lit up the sky with a quick succession of flashes, revealing the island just to the right of the plane. A beach was visible a little further along.

The red beacon could be seen clearly now. Once on the beach it picked up speed and easily outpaced the plane. Kicking up surf around it, it marked a path for Wolff to follow.

"Thanks," muttered Wolff. For a brief moment, he wondered if he should believe in angels after all.

The plane was descending quickly but was going to overshoot the beach. Wolff eased back on the throttle and the right engine sputtered. Cursing, he forced the throttle forward again to keep the engine alive. Hope for a second pass evaporated when the engine died anyway.

The plane dropped sharply. Wolff's stomach lurched and nausea washed over him once again. Forcing down the urge to vomit, he pushed forward on the wheel to send the plane into an even steeper dive toward the beach.

The descent was quick and the light guided him directly to the beach. Unfortunately, Wolff didn't have much control over the small plane and it struck the beach hard.

Jerked around in the seat violently, pain overwhelmed Wolff. He lost his grip on the wheel and the plane barreled forward uncontrolled.

It bounced over several rocks until it hit the soft sand. The front wheel sank instantly and the plane's momentum snapped it off. The plane's nose was thrust into the sand to plow a trench across the beach. Carried forward by inertia, the plane's tail threatened to overtake the nose.

Slamming into a large rock, the tail ripped free to skip across the sand. The plane's wings were crushed as the cabin somersaulted and rolled its way across the beach. The right engine tore away, flinging into the dark ocean to finally feeding its hunger. Fuel sprayed across the beach, and a trail of flames marked the plane's path. With fire leaping from the rear of the cabin, the plane came to rest at the edge of the water.

\* \*

Cold rain splashed through the broken windshield onto Wolff's face. The sting gave him just enough strength to open his eyes but it didn't help him register where he was or what had happened. His surroundings were dark, offering no clue. Lightning revealed water gushing through a broken windshield to quickly fill the cabin. A fire burned somewhere behind him. In the distance a red glow animated the shadowy trees into an army of wraiths. They moved in unison, coming to claim his soul.

Despite the fog in his mind, Wolff began to puzzle through his situation. He focused on his injuries and tried to ignore the red glow's army of wraiths.

He was trapped and his injuries were severe. His left side was numb and blood flowed from it to mix freely with the rising water. There was a bone protruding through the skin of his right arm. Blood flowing into his eyes stung. His left leg was pinned and twisted. Fire scorched his back.

The glow moved out of the forest onto the beach. It was to the left of the plane animating the shadows of the debris like it had done with the forest. The wraiths taunted Wolff.

Out of instinct he fumbled for the clasp holding him in his seat. Being submerged in the cold water made his arm numb and he couldn't open the clasp. As his strength drained, he allowed the arm to fall useless.

The glow was just outside the plane now. It had its army and they were coming for him.

Determined not to give up, he braced himself for the flood of pain and moved his right arm toward the clasp. Pain shot up the arm to blind him with a series of white explosions. It quickly sapped his strength, but he managed to pull his arm across his chest.

Even before the pain subsided, his fingers began to work the clasp. Anyone seeing him would have thought his efforts were as useless as him trying to pull a vault door off its hinges; but Wolff never listened to anyone about what he could or couldn't do. If a vault door had been in his way, he would have accepted that challenge as well.

"Again, again, again," he mumbled to himself as he pulled at the clasp. "Again…" His words faded to a whisper, but they were still loud enough to pull the glow toward him. He tracked it across the ground. Only when it was hovering over the plane did he bite back his words.

Like his body, his mind was failing him. Wolff worked on instinct alone now. As his surroundings faded and darkness closed in, his fingers continued to work the clasp. The cabin lit up brightly under a white light. The clasp gave way and Wolff plunged into the cold water.

Not yet defeated, he raised his head above the water and looked into the light. It blinded him, but he refused to look away. Using his left arm as a shield he stared into the light. The light came from the center of a red sphere about two feet across. The sphere pulsed and flared with each beat of Wolff's heart. As he watched, the pulse slowed, the sphere changed color to blue, to green and then back to blue. Blackness swallowed Wolff.

\* \*

Wolff's return to consciousness was a struggle but slowly he began to understand what was happening around him.

"Damn! Look at that…eyes are open!"

"…Blood…eighty-five over sixty…falling…extreme blood loss…"

"No s…I can see…No, get A-neg…Lots of it! Continue!"

"Collapsed lung…"

He tried to speak but all he managed was a gurgle that sprayed blood. Hands grabbed him and something was shoved down his throat.

"Second degree burns over thirty percent of his body, largely along his back. Third degree burns on the hands and along his left side. Compound fracture of the right radius."

He tried to move but found he didn't have the strength. A bright light penetrated his right eye, then his left. Behind the light was a masked face. Pain shot up his leg, but the tube prevented him from screaming. Slowly it subsided and the words came to him again.

"...fracture of the left femur and lower fibula. Fracture of his right hip..."

"No, no, no! I said the big needle! What am I working on here, a cat? I'm not a damn vet!" The voice paused and Wolff could hear mumbling. The doctor curtly cut the voice off. "I don't care what you think, I'm the doctor! Do as I say! You! Continue! You! You had better get me that morphine before you pull that leg again, he damn near came off of the table that time...I said continue!"

Faces appeared and disappeared. The flurry of activity was confusing and disorienting.

"Doctor?"

"I said continue!"

"Ahem..."

"Doctor? You have a visitor."

"I don't have time. Tell whoever it is to come back!" Briefly the face of a young man with dark brown hair appeared. The doctor snatched something from his hand and rudely shoved him aside. "Give me that, I'll do it!"

"Who is he?"

"I said come ba..." The doctor briefly paused as he looked up from Wolff. "Oh. It's you. Sir."

Suddenly everyone else pulled back and only the doctor remained over him.

"What are you idiots doing? We're not done here! This man is dying!"

A man's face appeared. He was dressed in an expensive dark suit and his cologne overpowered the sterile medical odor of the room. His hair was gray, but his clean-shaven face wasn't wrinkled. A blonde woman appeared briefly then quickly drew back. The man followed her out of sight.

"I need images. Plenty of them," said a female voice.

"We're busy! Come back later!" The doctor glanced up briefly and then turned his attention back to his work.

"Doctor, you will see to it that Heather gets all the images she needs."

The man never looked up as he spoke. "If all you want to do is identify his corpse then go right ahead. But if you want him to live then I suggest you let me do my job. And that means waiting until after he has been stabilized to take your images!"

"Doctor, I respect your desire to save this man's life, but you will allow Heather to do her job." The man briefly paused. Despite the stress and urgency of those around him, the man was calm. "Heather, do we have any leads on his identity?"

"No," said Heather. "All we know is he crashed a plane on the east end of the island. Apparently he missed the runway. We are tracing the plane's ID."

"Anything more?"

"There was no ID on him but we plan to work with visual identification. If he has a driver's license anywhere, we'll match it. We're working without prints at this point. Given the amount of burns and broken bones, we haven't pulled them yet. We were able to recover enough blood from the wreckage for a DNA analysis. We should have something in a few hours."

"Get what prints you can once the doctor has stabilized him." The doctor looked up at the speaking man briefly. "Most local law enforcement agencies still rely on them. If he is in any system, I want to know. Brief me in thirty minutes."

"Yes sir."

Wolff couldn't see her leave but he heard the woman's footsteps quickly fade from the room.

After a moment, the man spoke again. "Doctor?"

"Yes?"

The male face reappeared. "Is he meta-human?" The face hovered a moment, waiting for an answer. When none came, the man pulled back out of sight.

"Doctor, is he meta-human?" the man asked a second time.

Wolff wondered why the man would ask such a question. He knew what a meta-human was, but he wasn't one. From the way the man asked the question, the answer was more important than his life.

"We won't know for sure without tests..."

"Doctor. I know you don't need those tests. You knew the moment you laid eyes on him. Is he meta-human?"

"No, sir. I don't..lieve he is. But his injuries...extensive. I don't... how he is alive."

The voices were beginning to fade and despite Wolff's best effort, willpower simply wasn't enough.

"...we continue, sir?"

"For now...until the mark up.... I want to know who he is and why he is on my island."

Wolff struggled to hear the rest but the voices continued to fade.

"...crashing! Pressure plummeting...Get me that needle...Cart... now!"

\* \*

Diamond studied the blonde woman in front of him. She had entered his office a few moments earlier with a file in her hands and a curse on her lips. It really didn't surprise him. Heather Stone had worked by his side for years and he knew that she had the shortest temper of any of his employees.

"Is something bothering you, Heather?"

"I don't like the way the doctor treated you, sir. After everything you've done for him..."

"The doctor is one of the finest surgeons and meta-geneticists in the world, Heather. His experiments have produced results that no other geneticist has been able to duplicate."

"That's because no one else dares to." Heather muttered.

Diamond smiled but didn't correct her statement. "I'm sure your displeasure over the doctor's behavior wasn't the only reason you came to see me. Is that report for me?" Diamond pointed at the folder in Heather's hand. Given the level of technology available to them, printed documents were unnecessary, but Diamond knew that Heather preferred them. To satisfy him, she had most likely already made the information available through the Citadel's computers.

"Yes, sir," Heather passed the file to Diamond and began her briefing. "The DNA proved to be more useful than we expected. We got partial matches to several unsolved murders around the world. I had Curtis run him through Interpol."

"What did they say?" Diamond asked as he flipped casually through the file.

"The victims were all high profile individuals. The murders were all clean."

"Professional," Diamond corrected.

"Yes sir. Sir, you should know that Interpol wanted to know why we were asking about these cases."

"What did you tell them?"

"We said we were updating our cold case database and needed to fill in some of the details."

"Good. What did you find with the prints?"

"His name is Wolff Kingsley. Blood and DNA confirm it. We discovered several aliases scattered around the world. Most recently, Blaine Braxton, a real-estate trader out of Austria, who worked largely over the Internet. Neighbors knew the face but didn't know the man."

"A cover."

"Yes, sir. He was some kind of child prodigy. Intelligent, athletic, you name it. He has a master's in political science and a master's in mechanical engineering, an interesting combination. He spent time traveling the world right out of college, even spending some time with Tibetan monks. I haven't figured that one out yet."

"I suspect I know why," said Diamond as he flipped through the file.

When he didn't elaborate, Heather shrugged. If he wanted to tell her, he would.

"Extensive military training, including special and covert ops. Impressive record. You name the place; he's been there. You name the job; he's done it. He was the perfect soldier, and then he became increasingly difficult to control. There is no real explanation for it. His career ended with charges of insubordination. Unfortunately, he never showed up for the final decision. He simply vanished right out from under the noses of his escort at the Dulles International Airport. The military still wants him. They were interested in my investigation as well but I deflected them. My inquiry also sent up red flags in their computers, but the Citadel computers easily prevented any probes. The alias names pick up after that. Many are false. It will take weeks to trace through them all."

"Then you should get started. I want everything within a week."

"What?" Heather paused. She had never questioned orders before but she had already discovered enough to cause her concern. She leaned forward and spoke, "Sir, if you don't mind me saying, he doesn't belong here. If even half of what is in that file is true, he..."

"Your objection is noted, Heather. But I want to know everything there is to know about this man. Activate some of our deep-cover agents if you need to, but get me everything. Dreah has taken an interest in him."

"No disrespect sir, but Dreah takes an interest in everyone."

"Dreah's instincts are outstanding, Heather. I never ignore them." Diamond stopped and looked up. He could see the doubt in her eyes. It wasn't over Dreah's instincts, Heather knew them as well as he did, her doubt was the baggage Wolff carried.

"It isn't what she has said, it's what she won't say that troubles me," said Diamond. "I can see it in her eyes when she looks at him. It's why she sent Glip-2 up there to guide his plane in. It is why he's here. I want to know what that is."

# CHAPTER 3
# TRIALS AND TRIBULATIONS

"Awaken, Prisoner four, four, sixty-eight."

The voice startled Wolff. It was distant and faint. Was it speaking to him? Where was it coming from?

"Awaken, Prisoner four, four, sixty-eight."

This time it was louder. He turned but found nothing. Struggling to understand, he scanned the darkness, but could not find a source for the voice. It was mechanical and female, but there was nothing to explain it – no one, no objects, no light; nothing.

Holding his hand up, he found he couldn't see it. In fact, he wasn't even sure he was holding his hand up. He started to turn but realized his senses extended all around him. Only his thoughts existed in the darkness.

In the distance something sparked. It sparked again, closer. Each time it returned it grew nearer. It appeared electrical but there was no visible source for it. It simply appeared in the air and then vanished.

When the spark struck him, it startled him, but it wasn't painful. Instead, it left a tingling sensation that spread across his body, confirming that he at least had a body. The spark failed to light up the darkness.

Intrigued, he searched the darkness and found the spark some distance from him now. It flashed to his left, to his right, and then it flashed above him. It struck him a second time and he felt the tingle spread across his body again.

When it struck him a third time, he was prepared. He grabbed for it but it easily slipped from his hand. If not for the tingle that spread up his arm, he wouldn't have even known he had touched it.

The spark wasn't alone in the darkness now. An image flickered in and out across distant twisting storm clouds that disappeared without the light of the image. The image fascinated him but the clouds frightened him. Raging emotions warred against each other inside the clouds. The chaos was only dulled by the illumination of the image. It gave purpose to the emotions. It pushed most of them away and explained what remained.

It wasn't long before the spark struck him again. Now that he knew what to expect, he wasn't surprised when a second image appeared on the storm clouds.

It was difficult to make out the twisted images but each flash revealed a little more. Moving and playing out like a scene from a movie, both flashes revealed his past. However, he couldn't remember the scenes. A third strike by the spark revealed another image. A fourth strike revealed a fourth image.

Despite the strangeness of the phenomenon, something deep within Wolff understood what was happening. He didn't consciously control it, or understand it any more than he understood the images. It was a strong urge that reacted with a will of its own. Hesitantly, he acknowledged it. Immediately it captured his mind and pulled his thoughts inward. He found it impossible to concentrate on anything but the urge. It completely blocked out the storm clouds and the spark. As he remained huddled beneath the urge, the sparks intensity grew and it slowly penetrated his protection. At first it was only slight stings but then it became painful stabs. The urge pulled on every ounce of his strength to defend against the assault.

Wolff had no idea how long the attack lasted or when it ended.

\* \*

Heather stood at the observation window and watched silently. Except for Diamond and Wolff, the room was empty. It was always like this when Diamond took the steps he was taking today. Diamond kept his secrets closely guarded, and this was one of his closest. Recent events with the Sons of Mars had forced him to reveal this secret to some in order to save the life of Carol Estingdale. Carol was a popular and valuable member of his staff, and everyone had stepped forward to help find her. She was returned safely along with a diary she had been searching for. However, the rift left between Diamond and El Incindiaro still hadn't healed. The Mexican hero didn't like deception, and Diamond sometimes drowned in it.

Heather couldn't help but feel that Diamond's current actions, and thus the danger he faced, were her fault. She had failed him. She had learned all she could about Wolff Kingsley. For days she had pored over records and trailed false names to uncover his dark secrets, but in the end they had led her nowhere. Diamond didn't agree. He felt her work led him to someone he suspected existed for a long time, someone he had always failed to find a lead to, until now.

Dreah continued to insist Wolff was more than reports and false names. Heather didn't understand the need driving Diamond, or why Dreah had taken a personal interest in Wolff, but she understood the secrets she had uncovered. If Heather had her way, she would have buried Kingsley so deep under his sins, that even the worms would have had difficulty finding him.

Heather nervously chewed her nails as Diamond fixed his gaze on Wolff's bandaged forehead. It wasn't the secrets he could uncover, or even the depth to which he would go to uncover them, that scared her. It was the price Diamond would pay. Diamond was unique. He wasn't a meta-human, yet he possessed abilities that surpassed even the most powerful meta-humans. A monster lived inside his head that granted him his abilities, and every time Diamond used them, it left him weak and the monster stronger. Diamond had read dozens of minds before, but it scared Heather because at some point the monster would win in its struggle for dominance, and Diamond would be lost forever. It was a price Heather felt was too high to pay for someone like Wolff.

This was Diamond's second attempt to scan Wolff's mind. The first attempt had met with unexpected resistance, leaving Diamond weakened for several days. Over that time, Wolff's physical condition had improved, and Heather worried that his mental resistance had also.

Movement near the door to Wolff's room caught Heather's attention and she turned. Dreah glided smoothly across the floor to stand behind Diamond. The scent of flowers reached Heather as Dreah rested a gentle hand on Diamond's back. The tension in Heather's shoulders relaxed. Diamond wouldn't be facing the danger alone.

\*   \*

"Awaken, Prisoner four, four, sixty-eight!"

The words were a greater assault on Wolff's mind than the bells of Notre Dame to someone standing within their chamber. Instantly awake, he looked around but found only darkness. He had never experienced a darkness so deep before. He waited patiently.

The darkness pushed back and Wolff found himself illuminated. Glancing up he discovered that there was no visible source for the light shining on him. Glancing down he found himself naked and the floor beneath him as black as the darkness surrounding him. He couldn't feel the floor beneath his feet.

As he tried to understand what was happening, a spark flickered in the distance. It sparked a second time, then a third time. It reminded him of an electrical charge as it jumped to a different location each time. He realized he wasn't simply watching it. He was experiencing it. Even without touching it, it caused the hair along his arm to rise up. He was unprepared for it when it struck him.

The spark stung. Wolff immediately began to scan the darkness for the spark's source; it was the danger.

He tried to flinch away when the spark drew closer but found he could not. The sting was stronger than before. *Deal with the source*, he told himself.

An urge within him didn't wait for the spark to strike again. It reacted. At first Wolff tried to ignore it and to concentrate on his search for the source. He told himself it was just nerves because he did not understand what was happening to him. But the nervous itch didn't abate. It swelled upward and began to threaten his concentration. He didn't trust the urge any more than he trusted the spark. It wasn't him any more than the spark was. Yet, somehow it was familiar, and strangely, it offered protection from the spark.

Wolff was struck twice more and each strike was stronger than the previous one. Experiencing the spark went beyond just the physical pain expected from electrical current. It penetrated much deeper into his mind. It affected his sight and left him with spots dancing before his eyes. It penetrated his nose and left the smell of ozone in the air.

It penetrated his hearing and left a chorus of voices echoing through his ears. It was painful, but a pleasurable pain that left him wanting more. It was inviting where as the urge inside him was not. The initial pain of the sparks caused him to want to open up to the urge. The lingering pain made him want to bottle it up and to bury it deep within himself.

When the spark struck him again, the urge violently bucked and burst free from the weak restraints Wolff had begun to form around it. It formed a shield that completely deflected the next spark. Refusing to be deterred, the spark returned and grew stronger each time. Within moments, Wolff was driven to his knees by the onslaught. Each strike threatened to shatter his very existence. Each strike overwhelmed his senses. The blinding flashes, the burning smell, the intense pain, and the echoing sounds were all too much.

Wolff was stuck between the two opposing forces. It was a battle unlike any he had ever experienced, and beyond his understanding. He felt like a child cowering beneath bed sheets from monsters lurking just beyond the light. He began to lose consciousness.

A gentle hand touched his. Like a mother's grip, it penetrated everything with soothing reassurance. The smell of flowers overpowered the smell of ozone.

Wolff allowed himself the moment of relief the touch brought; immediately the battle shifted and the shield faltered. He panicked and pulled back from the hand, but it held his hand firmly, and gently. Embracing the hand would shatter the shield, yet the hand offered a safety and comfort all its own.

Wolff quickly considered his options. The assault was a violation of his deepest thoughts. Even though the shield offered defense, he couldn't shake the feeling that it wasn't safe either. The gentle hand was trying to guide him out from under the shield and into the full might of the assault. Yet, it offered the strongest feelings of safety. None of his choices seemed acceptable until he realized that without the gentle hand, he wouldn't have even had a choice. Without it, he couldn't have concentrated enough to distinguish between the pain of the sparks and the crushing weight of the shield.

Reaching up, Wolff grasped the hand and pulled. Light flooded his senses as the shield shattered. The assault immediately stopped.

Images flooded Wolff's mind. Each stood alone as a single moment, but together they formed his life. Each image was a thread running through a quilt. Alone they were weak and meant nothing; together they were strong, forming a complete image of his life.

Falling flawlessly into place, the visions of his childhood came together. Moments with close friends long forgotten brought a smile to his face. The thrill of victory from early sporting events caused him to tremble. The innocence of discovering girls were different from boys thrilled him. The disappointment of failure saddened him. The joy of friendship soothed him. Unfortunately, the names of anyone appearing in the visions disappeared as each image was replaced with a new image.

...His mother tucked him into bed, he heard every word of love she whispered. As she kissed him goodnight, he smelled her perfume and felt the soft brush of her hair against his cheek. Her smile lingered in his mind long after she turned out the light and pulled the door closed behind her.

...Remembering every detail, he stood before a large chalkboard filled with complicated mathematical formulas. Math came easy for him. The men gathered before him were astonished and he smiled over his father's pride.

...Wolff's father sat before a pale lamp studying a small metal coin. His glasses sat perched on the end of his nose and he held a coin under a magnifying glass with a pair of tweezers. Hidden in a corner, Wolff's knees cramped from remaining crouched. His father used a small brush to gently brush debris from the ancient coin. Wolff dared not move, he dared not speak, lest he disturb his father. Suddenly Wolff's patience paid off and his father's eyes lit up with the delight Wolff had been waiting to witness. His father had just discovered some secret held by the small object that time had attempted to erase from the history of man.

...Friends bullied each other until their fight spilled over to Wolff. His knuckles ached from the fight and he felt the disapproving stare of his father. His mother's gentle hand on his back eased both pains.

...His father taught him to shoot an air rifle and he experienced the joy of hitting the bull's eye for the first time all over again. It was a thrill lost to his mind for a very long time.

After his early years passed, his teenage years began to weave together; but they weren't as happy as his childhood, and they weren't as he remembered them.

A man he could not remember now appeared in the images. Unlike his friends, he couldn't even remember the stranger during the brief moments he appeared in the images. Unlike his mother, he couldn't hear the words the stranger spoke. Unlike his father, he couldn't see details of the stranger's face. No feelings of joy, anger, fear, or excitement accompanied the man.

...Wolff argued with Tabitha in a crowded mall. He couldn't hear the words he said or feel the anger twisting his face. The stranger watched silently, never moving, with his gaze fixed on Wolff.

...Silently, Wolff led his younger sister away from their mother's coffin. He didn't feel sorrow over her death. He should have. It should have been eating him up on the inside, but it wasn't. His father attempted to guide them into a row of seats but Wolff didn't even acknowledge him. Instead, he led his sister past the row and to a different set of seats. The stranger stood at the back of the gathered mourners. Like Wolff, he wasn't crying.

...Their relationship deteriorating with each word, Wolff argued with his father over college. Again, Wolff couldn't hear his words or feel the anger that burned in each one. His father persisted in the argument well after Wolff had given up on it. Wolff passed the stranger's image reflected in a windowpane as he stormed out of the room.

...On Wolff's first day of college, he felt no joy, no wonder. The man handed Wolff a stack of books and Wolff turned away from his family, never acknowledging his father's goodbye, or his sister's tears.

...Wolff chose to study in the library instead of going on a date with Kim. He never worried about missing it. As the man opened the library door for him, Kim's name faded along with the memory.

...Wolff sat alone in his dorm room with snow falling lightly outside the window. He casually tossed the wedding invitation into the trash. Like all correspondence from his father, he hadn't even bothered to open it. The man left no footprints in the snow outside Wolff's window.

...As Wolff moved beyond college and into the military, the man stopped appearing – at least in person. The effects he had on Wolff's life were still there, but his face wasn't. Each time Wolff faced the decision to kill, the scene slowed to a crawl and he never hesitated. All sensation was lost as he made his choice. All emotion evaporated.

...The chaos of war reigned around Wolff. Bullets flew over his head and explosions shook the ground. Dying people screamed. A sergeant, Wolff had known for years, ran next to him. A bullet instantly ended the sergeant's life, but Wolff never even blinked. He didn't feel any of it. He pushed forward killing without emotion; never stopping for a fallen comrade.

...Wolff's rifle flashed and an enemy fell. He stepped over a child still clutching its mother's hand and stabbed a second man. He dropped a grenade and rolled through the door as the room exploded behind him.

...Shackled and expressionless, Wolff walked toward a military transport. As in some of the other scenes, everyone but Wolff slowed to a crawl. Moving with ease and speed, he overpowered his escort and fled. Without hesitation, he climbed into the back of a limousine and came face to face with the stranger. For a brief moment the name of the man came to him. He was the Counselor. The name faded with the scene.

Only an occasional memory from that point forward was flawed with the presence of the Counselor. The rest fell perfectly into place. He remembered them as they occurred. The quilt of his life finished weaving with a fiery plane crash. Wolff collapsed to the stone floor and slipped into unconsciousness. It was done. His story was told; but it was flawed, and wasn't the story he knew.

\* \*

Heather sat across the desk and waited for her boss. Behind his desk, Diamond shuffled through several handheld computers. Each one held documents of a different nature. Some were related to the daily operations of Diamond Security Solutions, and others held information that even she wasn't privy to. Most of those relating to DSS she normally took care of, but he never failed to review them. It wasn't that he didn't trust her; it was simply in his nature to maintain control. He never fully relinquished it.

Glancing at her watch, Heather saw that Doctor McCoy was ten minutes late for the meeting. The level of disrespect the doctor showed Diamond infuriated her. She sighed heavily in her irritation.

Diamond glanced up at Heather's display of frustration. "That's the fourth time you've checked your watch in the last three minutes."

Heather looked up to meet his eyes. Unlike others who dealt with Diamond, she never hesitated to look him in the eye. He had once told her that it was the very reason he had recruited her to work for him as opposed to locking her up in a juvenile prison for trying to rob one of his medical labs.

Heather grimaced. "Dr. McCoy is late again."

"I am aware of that."

Heather started to speak again but Diamond continued.

"I have told you before why I tolerate it." Heather bit her lip to keep from objecting. "Dr. McCoy is gifted. As long as those gifts remain in our camp, his behavior can be tolerated. Besides, scientific experiments don't often work on a predictable schedule. I've been monitoring him in his lab." Diamond pointed to the wall to the right of his desk. An image of Doctor McCoy's lab appeared but it was empty. "Six minutes ago he completed a delicate procedure where he successfully forced an active meta-gene to return to a dormant state. If he can perfect the procedure, it will have significant value. He should be arriving in a few moments. Despite what you may think, his tardiness isn't a lack of respect. It is an act of prioritizing. I can respect that even if I don't always agree with it."

Diamond went back to studying a document before him, and Heather shifted in her chair. Just as he had predicted, the doctor arrived within two minutes. Heather kept her seat when he entered, but Diamond stood up and indicated a seat next to her.

Diamond took the initiative. "Sorry to bother you, Doctor, but I'd like to hear your report on Wolff Kingsley."

"Is my written report not good enough?" asked Doctor McCoy.

"I have read it, but I would like to hear it from you," replied Diamond.

The doctor looked annoyed. "Very well, sir. Physically, Kingsley will be fine. He will have some permanent scarring on his left side." Finished, the doctor sat back in his chair.

Not satisfied, Diamond said, "Mr. Kingsley had several useful physical skills before his arrival here. Do you think he will be able to maintain the same level of physical activity he had before the accident?"

"I do not know what type of activity Kingsley performed before coming here, so I cannot fully answer that question. However, if he maintains the apparent care he has previously taken with his physical conditioning, I would place him at ninety percent."

"Thank you, Doctor, but could you please give me a detailed run down?"

Doctor McCoy looked annoyed. He stayed in his seat for several moments, but Diamond didn't cave under his glare. Finally, the doctor got up and approached the wall to the right of the desk. He pulled a small computer out of his pocket and made some adjustments. The wall sprang to life with images of Wolff. His injuries were highlighted, and his vital signs streamed across the left side of the display. Starting with the injury to Wolff's leg, the doctor took the next fifteen minutes to explain in extreme detail the damage that Wolff had sustained. His report was nearly word for word from his written report.

Heather sat in silence and watched the display between the two men. It intrigued her. Diamond already knew the information and fully understood it. Yet, for some reason he was forcing the doctor to jump through hoops that the man obviously didn't want to jump through. Diamond clearly had some angle, and Heather watched intently hoping to discover it.

When he had finished, Diamond smiled at Doctor McCoy and said, "Thank you, Doctor."

The doctor grunted in response and turned to leave. The images on the wall disappeared and he reached for the door handle.

"Oh, sorry, Doctor. There is one more thing."

Doctor McCoy turned to face Diamond with the door partially ajar. He did nothing to hide the irritation on his face.

"Yes?" Dr. McCoy asked.

"Who will you assign to tend to Kingsley's recovery?"

Heather suppressed a smile. This was it. This was the real reason Diamond had summoned the doctor to a face-to-face meeting.

"Why?" Dr. McCoy asked suspiciously.

Diamond didn't flinch. "I know your schedule, Doctor. You're going to be extremely busy with your experiments for the next several days. You won't have time to monitor routine recovery of a patient. You'll assign it to one of your staff."

The doctor nodded. "You're right. I planned to assign the case to Dr. Ashan. I will, of course, monitor her work. I've done the hard part. And since Kingsley is not a meta-human, she should be able to handle it."

Diamond nodded. "She is very competent. However, I would like Brandon to handle it instead."

With the word *why* perched on his lips, Doctor McCoy frowned and stared at Diamond in confusion. Brandon was the youngest member of his medical staff. Diamond knew as well as anyone that he was still years away from completing his medical training. Despite the fact that the kid was gifted, Dr. McCoy doubted he ever would. There had to be something special about Wolff Kingsley for Diamond to make such a request. It intrigued the doctor. He decided not to object to the appointment or to question why. He could easily monitor the situation from afar.

"If that is what you want. As I said, Mr. Kingsley's recovery looks fairly straightforward. Brandon should be able to handle it. I'd still like to have Dr. Ashan monitor his work."

"As long as Brandon is the only member of your staff to have direct contact with Kingsley, you can assign whoever you want to be his supervisor."

The doctor nodded. "I understand, sir. Will there be anything else?"

Diamond shook his head and the doctor left the room.

Heather and Diamond sat in silence for several moments. When she realized he had nothing further to add, Heather got up to leave.

"Heather," said Diamond.

She turned to face him. "Yes, sir."

"Aren't you curious to know why I requested that Brandon attend to Kingsley's recovery, and why I forced the doctor to go through this charade?"

Heather didn't hesitate to answer. "I'm certain Brandon was Dreah's request. Although I don't know exactly why, I'm sure she has her reasons. And you rarely question those. As for the doctor, he would have avoided your order for Brandon had it come through any other means than face-to-face. And, after his display in the ER in front of his staff, well, sometimes you simply have to remind people who the boss is."

Without replying, Diamond returned to his work and Heather left the office.

\* \*

"Awaken, Prisoner four, four, sixty-eight."

He was groggy, and some part of his mind wanted to refuse. It wanted to remain in the darkness. Being stiff only fueled the desire to remain in the dark.

"Awaken, Prisoner four, four, sixty-eight!"

The voice was painful this time.

"Alright, alright, I'm awake," he muttered. Cursing, he sat up. Opening his eyes, he squinted through blinding light at the room around him. What he saw confused him.

A thin, green plastic mattress covered the black stone bunk he sat on. There were no other furnishings in the small room. He wore a pair of white pants. He had no shirt and no shoes.

The walls were made of the same black stone. The stone disappeared into the shadowed corners. The floor was also stone, and when he looked into it, he got the impression of staring into the dark void of outer space. He could see deep marbling and star-like patterns running through it.

Far above him was a single light. Its brightness caused him to cover his eyes and squint as he tried to peer around it at the room's ceiling. After a moment, he gave up and closed his eyes against the sting. When he opened them again, he marveled at how the stone swallowed the light.

"Enough to drive a man nuts," he mumbled to himself. Standing, he stretched. The floor was hard to his bare feet, but it wasn't cold. He took a step away from the bed toward the far wall. Placing both hands on it, he leaned forward to study the stone closer. Like the floor it was smooth and seemed to stretch on forever. The pale marbling also ran through it.

Wolff turned to face the bed. He strained to remember where he was and how he had come to be there. The only thing he could remember was a ball of fire rushing toward him. Staring at the small bunk, he wondered aloud, "Where am I?"

"You are in a maximum security prison for international terrorists."

The mechanical words stung him as they came at him from all directions. He hadn't expected an answer. Spinning, he frantically searched for a source but couldn't find one. The fog of his mind grew thicker, and he struggled with the reality of the room and the voice. They defied logic.

Cautiously, he asked, "Why?"

"You are a terrorist wanted in numerous countries. The charges against you include: terrorism, conspiracy to commit terrorism, first degree murder, and conspiracy to commit murder."

The words knocked the wind out of him and drove him to his knees. For several moments the room spun, and he fought against dizziness. He tried to see past the words to how he had come to be in the room, but each time he did the memory of the fireball overwhelmed him. Then it struck him, not only could he not remember how he had come to be in the room, but he couldn't even remember who he was.

"What...How...Who am I?"

"You are Wolff Kingsley, also know as Blaine Braxton, Wayne Finger, Bruce Kane, Steve Marston, Clark Siegel, and Kent Shuster."

Only the name Wolff Kingsley meant anything to him. It was the only thing that seemed real; he had no doubt it was his name. The room and the rest of the names held no meaning. The charges were another matter. He couldn't understand how he could be charged with such crimes when he didn't even know who he was.

Clutching his head, Wolff collapsed onto the floor. Pulling his knees to his chest, he tumbled into the dark void beneath him.

\* \*

"Awaken, Wolff Kingsley."

Wolff bolted upright on the small stone bed. It wasn't the first time the words had woken him and it wasn't the first time he had found himself in the strange room, but it was the first time the voice had called him by name.

He quickly noted a small chair sitting at the edge of the bed. A shirt was draped over it and a pair of white slippers sat on it.

"Rise and get dressed," said the female voice.

Wolff hesitated for only a moment and then rose. Standing next to the chair, he stared down at the shirt. As he took the shirt from the back of the chair, he glanced around the room and found nothing else had changed.

"Why?" he asked.

"Wolff Kingsley, get dressed," repeated the voice.

Wolff ignored the voice and kicked the chair across the room. It shattered against the wall. He began to search his room. He started with the mattress and completely shredded it in his search. The bed was fixed to the wall and didn't budge when Wolf tried to remove it. He got down on his hands and knees and studied every inch of the floor. It was flawless, so he moved on to the walls. The seam between them was also perfect. There was not a single joint or break he could exploit. Finally, he turned his attention to the ceiling.

Again the light stung his eyes as he tried to see beyond it. Using the room's corners, he tried to scale the walls but found the stone too smooth. He put the slippers on his feet but still couldn't get enough traction to climb. Using the shirt, he tried to hit the light. When that failed, he used his pants, but the light remained out of reach.

After several minutes, Wolff sat down on the floor, exhausted.

"Wolff Kingsley, rise and get dressed," said the voice.

Wolff ignored it. Sitting on the floor, he stared into the blackness of the opposite wall until it claimed him.

\* \*

Wolff had no idea how many times the voice woke him. Time had no meaning. His days were divided only by the voice, and he never bothered to keep count. He was never fed and never felt hungry.

Only escape had meaning. So everyday when the voice woke him, he searched his cell for a way out. When he found none, he cursed and started his search again.

Eventually, Wolff's anger turned into despair. It was a feeling he could not remember ever experiencing. Somewhere was the answer to his puzzle, but he couldn't find it. Lying on his back on the floor of his cell, Wolff stared up at the light far above him and felt like a rock trapped at the bottom of a well. He slowly became resigned to the fact that he would only be able to escape through some outside force.

\* \*

"Awaken, Wolff Kingsley."

Wolff wanted to ignore the voice but feared the voice yelling in his head. Sitting up, he took in his surroundings. They hadn't changed.

"Wolff Kingsley, get dressed."

Rising, Wolff stood beside the chair and stared at the shirt. There was only one course of action he hadn't tried. He didn't like it and had rejected it up to this point. It was a form of surrender. Reaching down, Wolff picked up the shirt and pulled it over his head. Sitting on the chair, he pulled the slippers onto his feet.

A deep rumble passed through the room. Wolff leaped to his feet and spun looking for a source for the sound. He quickly realized he wasn't hearing it, he was feeling it. It passed through his whole body. It felt like his head was pressed against a railroad track with a large train rumbling toward him. It originated from within him and echoed outward through the walls and the floor.

Across from the bed, the wall of his cell split open. The rumble continued until the wall stopped moving. A man stood silhouetted in the doorway. Slowly, he stepped into the room with the smell of exotic cologne preceding him.

The man was dressed in a tailored black suit that fit his slender frame perfectly. His shirt was a deep blue, and his tie was black with swirls of white and blue to match the shirt. His gray hair was short and neatly trimmed. He wore a silver watch on his left wrist and a silver ring with an onyx face in the shape of a diamond on his right hand. His face was hidden in shadow. Nothing about the man was out of place. Everything, including his step, was perfect.

Holding out his hand, the man said, "Hello, Mr. Kingsley. I am your counsel, and I'm here to help you."

Without taking the man's hand, Wolff stared at him. Even though the light of the room illuminated him as clearly as it did Wolff, his face remained hidden in shadow. Wolff felt like he had met the man before.

"Who are you?" asked Wolff.

The man dropped his hand. "Like I said, I am your counsel." Turning his back on Wolff, he exited the room. Wolff didn't follow, and the man turned back around to face him. He extended his hand toward the hallway to indicate Wolff should accompany him.

Wolff glanced at the hallway and quickly calculated his chances. He didn't know if escape was down the hall, but he did know he could take the man before anyone could come to his assistance.

"No, you can't," said the man.

He knew. Somehow he knew what Wolff had been thinking. It confirmed Wolff's fears.

"This way, Mr. Kingsley."

Deciding he had little choice, Wolff exited the room. Together the two men walked down a long hallway made of the same stone as Wolff's cell. The hallway had no visible light source and was dark. The man's face remained hidden in shadows. Behind them, Wolff felt the closing of his cell.

"Do you know what is happening to you, Mr. Kingsley?"

Wolff hesitated. He didn't want to admit it to himself, but he knew. "Yes," he said.

Wolff waited for the man to respond but he didn't. For a moment, the two walked in silence.

"This," Wolf added, "is all a dream. You are using it to hold me prisoner."

"That is very astute of you. I am glad you were able to pick up on it. It confirms some of the things we have learned about you. Although, it is not quite correct. Yes, this is all in your mind. But it is not a dream. It is real. It is a different reality than you are used to, but nonetheless, it is very real. You have to believe this is happening to you. Also, we are not using it to hold you prisoner. You are."

Wolff's face didn't reflect the surprise he felt. The man stopped, but Wolff continued for several steps. After a moment, Wolff turned to face him and the man continued speaking.

"It wasn't completely you, Mr. Kingsley. You need to understand that. This," and he again indicated the walls, "wasn't built by you, but it can be controlled by you." The man held up his hand to stop the protest forming on Wolff's lips. "Yes, you do have a powerful will, but what we encountered wasn't you. You need to understand that, Wolff. You need to accept it, or we can't move forward. It has been a part of you for so long, you have trouble distinguishing it from yourself. But just as you have seen his face in your memories, you can find the points in your life where you end, and he begins. You can find the cracks in these walls and make them into doors."

"You seem to have control over everything here," said Wolff.

"I am a man of considerable resources, and I can provide those resources to you, Mr. Kingsley. But I can only make small changes here and they won't last. I can show you the doors, but I can't hold them open. I can give you weapons you'll need, but I can't wield them for you. In the end, I cannot free you. Only you can do that."

Wolff narrowed his gaze at the man and considered breaking his neck. He doubted it would free him.

"Why would you want to free me?"

The man didn't answer, but Wolff felt the grinding in his head again, and further down the hall a doorway opened in the rock.

The man took up his pace again and Wolff silently fell in beside him. The new door led to a large round room. Except for a single chair sitting in its center, it was empty. A single bright light in the ceiling illuminated the chair. The man moved into the room and turned to face Wolff.

"Please be seated, Mr. Kingsley."

Wolff didn't sit.

The man smirked, and a moment later, Wolff found himself seated in the chair.

"Like I said, I can make limited changes."

Expecting straps to spring forth and tie him down, Wolff eyed the chair's armrests. After a moment, he glanced around the room. He was trapped well enough without them.

The man began to pace around Wolff.

"Why do you keep your identity hidden?" Wolff asked.

"Until we understand fully what we are dealing with in you, this is safer for both of us."

Wolff didn't respond and waited patiently for the man to continue, but he didn't. Instead the female mechanical voice filled the room.

"Prisoner four, four, sixty-eight, you are charged with Terrorism, Conspiracy to Commit Terrorism, First Degree Murder, Conspiracy to Commit Murder, and Trespassing. The charges are punishable by death. How do you plead?"

Anger flared in Wolff. He gripped the chair's armrests and started to rise. Instantly, his arms were locked down. Looking down, he found wrist straps secured him to the chair.

"Wolff Kingsley, how do you plead?" repeated the voice.

Wolff looked from the wrist straps to the ceiling. "Who charges me?"

"How do you plead?"

"How can you charge me? I don't even know who I am!"

"How do you plead?"

"I won't plead to anything until you answer my questions!"

Suddenly the light above Wolff flared brightly. It stung his eyes and burned his skin. Wolff clinched his eyes shut and tried to hide his face from the light.

"Wolff Kingsley, you are charged with Terrorism, Conspiracy to Commit Terrorism, First Degree Murder, Conspiracy to Commit Murder, and Trespassing. How do you plead?'"

Wolff refused to answer. He struggled to come to terms with his situation. Somehow he knew the charges were true, but he couldn't remember anything related to them. Again the light flared painfully, but he remained defiant.

"Some counsel you are," muttered Wolff. "I know you are in charge here. You've already admitted as much, so why don't we cut out the bull, and you tell me why I'm here."

The man stepped closer. "Very well," he said. "There is an instinct in you, Mr. Kingsley. It is an instinct that sets you apart and makes you a very dangerous man. We are here to kill that instinct, or at least help you get a grip on it. There are a series of steps we will take to do that."

"Torture," said Wolff.

"If that is what it takes."

Wolff was stunned. He hadn't actually expected the man to agree. "You intrude in my thoughts, manipulate my memories, and cloud my ability to discern reality from hallucination! And now you talk about torturing me and expect me to just accept it."

"No, I expect you to fight it. However, know that the longer you do so, the longer this will take."

"Perfect," mumbled Wolff. "So why don't we just get started."

"Do you remember killing the sparrow?" said the man. "You were ten. Your father had taught you to shoot only a year earlier. You and a friend named Freddie were target practicing. Do you remember killing the sparrow, Mr. Kingsley?"

Wolff remembered killing the sparrow. Before the man had asked the question, he could not have. Either way, he didn't see any need to admit it to the man.

"How did it make you feel, Mr. Kingsley? Did you stop to consider whether the sparrow suffered? Did you enjoy the kill?"

\* \*

The soldier was flung into the air as the metal ball struck him. He spun end over end before falling to the earth with the BB lodged in his abdomen. Freddie jumped for joy and cheered his pending victory.

"You'll never catch me now," said Freddie, as he handed the air rifle to Wolff.

Grinning, Wolff took the rifle and surveyed the battlefield. It was littered with green and gray soldiers. Many of them were missing limbs that had been blown clean off by the air rifle. Others lay charred or melted from attacks by firecrackers and gasoline.

"Not for long," said Wolff as he lay down in the dirt and took aim at a small gray soldier behind a mound of dirt positioned at the back of the battlefield. Before it was a trench dug by hand and filled with water from a garden hose. A small toy jeep with two soldiers hiding behind it lay overturned near a bridge of used ice cream sticks. They were more visible than the target Wolff had chosen.

As he took aim, Wolff couldn't help but imagine the scene as a real battlefield. Dead or dying soldiers lay everywhere. Black smoke rose from smoldering fires that had claimed several lives. The earth was charred and pitted where explosions had scarred it. Lately, Wolff had been thinking about real war a lot. He didn't know why, but he wanted to experience one. He wanted to feel the fear, the anger, and the pain. Of course, he knew his dad would never agree. College was everything to his dad. He would never agree to let Wolff join the military.

"Oh no!" shouted Freddie. "You'll never hit ol' Feldmarschall von Manstein."

Slowly Wolff took aim. If he could take out Freddie's general, he would get ten points. Several other targets would have been easier to hit, but he knew Freddie was a better shot than he was. The rifle was his, but Freddie was better with it. The only way he could hope to win the last game of the day was to take out the field marshal.

Freddie screamed next to Wolff's ear as he fired. The distraction was just enough to cause the BB to deflect off the dirt in front of his target. The field marshal fell out of sight. The boys raced forward to see if he had been hit. Freddie cheered when he found his soldier unharmed.

Tired, and with few soldiers surviving, the boys sat on the ground and surveyed the battlefield. Freddie had won, again. It wasn't a surprise, but it still bothered Wolff.

Wolff examined a green soldier that had suffered heavily as he listened to Freddie gloat over his victory. The soldier had been torn in half by a BB, and then his upper half had been charred from a firecracker blast.

Freddie finished his story and sat quietly, looking bored. Suddenly, he pointed the gun at a tree.

Wolff looked around to see what his friend was pointing the rifle at. When Freddie fired, a burst of feathers exploded in the tree. A small bird fell to the ground.

"I got it!" Freddie yelled. He jumped up and ran over to the bird.

Wolff got up and followed. When he got there, he found Freddie leaning over a sparrow struggling to draw breath. Its small chest fluttered with each difficult breath. After a moment, it stopped breathing and lay still.

"Why did you do that?" asked Wolff.

Freddie shrugged. "Why not? I've done it hundreds of times. Haven't you?"

"No," said Wolff.

"Try it," said Freddie.

Wolff looked at the small bird. He felt sorry for it. "No, I don't think I want to," he said.

"Chicken!" taunted Freddie. "Do it!" Freddie held the gun out to Wolff. When Wolff didn't take it, Freddie frowned and thrust it into Wolff's hands.

Reluctantly, Wolff looked around the yard for a target that would satisfy Freddie. It wasn't long before he saw a small bird across the fence in the neighbor's yard. If he shot it there, he wouldn't have to watch it die. Lying prone among the dirt mounds and dead soldiers, Wolff took aim.

Oblivious to the doom looming over it, the small bird sang in the late afternoon sun. Silently hoping it would fly off, Wolff waited for several moments. Freddie grew impatient.

As Wolff's finger tightened on the trigger, the image shifted, and the crosshairs focused on an older man dressed in a business suit. The crosshairs jumped and settled in time to see a spray of red coat the gold dress of a woman standing next to him. The woman screamed, and the man fell.

"What did you see, Mr. Kingsley?"

Wolff sat stunned. He couldn't find the words to answer.

"What did you see?"

Wolff turned to face the man. His teeth were clenched, and his words came broken and forced.

"It...it was a...small bird...a sparrow, I think. Only it wasn't a sparrow. It was a man...and I shot him."

"Who was it Mr. Kingsley?" The man asked.

"I..I..don't know," Wolff lied.

"Who was it?"

It had been his first hit for the Counselor. The man's name was Carlos Masquera. He was a Brazilian politician pushing for government reform. He had been a father of two. His oldest daughter, and personal assistant, had been the woman in the gold dress next to him. Later that same day, she had been found dead as well. She had drowned in her bathtub.

"Who was it?" The man demanded.

Wolff didn't answer.

"Who was it?" demanded the man calmly.

Wolff still didn't answer. He didn't know what to say. He didn't doubt that he had killed the man. The memory was real, but he couldn't remember actually doing it.

"Does it matter? There are others, lots of others." With each word spoken, Wolff's mind flashed with another hit. He couldn't remember any of them, but he knew they were real. "Do any of their names matter to you? Would you like to see them too?"

*A man was shot in the chest while giving a speech. A car exploded. A man's face was shoved underwater. A woman fell forward and a glass table shattered when she struck it.*

"Did they suffer? Maybe you have consoled yourself over the years by claiming they didn't. No one can fault your skill. Your aim is always true, but does that mean they didn't suffer?"

*A knife silently slit a throat. A child cried over the fallen body of her father. A rifle muzzle exploded, and blood spattered the interior of a car. A thin wire circled a woman's neck, and her tears smeared her mascara. Her pleas for help choked out by the wire.*

"Can you see their faces? Can you see their expressions? It is what you wanted, isn't it? Each one was in someone's way and they needed to go. Was it just a job to you?"

Hoping to block out the images, Wolff closed his eyes. It only served to make them clearer.

*A man fell from a balcony. A car veered onto a sidewalk and struck an old man. A fire raged and screams for help went unaided.*

Each hit ended in death. The old, the young, the rich, the important; they all died by his hand.

"Stop it!" screamed Wolff. "Make it stop!"

"Does it really matter who they are, Mr. Kingsley?" Despite Wolff screaming at him, the man didn't raise his voice. Wolff heard every word anyway. "Do their names change the fact that you are responsible for each one?"

The image of a crying child drove Wolff from the chair. His legs would not support him and he collapsed. Fire engulfed an old man and a small boy.

The images burned deep within him and his anger boiled. Wolff seized control of that anger and used it to turn the images against the man. The muzzle flashed, and the man's head exploded.

The images immediately stopped, and the man staggered. He grabbed the back of Wolff's chair to keep from falling. Panting for breath, Wolff rolled over onto his back. After a moment, the man regained his composure and moved out of sight.

"Who are you?" whispered Wolff.

"Despite your little act of defiance, that fact is still not our focus. However, I do think we are done for today, Mr. Kingsley. I will see you again tomorrow."

The man's footsteps faltered as they faded in the darkening chamber. Wolff felt a twinge of pleasure as the darkness claimed him.

# CHAPTER 4
## MEMORIES OF A KILLER

"I understand your concern, but he has to face his memories." Diamond knew his tactics looked like torture to Dreah. They would look like torture to anyone. However, Wolff Kingsley had to face the things he had done. Only then could they move on to freeing him.

Forcing Wolff to face his memories was only the first step. Beneath his conscious was his subconscious, and it was the dangerous part. He would need to kill the stalker that lay there.

"The alternative is prison, and we both know the Counselor would either get to him there, or free him to continue killing. I don't think any of us want either outcome."

Diamond still felt weak. Twice now, Wolff had resisted his mental probes and had even injured him. The first time had been mostly reflexive, and had been partially due to a trap placed in his mind by the Counselor, but the second time had been solely Wolff's indomitable will. The fact that the Counselor had gotten past it enough to gain control over Wolff impressed Diamond. The Counselor's mental powers rivaled his own. Even with the years that the Counselor had taken to do it, Diamond doubted any other mentalist could have done it. In addition, the Counselor had left no mental scarring. Usually, when a mentalist altered someone's memories, or will, they left behind scars or fragmented memories. Someone trained to do it could find those scars. Wolff had no such scarring.

"I still say he isn't worth it," Heather said. She knew neither Diamond nor Dreah needed to hear it; however, she was convinced Wolff Kingsley was a dangerous man. No amount of reconditioning would change the fact that he belonged in a prison, or dead.

Dreah didn't respond to Diamond or Heather. She knew no amount of pleading would change Diamond's course of action. She also knew he was usually right in such matters. But it wasn't the memories Diamond had already forced Wolff to view that concerned her. It was the memory yet to come. As for Heather, Dreah knew that the years of dealing with the criminal element had left her cynical. It was a trait often suffered by people in law enforcement. She wouldn't trust Wolff or anyone else until they had proven themselves to her.

\* \*

Wolff glanced at his watch and through his goggles saw the bright green numbers. The unaided eye would not have seen the display, but to him it was bright and its message was clear. It was almost time.

To confirm he was still alone, Wolff looked to his right, and then to his left. Except for the people contained in the paintings lining the hallway, the museum was empty.

The hall smelled of dust and age and was covered in burgundy carpet that appeared black in the dim light. Wolff wanted to take time to examine the art that surrounded him. It was a trait etched deep into his soul by his parents at an early age. However, he was on a mission, and currently that mission threatened his life. There was no time for sight seeing.

Something about the mission had bothered him from the start, but he had accepted it anyway. He hadn't heard from the Counselor for months. Suddenly, there was an urgent mission that left no prep time and called for the demolition of a museum, not Wolff's specialty. He preferred a high perch and a powerful rifle. Unfortunately, circumstances did not always allow for what he preferred.

Despite the odd conditions, he had accepted. Now he wondered why he had gone against his initial instinct. Things never worked out when he did that. At the time he had chalked it up to never turning down the Counselor. Now, he wasn't so sure.

Glancing at his watch again, he confirmed his silent count was correct, less than two minutes remained. He prepared to move.

\* \*

"Awaken, Wolff Kingsley."

Wolff groaned but sat up. He was back in his cell again. He glanced around to see if anything had changed. The chair sat at the end of the bed with his clothing draped over it. Attached to the wall next to it was a small washbasin made of the same black stone as the walls. A small mirror hung on the wall above the bowl.

"So tell me," said Wolff, "what is on the agenda for today? More torture?"

There was no reply.

Standing, he moved to the wall opposite his bed and searched it for the door that had opened in it the day before. He found a small seam running down the middle of the wall. It was still too tight to manipulate, but at least it was there.

Moving to the washbasin, he was relieved to find it filled with water. Bending over, he reached down and scooped up the cool water with both his hands to splash it across his face. The cold sting refreshed him. He breathed deeply and allowed the water to drip from his face and back into the bowl. The cold water caused him to shudder.

Reaching down, he scooped up the water again and splashed his face a second time. Instead of the cold refreshing sting, his face exploded with searing pain. He jerked back from the water and caught an image of his face in the small mirror. It was blackened and welted as if it had been on fire. His hair smoldered. The pain was intense, and the horror of his appearance only intensified it.

Clutching at his face, Wolff jerked away from the wall. His screams echoed through his cell as he collided with his bed and collapsed onto the hard floor. Instantly, the pain in his knees replaced the pain in his face. He took several deep breaths to regain his composure.

Eventually, he managed to struggle back onto the bed. He sat there silently and looked up at the water bowl. It was still attached to the wall and water was spilled on the floor around it. Standing up, he shuffled over to it and peered inside. The water in the bowl swirled with his blood and pieces of charred flesh.

Repulsed, he looked back at the mirror. His face was normal. Reaching up, he ran his finger along his left cheek. The charred flesh reminded him of something, but he couldn't quite place his finger on it. His back left shoulder itched and he reached around to scratch it.

He remembered the plane crash and the fire that had scorched him, but that wasn't the memory that plagued him now.

Moving across the room, Wolff picked up his clothing and dressed. As he slipped on his shoes, the deep rumble passed through his head and the door to the cell opened.

Wolff stood, and without prompting, joined the man in the hallway. "Who is the man? Who is the Counselor?"

"We will get to him. For now, let us stay with you."

Neither man spoke again until they were in the round room. The walk to the room was a little further than it had been the day before.

Seated once again in the chair, Wolff waited for the man to speak. His memories returned with each word.

"Your father was Felix Kingsley. He was a renowned British historian who focused on antiquities of ancient civilizations, notably technologies. Your mother was Elizabeth Bachmeier. She was German and taught European government. Both were professors at Oxford.

"You were born on April fourth, nineteen sixty-eight. You have one sister, Natalie, born on November twenty-first, nineteen seventy-five.

"Your mother passed away from cancer on June first, nineteen eighty. Your father passed away more recently."

The man stopped speaking and the room grew silent. He had walked out of sight to Wolff's right, and after several moments, Wolff began to think he had left the room.

Suddenly resuming from Wolff's left, the man said, "At an early age, you showed an IQ score just shy of gifted. You excelled in all subjects but particularly in the areas of logical reasoning. Against your father's wishes, you attended Cambridge. There, you majored in political Science, primarily political theory and philosophy. You earned your first master's degree at the age of twenty-three. You earned your second in mechanical engineering a few years later.

"Unfortunately, you grew apart from your father after your mother's death. In fact, you grew apart from everyone.

"Instead of attending your graduation ceremony, you set out to travel the world. You hadn't even bothered to tell your father, and he had actually showed up for the event. You told yourself at the time it was to study foreign governments first hand. I believe it was to avoid your father. You never spoke to him again.

"You settled down, in a manner of speaking, two years later in

February of nineteen ninety-four. You joined the Bundeswehr and were quickly accepted into the Kommando Spezialkräfte; or as it is better known, the KSK. Most of your missions remain classified to this day."

"You only state what I already know." Wolff said, and he did know it.

The man ignored Wolff and continued, "You quickly earned a reputation for always achieving your objectives, in spite of the risks or collateral damage, and there was plenty of that. Wasn't there, Mr. Kingsley? By ninety-six, your overly aggressive tactics were well documented. Aggression then became an inability to follow orders.

"It was June, your unit was part of a United Nations task force dispatched into Afghanistan. You were there to look into early violence connected to the Taliban. In your arrogance, you failed to comply with orders to secure a perimeter. Your team was killed. You were going to be court-martialed."

The man paused, but continued to move around the room, and Wolff paused to consider what he had said. There was something missing.

"That is when you met him. At least as far as you can remember."

The missing piece, it was the Counselor. Wolff waited patiently.

"Tell me about him, Mr. Kingsley."

Wolff was confused. He had hoped the man would tell him about the Counselor. His memories only returned to him as the man spoke. The Counselor was there but he couldn't remember him.

"Mr. Kingsley, did you hear the question?"

"Yes," replied Wolff. "But I don't know anything about him. I can't answer your question."

"Of course you can. We've shown you everything. All you have to do is open your eyes to him."

"I don't understand." Wolff said.

"Tell me about him," said the man.

"I don't know anything about him!"

"Yes, you do Mr. Kingsley. Focus on him. Focus on what he has done in your life."

Wolff didn't respond.

"You must do it yourself, Mr. Kingsley. I have shown you what

I can. Until you accept it and turn against him, we cannot move forward."

"I don't know him."

"Yes, you do. Now open your eyes and tell me about him."

A part of Wolff wanted to answer but he could not remember the Counselor.

Without warning, the man was suddenly in Wolff's face. Anger burned in his eyes, but when he spoke, his voice remained calm.

"Why are you protecting him? He has used you, manipulated you, your whole life. Look him in the eye and come away free."

"Why do you care? Who are you?" Wolff asked the man.

Instantly, the man was gone. He hadn't moved. He simply wasn't in front of Wolff anymore. His footsteps faded as he left the room. "The only hope you have left, Mr. Kingsley."

Wolff sat in silence as the words echoed through the room. Everything faded to black.

\* \*

Stepping across the hall, Wolff put his back against it and faced the corner he had been hiding behind. He inched to the right and peered down a short hallway. It was covered with the same carpet as the one he was in. Along each side were several small stands with the busts of famous writers and composers. In between each bust was a large window. At the far end stood a set of double doors covered with a thin curtain. A slight breeze ruffled the delicate fabric. Several dark figures moved on the balcony beyond. The laser sights of their weapons were clearly visible to Wolff's sensitive goggles.

One beam paused as it passed over him, but he ignored it. Even if they were using thermal, they would have had a hard time distinguishing him from the shadows, as long as he stood still. He wasn't a meta-human, but he could afford the best equipment.

Glancing at the last window on the left, he studied the source of the warning that had told him something was wrong. With the storm brewing outside, the staff had secured all the windows and doors before going home for the night. One of the soldiers had cut a small round hole in the glass. His gun barrel was now perched in the hole. It was that small hole that had alerted Wolff that something was wrong. The wind blowing through the hole had disturbed the thin curtains over the end doors. Wolff planed to reward the soldier for his blunder.

Wolff didn't bother wondering who had tipped them off. Only the Counselor knew where he was. It appeared their arrangement was over. Of course, knowing who didn't tell him why, but that was something he would ask the Counselor personally. Right before he killed him.

Almost time, Wolff told himself. Lightning briefly lit up the dark hallway and thunder echoed through the dark sky, but Wolff remained perfectly still and unseen. The smell of fresh rain blew into the house from the breached window.

\* \*

"Awaken, Wolff Kingsley."

As soon as he opened his eyes, dread filled him. Groaning, Wolff sat up on his bed. He was back in his cell.

Standing, he stretched. Glancing around, he froze. His room had changed again. A small razor and a comb rested on the rim of the washbasin. Glancing in the mirror, he noticed that his hair was ruffled and he needed a shave. Without hesitation, he shaved and combed his hair. He threw on his shirt, and as he pulled on his slippers, his stomach rumbled for the first time.

The doorway opened, but there was no one to greet him. Walking into the hallway, Wolff found it empty. He turned and headed down the hall, but also found the round room empty. He hesitated but then sat down in the chair.

"A man makes choices, Wolff."

Wolff didn't turn to the voice. "Get on with it already. I believe we were about to discuss the Counselor."

The man stopped moving and replied, "We are discussing the Counselor. Be patient." He picked up his pacing again.

"A man makes choices. Sometimes, we are pushed into those choices by forces beyond our control, such as with a soldier who kills on a battlefield. I believe that is something you have experienced. But, often we are not."

Wolff forced down the irritation that was growing inside him. The man continued pacing.

"There are factors that influence our decisions, but ultimately we are responsible for them. If you will, imagine an alcoholic."

Wolff gritted his teeth to keep from speaking.

"He too is responsible for his decisions; but, he has an outside influence that makes the decision whether or not to take that next drink extremely difficult. The alcohol constantly nags at him, pushes him, influences him.

"Let's say he takes that drink, he gives in to the urge. While driving his car home, he runs a stoplight and kills an eleven-year-old girl and her mother. Where does responsibility lie? Society immediately points the finger at him; all the while saying alcoholism is a disease that impairs judgment. In addition, it bombards him with images of drinking, and of its merriment, on television, it names its public venues after alcohol companies, and it only harks on the dangers of alcohol abuse after such tragedies as the girl's death." The man paused. "So tell me, where does responsibility lie, Mr. Kingsley?"

Wolff looked around at the man. He stood facing away from Wolff with his hands clasped behind his back. He never looked at Wolff, and waited patiently. Wolff turned away from the man and faced forward again.

"By your own words, with the man."

The man's footsteps echoed once again through the chamber. "Yes, it does. Do you know why? You do, don't you? It is because the choice was still his. Sure, it was a difficult one and he was influenced, but in the end it was still his. He knew the dangers. Going back to his first drink, it is unlikely it was forced on him; or his second, or his third. Those drinks were all his choices. He didn't become an alcoholic overnight."

Wolff considered the man's words and wondered how they applied to him, or to the Counselor.

"That's what you are, Mr. Kingsley, an alcoholic. You chose that first drink when you killed that sparrow as a boy. It awakened an instinct in you that came to the attention of the Counselor. Like the alcoholic, you knew the danger of that first drink. It is why you searched for a sparrow that you would not have to watch die. You differ from the alcoholic in that you never realized the Counselor was there to influence you in your second kill, or your third, or your fourth."

Confused, Wolff looked up at the man.

"The Counselor, Mr. Kingsley, he was your alcohol, your poison, your compulsion. He influenced you. Ultimately, you made that first choice, but you were unaware of his later influence, at least at first. On a deep level you became aware just like that alcoholic becomes aware of the pull of the alcohol. Unfortunately, he rejects the knowledge, and claims he has things under control, until it is too late and the alcohol has destroyed or taken everything from him. Sadly, he often continues to deny his dependence even then.

"But you did not. Some part of you rebelled against the Counselor, and he knew it. You grew beyond his ability to control effectively, and he attempted to cut you off in the only way he understands. He tried to kill you.

"Now you have to make a choice, Wolff. Will you continue to allow him to influence you, or will you break free? In order to do so, you have to acknowledge that he is influencing you.

"Who is the Counselor, Mr. Kingsley?"

"You seem to know more about him than I do. You tell me who he is."

"We have already covered that, Mr. Kingsley. Who is the Counselor?"

Wolff was tired of the man's game. "I don't know who he is."

"Think. Look into your memories and see him there. Ignore everything else and focus on him. Who is the Counselor?"

Wolff didn't respond. He didn't know the Counselor, and he doubted he could pull anything from his memories.

"Do it. Focus on your memories. Find the Counselor and pull him out of them."

Wolff wanted to hit the man, but instead he found himself thinking of his college days. He could see Kim's face and the effects the Counselor was having on him. When the Counselor's face appeared reflected in a window, he latched onto it. Kim and the rest of the scene faded, and all that remained was the Counselor. For several long moments, Wolff stared into the man's deep green eyes and began a battle of wills against the urge to turn away. He struggled for several moments, but in the end, he came up with nothing.

"Try again," prompted the man.

Shifting through his mind he settled on the memory of his mother's funeral. He ushered his sister into her seat and then sat down next to her. After sitting down, he turned and looked at the crowd. He immediately spotted the Counselor standing at the back. When their eyes met, Wolff became instantly uneasy. He became restless under the man's glare and wanted to look away, but he refused.

Wolff could feel the Counselor willing him to turn his attention back to the funeral. He could feel the hard seat beneath him demanding that he shift into a more comfortable position. He could feel his sister tugging on his arm. He could feel his father nudging him and quietly telling him to turn around. He could hear his mother whispering softly to him from her coffin.

*Please, Wolff. Look at me. I am here, Wolff. This is the last time you will get to see me, Wolff. Please, don't waste it.*

It was easy for Wolff to ignore his sister and his father, but his mother's words pulled at his heart with a strength that tore at his soul. He longed to look to her, to embrace her. Maybe, just maybe she was alive, and this was all a bad dream, a dream that her warm embrace could protect him from. His heart ached, and tears formed in the corners of his eyes.

*Please, Wolff. Look at me.*

Wolff wanted to scream. All he could hear was his mother. He wanted to look into her loving eyes one more time, and to tell her that he loved her. He wanted to know why he hadn't cried for her. He could feel the sorrow of her death now; but then, when it had counted, he had felt nothing. The pull was too much, and he started to turn his head.

"No, Wolff. She cannot help you. Only you can do this."

He no longer knew the voice of the man speaking to him, but he responded to it instantly, and forced his gaze to remain locked on the man with the green eyes. The horrible green-eyed monster willed him to look away, but he refused.

Long moments passed and Wolff began to sweat under the man's stare. The man's glare turned to anger and Wolff's discomfort shifted to pain. Wolff could feel the man's mind boring deep into his. The man could see everything about him, his past, his feelings, and his longings; even what he was trying to do now.

His mother's funeral collapsed into a swirl of colors that spiraled away into darkness. Only he remained seated in his chair with the Counselor's deep green eyes looming before him. He held those eyes and continued the battle of wills. The Counselor silently whispered to him to turn away, but he refused, and the green eyes began to lose their dominance. They shifted to confusion, and then to concern. Wolff lashed out with his anger, and they shattered.

Opening his eyes, Wolff said, "Marcus William Everett."

\* \*

Wolff began to plot his course along the hall. He could get halfway before his suit's camouflage would no longer conceal him from his enemy, and it became a firefight. His course set, he began to assess the danger the soldiers would pose along the path, and to plot the order of their deaths.

Wolff couldn't help but question his life, and the course it would take after tonight. He had been doing this for so long now, he wondered if he could even understand life without it. He wondered if he even wanted life without it. He didn't do this for the adrenalin rush or for any other reason that he understood. It simply was who he was and what he did, and it had all begun with the Counselor.

Holding his ground, Wolff lowered his head and focused his thoughts on remaining calm for the upcoming battle. Over the years, the Counselor had taught him several meditation techniques to calm his mind, and to help him focus. Some even allowed him to ignore pain. After a moment, Wolff raised his head and checked his targets to make sure they hadn't moved.

The footsteps next to Wolff were so soft that he nearly missed them. On reflex, and with one quick motion, he pulled his twin compact *Heckler & Koch USPs* from their shoulder holsters and spun on his approaching enemy.

Both weapons were pointed at the forehead of a boy who was just over three feet tall. Blond hair hung into his eyes and he was dressed in a soft green sweater and khaki shorts. He wore brown loafers, and carried a small teddy bear tucked under his right arm. Only his wide eyes indicated that the boy had even seen him.

"This isn't a good place to be right now," said Wolff.

"Grandpa!" yelled the little boy as he turned and fled up the hallway. He disappeared around a corner that less than a minute ago had been dark. Wolff considered chasing after the boy, but knew the countdown didn't leave him enough time.

\* \*

The day started for Wolff like countless others, the same voice, the same room. He had to admit he was grateful for the small changes that had begun to appear, however. First, he had a chair and change of clothes, then a washbasin, and today he had sheets on the mattress, and a small pillow. The changes indicated he was making progress.

As he finished dressing, the door to his cell opened. His counsel waited in the hallway.

"Come, let's walk, Mr. Kingsley."

Wolff exited the room and the two strolled slowly down the hall. It was brighter today than it had been yesterday. It still had no light source but Wolff could make out the edge of the floor where it met the walls.

The positioning of the round room had changed as well. Before today, it had been at the end of the hall. Today, it was through an archway on the right side. They passed it without stopping. Wolff didn't voice his curiosity. It was up to him to take each step, but the man controlled the pace.

When they reached the hall's end, Wolff felt the grinding in his head again as a door opened before them. Light spilled into the dark hallway and caused Wolff to shield his eyes. The man was unfazed by the light. When he was able to focus again, Wolff found a vast savannah spread out before them. He hadn't stepped forward, but he stood just outside the doorway.

A breeze bent tall brown grass in praise to the life giving sun. There was an occasional scrawny tree jutting up to claim its share of the light. Clouds rolled lazily by overhead and the sunset lit the sky on fire. It was a beautiful scene.

"The Counselor influenced you, Wolff. It started early, as you reached your teenage years. At pivotal points in your life, he nudged you, and concealed your emotions. As a result, your decisions were influenced. Not controlled, but influenced."

What the man was saying made sense, even if some deep part of Wolff still wanted to reject it. The Counselor was present at precise points in his life. At each of these points, Wolff had made decisions that had impacted his life for years to come. It still didn't explain why the Counselor had chosen him, but it did explain a lot about himself.

As if reading his mind, the man continued. "Why he chose you is why we are here. It is no different than why a leopard chooses which gazelle will be his next victim."

Wolff followed the man's gaze to spot a herd of gazelles. They strolled leisurely along, grazing on the dry grass and drinking from a shallow watering hole.

"It is because you stood out. Not because you had high marks in school. Not because you were a natural athlete. Not even because you scored highly on the IQ test your father subjected you to when you were only eight. All of these helped him select you, but it is not why he noticed you. You stood out because of your instinct. It is very acute in you. It lives deep inside you and makes you very dangerous. You stand out Wolff because you are a natural predator." Changing the subject, he added, "Do you see the gazelle on this side of the watering hole?"

Wolff glanced at the man. Despite the bright light of the sun, his face was still hidden. He turned back to the scene and easily spotted the gazelle. It was separated from the protection of the herd by the watering hole. It stood out.

"For whatever reason, it stands out, Mr. Kingsley. It is vulnerable to a predator. Do you see the leopard as well?"

Wolff had already spotted the leopard. Even though it lay hidden by the tall grass, Wolff had instinctively looked for it. Having spent his entire adult life in dangerous situations, it came naturally to him. It was easy for a target to hide, but it was harder for him to hide his effect on the world around him. Several years ago, one of Wolff's intended targets had known he was in danger and had attempted to flee. Wolff had found him not by looking for the man's credit cards or passport, but by looking for last minute passengers buying tickets out of the area. The man had used a fake name and had bought passage on a train at the last minute hoping to escape. He had not escaped Wolff. It wasn't the leopard that Wolff had spotted, but its effect on the environment around it. The grass pressed up against its body was stiff in the wind while the grass around it swayed freely.

"What do you think will happen, Mr. Kingsley?"

Wolff didn't answer. They both knew what was about to happen.

The leopard pounced and the gazelle bolted, but it was too late. The life giving water proved to be the gazelle's death. Its eyes filled with fear as its hooves dug deep into the soft bottom of the pool and its step faltered. Immediately the leopard was upon it. Even from their distance

Wolff could see the white of the creature's teeth as they flashed and sank deep into the gazelle's neck. The gazelle thrashed, but the leopard dug its claws in deep. They crashed into the shallow water, and within moments, the predator dragged its prey onto dry land.

"Have you ever wondered what it is like to be stalked, Mr. Kingsley?"

Wolff glanced at the man and said, "I'm not sure I know what you mean."

"Oh, I think you do. The question is simple. Have you ever stopped to wonder what it is like to be stalked by a killer? A killer that you know is relentless? A killer whose sole purpose is to end your life? A killer filled with an instinct that makes avoiding him impossible? Make no mistake, Mr. Kingsley. You are not the gazelle. Can you imagine the fear?"

Wolff stared at the man. "What's the significance of this? Shouldn't we be discussing the Counselor?"

"We are done with the Counselor, for now. You have broken through that wall. You have only two remaining obstacles, and facing both are for your own good. Alone, either one of them may prove fatal for you. Good luck with this one."

Confused, Wolff looked back to the leopard and then to the man again. The man was gone. The doorway and his stone prison were also gone.

The leopard growled deeply.

The sound chilled Wolff's blood. Slowly, he turned and found the leopard was only a few feet away. Blood from the fresh kill dripped from its jaws, only it wasn't a gazelle's blood. It was a young dark-haired man that Wolff had killed in South Africa. The body's throat was ripped out, and his eyes stared blankly up at the sky. It had been an unusually violent kill. The man had pleaded for his life. He had cried and prayed, but it had all fallen on deaf ears. In the end, he had fought back violently, and nearly won. The leopard stepped over the body and crouched in the grass to growl up at Wolff.

Wolff took a step back. He didn't want to believe in the danger the cat posed, but Diamond had told him that things around him were not a dream, that they were real. His senses had confirmed that things were real too. He had felt the coolness of the water, and the burning of his face. He had seen the darkness of his cell slowly retreat from the spreading light of his understanding. He had felt sorrow over his mother's death for the first time. He had felt hunger from days of captivity. He had felt the cold hardness of his cell's floor, and the downy softness of his mattress. He had experienced change by shaving. These things had all been real, and that meant the danger before him was real too.

The two slowly circled each other. A chill spread across Wolff's back and breathing became difficult. His vision grew dark along the edges, and the swaying of the grass made him nauseous. He tasted bile, and began to sweat despite the cool breeze. His heart pounded in his chest, and the leopard's growling was the only thing he could hear.

This was the fear felt by his victims. He could not even remember experiencing it as a young soldier on his first battlefield. The feeling of hopelessness from being trapped in his cell was nothing compared to this. This was worse, much worse.

He tried to swallow but found he couldn't. The fear had paralyzed his throat muscles. His legs were weak and he stumbled in the tall grass. If the feeling of numbness continued to spread, he would be easy prey for the leopard.

In the end, the dead man lying in the grass had turned his fear into desperation. Wolff knew that when faced with danger, the fight or flight response kicked in. His experiences had taught him there was a third alternative, to succumb to the danger, to give in, to lie down and die. Those that froze always succumbed to the danger. Those that found desperation panicked and fled, or they used it to fuel their fight. The young man he had killed had used it to fuel his fight.

Trapped in his own mind, Wolff had nowhere to flee to. If the watering hole was deep enough, it might allow him temporary escape, but Wolff suspected the leopard would simply lie in wait for him. Diamond had said he had to face this and Wolff doubted he would change his mind. That meant he was left with either succumbing or fighting. Wolff was determined not to die so he began to search for a way to fight the creature.

The trees were too far away to allow for safety, or to provide some sort of weapon. If he could reach the center of the pool, perhaps it would be deep enough to at least slow the creature down and give him an advantage.

The leopard growled deeper and bared its fangs.

As Wolff back-stepped into the pond, his foot sank into the soft mud. Without hesitation, he took another step. The leopard slowly followed. After only a few steps, the water came up to Wolff's knees and the leopard's belly. The mud and water slowed him but it didn't slow the beast. Wolff feared he had made a mistake in choosing the pool.

His leg brushed up against something in the water. Glancing down, Wolff saw a gnarled old tree lying beneath the surface. He started to dismiss it when light glinted off something metal buried in the mud next to it. Wolff thought of what his counsel had said early on in their meetings.

*I am a man of considerable resources and I can provide those resources to you...I can give you weapons you'll need, but I can't wield them for you. In the end, I cannot free you. Only you can do that.*

Before Wolff could decide what to do, he stumbled and the cat reacted. It leaped, but Wolff recovered quickly enough to dodge to the right and avoid the creature's dangerous claws. Wolff twisted around to face the cat again. In the deep water, it turned slowly to face him.

The cat didn't fear him and was playing with him. Its show of superiority caused Wolff to feel small and helpless. It further fueled his fear, and exposed a feeling of loneliness. Loneliness was a feeling that had always poked through the Counselor's programming but never enough to push him into action. It had always remained a small nagging that left him with the knowledge that he was going to die alone and with no one to cry over his coffin.

*You don't have to be alone, Wolff.*

The voice startled him. Like all the sounds he heard in this place, it originated from inside his head. It was female and the scent of flowers accompanied it. In it he found the sense of safety that had saved him from the mental assault.

Wolff took his eyes off the leopard long enough to look for the metal object in the water. It glinted brightly back at him. Using it would be pulling on his council's resources. Wolff feared it would tie him to the man, and he didn't know who the man was; but he didn't see any other option.

It took Wolff several moments to inch his way to the object. He faked another stumble to fool the cat into attacking and used his dodge to scoop the object up from the mud. As he turned to face the leopard again, he found himself clutching a long metal knife. Its bluish blade glinted in the light of the sun.

Armed, Wolff felt safer. He took several deep breaths to ease his fear and to push through the adrenaline-fused haze that threatened his vision. The beast advanced on him and he stepped deeper into the water. Sensing that the deeper water and the knife gave Wolff at least equal standing, the leopard hesitated. It slashed at the air between them with its claw, but when Wolff didn't give up his advantage, the leopard advanced again.

Wolff resisted the urge to attack. The leopard was still quicker and stronger so Wolff waited for an opening. Each step took him deeper into the water and increased his advantage. The beast didn't like the deep water, but it also didn't like its prey inching away either. Wolff remained patient, and allowed his training and instincts to take over. He knew the leopard would soon get tired of the game and attack. When it finally did, he would be ready.

After several tense moments, the leopard bared its fangs and growled deeply. The predator reared up on its hind legs and slashed at the air. Wolff dodged the attack, but before the leopard came down, he stepped under it and threw up his arm. The monster's teeth sank into the flesh of his forearm as the creature's weight crashed down on top of him. The two plunged beneath the water, and Wolff shoved his knife into the creature's underside beneath its right armpit. He twisted the angle of the knife and drove it deep into the creature's rib cage, and into its heart.

Despite the water, Wolff could feel the creature's lifeblood flowing over him from the deadly wound. The warm blood pushed the chill of the water aside as it spread, and the leopard's heart beat fast against its chest in rhythm with Wolff's own heart. Together the two hearts slowed. Their thundering softened until they beat as one. The still water grew dark and their indistinguishable hearts grew still.

Peace settled across the savannah and the sun sank beneath the horizon to plunge everything into deep shadow.

\* \*

*It's time*, Wolff told himself without glancing at his watch. Despite his focus on the upcoming battle, he heard the footsteps approaching this time.

"See grandpa. I told you there was a man."

*Damn*, cursed Wolff.

"You are trespassing! And judging by your outfit, you are up to no good. Leave here at once!"

The man's voice startled Wolff. He hadn't heard it in years. Against his instinct, he turned to face the man. Standing before him was his father. He was angry and held his walking stick high in the air, ready to strike Wolff with it. The small boy peeked out from behind his grandfather's legs.

Felix Kingsley was stooped with age and dressed in a pair of baggy tan pants and a blue striped shirt. He wore the same light tan sweater he had always worn to fight off the chill while working. Perched on the end of his nose was his old warped pair of wire-framed glasses. He held his smoking pipe in his left hand. He had given up smoking long before Wolff had gone off to college, but he had never been able to shake the habit of holding onto the pipe. His hair was thin and white. His face was unshaven and lined with wrinkles.

*Boom!*

The house shook as timers expired and a series of explosions went off in the basement. Explosions immediately followed them on the first floor, and then on the top floor. Wolff didn't have time to consider a reply to his father.

Felix pulled the boy close as the house shook violently. Fire erupted around the corner behind them, and they disappeared in the inferno.

Jolted by the heat and noise, Wolff turned and fled as the fire raced toward him. The heat scorched his back as he ran down the short hallway toward the doors at the end. He opened fire with both of his pistols, and despite the rumbling house, the soldiers returned fire. The fire chasing Wolff consumed what the bullets didn't destroy.

The doors exploded outward, blasting everyone with glass and debris. The soldiers dove for cover as the flames enveloped them. Wolff was flung from the fireball to sail over the balcony. An airship hovering above the museum was engulfed by the fire and exploded. Shrapnel pierced Wolff's left side and he was sent tumbling out of control into the churning surf far below.

\* \*

Wolff crashed to the stone floor. He lay stunned for several moments before finally rolling over. Pain shot through his side and he winced. He coughed, and blood splattered the stone around him. Sweat glistened across his naked body and he struggled to catch his breath. His left arm ached, and bled where the leopard's fangs had ripped his flesh. Blood flowed freely from the shrapnel wound in his side. He was covered with bruises and cuts.

His father and the boy had been real. He had killed them both. At the time, standing before them, their deaths had meant nothing to him. Even in his flight to freedom, he had been more concerned with the Counselor's betrayal. Now that he was finally free from the man's influence, the emotions of what he had done, not only to his father and the small boy, but to countless others, came crashing down on him. Overwhelmed by emotions Wolff hadn't felt in years, he curled into a ball and wept.

*   *

"Wolff Kingsley, stand up."

Wolff heard the voice, but ignored it. He didn't care what they did to him now. Not even death was lower than he felt at that moment; it would have been a release.

"Wolff, please stand up."

It was the first time the voice had made a request. It was still feminine but it no longer sounded hollow or mechanical. It was the voice that had offered him safety. Slowly, he responded and sat up. The bleeding of his wounds had subsided, but they still burned with pain.

Glancing around, he saw that he was back in the round room. The single light illuminated it, but the walls had retreated completely into shadow. The floor around him was wet with a mixture of water and blood. The chair was gone.

As Wolff struggled to his feat, footsteps echoed in the chamber and his counsel walked up next to him. The man's face was no longer shrouded in darkness. He was in his sixties but his face was free of wrinkles. Wolff knew him instantly. Samuel Joseph Diamond was a very rich and powerful man. Obviously he was more powerful than most knew.

"What you have experienced here may prove more than you can handle, Wolff. You haven't experienced deep emotions since you were a boy. The Counselor kept them bottled up inside you, and it made you a different man.

"You won't remember all of this at once. After you wake, it will come to you over several days. Take it in slowly and digest each piece. Hopefully, you can adjust to it. If you can't, it will kill you."

The man held out his hand, but Wolff ignored it. Turning, he started across the room and forced a door to open in the darkness ahead of him. Bright light flooded the room. Without looking back, Wolff exited into the light.

# CHAPTER 5
# DIAMOND SECURITY SOLUTIONS

Aegis inhaled deeply and the smell of flowers and grass filled his nostrils. He allowed the breeze blowing over him from the garden below to cool him before turning and starting toward an elevator. As he approached it, the doors opened automatically. Without hesitation, he entered and pulled a small handheld computer out of a belt pouch. The doors closed and the screen of the sidekick lit up to display a list of names along with the status of each one. Aegis easily found the name of the individual he was searching for, and as usual his status was unknown. "Damn," Aegis cursed.

Slipstream rarely showed up for mission briefings, and with him it was tolerated. Slipstream and Diamond had a special understanding, but that didn't mean Aegis had to like it. Even if Slipstream was the most powerful man on the planet, it still strengthened the team to have him show up for team briefings. Aegis hit several keys on the computer's screen and set it to automatically record the briefing and to forward it to Slipstream's commlink. He knew the hero could listen in even if he wouldn't show up.

Aegis tapped the screen again and the display changed. "Butch," he said aloud. Instantly the computer sent a ping to Butch's identical device.

*Shring!*

In response to the soft bell, Aegis tapped his device and Butch's face appeared on the screen.

"Yeah, boss?" Butch said.

"Team briefing in the ops center in five. Can you be there?"

"Can do," replied Butch.

"Good, see you there," said Aegis. The screen went blank.

Butch wasn't a field agent but he served as the team's primary pilot. The last report Aegis read on the *Egress* indicated there was some mechanical problem with the pod. He wanted an updated status and he wanted it directly from Butch. No one got a better response from the pods than him. Aegis couldn't explain why but the pods just seemed to like the man.

Aegis exited the elevator. His blue metal boots gleamed yellow in the Citadel's bright light and echoed through the Citadel's sterile corridors. His blue pants were loose and functional, and a gray metallic chest plate mostly hid his matching blue shirt. Atop his head was a matching gray helmet. A utility belt with several compartments was cinched around his waist. Inside the pouches Aegis kept a variety of items experience had taught him he just couldn't do without. Among the items were a small tool kit, a flashlight, video and audio recording devices, first aid equipment, a re-breather with two minutes of fresh air, and several small mini-grenades. His DSS sidearm hung from the belt. It was one of the most advanced particle weapons money could buy and Aegis liked the fact that he could adjust the power settings to suit his needs. The *Aegis*, his shield and legacy, was strapped to his back.

As usual heads turned to watch him as he passed. Despite having been a hero all of his adult life, he had never gotten used to the fame, and doubted he ever would. He wondered why his co-workers considered him a celebrity. Most of them possessed amazing abilities of their own. They could bend steel bars in their bare hands, or calculate the quantum signature of the universe with a piece of paper and a pencil; yet, they still acted like dreamy eyed kids when he walked by. He just didn't get it.

As he approached a t-port, the doors opened automatically and he stepped aboard. Within moments, the doors cycled and he exited into the briefing room.

Even though he hadn't summoned half the people present, the room was full. Keeping a mission secret was like keeping a developing movie out of the hands of its fans. It just didn't happen. Given the importance of this mission, he was surprised the room wasn't bursting at the seams.

As Aegis was about to address the room, Clara, who had been talking with Butch, thrust a sidekick in front of him and tapped the screen. He couldn't help but notice the sparkle in her eyes as she pointed at the device. Her eyes always sparkled like that, but to him they seemed unusually bright when she was speaking to him. Holding up his own sidekick, Aegis reviewed the roentgenogram image she sent him from her device.

"As you ordered, boss," said Clara.

"Thanks," replied Aegis. The live x-ray image showed a single figure moving about a very cluttered two-story structure. The image didn't identify what cluttered the house but it made a virtual maze of the interior. Aegis tapped the image, and it pulled back to show the estate surrounding the house. It was deserted except for the single figure. That matched the target's MO. Any target that could elude Diamond for nearly thirty years had to stay off the radar somehow.

Admiring the accuracy of the satellite image, Aegis started toward the front of the room. He was relieved to see that Clara had turned her attention back to Butch. The man had beat Aegis to the meeting. He obviously had been present before being summoned. Glancing around, Aegis noted nearly everyone had arrived ahead of him.

Stronghold's booming laughter immediately drew Aegis' attention. Even if the kid had been silent, which was extremely rare, he would have been hard to miss in any room.

Stronghold stood over seven-feet tall, and was as broad as an elephant. His body was covered in fine dark red fur that he kept trimmed short except for long tuffs along the sides of his chin, at his elbows, and on his wrists. Large incisors jutted up from his broad mouth. His ridged nose was large and flat. His overlarge ears were pointed, and a broad bold eyebrow overshadowed his small yellow eyes. His four well-muscled arms rounded out a monstrous appearance that only a mother could love. Stronghold wore a pair of black DSS uniform pants. His dark blue and grey uniform shirt had the sleeves removed and was open down the front. Stronghold was the team's primary muscle, and he was capable of squeezing the air out of a pair of diamond-crafted lungs with each of his four arms.

Stronghold was a good kid, if a bit naive at times, and his appearance gave no clue as to his attitude. He loved being a meta-human, and was rarely seen without a smile on his face. His bestial features initially startled anyone who encountered him. Over the years, he had learned to erase that fear through his behavior. Today most people saw him as a hero; especially young children. He made regular appearances on children's television programs, and often made personal appearances in children's hospitals. If the adults of the world tried to lock him away out of fear, their children would no doubt form a protective barrier around him.

Unfortunately, he was one of the youngest members of the core team, and his behavior often reminded Aegis of that. He was prone to clowning around and rarely took anything seriously. The more dangerous a situation was, the less seriously he took it. To Aegis, this was a poor quality in a soldier. Thankfully, the kid brought several positive qualities to the team. For one, he was capable of thinking outside the box. Unique situations rarely confused him. Perhaps this trait was due to his love of being a meta-human, or perhaps it was due to his extensive comic book collection. Either way, it was a unique asset. Of course, Aegis liked that he was loyal to a fault. The kid followed orders without question, and Aegis preferred loyalty to brawn in his soldiers any day. In Stronghold, he got both.

Paragon stood leaning against a wall with his arms folded across his chest. Even though the chairs in the Citadel had all been designed with his wings in mind, he claimed they were uncomfortable to him, and he usually stood during team briefings. Paragon's magnificent wings were white with light brown plumage and with a wingspan of twelve feet. They granted him the ability to fly. When unfurled, they made even the biggest skeptic want to believe in angels.

As usual, Paragon wasn't wearing a shirt, and his faded blue jeans sat loosely on his hips. He wore a pair of well-worn sandals, and his long wavy hair hung below his shoulders. The golden locks were the envy of many a young woman. Paragon had the slim well-muscled form of an Olympic swimmer. Only a single tattoo on his right deltoid marred an otherwise perfect body. The tattoo was of a simple Christian design that depicted a cross on a rocky hillside. The cross was slightly tilted to the left and was flanked by two smaller crosses.

It used to bother Aegis that Paragon never wore a uniform, much less clothing. A uniform was identity and unified a group in a single cause. Of course, Paragon had reasons for not wearing clothing beyond appearing as the sexiest man alive. He possessed a sword with magical properties and through it he could summon a suit of medieval armor to protect him. Thick clothing didn't fit well under the armor, so Paragon only wore the essentials.

Paragon was a little strange even among this crowd, but he was also one of the finest soldiers Aegis had ever worked with. Despite the fact that the young knight thought too highly of himself, and claimed to have known the legendary King Arthur, he was a damn fine warrior. Given that Paragon was a meta-human and King Arthur would have lived around the third to fifth-century, it was unlikely the two had met, unless one allowed for the possibility of time travel.

Aegis thought very highly of the young warrior, he just wished he could convince the knight to carry a sidearm along with his sword. Despite his eccentric behavior, there was no one Aegis would rather have guarding his back.

El Incindiaro was a man past middle age. He had disheveled black hair with streaks of gray spreading through it. His face was in need of a shave, tanned, and worn with years of battle. His eyes were dark, but sharp and never missed a detail. He was currently wearing a DSS field uniform with a dark blue jacket with gray padded shoulders and cuffs. Along the neckline, a black undershirt could be seen. His pants and boots were black. He wore a DSS sidearm strapped to his right leg. The DSS logo was emblazoned on the right side of the uniform's chest. From time to time, fire danced across his arms and torso. The dangerous element matched his fervent personality.

Incindiaro was currently arguing with a male technician, who Aegis knew had no business being in the room. Most likely, they were arguing about some conspiracy theory Incindiaro was currently troubled with. Incindiaro had more experience as an active meta-human than most of the team; but the man's desire to pin every wrong ever done solely on bureaucrats, was a concern. It was that paranoia that had originally brought Incindiaro to DSS.

Incindiaro had been Mexico's primary hero until he discovered government cover-ups and corruption that had resulted in the deaths of many young men and women, all to create him. As a result, he joined Diamond Security Solutions. It cost him a lot of prestige with his people, but Incindiaro had learned to live with it.

Over the last few years his paranoia had only gotten worse; and recently, he had even come into conflict with Diamond over it. Of course, Aegis knew it had only been a matter of time. When the Sons of Mars took Carol Estingdale captive, Incindiaro had stepped up like everyone else to rescue her. Unfortunately, he had learned some of Diamond's secrets during that incident. Incindiaro hated secrets, and the incident had left him with a bad taste in his mouth. Aegis hoped the two could come to terms before their dispute gravely affected the team. Incindiaro was a good man, and Aegis would hate to lose his experience; but Aegis knew Diamond would not tolerate El Incindiaro if he continued to cause conflict.

Envoy sat at the head of the room. She was dressed in a DSS field uniform that matched Incindiaro's. Her hair was cut short, like any good soldier, and she wore no makeup or jewelry. Her dark brown eyes darted from person to person. They only briefly met his before laughter across the room drew them away. Aegis knew she was running through the names of everyone in the room, and guessing as to who was supposed to be there and who wasn't. Her list would be more comprehensive than his. Aegis smirked briefly because he knew, if he hated groupies, Envoy loathed them. Yet her face never revealed her feelings as she assessed everyone, one at a time.

Envoy was his second-in-command; and next to Slipstream, the most powerful member of the team. Her right arm was bonded with an alien artifact that allowed her to channel energy on a scale that dwarfed a small star. She had served under him in the US Army from her first day in the field. Together the two had been all over the world, and faced nearly every danger known to man. When Aegis left the Army for DSS, he left Envoy in charge of the squad. Less than a year later, the squad encountered a metal alien artifact. The artifact became twisted around and through Envoy's arm, physically and mentally bonding her with it. She was left with little use of the limb. She couldn't move her elbow, wrist, and most of her fingers.

The Army had quickly learned the metal artifact was sentient. It resisted any attempts to be removed from Envoy's arm. Aegis and Diamond had called in numerous favors to get Envoy recognized as a person and not an item owned by the military. It was the first, and only time, Aegis had questioned his military superiors, and he had nearly torn a base apart searching for Envoy when she disappeared immediately following the incident.

Despite concern for her superior's motives, Envoy had remained with the Army until her original contract with them was up. During that time, she spent more time as a guinea pig than as a soldier. If they had treated her better, she would have remained. Aegis hadn't wasted a moment bringing her aboard DSS.

As for the alien metal, it responded to Envoy's mental commands, and was capable of communicating and controlling nearly any piece of mechanical or electrical equipment. In addition, the metal was intelligent and capable of independent action. It could project data and information across her vision, scan an area for life signs or energy readings, track a target independently of her, react on its own to defend her, and even move her if she was knocked unconscious. It swallowed any data it came in contact with like a black hole swallowing up light. Anytime it encountered a new computer it automatically downloaded all the information within the new source unless Envoy restrained it. This effect was a concern, and in the ten years Envoy had been bonded with the artifact, they had not determined why it did this.

Pulling on the metal's internal energy source, Envoy was capable of creating force shields, generating life support for interstellar travel, and of directing bursts of energy powerful enough to disintegrated objects it touched. The artifact made Envoy a very powerful meta-human, but it wasn't why Aegis had recruited her.

Envoy was the best soldier he had ever known, and she possessed leadership skills that were superior to his own. She was a natural tactician and he had recruited her to keep him, and Diamond, in check. She reviewed every order he gave, checked every detail of a plan, and evaluated every team member. She was ready to replace him, and he knew the day would come when she would do so.

Of the twenty-seven people in the room, Wavefront was the loudest, and rounded out the team's core. The Aussie was dressed in a pair of wrinkled black DSS field pants. His scuffed, untied and dusty boots were propped on the briefing room's central monitor table. The boots left the table's glass surface scuffed and dirty, but the documents related to the day's mission could still be seen and read. Wavefront's uniform shirt was nowhere to be seen and he wore an old brown leather vest over an off-white t-shirt. An image of a small white lab mouse with an overlarge head, and a taller mouse with its tongue hanging out the side of its mouth, was depicted on the front of the shirt. It had the caption, "*What we gonna do tonight?*", printed under the picture. Wavefront's trademark cattleman hat rested on the table in front of him. He was unshaven and his hair hadn't seen a proper cut in weeks.

Aegis never thought of Wavefront as a soldier, and never would. He was the best friend who slept on your couch and never went home. Aegis smiled as he remembered their first meeting.

While mourning the death of a fellow soldier, he and Envoy had gotten drunk in a bar they had had no business being in. When a confrontation broke out with the locals, an equally drunk Wavefront stepped up with them to challenge him and Envoy. Then, when one of the locals made fun of his Aussie accent, he had not only turned on them, but he had actually thrown the first punch. His drunken fighting skills proved even less effective than those of Aegis and Envoy. All three of them spent the night in the hospital emergency room trading stories all night long. After that, Wavefront had made himself a permanent fixture in Aegis' life; serving as best man in his wedding to Lauren, serving as a god-father to his daughter, Alexis, acting as a teammate in times of need, and being his best friend when Lauren had died. There was no one more loyal to Aegis.

Wavefront possessed the ability to see across a wide range of the visible and invisible spectrum. Invisible or camouflaged objects stood out to him. He could distinguish objects simply by their heat signature, view patters of radiation and energy that others couldn't, see things a mile away as if he held them in his hand, see in total darkness, and view things in detail down to their cellular level. He was even capable of seeing through solid objects. It made surprising him at Christmas and on birthdays nearly impossible. His hearing made it just as hard to keep secrets from him. He could hear sounds from greater distances, hear through sound proofed walls, and hear frequency levels beyond normal hearing. He never needed a device to pick up radio signals, and had even learned to *hear* the team's extra-dimensional commlinks as long as one of the devices was within a few yards of him. Wavefront's nose could detect and identify nearly any scent, and he could track a target through smell alone.

In addition to his meta-human powers, Wavefront possessed a belt of mysterious origin. The belt could project very powerful force fields, granted limited telekinesis, emitted a burst of sound that shattered objects and deafened people, and generate a burst of force that pushed objects away from it. Wavefront often joked that he had thrown the belt together from bits and pieces, but Aegis knew better. Wavefront was a techno-genius but the belt was alien in origin. Aegis was sure of it.

Several years earlier, Wavefront had simply disappeared while visiting his homeland of Australia. Aegis had searched for him extensively, but there had been no trace of him. He had always lived mostly off the grid, without credit cards or even a driver's license, but this time there was absolutely nothing. Even the Citadel computers had been unable to find so much as a glimpse of him on any traffic or security cameras worldwide. After several months, he had simply turned back up. He claimed he had been on a walkabout through the backcountry, but Aegis doubted his story because he had returned with the belt. Regardless of its origin, with it Wavefront could withstand a direct assault by an entire armada.

Now, despite his rough exterior, Wavefront served as the team's conscience, its computer hacker, and as its med-tech. Aegis made a mental note to be sure and pressure Wavefront to wear a proper uniform for the mission.

As expected, the last member of the core team wasn't present in the room. A quick glance at the monitor table showed him that Slipstream was currently crossing the Atlantic. Slipstream was a loner, but damn powerful, and extremely loyal to Diamond. Aegis knew what formed that bond. It was a secret more closely guarded than the President of the United States. Nevertheless, Aegis believed in team unity. Slipstream's lack of presence at important events undermined that. Unfortunately with him, Diamond tolerated it; and since he did, Aegis had no choice but to do the same.

To the world, Slipstream had been an active meta-human in some form or another for more than forty years. Aegis knew it was much more. He was the first of Diamond's meta-humans, and the most powerful. The Homeland Advisory System classified Slipstream as a rank two, red-level threat. There were fewer than a dozen or so meta-humans who carried that much power, and Aegis had witnessed Slipstream take two of the others down alone. When Slipstream unleashed his power, whole cities were in danger of dying. Thankfully, he had learned to hold himself in check. Fear of civilians being hurt was the only thing that Aegis had ever seen defeat the metal warrior.

Slipstream was barely human. His skin was covered in an unclassified blue metal. It gleamed like chrome and was denser than anything found on earth. His eyes were large and completely black. He couldn't see through those eyes, however. He was blind. Using a form of spatial awareness, Slipstream was capable of *seeing* up to two miles in every direction around himself. The detail was vague and there was no color, but Slipstream had come to understand it and to fully understand it. Through his eyes, he could project beams of energy that were some of the most destructive on the planet. With them, he could punch through mountains.

Surrounding Slipstream was a frictionless aura that prevented him from coming in contact with solid objects, but allowed him to manipulate his own gravity well. He could operate in nearly any environment without restraint, including zero-g, or within the high gravity of planets like Jupiter. He was just as comfortable *standing* on the ceiling as he was on the ground, or at the center of the earth; and he didn't need to breathe, eat, or sleep. He was also capable of traveling at speeds that exceeded mach ten. Aegis was glad he was on the side of the good guys.

Overall a good team; powerful, smart, and experienced. The best Aegis had had the pleasure to work with in over twenty years of service as a hero and as a soldier.

Despite its importance, the day's mission was expected to be simple, and Aegis had considered taking some of the lesser-experienced members. But after reading the mission specs, Envoy had put her foot down. Anytime one of the Nine was involved, Envoy expected the worst. Aegis had summoned them anyway.

The need for Shadow Spirit depended on the report from Butch. If Butch reported the *Egress* was fully operational, the Spirit wouldn't be needed. If the ship wasn't ready, then the Spirit would be used to teleport the team to the target site. Aegis hoped he wouldn't be needed.

The Spirit currently stood in the back of the room shrouded in his dark cloak. The shadows of his hood hid his ebony face from the bright light of the room. The corner where he stood was the only spot in the room where there were actual shadows.

The Spirit was a mystery to Aegis. He always remained beneath his dark cloak, and unless directly addressed, never spoke with anyone but Dreah. When he wasn't needed for a mission, he could be found secluded in his chambers. He wasn't human, that was about the only thing Aegis understood about him. His mere presence in a room reminded Aegis of that. According to Dreah, the Spirit betrayed his people to obtain his mastery over shadows, a forbidden magic to his people. When he was caught, he was tortured and branded with skin as black as obsidian to forever mark him as a traitor. If the story was to be believed, he spent the next thousand years as a servant to his people to atone for his sins. If Dreah had ever revealed to Diamond how she knew the Spirit's story, Aegis was unaware of it.

Several months ago, the Spirit simply showed up in the Citadel, claiming that the darkness was spreading and he would be needed. Before that moment, no one or nothing had ever succeeded in locating the Citadel or penetrated its defenses. Only Dreah had prevented a dangerous flare-up by Diamond. Once he got over his initial anger, Diamond had found use for the Spirit's ability to breech dimensional barriers to go anywhere he wanted. The Spirit had asked for nothing in return for his service. Of course by keeping the Spirit close, Diamond kept the only being to ever penetrate the Citadel's defenses close at hand. Despite what Diamond may believe, Aegis doubted the Spirit was under his thumb.

Heather, or Fluxstone, wasn't a member of the core team, but only because she chose not to be. However, she never missed team briefings. Heather served as Diamond's right-hand and thus, nothing went on in the Citadel that she didn't know about. She owed him her life and never failed to follow his orders. Also, as the chief public relations officer for all matters involving DSS, she often needed briefing information. Briefings supplied facts that would be needed by the press, or they contained vital data that was best kept out of the hands of the public. Either way, only by attending the briefings could Heather keep track of which was which and serve as Diamond's voice.

Glancing up, Heather's eyes caught his and she smiled. Aegis smiled back as his heart jumped a beat. Due to work, he hadn't seen her in a couple of days. As her fiancée, he couldn't help but marvel at her beauty. As always, she sat straight backed in her chair as she reviewed documents in front of her. She was wearing a red business jacket and skirt. Her shirt was white and a loose button at the top revealed her large breasts. She wore light red lipstick and only a touch of eye shadow. Her blond hair was cut short, and Aegis could see she wore the simple diamond earrings he had bought her during a private weekend shared by them in Monte Carlo. Even from across the room, Aegis could smell her usual perfume.

To most, Heather would never win a beauty contest. She wouldn't be labeled as ugly, but she was as tall as a man and nearly as broad shouldered. She was not slim, but well muscled from years of working as a meta-human operative. She didn't walk with poise and grace, but with purpose. To Aegis it didn't matter, he was in love and she was beautiful.

Q-Zone, Aegis hated that moniker, sat next to Heather and was making every attempt to speak with her. She was doing her best to ignore him even as she smiled at Aegis. Q-Zone wasn't dressed in a typical team uniform. It was the same basic design but the colors were different. Instead of dark blue and gray, the jacket was burnt orange across the shoulders and a lighter blue across the chest and sleeves. It had a large collar and had only the top two buttons secured to allow it to flare open just below his chest to further reveal the black undershirt beneath. The pants were a matching blue and his boots were black. It was only one of several color combination that the kid often wore. He usually topped it off with the dark shades he was currently wearing. The endorsement from the sunglasses had earned him millions.

Q-Zone was a prime example of just how deep Diamond's pockets were. When the kid had first come on the scene, he had quickly come into conflict with DSS, and had single handedly defeated an entire field team. Aegis had argued against paying the kid a multi-million dollar salary, but in the end Diamond had paid it. So far the salary had only served as an insurance policy to keep the team from having to face the kid in the field because Aegis had so far refused to assign him to a field team. To Aegis, money didn't buy loyalty, and it was not a reflection of positive character. Q-Zone was arrogant, failed to follow orders, took every opportunity to showboat, and embraced the life of a celebrity. The sunglasses were just one example of that life. Over all, Aegis didn't consider Q-Zone team material, and as long as Q-Zone wasn't complaining and Diamond was satisfied, it would remain that way.

Nevertheless, Aegis couldn't help but shudder at the kid's level of power. His ability to manipulate the time-space continuum was beyond anything Aegis had ever witnessed. In the blink of an eye, he could walk across the country. As he was often fond of doing for any lady who caught his eye, he could cause a flower to bloom for a hundred years, just for her. When he sat his mind to it, Q-Zone was capable of just about anything. Even with a limited range on his powers, he was one of the most powerful beings on the planet, and Aegis couldn't help but fear him.

The twins were known as Duo. They were dressed in DSS field uniforms and each of them wore a DSS sidearm. Brian and Kandi were like a set of magnets. Even now, he was on one side of the room and she was on the other. Together, they were working to control the chaos their powers created when they were in close proximity to each other. Oddly enough, it was also this repulsion that enhanced their telekinetic abilities. The closer they were, the more powerful they were, but also the more turmoil they created around themselves. The static was often powerful enough to send cars flying or to crack concrete walls; but when they worked together, it was powerful enough to topple skyscrapers.

Kandi had been a hero for several years. She had started her career as a sidekick to Lady Cobalt. It was illegal for underage children to act publicly as meta-humans, but it wasn't the first time Lady Cobalt had violated such laws. Even now Lady Cobalt continued to operate unsanctioned by the government. As for Brian, his powers had manifested later than Kandi's, and coincidentally, it had been during an outing with Lady Cobalt that Kandi had rediscovered her long lost younger brother. Use of her powers caused his to manifest. Now they worked for DSS, and only Brian's lack of experience kept them off a core team. It was a decision Aegis was ready to reverse, and why he had them attend team briefings.

Carol Estingdale rounded out the last of the people Aegis had summoned. It was due to her work that today's mission was possible. She didn't know it yet, but she was present for a specific reason. Aegis knew she wouldn't like it when he sprang it on her.

Aegis couldn't help but like Carol. She was shy, smart, friendly, and would give you the shirt off her back while asking for nothing in return.

She was the proverbial girl-next-door that all guys ignored until it was too late, and Carol had grown only more charming as she had aged.

She was an archeologist who specialized in early colonial America and was more at home pouring over dusty books in dimly lit libraries than she was traipsing around the world as a superhero. Given her unique abilities, Diamond found this disappointing. He had originally recruited her for her archeological skills, but he would have preferred to take full advantage of her powers. To Aegis, that just wouldn't have been Carol, and Diamond's money hadn't been able to change it.

Carol possessed a unique energy that manifested in ways only limited by her imagination. The pink energy took on physical forms like the ones you would expect to find in a children's faerie-tale book. But more importantly, they took on personalities and remembered things that they had experienced in a previous summoning. Each one was different and adored her. Aegis had witnessed small pink faeries buzzing around her like busy worker bees, he had seen small fire-breathing dragons that acted like jealous cats when anyone got near her, and he had seen her ride upon the back of a winged unicorn that had more nobility than any king. Her powers were the closest known meta-human powers to generating actual life. The team had come to lovingly calling her Dr. Dweomer, but Aegis doubted she would ever fully embrace that life, and it made him respect her all the more.

Other than Butch and Clara, the rest of the people in the room were various scientists and minor team members who possessed too much security clearance for their own good. Some, like the lab tech Wavefront was flirting with, were more akin to groupies.

As Aegis reached the end of the table and the podium, his hand instinctively found Heather's for a brief moment. Also instinctively, it quickly released hers. Public display of affection when in uniform was something the military frowned on, and it was an old habit he found hard to break. Of course, Heather's usual demeanor about such things was even stiffer than his so it never created a problem for them, or prevented them from showing affection when they were alone.

As he sat his helmet on the table next to the podium, Aegis said, "Everyone out. If I didn't summon you, get out." Grunts and grumbling filled the room at the command. Everyone had known Aegis would issue it, but they put on a show of protesting anyway.

Only Kahori didn't react to his order. She was speaking with Kandi and pretended not to notice. Aegis considered confronting her directly but decided against it. Kahori had the run of the Citadel and there was no secret she didn't already know, or could get anyway.

Kahori was only eighteen and Diamond's goddaughter. She had grown up around Aegis and the team. To everyone she was a little sister, and even though she wasn't an official member of DSS, she wanted to be. Everything she did was to earn her that position. Aegis had no doubt she would succeed some day. Instead of removing her, he decided to find a use for her.

As everyone crowded the door to exit, Aegis saw Meta-man waiting patiently just inside the entryway. He made eye contact with Aegis and smiled. Despite the briefings importance, Aegis hadn't expected the hero to make it. Being the leader of the United Nations International Taskforce kept Meta-man busy. UNIT was often deployed to some remote corner of the world dealing with an international incident. The political fallout was often worse than the incident itself.

However, Aegis also knew that Meta-man wouldn't want to miss anything involving the Nine, especially the Missing Man. Meta-man was the world's oldest operating meta-human. He was also one of the most popular in the U.S. He had served openly during both World Wars, and often operated as a special advisor to the White House on meta-human affairs. In the sixties, he had helped set up the Homeland Security Council's advisory system on meta-human operatives. He had been the US representative to UNIT since its founding. Meta-man was well known in almost any circle. What wasn't known was that he was also one of the Nine, the world's very first meta-humans, and he was over four hundred years old.

Meta-man was among a small number of people not employed by Diamond who knew about the Citadel's existence, and he was the only one who could come and go unescorted. Meta-man's refusal to accept Diamond's methods formed a barrier between the two, but Meta-man's contacts and Diamond's resources gave them both reasons to maintain their association.

Along with the ability to fly, Meta-man possessed vast super-strength and a physiology that adapted to his environment. It made him highly resilient to attacks as his body adapted to them and prevented further damage. In addition, he was capable of mimicking the meta-powers of those around him. These abilities combined with his vast experience, gave reason for Aegis to fear battle against him more than he did against Slipstream. Meta-man had an understanding of how to best utilize meta-powers that far exceeded anyone else, including Diamond.

As Meta-man approached Aegis, his patriotic metal costume gleamed in the light, and he appeared every bit the hero he was. The red, white, and blue outfit was just as much a symbol for Meta-man as it was for the country. As a boy, Aegis had watched his exploits on TV. He might have still had one of his old action figures tucked away in a shoebox somewhere. When Meta-man finally reached him and extended his hand in greeting, Aegis couldn't help but feel like one of the groupies he hated.

"Alex," said Meta-man.

"John, glad you could make it." The two shook hands. To Aegis, Meta-man looked just as majestic in person as he did on TV. Even so, Meta-man always treated him as an equal when shaking hands, and as a leader when serving as a team member.

Without another word, Meta-man took a seat next to Envoy. She immediately handed him a computer with documents related to the mission. He wouldn't interfere with the briefing. Despite his personal interest, Meta-man was an outsider to Diamond Security Solutions and knew Aegis was in charge. If he objected to something, he would say so privately to Aegis after the meeting.

As everyone sat quietly waiting for Aegis to begin, he tapped several buttons on the podium and instantly the wall to his right changed from a rich wood paneling to a series of images that completely covered it. The images displayed data on the weather, the target, the location, and each team member.

"Our primary target is here," he said as he pointed to the imaging wall. The room grew quiet and all ears tuned to Aegis.

As if reading his thoughts the images on the wall adjusted. A map zoomed from an orbital shot of North America to a close up view of a mansion located near Williamsport, Pennsylvania, and to the grounds surrounding it. Like the earlier image from Clara, the image was live. A second image rotated a three hundred sixty-degree view of the house. As it moved, the computer automatically highlighted potential entry and exit points.

"The residence is listed to one Charles Stein. Unfortunately, we have no picture of Stein. It appears he has never been photographed. In fact, from what we can tell he has never left the estate grounds. We don't know who he is, or where he comes from. We wouldn't even know that he is at the estate if it weren't for the live satellite feed. He has no driver's license, and his English birth certificate is a fake, as is his father's. The man doesn't exist."

Everyone looked confused but waited patiently for Aegis to continue.

"You all recall that several months ago we encountered the Sons of Mars." Several members of the team become visibly angry at the mention of the mercenaries, and Carol turned pale. Aegis couldn't blame them. Carol's abduction by the meta-human mercenaries had been a trying time for them all. He wasn't the only one who thought of her as a sister. "Fortunately, we were able to recover Carol without sustaining serious injuries. We were also able to assist her in completing her mission to acquire the Dare Diary. As many of you know, Carol had been searching for that diary for years.

"The diary proved to be the missing link we were looking for to meta-humans. It confirmed our suspicions involving Roanoke Island. By combining the intelligence we gathered from the Sons of Mars with the information Mr. Diamond learned from the creature known as Fetch, we have learned of Mr. Stein. After working through a series of dummy corporations and false names, we have determined he owns the Renaissance Corporation, or at least his family does. Our search for the diary seems to have pulled him out of seclusion, and we got just enough info to find him." Aegis paused; he knew his next words would light up the room. "The complete relationship is still unknown, but we suspect that Charles Stein may be a lead to the Missing Man."

Everyone turned from the monitors to Aegis, including Carol, whose mouth fell open as she did so. Buzzing filled the room as everyone tried to speak at once.

"Hooly dooley!" shouted Wavefront.

"We didn't piece it together until recently. We want to talk to Stein, or whoever is posing as him. We are looking for any information he may have about the origin of the Dare Diary, and the Missing Man."

"It's about time!" exclaimed Incindiaro. "We've been chasing that ghost for years. I'd begun to think he was a figment of Mr. Diamond's imagination."

"Are we sure?" asked Carol.

"Yes," replied Heather, "and if he is connected to the Missing Man, we may be able to confirm the last of the bloodlines."

"I've never understood why that is so important anyway," said Stronghold.

"You wouldn't." Incindiaro jeered. "If it isn't smothered in butter or layered with chocolate, you don't understand it." The room burst into laughter.

"Stop! We are not going down that road today." Aegis was determined to keep the meeting in line in front of Meta-man. "Let's be serious. The bloodlines are connected to all meta-humans; you, me, all of us. They trace back to the very first meta-humans, the Nine. Through them we have a better understanding of ourselves, and gain the ability to predict who has the potential to develop meta-powers. As you know Mr. Diamond is convinced there is some purpose to our creation. By tracking the bloodlines, he hopes to find that purpose."

The buzzing in the room picked up again as Incindiaro smiled and held out his fist for Stronghold to swat with his own. The two were buddies and Incindiaro's comments hadn't angered the kid.

Turning to Carol, Aegis continued, "Carol, I want you with us on this one. If Stein is a connection to the Missing Man, your knowledge could prove useful, and your understanding of the diary could be important."

"Me? Are you sure?" Carol responded. She trusted his judgment, but Carol was confused as to why Aegis would ask her to come along. "What about Dreah?" she asked as she looked around the room, noticing for the first time that Dreah wasn't present.

"Dreah has other matters that require her attention right now." He was grateful she hadn't openly objected. He continued without giving her the chance to do so. "Butch, is the *Egress* operational?"

Butch stepped forward from the back wall. "Hard to say, boss. As you know, the tech has been stubborn. I don't like the length of time it's taking the inner doors to seal. All readouts are good, however. I'm pretty sure the problem is connected to the emergency override system."

"Can we use it?"

Butch knew Aegis was looking to him for a judgment call so he made one.

"Yes, boss, we can."

"Good, get her prepped and in-route to Pennsylvania as soon as possible." As Aegis paused to shift his notes, Butch exited the room. The wall images shifted again as he continued. "As for security, the estate appears to have none to speak of. There is a perimeter wall but it is in disrepair. Satellite imaging is picking up limited electronics." The image revealed a dull gray image of the house. Except for a series of power cables that extended from the edge of the property to a room in the basement, there were no areas highlighted. "There is electricity but it appears to only be in use in this single room in the basement. The house is heated by fireplaces and lit by candles and oil lamps. Stein appears to be the only occupant."

"What's the plan, boss?" asked Incindiaro.

"We go in soft, Paragon, Carol and me. The rest of you will wait with the *Egress*. I want Stein on the friendly side. I want a simple question and answer session."

He paused and looked out across the group. "Any questions?" Aegis cursed under his breath when Kahori's hand shot up. He had forgotten to address her.

"What about me, Aegis? Do I get to go? The mission seems pretty straight forward, so it's probably safe enough."

Aegis turned to Kahori and smiled. "Sorry, Kahori. You still aren't cleared. However, I would like for you to do some more digging on Stein. If there is anything on him out there, I'd like you to find it. Stand by in the operations center for easy contact in case you come up with anything." It was an assignment that any operations technician could handle and Aegis doubted the young girl would be fooled by it. To his disappointment, she wasn't.

"Is it my age? I turned eighteen two months ago. I'm a legal adult now, you know."

"Kahori, you know mission clearance comes through Heather and Dreah. Once she clears you, we will discuss it. Anyone else have any questions?" Aegis didn't pause long enough to give anyone the opportunity to actually ask. "Good, meet at the pod chamber in twenty minutes."

As everyone rose to leave, Aegis dodged Heather's glare and turned his attention to Meta-man. Kahori made a beeline straight for Heather.

"Are you coming, John?"

Standing up, Meta-man responded, "As important as this mission is, I can't. We have an issue brewing between the Central African Empire and Cameroon. It's some kind of border dispute. Kilimanjaro feels that we should intervene before the situation escalates, and I'm inclined to agree. I just wanted to hear what you had to say, and to read these." Meta-man held up the small computer Envoy had given him. "It's pretty conclusive. Do you think he is the Missing Man?"

"I'm withholding any conclusions for now, John, but evidence indicates that he is connected to him somehow. Are you sure you don't want to come along?"

Meta-man smiled at Aegis. "I'll have to trust you to handle it, buddy."

Aegis smiled back. He knew how much Meta-man hated dealing with CAE. The Negus ruled it. He was extremely powerful and insane, and that was not usually a good combination. The first and only time the two had clashed, the Negus had defeated Meta-man and the rest of the UNIT field team sent to stop him.

The Central African Republic had been embroiled in a civil war for years. The world begged the United Nations to intervene as civilians were caught between the two warring factions and hundreds were being slaughtered each day. Meta-man and a peacekeeping force were on the border and eager to intervene, but politics kept them out. Suddenly, the Negus appeared on the scene and singlehandedly defeated both factions in a single day. He publicly executed all the leaders and threw their supporters to the people like scraps to starving dogs. He claimed the throne for himself, denounced the lack of action by the United Nations, renamed CAR the Central African Empire, and created a political nightmare for the world. Eventually, Meta-man and his team were ordered to intervene. They lost. Now, CAE was a nation to be reckoned with. It was prospering under the Negus, and even though he ruled harshly and absolutely, the people loved him and followed him eagerly. To the people, he had saved them while the rest of the world had stood by and done nothing. Aegis knew that despite his personal interest in the case and in the Missing Man, duty would keep Meta-man away.

"Duty before desire. The curse of a soldier. Good luck with the Negus."

"Don't worry. We aren't looking for a fight this time. It's Cameroon that's stirring up trouble and it is not very wise of them. I have some down time put aside. As soon as we get this mess with the CAE sorted out, I'll take it and return to see what you've come up with."

Aegis slapped his friend on the shoulder and Meta-man turned to leave. Meta-man still held the sidekick containing the Missing Man documents but Aegis didn't ask for it back. If necessary, he would deal with Diamond over it later. He turned to find Envoy waiting for him.

"Any questions before you go, Envoy?"

"Just one, sir. What's the deal with Dreah? Given this involves the Missing Man, I'm surprised she isn't here."

"She's with Diamond. She didn't tell me what they were doing, but I suspect it involves our guest in the infirmary. You know how Dreah likes strays. I assume it is also why Glip-2 isn't here."

Envoy's brow furrowed. "But the importance of this mission, Alex. One of the Nine! We have been looking for this man for years."

"I know. I found it hard to believe too. Something about this man has her attention."

Envoy shrugged. "Okay, any last orders?"

"No. See you in Pennsylvania."

"Very well, sir. I'll head out immediately." Envoy turned and headed for the exit.

Turning to Heather, Aegis found she had finally pried Kahori's claws from her arm. "Sure you don't want to come along? We haven't seen each other for a couple of days, and you've been a part of this for as long as I have."

"Longer than you," corrected Heather as she poked Aegis in the chest. "You'll have to bring back the big man's info without me. I've got to deal with the fallout from the little she-devil going to him. Again. And the next time you throw me before her like that, I'll beat you silly."

"Heather, Kahori is a resourceful girl. She is strong, intelligent, and has the right qualities for this. We aren't going to keep her grounded forever. Lock up a teenager and you're guaranteed to get just the opposite of what you want." Aegis took a step back as Heather threatened to take a swing at him. "Hey, I support you and the old man does too. She is still too impulsive for fieldwork. I'm just warning you what happens when a teenager gets restless."

Sarcastically, Heather replied, "Thanks for the advice, father-of-the-year."

Aegis flinched. "Ouch! Sore subject."

"Sorry." Heather looked genuinely remorseful. "Okay, just remember I'll kick your butt next time." Heather looked frustrated and crossed her arms under her chest.

Aegis smiled. "You sure there isn't another reason you don't want to come along?" Heather's glare deepened. "He is unconscious you know."

"I don't trust him. He is why I've been so busy lately. I don't care what Dreah says. I don't think he belongs here. He's dangerous and unstable. We can't trust him, and as long as he's here, we're all in danger. Alex, if you would just look over the file I'm sure you would agree with me."

"Whether I agree with you or not doesn't matter. Diamond will make his decision with input from you and Dreah. Don't fret so much about it. Look, I've got to get prepped. We'll talk when I get back."

Aegis kissed Heather briefly and turned to leave. When he glanced back, she was still scowling but she had turned her attention to some document displayed on the conference room table. Most likely it was connected to Wolff Kingsley.

\* \*

There was no doubt about it, Aegis hated what others had come to call shadow-sliding; yet, he could not deny that it was the quickest form of transportation available to a field team. It took longer to gather a team in the pod bay than it took to complete a slide. Its accuracy was even better than its speed. Shadow Spirit simply locked on to someone he knew and teleported everyone to their location. Today that would be Envoy. With her speed she would be in Pennsylvania by now.

Using Shadow Spirit caused Aegis concerns about the team's security. If the Spirit ever left Diamond's employment, there would be no way of stopping him from tracking any of them. Aegis trusted Dreah's instincts, but he still didn't like the secrets surrounding the man.

The team was gathered in the pod bay by the time Aegis arrived. Jonesy was arguing with Butch and the rest of the team was looking on with amused smiles. The two men were standing over Butch's

*Harley-Davidson* motorcycle. The pearl and grey bike was in pieces and spread all over the bay. Glancing toward the *Egress* doors, Aegis saw the readouts of the monitors indicated the systems were normal.

It was hard to call the *Egress* an airship. It was actually a room of the Citadel that wasn't directly attached, and it could be moved. Once it was in place, the doors were opened and you walked from the Citadel into the ship, and then out of the ship to your destination. Aegis left the complicated extra-dimensional physics to the scientists. He tried to think of it as a teleportation gate, but even that made his head hurt. Teleportation was an extremely complicated science.

"Gentlemen," Aegis interrupted them.

"Hey boss, *Egress* is fine. The readouts were fuzzy when I first got back down here, but they are fine now. I'd been in Pennsylvania by now if it wasn't for Jonesy-boy here picking a fight."

"He doesn't know!" Jonesy pleaded. "He's been working on his bike, not the pod."

"Yes I do, and no I wasn't. I know this tech. It's fine. She's fired up and ready to go. I was just about to head out when Jonesy-boy showed up and picked a fight." Butch took a step forward. "He is lucky he hasn't gotten what he wanted."

Jonesy took a step back and glared at Butch. "He is no scientist, Aegis. Let me check it out."

Aegis grunted. He had little patience for wasting time with arguments; quick decisions usually helped him avoid them. Cutting off the argument, Aegis said, "Jonesy, take a quick look at the readouts. If you find anything unusual, let me know." Butch started to protest but Aegis held up his hand to silence the man. "A fresh pair of eyes may spot something you've overlooked." Butch held his protest as Jonesy moved around him to the control console. It took longer than Aegis would have liked for Jonesy to finish his inspection.

Jonesy frowned and looked to Aegis, and then Butch. "All systems are registering normal."

Butch smirked. Aegis ignored it, but Jonesy scowled.

"Butch, you know the location. Head out. I want this mission dealt with so we'll shadow-slide there. Envoy should be on scene by now. We'll have the *Egress* on hand for the return, or in case backup is needed. Jonesy, I want you to stay on standby in the operations center." Aegis turned away from the two men and said, "Everybody get ready."

Everyone was accounted for except Slipstream. Incindiaro and Stronghold were engaged in some argument, most likely one of Incindiaro's conspiracy theories. With reading glasses perched on the end of her nose, and a lock of brown hair tucked behind her ear, Carol flipped through a book. Paragon stood with both hands resting on the hilt of his sword. Twitching for the freedom of the open sky, only his wings moved. Classical music punched through his wireless headphones. Paragon was a strange mix of the modern and ancient worlds, with a whole lot of chivalry thrown in. Wavefront was just the opposite of Paragon and paced with unease and boredom.

Within a few minutes, Envoy reported that she had arrived, and the team gathered for the shadow-slide. Silently, Aegis wished for the comfort of the *Egress*. The temperature was always seventy-two degrees, fresh air breezed through the cabin, the seats were plush, and no matter how fast it traveled, it felt like you were still sitting on the tarmac. The ship flew at speeds no terrestrial craft could achieve and it held an entire field team. Butch was currently developing four more pods. Aegis had no idea how far along that project was and he didn't even claim to understand it.

As everyone gathered around Shadow Spirit, Aegis couldn't help but dread what would come next. As far as comfort was concerned, shadow-sliding was the yin to the ship's yang. As shadows engulfed them all, the room faded from view.

The darkness was the worst part and the part you experienced first. Nothing was darker than the Spirit's cloak—not the bowls of the earth, not blindness, not the vastness of space, nothing—and Aegis had experienced them all over the years. There was simply no light within the cloak and it scared him beyond anything else he had ever experienced.

The cold came next. It wasn't the sharp sting experienced from the opening of a sub-zero freezer, but a slow bone-numbing chill that seeped into the bones and hung on there for hours afterward. It reminded Aegis of too many lonely nights spent on guard duty during cold wet winters.

Aegis allowed himself a smile as his mind raced through the effects of the shadow-slide. Time was different with each one. Others never spoke of this part but Aegis experienced it each time. Even now he was beginning to feel like he could have recited Homer's *Iliad* and still had time left over for a cup of coffee. Sometimes a slide seemed that way; sometimes it seemed as quick as a blink.

Jonesy insisted the effects Aegis felt were just tricks of his mind. He claimed that a person was suspended during a slide. That his mind didn't exist; so there was no way he could experience the darkness, the cold, or the time distortion. How could his mind not exist yet play tricks on him at the same time? To Aegis it confirmed that there were some things that science just couldn't explain.

# CHAPTER 6
# THE MISSING MAN

The team appeared next to a large tree. As his eyes adjusted to the light, Aegis saw Envoy shudder. She stood before him with Shadow Spirit's cloak flowing from her shadow. She never complained about being used as a mark for the Spirit, but Aegis knew she hated it. She had the same reservations he did about the Spirit's loyalty. Their current mission wasn't time sensitive so perhaps he should have waited for the *Egress*. Aegis had come to rely on Dreah's instincts so much over the years that he often failed to stop to consider how others were affected. It was a way of thinking he would have to reverse.

"Control, status on Only Child?" Aegis asked into his commlink.

"Only Child is in route. He's tearing up the countryside to get there, boss."

"Roger. Status green." Kahori had exaggerated. Slipstream was fast, second only to Envoy, but he had no wake. He didn't create so much as a whisper when he moved. As for Kahori, she shouldn't have even been on the commlink. Of course, he would have to give Clara or Curtis a pass. It was his fault she was even in the command center. "By the numbers, folks. Carol, Paragon, with me. Paragon, we don't want to spook the man. The rest of you remain here. When Butch arrives, tell him to keep the *Egress* warmed up."

Aegis headed for the gate. Without speaking, Paragon thrust his sword into the ground. It gleamed in the sunlight as he left it there. He would be able to instantly recall it later if he needed it. Carol hesitated, but followed when she received a nod from Envoy.

Aegis pressed the intercom and waited patiently. After a minute he pushed it again. After another minute, he began to get irritated and pressed it harder.

H-hello?" The voice that issued from the old box was muffled and static filled.

"My name is Aegis. I'm with Diamond Security Solutions. I'd like to speak with Mr. Charles Stein, please."

"Huh, why?"

"The matter is confidential. I'd like to speak with Mr. Stein about it directly, please."

Only static issued from the intercom.

Frustrated, Aegis stepped forward and leaned into the box. "Hello? Did you hear me?"

Finally the voice returned.

"Hum, well, let's see...Mr. Stein is busy right n-now. Could you come back another time? Tomorrow, perhaps?"

"No," said Aegis. Irritated, he glanced around at the others. Paragon was unfazed by the delay, and a large insect buzzing around her head distracted Carol. Looking to Envoy, he held up one finger and then two. "One or two?" he said softly before turning back to the intercom. "This is a vital police matter, and I know Mr. Stein is present in the house. I can get a warrant to take him into custody if necessary, but I would prefer to just speak with him." The warrant was a bluff. Aegis had no probable cause for one, but he hoped the man on the other end of the intercom didn't know that.

"Into custody? Oh my! Th-th-that wouldn't be good at all. Hold on."

As they waited, Envoy stepped up next to Aegis and pointed at her sidekick. The image of the house still showed only one person inside. "Control, Wavefront, and I still agree that there is only one occupant."

Aegis nodded and turned back to the intercom. Grunting, he pushed the button and said, "I'm out of patience. Open up the gate now or I'll knock it down."

Carol glanced at Aegis in shock. As the lock on the gate clicked,

Paragon glanced at Envoy and she shrugged. The trio started through the gate.

The place was deserted and the old buildings dotting the grounds were dilapidated. The fields were overgrown with weeds, and rotted fruit lay under the trees. There were no footprints or car tracks in the road, and the grass hadn't been tended to in years. The footsteps of the heroes kicked up a cloud of dust as they walked in the hot sun.

Glancing around the estate, Aegis stumbled when his foot caught on a large rock jutting up from the road. "Damn," he cursed as he checked his boot for a scuff. He only managed to get his hand dusty.

Paragon waited patiently for Aegis to continue up the road. After a moment, Aegis cursed and then continued the march. "You seem unusually agitated today," said Paragon.

Aegis glanced at his friend and then at the house that now loomed over a rise in the road.

"Sorry. I've got a lot on my mind."

Paragon smiled. "I do not mean to judge you my friend, but I am concerned."

"I know. It has just been stressful lately. Mr. Diamond has been distracted, and I don't mean just by the man in the basement. He's neglected some routine duties that I've had to pick up. I fear his voices are plaguing him."

"They are. And Heather?" asked Paragon.

"You know me too well, my friend. Heather has been badgering me over this wedding thing. She hates the planning, but she can't stand the thought of it not being completed. She's determined to find an exotic destination for the honeymoon. Work has prevented us from seeing each other long enough to talk, and her disagreement with Mr. Diamond over Wolff Kingsley has really been bothering her." Aegis waved his hand at a large buzzing insect to shoo it away from his face. "Of course, I've been to almost every corner of the world, so Heather's search for a honeymoon location isn't going well. Which only irritates her further. She wants to go somewhere *special*."

Paragon smiled again. He knew Heather well enough to know that she would be stubborn about such things. It was well known that she was one to become irritated easily. As for Diamond, he too had noticed that things were not right with him. Diamond's breath held the odor of alcohol almost constantly now. His grip over the team was slipping and Diamond didn't seem to notice.

"Any concerns with the mission?"

Aegis sighed. "No. Trust me, friend, it's mostly personal. In fact, I look forward to a challenging mission. Maybe even a good fight. Thank you for your concern, but I'll be fine."

"Careful what you wish for."

The two men chuckled and continued up the path in silence.

The thought of the upcoming celebration for Aegis and Heather made Carol sad. She was happy for them, but as she was now thirty-five, it made her feel like an old maid. As a kid, she had always pictured herself with a white picket fence and several small children. It was something she had once desperately wanted, but she had spent much of her youth poring over old tomes in dark libraries. As a result, she had missed out on the socializing that formed relationships. At the time she had told herself that she was young and that she had plenty of time. Now that time had slipped by, she was left with regrets.

Paragon's flexing wings drew Carol's attention away from her thoughts. She had noted years ago how he constantly flexed them, especially when he was under the open sky. She knew he was more at home in the sky than on the ground. He loved to fly.

Under the light of the sun, Carol marveled at the soft sheen of his feathers. Each one stood out and appeared radiant to her. Slowly she traced them to Paragon's broad muscular shoulders where his golden locks drew her eyes. Thoughts of his soft hair caused warmth to spread through her.

Suddenly, Carol tripped on her own foot and stumbled. Both men quickly turned to face her.

"Carol, are you alright?" asked Aegis.

Embarrassed, Carol realized the warmth that had spread through her was still present in her face. Shyly, she pretended to adjust her hair while hiding her cheeks with her hand. "Fine, I'm fine, Aegis. I just stumbled on a rock. I wasn't watching where I was going."

Satisfied, the two men turned and continued toward the house. Carol quietly followed.

The house was a crumbling three-story colonial mansion. The grimy windows were large and covered with thick curtains. The porch arched over the front yard but had holes in it, and it creaked loudly when they walked upon it. Little paint remained on the building's sides, and the roof was in desperate need of repair.

When they reached the front door, a man opened it before they could knock. He was Native American, old, and dressed in a suit that matched the colonial setting. He admitted them without speaking. Paragon frowned when he passed the man. Noting Paragon's expression, Aegis loosened the straps holding his shield on his back for easier access and watched the man more intently.

They were led into a dark foyer where the man gestured to Carol's sweater. She graciously declined, and pulled it closer around her. The sun outside had been unseasonably warm, but the shadows inside the house gave her chills. When the man turned to Aegis, he shook his head no. He only had his shield, and he wasn't about to give it up. Paragon had nothing. Aegis was grateful he was at least wearing a shirt, even if he was still only wearing a pair of sandals. The shirt was also a DSS uniform shirt, an added bonus since Paragon claimed the material made him itch.

The man led them past a grand stairway and into the interior of the house.

Thick curtains covered the large windows. Made darker by layers of dust and cobwebs, shadows clung to every corner. Oil lamps lit the rooms and cast a sorrowful mood over everything. The air was filled with the smell of dust and the exotic scents of burning oils. The floors were wood and well worn.

The house was cluttered, Aegis knew no other way to describe it; but strangely enough, the clutter had order. Stacks of books, newspapers, magazines, paintings, pottery, and other types of artwork sat everywhere.

Carol's breath caught in her throat when she recognized art coated in dust that had been lost to the world for generations. To her they were like drowning children crying out for her to save them, and it pained her to leave them to the horrors of the dust.

The stacks of clutter had larger books or items on the bottom, smaller objects on top. Many were color-coded. There were works of fiction, encyclopedias, old school textbooks, biographies, and works of nonfiction. Many appeared ancient, and Carol cringed when she found a stack clearly a hundred years old with candle wax clinging to their delicate spines.

They were led to the right through a doorway. The next room was no different. Only the large fireplace along the left wall was devoid of the organized clutter. They passed through a door beside the fireplace and into an even larger room. This room was two stories tall, and its walls were lined with bookshelves. Even more books were stacked all around the room. One corner of the room was completely hidden by a wall of stacked books. An area in front of a large bay window was the only part of the room free of clutter. A single sofa and an overstuffed chair with a small table between them sat in the area. A single book lay on the table next to a large oil lamp that burned brightly.

The man never spoke a word and closed the door behind himself as he left. Ever the vigilant guard, Paragon took up a position near the door while pointing out a second door in the far corner and a third door on a balcony overlooking the room. Aegis nodded and moved over to the bay window. He pulled the curtain aside to allow light into the room. Dust showered him. Carol tried to examine everything by the dim light.

"Paragon, what disturbed you about the butler?" asked Aegis.

"He was not there," replied Paragon.

"And that means what?"

Paragon shrugged. "Hard to say. He wasn't undead, but he was definitely of the spirit world. I have a feeling I have met him before."

"Understood. Envoy," said Aegis into his commlink. She responded immediately. "Give me an updated status on number of occupants for the residence."

"Just four. You, Carol, Paragon, and our target, who is currently on the second floor."

"Rescan, please," replied Aegis. "We were let in the front door by an elderly butler."

After a short pause, Envoy replied, "Readings are the same, Aegis. There are only four signatures. Wavefront agrees. Control, your assessment?"

"I confirm, only four people in the house. No other bio-energy signatures anywhere on the estate." replied Curtis.

"Copy," said Aegis. "Paragon said he was a spirit and he seemed familiar. Stein may have abilities of a magical nature. Envoy, keep the guys on their toes."

"Roger," replied Envoy.

"Roger," replied Curtis.

"I think I saw a Gilbert Stuart in the foyer," said Carol, changing the subject as she picked up the book from the small table and carefully opened it. "This book was printed in seventeen hundred and thirty-nine. Amazing."

"And dusty."

Carol smiled at Paragon and continued her forage. Paragon watched over her. Despite his jest with Carol, he was tense and his eyes studied every detail of the room. It was unlikely anything would escape his notice.

Suddenly Carol gasped. Aegis was across the room and beside her before she could speak. His shield was thrust between her and the wall of books before her. Paragon stepped forward. His corded muscles tensed and his wings flexed.

Behind the books was as a fifteen-foot bronze statue of the Minotaur. Its Greek design was as out of place in the colonial mansion as clown at a funeral. The statue's tarnished metal was well worn and pitted with age. Numerous scratches and dents marred its surface. The monster bulged with exaggerated muscles, and horns as large as a man's leg swept outward from its forehead. The tip of one of the horns was missing and the horn ended in a jagged break. The legs of the thing were bent backwards like an animal's, and it had massive cloven hoofs. The metal behemoth's right hand rested on a large battle-axe with a head larger than a man. The blade was as tarnished as the rest of the statue and had a large chip along its edge. The floorboards beneath the massive statue sagged and were cracked.

"Impossible." Carol ran a hand along the rough metal. "I'd swear it was authentic, but I've never heard of one surviving that is anywhere near this large."

Suddenly, Paragon moved and was standing next to Carol and Aegis. Aegis reacted and stepped before Carol. The *Aegis* was held before him.

The man on the balcony appeared startled by the sudden movements, but he recovered quickly.

Nodding at Carol, he said, "You have never heard of one that large at all, Miss Estingdale." His voice cracked with age when he spoke.

\* \*

"What's happening?" asked Envoy.

Wavefront didn't answer right away. "They are in a large room on the backside of the house. I can't locate the man Aegis says led them there. Bloody hell, this place is cluttered. It's screwing with my depth perception. I think they are examining a stack of books, but I'm having trouble making out what's behind them."

"Keep an eye on them. Control, this is Envoy. Status green."

The glow of Wavefront's eyes intensified as he adjusted his vision to keep tabs on the party.

"I'm bored." Stronghold sat under a tree with his chin resting in his large hands. "And I'm hungry."

"We follow orders."

"Easy for you to say, you don't have the appetite of a whale."

"Rations are on the *Egress*."

"You ate twice before we left," remarked Incindiaro.

Stronghold smiled, and grunted, at Incindiaro as he rose and entered the ship.

Incindiaro turned to Envoy. "Leader-man isn't the best negotiator. Didn't he start a war once? Perhaps you should be the one in there."

"Don't sweat it, Basilio. He'll do fine. He chose Carol and Paragon because he isn't looking for a fight." Envoy didn't feel as confident as she tried to sound.

\* \*

The old man was stooped with age. He wore a ruffled colonial outfit with dark pants and black boots. In his right hand, he held a small glass that contained ice and a caramel colored liquid. He took occasional gentle sips from it.

Without moving, the man glanced around the room, and then settled his gaze on Carol. "Born of Pasiphae and the Cretan Bull. Cursed due to his father's greed and his mother's sexual sin, or so some legends say. When it comes to Greek mythology, the stories are so modernized it's hard to know for sure."

As the man started down the stairs, his eyes darted between his three guests and the room around them. They never lingered on anything for more than a moment. As the man approached Carol, his eyes briefly met hers, and he extended his hand to her. "I assure you, it was crafted long before the fall of the Roman Empire, and it is more authentic than the shield carried by your friend." As Carol shook the man's hand, his eyes darted to and lingered a moment on the *Aegis*.

Aegis reflexively shifted the shield away from the man. His free hand gently touched its metal surface.

His eyes back on Carol, the man smiled and continued. "Charles Stein, pleased to meet you, Miss Estingdale, graduated George Washington University, *summa cum laude*."

Stein then turned to Aegis and extended his hand to the hero. Aegis hesitated, but Stein only smiled at him and waited patiently with his hand extended. Aegis glanced at the man's hand and watched as it began to twitch slightly. Just as Stein's eyes darted to a stack of books and he started to turn to them, Aegis grasped the hand. Stein was instantly pulled back to the conversation by the grip. Despite the man's age, Stein had a strong firm grip

Looking Aegis in the eye, Stein said, "Alexander Diogenes, born of Zeus, son of the second Aegis, and his lovely wife, Artemis, also known as Theodore and Kristina Diogenes."

When Aegis released his grip, Stein turned to Paragon. "Of course, let us not forget Sir Lawrence Pentacle, knighted by King Arthur himself. It is an honor, Sir Knight." Stein slightly bowed his head at Paragon, but he didn't move across the room to shake the knight's hand. Paragon nodded his head in acknowledgement.

"You know us."

Turning back to Aegis, Stein said, "Of course, Mr. Diogenes. Come, sit."

Stein moved across the room and sat in the large dusty chair with his back to the bay window. Carol slowly sat across from him on the couch. Paragon remained by the door. Aegis approached the couch, but didn't sit. Stein obviously knew more about them than they did about him. It put them at a disadvantage.

After a moment, Stein smiled at Aegis and again said, "Please, Mr. Diogenes, sit. You have exactly six minutes thirty-two seconds to tell me why you are here."

Aegis frowned. "What happens in six minutes thirty-two seconds?"

"Six minutes twenty-nine seconds. Time is always moving, Mr. Diogenes. But to answer your question, you will leave."

Aegis moved around to the front of the couch, but still didn't sit.

Carol glanced up at him, but Aegis hadn't taken his eyes off of Stein. She turned back to their host and found the man's eyes darting around the room. He seemed to have forgotten all about Aegis, even though the hero still towered over him. After a few moments, Carol cleared her throat to draw Stein's attention to her. When the man's eyes locked with hers, she waved her arm around her and said, "How did you come by all this? Some of it is… priceless."

Stein looked confused for a moment and then he caught sight of Aegis and quickly recovered. "Priceless?" He said. "No, no, my dear. Nothing is priceless. You only have to accept what is offered. But as for all this, I've been collecting for some time. My father before me, his father before him."

Stein's clothes were dirty and wrinkled. Age had brought a twitch to his left hand, and thinned his graying hair. His teeth were yellow and crooked, and Aegis could smell his breath from where he stood. Oddly, Stein continued to be distracted, as if he were listening to two conversations at once. Each time silence settled in the room, the man's thoughts were pulled elsewhere. Only by engaging him directly, could Carol hold his attention. Aegis doubted he was the Missing Man. If he was, he didn't share the same longevity that the others shared. Stein was at least eighty years old.

"If you know us, then you know why we are here," Aegis said.

"Of course. I feared you would come months ago. But just in case I've missed something, Mr. Diogenes, humor me. Six minutes, eleven seconds."

"Very well." Aegis said. "Recently we found a diary that used to belong to someone we know."

"Unlikely." Stein locked eyes with Aegis. A look of intense anger flashed through them. "The owner of that diary died many years ago. It has been in my family's possession ever since." Stein's face relaxed, and his eyes left Aegis to jump around the room from object to object once again. As if seeing Paragon for the first time, Stein mumbled one hundred seventy-four.

"Then you know of which diary I speak."

Distracted, Stein didn't respond right away. When his eyes focused on the room again, he said, "Of course. It was mine, and on loan to a museum until you stole it." Stein glanced at a stack of books and mumbled again as he reached out and switched two of them in the stack.

Aegis stood. "We made an offer..."

Stein's eyes darted to him. "Which was refused. Now, please, Mr. Diogenes, sit down. Five minutes forty seconds. I can assure you, I am no super villain seeking to destroy you with an army of minions, or a set of complicated diabolical deathtraps."

Hesitantly, Aegis sat down on the edge of the couch next to Carol.

"Better. Now, please continue," said Stein.

"If you claim the diary, do you also claim connection to the Sons of Mars?"

"Sons of Mars, the Mamertines, mercenaries of Italian origin, around three hundred BC, fought in the First Punic War. No. I'm afraid I am not that old, despite what you may think of my appearance."

Stein was breathing heavily and sweating profusely.

"The diary, Mr. Stein," said Carol, "it described a remarkable event. An event that others have claimed knowledge of, but none has ever proven. The events described in that diary changed human destiny."

Stein didn't reply. Aegis doubted he was even listening. He had never encountered behavior like Stein's. Perhaps, Stein was under some form of mind control by the Missing Man.

"That event created nine extraordinary people. We know who five of them are, and we have been able to track several others through history, through their descendants." Stein's eyes met Carol's and lingered there. "Mr. Stein? One line remains hidden."

"Six hundred twenty seven," he mumbled with a look of fright. His twitching hand had spilled his drink in his lap, but he had not noticed. His eyes darted from Carol back to the room.

Concerned, Carol eased back on the couch, and glanced briefly at Aegis. She could see doubt in his eyes that Stein was the Missing Man. She felt otherwise. Stein's behavior was odd, but she could easily think of a dozen different psychoses to go with his recluse behavior to explain it. "We also don't know why, Mr. Stein. Why did it happen? What purpose does it serve? Do you know?"

Stein stopped again, and glared at her. For a moment, he focused on her. "No purpose you can understand." Suddenly he got to his feet and crossed the room. Leaving it open, he exited the door opposite

Paragon. As he went, he mumbled loudly to himself. He called over his shoulder, "Three minutes six seconds." Paragon started to follow, but Aegis stopped him with a wave of his hand.

Stein stopped before a stack of books and took two from it. He readjusted the stack and entered the library again. He placed the books on the table before Carol and then climbed a ladder. He pulled a book from the top shelf, and then he moved the ladder and pulled another book from halfway up the wall.

"Two minutes twelve seconds." Stein arranged the books on the table from largest to smallest, and then he opened two of them at the same time using both hands. The twitch of his left hand slowed him, but he managed to get both books open. As he flipped the pages, his eyes danced over the books and he continued to mumble. Finally, he tapped each book with his fingers. Then he repeated the process with the other two books.

"Here, my dear. If...If you want to know about genealogy, these books will help." Mumbling to himself, Stein turned away from Carol and stumbled across the room to the large bay window. Carol had to strain to hear what he was saying. "Gregor Mendel, Wilhelm J-Johannsen, Hermann M-Mu-Muller, early ex-experts in the fi-f-field. As for them, there is nothing. I made sure of that..." His last words were lost as he rustled the curtain covering the large window.

Carol picked up one of the books and scanned the page as Stein stood facing away from them, still mumbling. She then scanned the page from the second book. With a look of surprise, she turned to Aegis. "He's quoting the pages. He's quoting from all the books at once, Alex."

Having had enough of the man's eccentric behavior, Aegis activated his silent alarm. The yellow alert would bring the others without causing them to come crashing through the walls.

Aegis stepped forward. "What did you mean Mr. Stein, when you said, *there is nothing, I made sure of that?*"

Stein quickly turned on Aegis. The wild look in his eyes made Aegis think he was going to attack. The expression disappeared as quickly as it had come, and Stein slowly turned to Carol.

"My dear, I c-c-c-can assure you. That diary is utterly ridiculous. The events are absurd. No, no historical value whatsoever. The ramblings of a c-cr-crazy woman. One minute eigh-ei-eight seconds." His last words seemed almost like a plea to the heroes.

\* \*

"Move!" Envoy said. The activation of a yellow alert and the sudden disappearance of Paragon's sword indicated danger. The world around her blurred as the alien artifact on her right arm responded to her mental commands. She cleared the distance to the house in less time than it took her to issue the order to the others. Hovering over the house, she amplified the sounds issuing from inside. Other than the voices of Aegis and Stein, the house was silent.

"Stronghold, let's move!" yelled Incindiaro over his shoulder as he darted after Envoy.

Stronghold poked his head out of the airship and grumbled when he saw Incindiaro pushing his way through the gate. Wavefront was climbing over it. Stuffing a sandwich into his oversize mouth, Stronghold leaped from the ship. A second leap took him a quarter of the distance to the house.

Wavefront sat on the top of the gate and grunted as it swung open beneath him.

Incindiaro sprinted off after Stronghold. Wavefront started to descend but slipped and fell. His shirt caught on the fence and ripped. "Bloody hell," he mumbled as he dangled helplessly from the fence. A moment later the shirt finished ripping, and he fell to the ground. He scrambled to his feet and darted off after the others.

"Humph. Must'a stumbled upon a nest of angry hornets," mumbled Butch as he watched the heroes race off. Turning around, he started for the airship. He glanced at Shadow Spirit, who was still poised like Death beneath a tree. He started to speak to the man, thought better of it, and entered the ship without a word. The ship's systems responded to his presence and the door closed.

A moment later, Shadow Spirit melded with the shadow of the tree and somewhere near the house, Stronghold shivered as the Spirit emerged from his shadow.

\* \*

"Fifty-two seconds." Sweat dripped from Stein's nose.

Aegis was convinced the man suffered from mind control. If Stein was a meta-human intellect, his behavior was the strangest Aegis had ever encountered. Perhaps he could convince Stein to grant them more time. If that failed, perhaps he could convince Stein to speak with Dreah.

"B-before you ask, Mr. Diogenes. No. I n-never l-leave the house. M-Mike could you come in here, please? Our...our guests should be leaving."

*Telepathy*, Aegis told himself. *It must be some form of telepathy.*

"No, you only have forty-five seconds left. No more time. I-I am not reading yo-your mind either. One th-thousand six hundred twenty-one."

The door next to Paragon opened and the butler came in. The temperature of the room dropped noticeably. Sword in hand, Paragon turned to face the man. As he stared into the man's dark eyes, he couldn't shake the feeling that they knew each other. His breath formed a cloud in the air before him.

Carol stopped scanning the books and stood up next to Aegis. "You've muttered several numbers, Mr. Stein. What is one-thousand six hundred twenty-one?"

Stein didn't turn to face them. Something outside the window had his attention. He rubbed his twitching right hand and mumbled, "One-thousand six hundred twenty-o...one to one t-that you won't l-leea-leave. Thirty-five seconds."

"Mr. Stein..."

"No! Ms. Estingdale...you may not return later! Take the books and go, nothing more! Please! Please, go," he pleaded.

Carol held the books to her chest and glanced at Aegis. Aegis looked at Stein and then at the butler. The tension across the shoulders of Paragon told him they were in danger.

"Only Child on sight in t-minus ten seconds," said Kahori over the commlink.

Aegis tried to ignore her. He was at a loss. Stein was responding to his thoughts quicker than they occurred; yet, Stein denied reading his mind.

"Seven, six, five..."

Aegis wished Kahori would shut up.

"Drop it, Control!" Envoy interrupted and the commlink went silent.

Gripping the curtain tightly in his trembling hands, Stein stood silently before the window with dust raining down on him. Suddenly, he stopped shaking and mumbling, and stared out the window. His eyes grew wide with freight and spittle dripped from the corner of his mouth. "Mm...mm," he stammered and stumbled backward. The curtain ripped free from the window and Stein was sent tumbling over backward. He crashed into several stacks of books and scattered them across the floor.

Scrambling away from the window, Stein mumbled incoherently. Terror was etched on his face and tears streamed from his eyes. The tumbling books caused him to panic more.

Aegis leaped to his side and grabbed Stein's wrists. The old man fought against him with surprising strength. Concerned, Aegis glanced up and saw Slipstream through the swaying curtain. The metal warrior stood before the window with dark energy leaking from his large black eyes.

"V-v-vvvallo... mihi," Stein stammered. Spittle sprayed Aegis with each word. "Vallo m-mihi!"

Metal shrieked from behind the wall of books.

*Crash!*

As if desperate for freedom from eons of sleep, the Minotaur statue burst from the wall of books. As it moved, metal creaked and groaned, and mountains of books flew in every direction.

Screaming, Carol dropped to her knees and threw her hands over her head to shield herself from the books. Ignoring his own peril, Aegis leaped in front of Carol to protect her.

Paragon desperately wanted to turn to his friends, but forced himself to ignore the books pelting him. Fearing the man before him was the greater threat, Paragon kept his eyes locked on him. The butler also ignored the chaos enveloping the room and kept his eyes focused on Paragon.

The massive Bull glanced only briefly around the room before settling his metal eyes on Aegis. Even the movement of its eyes echoed through the room as they rolled inside its metal skull. Aegis stood over Carol and held the shield up to protect them. Metal creaked and groaned as the Bull swung its massive axe.

*Clang!*

\* \*

*Crash!*

The window shattered and Aegis hurtled past Envoy. "Some negotiator," she mumbled.

Energy leaped from Envoy's outstretched hand and the building's wall disintegrated. Easing forward, she peered into the darkness and barely dodged the Bull's deadly horns as it charged through the opening.

Slipstream didn't move from the metal monster's path, and the Bull's massive hooves trampled him into the ground.

\* \*

The sounds of battle behind Paragon gnawed at his soul. Unfortunately, Aegis would have to deal with it. The horror before him was far worse, and would consume them all if he turned his back on it.

"It has been a long time, knight," said Mike. The air around him grew colder with each word.

Frost formed on Paragon's sword. "I would not have expected to find you here," he replied as calmly as he could.

\* \*

Carol pushed books aside and looked around her. Behind her the Bull dominated the hole in the wall as it swung its massive axe at Envoy. She darted around the creature like an annoying mosquito stinging the metal beast with blasts of energy that left glowing red patches where she hit it.

Turning back to the room, Carol found Stein babbling and crying as he clawed toward a doorway. He continued to knock over stacks of books in his path. Carol raised her hand and three glowing pink lights floated in the air in front of her. A moment later, a single small faerie materialized out of each of the glowing lights. Their songs of admiration for Carol sounded like a thousand tiny bells. Pointing at Stein, she waved for them to follow him. They spiraled around her head and then darted after Stein as they giggled loudly and playfully. They left a trail of glowing pink sparkles suspended in the air to mark their path out of the room.

Noticing the fog of her breathing for the first time, Carol looked up in time to hear Paragon address the butler. His words chilled her more than the cold air surrounding her.

"Winter Eagle," said Paragon. Careful not to slip on the frost-covered floor, he took a step backward. "Why are you here, monster?" He raised his sword higher in defense. His wings flexed to better balance him on the slippery floor.

A glowing white light quickly spread from his sword, up his arm, and over his body. Once it had enveloped him completely, it flashed and was gone. Paragon stood before Winter Eagle wearing a suit of medieval plate mail armor. The steel armor was magically enchanted like his sword. It had a slight blue tint and covered him from his shoulders to his feet. He had chosen to forego the helmet, leaving his golden locks to fall loosely around his metal-clad shoulders. His wings extended outward behind him and caught the rays of the sun. He was the archangel Michael with the light of Heaven shining down upon him while he faced down the Prince of Hell.

Winter Eagle took a step forward and Paragon took a step back. Winter Eagle circled to the right but stopped when he saw Carol lying on the floor behind the hero. Carol was visibly shaken, and Winter Eagle could taste the fear in her heart. The air grew colder. "You know that no enchantment can stop the power of my touch. Your magical armor will not protect you."

"It doesn't have to," replied Paragon. "My sword will do that." To emphasize his words, he gripped the sword tightly with both hands, and leveled it at Winter Eagle.

Winter Eagle glanced briefly at him, smirked, and then looked back at Carol. "My business with the old man is none of your concern. Although I must thank him for giving me the opportunity to finally slay you." Winter Eagle blew gently on the air, and a cloud of cold rushed toward Carol.

* *

*Boom! Boom!*

As Envoy circled around the Bull and blasted it with waves of energy, Slipstream pounded it with his metal fists. The Bull's charge had not even fazed the metal hero. Now the shock waves from his blows caused the house to shudder and the ground beneath the behemoth to crack and split.

*Fathoom!*

Stronghold's leap brought him down on the Bull's head. The metal creature was driven to its knees by the impact but showed no sign of pain. Stronghold pressed his advantage with a series of blows that caused the bull to stagger as it tried to recover from the initial attack. Wildly it swung its axe.

Slipstream easily dodged the attack and returned with a blow of his own strong enough to rip a hole in the side of an aircraft carrier. He followed up with a blast of energy from his eyes that tore through the creature's metal chest, and out its back to slice a section off the roof of the house. The energy blast disappeared into the clouds hovering high overhead.

Shadow Spirit stretched his hands out toward the Bull and creature's shadow began to move independently of the metal monster. The shadow reached up to wrap around the Bull's limbs, slowing its movements. Sweat beaded on Shadow Spirit's forehead as he mentally struggled to restrain the creature.

\* \*

Carol screamed and covered her face with her arms as the cold air rushed toward her.

Paragon thrust himself before her and ice coated his metal armor as the cold enveloped him. He stifled a scream as the cold penetrated his body, and began to freeze the life out of him.

"Winter Eagle!" screamed Carol into her commlink when she realized Paragon had blocked the attack. She reached out with her hand and grasped his leg. The cold metal stung her hand. Carol's eyes glowed pink as she pushed energy through her hand and into Paragon. Together, they fought the deadly effects of Winter Eagle's icy breath.

Winter Eagle watched the two struggle against his attack and smiled at their desperation. It didn't matter to him if Paragon or the woman died first. It would bring him joy to witness Paragon's despair over failing to protect her. The guilt would crush the knight, and Winter Eagle would have thrilled at seeing it in the knight's eyes just before his death.

"Good," he mumbled as the two heroes began to defeat the attack. He wanted to relish the knight's death.

Taking a step back from his enemy, Winter Eagle summoned

the power within him. Euphoria washed over him. He hated being constrained to human form. It denied him the power and majesty of his true self. Winter Eagle's body faded and shifted into a large ghostly eagle with blue-fringed white feathers. Ice coated everything his incorporeal form touched.

\* \*

Startled by Carol's transmission, Envoy failed to dodge the Bull's axe. It left a gash across her left arm. Cursing, she rose higher in the air over the Bull. Another inch and the attack would have severed the arm. She could feel the artifact shifting energy to stifle the flow of blood. The arm would be so stiff tomorrow, she would barely be able to use it.

"Control! Red-level threat! Winter Eagle is on site! I repeat, we have Winter Eagle on site! Second subject is unknown and an unclassified threat!" The radio lit up with chatter as people responded to her transmission. Envoy knew the threat Winter Eagle posed and feared backup wouldn't arrive in time. "Spirit, engage Winter Eagle! Slow him down!"

Shadow Spirit hated taking orders from anyone, even when it was someone he viewed as an equal, like Envoy. Nevertheless, he dropped his control of the Bull's shadow and melded with it. Inside the house, Carol cried out as he pulled himself from her shadow.

Free from the restraint of its shadow, the Bull rose to its feet.

*Clang!*

The Bull's massive axe rang out as it cleaved Slipstream's shoulder. The hero was knocked to the ground by the attack, but never faltered with his own attack. Energy blasted upward from his eyes to rip through the metal monster's shoulder. Unlike the Bull, Slipstream felt the pain of his injuries; he just chose to use it to fuel his own attacks.

\* \*

Stunned, Aegis failed to roll with his landing, and now he climbed unsteadily to his feet. Incindiaro ran past him with flames billowing around him as he built them into an inferno. With a burst, the flaming hero lifted from the ground and soared through the air. His flames lit up the sky as he fired a second burst to soften his landing. Immediately, he launched himself into the air again. He couldn't fly, but by utilizing the burst of flames, he could clear large distances quickly.

As Aegis worked to catch his breath, Wavefront gripped him across the shoulder. "You okay, mate?"

As Aegis tried to choke out a response, he noted his friend's torn shirt and the large bleeding gash down his back. He raised his eyebrows in question, and Wavefront responded to the unspoken request.

"Never mind that, mate. Weren't me favorite shirt anyway. I see you took one for the team. Aye?"

Aegis managed a smile before taking a series of deep breaths and then charging after Incindiaro. With his speed, he easily overtook the other hero. With one great leap, he cleared the last hundred feet and brought his shield down on the Bull's head.

\* \*

Shocked to see the axe penetrate Slipstream, Envoy shouted into her commlink "Code red! We have a code red meta-threat! Unknown is code red!" Only half a dozen meta-humans possessed enough power to penetrate Slipstream's metal skin. The Bull was a new threat to add to that list.

As Slipstream's repeated energy blasts drove the Bull back, the hero climbed to his feet. For a moment, the two traded blows; and then the Bull stooped down, swung its massive axe in a sideways arch, and struck Slipstream solidly.

*Boom!*

Slipstream hurtled from the battlefield.

"Damn!" Envoy cursed in shock as she watched Slipstream disappear into the distance. Given his gravitational aura, he rarely took knock-back from a blow. It was testimony to the Bull's tremendous strength.

Turning back to the battle, she watched as the Bull slammed its massive fist down on Stronghold. The blow drove the kid to the ground. Incindiaro's flames engulfed the Bull's leg and after a moment the metal grew soft and started to buckle. Aegis took a step back and threw a bolt of lightning that struck the Bull across its face. Stronghold used the distraction to roll to his feet and move around behind the metal behemoth.

\* \*

Winter Eagle flexed his wings and hovered over the heroes. The freedom of his spirit form always excited him. Nothing, not even gravity restrained him.

Without warning, he swung one of his wings at Paragon. When the hero ducked the attack, Winter Eagle lashed out with his claw at Carol. She screamed and tried to roll out of the way. Shadow Spirit spread his cloak over her.

Even through Shadow Spirit's protection, Carol could feel Winter Eagle's cold touch as his claw passed over her. The Spirit didn't even shudder from the cold and Carol feared he might have even envied it. His cloak was nearly as cold as the monster threatening them.

Paragon recovered first and stepped bravely forward to swing his sword. As it sliced through Winter Eagle's wing, ice instantly coated the blade and Paragon's arm.

Winter Eagle screamed and pulled back from the heroes.

Ice cracked and broke free from Paragon's arm as he waved his sword at the creature, and said, "You never did like my touch any more than I liked yours, beast."

\* \*

Seizing the Bull around its waist, Stronghold heaved and pulled it over backward.

*Thumph!*

As the Bull slammed into the ground, its axe struck the house. The structure shook violently as wood splintered and cracked. Stronghold recovered from the grapple and pulled himself up onto the Bull's chest.

*Boom! Boom! Boom! Boom!*

With all four fists, Stronghold began to pound the creature. The Bull's metal buckled under the assault.

Without rising, the Bull swung its axe across its chest. Stronghold dodged the axe blade but the large shaft caught him across his forehead and sent him tumbling into the dirt.

Aegis avoided the return swing of the axe as he rolled away from the Bull. The hero came up on his knees and the hairs along his arm stood up as lightning tingled across his fingertips, and leaped across the ground to strike the Bull.

*Kaboom!*

The force of the impact caused the rising Bull to crash back to the ground.

\* \*

Pulling his cloak tighter around him, Shadow Spirit moved away from Carol to join Paragon. Winter Eagle floated in the air before them with his wings spread menacingly. Ice grew thick in the area around the creature as the temperature in the room continued to drop.

Screeching, Winter Eagle spewed a cloud of cold breath at Paragon. Shadow Spirit flung his cloak before Winter Eagle, and the icy death disappeared into it. Winter Eagle pulled up from his attack before he was also swallowed up by the cloak's darkness.

Paragon swung a wide arch with his sword and sliced through Winter Eagle's belly.

Screeching from the pain, Winter Eagle rose toward the ceiling and out of reach.

Carol was scared out of her mind as she watched the battle between her friends and Winter Eagle. She did her best to keep the two heroes between her and the evil creature. She had never even seen Winter Eagle before, but knew he was deadly. Usually nothing less than an entire field team faced off against him.

"Aegis," she pleaded, "We need help in here!"

\* \*

*Kaboom!*

Aegis threw another bolt of lightning at the Bull as Carol's plea came over the commlink. He felt a pang of guilt for dragging her into danger. She wasn't used to battles with super villains, and Winter Eagle was one of the worst. Envoy had been right to worry about the mission.

Quickly running several battle scenarios through his head, he responded. "Water, Carol! Drown him in an ocean of water!" Winter Eagle had never successfully been stopped before, and it had been several years since anyone on the team had faced him, but Aegis had included battle plans for the meta-human into training sessions. Unfortunately, the scenario he was suggesting was untested.

\* \*

Carol glanced around the room and wondered where she was going to find a bucket full of water, much less an ocean. Suddenly, Envoy hurtled past her to crash into the room's inner wall. Fearing the worst, Carol darted for the hole and found Envoy already crawling from it. Envoy gritted her teeth as she pressed her hand against her side where blood seeped between her fingers.

Carol started to place her hand over Envoy's but the woman shook her head. "Don't worry about me. I'll heal." Glancing around, she watched as Paragon dodged another attack from Winter Eagle. "Find that water!" Not waiting for Carol to respond, she flew from the house to attack the Bull again.

Carol felt overwhelmed. She glanced around to see Shadow Spirit fail to block an attack with his cloak. He fell back clutching his frozen hand, and Paragon was left to face their foe alone.

\* \*

Wavefront activated his force field and darted beneath the Bull to Stronghold.

*Thoom!*

He ignored the metal monster's attacks as they bounced off his force field. Kneeling over Stronghold, he quickly scanned the kid using his small sidekick. Stronghold groaned as Wavefront touched the deep gash across his forehead. The kid wasn't unconscious yet, but the concussion would soon render him that way.

Wavefront pulled a small patch from a belt pouch and slapped it over the wound. The adhesive patch would act as a bandage while the nanites contained in the gel on its surface entered Stronghold through the injury. The gel would also serve to sterilize the wound. Each of the heroes already had just such a patch on them somewhere, including Stronghold, for a quick release if necessary. Wavefront had forgone using the kid's pouch since he was already next to him to prevent further attack with the force field. The kid's patch would still be available if needed in the future and Wavefront wasn't close to him.

*Thoom!*

As the nanites hit Stronghold's blood stream, some of them immediately began to stitch his wound. Some dispersed throughout the giant's body and began feeding Wavefront's sidekick detailed information about Stronghold's medical condition. Wavefront monitored their progress. Once he was satisfied their stitch would hold, Wavefront punched several keys on his sidekick and issued new orders to the nanites. The small robots injected a micro stream of chemicals into the young giant that quickly stimulated him. Stronghold's eyes fluttered opened.

*Thoom!*

Stronghold jerked fully awake as the Bull's large axe deflected off the force field right above his head. Wavefront grinned and continued to ignore the attacks. "I know! Thrilling, ain't it. It's even better with the adrenaline push I just gave you. Aye?" Stronghold only grunted in response and rubbed his aching forehead.

\* \*

"Where is my back-up?" yelled Aegis into his commlink

*Kaboom!*

His lightning bolt pulled the Bull's attention away from Wavefront and Stronghold. He rolled to the right as the Bull responded by swinging its massive axe at him. Every move the statue made caused it to creak and groan. Aegis wished it was as slow as it sounded.

"Doors cycling now!" replied Butch.

Recovering quicker than his enemy, Aegis rushed forward and leaped upon the Bull's shoulders.

*Wham!*

His shield bounced off the Bull's head and caused it to stagger. Aegis raised it for another strike.

\* \*

Slipstream struck the ground and plowed a furrow for over three hundred feet before he slammed into a small grove of trees. The trees were ripped from the ground as they broke and shattered. Dirt was thrown hundreds of feet into the air.

The attack had stunned Slipstream and prevented him from adjusting his gravity field to halt his flight. The impact had only been an inconvenience. Nevertheless, he allowed himself a moment to clear his head before gripping a tree lying across his chest and casually tossing it aside. As he rose to his feat, he flexed his muscles and focused his sonar. It twisted and warped until the estate, and the metal behemoth, three miles away came into view.

"Incoming," he said calmly into his commlink.
*Boom!*
The sound barrier shattered as Slipstream exploded from the grove at full speed. Energy from his wound stretched out behind him to mark his path.

To Slipstream, the world around him always seemed to move in slow motion when he focused on his speed. To the world, his charge was instantaneous; but to him, it seemed to drag into several moments.

The edge of his vision became distorted. Tightening his sonar on the Bull caused everything else to blur out of existence. The Bull's torso became clearer and clearer as his focus grew tighter and tighter.

\* \*

*BOOM!*
Slipstream blasted through the Bronze Bull. The metal monster shattered and flaming metal flew in all directions. Large chunks struck the house and scattered across the yard.

Aegis barely had time to backflip away from the monster in response to Slipstream's warning. As he landed, he used the *Aegis* to prevent several pieces of debris from striking him.

Incindiaro watched with wide eyes as the Bull's axe spun in the air several times, and then bury itself in the ground mere inches from his foot.

"Well, why didn'a he do that to begin with?" asked Wavefront. He stood unconcerned among the raining chaos, watching it.

Still lying on his back, Stronghold watched through folded arms to ward off the danger that Wavefront's shield already protected him from.

From above the destruction, Envoy threw a bolt of energy to disintegrate a large chunk of metal before it could hit the already unsteady house.

Slipstream's momentum carried him nearly two miles beyond the battlefield before he stopped.

Winter Eagle's cry from inside the house forced the heroes to swallow their sighs of relief.

\* \*

Startled by the explosion outside the house, Carol jerked back from the shuddering wall. When the house didn't collapse, she placed her hand back on it and her eyes glowed again as she traced the source of the water in the pipes. Nervously, she glanced around to make sure Winter Eagle wasn't about to attack her from behind.

Winter Eagle and the two heroes ignored the shaking house, and continued to attack one another. Protecting Paragon with his cloak, Shadow Spirit floated over the winged warrior like a dark guardian. Winter Eagle continued to coat the room in ice with his frozen touch.

*Kaboom!*

Lightning flashed across the room to halt Winter Eagle's latest attack as Aegis rolled through the hole in the wall and came to his knees.

Unhurt by the electrical current, but momentarily blinded by the flash, Winter Eagle pulled back from the heroes. When his vision cleared, he glared down at Paragon and Shadow Spirit just as Aegis moved in front of them. His hate filled eyes lingered on Paragon for a moment before turning on Aegis. The monster's ghostly form showed several wounds where Paragon's enchanted blade had struck him.

"I don't know what your reason is for being here, Winter Eagle," said Aegis, "but your agreement of immunity with the government will not be honored here."

On cue, books lifted from the floor and began to swirl around the room to signal the arrival of backup. Duo glided silently into the house. The eyes of Kandi and Brian glowed brightly, and their close proximity to each other created a storm of chaos that flung the books about. Fenrir bounded into the room after the twins. In wolf-hybrid form, he bared his fangs and snarled at Winter Eagle. His claws splintered the wood floor. With her energy shield flaring and incinerating anything it touched, Envoy flew into the room. A moment later Slipstream slid quietly in behind them. Wavefront peered around the corner and held his sidearm in his right hand. Behind him, Stronghold grumbled about being left out.

"You are right about one thing, cretin. You do not know my reasons for being here."

"Cretin? That th'worst insult you got? My mom's dirty old socks are more insulting."

Envoy glared at Wavefront, but quickly turned back to Winter

Eagle. Aegis ignored him. Winter Eagle didn't. His gaze shifted to Wavefront and his features twisted with rage. Wavefront shrugged in response.

After a moment of silence, Winter Eagle focused back on Aegis. "You will leave this place, or I will leave your frozen flesh shattered on the floor." Winter Eagle breathed out a cloud of cold and the temperature in the room fell even more as snow began to fall from a cloud forming over the heroes.

Aegis held his ground. "I will not give in to your demands, Winter Eagle. Our business is with Stein."

"I know your business!" screeched Winter Eagle. "Your business binds me here! He has refused your requests! Go or die!"

Aegis didn't want a confrontation with Winter Eagle. He didn't fear the legal repercussions for arresting the man, but he did fear Winter Eagle killing one of his people. Winter Eagle wouldn't hesitate to, and despite his show of force, Aegis knew only Paragon's sword, or possibly the Spirit's shadows, were any real threat to the creature. His incorporeal form would protect him from the rest of them. Only a slight rumbling through the floorboards of the housed stopped him from actually considering retreat. *Bless you Carol*, he thought.

Stalling, Aegis glanced around and motioned everyone to step back. The team hesitated, and he motioned a second time. "Back up," he said. His eye caught Paragon's, and he knew the warrior's heightened senses could also detect the rumbling beneath the house.

As several folks began easing backward, Wavefront said, "Bloody hell, boss. You ain't seriously considering backing down from this bloke are you?"

"I have to agree," said Incindiaro. "This monster has killed too many people to be allowed to remain free. I don't give a damn what immunity the government grants him on his reservation. He isn't on it."

As the vibrating under the house reached a level everyone could feel, Aegis smirked and responded, "No, I'm not."

*Kaboom!*

Lightning arched from Aegis to strike Winter Eagle as Paragon threw his sword.

The lightning distracted the creature and the sword sliced through Winter Eagle to bury itself in the wall behind him. The monster screeched and plummeted from the air as the house rocked from the force of the water building in its pipes.

Bursting from the walls and floor, water poured into the room. It froze instantly, and even Incindiaro worked frantically to avoid its deadly touch. The rushing water flung chunks of ice about the room to pelt them all. Winter Eagle screeched and flailed about as he was blasted from every direction.

Carol fought for control of the water as she forced it up from the ground and from the pipes. It was the first time she had tried to control such a large volume of any of the elements, and it quickly sapped her strength. The house was shaking violently and icy water was blasting her along with everyone else. Ice was forming in her hair and her clothes were becoming stiff. The cold stung, but it wasn't enough to fight off the exhaustion that quickly overwhelmed her. Within moments, Carol collapsed.

\* \*

Warm hands woke Carol and she opened her eyes to find Incindiaro melting ice that coated her right leg. Paragon's right hand rested gently on her stomach, and his warm touch pushed back hypothermia and healed the frostbite that threatened to take her extremities.

"That should be enough," said Incindiaro as he rose. "You will be fine." When Carol smiled at him, he turned and started for the *Egress*.

Carol turned from him to Paragon and found him smiling at her.

"I owed you one," he said as he winked.

Carol smiled and struggled to prevent warmth from spreading through her cheeks. She felt awkward and embarrassed by his touch, and she was grateful when voices pulled Paragon's bright blue eyes from her to the scene behind them.

Members of the team were milling about the remains of Bronze Bull. The Bull's axe still sat where it had buried itself in the ground after Slipstream tore through the Bull. Debris from the shattered Bull, and from the damaged house, was scattered around the yard. A nearby tree had been uprooted and lay on its side with ice clinging to its branches. The ice was starting to melt in the hot sun to form pools of water. The team's footsteps were quickly turning the water muddy. TASC had arrived on the scene, and Envoy was instructing the lieutenant in charge on how she wanted the perimeter set up for a search the estate's outer structures.

"What is it?" asked Stronghold as he picked up a piece of the Bull.

"It's not technical or mechanical," said Envoy.

Wavefront's eyes glowed as he took the piece from the giant and studied it. He then glanced around at several larger pieces. "I'd think meta at th'core. But unlike any A've ever seen before, that's for sure. Maybe it was some kind of soul-meld. There are metas with th'ability to jump bodies. But, the metal is reacting strangely enough. It's alive, I think. Th'torn edges are starten to mend. Given time, they'll reform completely."

Glancing around again, Wavefront saw Slipstream among the debris. Energy still leaked from his wounded shoulder. "Sorry, mate. I don't know what to do about that. Maybe the Doc can help ya." Slipstream didn't respond as he picked up a large piece of the Bull, and headed for the *Egress*. Wavefront chuckled and went back to examining the piece of the Bull he held.

Suddenly, Carol jolted up. "Stein?" she asked.

Paragon pushed her gently back down and continued to heal her, "Don't worry. Aegis easily followed the faeries straight to him."

"How is he?" Carol asked.

Paragon frowned. "I fear our visit has harmed him."

"Winter Eagle?" she asked.

Paragon pointed over her shoulder, and said, "See for yourself."

Slowly Carol turned to the house. "Huh?" she exclaimed as her breath caught in her throat.

The water had instantly frozen as it touched Winter Eagle, and had punched through the wooden walls. The monster had tried to flee, but he had been caught by his own icy touch. The white ghostly form of Winter Eagle was suspended inside a geyser of ice that spread outward over the yard. His wings were spread wide and his beak was open in mid scream. His large claws gripped the frozen air and his ghostly form blended well with the ice to make a magnificent ice sculpture. The ice glinted and sparkled in the rays of the setting sun.

"Frozen. Dr. Dweomer saves the day." Paragon smiled at Carol, and she again fought again to keep from blushing. She turned away to avoid his eyes, and saw Aegis exit the house with Stein in tow.

The old man was hunched over and babbling incoherently. He ignored everyone and everything around him. Aegis had to guide him across the lawn to the *Egress*. Laughing, the three faeries circled Stein, and then darted over to Carol. The sounds of bells filled the air as they landed on her and chatted enthusiastically to her. One of them peeled Paragon's hand off her, and stuck its tongue out at him. Carol smiled at it and Paragon laughed.

After a few minutes, Aegis walked over to Carol and kneeled beside her. One of the faeries chattered jealously up at him. He ignored it. Glancing at Paragon, he said, "Could you give us a minute?" Paragon nodded before rising to leave.

"I'm sorry," said Aegis after they were alone. "I shouldn't have forced you to come along."

Carol smiled. "No, you shouldn't have," she replied. "But," she quickly added as Aegis was about to speak again, "if I'm going to continue to hang out with you and the zoo crew, I should learn to expect situations like this, and I should be better prepared."

Aegis considered her words and nodded his agreement. "Your powers are unique and some combat training would do you good. You would be welcomed on the team." Glancing around, Aegis waved at Paragon. "I'm sure I can find a volunteer to train you."

Before Carol could respond, Aegis smiled and rose. The faeries chimed in their agreement with him as he walked away.

# CHAPTER 7
## THE GARDEN

"...Burns over thirty percent of his body. They are healing nicely but he can expect major scarring across his back and left arm. The injury to his left side was very severe. Something jagged ripped through it pretty good. He lost a lot of blood. It's a miracle he survived it at all. I would think he was meta-human. But the Doc says no, and the tests are negative. I don't know though. Maybe he is a new type of meta-human. Maybe I should revise the tests to make sure. To survive..."

"Brandon," interrupted a female voice.

"Oh, sorry." Brandon sounded embarrassed. He cleared his throat and continued. "He should be coming out of it before long. We've done all we can so it's going to be up to him now. He may have a limp the rest of his life, and his left side is going to keep him down for a while still. Some rehabilitation will help. We've stopped keeping him under, and given his level of brain activity, he should be waking up soon."

Wolff contained his surprise and didn't flinch. He didn't know who was speaking, but it appeared they were monitoring him closely. He felt in better condition than they seemed to think he was in. Keeping that to himself would be to his advantage.

A hand was placed on Wolff's shoulder, and the female spoke again. "I wouldn't worry too much, Brandon. He will be awake soon enough." The hand gently squeezed before withdrawing. There was the rustle of soft clothing followed by the scent of flowers. As the sounds faded, so did the scent.

A moment later, Brandon bent over Wolff. He mumbled to himself as he adjusted Wolff's bed into a sitting position. "I'm lad she knows you'll be okay. Of course, she isn't the doctor. That would be me." As if interrupted, Brandon went quiet. "I am too a doctor," he argued. "No Sarah. I..." He paused again. "I am too a doctor. I don't have the diploma...A piece of paper does not a man make...No, of course I wouldn't say that to the doctor's face. Why? He's not here is he?" Brandon sounded alarmed. "Sarah! That's not funny!" Brandon withdrew from the bed. "No. It's really not..." Brandon's one-sided argument faded as he left the room.

Wolff dismissed the kid, and the strange conversation before it could fade completely into the distance. He could neither understand it, nor did he care. His situation was more important.

Wolff couldn't remember where he was, or how he had come to be there. The only thing he knew was his name. For several minutes, he fought against the fog in his mind and struggled to remember more. The harder he fought, the more confused he became. His head began to hurt from the strain, and frustration set in, followed by anger. The anger was sharp and overwhelming. Wolff quickly decided he would have to settle for just his name for now.

Wolff forced his thoughts inward and concentrated on his condition. He tuned out the bed, the odors of the room, his memory loss, and the kid. Soon all that remained was his body.

His left leg was swollen and stiff. Having experienced broken bones before, he recognized the condition. His back was tender, and even slight movement caused stinging pain. The bandages on his left side itched, and it hurt when he tried to move. Across his shoulder and left forearm the skin was tight and also bandaged. A bandage was wrapped around his head and covered his left eye. Most likely as a result of medication, his pain was dulled and he felt a little lightheaded. He concluded that his injuries had been severe at some point. He had no idea how long he had been unconscious, but judging from what Brandon had said, it had been several weeks.

Turning to his memory again, Wolff found it still escaped him. He knew he was Wolff Kingsley, but he couldn't remember anything else. It was a strange feeling to know his name, but not know who he was. Suddenly, a thought struck him. His memory would return. The thought unnerved him because it wasn't his. He knew it was true, but he didn't know why.

Without opening his eyes, and keeping his breathing steady, Wolff turned his senses outward to the room. The bed was soft and the sheets held the sharpness of being new. The room smelled of alcohol, but there was no hiss of oxygen, and no beeping of machines that usually came with a hospital. There was the soft hum of florescent lights, and he could feel their brightness on his right eye. In the distance, he could hear the echo of footsteps and people speaking softly. He focused on the voices, but they were too soft for him to understand.

Deciding he was alone in the room, Wolff slowly opened his right eye. His vision was blurry, and it took him several moments to blink it clear. Confusion hit him when he found a small sparrow perched on a swaying branch before him.

The sparrow studied Wolff as intently as he studied it. It appeared so close Wolff could have reached out and touched it. At first he thought the room's wall was missing and the tree extended into the room. Then he realized he couldn't feel the breeze blowing the tree limb, or hear the rustle of its leaves. When the bird chirped, Wolff couldn't hear it either. Looking closer, he determined there had to be a window between him and the bird, but it was so clear, he couldn't see it at all. Looking at the corner of the room, Wolff found there were no rails or seams for the window, and it ran the entire length of the wall.

Beyond the bird was a garden. It was filled with large and small trees, a rainbow of flowers, and lush green grass. Sunlight brightened it all and created lazy shadows. Wolff quickly got lost in the peaceful view. The room disappeared, the voices completely faded, and his injuries became unimportant as the moments silently slipped by.

Sudden movement jerked Wolff's eyes back to the branch. It swayed, but the small bird was gone. Scanning the shadows, Wolff found no sign of it.

Sighing, Wolff turned his attention to the room around him. The walls were white but faded to blue at the corner of his vision. The blue disappeared and only the pale white remained when he turned his head to focus on the wall. In addition, the walls had no pictures or objects on them. There was no sink, no restroom door, and no medial equipment.

Other than his bed, the room was empty. The left wall flashed and blinked with a display of his vital signs. The monitor appeared to be a part of the wall. As with the window, there were no seams or breaks to indicate where the wall ended and the monitor began. Even though there were no attachments on his body, the readings adjusted when he shifted in the bed. He held his position as still as possible to avoid disturbing the readings.

Over his left shoulder, dim light spilled into the room through a doorway. The voices came from that direction. The room had a soft hum, but there was no visible source for the sound. He had originally attributed it to fluorescent lights, but there were no lamps or other visible light sources in the room.

The ceiling was the same color as the walls and it also faded to blue when he didn't look directly at it. Glancing back to the garden, he rejected the idea that the sunlight was enough to light the room. The light from the doorway was brighter than that of the room, but cast no apparent shadows. The monitor inset in the wall wasn't bright enough either. There simply was no light source that could account for the brightness of the room.

Glancing back at the garden, he considered how sharply it contrasted with the room. The garden was full of vibrant colors and motion while the room was still and void of color. Wolff preferred the garden.

\* \*

Aegis leaned back in his chair and studied the documents before him. The wall beside him held the same images, but he preferred the smaller screen of the sidekick. He had been going over the files for hours, and his eyes ached from the strain.

"Hey there, lover."

Aegis looked up to see Heather standing over him. She had entered without him noticing. That was a sure sign he needed sleep.

Placing the small computer on the table, he smiled and said, "Morning, gorgeous."

"You've been locked up in here all morning. I thought you could use a break."

Aegis smiled. "That I could."

Heather sat down across from him and picked up the device.

"So, he is the Missing Man."

"Yes. Dr. McCoy has confirmed the DNA markers, and I've already spoken with Meta-man. The situation in Cameroon isn't settled yet, but he thinks it will soon be stable enough for him to return."

"Dyonis Harvie," said Heather as she read the file.

"Yes. That's his real name, and he is one of the original settlers of Roanoke Colony."

"Does Dreah know who he is?"

"Through the diary only. Even though Eleanor was married to Ananias, Harvie was obsessed with her. It's unclear what he knows, but what we have learned so far is that he killed every one of his descendants. Then he erased as much evidence as he could of their existence. His family tree is dead. That's why we couldn't find any trace of it. The fact that the diary survived can only be attributed to his fixation with Eleanor. He couldn't bring himself to destroy it."

"Every one of his descendants?" asked Heather.

"Yeah. We just got lucky to discover his line in the first place. The books he gave Carol had their names scribbled in the margins. We are pretty sure he listed them all. Maybe it was a desperate cry for help."

"That's horrible. What kind a man does it take to kill over five hundred people? His own descendants even."

"I don't know. Diamond doesn't either. Harvie's mind is a mess as a result of some deep psychosis. We don't know if it is intentionally self induced, or just a result of being extremely paranoid. Then again, it could be some sort of mental defense mechanism. Either way, when combined with his long-term isolation, you get a mass murderer. He may have known what his descendants could become, and feared it. We believe his reaction to Slipstream was confirmation of that."

Heather's brow furrowed. "That goes against what we know of the other Nine. All of them were in perfect health, mental and physical, and they have handled the stress of this pretty well. Why would he be different?"

"Unknown. Maybe he was as stable as the others initially. We may never know. But remember, we haven't discovered all the Nine yet. We know of their family trees, but counting Harvie, we now only know the full identities of six of them. Diamond suspects his condition was brought on after the incident, maybe as a result of it. He simply couldn't handle it. Maybe he remembered more than the others. Neither Diamond nor Dreah can keep his condition under control."

"What about meta-powers?"

"Maybe the psychosis, but there is no evidence of it, or any other kind of meta-activity. Other than his longevity, of course. It seems to be shared by all the nine."

"That's odd," said Heather. "The others are all unique, and powerful." She glanced down at the documents on Harvie.

"Yes. That's just one more mystery about this whole affair that we may never solve."

Aegis stared at Heather across the table as she read through the information on Harvie. Her brow furrowed and she squinted. It made him smile. Her intensity was one of the things he loved most about her. She was even more serious than he was. He suddenly felt a longing to spend time alone with her. *Just a weekend*, he said to himself. One quite weekend alone wasn't too much to ask. Given Diamond's belief that a disaster was fast approaching, he doubted that would happen any time soon, even with the wedding fast approaching.

"What about Winter Eagle?" he asked.

"He's a bastard," replied Heather.

Aegis smirked. "I know that. Any idea why he was with Harvie? It is unlike him to work with anyone he doesn't control."

"None, and he isn't talking. Can you believe his lawyers have already filed petitions for his release? How did they even know we had him? I'm not even through arranging his release to federal authorities."

Aegis chuckled.

"Maybe we should just keep him locked up down in the dungeon. Forever!"

Aegis knew how she felt. Even before becoming Winter Eagle, Shoshone Mike had a history of being a very violent man. Unfortunately, it was those early days that had earned him his legal clout. As part of the federal government's treaty with him, he had near sovereign immunity as long as he was on his reservation. When he wasn't, he had a team of lawyers that usually kept him out of prison.

"How about the Bull?"

"We have nothing on him. Winter Eagle is claiming him, however. We'll fight it in court, but who knows. Even though Envoy reports disintegrating some of his pieces, he has nearly put himself back together, too. If he turns out to be sentient, it will be a complicated matter that will tie up the lawyers for months, maybe years."

Heather looked as weary as Aegis felt.

"What about you? Do you need any help with the planning?"

Heather brightened and smiled at him. "I took your advice and turned some of it over to Kahori and Maria. The girls saw it as an opportunity to go shopping, so they jumped at the idea."

Aegis smiled and allowed the two to share a pleasant moment.

"Have you stopped worrying about the man in the basement yet?"

Heather frowned, and Aegis instantly regretted having asked the question.

"He's going to live," she replied. "At least for now."

\* \*

Each time Wolff woke, he continued his charade. He studied his surroundings, and then he worked with his memories. He knew he couldn't keep up his pretense for long so he took advantage of it while he could. He felt himself getting stronger each day, and knew the monitors recorded it.

As he had suspected, his memory returned. It was slow at first, and then it came in waves. He found he could even force certain memories when he concentrated hard enough. He didn't like everything he found, but he kept pushing forward anyway.

He spent much of his time on the Counselor, Marcus William Everett. At least that was the name Wolff knew him by. It wasn't the one the Counselor had given him, but one Wolff had uncovered on his own. He knew who the Counselor was, and he knew how to get to him; but for now, he would remain content with just reviewing every detail he knew about the man. Patience wasn't something the Counselor had instilled in him, it was one of the reasons the Counselor had recruited him.

Wolff couldn't help but wonder how his life would have been different without the Counselor's interference, and he couldn't help but wonder how many others the Counselor had chosen. How many had been manipulated to fit his twisted needs? How many had he turned into killers?

Despite the fact that Wolff hadn't thought of his mother in years, he found his memories of her exceptionally lucid. She tucked him at night and whispered hope and love to him. She sat next to him at the table and smiled at him as he ate his favorite meal. He sat in her lap as she read his favorite children's book, *"Stand Back", Said the Elephant, "I'm Going to Sneeze!"* They sat on a pier and ate ice cream. He stood before her coffin and his younger sister took his hand.

His memories of his father were not as he remembered them. They had been full of anger and neglect. Now, he remembered the good more than the bad. Instead of his father holding him back, he now saw a father who offered cautious advice and sound counsel. He remembered his father patiently teaching him how to use the air rifle. They had spent hours practicing, and what he had remembered as harsh words of criticism were now soft words of direction. Their conversation about Wolff's choice of colleges changed from his father telling him where he would go, to him revealing the benefits of certain schools over others. His memories still weren't of a perfect father, but they were of a different man. The twisted memories revealed to Wolff just how much influence the Counselor had had over him.

Wolff remembered childhood friends he hadn't spoken to in years. Memories of Freddie were chief among them. He didn't know if they were there because of his experience during Diamond's mind probe, or if it were because Freddie was someone he would have called a true friend. He actually found himself wondering what had happened to Freddie after all these years.

Old girlfriends filled him with the joy. If pressed on relationships before the mind probe, he would have only remarked on the pain and trouble they brought. He would not have remembered the tingle that spread through his body when a pretty girl kissed him. Before now, he could not even remember the cause of the argument that had led him to break up with Tabitha at the mall in front of other people. Now he knew it was because he had been selfish, and the Counselor had simply used that moment to push him away from the relationship. Kim had nearly broken through that wall when he was in college, but the Counselor had stepped in and prevented it.

How different would his life have been without the Counselor? There were no guarantees that it would have been a better life, but it would have been his life.

Along with his memories came emotions. They were something Wolff wasn't prepared for. For years the Counselor had suppressed them in him – guilt, anger, hate, love, joy – and now they threatened to overwhelm him. They were unexpected and hit him with such force he was left reeling.

He tried to suppress them through meditation, but that only brought on images of the Counselor, and thus more emotion. It was only through the small sparrow that he learned how to deal with them. It returned often, usually when he needed it most, and drew his attention to the garden. He found the garden calmed him and brought him peace by allowing him to slowly deal with his emotions, without suppressing them or using the Counselor's meditation.

\* \*

The day started out like any other, and at first Wolff thought nothing had changed, but then he noticed a small table to the right of his bed. On the table were two newspapers. A picture dominating the front page of one paper showed a large burned out structure. The headline was hidden.

It caused him intense pain, but Wolff managed to reach out with his right hand and to turn the paper just enough to read the headline.

*"Museum Curator and Grandson Killed in Explosion"*

Wolff wasn't surprised by the headline. He remembered the incident now, every grisly detail. Wolff tried to read the article.

*"World renowned archeologist Felix Kingsley and his grandson, Carl Weston, are the only known dead in a terrorist attack on the Bodega Museum of Ancient Science and Technology in Bodega Bay, California, three days ago. It is unknown if the attack was directed at the museum or at Kingsley. The museum was known to house several priceless artifacts. Whether or not they were stolen is currently unknown. Kingsley is reported to have angered a number of groups with the relentless dedication with which he pursued his passion. Some outspoken groups say that the artifacts Kingsley acquired during his career were never meant to be his, and were stolen from their legitimate owners – the descendants of the ancient civilizations that created them. The police have not ruled out retribution by one of these groups..."*

Wolff knew the truth. The attack had not been directed at Felix Kingsley, his grandson, or the museum; it had been directed at him.

*"...Police have identified the body that washed up on the rocky beach below the museum yesterday as that of the terrorist responsible for the attack...."*

The words stunned Wolff. Dead? How was he dead?

"...*Police reported a shootout with the suspect just moments before the explosion. His name is being withheld at this time...*"

The article went on, but the rest of it was blocked from Wolff's view. Looking at the second newspaper, he found it was dated three months after the first paper.

Wolff knew his pretense was up. The papers meant his captors knew he was awake. He had planned to wait until tomorrow, but now he needed to move up his plans to test his strength, and to test his prison. He began to shuffle to the edge of the bed.

"Whoa, there big guy!"

Wolff recognized Brandon's voice. Appearing over Wolff, the young man placed his hand on Wolff's chest and gently pushed him back down. Wolff doubted he could have resisted the kid's strength even if he had been fully healed.

"I don't think you are ready for that just yet, sir."

Once Wolff was lying down again, Brandon pulled a small digital device out of his lab coat and began running it through different displays. It was about twice the size of a handheld PDA but appeared to be much more sophisticated. Its casing was a pale white and it had a series of bright blue circles along the top that shone with an inner light.

Stepping toward the wall that displayed Wolff's vital signs, Brandon pushed a button on the small handheld computer and instantly a panel of buttons materialized in the air before him. The multi-colored panel appeared etched on an invisible surface. Brandon stuffed his computer in his pocket, and began adjusting the buttons on the panel. The wall image responded. Wolff knew such virtual panels existed, but those he had encountered before all needed a medium of glass or plastic for the images to be projected onto. There was no such glass for this panel.

"You've been through a lot of trauma." Brandon looked at Wolff and grinned. Then he turned his attention back to his handheld device and started back toward the bed. The virtual panel disappeared, and the images on the wall beeped and flashed before settling down again. Brandon noticed Wolff watching the handheld device, and his grin broadened.

"It's a sidekick. Cool name, huh? I named it. Well, I guess I didn't officially name it. It's more of a nickname actually. Pretty cool though, better than the original name for it. MOM, Mobile Operations Monitor, or PAL, Personal Assistant...something-or-another. Trust me, it was lame." When Wolff didn't respond, Brandon took his silence for confusion. "You know, like in all superheroes have a *sidekick*?" He emphasized the word and waved the device. "Well, this little buddy can do much more than your average *Robin,* and it doesn't wear tights!" His grin threatened to spread off his face as he continued to wave the device in front of Wolff.

Brandon was young, maybe twenty, and hadn't escaped the horror of acne yet. He was thin, and had shaggy brown hair that he kept pushing out of his bright blue eyes. He had a perpetual grin tattooed on his face. He wore blue scrubs, a white lab coat, and his shoes were covered in paper slippers. A nametag with his picture was clipped to the lab coat. There was a small metallic diamond pin in the lower left corner of the nametag.

"So, how are you feeling today? Judging by your level of activity, you must be feeling pretty good." Brandon turned much of his attention back to the sidekick, but kept talking as he worked. "Vitals are excellent, considering the trauma you went through. How is your memory of that anyway?" Expecting a reply, Brandon looked at Wolff and paused. Uneasy silence settled between them.

"Well, okay then. Guess we'll have to see for ourselves." Brandon pulled a penlight from his pocket and held it up to Wolff's right eye. The light stung. Uncovering Wolff's left eye, he repeated the examination. It stung worse than the right eye.

Stuffing the bandages into his pocket, Brandon said, "I don't think we'll be needing those anymore." Several minutes later, he had removed the bandages from Wolff's left arm and shoulder. He tested the pink skin, and appeared satisfied.

Throughout the examination, Brandon talked. At some points, he spoke about things at random. At other times, he focused on events of the world, primarily on who won what sporting event. At other times, he focused on Wolff's injuries.

"Much better," he mumbled as he examined Wolff's side. "But I think you will have some issues with this one for a few more weeks still. Should heal completely though. I must say we are pretty impressed with your recovery."

Brandon finally stepped back. "So, er...sir, any questions of me?" The kid waited a moment, but Wolff didn't say anything.

"All-righty-then. I guess we'll just call him Mr. Patient, huh Sarah? He must be the strong silent type." Brandon winked at Wolff. Wolff glanced around to see who Sarah was, but there was no one else in the room. "Questions?" asked Brandon.

"No," mumbled Wolff.

"Ha! See, I knew you could talk." Brandon danced a little circle, and then turned back to face Wolff. Moving around the bed, Brandon picked up the newspapers, and tucked them under his arm. Heading for the door, he said over his shoulder, "We'll see you in a few minutes. I need to get a device from the lab. I wouldn't try to get out of bed if I were you. The nanites have started rebuilding muscle tissue but they can't do it all, and I doubt you have the strength to support your own weight. You won't be able to stand on your own for a few days still."

Wolff wanted to concentrate on the kid, and his situation, but after he was alone in the room the weight of his past crashed down on him. His vision darkened, and the room spun. He felt nauseous and a dull pounding in his head. His side stung, and the skin on his arm itched. His anger over his captivity was crushed beneath the weight of his grief over his father's murder. He felt the repressed sorrow of his mother's death, the regret over his sister's son, the pain of every relationship break up, the disappointment of every lost dream. After three days of trying to come to terms with everything, he didn't have the strength to fight it. For the first time in years, Wolff wept until darkness claimed him.

*Swhoosh!*

Wolff jerked awake. He hadn't meant to fall asleep. He quickly glanced around for the source of the sound, and found a man standing at the end of his bed. The man had his back to Wolff and faced the garden. He was dressed in a dark suit and his grey hair was short. Without turning, he spoke.

"Good afternoon, Mr. Kingsley. I am glad to see you are awake."

The man's voice was familiar. As he turned, light glinted off his silver watch and onyx ring. It was the faceless man who had guided Wolff through his memories.

The man approached the bed. "How are you feeling? You look remarkably better than when you first came to us. Of course, we have the best medical doctors here." The man smiled as he gripped the footboard of the bed. "You are a testament to that now."

"What now?" Wolff asked.

"That is just what I expected from you, Mr. Kingsley, straight to the point. Since you asked, there is a matter we need to discuss. Your response will determine what is next."

The man released his grip on the bed, and started pacing the room.

"I should introduce myself first. My name is..."

"Samuel Diamond," Wolff interjected.

The man didn't bat an eye. "Yes, Samuel Joseph Diamond. Folks around here call me, Mr. Diamond. Now, it appears, by chance actually, you crashed your plane on my island."

"Your island?" responded Wolff.

"Yes, my island." Diamond continued pacing, but altered his course to circle the bed. "This is a very special place." He gestured at his surroundings. "I have a lot of extraordinary people working for me."

"Meta-humans," said Wolff.

"Most aren't, but yes, many of them are indeed meta-humans.

"I know who you are Mr. Kingsley, or were. I guess it depends on perspective. By now, the memories of our walk through your mind have come to you. At first you probably dismissed them as a dream, but by now you know them for what they are. Don't fool yourself. I know everything there is to know about you. You have no secrets."

With or without the dreams, Wolff could have surmised as much. The newspapers had confirmed it.

"The Counselor built up some very valuable skills in you. He then dumped you when you were no longer useful to him. Now, to him, and to the world, you are dead." He paused to look at Wolff. "That can be a very powerful hand to hold, Mr. Kingsley."

Wolff remained silent and watched Diamond closely.

"Considering certain mitigating factors, and I believe we both know of whom I speak, you are faced with a choice. I always look for the benefit to be found in any situation. I encourage you to do the same. You are left with the choice, Mr. Kingsley. You can be dead as the world believes, or you can come to work for me."

Anger flared in Wolff. He had spent most of his life manipulated by the Counselor. Even before he knew the man existed, the Counselor had influenced him. He had poked and pushed Wolff into making decisions that would give him the skills and knowledge needed to make him an assassin. Then without even knowing it, Wolff had agreed to work for the man. Now Diamond was forcing him into making a decision, but not leaving him with any options. With the only alternative being death, it left Wolff as manipulated by Diamond as he had been by the Counselor.

"Think about it, Mr. Kingsley. In exchange for your services, I can provide you with all you need and more. Understand, the Counselor's needs are different from my own and if you choose to work for me, you must find a way to leave your past behind you."

Wolff cursed through gritted teeth, "You expect me to trust you when you and your damn doctors have thoroughly screwed with my mind!"

"Think rationally, Mr. Kingsley. Don't answer out of emotion. Take some time to consider the offer." Moving to the doorway, Diamond paused again. "You can't always believe what you read in the paper; and then again, perhaps you can."

Talking to himself, Brandon barreled around the corner and nearly collided with Diamond. The taller man had obviously anticipated the startled kid, and easily caught him.

"Take care, and I hope you continue to feel better." Diamond patted Brandon on the shoulder. "Brandon here will take good care of all your needs. He's a special kid. Take the time to introduce yourself to him. You could be with us for a long while."

As Diamond left the room, Brandon said, "B-Bye Mr. Diamond. Good to see you, sir." Diamond didn't respond to the kid, but waved over his shoulder. Turning to Wolff, Brandon grinned. "Great guy, Mr. Diamond. He gave me this job when no one else would. I owe him a lot."

Wolff glared at the kid before dropping his head back to his pillow. Brandon seemed oblivious to the tension between Wolff and Diamond. He pulled a device out of his pocket and placed it against Wolff's side. It beeped loudly as Brandon explained what he was doing.

"I'm adjusting the programming of the nanites in your blood. Up until now they have concentrated on monitoring your vitals, and delivering medication to keep your muscles from experiencing full atrophy, and to keep you from suffering bedsores. Doc McCoy wants you on some solid foods so I'm easing off on that part of the programming for now. You'll start to feel hungry soon. If you start feeling pain let me know and I'll readjust the programming again...So, what do I call you anyway?"

Wolff ignored the kid as he stared into the garden and replayed Diamond's words in his head. On a branch before him sat the small sparrow. It watched him as he watched it, and his mind wondered back to where it had all began for him. Pointed at the sparrow, the barrel of the air rifle stretched out before him. Even if the bird had been aware of the danger, Wolff knew it would still have been as helpless as he was feeling. Helpless. Cornered. Flee or die. How different would his life have been if he hadn't taken that first shot?

"No options," Wolff mumbled to himself. "A sparrow with no options."

"What was that?" asked Brandon. "Sparrow? Odd. But, okay with me if that is what you want to be called. Never heard of anyone named Sparrow before. Of course, I've heard worse around here." Brandon paused to laugh. "Oh, what Sarah...Oh, sorry. That was not at you. I just knew this one guy who wanted to call himself, Colossal Lad. Lame. I mean, who did he think we are anyway? A group of teenage superheroes hanging out in a clubhouse shaped like a rocket ship? Lame!"

\* \*

Over the next few hours, depression sank into Wolff. It was something he had never experienced before, and it had a full grip on him before he even realized it existed. The more he thought about the sparrow and its options, the deeper he slid.

The first option was to flee. Anger nearly overwhelmed him when he realized that the escape would only free him from the walls around him. Once outside, death would still pursue him from the Counselor and from Diamond. He also knew freedom from the walls would do nothing to purge him of the image of his father and nephew being consumed by the inferno. The image made him want to kill the Counselor even more, but he knew he would need months of recovery before he could do so. His needs wouldn't only be physical. Diamond and his team had pretty much taken care of that while he had slept. No, his recovery would include finding resources and setting himself up in a safe location. With the Counselor and Diamond looking for him, that would be difficult. The Counselor had shut every door behind him, and Diamond was capable of shutting every door before him. In addition, the retribution would do nothing to console his sister's sorrow, but Wolff was pretty sure it would ease his.

All the dangers of escape led Wolff to consider the sparrow's other option. Death. Diamond had been clear about that option. Wolff didn't know if Diamond would pull the trigger himself but he had no doubt Diamond could do so. Diamond could also just reach into Wolff's brain and shut it off; or worse, leave Wolff trapped in the black marble prison. Diamond had said the prison was of Wolff's creation, but he had no doubt that Diamond was capable of recreating it. Thoughts of his sister's grief made him long for the prison.

Unlike the sparrow, Wolff had a third option. He refused to consider it, but he at least acknowledged it existed. He could work for Diamond. The thought of being forced to cooperate caused Wolff's anger to nearly overwhelm him. He was free and being chained again was unacceptable. He was determined to remain free. He rejected the option without exploring the possibilities.

The endlessness and hopelessness of his options drove Wolff into depression. Emotionally, he just wasn't strong enough to deal with everything.

\* \*

"Good morning!" said Brandon as he entered Wolff's room the next day. "How are you feeling today?"

Doing his best to ignore the kid, Wolff didn't answer. He was groggy and tired. He hadn't slept much, and it made him irritable. Brandon seemed not to notice.

"I hope you slept well. I've got breakfast here for you. Eat up. We have several tests to run today."

Brandon sat a tray on the stand next to Wolff's bed, and then moved over to the wall to activate the virtual console. Wolff didn't move and kept his back to the kid.

"So, what interests do you have?" Wolff could hear the beeps of the buttons as the kid hit every one. "I love sports myself…No. I didn't play. I've never been very good because I don't have any coordination. I usually trip over my own two feet…I don't see what that has to do with sports. No, it doesn't…Okay, okay. I misplace things a lot too, apparently. Although, I don't see what that has to do with sports, but if you do, okay…You are always right after all."

Like yesterday, the kid was speaking with someone that Wolff could not hear. He considered rolling over to see who it was, but doubted it was worth the effort.

"I know you are awake, and you need to eat. Come on, Sparrow, roll over."

*What? What did he call me?* Confused, Wolff raised up just enough to look over his shoulder.

"He lives!" Brandon grinned broadly. "Told you."

As he suspected, Brandon was the only one in the room. Wolff looked at Brandon and asked, "What did you call me?"

Brandon was about to scan Wolff with the sidekick but paused. He looked at the floor, and then back to Wolff, "Sparrow. That is what you told me to call you yesterday? Isn't it?" Before Wolff could respond, Brandon rolled his eyes and sighed. "Yes, it is," he said.

Wolff didn't care what the kid called him. Most of his adult life had been spent under alias names, and a few more days or a dozen new names wouldn't matter. If Diamond had wanted Brandon to know his real name, he could have just used it himself. Besides, he had more important matters to puzzle over. Although he had to admit, he kind of liked the name and the strange connection it had to his situation.

Realizing Brandon was still mumbling to himself, Wolff narrowed his eyes and asked, "Who are you talking to?"

Brandon flushed and immediately took a step back. "Oh…Umm… Sorry about that. You are new around here so you don't know. It's my sister, Sarah."

Wolff raised his eyebrow in question.

Brandon looked nervous and held the small device up next to his head. He moved it in a circular motion as he said, "Kind of weird, I know. I can hear her up here, sometimes. Sorry."

Wolff grunted and lay back down on the bed. Nervously, Brandon stepped up next to him and held the sidekick over him. For the next several moments, he was quiet and Wolff was grateful. When Wolff looked at him, Brandon grew nervous and turned away.

While Wolff ate, Brandon worked with the nanites in his body. Breakfast consisted of a dirty white pudding that was easy on his stomach, but it wasn't very filling. Holding the spoon up, Wolff scowled at the bland concoction.

"It's not very tasty," he grumbled.

Brandon laughed. "No, it isn't." He never took his eyes off the monitor as he spoke. "Don't worry about that though, it has all the nutrients you will need. It has more protein than a steak dinner, more fiber than a cup of beans, all with none of the flavor!"

Wolff's stomach rumbled, and he glanced at it.

Brandon laughed. "Don't worry, that's normal too. It will only be for a few days and then you'll be on solid food." Taking Wolff's grumbling as a sign that he wanted to talk, Brandon spent the next several minutes telling Wolff about his college days, and how he had actually tried out for the basketball team. Suddenly, he grunted and said, "No!"

Wolff instantly knew that Brandon had dropped from the conversation to speak with the voice in his head. It was slightly irritating, but Wolff didn't interrupt. So far, he wasn't sure if Sarah was just Brandon's imagination, or if somehow she was real, but he knew that Brandon was distracted and vulnerable when he spoke with her.

"He doesn't want to hear about that." Brandon fell to mumbling as he adjusted his devices and continued running tests on Wolff.

\* \*

Much to Sparrow's disappointment, Brandon visited often over the next few days. When he wasn't speaking to Sparrow, he talked to Sarah, or to himself. The imaginary Sarah liked to argue with the kid. No matter what Brandon felt was best for Sparrow, she argued against it. Of course, Brandon seemed to like the arguing, and even took opportunities to pick fights himself.

Brandon continued to call Wolf, Sparrow, and he never corrected the kid. He had mixed feelings about it but he had taken the time to consider it, and he was pretty sure it was a safe alias. The less Brandon, or anyone, knew about his past the better. It would help him avoid questions and help him earn trust. Diamond knew the truth, but Wolff was pretty sure he hadn't discussed it with anyone.

Brandon showed Sparrow the sidekick and explained many of its functions. It was tied to the main computers of the complex, and was used much like any PC on a network, but it was far more sophisticated than most computers Sparrow had encountered. It responded to voice commands and to touch operation. With it, the Internet or pretty much any television station he wanted could be viewed. The images could be viewed on the sidekick, or projected on the room's walls.

The sidekick could also be used to close out the view of the garden, and to replace it with a view of just about any thing Sparrow wanted. Brandon claimed the garden was really beyond the transparent wall, but it could still be changed. Sparrow left the view of the garden. It reminded him of the freedom he so desperately craved, and its calming effect still helped him deal with his emotions.

Through the sidekick or with simple voice commands, Sparrow also learned to adjust the lighting in his room. Claiming Sparrow's security clearance was too low, Brandon would only hint at some of the sidekick's other features.

By the end of the first two days, Sparrow was also up and out of the bed for the first time. By the end of the third day, he had taken two full laps around his room. Brandon and the nurse who assisted him were surprised by the speed at which he recovered.

"No Sarah, I don't think that would be best. He is not ready to wander the halls."

Sparrow allowed Brandon to help him onto the bed and took advantage of the kid's distraction. Slipping his hand into Brandon's pocket, Wolff withdrew the kid's sidekick and slipped it under his pillow.

When Sparrow was safely on the bed, Brandon took a step back and glared at his patient. His brow furrowed as he placed his hands on his hips. Sparrow had been caught.

"Tomorrow. Yes, I think tomorrow would be best." Suddenly Brandon's face changed and he smiled at Sparrow. "Sarah thinks you should walk the hallways today, but I think we will start that tomorrow...Nope! It's my decision." Without another word, Brandon turned toward the door. Just as he was about to leave, he turned and said, "See you tomorrow, Sparrow. I've got tickets to a hockey game in New York tonight." He grinned broadly.

Sparrow sat in silence and waited several minutes to ensure the kid would not return. Easing himself from the bed, he moved across the room to a small chair. Pulling up the cushion, he mimicked what he had seen Brandon do, and turned off the sidekick's power. The blue screen went dark, but when Sparrow tilted it, the blue shifted and moved like water beneath a glass. Wolff shrugged it off for now, and slipped it beneath the chair's cushion.

* *

The next day when Brandon returned, Sparrow didn't mention the sidekick but it wasn't long before Brandon missed it.

"Darn," he mumbled as he checked each of the large pockets on his lab coat.

"Huh?" Sparrow faked interest as he ate his pudding.

Brandon looked up at him and grinned sheepishly. "I seem to have lost another one."

Sparrow put his spoon down on the tray and placed the tray on the table. "Lost what?" he asked as he wiped his mouth with a cloth napkin.

Brandon looked embarrassed. "Another sidekick…Huh? No! I didn't leave it in the dining area." Brandon started for the door as Sparrow picked up the morning paper. "I'll be back," Brandon called over his shoulder. "I've got to look for it." The rest of his words were lost as he walked down the hallway.

It was an hour later when he finally returned. By then, Sparrow had fully read the paper, and was ready for his morning exercise.

"Find it?" he asked as he sat up in bed.

"No. Sarah's pissed," said Brandon as he led Sparrow out of his room and into the hallway. "She's threatening not to let me have another one. Mr. Diamond will probably be angry too."

It wasn't lost on Sparrow that it had only been because of Sarah distracting Brandon that it had been so easy to steal the sidekick in the first place.

* *

The hallways were made of the same white material as Sparrow's room, and again, there was no visible source for the lighting. Some hallways were dark while others were lit up as brightly as a hospital corridor. The corridors that were dark were usually stark while the ones that were lit up were decorated with artwork and potted plants that seemed to thrive in the strange lighting.

Doorframes slightly protruded from the walls to mark other

rooms. Along each frame were numerous one-inch wide bubbles of transparent glass that revealed a blue liquid beneath. The liquid wavered and reflected light like the sun off the surface of a blue swimming pool. It made the liquid appear to be alive, and Sparrow thought of it as liquid light. The sections varied in length and their patterns were different from door to door. A round bubble appeared in the center of each door. It was surrounded by a series of overlapping circles. In some of the doors, the liquid light was dark.

On the morning of the sixth day, Brandon was bursting with joy and claimed he had a surprise for Sparrow. He grunted in response and declined. He was becoming more depressed, and wasn't in the mood for Brandon's bubbly attitude. Of course, Brandon wouldn't relent, and he finally rolled over just to shut the kid up.

After two laps down the hallway, Brandon led Sparrow to an open doorway across from his room. The door puzzled Sparrow. He was certain it hadn't been there the day before.

"What do you think?"

Sparrow turned away from the blue pattern around the door and looked into the room. Inside he found a large weight bench and a whirlpool bath.

"The whirlpool bath and hand weights are part of normal rehabilitation. Since you are progressing faster than expected, I thought we'd go ahead with them." Brandon smiled at Sparrow as he waved his hand at the room. "The weight bench is Dreah's idea. She says you will need it."

Wolff examined the room and asked, "Who's Dreah?"

Brandon was stunned. "You haven't met Dreah yet?"

"No."

"Wow! That's odd. I guess she's been busy. I haven't seen her around much either." Brandon scratched his head as he looked at Sparrow. "Anyway, she said you would need them. I tried to tell her heavy weight training wasn't for a while yet, but she insisted." Brandon squinted. "Wow! I can't believe you haven't met Dreah yet. She is my favorite person in the whole world, you know. She always seems to know just what anyone needs. She is so easy going. You can talk to her about anything. She even understands Sarah...when others don't. Okay, okay, Sarah. We won't talk about that." For the next several minutes, Brandon rambled on about Dreah like a kid reminiscing about his first love.

An hour later as Sparrow relaxed in the tub, he examined the stolen sidekick. He hadn't turned it on yet, but he had cracked the casing to examine the interior. Its design was unlike anything he had ever seen before. He couldn't figure out which piece was the processor, or even the power source. He had no idea how to use it.

Setting it aside, he turned his attention to the weights and again was disappointed. The weights were not what he would have requested. It was built for heavy lifting. He preferred lower weight and more repetition. He avoided bulk. Perhaps Dreah didn't know everyone as well as Brandon thought. In addition, something was wrong with the design of the bench.

The sidekick and weight set did nothing to push Sparrow's depression aside. They only frustrated him further. The next day he was slow to respond to Brandon and only barely noticed his exercises. The day after that, he wouldn't even speak with Brandon.

* *

Feeling like a caged animal, Sparrow paced the room. Diamond's proposal was tearing at him, and he hadn't slept the previous night. He couldn't find a way out of it, and his memories of the museum were causing feelings in him he didn't know how to deal with. Stopping before the window, he watched the waving branches and found that even they irritated him.

"Good morning!" called Brandon from the doorway behind him.

Sparrow flinched but didn't turn around to face him.

"How did you sleep?"

Growling, Sparrow tightened his fists. "Get out," he growled through clenched teeth.

"I slept like a baby. I worked late in the lab. I always sleep well after a long night of work."

"Get out!" yelled Sparrow.

"What?"

Slowly Sparrow turned around. "I said get out!"

Brandon didn't flinch. "Sorry buddy. But we have work to do."

Stepping forward, Sparrow glared at Brandon. For the first time, Brandon realized that Sparrow was angry, and took a step back.

"Umm, sorry, but we really should run a few tests. No, Sarah. I don't think…"

"I said get out!" yelled Sparrow. Suddenly, he grabbed the tray from Brandon's hands and hurled it. Brandon ducked aside as the tray sailed past him and struck the wall by the door.

"Get out!"

"But,...Sarah, no!"

At the mention of Sarah, Sparrow's anger flared. "Get out and take that bitch with you!" He stepped forward and raised his arm to strike Brandon.

Brandon quickly backed toward the door. "Okay! Okay! Take it easy! I'll, uh...I'll see you a little later today. Okay?" He quickly disappeared through the door without waiting for an answer.

Sparrow turned around and glared out the window. *Damn!* He cursed.

Turning away from the window, he reached into his shirt and took out the sidekick. He glared at it a moment, and then slammed it against the wall. Turning, he exited his room and entered the weight room.

Stopping in the doorway, he glared at the weights. Eventually, he sat down on the bench and picked up a small hand weight. After several curls, he threw it against the far wall. It landed in the tub.

Reaching up, he pulled himself up by the weight pulleys. They creaked, causing him to stop and glare at them. His eyes raced over the pulleys and ropes as his mind studied their design. It only took him a minute to realize the bench was indeed put together wrong. Considering several adjustments, he started dismantling the system.

Two hours later the weight bench was scattered across the room and out into the hallway. Sparrow began shifting the pieces when Brandon walked around the corner.

"Wow! What's this?"

Sparrow ignored him.

"Can I do anything to help?"

Without looking up, Sparrow said, "You could get me a screwdriver."

Brandon laughed. "Well, what do you know? I just happen to have one right here." Reaching into his back pocket, Brandon pulled out a screwdriver and handed it to Sparrow. Without looking up, Sparrow took it and continued working. Brandon began whistling loudly as he left the area.

When Sparrow finished his project, he stood staring at the bench.

He felt better. The weights had been intended as a mental exercise, to distract him from his emotions and discomfort. Perhaps Dreah knew him better than he thought. Sitting down, he spent the next two hours working out, and slowly his mind cleared.

\* \*

It was late and Sparrow was certain Brandon wouldn't return again before morning. Exiting his room, he started down the hall. He studied everything as he went. Of course, as part of his therapy, he had been in these early hallways before.

Reaching the end of the hall, Sparrow turned right. By his calculations it should have been the most direct route to the garden. Disappointingly, the new hallway was no different from the previous one, and branching off from it were several other identical hallways. Sparrow took time to examine a few of the many doors he found; those that were dark wouldn't open, those that did open only revealed only empty rooms.

*Swhoosh!*

Sparrow froze. He stared down the empty hallway and listened. The sound didn't return. He considered following it, but it appeared to lead away from the garden. *Tomorrow*, he told himself as he resumed his search for the garden.

He was about to consider backtracking to one of the side passageways when he felt a slight breeze. He closed his eyes and concentrated on the breeze. It was coming from the direction he was headed, so he doubled his pace.

Stopping at another intersection, he closed his eyes and turned until he felt the wind on his face again. Opening his eyes, he saw an arched exit about forty feet away. Beyond the exit, Sparrow saw the garden. Already, the sun was setting, and the flowers were casting long shadows. He moved forward and stopped at the entrance.

The immensity of the place was overwhelming. There were trees of all types and vast arrangements of flowers blanketing the ground beneath them. Even in the fading light, the array of colors would bring shame to any rainbow, and the many fragrances that fought for dominance on the wind didn't overwhelm his nose. Insects and bees buzzed between the many plants. Dim lights lit a stone path that twisted through the garden. The window of his small room had not done the place justice. Sparrow stepped forward onto the path. For days the garden had been calling to him. That call was overwhelming now.

*Swhoosh!*

Sparrow turned to look back up the hallway. The source of the sound remained hidden, but it indicated he was being watched. Sparrow turned back to the garden. "Whoever you are, you'll just have to wait." He started forward.

Glancing around, he saw the walls of the garden extended out of sight. Following them up, he grew confused. Instead of stars, Sparrow saw a large glass dome towering over him. Beyond the clear dome was rock. There was a large opening in the center of the dome and it extended up through the rock. Light filtered down from it. The opening was over one hundred feet across.

Shaking the view from his mind, Sparrow bowed his head in defeat. The garden wasn't the escape he had thought it was. Lifting his head again, he looked around and took in the vastness of the area. Determined it wouldn't be a permanent defeat, Sparrow started forward again. Keeping his eye on the shaft, he took the path that angled toward it.

The shaft came more into view the deeper into the garden he went. It was immense. There were at least five floors above the garden. Fifty to one hundred feet separated each one and a couple of the floors were at least a hundred feet tall. Bright light blazed from each one. They were connected by a series of five elevators that were positioned around the edge of the shaft. Only one of the elevators was moving. The ceiling of the shaft was too far away for Sparrow to make out any detail. The entire structure, including the garden, was buried underground.

The sound of a dove cooing pulled his eyes from the shaft. Turning, Sparrow faced the center of the garden. A small meadow overflowing with flowers and clover spread out before him. In the very center was a large tree with light blue blossoms. The light from the shaft illuminated the tree.

Sparrow's breath caught in his throat at the sight of a woman sitting just under the edge of the tree. She had long silky black hair that spilled around her to touch the ground. Her skin was pale and she wore a thin white gown. She had large dark eyes, and she played with the grass with her slender toes. Around her neck was a silver necklace with a pendant in the shape of a small bird taking flight. She sat with practiced poise that went undisturbed by even her own movements. A dove rested on her outstretched hand. It eyed her and cooed to her.

Feelings of sorrow welled up inside Sparrow at the scene before him. His very presence tainted it. Before him was peace, love, and life. He was evil, hatred, and death. He wanted to turn away in disgust, but found the scene pulled at him.

The lady held her hand high, and the dove took flight. She smiled as it circled her and the tree. Her outline blurred, and mist flowed from her. The mist hung around her like a halo. In an instant, she was gone. Dozens of small sparrows burst from the mist to flutter in all directions before forming a flock to circle the tree, and to rise high into the air.

A single bird darted from the flock straight for Sparrow. It turned away at the last moment, and circled around him. As he watched, it rejoined the flock as they soared upward toward the shaft. When they reached it, they broke apart and descended among the trees as darkness settled over the garden.

Slowly, Sparrow turned and started back to his room. The scene had been one of the most beautiful things he had ever witnessed. He knew the image would remain with him forever.

# CHAPTER 8
# ON THE MEND

The next day, Sparrow again walked the hallways. He stopped by the garden briefly, but quickly moved on to areas he hadn't previously explored. To his disappointment, most rooms remained locked and he found no elevators or stairs.

*Swhoosh!*

Sparrow stopped and took a step back to study the hallway he had just passed. It was empty. The sound was the only thing that had distinguished it from any other. Turning, he proceeded down it.

When he came to an intersection, he turned in a circle, but saw nothing. Listening closely, he heard the distant sound of a door opening. Moving as quickly as he could, he followed the sound.

Turning the next corner, he stopped. Sixty feet down the hallway a two-foot wide silver globe floated in the air. The globe pulsed white every few seconds and appeared to be spinning. The light of the hallway flared with each pulse.

The globe's surface turned blue and the pulse increased in intensity. Then the globe sped off out of sight. Sparrow sprinted forward, but by the time he got to the intersection, the globe was gone.

\* \*

"I had an encounter earlier today."

"Really," replied Brandon. "With whom?"

"I was hoping you could tell me that."

Puzzled, Brandon looked at Sparrow.

"It was a globe, about two feet wide. Glowed and pulsed."

Brandon laughed. "Oh don't worry about him. That's just Glip-2. Even when you don't see him, he's always around here someplace. He's security, and handyman, I guess. Whatever is needed. He zips around this place all the time."

"Security?" Sparrow questioned.

"Yeah. He is tied to the computers that run this place. They thought for a while he was the AI itself, but I guess he's sort of developed along side it. He knows every hallway and access tunnel. It's amazing how quickly he can go from one place to another, and you never see him coming. I don't see how he doesn't get lost. I do all the time actually."

"You mean he is a computer."

Brandon stopped adjusting the device again and looked at Sparrow. "No, not really. I don't think I'd call him that. He's pretty cool, though. He tells some of the best jokes. You should get to know him. I owe him ten bucks. Lost a bet...I do not always lose...Ugh! Sarah, stop that. I've been known to win from time to time." Sparrow let Brandon get lost in his argument with Sarah as he considered the addition of Glip-2 to security.

\* \*

The next day, Sparrow searched for Glip-2, but the globe didn't make an appearance until he changed his tactics and started trying to open every door he came to. He made sure to try all the ones he knew were locked.

*Swhoosh!*

He immediately set off down the hallway after the sound. Spinning around the corner, he was disappointed to find the globe already gone. Hurrying to the next corner, he was again disappointed.

For an hour Sparrow listened for the globe, and followed it as best as he could. Each time the globe was gone when he turned a corner. Each day he returned to the game of cat and mouse with the globe, but it always remained just out of sight.

\* \*

"Today is the day, big guy!"

Sparrow looked up as Brandon walked in. "For what?"

"For your new room. You've healed pretty quickly. Physically, you are sound. There isn't much more I can do for you. So if you are ready, I'll take you to your new room." Sparrow quickly packed up his few belongings, along with the stolen sidekick.

As they walked, Brandon talked. "We call this place the Citadel. As you've most likely guessed, we are underground. Mr. Diamond owns the whole thing. This lower level is mostly empty. Medical is down here, but with Paragon on the team, it is only used for extreme injuries. Dr. McCoy has his lab down here, too, but he doesn't like to be disturbed when he's working. And he's almost always working. And then there is the garden, of course. If you'd like, we can stop by there before going up."

Sparrow shook his head no. He was eager to see more of the Citadel. He had already explored the lower level extensively, escape would not be found there. It would be found through another level.

Just before they turned the first corner, Brandon stopped in front of a door that had previously been dark. The liquid light bubbles were lit up now. Before Sparrow could say anything, the door opened. Beyond it was a small area that resembled an elevator. Brandon waved Sparrow forward and then followed. As they entered, the door closed and a virtual panel lit up on the wall to the right of the door. Brandon touched several buttons.

"I know what you are thinking, and yep, it was hidden from you. If you aren't supposed to use it, you probably won't find it, and you were restricted to Medical before today. That's just the way things work around here." Sparrow waited for the elevator to start moving, but it didn't. "Anyway, don't worry. Your security clearance has been upgraded. You'll have access to most of the floors, and all that you'll need. It's only basic clearance, but it will get you around. Two, one, and..."

*Shring!*

The elevator doors opened. Brandon stepped out and turned to face Sparrow with his usual smile plastered across his face.

"I'll bet you twenty, you didn't find Dr. Ashan's lab either." Sparrow didn't respond to the bet, and eyed the virtual keypad, before looking around the small chamber. The kid shrugged and continued.

"It's not really an elevator."

Interested to hear more, Sparrow looked at Brandon, but didn't exit the small room.

Brandon took the opportunity to explain. "We call it a t-port, officially. I usually just refer to it as a port. Easier that way. It acts pretty much like an elevator. The Citadel contains eight or so floors and the ports move you from floor to floor, just like an elevator would. However, it can also move you from location to location on the same floor. Some of the floors are quiet extensive. But, there are no shafts, no wires, and no gears. It is actually a form of teleportation, hence the name. There are a few real elevators, but they are centered on the central shaft. You'll see them. As for the ports, the trip always takes exactly nine point sixty-three seconds no matter how many floors you are moving. That is provided your security clearance grants you access. Don't ask me why. It's a level of dimensional physics that is way out of my league."

*Damn*, thought Sparrow. No elevator shafts meant potential escape routes were cut off. As for the upgraded security clearance, Sparrow wondered if it meant Diamond was taking his silence as an acceptance to work for him.

The hallway hadn't changed but Brandon seemed to know where he was. He turned and started down the hallway, waving at Sparrow to follow him. Glancing again at the elevator keypad, Sparrow grunted and hurried to catch up.

"This floor is mostly maintenance and storage. It is the first of the major levels and it is huge." As he spoke, Brandon smiled. He was enjoying the opportunity to display his knowledge of the complex.

After wondering down several hallways, the two exited into a large spacious area that surrounded the open shaft. Moving over to the glass railing, Brandon looked down. Sparrow followed. Below them was the opening to the garden. Above them were several floors. Unlike the first time Sparrow had seen the shaft, sounds echoed down from above. He could see people moving about and elevators moving up and down.

Smiling, Brandon said, "Impressive, isn't it. I love to stand at the edge and just watch people. Can you smell the garden below? Awesome! I so love working in this place. Above us, on the island is a resort that caters to Mr. Diamond's rich friends. It's a real luxury place. They have no idea the most advanced facility in the world is below them."

*Hidden in plain sight*, thought Sparrow. *How much damage would be done to Diamond's operations if the Citadel were exposed?*

Seemingly disappointed, Brandon sighed and started toward an elevator that overlooked the central shaft. There was no panel or button to summon it, but it arrived anyway. The elevator was made of the same clear glass as the railing. It was noiseless and had no visible moving parts.

After they entered, a virtual panel offered Brandon several choices. "If you don't have access to certain levels, the choices won't appear on the screen. It knows where you can go and where you can't."

*What good is such security in a building that houses people who can fly and has a large open shaft in its center*, wondered Sparrow. He didn't voice the thought.

The first level they stopped at contained several labs, most of which would be off limits due to Sparrow's limited security clearance, but the level itself wasn't restricted. They took a quick tour of a robotics lab and a larger lab working on military grade body armor. Neither was off limits to Sparrow, but the engineers were agitated by their presence.

They visited a small lab Brandon claimed was assigned to Sarah. It was disorganized and cluttered. Several sidekicks lay disassembled on one table, and a large robotic arm on another table was swinging round and round. There were several pieces of medical equipment in various stages of repair scattered around the room. Despite the room's appearance, Brandon spoke about it with pride, and even showed Sparrow several small experiments he worked on himself when Sarah allowed him.

Unfortunately, Brandon claimed Sparrow's clearance wasn't high enough for them to tour the higher-level labs. Brandon's eyes sparkled when he spoke of the wonders those labs would hold for him someday.

Several minutes later, they exited another t-port and headed for an area around the central shaft. A section off to the side had several comfortable looking chairs and the wall displayed a football game. A man wearing a floppy cowboy hat crumpled to the floor when a team scored a touchdown. A blue-skinned man with horns on his head bent over the man laughing. The area also had numerous tables and chairs. Several of the tables were occupied. Sparrow's stomach growled at the smell of grilling hamburgers.

"This is a common area." Brandon said as he pointed toward the area.

"There is a common area on each housing level, but this one gets the most use. Over there are tables for eating, I'm sure you can smell the food from here. We've got pretty much anything you can want. A menu is provided a week in advance, but they take requests. Just get them in as early as you can. Of course, you can eat in your apartment, but Mr. Diamond prefers us to socialize as much as possible. Follow me and I'll introduce you to Bob, the cook. They say he was working for a really expensive restaurant in New York before coming here. All I know is he grills one mean hamburger."

Suddenly, Brandon spotted someone he knew and waived heartily. "Hey Heather! Hey Alex!"

The couple at the table turned and looked at them. Heather was blond and dressed in a white shirt, purple jacket and skirt, and black heels. She started to wave, but stopped when she saw Sparrow. Instead, she scowled. The man Sparrow recognized immediately. Brandon had called him Alex, but Sparrow and the rest of the world knew him as Aegis. Memory of their first meeting sprang to mind as Aegis raised his hand and waved. The meeting had not gone Sparrow's way. If Aegis recognized Sparrow, he didn't show it. Aegis leaned over and said something to Heather, and she reluctantly waved.

"Hey, Brandon. Are you showing our guest to his apartment?" asked Aegis.

"Yep. And I'm giving him the grand tour!"

Brandon's voice cracked with excitement as he spoke with the couple.

"Good," replied Aegis. "You're in good hands," he said to Sparrow. "Hope to see you around."

"That's Heather and Alex." Brandon said as he led Sparrow into the kitchen. "They are engaged. The wedding is planned for next month. Mr. Diamond has reserved the entire resort for the ceremony. He is throwing a really big shindig. Okay, okay...Sorry. It's not a shindig, it's a wedding...There. Happy?'"

"Her name is Heather?" asked Sparrow. "Does she have a code name?"

"Code name? Oh, of course she does, although she doesn't use it much. She works directly for Mr. Diamond and doesn't do field work. Come here, let me introduce you to the cook."

Sparrow stopped and glanced back at the dining area. When Brandon realized he had paused, he glanced back at Sparrow. "Her code name is?" asked Sparrow a second time.

"Oh, sorry. Fluxstone. She is known as Fluxstone."

Entering the kitchen, Brandon introduced Sparrow to Bob the cook. Bob had been injured in a major accident that had left him paralyzed from the neck down. He moved about the kitchen in a large wheel chair with pots and pans flying around his head. He flipped burgers with his mind stirred pots of simmering stews with large spoons that he never touched. Despite his condition, he was a pleasant jolly man who thrilled at giving Sparrow a tour of his kitchen up until he caught Brandon sampling a pot of sauce with his finger. Threatening to force feed Brandon hotdogs for a month, he ended the tour by running the kid out of the kitchen.

The tour continued for another hour. Brandon showed Sparrow how to place lunch orders, and where to find the full size movie theater. The theater took requests as well and ran a picture every night. The gym was designed for meta-human field agents. The pool was Olympic size, and the running track was a quarter mile long. There wasn't much chance of Sparrow breaking the weight equipment.

Finally, they wandered back through the dining area and down a side hallway with conventional doors. They were the first Sparrow had seen on the tour.

"It's meant to give you a feeling of normality. You may have noticed this place is anything but normal. I don't see the problem myself. I love this place," explained Brandon to Sparrow's unasked question.

As they rounded a corner, Sparrow stopped in front of a door that didn't fit in with the others. It had the strange liquid-blue light bubbles like all the doors of the lower levels.

"Slipstream," said Brandon.

"Slipstream?" replied Sparrow.

"Yeah, he doesn't spend much time here, and he isn't much into socializing. I haven't heard him say two words in the two years I've been here."

Sparrow stared at the doorway for a moment, and then turned to follow Brandon. He knew the name. The door was one to stay away from.

Finally, they reached a light colored oak door identical to millions across America. Brandon grinned and held out his hand toward the door. "Home sweet home," he said.

Sparrow hesitated, but then reached forward. The door swung open without him touching it.

"Oh," Brandon cringed, "Sorry about that. The door looks conventional, but isn't of course. You can have it work normally though if you want."

Sparrow stepped into the dark room and it lit up in response to his presence. He knew the place. He had often retreated to it between missions. It was the only luxury he had ever allowed himself over the years. The real apartment was in the small mountain village of Hallstatt in Austria. This one appeared nearly identical. Anger flared in Sparrow, and he turned on Brandon.

Not reacting to the anger in Sparrow's face, Brandon continued to smile and said, "Dreah decorated it, and I hope you like it. It looks bigger than mine." Brandon glanced at his watch. "Sorry, but I gotta go. I have a report to write for Dr. Ashan. It's been fun and I hope to see you around. By the way, I left a work out schedule for you on your sidekick." Waving, he turned and left Sparrow standing in the doorway.

Sparrow watched Brandon disappear down the hallway. Slowly, he turned back to the room, and the door closed behind him.

He struggled with a mixture of emotions. He felt joy over finding a part of him that he thought had been lost. He felt confusion over the identical nature of the two apartments. He felt anger over his inner most thoughts being violated.

Sparrow knew now that the apartment had been the first thing to penetrate the veil placed over him by the Counselor, but it had also broken a primary rule set by the Counselor. The apartment established a persona and a persona was forbidden. Personas could be tracked.

Like the original apartment, this one was spacious. The walls were covered in light wood paneling, and the dark wood floor was covered with large black rugs. There was a small kitchen area just to the left of the entryway. The matching appliances were new and the area was spotless. A sidekick sat on the counter.

Beyond the kitchen area was a small table with two chairs. Beyond them was a brown leather couch with wood end tables at each end. Each table had a small lamp. The left table also had a stack of magazines. Two dark overstuffed chairs flanked the couch. The wall beyond the couch had a large fireplace in the center with a large television to its left. There was a full bookshelf to the right. A thick curtain covered the room's left wall. Bright light peeked out from around it. Beyond the curtain in the real apartment, was the calm Hallstätter See. The only doorway out of the main room was on the right wall. As Sparrow started through the only doorway out of the room, he glanced over his shoulder at the curtain.

Sparrow found a short hall that ran left and right. There was a door at each end. Directly in front of him was a third door. He reached forward and pushed it open.

The bathroom was nearly twice the size of the original, and was laid out differently. Instead of a single small tub with a showerhead, it had a large shower stall with two showerheads. The shower's walls were clear glass along the top half and opaque along the bottom. On the right wall there was a large whirlpool tub with room enough for three. It had a large sparkling facet. A counter with two sinks ran along the left wall with a full wall-length mirror over them. There was a single porcelain toilet hidden behind a short privacy wall. The room's light brown stone tile matched that of the original apartment. A single rug and a stack of towels matched the tile.

Except for the large walk-in closet that was filled with a variety of clothes that were just his size, the master bedroom was just as he had left it. A large queen bed dominated the room. It sat along the back wall and had the same brown and white comforter that he had used in the original apartment. The headboard was made of solid oak and stained dark. It was an antique that he had picked up years ago on a whim. Twin nightstands flanked the bed and there was a small lamp on each one. A five-draw dresser sat along the right wall and a mirrored double dresser rested along the left wall. A cedar chest sat at the end of the bed.

Stepping forward, Sparrow lifted the lid to the chest. It was packed full with many of his belongings.

Sparrow turned and exited the room without closing the chest. As he passed the doorway to the main room, he glanced at the curtained window in the main room, but continued on to the spare bedroom.

It was void of the expected furniture. Instead, it had a desk on the left wall. A large computer monitor sat on the desk. The modified weight bench filled the rest of the small room.

Sparrow sighed heavily and returned to the main room. Lost in thought, he stood over the back of the couch and ran his hand over its soft leather. He considered sitting on it, but decided that doing so would be accepting the apartment's existence. Accepting the apartment, would be accepting Diamond's offer.

Turning, he faced the curtain. He stood in silence for several moments before moving over to stand before it. Slowly, he reached up and gripped it in both hands.

"He may be able to make me disappear, but not even Diamond can change what is on the other side of this curtain," he mumbled to himself.

He threw the curtain open. Before him was a small wooden balcony with the Hallstätter See beyond it. The mountain lake glistened in the morning sun. To the left and right of the lake stood the snow covered wooden buildings of Hallstatt with wisps of smoke drifting upward from their stone chimneys. A small charcoal grill sat on the snow-covered porch along with a small outdoor table. Two olive colored lounge chairs offered a relaxed view of the lake. Gently, Sparrow reached up and laid his hand against the glass. It was cold to the touch.

Sparrow's head spun, and he felt sick. Staggering backward he collapsed on the couch and sat there for the next hour, staring at the sliding door's wooden handle. As much as the desire burned in him, he refused to get up and pull on it. A part of him just wasn't ready to see if the scene beyond the glass was somehow real.

Despite feeling violated, he slowly took control of his anger and actually found serenity in the view.

\* \*

A knock at the door brought Sparrow out of his trance. The knock came a second time before he moved. Rising, he started across the room. When he reached the door, he griped the door's knob, but glanced over his shoulder at the glass wall. There was a third knock before he turned away from the window. Sighing deeply, he pulled the door open. His breath caught in his throat at the sight of the woman from the garden standing before him.

She still wore the same loose fitting white dress. It clung to her small bosom and flowed down over her slender hips to reach the floor. The opening at the neck reached down below her breasts and revealed the silver pendant around her neck. Her black hair cascaded over her shoulders and past her waist. When she moved, the light turned to silver waves that washed over its glossy surface. Her skin was pale, delicate, and flawless. No wrinkles, marks, or blemishes marred her features. Beneath her dark eyebrows were black pools of laughter, shadowed by long eyelashes. Her full lips were painted red. She wore simple cloth slippers on her feet and held a battered old leather book in her hands.

She smiled and said, "Hello, Wolff. I'm Dreah." She held out her hand.

Sparrow didn't initially respond. He was too shaken by her beauty. Her features had been shaded in the garden, but now in full light, they stunned him. He doubted he had ever seen a more beautiful woman.

Dreah raised an eyebrow in amusement, and Sparrow realized he had been staring. He flushed with embarrassment.

"Sorry." Cursing to himself, he stepped back to allow her to enter.

Dreah lowered her hand and moved inside. Sparrow closed the door behind her. Dreah glided across the room until she was standing behind the leather couch. Slowly she ran her hand along the very spot Sparrow had recently done the same. Finally, she turned to face him. Waving the small book around the apartment, she said, "I hope you like it."

"It's fine," Sparrow lied. He still felt anger over the apartment, but he had had enough time to wrestle with it before Dreah's arrival to keep it under control. As for Dreah, a beautiful woman had never unnerved him before, and he didn't like it.

"If you are wondering, the artwork is yours. Your place in Austria went up for sale so we purchased it and shipped it here. You will find everything is as you left it."

"Thanks," said Sparrow as he took up a position behind the kitchen counter. It formed a barrier between him and Dreah, and brought him some relief. "Given that we are underground, it is not what I would have expected." His eyes darted to the large window. It had started snowing outside.

Dreah smiled, "Yes, this place does take some getting used to." She paused and smiled as she also glanced at the window. Turning again to Sparrow, she said, "Don't worry, it's an illusion. The lake and the village are not actually beyond the wall."

Sparrow managed a smile. "That's a relief."

Dreah's smile broadened. "I hope Brandon got you everything you needed."

"He did," replied Sparrow.

"And he showed you around?"

"Yes, he did."

"Good. He can get distracted sometimes, and he is bit trying. But he is a good kid, and..."

"And he has a special talent for tolerating people," interrupted Sparrow.

"Yes, he does. The kid is special."

Uneasy silence settled between them. Sparrow's discomfort continued to grow with Dreah's dark eyes focused on him. She continued to smile and maintain her delicate poise.

"So, if you need anything, I hope you won't hesitate to call on me. I understand that all of this can be unsettling. To tell you the truth, I am only comfortable in the garden myself." Dreah started forward. She passed Sparrow still hiding behind the counter, and stopped before the apartment's door. She waited patiently.

Realizing she was waiting for him, Sparrow left the safety of the kitchen and quickly opened the door. Dreah stepped into the hallway and turned to face him.

"Wolff, please don't hesitate to come see me. I want to make your stay here as easy for you as possible. What we have is yours to enjoy, so please don't lock yourself up in there. Allow yourself to get out and mingle with the others. I'm sure it will do you a world of good. I look forward to us being friends."

"Me too," Sparrow managed to say.

Dreah smiled and turned to walk away. Abruptly, she turned back around to face him. "Sorry, I almost forgot." She held out her hand. In it, she held a silver chain with a small silver pendant dangling from it. The pendant was a triangle and circle looped together. Inside the shapes was a three-pointed triquetra.

"I'm not one much for jewelry," he said.

"I know. But please take it anyway. When I got up this morning and saw it, I thought of you. I think you will need it."

Slowly, Sparrow reached out and took the pendant.

Dreah smiled and then turned to leave. Sparrow's eyes lingered on her as she left. Her movements were graceful and her dress swayed around her slender body. Her slippered feet made no noise on the hard flooring. The hallway brightened as she passed through it.

Just as Dreah was about to round a corner, she turned and waved gently. Feeling overwhelmed, Sparrow barely managed to wave back as he retreated into his apartment, and slammed the door shut behind him. For several moments he leaned against the door with confusion overwhelming him. Dreah had awakened urges in him he hadn't felt since college, and it worried him.

He felt metal pressing sharply into his flesh. He glanced down and opened his hand to reveal the pendant lying in his palm. Briefly, he wondered if the Citadel was more than captivity after all.

\* \*

Sparrow spent the first night in his new apartment alone. The only thing he did not find in the cedar chest was his weaponry. He inventoried the gear, and set his climbing gear aside along with a small dart gun used for driving spikes into rock.

The refrigerator was fully stocked and he patched together a quick dinner of fried rice and teriyaki chicken. He found a pair of chopsticks in the silverware drawer. Afterward, he lit a small wood fire and stared into it for an hour as he wondered where the smoke went to as it disappeared up the narrow chimney.

Eventually, he forced his mind away from the smoke and to his dilemma. He felt like a captive and was confused by the effort being made to make him feel welcomed. He had no doubt he would find a way to escape the Citadel, but he feared facing his growing emotions once he was free. In the Citadel, his environment was controlled; not ideal, but controlled. Outside he would be bombarded with sensory input that would be overwhelming. Perhaps Diamond had considered this, it explained why he was locked down. Unable to understand his situation, Sparrow eventually turned his attention to another source for answers.

The computer in his office looked conventional, but it wasn't. It operated on the same complex level and with the same tight security. The wall behind the computer could be used to display information, but Sparrow stuck to the small monitor screen. He spent several hours learning to navigate the system, and testing the security. In the end, he found more frustration than answers. He finally gave up and turned in.

The next day, he fixed a small breakfast of coffee and toast while he scanned the news. He then exercised for an hour. After a shower, he turned to the computer to search for information on Diamond, and those he could expect to encounter in the Citadel.

The internal system contained some data but most of it was blocked to him. He tried to skirt around it but couldn't. The external Internet had lots of detailed information on Diamond and Diamond Security Solutions, but he suspected sifting through the propaganda for the truth would take days.

Diamond was a lawyer, businessman, and philanthropist. His money had been earned the old fashioned way, inherited from his father. Diamond Enterprises was worth billions. However, Diamond had turned the company into a different direction from his father. Moving away from real estate and law, Diamond focused on aerospace, medical facilities, and genetic research. His company held several patents in the avionics field, and owned numerous hospitals, research facilities, and even a company responsible for the collection and storage of blood and plasma for emergencies.

Diamond's influence on the medical field was prodigious. A man could change his face, or even his fingerprints, but he couldn't change his DNA. Diamond had volumes of information on people, and their capabilities. It made hiding from him nearly impossible.

He was disappointed to find no information about Dreah. She was mentioned but no one knew her. She only appeared in a few pictures, and there were no fan sites dedicated to her. In the few pictures Sparrow found, she always appeared the same. As the others around her aged, she remained flawless.

Heather Stone, or Fluxstone, had only scowled at him in the common area. She was widely known, and had been an active meta-human for several years. Her association with Diamond was well documented and she often accompanied him to important functions. She served as the chief public relations officer for Diamond Security

Solutions. Most believed she was Diamond's personal assistant, while others believed she was his daughter, and still others speculated that they were lovers. Regardless of the relationship, her influence on the team was well documented. There was plenty of information on her abilities as well. She possessed the ability to increase her density and thus enhance her strength. The upper limit of her strength was unrecorded, but he found pictures of her supporting a 747. She could also drop her density low enough to allow her to walk through walls. Her powers made her dangerous, but her influence on Diamond was Sparrow's greater concern.

Out of hope to explain the young man's odd behavior, Sparrow spent several minutes researching Brandon. Despite his annoying behavior, Sparrow had come to like the kid. He had a personal page on several social networking websites, but there was no other information on him. Most of the information Sparrow found, he dismissed because most of it came from the kid's own inflated ego.

He found even less information on Sarah. She had been a prominent physicist, but had died in a lab accident. Sparrow found a newspaper article on her funeral with Brandon in the picture along with Dreah and Heather. If Sarah had been a meta-human, there was no mention of it.

Many of the other names Sparrow found connected to DSS were familiar to him. The team was well known and its exploits exceedingly well documented. Of course, Sparrow now knew Diamond on a level that the world didn't. He figured the information available to the public was what Diamond allowed them.

Eventually, Sparrow left his room to explore the Citadel. He pushed the boundaries of his security clearance everywhere he went. He tried doors and t-ports at every turn. He visited the garden and Brandon's lab. He took the opportunity to pocket several small tools and to study the sidekick pieces, while Brandon rambled on about the mechanical arm that would not stop spinning. When time came for lunch, he ate in the common area. The kitchen took his order as Brandon had predicted. The *Hacker-Pschorr Dark* was room temperature, and the sirloin was medium rare. The vegetables were steamed and seasoned to perfection.

It wasn't hard to spot Glip-2 as the globe slowly rose over the shaft's edge to watch him. It hovered there and then disappeared. A short time later, the lights of a hallway branching off from the common area pulsed. A moment later, Glip-2 flew around the corner. When it disappeared again, Sparrow immediately left the table. He watched from the kitchen as the globe reappeared a third time. It floated around the common area searching for him, and then darted off. Sparrow followed, and the two took up their game of cat-and-mouse again. Other than fooling Glip-2 in the common area, the globe proved too fast for Sparrow to fool again.

Glip-2 darted along the hallways with ease. It disappeared from empty hallways and reappeared in areas Sparrow had been standing moments before. The doorways and areas Glip-2 used were hidden and denied him by his security clearance. Using the stolen sidekick, Sparrow began mapping the globe's path.

\* \*

The days passed slowly for Sparrow as he explored the Citadel. Any time his emotions started to get the best of him, he visited the garden. Eventually he set out to meet the others. His observations of the others had taught him where to find them at any time of the day. Most had full time jobs and others came and went as they pleased; but to someone trained as Sparrow was, they were all predictable. Today, he knew where Heather would be, and for how long.

He arrived in the gym at exactly seven o'clock and spent the first hour swimming laps in the large pool. Heather arrived at eight. Unfortunately, she wasn't alone. Normally she would spend the early hours working out alone, and that was why Sparrow had chosen this time of the day to meet her face-to-face. Next to Glip-2, he considered her his biggest obstacle, and had hoped to assess her true intent. The presence of the others complicated his plan.

There was nothing in the computers, and very little Internet information, on the young woman who entered the room after Heather. Kahori Tokushima was eighteen, athletic, and popular. Brandon claimed she was Diamond's goddaughter and that her parents were dead. Throughout the day, she could be found nearly anywhere in the Citadel, laughing and speaking with everyone.

Latisha Anderson, Envoy, was a solider like Aegis, and looked every bit one. Her hair was shaved like a cadet fresh out of boot camp and she was fit. Her right arm had a dark metal object intertwined around and through it that granted her the ability to manipulate vast amounts of energy. It also left her limited use of the arm. The Internet loved her, but she continued to choose the life of a soldier instead of that of a celebrity.

Jack Turley, Wavefront, contrasted sharply with the others. He needed a shave and his clothes were baggy and dirty. He puffed a cigarette that earned him the wrath of Envoy every time he blew smoke into the air. A floppy cattleman hat was the Aussie's trademark. He had actually done commercials in the past to sell them. He brought the rugged culture of an outdoorsman to life. Despite the fact that he looked like a hillbilly, and never graduated high school, Turley was very intelligent. According to his file, he was a wizard with computers and advanced technology.

Lawrence Pentacle, Paragon, spread his wings as he entered the large room. None of the corridors of the Citadel were cramped but the man instinctually sensed the freedom of the large room. Paragon was dressed only in a pair of baggy blue jeans. His hair was long and well groomed. His personal code of honor was like the knights of fiction. It was a weakness that could be exploited simply by placing an innocent in danger.

The last individual to enter gave Sparrow pause. Slipstream was counted as one of the most powerful meta-humans on the planet. Personal information on the man was non-existent. His powers and exploits were well documented, however. He first appeared officially just over forty years ago. However, Sparrow suspected he was connected to several deaths in a small town in Kentucky thirty years earlier. The details of that incident were sketchy, and Diamond shielded the metal-skinned man from any questions related to it. Slipstream walked several inches above the floor, and through a sonar-like sense, he saw everything in the room without turning his head.

Sparrow pretended to ignore the group as he finished his laps and began to dry off. With the addition of the unexpected guests, he decided to put his plan off for a later date.

The group gathered by a mat near the pool. Fluxstone and Kahori moved onto the mat and the others circled them. Fluxstone towered over Kahori. The larger woman was well muscled and Kahori was slim and thin, giving Fluxstone at least a fifty pound advantage. Sparrow suspected any sparring would be over quickly.

"Okay, little girl. Let's see what you've got." Fluxstone said as she back stepped onto the map and flexed her muscled arms.

"Twenty on the Amazon," said Jack he as looked around at his friends and pointed at Fluxstone.

"You're on," replied Envoy.

"You?" said Wavefront as he turned to Paragon.

"No, friend. I do not bet, especially on an outcome between two friends."

Wavefront looked disgusted, and turned to Slipstream. Shaking his head, he said, "You don't have any money." Turning to Sparrow, he yelled, "How 'bout you fella? Care to wager a dollar?" To the others, he mumbled, "Bloody, work with me here guys, we can take'em for all he's got."

Sparrow simply shook his head no. Fluxstone frowned at him, and then looked back to Wavefront. The Aussie either ignored her or didn't notice the glare.

From the mat, Kahori said, "Hey Jack, Brandon said you were broke. He said you owe him a hundred bucks. When did you get money?"

"I have some in me private stash, little lady. Don't you worry."

"Basilio said he is in for the going bet. He said to bet on whoever Jack wasn't betting on," said Envoy.

Everyone laughed.

"Aw, that hurts now. Can't a guy have a string of bad luck?" Wavefront said in response.

"Your luck is always bad, Jack," replied Envoy.

"If you people are done, can we get on with this?" Fluxstone's mood had soured, and she kept glancing in Sparrow's direction.

"Slow down, sugar, we'll get to you soon enough. Let's see, that's me a'betting against all of you. Bank, darlin, bank. Hey! No coaching!"

Having pulled Kahori to one side, Envoy held her hand up to Wavefront with the middle finger extended. When she finished whispering to Kahori, the young girl rejoined Fluxstone in the center of the mat. Fluxstone did not seem to mind the coaching.

Envoy stepped between them, looked at each in turn and raised her hand.

"Wait!" yelled Butch from the doorway. He charged across the room waving money in the air. He looked like he had just rolled out of bed. "Twenty on little sister!" He stopped next to the others, smiling. "Brandon told me you'd be here! I can't believe you didn't wait on me!"

"I'll take that bet," said Wavefront.

"I only get Jack. That is insulting," said Fluxstone.

"Hey, I've got to take care of my little girl. Besides, she's been practicing," grinning Butch nodded at Kahori.

Before anyone could interrupt again, Envoy dropped her hand and said, "Go!"

Despite his decision to leave, Sparrow watched from the sidelines. It was still an opportunity to learn something about Fluxstone.

She was experienced. She circled the smaller quicker girl and allowed Kahori to lead as she waited for an opening. Even without her powers, her size and strength would end the match if she got her hands on Kahori.

Although skilled, Kahori was inexperienced. Making it an easy handhold for any opponent, her hair was long and tied in a ponytail. She didn't pace herself, and her breathing quickly became labored. She was much quicker, but Fluxstone's experience easily countered it.

Except for Slipstream, the group cheered from the sidelines every time one of the women gained an advantage. With his arms crossed over his chest, Slipstream stood behind the others and watched the match like a disapproving father.

Kahori made an attempt to leg sweep Fluxstone. She caught her foot on the mat and stumbled. Fluxstone took advantage of the mistake and immediately grabbed for the smaller girl. She realized it was a ruse too late as Kahori rebounded from the blunder, caught Fluxstone by the front of her sweatshirt, rolled backward, and heaved the heavier woman out of the ring.

Cheers erupted from everyone as they rushed forward to congratulate Kahori. In their excitement, they nearly missed Wavefront trying to sneak out of the room.

"Where do you think you're going?" Fluxstone called after him from her sitting position outside the ring. "I lost fair and square."

Wavefront cringed and froze in mid step. Turning, he shrugged. Paragon and Butch didn't give him time to make an excuse. They tackled him. After a moment, Butch stood up with Wavefront's wallet in hand. Handing it to Envoy, he and Paragon protected her from Wavefront.

"No fair," said Wavefront, looking as insulted as he could.

"You hillbilly! You're twenty short! You made a bet you couldn't cover!" Envoy held up the empty wallet and waved a couple of bills in the air.

Wavefront cringed again under everyone's glare.

"Sorry, mate. Had to make a beer run last night. You know how it is."

"Sorry, hillbilly," said Envoy as she tossed the wallet to the ground. "Everyone knows that Bob keeps a wide assortment of beer on hand."

Looking up from her conversation with Kahori, Fluxstone broke in, "His hat has his private stash. It's inside the inner head band."

"Bloody hell, woman! You don't violate a man like that!"

Before Wavefront could move, Butch snatched the hat and handed it to Envoy. Paragon held Wavefront back as he protested.

"That's not fair! Thief!" he yelled.

Envoy wrinkled her nose as she reached inside the grimy hat. A moment later she grinned and pulled out a roll of money. "This should cover your bets today, and the rest I'll turn over to Brandon for you." Laughing, she tossed the hat back to Wavefront.

He jumped for it but Paragon flexed his wings and the rush of air sent the hat sailing over everyone's head. As Wavefront flailed for it, he slipped and plunged into the pool. Everyone roared with laughter as he stood up in the water with his soggy hat on his head.

Sputtering, he said, "You'll regret that Sheila! That there is the money I've been saving for your wedding present!"

Laughing, Heather replied, "That's okay, Jack. Seeing you finally take a bath is all the present I need."

Sparrow chuckled at Wavefront's misfortune, and realized even Slipstream had cracked a smile. Wavefront grumbled as he climbed out of the pool. Kahori had started prancing around the mat, challenging the others to a fight. They all merrily declined.

Sparrow had seen enough and started for the door.

Kahori called after him. "Hey mister, how about you? I'm feeling lucky. Care to spar a few rounds?"

Sparrow glanced back and saw the young girl dance a couple of steps as she held her hands up in a boxing stance. As she threw a punch, she grinned. The others stopped harassing Wavefront to watch.

"No thanks. I just spent an hour in the pool." Sparrow said.

"You hear that guys? The old man is afraid of a little girl," Kahori teased.

"Never mind him. He shouldn't be here anyway," Fluxstone said to Kahori.

"Anyone? How about you, Paragon?" Kahori continued to tease as she looked at the others. Paragon threw up their hands in mock fear and shook his head no.

Sparrow stood and watched as Fluxstone turned the conversation away from him. *No*, he screamed at himself. *Never change a plan. Stick to the plan. Never change a plan!* But anger flared within him when he saw Fluxstone glaring over her shoulder at him. He turned and started toward the mat.

"Okay, I'll go a round." Sparrow dropped his bag and kicked off his shoes. The others turned to face him.

Fluxstone stepped forward to block his path. "Go away," she said.

Sparrow stopped, and the two locked eyes. Logic screamed at Sparrow to walk away, but the anger he was feeling toward Fluxstone pushed him headlong into the challenge.

"Double or nothing!" shouted Wavefront. "Ma'bet's on the new guy!"

At first no one responded to Wavefront's challenge, then Fluxstone spoke up over her shoulder, "I'll cover you, Jack." She never took her eyes off Sparrow.

He allowed Fluxstone her moment, then sidestepped her and moved to the center of the mat. Behind him, her eyes bored a hole into his back, and he wondered just how far he could push her.

Envoy stepped up to Fluxstone and spoke quietly to her. After a moment Fluxstone relaxed her glare and moved to the edge of the mat. She kept her arms folded across her chest. The others moved aside to watch as well. Not waiting for someone to tell her to start, Kahori quickly circled Sparrow.

"Are you sure you want to do this, old man? I took it easy on her." Kahori smirked.

Sparrow's only response was to take up a defensive stance.

"Watch'er feet, mate. Ay'pack as mighty a punch as any you can land," coached Wavefront from the sideline.

Kahori took immediate control of the fight. She was more experienced than Sparrow had thought. She barely gave him time to consider her tactics as she pressed him over and over, and changed her style with each blow. She connected with two quick kicks to Sparrow's right side that nearly stunned him. Another kick tapped his left side. It was light and had been meant as a warning. She knew more about his condition than he had guessed. Kahori smirked, and held her hands out to her side in a gesture of innocence.

Sparrow was not used to prolonged combat. If he went more than two blows with his opponent his advantage was lost. However, this bout continued to drag out, and he began to feel the weight of his injuries. Only by focusing deeper and deeper on the combat was he able to block out his pain. Around him the cheers faded. Eventually, Sparrow lost himself to the moves and countermoves. Sparrow's punches became harder and deadlier.

Kahori lashed out with a high kick that Sparrow easily ducked. Spinning, she rolled over his back. She landed on the other side, and lashed out with a kick to his face that he barely avoided. Kahori backed off and danced before him.

The two locked eyes and the look in Sparrow's eyes caused Kahori to hesitate. Sparrow immediately lashed out with a high-kick that Kahori barely avoided.

"Ooo!" yelled Wavefront.

"That was a close one, little sister," cautioned Butch. "Be careful."

"Don't worry. I've got this," Kahori replied confidently. She had already recovered from the attack.

Sparrow hadn't noticed the exchange. He remained focused on Kahori, and eyed her as she danced back and forth in front of him. Something had changed about her tactics. Instinctually, he knew her last move had been a distraction.

Sparrow leaped, twisted, and lashed out with a roundhouse kick. He connected with the opponent sneaking up behind him. She was sent sprawling across the mat. Sparrow landed facing Kahori.

The cheers from those watching died instantly. Kahori's eyes widened with surprise.

"You bastard!" screamed Fluxstone as she dashed forward onto the mat.

Seeing her out of the corner of his eye, Sparrow prepared for her to assault him. Instead, he found her leaning over the unconscious form of the opponent who had tried to sneak up behind him. It was an exact duplicate of Kahori. He knew the others still stood around them, but he could barely acknowledge them. Anger blinded him, and it took all his strength to keep from attacking Kahori.

"You could have killed her with that hit!" Heather stood up and advanced on Sparrow. He did a back-step and turned to face her while keeping the rest of the group in view.

Paragon kneeled next to Kahori and placed a hand on her. Envoy stepped in front of Fluxstone and placed her hand on the larger woman's shoulder to restrain her. Her brow furrowed as she noted the wild look in Sparrow's eyes. Everyone stood on edge.

"It's my fault," said Kahori as she stepped past Sparrow and in front of the two women. She looked down at her doppelganger. Under Paragon's touch, she had started to stir. Turning to face Sparrow, Kahori said, "I tried to trick him. It had been a fair fight." Turning back to Fluxstone, she insisted, "It's okay. It was my fault." She bent down over her doppelganger and placed her hand on it. It dissolved away. Standing back up, she turned to Sparrow. She wiped blood from the corner of her mouth that had not been there before absorbing the doppelganger, and managed a smile. "Sorry."

"Yes!" screamed Wavefront. Startled, everyone jumped. "Pay up suckers! That was awesome, mate! I've never seen that trick fail before. Yes!" Despite Wavefront's enthusiasm, everyone else remained subdued. As the group broke up, Envoy led Fluxstone and Kahori out of the gym. Paragon followed them.

Sparrow struggled to push down his anger, and to keep himself restrained. All he wanted was to lash out at everyone, but instinct held him in check. He had allowed himself to become so engulfed in the combat that his control over his emotions had slipped.

Slowly, he pulled his anger under control. It left him drained, and his knees weak. With shaking hands, he quickly gathered up us things and allowed Wavefront to lead him toward the exit. Butch followed them.

Wavefront slapped Sparrow across the back.

"Congratulations, mate," he said. "I love that little girl but she had that comin. Side's, I needed the win! M'name's Jack. Yours?" he asked.

"Sparrow," he mumbled as he swallowed the urge to kill the man. Keeping his eyes focused on the white floor, and his mind focused on his emotions, he allowed Wavefront to lead him toward the door. He was at a loss to explain what had happened. He knew he hadn't experienced true anger in years, but the way it had taken control of him shocked him. If he was going to function at all now, he had to find a way to control it.

Suddenly, the three men found their way blocked. Slipstream stood before them with his arms still crossed across his chest.

*Boom!*

The impact caused Sparrow's ears to ring. If the strike had been intended for him, he would never have dodged it. Slipstream's hand was embedded four inches into the wall. The wall flaked and crumbled around the hole. His stare was focused on Sparrow. Without a word, he withdrew his hand, turned toward the door, and left the room.

Sparrow picked up a piece of the strange material as Butch mumbled behind him, "I didn't think the walls of this place could be damaged like that."

The piece of wall was porous and lightweight. As Sparrow studied it, it crumbled and turned a dull gray. Looking back to the wall, he found that the area around the hole was also dull in color. Slipstream's threat was obvious. *Don't mess with Kahori.*

Wavefront broke in, "Don't mind him mate. He's a little tightly strung. The wall will heal soon enough or else Glip-2 will come along and fix it. Likely, he already knows about it. Come on, you can buy me a beer. Care to join me and me new mate, Butch? Here mate, have a rollie." Wavefront held out a small hand-rolled cigarette to Sparrow. Sparrow didn't hear Butch's response and ignored the cigarette as he rolled the piece of wall over and over in his hands. Wavefront escorted him from the room.

A few minutes later the three men sat in the common area enjoying a beer. Sparrow was actually starting to relax, and his hand had stopped shaking, when Aegis interrupted them.

"Hey," said Wavefront. "Sparrow, this here's me best mate, Alex.

Alex, this here's me new mate, Sparrow. Careful Alex, he has quite a kick."

Aegis grabbed a chair, spun it around backwards and sat down. The shield on his back would have prevented him from sitting comfortably in the chair otherwise.

"Jack. Butch." Aegis nodded to each man as he greeted him, and then he turned to Sparrow and extended his hand. Sparrow didn't hesitate to take it.

Almost immediately Wavefront and Butch launched into telling Aegis about the incident in the gym. Aegis humored his friends and even asked a few questions that allowed them to embellish the story.

"Bam!" shouted Wavefront. "Little sister went down. Out like a light!"

Aegis smiled at Sparrow. "She's tried that trick before. It usually works for her, but I've warned her against trickery in combat. Taking advantage of a moment can be tactful, but relying on your enemy to miss your slight of hand is dangerous. I'm glad to see she finally got caught. With it being on the sparring mat, maybe it will be a lesson learned." If Aegis was upset over Sparrow knocking out Kahori's doppelganger, he didn't show it. "How did you know?"

Sparrow shrugged. "Instinct mostly. This place is crawling with meta-humans, and I've seen her all over."

Aegis nodded.

"Heather was a bit of a'snot," said Wavefront.

Aegis frowned and turned to Wavefront.

"She seemed to have a beef with ol' Sparrow here." Wavefront waved his hand toward Sparrow. "She was rude, more than normal that is. I thought she was gong to hit'em after the match."

Aegis nodded at Wavefront. Looking to Sparrow, he said, "I'm sorry about that friend. Heather has been under a lot of stress lately."

Sparrow nodded. "No harm done."

"Oh! Pardon my rudeness, buddy. You don't have a beer. What would you like?" asked Wavefront to Aegis. Without waiting for a response, he waved to the kitchen staff to bring a new round. Instead of three fingers, he held up four.

Shaking his head, Aegis said, "No thanks, Jack. I'm on duty. In fact, I'm headed out on an assignment in a couple of hours."

Jack suddenly got serious. "Mission?"

"Yes. Security detail on a politician in Paris."

"I'll get m'gear," said Wavefront as he started to rise. Aegis pushed him back down into the seat.

"No need buddy. El Incindiaro and Stronghold are already prepping. Slipstream will join us in Paris. We're augmenting a security team that's already in place. The client's people limited our numbers. Besides you're on down time, and I'm ordering you to stay on it."

"Blimey! You gonna leave me behind?" Wavefront looked injured.

"Don't go there. You know the rules. Down time is mandatory. Besides, don't you have to plan a certain party that you've been told not to plan?" Wavefront broke into a broad grin. Butch looked away and whistled innocently. Aegis chuckled. "Heather knows what you are planning, and you know she has forbidden it. Absolutely no strippers, Jack. She will break your legs and mine."

Wavefront leaned forward and said in a loud enough whisper for everyone to hear, "Don't worry mate. I've planned many a bachelor party and there ain't no Sheila ruined one yet. B'sides, you ever seen a stripper who can fly? It's enough to send a man into hysterics." Wavefront looked at Sparrow and grinned ear to ear as he added, "Hotter than sin, mate!" Sparrow couldn't help but grin in response.

"Read my lips, Jack. No strippers." Wavefront only smiled and winked. Changing the subject, Aegis turned to Butch. "Prep the *Egress*, Butch. Be ready at ten hundred hours."

"Roger boss," said Butch as he downed the last of his beer. He then rose and left the table.

"Jack, I am expecting Meta-man to arrive here tomorrow. Let him know I'll be back in a couple of days, please." Aegis received a nod from Wavefront and then rose from his seat. Turning to Sparrow, he said, "It was good to meet you. I hope to see you around." Waving, he walked away from the table. Calling over his shoulder, he added, "No strippers, Jack!"

Wavefront laughed and raised his bottle in salute to his friend.

# CHAPTER 9
# UNE VILLE ALLÉE

Sparrow laid the faceplate of the stolen sidekick on the table. He compared the internal parts with those of his assigned unit. As he suspected, they were identical. It had taken him several days of studying the device to learn anything about it, and he still didn't understand most of it. It was alien and its parts didn't resemble those of any man-made computer he had ever used. It was only by pulling out parts while using the device that he learned anything about it. He had considered pulling up information on the sidekick from the Citadel computers, or asking Brandon about them, but had decided against both ideas. He had no way of hiding what he did with the Citadel computers, and he didn't want anyone suspecting he was tampering with a device.

Sparrow pulled a small bulb out of the sidekick. It had the same blue liquid light found in all the doors. Even removed from the device, the light in the bulb flashed brightly. He picked up a piece of gold foil and wrapped it around the bulb before inserting it back into the sidekick. He had tried leaving the bulb out of the device, but it wouldn't function at all without it. When the bulb clicked into place, the faceplate lit up, but a single blue light on the front of the device stayed dark.

The bulb was an antenna that connected the sidekick with the Citadel computers. From what little Sparrow could understand, the sidekick used dimensional folding to communicate with the Citadel, or any other communications device, over astronomical distances.

It was technology way beyond anything he could explain. The gold foil blocked the signal. It caused him to loose access to the Citadel's extensive memory banks, but it also prevented Glip-2 from tracking the device. He still had access to the sidekick's internal memory, he could still use of the device's scanning capabilities, and he could still use external probes to connect it with other computers or electronic equipment, which it could then hack or manipulate.

* *

Sliding along the wall, Sparrow peered around the corner. As his map predicted, Glip-2 was gliding toward him. Quickly, he retreated up the passageway and into the common area surrounding the central shaft. He leaned against the glass just as Glip-2 came out of the hallway. The globe glided past him and over the side of the shaft to disappear. Smiling, Sparrow turned and headed for his apartment.

Sitting at his desk, Sparrow drew the latest portion of his map on the stolen sidekick. He then picked up a diamond shaped pin and examined it. The bottom of the pin was marked with a blue dot. He placed it by itself at the edge of the desk next to an armband and his modified dart gun. He felt a pang of guilt, but quickly pushed it aside. He was going to do what he had to do. Diamond had left him no other choice.

The pin belonged to a scientist in the robotics lab. Over several days, Sparrow had pocketed five pins from five different staff members. The pins were at the center of security. Different security levels were encoded on the pins. The t-ports and the doorways acted as checkpoints that monitored the pins. If a pin failed to meet the required security level, the door simply wouldn't open, or was even dark.

Unfortunately, his first attempt to test the pins failed. Glip-2 came running when Butch passed a checkpoint with a pin Sparrow had switched for the man's own. His theft of pins had been restricted to individuals of roughly the same height and build as himself after that. He even went so far as to choose similar hair and eye color. He didn't know if his plan would work because he didn't know if the checkpoints also monitored a person's bio-signs. What he did know was that he didn't normally wear a pin, and the doors seemed to respond to him when he approached.

Hoping to compensate, Sparrow had pieced together the armband from various parts picked up from Brandon's lab. It ran on technology far below that of the Citadel, and it was uncomfortable to wear. Using the sidekick, he had scanned the bio-signs of the people the pins were stolen from. The armband was designed to imitate their heart rate and blood pressure. He had no idea if it would work, but his sidekick picked up the armband's pulse over his own heart rate. It only needed to keep Glip-2 at bay for a few minutes.

Sparrow hadn't found any additional security beyond the checkpoints. Given the importance of the Citadel to Diamond, he was puzzled by the slack security. He would have expected security cameras, facial recognition software, and even retinal scanning; and those were only conventional technologies he could understand. The Citadel was alien and its capabilities were unpredictable. He would need to expect anything.

*Tomorrow*, Sparrow said to himself as he rose and headed for the shower, *I will put Glip-2 to the test, and find out if there is a way out of this place.*

\* \*

Aegis stretched as he stood up from the chair. He would have preferred the comfort of the *Egress* but he knew his job, and he always took it seriously. He needed to stay close to the subject. Incindiaro had already expressed his disgust with Facet's politics so it was best to keep him at a distance, and Facet had refused to allow Slipstream or Stronghold into the same room with him, so that left only Aegis for the close contact work.

To the client, Aegis was to provide security from death threats. Death threats to controversial politicians like Marc Facet weren't uncommon, but when they came from meta-humans they were usually taken seriously. Facet's politics were unpopular with the meta-human community, and they were starting to protest loudly against him.

To Diamond, the mission was much more. For months, Diamond had been trying to get close to Facet. Facet was one of the first targets that Diamond had identified, and he had proven to be the most difficult to get near. This was the first time they had gotten within fifty yards of the man. Aegis had little doubt Diamond was connected to the death threats that had gotten them here.

The rally was planned for four, and if it went as planned, Diamond

Security Solutions might earn a permanent spot on Facet's security force for the first time. It would be much easier to keep an eye on him after that.

Pouring himself a cup of coffee, Aegis took a moment to dwell on the deep smoky aroma. He smiled at the dark-roasted liquid swirling in his cup. Dark strong coffee was one of his vices. He never got on missions deep in steamy jungles, so he always treated himself when he could. Apparently, Facet didn't skimp on the good stuff.

Striding over to the apartment's entrance, he peeked at he guard stationed outside the room. The man was asleep. After kicking the guard's chair to wake him, Aegis sat down at a table and glanced out the window at Paris. The city was coming alive with the dawn.

* *

The next day, Sparrow rose early. The halls were empty and only the cooks were up preparing for morning breakfast. He had two hours before the crowd would start arriving.

Sparrow took the elevator to the Citadel's top floor. Moving quickly through the corridors, he headed away from the shaft. After several turns he stopped. Ahead of him was a t-port he suspected was not connected with the rest of the system. He had witnessed Fluxstone and Diamond use it, and the control panels of the other t-ports didn't have this t-port as a possible exit.

Reaching into his pocket, he pulled the small pin out and tacked it to his shirt. Adjusting the armband concealed beneath his sleeve, he started forward. The t-port opened.

The port's control panel only offered two destinations. One was dark so he chose the second one. Just over nine seconds later the doors opened again and Sparrow walked out into a circular room with a single hallway leading away. Spinning, Sparrow saw that the walls of the circular room were covered in thick red tapestries trimmed with gold thread. Embroidered on each tapestry was a large golden tree. In between the tapestries hung large paintings.

The painting immediately to the right of the elevator was framed in grey stone. It showed a dark man dressed in animal skins standing over a fairer unprotected man lying on the ground. The darker man held a large stone high over his head and his foe begged for his life.

The second painting, framed in bronze, showed a hero wearing crude bronze armor. He held two struggling men high off the ground by their necks. Behind him was an immense city protected by a large wall decorated with bronze lion heads.

A king astride a great white horse surveyed a large army in the third painting. The king was tall and had hair of fine gold. His cloak was blue, and he carried a sword with an elaborate gold hilt. Next to the king, a man held a standard with a golden eagle etched into it. The frame was made of dark, almost black, wood carved into fine roses.

The next picture showed a man resting a large claymore across his shoulder. He stood in the center of a stone bridge, and faced an army. The frame was made from hundreds of small stones patched together.

The painting after that was framed by hundreds of small pieces of faded driftwood tied together with twine. It showed an African American man dressed in a flimsy shirt and dirty trousers. He carried a large steel hammer in one hand and a pickaxe in the other. He walked barefoot next to a railroad track.

Next came a frame of polished black stone that housed a picture of the hero known as Meta-man. He stood fearlessly upon a mound of devastation in the center of a large metropolitan street facing a large creature made of earth and debris. The hero wore a tattered US military uniform. The architecture of the buildings and the cars that lay overturned in the street indicated the scene was from the early nineteen hundreds.

The last picture didn't have a frame. It featured a human silhouette with blinding light flaring around it. The edges of the silhouette were blurred just enough to prevent Sparrow from deciding if the painting was of a man or a woman.

Sparrow took only a moment to consider someone's loose interpretations of the ages of man before he turned and moved toward the hallway.

The hallway was fifty feet long and ended at a set of double wooden doors. Along the right wall were three small stands. Atop each was a glass dome. Under each dome was an object that floated in the air. A solemn tune filled the hallway.

The object rotating under the first dome was a metal mask that was twisted and scratched. There were traces of blood inside the mask. A plaque attached to the pedestal read, *2000, Gear, Metal Clad Hero and Friend.*

The next pedestal had a single red rose in full bloom. There was no dirt or water for the stem, but the flower appeared real. The plague read, *2002, Floret, Her petals shall bless us forever.*

Under the last globe was a small broken and twisted unidentifiable metal device. It had a small speaker that issued the soft music filling the hallway. The plague attached to the pedestal read, *2005; Vox; A good friend; Her song silenced by the mark; Its beauty forever lost to the dark; In her memory, we make a choice; Revenge we disdain, Heroes we remain.*

Sparrow took less time to consider the memorials to fallen heroes than he had the paintings. He pushed on the double doors, and they swung inward.

The room before him was lavish. It was out of place in the high tech Citadel. It was paneled in wood and decorated with expensive art and antique furniture. Several small oil lamps and a large fireplace cast a somber mood to match the music in the hallway. Thick curtains covered windows that didn't actually reveal the outside. Dark burgundy carpet blanketed the entire room. The room was elegant, soft, and comfortable.

A large bookcase lined one wall. Running along the spines of the books, Sparrow found a virtual who's who of the literary world; new, old and ancient biographies and autobiographies, novels, textbooks and essays. Many of the covers were old and worn. He stopped at one that had become so worn with age it couldn't be read. Removing it, he glanced at the cover. It read; *Memories De La Vie Privee, 1791.* Understanding the value of the book, but doubting it was an original, he placed it gently back on the shelf.

Moving around the furniture, Sparrow glanced at the fireplace, and then above it at a large painting that dominated anyone's view in this part of the room. At first, Sparrow thought the picture was of Diamond, and he felt contempt for the man's arrogance. Then he realized it was of a close relative, possibly his father. Glancing at the gold plate attached to the bottom of the frame, he read the name, *Gaius Coltar Diamond.*

Sparrow turned away from the painting, and his eyes fell on a pedestal beside the fireplace sitting alone in the shadows. Lying under the glass dome was the small tattered book Dreah had been carrying the day she had visited him in his room. It was open, and a pale lamp illuminated old yellowed pages. Sparrow scanned the cursive script.

*Aug. 18, 1587*

*I can't express the joy I feel. I find myself in this new world, overwhelmed by the beauty of it. Then, God sees fit to bless me with an even greater beauty. My little one was born today, in what had promised to be a dark day; but now, Ananias calls it the most beautiful day we shall ever experience. By his affirmation, she is truly an omen that we shall survive this new but dangerous world...*

Sparrow silently cursed at the sound of someone approaching him from behind. He wanted to finish reading the diary.

"I wouldn't get too comfortable," said Fluxstone. "You don't belong here."

Although he was surprised it was Fluxstone, he didn't turn to face her. Maybe his actions in the gym had pushed her too far and she was keeping an eye on him now.

"Perhaps you're right. Time will tell. For now, I'm here aren't I?" Sparrow didn't look up from the diary, but instead watched Heather through her reflection in the glass dome. The couch stood between them but Sparrow doubted it would slow her down.

"I don't trust you, Kingsley."

Sparrow turned to face her for the first time, and replied, "I'm not looking for your trust, and judging from your lack of stealth, I don't need it either."

Fluxstone clenched her fists and moved around the edge of the couch. "Care to try your trick from yesterday on me? I'm not a kid who will underestimate you!" Her skin rippled.

"Heather!"

Without hesitation, Sparrow took his eyes off Fluxstone to look at Diamond. He had entered from the same hidden door next to the fireplace that Fluxstone had.

Fluxstone kept Sparrow locked in her venomous stare.

"Heather, please go on ahead to the ops center." Despite the building tension and Fluxstone's obvious anger, Diamond was calm. "Aegis and the others should be preparing for the rally by now. Go run operations until I get there."

"I'll be watching you, Kingsley." Fluxstone glanced at Diamond before turning and exiting the room through the double doors.

Sparrow watched as Diamond walked around the couch to stand

before the fireplace. For several moments, he didn't speak and stared into the fire.

"My father," he said holding his hand up to the painting. "He was probably what you think I am. Arrogant. Egotistical. Greedy. Yes, in some ways I am like him, but in others we are vastly different. This sherry room is to remind me of that."

Sparrow didn't respond, and Diamond didn't seem to expect him too.

"I was raised with a silver spoon in my mouth. I didn't care who I hurt, or how. It was during some of my meaner days that I found this place. I teased a local girl with a ride on my father's yacht. When she arrived at the dock, I pulled away and left her in tears. She wasn't my kind. She wasn't rich. It had all been a joke meant to humiliate her. Little did I know how that little adventure would end."

\* \*

Samuel couldn't stop laughing. "Did you see the look on her face? She actually thought we were going to take her with us." The others laughed with him. Even if they had found his actions mean, they wouldn't have said so. After all, it was Samuel's yacht, and he could have left them all behind too.

As they sailed out of the harbor, the friends retreated downstairs and the captain took over the controls. Several hours later, they dropped anchor off the shore of a small island. Their party lasted long into the night.

The next day, Samuel stood next to the railing and helped Amanda into a small boat. "I don't know about this," she said. "I didn't bring any hiking shoes, and these heels cost me four hundred *somalians*."

From the boat, Jessica replied, "Oh, stop whining. It's all you have done since we left dock yesterday. Besides, I'm getting bored. I want to explore the island. And it's *simoleons* not *somalians*."

"What do you think, Terry?" asked Samuel.

His friend looked up at him, started to answer, then dropped his head over the side of the small boat and vomited.

Samuel laughed. "You never could hold your liquor!"

The four friends didn't explore much. By the time they got off the beach, both girls were complaining, and Terry had gotten sick again. Retreating back to the beach, they ordered the captain to set up a small camp. After dinner, they spent several hours around a blazing fire, and when they were drunk and exhausted, they retreated to their tents.

* *

Samuel sprang up. Panting, he fought to understand what was happening. His head throbbed, and he felt sick. Beside him, Amanda groaned. Kicking out with her foot, she gouged his leg with her toenails.

"Ouch!" Samuel yelled as he jerked away from her. Leaping up, he staggered out of the tent.

"It's too early," Amanda groaned as she rolled over and went back to sleep.

Samuel stood on the beach and listened to the sounds of his sleeping friends. Even though the sun hadn't started to rise yet, he knew his pounding head would prevent him from getting back to sleep. Bending over, he rubbed his temples.

A drop of blood fell from his nose to strike the sand.

Puzzled, he rubbed his nose, and pulled his hand away bloodied. Staring at it, he staggered and fell backward into the sand. Confused, Samuel wondered if he was dreaming. Even with a full moon, the beach was too bright. The surf sounded like thunder crashing against the sand. Despite the warm night air, he shuddered with a chill when a breeze hit his sweat-streaked spine.

He glanced up, and the moon's bright light stung his eyes. He had to rub them for several moments before he could see clearly again. Leaning forward, he placed his finger against the side of his nose and blew hard. Dark blood painted the sand. He repeated the process with the other nostril, and more blood darkened the sand.

Glancing around the beach, he found the small boat beached several yards away. Early in the evening, the captain had taken it to return to the yacht. Now the waves rocked it against the sandy shore. A moan caused him to dismiss the boat and turn back to the tent. He stared at the closed flap and it grew silent inside. Amanda had fallen asleep again.

"Eeaaaa!" screamed Amanda.

Jumping forward, Samuel flung the tent flap back. Amanda lay curled in a ball with her arms wrapped around her legs. Blood flowed from her nose to pool in front of her. She shuddered and sobbed in her sleep.

"Amanda! Amanda!" Samuel shook her as he called her name, but couldn't wake her.

Running to the other tent, he dropped in front of it and ripped the zipper up. Moaning coming from inside the tent caused him to hesitate. Slowly, he pulled the flap back. Choking on his own blood, Terry lay on his back. Jessica lay across him, blood flowing from her nose and onto his chest.

Samuel rose unsteadily to his feet, and backed slowly away from the tents. His head swam with confusion. Turning, he fled toward the boat. Splashing through the water, he grabbed the edge and hauled himself into the craft. He landed on the body of the captain, crumpled in a pool of blood.

Samuel shrieked and scrambled out of the boat. He fell into the water and the strong waves crushed him to the sandy ocean floor. With strong hands, the surf held him under the water until he lungs threatened to burst. Only when the ocean pulled back to breathe itself did the grip relax enough for Samuel to push himself above the water's surface. He gulped handfuls of salty air and dragged himself up onto the sand. He stumbled to his feat. Without even looking at the tents, he fled the beach. He had no idea where he was going, and sought only to escape the fear that gripped him. The hours blurred as he ran, and the sun rose high over the island.

Some time later, Samuel found himself sitting on a rock and clutching his head. It still pounded, and he struggled to catch his breath. His nose had stopped bleeding, but he was exhausted. He was dizzy, and his vision was still blurry.

In his flight, he had clawed his way up the side of a small mountain, but he couldn't remember doing so. The white sand of the beach far below was radiant in the midmorning sun and stung his eyes when he looked at it. The tents fluttered under a soft wind, but there was no sign of life.

Hungry and weak, Samuel struggled to his feet, and started down the mountain. He didn't understand what had happened to him, but he knew he didn't want to spend another night on the island.

*Swhoosh!*

Samuel glanced around for the source of the noise. He was alone, so he started down the mountain again.

*Swhoosh!*

Samuel turned around quickly, but the motion made him dizzy. He stumbled and nearly fell. The pounding in his head increased. Grunting, he pushed aside his curiosity, and started toward the beach. He wanted down the mountain, and off the island.

*Swhoosh!*

Samuel froze. Slowly, he turned around again. It took him several moments, but finally he spotted a small crack in the mountain just beyond where he had been sitting. He hadn't noticed it earlier. Slowly, he approached it.

He kneeled next to it, but could not see inside. He lay down on his stomach and inched over the edge. Below him was a small barren cave with a dirt floor. There was no source for the sound, but, strangely, it was bright inside the cave.

Uneasiness crept into him, but his curiosity kept him from fleeing.

The cave looked like any of a dozen others scattered across the islands in this part of the ocean, but there was something about this one that forced him to examine every nook and cranny. The detail he saw in every grain of sand, marveled him. The walls were cloaked in shadow, but he could see the insects in even the darkest corner.

Suddenly, the fear from the night before washed over him like a wave. It left him paralyzed. Desperately, he wanted to climb to his feet and run, but he couldn't. He wanted to look away, but he couldn't. Somewhere below him in the cave lay the source of the previous night's horror, and it wanted him.

Through the fear, the cave spoke to him. It was only a whisper, but it called for him to enter the cave. The compulsion grew until it was overwhelming. Against his will, he reached out and grabbed the rock below him. He pulled, and slid toward the crack.

"Help!" screamed Samuel, but there was no answer.

His arms worked independent of his desires and slowly dragged him into the cave. When he cleared the crack, he fell twenty feet to the cave's floor. The impact knocked the wind from his lungs, but before he could catch his breath, his hands gripped the rocky wall and pulled him to his feet. As he gagged for breath in the stale dusty air, his legs carried him deeper into the cave. Blood flowed from his nose, and his head pounded harder than ever. Samuel glanced over his shoulder at the cave's entrance as he was dragged around a corner and out of sight of it.

The cave grew brighter and began to pulse the deeper in the cave he went. Rounding another corner, he was blinded by the intensity of the pulsing light, but his limbs refused to shield him from it, and his eyelids refused to respond. Through tears, he saw a red glow appear in the white pulsing light. It began to pulse along with the white light.

His hand scrapped against the rocky wall but refused to save him.

"Help me!" Samuel screamed.

The rocky wall became smooth against his hand, but it still refused to save him.

"Hel...Aaiiee!"

A piercing scream sliced through his head.

Samuel's body was released from the mental grip, and he collapsed to the white stone floor. He pressed his hands hard against his ears, but it did nothing to stifle the sound bouncing around inside his head. Desperate to escape the assault, Samuel clawed his way across the floor. Struggling to his feet, he turned to flee, but ran into something solid. Dark spots exploded across his vision, and he collapsed to the stone floor again.

Through the pain, Samuel looked up and found a tall man standing over him. The pulsing light gleamed off the man's naked metal body. His eyes were dark voids that swallowed up the blinding light. The source of the red pulse hung in the air just over his shoulder. It appeared to be a globe about two feet across.

The pain intensified and nightmarish visions blinded him. He saw thin frail creatures with white wispy hair, and large black eyes. Burning flares and a deep darkness. Nine shafts of bright light with large and small victims. The black-eyed creatures pawed at shafts of light. The victim's screamed, and their anguish echoed through Samuel's skull.

Samuel's body became numb and he began to black out. Out of desperation, he pulled on the last of his strength and rolled over, only to come face-to-face with one of the black-eyed creatures assaulting his mind. In his mind, it was a frail creature but now it was a shriveled dry husk curled into the fetal position and lying on the floor next to him. Only a few strands of white hair grew from its waxy scalp. Its large black eyes were sunken into its skull, but they still held just as much evil as the tall metal man, and they swallowed what remained of his free will.

He wanted to look away from those eyes, but found he couldn't. He had no strength left. He was defeated.

*Fwssh!*

A flash of energy struck the creature and it was flung away from Samuel. It slammed into the cave wall, and its dried husk shattered.

The assault on Samuel's mind stopped.

Reeling, but desperate to flee, Samuel climbed to his feet and staggered away from the broken creature. His legs were too weak, and he stumbled into the metal man again. Looking up, he found the metal man staring down at him. Dark energy leaked from his eyes, and his face was twisted with rage.

The light of the room shifted as the red glow moved around them and toward the alien. Samuel tore his gaze away from the man to watch the glow cross the room. The red globe's pulse slowed as it hovered over the shattered alien. Just when Samuel thought the pulse was going to stop altogether, the red globe flared brightly.

\* \*

"Glip-2 attacked me then, and I fled the cave. I managed to make my way back to the others in spite of my condition. We left the island and the captain's death was ruled a brain aneurism. We tried to go on with our lives and never spoke of it, even with each other. After awhile, they forgot, but I didn't. They all died young. Terry had a brain aneurism less than two years later. He dropped dead on the tennis court one afternoon. Amanda died from a brain tumor five years after that. Jessica threw herself off a balcony in downtown Los Angeles after hearing of Amanda's death. She had been suffering from depression and suicidal tendencies since the incident."

Sparrow stood silently and listened patiently. He wasn't sure what to make of the story, and he didn't understand why Diamond was revealing it to him. During the story, Diamond had never looked at him and had stared into the fire as if the events were playing out in the crackling embers before him.

"It was desperate, dying. That much I know, but its motivation for attacking us remains hidden from me. We were too far away on the beach, and it only woke me with its initial assault. I don't know why. Maybe the alcohol had some affect. Maybe I was stronger willed. When I abandoned my dying friends, I fled straight to it without even knowing it. Once I was inside the cave, its assault overpowered me.

"Several years later, I bought the island and returned. Glip-2 was still here, protecting the body of the creature. It took me several attempts to get past him. It was only after I learned he was susceptible to the abilities the alien had left inside me that I succeeded.

"Slipstream was still here as well. The creature's attempt to dominate me that day had freed him just enough for him to lash out at it. Unfortunately, after suffering under the creature's dominance for nearly forty years, he was lost even to himself. It took Dreah months just to break through to him.

"I began to work through as many of the images as I could. I still don't understand most of them, and I experience fresh ones from time to time. They led me to where I am today." Diamond paused.

"Where is that?" asked Sparrow.

Looking from the fire to Sparrow, Diamond replied, "At war." He straightened his jacket and turned back to the fire again. "I built this place with their technology, and I use the knowledge they left in my head to prepare for them. I don't know when it is going to happen, but I know it will happen again, soon. Slipstream is a direct product of their actions a long time ago. People died then, and people are going to die again. I will do whatever I have to do to stop them. No price is too high, and no life is too precious." Looking up at his father's picture, he continued. "Like him, I am a driven man. But, unlike him, my drive isn't for me. It's for others. His picture reminds me of that."

Turning, Diamond headed for the doors.

"Why do you tell me this?" asked Sparrow.

Diamond stopped and turned to face him again. "Trust. I tell you because of trust." He started to turn away again, but stopped. "I guess I should adjust your security clearance. If nothing else, it may keep Heather from killing you."

Sparrow watched the doors close behind Diamond, and stood in silent thought long after he was gone. Before exiting the room, Sparrow tested the secret door but found it locked.

\* \*

As Sparrow rode the t-port down, he replayed Diamond's story in his head. It obviously wasn't complete, but Sparrow suspected very few people had heard the whole thing. Trust wasn't blind, and Diamond had taken a leap of faith to open up at all. It was an indicator that Diamond wasn't out to mentally control Sparrow, but it didn't mean Diamond wasn't still trying to manipulate him. The story could have been a complete fabrication designed to gain Sparrow's trust.

To Sparrow, Diamond was like a religious fanatic waiting for Armageddon. They had waited for thousands of years, and their apocalypse still hadn't come. Diamond's story indicated that he had been waiting for his for most of his life. Sparrow wondered if it would ever come.

Nevertheless, as Diamond had said, he was at war. That made him a dangerous man who would go to great lengths to protect his cause, and Sparrow suspected that including killing someone who was in his way.

When the t-port door opened, Sparrow headed toward the central shaft.

*Swhoosh!*

Sparrow froze. Lost in thought, he had forgotten the rest of his morning's plan. He had broken security, and possibly found a way out of the Citadel, but he hadn't defeated Glip-2. Fluxstone had likely turned Glip-2 on to his breach by now. Since Diamond probably hadn't adjusted his security level yet, it meant the t-port was still off limits to him. Even if Diamond had adjusted his security clearance, it didn't mean Glip-2 would respond without violence.

As he rounded the corner, he saw the globe suspended over the shaft. It glowed red and pulsed rapidly. Several worried people watched the globe from a distance and talked hurriedly among themselves. For a moment, the two faced off. Sparrow broke the standoff by acting first.

Moving toward an elevator, he watched Glip-2 closely. The globe didn't visibly respond, but the elevator didn't open for Sparrow either.

*That confirms Glip-2's ability to directly control access,* thought Sparrow. *Unfortunately, that also makes things more difficult.*

Shrugging, he started around the shaft toward a hallway on the far side. Glip-2 followed slowly. As Sparrow rounded a corner out of sight from everyone, he spun to wait in the middle of the hallway.

When Glip-2 rounded the corner, Sparrow was waiting for him. The two faced off again, and neither of them moved as seconds dragged into minutes. Sparrow began to doubt he could hold his stare longer than the globe. Everything he had learned so far had told him Glip-2 was alive. It wasn't a machine. If it was alive, it could be distracted, or intimidated.

Sparrow was about to break off the challenge when he noticed Glip-2's pulse slowing. Soon it matched Sparrow's heartbeat. A moment later, the globe's red glow faded to blue, after another moment, Glip-2 floated away. As the globe retreated, Sparrow followed. At first, Glip-2 ignored him, but then they returned to their game of cat-and-mouse.

Sparrow didn't plan to make the chase long. He had studied his maps extensively so it was only a matter of a few minutes before Glip-2 repeated a pattern he knew. As the globe rounded a corner Sparrow knew ended with a dead end, Sparrow turned and darted in the opposite direction.

As Sparrow darted out of the hallway and toward the central shaft, he nearly collided with a man. He ignored the man's complaint and dashed for the shaft. Pulling the altered dart gun from the small of his back, he attached a steel line from under his belt to it. As he reached the shaft, he leaped over the railing and fired the small weapon.

A steel dart erupted from the gun and struck the wall high above him. Immediately, the gears in the gun activated and reeled the rope tight, and Sparrow was hauled upward. The momentum of his leap swung Sparrow wide over the shaft. As he cleared the next level, he released the gun and rolled with his landing. People gathering for an early breakfast were jolted from their activities by his sudden arrival. He ignored them and sprinted down a passage.

Forcing his breathing under control, Sparrow skidded to a halt and stood in the center of the hallway. He crossed his arms and waited. Moments later, Glip-2 zipped around the corner and nearly collided with him. The globe flashed red, but immediately changed to blue again. The two faced off again. After only a few moments, Glip-2 faded to green and then off down the hallway.

Retracing his steps, Sparrow entered the common area. He felt silly over his flamboyant behavior, but he ignored the heads that turned to watch him. He retrieved his zip gun from the man he had nearly collided with and started for an empty table. The man watched Sparrow suspiciously, but Sparrow ignored him. Sparrow sat down, and as he retracted the steel cable, he spotted Fluxstone glaring at him from across the area. Scowling, she left with her morning coffee in hand. Smiling, Sparrow ordered breakfast.

\* \*

The elevator opened and Kahori exited. She glanced around the common area and saw Sparrow sitting alone. She felt a pang of guilt over the incident in the gym and, after hesitating a moment, crossed the floor toward him.

"Hi," Kahori said nervously as she approached the table.

"Good morning," replied Sparrow as he stood to greet her.

Kahori smiled shyly, and then cast her gaze downward. She twirled her fingers nervously before looking up and saying, "I'm sorry about yesterday. I shouldn't have tried to trick you."

"Think nothing of it. All is forgotten, as long as you will forgive me." Sparrow indicated a seat for Kahori and sat back down himself.

Kahori rubbed her jaw as she sat down and smiled. "Forgiven."

"Is this the real you?" asked Sparrow.

Kahori laughed, "Yeah, it's me. How did you know anyway?"

Sparrow shrugged, "Instinct mostly. I've learned to read people over the years. Besides, I've seen you all over this place. Either you moved around without the t-ports, or you could be in more than one place at once. I've learned to expect the unexpected when dealing with meta-humans."

Kahori smiled. "That was a pretty good move you used. I've studied under several masters, but I don't think I've seen it before. Do you think you could teach me sometime?"

For a moment, Sparrow hesitated. He remembered the state that had overcome him during the fight, and he was afraid of it. Samuel's story hadn't changed his plans, and he was pretty sure killing young girls wouldn't be a good move for him either way. "Perhaps," he replied.

Immediately, the tension broke and Kahori smiled. "Cool. Thanks. By the way, I'm Kahori, or Lady Gemini."

For several moments, the two sat in silence. Sparrow wondered if he and his sister could ever share such a quiet moment again.

"So, how do you like the place?" asked Kahori.

"It is...interesting." Kahori smiled at him as Sparrow continued, "There is a lot to see."

"Yes, there is."

Kahori's smile broadened. She was at ease with people. It didn't matter if they had blue skin or fur, or were killers, as Fluxstone claimed this man was. Fluxstone had warned her to stay away from him, but Kahori insisted on making her own judgment.

Sparrow allowed the conversation to drift as Kahori opened up to him about how her age was keeping her off of field teams. Her bout with Fluxstone had been a test, which she felt she had passed. However, Fluxstone had pointed out her defeat by Sparrow was a valuable lesson, and a failure. As typical with any teenager, Kahori felt adults just didn't understand her.

"It's just not fair," said Kahori. "If they would just give me the chance. Dad is just being stubborn. If only..."

*Swhoosh!*

Glip-2, glowing red and pulsing rapidly, zipped past and out of sight.

"What do you think that is all about?" Kahori asked.

Sparrow didn't respond. Several people gathered in front of the video wall had captured his attention. Slowly he rose to his feet and started for the area.

Kahori sat confused. Turning in her seat, she watched him. A moment later she got up and followed.

None of the people spoke, and a tear ran down one woman's face as she raised a trembling hand to cover her mouth. The image on the wall showed a woman reporter. Behind her was the skyline of Paris with smoke rising from several spots around the city. A red banner scrolled across the bottom of the screen. It read, *Breaking Story: Paris; A Dead Zone. City Under Quarantine.*

"*...I say again, this is a breaking news story. Tragedy beyond compare has struck the city of Paris.*" The reporter disappeared as the view zoomed in on an aerial shot of the city. The woman continued talking, but her voice was broken by emotion. "*Authorities...are unsure what has happened at this time...They cannot establish communications with anyone in the city. The French military is currently setting up checkpoints, and preventing anyone from entering. As you can see, fires are burning throughout the city,* *and traffic has come to a standstill. Nothing...is moving in the streets. M... millions are presumed dead."* The camera zoomed in to show bodies lying along the streets and cars crashed into each other. *"B-Bodies are...lying everywhere. Oh my God! I can't do this..."* The woman's commentary died as the reporter dropped her mike and fled the stage.

Everyone in the common area was stunned to silence.

"Aegis," whispered Kahori. Sparrow looked at the young girl and saw her eyes tearing up. Her voice shook. "Aegis is there."

Before Sparrow could reply, a flock of birds sailed up the shaft and over the railing. Mist filled the air between them and the birds coalesced into the form of Dreah. Even from the distance, Sparrow could see she was crying.

"Come," Dreah said to Sparrow and Kahori. She then turned and charged down a hallway. Kahori and Sparrow had to run to keep up.

As they reached the t-port Sparrow had used to find the sherry room, the doors opened and they stepped aboard. As the doors closed, Kahori could no longer control her emotions and began to sob. Reassuringly, Dreah took the young girl's hand and she then took Sparrow's in her other hand. She then closed her eyes and took a deep breath. Sparrow didn't have time to consider the implications of the contact because chaos assaulted them as the t-port opened.

# CHAPTER 10
## AFTERMATH

"What do you mean, you still can't get any readings!" screamed Fluxstone. "Our systems can withstand a nuclear hit!" She looked ready to strike Jonesy.

There were over twenty people in the large room. Each one worked frantically at some task and sought to avoid Fluxstone's wrath. Even with Fluxstone yelling, the talk and buzz of the room threatened to drown her out.

Jonesy's back was to the t-port and he stood before the tall woman with several sidekicks in his hand. A technician ducked past him to hurry across the room.

"The systems are still down! The energy pulse disrupted all the electronics in the city, including ours. Their commlinks are most likely fried! I can't explain it at this point." Jonesy screamed back at Fluxstone. She didn't intimidate him.

Frustrated, Fluxstone threw up her hands and looked around the room for someone else to torment. No one dared to glance in her direction.

Dreah moved quickly across the room to join Fluxstone. As Dreah wrapped her arms around the woman, she whispered softly. Slowly, the two women sat down on a low cushioned couch. Fluxstone hung her head, and her shoulders shook as she began to weep. Dreah hugged her close.

Kahori hesitated a moment and then started across the room. As she walked, several doppelgangers split off from her to join various conversations. When she reached the far end of the room she sat down next to Fluxstone and wrapped her arms around the larger woman.

Sparrow quietly leaned against the back wall. Without interfering, he studied the chaos saturating the room.

The left wall of the room was filled edge to edge with graphs, live video feeds, and images of Paris. Photos of Aegis, Incindiaro, Stronghold, Slipstream, and Butch were in one corner. The words, *Status: Offline*, were displayed under each picture. The far wall and the right wall were paneled in rich wood, and an image of a large rotating diamond dominated the center of each. A large table standing in the center of the room had a glass surface that displayed images as brightly as any computer screen. Twenty plush chairs surrounded the table and a podium stood at the far end with a low cushioned bench along the wall behind it.

Despite its large size, the room was crowded. Most of the men were dressed in white lab coats, but Sparrow recognized a few.

Wavefront worked frantically with several technicians to adjust a blurred image that dominated one section of the wall. When it disappeared in a field of static, he cursed and threw his hat at it.

A male and a female, both with bright red hair and dressed in matching white and burgundy leather costumes, shifted through files and papers displayed by the table's monitor-like surface. Sparrow knew them as Duo. Several sidekicks of various sizes floated in the air around their heads.

Sparrow shifted his position to move out of the way of two men who hurried by.

Suddenly the atmosphere of the room shifted as a door on the right wall opened. Everyone turned and their conversations quieted as Envoy and Paragon entered the room. Paragon took up a position beside the door, and Envoy moved into the center of the room to take instant charge of the chaos.

"Okay, people. This will get us nowhere. Jonesy get me an energy signature on that pulse." Jonesy shook his head and stated to speak, but Envoy interrupted him. "No! I will have none of your excuses. Get it. You two," she said as she pointed at two technicians, "pull up all video and bio feeds from the team's commlinks, and put them there. I want to review them in two minutes." She pointed to a section of the wall. As Envoy went around the room, she issued orders and people responded. When she got to Sparrow, she skipped him and moved on to Paragon. She asked him to review current news feeds out of France. She wanted to know the minute anyone entered the quarantine city. Power sources and technology were coming back on line as systems reset and rebooted themselves. She sent one technician to find Shadow Spirit, and two technicians down to the pod bay to gather as much information as they could on the status of the *Egress*.

The noise level remained high, but under Envoy the chaos of the room was quelled. Even the wall of images took on order as they were shifted and categorized. When the door on the right side of the room opened again, the room fell silent. Diamond stood there with Glip-2 hovering behind him.

"I didn't expect it to be this big." His voice was calm and his face was expressionless. No one spoke and he moved to stand beside Fluxstone. He placed his arm around her shoulder, and turned to survey the room.

"Ready, sir," Envoy said. Turning back to the room, she said, "Clear the room please. Only those with Omega clearance remain. Thank you for your help up to this point. I will brief you later." Without a word, several people got up to leave. One of Kahori's doppelgangers left with the crowd while the rest rejoined Kahori. Sparrow turned to follow the people out of the room.

"Not you Sparrow, remain please," said Envoy.

Sparrow turned to Envoy and she briefly met his eyes before turning her attention to a monitor. Sparrow scanned the room, and saw that several people glanced at him curiously. They were also puzzled by the request. Finally, Sparrow's gaze fell on Diamond, who nodded his approval. Seeing this, the others turned back to their tasks. No one questioned him.

Fluxstone was watching Sparrow too. Her eyes were red and puffy, but despite her obvious grief, she hadn't missed the exchange. Judging by the glare in her eyes, she disagreed with the decision.

Even with the room cleared, there still weren't enough chairs to go around. Diamond took his hand off Fluxstone and stepped to the head of the table.

"Twenty minutes ago, Paris was hit by an attack centered in the

*Champ de Mars*. We knew this would eventually happen, but not when. And we didn't expect it to be of this magnitude. Unfortunately, we weren't ready, and as a result, we suspect millions are dead." Diamond paused and glanced at Fluxstone. Despite the grief in his eyes, his voice remained calm and stoic. "What we are about to review will not be easy to watch, and anyone who thinks they won't be able to bear it is free to leave."

He paused and glanced around the room. His eyes met those of everyone, even Sparrow's. No one moved.

Moving around the podium, he took the seat at the head of the table. "Wavefront, cue it up."

"The video and much of the audio will be from the Paris team," said Wavefront. "The rest is from live video feeds we've captured from the city. A've filtered out most of the junk."

"Heather?" asked Dreah.

Everyone turned to the two women.

Fluxstone glanced at Dreah, and then glared at everyone else in the room. "I'm staying."

Sparrow watched as Dreah looked at Diamond. Her eyes were filled with sorrow for the woman. Diamond's face didn't reveal his thoughts and he turned to the wall. Dreah sighed and pulled Fluxstone closer as she turned her eyes to the wall as well.

Most of the images on the wall were pushed back to the edge, and five distinct feeds filled the center. Each one had a label that matched one of the missing heroes. Bio-signs were attached to each one. Under the video feeds was a box labeled *Egress*. It showed the power levels of the pod and the status of its various systems. All transmissions between team members and control were translated into text and scrolled across the very bottom of the display. Finally, a screen monitored and displayed all transmissions of local police and Facet's security forces. A time stamp across the top of the wall started counting at fifteen fifty-eight as the images started moving in sync. The room darkened.

\* \*

Aegis studied the *Eiffel Tower* briefly before turning and entering the park. Observing people as they entered, Incindiaro stood at the entrance to the restricted area. Munching on several candy bars, Stronghold watched from the right side of the stage. Slipstream stood behind the stage, and never moved or shifted. As people passed him by, they stared and whispered among themselves. He ignored them. Butch flipped over another card onto the *Egress'* control panel and grunted. Picking up all the cards, he shuffled them and dealt himself another game.

"Status green," Aegis said over his commlink

"Roger," replied Curtis.

Aegis and his team relayed routine status checks as the minutes ticked by. At three minutes past the hour, Facet's aid took the stage and began a speech. The only thing out of the ordinary was a dark cloud developing over the city. At five minutes past the hour, the man finished introducing Facet, and the politician took the stage amid cheers from the crowd. Incindiaro booed, but the howling wind drowned him out. Facet had to shield the microphone from the wind to be heard.

"Control," said Aegis. "Run a check on meta-humans with weather control. See if any of them are active in the area, or if they have a specific beef with Facet. The weather report for the day didn't predict bad weather." The dark clouds forming over the city made Aegis uneasy. Growing fear gnawed at his gut.

"Roger, Aegis. Stand by," replied Curtis.

Aegis took advantage of the moment to investigate a group of young adults who were starting to get rambunctious. When he approached them, they immediately ceased their activities and dispersed into the crowd. Aegis turned his attention back to the stage.

"Aegis, I have that requested info."

"Roger," replied Aegis. "Go."

"One match. Code-named: Éolienne, or Windmachine. He's an android currently in custody at Euro-Block."

"Roger. Thanks. Send his picture and bio to our sidekicks, as well as to local law enforcement. Contact the Block and make sure their guest is still there. They have been known to lose one from time to time."

"Roger, Aegis."

*Shring!*

Even as the transmission ended, Aegis' sidekick alerted him to the incoming information. He glanced at it to see the image of Éolienne. The android had a gray face devoid of emotion. Its eyes were lifeless and had no pupil or iris. It had no nose, and its mouth didn't reveal emotion when it moved. The android had large round cups on the side of its head instead of ears. It had no hair or facial marks, but black painted markings came over the top of its head to form a point just above its brow. The black formed sharp stripes along its jaw near the corner of its mouth. The black ran down its neck to its torso where it alternated with the gray to highlight physical features. Its legs were black. A large mechanical apparatus that appeared to be part of the android's body dominated its back. As the image of the android rotated on the sidekick, the small machine automatically highlighted various systems. Aegis fixed the image in his mind, and then returned to his patrol.

Thunder rolled across the sky.

"If it rains, I am not spending the night in the same room as the kid," said Incindiaro.

"It's not my fault I have all this fur," replied Stronghold.

"No one is blaming you, kid. It's just that you smell like a wet dog after you've been in the rain."

Butch laughed at the remark. Slipstream tilted his head back to stare up at the forming storm. Aegis ignored the comment and moved up onto the stage.

"Control, are you getting this? Facet is sweating profusely. Get a thermal reading on him."

The city darkened further and the thunder lasted for several seconds as it reverberated across the sky.

On the monitor wall, an image of Facet pulled apart from the primary feed and focused on his face. He was sweating, looked pale, and was shifting back and forth on his feet. His eyes were sunken and dark. The image shifted to thermal and revealed Facet's temperature at thirty-eight point two degrees Celsius and rising. The air temperature was twenty-three point six degrees Celsius and falling.

"This wind is really picking up," said Stronghold.

Flying paper slapped him in the face, and people ducked to shield their eyes from swirling debris. People were starting to leave, and Facet joked about the weather. It did nothing to calm the growing fear.

"People, check out the clouds," said Curtis.

Incindiaro tilted his head back. The clouds were dark and swirled violently around a single spot in their center. They caused fear to ache in the pit of his stomach. The center of the clouds began to sink into themselves and to form a vortex. "That could be a problem." He shuddered as the wave of fear grew stronger.

Aegis and Stronghold looked up at the clouds.

"Slipstream, this is control. Status, please?'

"We'd better see about shutting this thing down," said Aegis. A loud clap of thunder nearly drowned him out. Aegis bent his head and cupped his ear trying to hear what was being said over the commlink.

"It's nice and comfy from where I'm sitting," bragged Butch.

"Facet will never go for that coming from us, boss," replied Incindiaro.

"Cut the chatter. Control, repeat message," said Aegis.

"Slipstream's vitals are spiking, and he's focused on the clouds," Curtis said.

Aegis looked back to the stage, and then up at the clouds. He didn't know what was causing the bad weather, but he was sure it wasn't Éolienne generating the fear. The android had never demonstrated any type of emotion control ability in the past, and the clouds were definitely generating fear. Of course, that didn't mean that the android hadn't aligned himself with some other super villain that could. "We're shutting things down. Stronghold check on Slipstream." Looking around, Aegis found people already deserting the park, and it wasn't because of the wind.

"Roger, boss," replied Stronghold. He turned and started his way through the crowd. People parted before the giant.

Before Aegis could interrupt the proceedings, Facet spoke up. "Sorry folks, but it looks like the weather just isn't going to cooperate today. Please, everyone let's all get indoors." Facet waved at his people who immediately responded and started ushering people out of the park.

"Wonders never cease," said Aegis. "Watch the crowd for panic as they exit. Facet's people should be able to handle things. Basi..."

*Ka-Boom!*

Aegis was flung backwards as the stage exploded. Incindiaro ducked and Stronghold was knocked into a crowd of people. Power sources were disrupted and most of the electrical equipment in the park went dark. The crowd panicked and fled.

Scrambling back to his knees, Aegis turned toward Facet and the center of the stage. Before him was a wide shaft of energy blazing from the vortex in the clouds to the center of the stage where Facet had been standing. The blazing energy incinerated anything it touched. There was no sign of Facet.

Aegis had no idea what he was witnessing, but he feared it was connected with Diamond's prophecy. If the end result was anything like the one that occurred years ago with Slipstream, everyone in the park was in danger. Over the roar of the shaft, he shouted, "Code Omega! We have a code Omega! Evacuate the park!"

Incindiaro started toward the stage, but the fleeing crowd blocked his path.

Stronghold did his best to rise from the pile of panicked civilians while trying not to crush any of them.

Slipstream staggered under an unseen attack, and dropped to his knees. Without taking his eyes off the clouds, he struggled back to his feet; only to be driven back to his knees again by the next round of thunder. Every burst from the clouds caused him to spasm. Energy leaked from his eyes, and his muscles bulged as he strained against the influence of the clouds. He could feel the full force of each lightning strike as if he were the target. He could feel the searing pain of the energy shaft engulfing Facet. He knew the pain. He knew the clouds.

Following the shaft of energy up from the center of the stage to the clouds, Aegis found the full source of the fear. It emanated from the clouds, the sheer overwhelming force nearly caused him to flee. The clouds were evil, and growing stronger with each passing moment. Angrily, they twisted and flexed.

Aegis had faced all kinds of enemies over the years, but this one stretched over an entire city. He didn't understand it, and he didn't know how to fight it. Aegis wanted to look away, to flee from it; but it held him transfixed. It captured his mind, and defeated him without a battle.

Movement in the corner of his eye saved him.

*Clang!*

A large piece of the stage bounced off the *Aegis*. The hero had seen it just in time.

Glancing around he found that he wasn't the only one captivated by the cloud. Numerous people lay cowering on the ground. Tears ran from eyes they wanted to gouge out to prevent them from seeing the clouds. He felt pity for them, but had no idea how to help them.

He started to issue a warning to the team about the clouds, but was interrupted by one of Facet's bodyguards extending a hand toward the energy shaft.

"No!" screamed Aegis. The bodyguard glanced at the hero.

A flare burst from the shaft and punched through the man's chest. He collapsed, and the blazing flare circled the stage. When it neared the shaft of energy again, two more flares burst from the conflagration to join it. They twirled around each other and circled Aegis.

Stronghold finally freed himself from the pile of bodies, and after climbing to his feet, leaped onto the stage. He stood at the edge of the energy shaft and peered into the pit it was boring into the ground.

*Rruummmble!*

Stronghold's commlink sputtered as he screamed over the shaking stage, "It's punching a mighty big hole into the ground! No sign of Facet!"

Suddenly, one of the flares flashed toward him, and speared his lower right arm. He screamed and dropped to his knees, cradling the injured arm to his side. It was blackened and burned clear to the bone. A second flare darted toward his exposed back, but he was oblivious to it.

Aegis leaped across the stage and threw up his shield between Stronghold and the flare.

*Clang!*

The flare bounced off the *Aegis* and circled around the two heroes. Another flare joined it. Together, the two flares attacked Aegis and Stronghold in a relentless barrage that Aegis was hard pressed to block.

*Clang! Clang! Clang!*

"Move people! Move!" shouted Incindiaro.

Ignoring him, the civilians continued to crowd him. They jolted and shoved him as he struggled to get around them. Many had collapsed to the ground in fear of the cloud and were being trampled by their fleeing friends. Incindiaro could feel the fear pressing down on him from above, but refused to look up.

"Mierda! No hablo Francés!"

Stopping, Incindiaro extended his hands out in front of him, fire leaped along his arms. The heat of the fire pushed the people back, and Incindiaro allowed the flames to engulf his body. With everyone pulling back from him, he ran forward.

A flare streaked from the stage toward him.

"Down!" he screamed at the fleeing civilians.

Blazing fire leaped from him to blanket the area between him and the flare. Unharmed, the flare punched through the flames, and struck the hero. Incindiaro was flung backward by the force of the attack. He crashed into a large fountain and lay still. The flare circled around him before darting back to the stage.

Slipstream convulsed and collapsed to the ground. His heart pounded in his chest and a seizure engulfed him. The intensity of the attack increased, and Slipstream's enhanced physique gave way to cardiac arrest.

The clouds groaned and flexed as they circled around a dark center large enough to swallow the park.

Those of the crowd still on their feet, attempted to flee in all directions. The wave of fear generated by the clouds fueled their panic. Many didn't know which way to run, the fear was all around them.

The gates and fences guarding the park were pushed down, and in several places people trampled through bushes and hedges. The windows of buildings burst under the gale force of the wind, and loose items were sucked from the buildings to rain down on the city. A large bus was pushed over to crush fleeing civilians. A statue in the center of the park shattered as lightning struck it. Fire blazed from wrecked vehicles, and people dodged the flames as they struggled to escape.

Aegis watched the flares closely, but took a moment to glance toward the energy shaft. There was no sign of Facet in the blazing energy. Looking around the park, he found too many people still in danger.

Shoving Stronghold off the stage, Aegis blocked a flare before joining him on the ground. As Aegis landed, he rolled and deflected a second flare away from Stronghold. The third flare speared Aegis in the right leg. He screamed, and collapsed to his knees.

Aegis forced himself to his feet, but stumbled, and was nearly hit by the flare again. Slowly, he gained his footing and began to retreat with Stronghold. The giant youth grabbed a large part of the stage and held it up as a shield. The wind threatened to tear it from his hands.

Aegis turned to him and screamed, "Run!"

Instead of fleeing, the kid swung his makeshift shield at one of the flares bearing down on them. The stage shattered as the flare blasted through it. Unhindered, it plunged through the young giant's chest. He collapsed.

Aegis stood over his friend's body for only a moment before all three flares forced him to roll to safety. He successfully dodged the first two, but the third speared his right leg again.

"Control...We need immediate evac! I-Incindiaro and Stronghold are...down! We need immediate evac!" screamed Aegis into his commlink.

Despite being in pain and out of breath, he managed to climb to his feet. Immediately, a flare penetrated his left shoulder, and he collapsed to his knees. A second flare followed the first, but due to his injured shoulder, Aegis was unable to raise his shield to defend himself. The flare speared him through the chest. He collapsed before the flaring energy shaft.

The shaft pulsed and started spewing balls of fire in every direction. They set fire to everything around the stage. The shaft pulsed brightly, and a ring of energy burst from its base. Cameras died as the ring washed over them. When the ring hit the *Egress*, power readings on the craft bottomed out, and Butch's readings on the monitor wall in the conference room went off-line like the others.

\* \*

No one spoke. Heather and Kahori sobbed. Even Envoy's stoic exterior had been cracked by the horror of the events that had unfolded before them. From the moment the shaft of light had appeared, just over a minute had elapsed. The bio-signs of each of the heroes had flatlined before the monitors had gone off-line. Many of those in the room burned with the desire to charge off to Paris to rescue their friends, but hoping they were still alive, would be denying the truth.

Diamond cleared his throat, and slowly the room turned to face him. Behind him, the wall shifted from the team's off-line cameras to several live news feeds of Paris. For a moment, Diamond looked overwhelmed, then he took a deep breath and stood tall.

"We are, of course, still analyzing the data from the event, but at this point we believe the team is dead, along with the rest of the city. We will send in a team as soon as we confirm it is safe enough." The room remained silent. "Many of you have been with me on this for a long time, some of you for years. I'm sorry we weren't ready. I'm sorry we couldn't prevent it." Diamond paused and glanced at the video wall.

Fires burned all over Paris. The energy shaft had started those in the park. The rest were a result of damage caused by the lightning and the wind. Bodies lay everywhere, and nothing moved. Even the wind had ceased blowing. The city's structures still stood, but those near the park had shattered windows and large fires worked to gut them. Cars sat in pileups on every street and debris littered the ground.

Diamond cleared his throat and continued. "Some of you already know what we are doing here and why. Some of you don't, and it is time you did.

"We don't know when they came to Earth, but we do know of several spots across the globe where they have visited." The images behind him changed and a globe of the earth appeared. As it rotated, several spots blinked. "Wherever they visit, they leave behind a zone of death. The biggest zone before today occurred here, Roanoke Island." The globe stopped rotating and the image expanded to show a detailed map of an island off the coast of North Carolina. "Many scientists believe it was just a time of extreme drought in the area that killed the vegetation. They are wrong.

"The colony was settled in fifteen eighty-seven. After only a few months, John White left the colony and returned to England for supplies. Due to various reasons, he didn't return for three years. His daughter, Eleanor Dare, had disappeared along with one hundred and fourteen other colonists.

"Nine of those colonists reemerged sometime later. They were confused, and some had lost all memory of the colony. They had been changed, and even if they had realized it, there was nothing they could have done about it. They passed those changes on to their children through their DNA. Meta-humans were born of that DNA.

"Many of those early meta-humans are believed to be simple folk lore today. I know better." The images shifted again and nine family trees appeared. Eight of the trees had a trunk that ran through the center that was thicker and bolder than the limbs. The trees rotated and at several spots along the different branches, points flashed and names and data scrolled across the screen. "Through birth records, medical records, and personal information we have been tracking these family trees. Most of you know this. You believe it is so we can predict who has the potential to develop meta-human abilities. This is true. Every meta-human alive today can be tracked to one of the original Nine. What some of you don't know is that it was also so we could try and prevent today's incident.

"When I was a teenager, I found this place. In it I found one of the aliens. From it I learned some things about it and its kind. Except for the center trunk of each family tree, the aliens care nothing about humanity, meta-humans or otherwise. The center trunk of each tree carries the purest alien DNA. Collecting the strongest traits of humanity, it snakes its way through us. Each generation passes it on to their first-born, and it becomes stronger."

The smallest of the family trees expanded to fill the screen. "Until recently, we were missing this family tree altogether. With the recovery of the diary of Eleanor Dare, and with information gathered from the Missing Man, we now believe this line is extinct. The Missing Man destroyed it. He was the oldest of the original nine and he remembered enough of the incident to fear, and hate, the aliens so much that he killed every descendent he had; over six hundred men, women, and children. His name is Dyonis Harvie." Harvie's name appeared at the base of the small tree.

Diamond glanced at Glip-2 and the images shifted in response to highlight a second tree. The name at the bottom of the tree read *John Sampson, Jr. (Meta-man)* and the trunk was shorter than the rest of the tree. "As you can see, this tree has the trunk cut short. The man's name was William Clark and he died in a house fire along with the rest of his family in nineteen thirty-five." The image shifted again. This time it brought up a black and white photo of a man named *Kevin Clark*. A branch running parallel of the trunk blinked and expanded to end with Clark's name. "Nineteen thirty-nine, a small town in Kentucky experienced a similar event to the one today. Every living thing within a mile of Clark's home died; people, animals, plants, everything. You people know the result of that event as Slipstream. He was a cousin to William Clark." The image of Clark slid right and an image of Slipstream appeared. The computer compared several features on each face and then the word, *Match*, flashed over the images. "Kevin was not the intended seed, William was. We do not know why the event was centered on him. However, we ran a DNA analysis of Kevin and William, and their profiles were very similar."

The image wall shifted again to reveal a dead jungle. Skeletons littered the ground. In the background, a large animal hide was stretched across a stick frame. The image on the hide showed a shaft of light, and people lying dead around it. A small red globe hung in the air above the bodies.

"The final tree of this alien leads us to Africa where the center stalk is lost, but we found evidence of a similar event. We believe it ended with the creation of Glip-2, just as the Kentucky incident ended with the creation of Slipstream.

"From the information gathered from the alien I encountered, and through these family trees, I have tried to predict when an incident would occur. I knew there was the potential for multiple deaths, but nowhere near a scale such as this. For the past forty years, I have dedicated my life to preventing it. I swore to stop it. I failed.

"There were three aliens who took nine people from Roanoke. We know this. We can account for two lines cut short, and believe a third line is also dead. A fourth line ended today in Paris. That leaves five potential incidents looming over us just like the one today. Five more cities will die and with them, millions of people."

The room remained silent as Diamond finished his briefing. The wall behind him shifted again to reveal the nine family trees. Four were subdued in color while the remaining five were bright.

With his emotions unleashed, Sparrow was feeling the weight of the situation on his shoulders. He was surprised by just how upset he was, and it unnerved him. He struggled to push the feelings down deep. As he did so, he glanced around the room to see how the others were doing.

Sorrow was evident on everyone's face. They all knew the men who had died, and the death of five good friends at once was a weighty burden to bear. Diamond stood at the podium watching everyone. His face was expressionless. With his head bowed, Paragon stood by the doorway he had entered earlier. His long hair fell down around his face, and Sparrow could hear him whispering to himself. Wavefront sat on the edge of his chair with his floppy hat balled up in his hands. His jaw was tight, and his eyes glassy. Envoy stood rock solid again, but not as expressionless as Diamond. Her sympathetic eyes darted from person to person. Duo sat side by side at the table. They both appeared tired and weary. Kahori and Fluxstone were both openly sobbing. Fluxstone was also staring at a picture of Aegis on the monitor wall, and Kahori sat with her face buried in Fluxstone's arm. The various scientist and technicians in the room all displayed varying degrees of emotion. Some were openly upset, while others stoically concentrated on computer screens before them.

Watching the sorrow of the room released memories in Sparrow of his mother's funeral. In that instant her death crushed him. The wind was knocked from his lungs, and his face flushed. Wrestling against the blow, Sparrow lowered his head and struggled to prevent his emotions from overwhelming him. After only a moment, he felt a gentle hand touch his chin and lift his face. Across the room his eyes met Dreah's. She looked weary, but he could feel her strength lifting him up. His sorrow subsided and his breathing slowed. He was in control again. Dreah held his eyes a moment longer, and then she lowered her gaze and hugged Fluxstone close to her again. She visibly slumped lower on the couch.

Sparrow was suddenly self-conscious about his momentary loss of control. He quickly reached forward and took a sidekick off the table. He began to thumb through images of the event and shifted his mind away from the sorrow. After a few moments, he faced the situation as an outsider again. In his mind he began to puzzle through the event and Diamond's words.

"How much of this did Alex know?" asked Jack through clenched teeth. "Did any of them know today was a death trap before they walked into it?"

Everyone turned to Jack and then to Diamond, but it was Dreah who answered. Her voice cracked as she said, "Alex knew everything we know, Jack. You already knew most of it. But no one knew when or where it was going to happen. I knew it was coming. I've seen it looming over us in my dreams. I didn't know when, but I suspected it was upon us. I spoke to Alex about my fears before he left. His only response was, *then we will deal with it as best as we can.*"

Dreah choked on her sorrow and Diamond jumped in.

"The mission was to get next to Facet. Nothing more. Even if Aegis had known what was going to happen he would still have gone. Incindiaro and Stronghold would have followed him. You or I would have done the same. They didn't go in unprepared or unwilling. Blame me if you need someone to blame, but I ask that you help me finish this. It's what any of them would do."

The room fell silent. Wavefront tried to hold Diamond's eyes, but couldn't and looked away. No one knew Aegis better than he did, and he knew Diamond was right. Aegis would have still gone. No matter what the danger was. In fact, he would have charged in, willingly sacrificing his own life, for just a glimmer of hope to rescue even one civilian from that park. Even after recognizing the event as having potential citywide impact, Aegis had remained to help his friends, and give the civilians a chance to escape.

"What do they want with us?" asked Kandi.

"Why are they here?" added Brian.

This time Envoy answered, "That eluded us for some time. Maria gave us the most plausible answer."

Everyone turned to a young Hispanic girl who sat in one of the chairs. Throughout the entire meeting she had not uttered a single word, and her face didn't reveal what she was feeling. She had her feet in her chair and one of her arms wrapped around her knees. She stared blankly at the monitor wall, and chewed slowly on a lock of her dark shoulder-length hair. Her skin was smooth and tanned. Her eyes were pools of chocolate, and her fingernails were short and unpainted. She wore a dark shirt with back, red, and white swirls, and a pair of expensive black pants. Her high-heeled shoes were black.

Sparrow paused in his review of the sidekick to study the young girl. He hadn't noticed her earlier and briefly wondered how he had missed her. Despite her small stature, she actually stood out among the uniformed heroes and technicians. Yet she had gone unnoticed. When Envoy spoke again, it pulled his attention away from Maria.

"We've had many theories. We are still consider some of them as possibilities, but for the past couple of years we have operated on the belief that Maria's reasoning is correct." Envoy paused before answering the question. "It's reproduction."

The room erupted in confusion.

"Bloody hell," grunted Wavefront as he stood up.

"Not possible," said a female scientist.

Envoy held up her hand to silence the room, but it did no good.

Everyone had something to say and none of them seemed to accept the reasoning.

"Maria is usually right, we all know that..."

"Yeah, right. Reproduction? Come on, Envoy. That's ridiculous!"

"Why us?"

"I guess we aren't the dominant species on the planet after all."

"It's not so hard to understand, really."

"Why would they need to destroy a city to do this?"

"How do we stop it?"

"Wait..."

"I just don't believe it."

"I said wait! Hush!"

Everyone turned to Envoy. She was leaning forward and had placed her hands on the table in front of her. She was looking at Maria. "Did you say something, Maria?"

For several moments the young girl didn't speak. When she did she didn't look at anyone. "I said it's not so hard to understand." Maria's stare at the monitor wall never wavered. Her face remained expressionless. She continued to chew on her hair as she spoke. "Many species use other species for the same purpose, although on a simpler premise. The cowbird lays its eggs in another bird's nest. The host mother raises the chick as her own. The cowbird chick is even known to cast its adoptive brothers and sisters out of the nest to survive. When the chick matures, it is still a cowbird; not one of its adoptive parents. But it too deposits its eggs in another nest. To the aliens, the Nine were a nest to deposit their eggs. Only our arrogance prevents us from accepting that there are things out there greater than we are."

Sparrow narrowed his eyes as he studied Maria. She hadn't moved, and it still puzzled him as to why he had missed her. Everyone began to bombard her with questions, but she ignored them.

*Meta-humans*, cursed Sparrow silently to himself.

As if she had heard him, and Sparrow realized she might have, Maria turned and looked him in the eye. In an instant, her brown eyes drank in every detail about him. She then turned her attention back to the monitor wall, and began to chew her hair again. Sparrow shuddered.

Maria was apparently finished with her analogy, but the people in the room weren't satisfied. Tempers flared and questions erupted from everyone.

Diamond took control. "People, quiet!" Everyone slowly responded and the room grew silent. "Maria's analogy merely summarizes the basic concept. It's much more complicated than that. For example, to us each generation has to start the reproductive process all over again. If Maria's theory is correct, then each human generation is simply another stage of development in a single alien offspring.

"The aliens altered the original Nine. How? We don't know, but even our society has learned to manipulate genes to produce the traits we want, or to suppress the traits we don't want. For all we know, it's a natural process for them. Perhaps it is something they have learned to do through science. We do not know. The event that started this was too long ago to study with any accuracy, but it doesn't change how it appears to end.

"The alterations to the DNA of the Nine have been passed down over the generations. With each generation, it takes the best of its hosts and becomes stronger. We believe the alien DNA has now reached a peak, the point at which it is ready to mature. Today's event appears to have been one of those seeds maturing. It appears to be similar to the process that results in the development of a meta-human's abilities, but on a much larger scale.

"We know that for a meta-gene to become active it has to be charged with energy. Thermal. Electrical. Light. Chemical. Even Nuclear. Sometimes the type of energy plays a role in the meta-powers developed, but often it doesn't."

As Diamond spoke, the wall behind him began to display images that emphasized his words. Meta-humans of all descriptions flashed along with newspaper stories tied to each one. There were images of explosions, vats full of chemicals, lightning strikes, burned out buildings, scientific laboratories, and even a large swirling multi-colored energy vortex.

"Often similar abilities are shared or passed along from parents to siblings. Sons inherit a specific set of meta-powers from their fathers, who inherited the same set of powers from their fathers. This is no different than children sharing the same hair or eye color as their parents.

"What activates a gene in one person often kills another under identical circumstances. Attempts to duplicate these random events have proven fatal, or resulted in deformities and horrible mutations almost every time. I believe now that these failures are because the energy needed to properly activate a meta-gene is special. Unique. The activation of the average meta-gene is a fluke caused by the incorrect energy type being combined with impure, or bad alien DNA."

*Bad DNA?* Sparrow had never heard of the meta-gene described as bad DNA before. Most often meta-humans were looked at as the most pure, or as superior because of their special abilities. If what Diamond was saying was correct, then only a person who didn't carry the meta-gene was truly human. Meta-humans were hybrids or worse. The revelation had a perverse ring to it, and Sparrow liked it.

"The event that occurred today combined the energy in its pure form with the purest alien DNA. They are extremely rare, but there are even events where a meta-gene matured and people around the meta-human died mysteriously. No marks, no burns, no signs of the cause on their lifeless bodies."

"So Facet is still alive," said Wavefront, "but one of these aliens now."

The group's discussion turned to Facet and the possibilities of him being alive. Where was he now? Was he alien or human? If a similar event created Slipstream, was he alien or human? Were the people along the trunk of each tree human, meta-human, alien, or some sort of hybrid? The discussion abruptly ended when a young scientist in the back of the room asked about the identities of the remaining seeds.

"We believe we have identified each of them. We can never be one hundred percent certain but we are pretty sure of their identities after today. The same criteria that identified Facet was used to identify them, and their parents before them." Turning toward the right, Diamond faced the monitor wall. It shifted and five pictures along with data about each one was revealed. One by one, Diamond briefed the room on them.

"Elaina Fuentes is a young pop singer out of Buenos Aires." The images of Fuentes showed the young rock star from various concerts along with images of her clashing with police. "She rocketed to stardom when she was just seventeen. Within five years, she gained a world wide following whose behavior borders on that of a cult. Recently, she shifted her focus from music to being a thorn in her government's side as an outspoken activist against what she sees as unjust government corruption. Her popularity has prevented her government from silencing her.

"Douglas Austin is currently the mayor of Denver, Colorado." Austin was a man in his thirties. He stood in a park with large gray mountains in the background. He held a spatula and was wearing an apron. He was shaking hands with an elderly man dressed in a suit. "Austin is in his second term, and is currently making preparations to run for governor of the state. His popularity rating is the highest the city has seen in fifty years."

The next image was of a woman nearing fifty. She stood in front of a fleet of shipping trucks. After a moment, commercials featuring her and the shipping company began playing. "Lariza Nazarov runs an international shipping company out of Moscow. *Unprecedented Shipping* was founded in nineteen fourteen, and has been in her family ever since. She took the company from her father in a hostile takeover twenty years ago, and under her the company has doubled its revenue and even swallowed up two of its biggest rivals."

Diamond paused as the wall shifted again. "Thomas Aikin is a member of the House of Commons for Great Britain." Aikin was dressed in rich suits and was always pictured with other prominent individuals, including the Queen of England. "His politics are loved by the masses, and he often takes on big corporation and corruption. He is expected to be a candidate for Prime Minister in the next election.

"Yeorgi Lekkas is a wealthy businessman out of Athens, Greece. He runs a conglomerate with holdings scattered across the city. As a person with major connections to the local mafia, he is closely watched by the police." Many of the images of Lekkas were old newspaper photos. The headlines reflected the legal troubles one would expect of a man connected with organized crime.

"All of these people possess similar traits, and all of them possess genetic markers going back to the Nine. Since we do not have all the Nine to compare to, we can't be absolutely certain. But their genetic markers are different, and can be traced back several generations.

"None of them are active meta-humans. Only Nazarov has been exposed to an event that could have resulted in her meta-gene being activated. It wasn't, and yet she survived it. If any of the others have experienced such an event, it is not recorded. While many of their close relatives often do, none of the individuals in a family tree's core trunk ever develop meta-powers.

"All of the candidates are first born children, resilient, and extremely healthy, despite often having younger siblings who were physically or mentally disabled. Austin was involved in an automobile accident as a kid that killed the four other people in the car. Despite a sickly younger sister, there is no record of Fuentes suffering from anything other than the common cold.

"The candidates all display a higher than average IQ, and are extremely charismatic. All of them hold positions of power, and at least one of their parents displayed similar characteristics. Currently none of them have children, although rumor surfaced two days ago that Nazarov might be pregnant.

"Several years ago, I attempted to warn our government of this threat. Word quickly reached me that certain people within the government were calling for measures that I felt would have only complicated matters. I cut off contact with those people, and as a result, very little progress has been made to deal with the situation beyond this room. I fear the disappearance of the seeds, so we have been hesitant to reveal their identities. The information that has been revealed has been restricted to the highest levels of government and without solid proof, they haven't acted."

Silence briefly settled over the room as everyone began to question the tactics Diamond had used up to this point. Many felt it was morally wrong to keep the information from the potential victims. Speculation also turned to whether the same level of devastation would occur if a parent who previously had been at the top of their family's chain triggered the event.

Envoy was pulled from the conversation by a beep from her intercom. She frowned as she accessed it. After a moment, she spoke up. " Quiet everyone! We have a situation in the pod bay." She shifted the communication to the display wall and a technician appeared. "Start over with what you told me, Ted."

"Yes ma'am. We've been trying to access the *Egress* since you sent us down here. We've had no success. Two minutes ago, the readings on the *Egress* changed. It was nothing we did. The pod still doesn't have full power, but the door system is getting power from somewhere, and we think it is trying to cycle from the other side."

Jonesy got up and approached the video wall. Touching the screen, a virtual monitor formed in front of him and through it he brought up a display that showed the power ratings of the *Egress*. As he studied them, Envoy asked, "What do you think, Jonesy?"

"Hum. Readings are minimal but definitely connected to the door system. The pod itself is still dead. The readings are low, maybe equivalent to ten volts. Car batteries have a higher rating. Nowhere near enough to cycle those doors. The doors can't be cycled without power to both sides. If boosted somehow, we may just get them open."

"Could it mean someone is alive?" asked Kahori with hope in her voice.

Jonesy looked at her, "Don't count on it."

Envoy frowned at Jonesy as Diamond said, "Get down there. See what you can do to boost that power. Get those doors open."

Jonesy didn't protest as he turned and left the room. Envoy followed and spoke hurriedly into her commlink. The room fell into whispers as everyone waited. If anyone had concerns about contaminants seeping from Paris into the Citadel through the doors, they didn't express it.

When Envoy and Jonesy appeared on camera in the pod bay, the two technicians were pushed aside by Jonesy as he began to adjust the door controls.

"Not enough power," Jonesy said. "I don't see how to boost it more from this side. Maybe if I had a week to study the design closer..." His voice dropped off to mumbling as he frantically adjusted the controls.

Brandon and two medical assistants entered the pod as Envoy stepped forward and placed her hand on the pod doors. Her eyes glowed as the artifact on her arm reacted to her mental commands. A glow quickly spread down her arm to her hand and into the door. The blue circular apparatus in the center of the door lit up as she pushed energy into it. A moment later the floor and ceiling of the room began to spin, and power ratings on the monitors jumped. The door suddenly popped open and an arm fell through the opening into the room. The mechanism sparked and the blue apparatus went dark.

"Butch!" said Brandon as Envoy pulled her hand away from the door. Kneeling next to the door, Brandon grasped Butch's hand in his own.

From the other side of the door, they could all hear Butch laughing.

"I knew that alternate system would come in handy! Someone tell ol' Jonesy' boy I was right!"

Envoy pushed on the doors to open them further, but they wouldn't budge. Without power, they were stuck. She stepped back to summon energy from the artifact again but Brandon stepped in her way.

A medical assistant kneeled down next to Butch and spoke softly to him as Brandon grabbed the door and pulled against it. For a moment nothing happened, then metal ground against metal and the door peeled back. The medical assistants immediately began checking Butch for injuries. After a moment, Brandon lifted the larger man and placed him on a gurney. Butch's shirt was stained with blood, and he held a car battery to his chest. It was connected to three other batteries, and Brandon had to sever the cables before Butch could be wheeled away.

Everyone in the conference room cheered as Butch gave thumbs up before disappearing off screen. Envoy disappeared into the *Egress*, and her voice issued over her commlink moments later, "The outer doors are sealed and the power is dead. There is no threat of contamination."

For several moments everyone rejoiced. Sparrow turned his attention back to the videos on the sidekick. Vaguely, he heard the conversations but he tried to ignore them. Everyone began to speculate about Butch's survival. If he had survived, maybe others had as well. The conversations went in circles as everyone presented their own outlandish theories. After several minutes, Sparrow became annoyed and glared at everyone over the edge of the sidekick.

"Do you have something to add, Sparrow?" Diamond asked.

Looking at Diamond, Sparrow realized he had seen the glare. *I really need to learn to control these emotions*, he told himself. Everyone turned to him, and for a moment he felt an urge to crawl under the table. Pushing it aside he said, "Actually, yes I do." As he stepped forward from the back wall, Fluxstone jumped up from the couch.

"Who the hell do you think you are?" All heads turned to her. Fluxstone shook with anger. "You didn't know any of them! What makes you think anything you have to say is important?"

Dreah rose beside Fluxstone and tried to coax the woman back onto the couch, but Fluxstone was fuming and would not allow Dreah to comfort her.

For a moment Sparrow considered strangling her. Holding up his hand in defense, he said, "Look, I'm not trying to interfere. I was just asked if I had anything to add."

"No one cares what you have to add!" screamed Fluxstone.

Sparrow glanced around at everyone. Several of their faces seemed to agree with her. "Fine," he said as he moved back to his spot along the wall.

"I care," said Diamond. "Heather, please be seated."

Fluxstone looked as if she were going to explode. Dreah laid a hand on her shoulder, and she reluctantly sat back down onto the couch. Diamond nodded at Sparrow.

Sparrow moved to stand before the imaging wall. He worked with the sidekick in his hand, but he couldn't get the results he wanted. Glip-2 floated over next to him and instantly a mixture of video feeds from the heroes and various news stations filled the wall. Sparrow glanced at Glip-2 and then turned to face the room.

His heart leaped into his throat. Sparrow hadn't spoken in front of a crowd since college, and was suddenly frightened by the thought of it. He knew instantly that fear was one emotion he wanted to push back into the Counselor's box and forget about. Glancing around the room, he caught Dreah's eyes. In them he found strength.

"I don't want to diminish the relationship anyone had with these men, nor do I want to diminish anyone's position here, but I've been sitting here listening to all of you and it makes my head hurt. Each of you has a theory about why this happened, but none of you are looking at what actually did happen. I don't solve a puzzle with theory. I start with the facts, with what I know. That's what you should be doing here." As he tapped the sidekick, the videos all jumped forward to the spot where the three flares initially erupted from the shaft of light.

"These three flares all responded to the environment around them. Looking at the video, I see no sign of anything or anyone exerting control over them." To illustrate his point the video showed an image of a flare as it zipped toward the front of the stage, but then suddenly altered course to charge Incindiaro. He stopped the video before the flare killed the man. "This flare targeted Incindiaro while ignoring all the people between it and him."

"Here," Sparrow said as he tapped the sidekick and a new image appeared on the screen. The three flares twirled around each other before breaking off again. "We see all three flares responding not only to the environment, but also to each other.

"Here, they respond when Facet is directly threatened." The image shifted again to show a flare attack a security guard. The gruesome image clearly showed the flare bursting from the guards back. The image shifted again to show Stronghold land next to Facet, a flare immediately responded to his presence and speared his arm. Stronghold's camera focused on the charred and bloody wound.

Again Sparrow punched the sidekick and the images shifted. "The flares assessed and reacted to threats against themselves and Facet." Sparrow pointed at a bodyguard with a gun standing near the front of the stage. "This flare ignored this guard and went after Aegis." The images shifted to show a flare spear the hero's leg. Sparrow pointed at a group of people fleeing the scene. "This flare ignored seven civilians, and attacked Incindiaro who was further away than they were."

The images changed one final time, and Aegis could be seen kneeling over the body of Stronghold. The flares were inches from striking the hero. "Look at this with your eyes, and not with your emotions. These three flares worked in unison to attack Aegis, while ignoring everyone else in the park. The first flare dived low and pulled his attention." The images moved forward in slow motion to show the flare spear Aegis. "The second flare struck him in a vital spot. Without his shoulder, he couldn't use his shield to defend himself or anyone else." The images moved forward again to show the flare rip through the shoulder. The image froze as the last flare struck him. "They targeted Aegis because he was the greatest threat. You can bet they will do so again in London or Buenos Aries, or wherever you may encounter them again."

Sparrow turned back toward the wall and brought up one final image. It was a view of the energy shaft from Aegis after he was down. Sparrow expanded the image to fill most of the wall. He advanced the time stamp to the point just before the ring of death was cast across the park. He then dimmed the brightness of the image. A silhouette of Facet with his arms extended out to his side could be seen within the shaft of light. His head was thrown back and he screamed up at the sky. A round two-foot wide globe was positioned just above his head.

Tossing the sidekick onto the table, Sparrow said, "This incident ended with the death of Paris, but how it began seems of much more interest to me. I would rethink how that African incident ended if I were you."

Everyone sat in silence and stared at the image of Glip-2 frozen just above Facet's head.

# CHAPTER 11
# RECOVERY OF LOST FRIENDS

Of everyone in the room, Diamond was the most stunned. For most of his life he had shifted through the memories in his head, and he thought he understood them all. Now he knew he didn't. For the first time in years, he had no idea what to do next.

As for Glip-2, he hung silently in the air shifting rapidly through colors; red, blue, green, silver, green, blue, red, blue, red. Everyone knew what individual colors meant, but when they came in flurries no one knew how to read them. An empath even had difficulty reading him. It was impossible to tell if he had just been exposed as a traitor, or if he was as surprised as everyone else.

"I think we need to back up and regroup here people," said Envoy. Her tone was flat and commanding. She had returned during Sparrow's revelation and had not heard all of it, but she had heard enough to see the fingers being pointed at Glip-2. She knew that division in their ranks would be devastating right now. "Let's not jump to conclusions just yet. Glip-2 has been with us from the beginning, and we know he was here in the Citadel during the event."

"I can guarantee you he had no direct connection with this, and that he has no memories from before I came to this island." Diamond still looked confused, but even he had difficulty hiding his surprise when he looked at the globe.

Dreah added, "Glip-2's loyalty should not be questioned."

Sparrow turned his attention from Diamond to Dreah, and found her glaring at him. He didn't know how to read her at that moment. She sat as straight backed as always and her face was as soft as before, but he eyes held a dangerous look that confused him. Movement from Glip-2 pulled his eyes from her.

Despite those defending him, Glip-2 floated toward the conference room door and disappeared into the t-port. Along with the rest of the room, Sparrow watched him go in silence. He felt a pang of guilt, but quickly pushed it aside.

For the first time Paragon spoke, "Latisha, the news is reporting that the military is preparing to send the first reconnaissance team into Paris. It probably means there are already teams there that the media doesn't know about." Paragon had continued to monitor the news feeds as Envoy had ordered earlier.

Before Envoy could respond, Diamond regained his composure and stepped forward. "Envoy, put together a team. I want to reach our people before they do. Let's recover our friends. Be sure to pull environmental data. Let's find out what we can, and do it quickly. No contact with the French."

Envoy went to work immediately gathering a team. Several of those in the room quickly filled in the space around her to volunteer. They all felt they had a personal or professional reason to go. She chose several of them and used her sidekick to send messages to others that weren't in the room.

"Let's get Jonesy back up here to monitor science and tech. Kahori, report to special ops and run some extraction scenarios. I want to be prepared for anything," concluded Diamond.

Sparrow glanced at Diamond and saw that his mask had returned. He was again the faceless man from Sparrow's dreams. Everyone responded to his commands without question. *Is it loyalty or is it mind control?* Sparrow wasn't sure which just yet.

Diamond started for the doorway in the left wall of the room as the wall shifted in appearance. The wood paneling disappeared and the wall turned white, and then it became transparent, revealing a large command center on the other side.

The room was huge. The far wall was one large monitor screen with dozens of images. It stood over thirty feet tall and wrapped around the entire side of the room. It displayed the devastation of Paris and hundreds of events related to it occurring all around the world. Even though only a little more than an hour had passed, riots were already breaking out as news spread. Saint Peter's Square was crowded with mourners seeking divine guidance. Four different doomsday cults spreading their rhetoric about the event were being monitored. One view showed the status of the world's financial markets through the various stock exchanges. They had been shut down in the wake of the incident to avoid a global meltdown brought on by panicked investors. One entire section was dedicated to the chambers of several governmental bodies already in emergency sessions.

Beneath the monitor wall were three separate monitor stations. Each station was curved to give the user as much access to the monitor wall as possible. Extending out over the three stations was a catwalk. A central console sat at the end of the catwalk.

As Sparrow watched, Diamond took up a position on the catwalk overlooking the room. Kahori approached him. She split and a doppelganger disappeared to the right through a single door. Kahori pointed after Envoy and spoke quickly with Diamond. She was on the verge of tears. Diamond shook his head no as he turned to look back into the conference room.

"Okay people," said Diamond from the balcony, "I know everyone is still emotional. However, let's remember there are five other cities in danger. Let's do our jobs." Already three people sat at the consoles and Diamond moved out over them. The lights in the room dimmed and the wall separating it from the conference room began to close and to shift back to a solid color.

Turning to Envoy, Diamond said, "Envoy, bring it back."

Envoy didn't respond to the order and Sparrow wondered what *it* was. As the wall finished closing, his eyes met Kahori's. Her eyes held longing to follow the team.

Most of the people in the room had cleared by now. As Envoy crossed the room toward Sparrow, she said, "You're with me, Sparrow. I want your eyes on the ground." She didn't bother to wait for a response.

Sparrow considered his options as the twins, Wavefront, and Paragon entered the t-port behind Envoy. He couldn't help but feel a strange curiosity about what had happened in Paris, but he didn't know that he was up to playing hero. Deciding against pushing Envoy, he stepped aboard the t-port.

Before the doors closed, Fluxstone also stepped aboard. Her eyes passed over Sparrow before locking with Envoy's. "I'm coming," she said.

"Are you sure that's a good idea?" asked Envoy.

"Do you think you can stop me?" replied Fluxstone.

Envoy frowned but didn't answer, and the group fell into silence.

When the t-port opened again, Sparrow knew he hadn't seen the area before. Everyone immediately proceeded to the right. Reluctantly, Sparrow followed.

They passed several open doorways that led into small conference rooms before entering a larger conference room at the end of the hallway. Several people already waited for them and everyone proceeded around a wall on the left as Envoy spoke.

"Okay people, all of you know what has happened. Just over an hour ago, Paris was hit by something big. Some of our people were there. We are going in after them. We don't know what to expect so I want everyone in an enviro-suit. Check the gauges to make sure everything is functioning. You have five minutes to suit up."

Around the wall Sparrow found everyone in various stage of undress. Fluxstone stood in one corner with her shirt lying on the bench beside her. Like many others in the room, she didn't worry about modesty as she dropped her pants and began to put on the enviro-suit.

"Here, you will need this," said Paragon as he handed Sparrow one of the suits. "Don't worry, I'll show you how to put it on."

The suit was made of a material that reminded Sparrow of leather. The deep green material was thick, had stiff padded elbows, and was cool to the touch. There was an apparatus that slipped over his head to rest on his shoulders. He was given a helmet with a glass faceplate that attached to the apparatus to form a seal. Paragon had gotten the size correct, but it was tight; which explained why everyone else in the room had shed their outer garments before suiting up. Soon everyone but Envoy and Paragon were dressed and they all followed Envoy out of the room.

As they passed into another hallway that ran behind the briefing rooms, Paragon handed Sparrow a belt. The belt had several pouches on it and a sidearm that Sparrow recognized as a DSS blaster. It looked like a normal firearm, but Sparrow knew it wasn't. Following the lead of the others, Sparrow belted it on.

The hallway looked like any other hallway in the Citadel but smelled of ocean water. The first door they passed revealed a large bay with white walls that faded to natural rock toward the back of the room. A large pool of water covered most of the floor. Poised above the water were two large platforms and on each was an airship belonging to Diamond Security Solutions. The airships had been the team's primary form of transportation prior to the pods. They were both still capable of flight, and were kept readied and fueled at all times.

Envoy ignored the room and continued to the end of the hallway to an even larger room. As Sparrow entered, he recognized the room as the one Envoy and Jonesy had disappeared into to rescue Butch.

The room was circular. It was over two hundred feet across and one hundred feet high. Covering most of the floor and ceiling was the same circle and blue light design that was in the center of the Citadel doors. The far wall had four large bay doors. Each door had the circle design in its center. The middle right door was peeled back where Brandon had ripped it open earlier.

Everyone walked around the circular design in the floor, and Sparrow followed. He felt like an astronaut about to embark on a spacewalk across the surface of a starship.

After speaking with a technician stationed at a large monitor station, Envoy approached the group. "Earlier we dispatched the *Exodus* to Paris. It should be in position in less than two minutes." She paused and looked at two young men, "We will land two blocks from the park. We don't know exactly what to expect. Mason, as soon as we are on site, organize the set up of the equipment and take readings on everything. I want to know if the damn dust on the ground has moved even a millimeter since the incident. Duo," Envoy paused long enough to hand Brian a sidekick, "here are the coordinates of the *Egress* and your instructions. Paragon, get airborne and keep tabs on anyone approaching the park, especially that military unit. Fluxstone, Fenrir, Wavefront, and Sparrow, you stay with me. Shadow Spirit will remain on standby for a quick evac. Any questions?" No one spoke. "Find a partner and stick together. We don't know what to expect from the locals. It's possible some survived. If they did, they may be hostile. No contact. Pull back to the *Exodus* and pull out."

While they waited, Kahori entered the room. Envoy moved over to speak with her. As Sparrow watched, a look of disappointment crossed the young girl's face. Envoy seemed to sympathize with her, but ultimately shook her head no and gave the young girl a hug.

Sparrow stood silently among the others and studied the room. He had no idea what was about to happen, but he understood that somehow they were about to be transported to Paris. Someone spoke next to him.

"We are waiting for the doors to cycle."

Sparrow looked to his right and found it was Wavefront speaking. He was still angry and his eyes were filled with sorrow. He stared at the doors, but Sparrow doubted he saw them.

"See th'series of blue lights across the top of each door? None of them are lit up. If one is lit, the door is safe to cycle. As the door sets, the lights across the top continue to light up. When they are all lit, the doors are ready. The greater the distance to the pod, the longer it will take them to light up."

Sparrow glanced at the series of lights. As Wavefront had indicated, none of them were lit.

"Ya can't open this door and the outer door of the pod at th'same time. It's a security measure, but also a safety one. It's a bad thing for them both to be opened at th'same time."

Sparrow started to ask why, but suddenly the first of the lights lit up and immediately the matching device in the center of the door began to spin. The floor and ceiling of the room began spinning as well. The outer rings of each design spun clockwise and the inner rings alternated counter to and in sync with the outer ring. Watching the room spin brought on a wave of vertigo, and Sparrow was thankful the phenomenon lasted only a few moments.

*Shring!*

The bell echoed through the room to signal that the door to the *Exodus* was ready to be opened. Before the sound faded from the room, the door began opening.

Everyone moved through the door as they placed their helmets on their heads and activated the seals. Envoy accessed the artifact on her arm and a glow surrounded her. She lifted gently off the ground and glided to the front of the group. Paragon placed an earpiece in his ear, and waited patiently. Wavefront remained distracted by distant memories. Duo stood on opposite sides of the room, and Fenrir growled deep in his throat.

Sparrow would have expected everyone to be as nervous as he felt. He was disappointed to find that most of them waited with a calm eagerness instead. They had all experienced things beyond his imagination, and despite the sorrow they felt over their friends' deaths, this was simply another opportunity to explore the unknown.

The door closed behind them and only the light from the blue liquid door designs filled the room before the entire chamber lit up brightly. The room looked like any other in the Citadel. The walls were white and the floor gleamed even though there was no visible light source. To the right of the room, there was a set of short steps that went down into a passenger area. The lower area had five rows of seats with four seats in each row. Dividing the seats in two, an isle ran from the steps down the middle. There was also a set of set of steps that led up to the cockpit area above the passenger area. A man Sparrow didn't recognize leaned out of the cockpit. Behind him, there were three seats and a glass surfaced console that looked like the conference room table. It was lit up with numerous lights and blinking displays.

The man gave Envoy thumbs up as the dial in the door to the Citadel spun. The blue lights all went dark. A moment later, a large door on the opposite wall opened up, and a ramp slid down to the ground before them. The fading light of the Paris sun filled the room.

\* \*

Impatient, Diamond paced the catwalk. Several lights flashed on his station, but he ignored them. For the past hour calls had been coming in from world leaders demanding to know what he knew about the Paris incident. No one had missed his team at ground zero.

Jonesy sat at station one. His monitors flashed with readings from Paris. So far he hadn't detected anything that was dangerous. Which, given the level of death they were dealing with, caused him even more concern. An incident that big should have left some evidence as to what had caused it.

At station two, Clara reviewed video footage from around the world. Her eyes sparkled brightly in the dimly lit room. Panic was infecting major cities like a plague. Already, people were fleeing large metropolitan areas, rioting was occurring on a large scale, and doomsday cults were predicting which city would be next. Clara paid particular attention to the five cities they suspected would be next.

Curtis, at station three, monitored as many radio, telephone, and Internet communications as he could. He paid particular attention to the governments of rival nations, and to any communications that mentioned Paris or France. When an indicator light on his console lit up, he shifted his focus to the Paris team and said, "We are on the ground, sir."

\* \*

Everyone stood in silence. Death hung over the city like thick fog over a cemetery. Bodies lay crumpled everywhere; in the streets, on the sidewalks, against buildings, and even behind the wheels of cars. Dead animals lay next to their masters, and plants drooped as leaves fell from dying stalks. Not a single bird sang, and even the wind lay still as if to show respect for the dead blanketing the city.

Paragon was the first to recover from the horror. He kneeled over the body of a young girl. Lifting her into his arms, he placed his hand upon her chest. A glow passed from his hand to surround her. After a few moments he pulled back his touch, and gently laid the body down on the pavement again. Standing over her, he shed a tear while praying for her soul.

As she spun in a circle, Envoy's eyes glowed. The artifact on her arm recorded environmental data and displayed it for her to see. "Initial readings are safe. No background radiation or contamination. If you choose, you may remove your helmets."

Several people did, including Sparrow. Others didn't and began to spread out to go about their assigned tasks. The team of scientists began to set up their equipment. Duo took flight and circled above the team. After receiving a nod from Envoy, they flew off toward the south.

Envoy turned to Paragon and said, "Paragon, get airborne and see if you can spot that military team. I'd like to make sure they don't surprise us."

Paragon didn't respond but flexed his wings and took flight. Without circling, he headed off to the west.

"Okay, let's go. Remember, if you encounter anyone you are to pull back. Do not engage. Sparrow, Wavefront, and Fenrir, follow me." Turning toward the *Champ de Mars*, Envoy lifted off the ground and flew toward the park. She cursed when she saw that Fluxstone was already a block ahead of her.

\* \*

"Operations mode," said Diamond. "Satellite feed in A-6 through D-15." Immediately an image of a globe leaped off the wall. As it rotated, a satellite orbiting it blinked. A satellite feed of the team on the ground appeared in the center of the monitor wall. The 3D globe retreated back to its spot in the upper right hand corner of the wall.

"Lady Gemini?" Diamond paused and waited for a response.

"Yes, sir?" She acknowledged from the special operations room off to his right.

"Kahori, factor scenarios with aggressive survivors."

"Copy," she responded.

"Status," said Diamond.

"Equipment is up and running. Initial readings are coming in," said Jonesy from station one.

"All team members are green," said Clara.

"No interference expected from the military at this time, sir. They are still over a mile away," said Curtis.

As he listened to the status checks, Diamond finished typing his message and instantly it was projected to the monitor before Jonesy. After reading it, Jonesy adjusted his screen and the right side was filled with the image Sparrow had generated of Facet with Glip-2 poised over his head. Readings began scrolling across the screen as he subjected it to any and all filters he could imagine.

\* \*

Envoy landed in front of Fluxstone. "Stop, Heather! I let you come along, now you stick to procedure. Let's do this together."

Fluxstone glared at Envoy and her skin rippled. Envoy didn't miss the change in Fluxstone's features, and feared her friend might actually attack her. Paragon landed next to Fluxstone and placed his hand on her shoulder. Fluxstone glanced at the knight, and found compassion in his eyes. She sighed and nodded her agreement.

Paragon turned to Envoy, "We have ten to fifteen minutes before the army reaches the park. It looks like they suspect it to be ground zero. They are making a beeline straight here." He paused and grinned,

"Latisha, there are survivors. They appear frightened, but they are there, hiding in the shadows."

Envoy nodded as Sparrow and the others caught up with them. She turned to Fenrir, "Scout the perimeter."

Fenrir nodded at her and shifted from a wolf-hybrid form into that of a large wolf. He shrugged off the rest of his enviro-suit and threw back his head to howl. A moment later, he bounded off through the trees and out of sight.

"Envoy, this is Duo. *Egress* is powerless. Charges planted. We're returning to your position."

"Roger Duo. Give me a quick once around the park on arrival. Fenrir is scouting."

"Affirmative," replied Kandi.

"Control, did you copy last? You are a go to permanently seal the inner door of the *Egress*."

"Affirmative," replied Curtis. "We copy charges are in place for initiation upon evac."

"Control, Paragon reports survivors. Numbers unknown, but there are survivors."

"Roger that, Envoy!" Curtis couldn't contain his excitement at the news.

The small group took up position behind a series of trees and waited. Fluxstone remained impatient, but held her ground. Paragon's touch had calmed her, but it couldn't heal her heartbreak. Within moments, the twins circled overhead and then sped off to circle the park.

Less than two minutes later, Fenrir reported in. "I have moving targets. Looks like three of them, mother and two children."

"Same here," said Brian. "Single male. He looks to be searching the bodies. Can I throw him through a window?"

"Negative, Brian." Envoy wanted to give him permission, but held her tongue. "Control, please advise."

"Mission parameters still stand. No contact," said Curtis. "Satellite feed indicates the military is closing on your location. They have numerous contacts. Stay on plan."

Before anyone could stop her, Fluxstone rose and ran for the park. Paragon took flight after her.

"Damn!" cursed Envoy. "Roger, Control. Duo, maintain perimeter and keep us notified. We are going in." She took flight, followed by Wavefront and Sparrow on the ground.

Fluxstone ran past the body of Incindiaro and to the stage. Paragon maintained an airborne vigil over her. Envoy dropped out of the sky next to Incindiaro. She extended her right arm toward him and the artifact scanned his bio-signs. He was dead. With a tear in her eye, she rose and followed the others.

Fluxstone dropped to her knees next to Aegis. He lay as the video feeds had shown. Slowly, she reached out and took him in her arms. As she cradled him, Paragon landed next to her, and placed his hand on her shoulder. When Envoy arrived, she knelt next to her long time friend, and bowed her head in mourning. Wavefront dropped to the ground to hug Fluxstone and Aegis. Sparrow stood behind the group quietly.

Several moments passed as Fluxstone cried over her lost lover.

Fenrir soon joined them in the center of the park. Shifting to his hybrid form, he adjusted Incindiaro's body before covering it with a sheet. He then moved to Stronghold, and respectfully covered him as well.

After several minutes, Envoy stepped aside, wiped the tears from her eyes and cleared her throat. "Duo, get down here, and take our friends home. Mason, what's your status?"

Mason replied, "Status green. We've got all we are going to get."

"Roger, I've got readings from ground zero. Get your team out of here."

Duo landed next to Envoy.

"Duo, get Stronghold and Incindiaro back to the pod, please. We'll take care of Aegis."

The twins were melancholy, but obeyed Envoy's orders. Gently, they reached out with their minds and lifted the young giant off the ground. They took care to keep him in the position Fenrir had placed him. Moving to the park entrance, they picked up Incindiaro and drifted back toward the *Exodus*.

\* \*

"We have a problem," said Lady Gemini on her direct feed to Diamond.

"Explain," said Diamond.

"A second team is approaching from the south."

As she spoke, she shifted a series of images to his console. They all showed an empty street. Lady Gemini altered the feed, and several blurry paths through the image appeared.

"Their invisibility is good," reported Lady Gemini, "but I'm better."

"Origin?" asked Diamond.

"Unknown. No markings, but I'll bet your next paycheck they aren't French though," she replied.

"Have they spotted our team?" asked Diamond.

"Affirmative. They shifted their pattern back toward the park after Duo left."

"Numbers?" said Diamond.

"I'm counting five squads of five."

"Patch over and run tactical. And Kahori, good catch."

"Welcome, daddy'o," she said as she took control of the command console.

\* \*

"Tactical to Alpha Team." Lady Gemini's voice broke up the memorial. "You have five squads of five approaching from the south. They are using stealth. Their association is unknown. Believed hostile."

"Roger, Gem." With her military exterior once again in place, Envoy turned to the others. "Sorry folks. We've got a team advancing from the south. We have to step this up. Wavefront, prepare Aegis for transport. Paragon, get behind the stage and check for Slipstream." Everyone responded to her orders while Envoy turned and began a search of the area.

Sparrow followed Envoy away from the others. "What are you searching for?"

Without looking at him she replied, "The *Aegis*. It's not here, but it should be right next to Alex. It's missing."

Sparrow stepped in front of her, and she stopped to meet his gaze. "You mean to tell me that shield is the true purpose of this mission? Diamond doesn't give a damn about these people does he?"

Unfazed by his aggression, Envy looked away and continued her search. She said, "Don't do that."

"Do what? Question Diamond?"

"Don't think you understand him. Mr. Diamond is a complicated man. I've been working for him for years, and I still don't understand him. You couldn't possibly come close after knowing him for only a few weeks. No one could. And yes, the shield is our primary objective. You saw the footage. The *Aegis* was successful at stopping those flares, and you're the one who pointed out that we're going to be facing them again." Stopping, she finally looked at Sparrow again, her face hardening. "And DSS is a military operation under my command, Sparrow. We follow orders when we're in the field. You were a soldier. If you can't understand Diamond, you should at least understand that." She held his eyes a moment and then turned back to her search.

Envoy was correct. The shield had been effective when everything else had failed. Sparrow had just been looking for a reason to question Diamond. If Diamond could somehow replicate the shield, his people would stand a better chance next time.

Sparrow looked back to Envoy. She was a soldier and this was a mission. He could understand that. He knew she would grieve after the battle. As for Diamond, her loyalty could again come back to mind control.

He started to turn away when the grass next to Envoy depressed and then rebounded. As he watched, it happened again. Someone or something invisible was paralleling her. Pretending to join in her search, Sparrow circled around Envoy while watching the ground for signs of movement.

\* \*

With classical music playing in his ear, Paragon wondered just how many friends he could stand to lose before he was pulled under by the grief. Only one leader had ever stood out above Aegis. People thought the man a legend, a myth, a child's tale. But Paragon knew the truth. He had been a man of honor and loyalty, filled with passion. Paragon had failed to protect him too. That had been a long time ago, and Paragon had come to think he would never serve another. Then he had met Aegis, and his hope had been renewed. Too many great men fell in the war against evil; and yet, evil survived.

On the other side of the stage, Paragon found the ground was littered with bodies. Many of them were covered with debris. He began to wonder if he would have to shift the debris to find his friend, but then he spotted the metal hero lying in an area by himself. Slipstream lay on his back with his large round eyes staring up at the sky. Paragon knew his dark eyes never closed, and were no indication of his status. With sunlight gleaming brightly off his metal body, there were no visible signs of injury.

Paragon landed next to his friend and kneeled down. He moved his hand over the warrior and extended his senses outward. At first all he felt was the cold metal that encased the man. Then deep within the man's chest he felt Slipstream's heartbeat. With the soft beat came the rush of warm blood. Paragon felt his own lungs fill with life at the touch. Relief filled him and he reached out to pick up his friend.

Slipstream hand shot up to clutch Paragon's wrist.

*Crack!*

The bones in Paragon's wrist snapped.

\* \*

As Envoy turned, Sparrow leaped for her. The only thing she had time to do was brace for the impact. He collided with something between them and tumbled to the ground struggling with it.

"Control, we have hostiles on scene!" shouted Envoy as she surrounded herself with a force field. A flash of energy rebounded off it. She returned fire and an invisible target screamed as her pulse disintegrated the bush the attack had originated from. The man's invisibility dropped and he crumpled to the ground.

"Tactical soldiers in stealth suits on scene," said Envoy as her eyes began to glow and she scanned the area for heat signatures. "No identifying marks and there is nothing on thermal. Wavefront?"

*Boom!*

Paragon's body shattered the last remaining portion of the stage wall. He sailed over everyone's head to crash into a large marble statue. The statue shattered and the hero was left tumbling across the ground.

"Paragon's down. Unknown assailant!" screamed Envoy into her commlink. In a blink she was next to the down warrior. At her touch, he groaned and rolled over.

Curious, Wavefront turned in the direction Paragon had come from. His eyes widened with surprise. "Slipstream looks bloody pissed!"

Slipstream stood behind the destroyed stage. Energy blazed from his eyes. His face was contorted with rage. His muscles bulged and his fits were clenched tightly.

Envoy glanced from Paragon to Slipstream. Like the others she was confused. Satisfied that Paragon would survive, she focused on Slipstream. Instantly, she was across the park and hovering over him. She could feel the energy blazing from his eyes through her force field.

\* \*

Sparrow tried to track what was going on around him even as he struggled with his invisible assailant. His attack had caught the man by surprise and Sparrow had quickly wrapped his arms around the man's neck. The soldier's struggle began to lessen, but pain erupted along the left side of Sparrow's face. He lost his grip on the man and rolled away. He came up in a crouch before his invisible enemy. He kept his eyes focused on the ground to track them. An instant later, he dodged to the right as an energy blast tore up the ground where he had been.

\* \*

"Six more," said Wavefront as he turned his attention away from Envoy and Slipstream. His eyes glowed. "One to the south, nine meters." An energy blast from that direction struck an invisible shield around him. Wavefront grinned, "You think I'm a bloody drongo! I cheat." Drawing his sidearm, he shot the invisible target. "Scratch one. Who's next? I'm a'spewin for a fight!" As he advanced on the enemy, several blasts from different directions bounced harmlessly off his shield and he returned fire.

\* \*

Fenrir howled as his keen senses picked out a target. An instant later, he leaped upon the man and his claws ripped into the helpless man's armor and gear. He leaped at another enemy even before the first one hit the ground. Energy blasts burned away patches of fur from his body but he barreled forward unhindered.

\* \*

Envoy poured as much energy as she could into her force field. She knew if Slipstream attacked her, she would need it. Suddenly his face relaxed and he turned to face her. The movement was unusual for him, and it unnerved her. An instant later he was gone and standing over Paragon. She sighed with relief. If he had chosen to attack her with such speed, he would have struck her without her having had a chance to react.

\* \*

Slipstream held out his hand to Paragon and assisted the winged warrior to his feet. Paragon's sword appeared in his hands, and his wounds began to heal.

Smiling at Slipstream, he said, "Sucker punch, huh?" Slipstream's face didn't reveal what he was feeling, but Paragon knew it was regret. It seeped from the man and Paragon had no problem detecting it. "I don't remember teaching you that one."

\* \*

Wavefront's force field easily held the blasts from his enemies' energy weapons at bay while it allowed his own weapon's energy to pass. He longed to pommel them, but when they realized their weapons were ineffective against him, they avoided contact. He had to settle for kicking the ones he gunned down.

\* \*

Fenrir barely held his animal instincts at bay as he carved a path of pain through the soldiers. His growls grew deeper as he longed to sink his teeth into their flesh. It was a desire that had been growing stronger in him since he had lost the ability to resume his human form. It had become a constant gnawing in his gut. Now, he found he was barely able to keep himself under control as the anger over his lost friends, and the powerful scent of the soldiers' fear mixed with their blood, threatened to overwhelm him. Dreah feared him losing control completely and had been working to keep him from field missions. Knowing the nature of this one, he doubted anything would have kept him from it.

Howling, he leaped at his latest target. Terrified, the man tried to flee, but Fenrir's clawed hand caught him in the side and hurled him twenty feet through the air. By the time he landed, Fenrir had already found another target.

\* \*

"At your ten, Envoy!" said Lady Gemini over the commlink.

Envoy lashed out with a wide burst and her target was blown backward.

"One at your three and another at your six. Two flanking Sparrow at twelve and six."

Sparrow turned and dropped as an opponent lashed out at him. An instant later a second opponent tackled him.

"Patching tactical to your sidekicks," said Lady Gemini.

Envoy lashed out with another wide burst, but didn't hit anything. She was impressed by the stealth technology used by the soldiers. Usually, her artifact would have punched through it by now.

*Shring!*

Envoy's sidekick announced the incoming data and she reached out to it through her artifact. Lady Gemini's images of their opponents appeared before her vision. Immediately Envoy's artifact analyzed the images and began streaming data on the strengths and weaknesses of the soldier's technology across Envoy's vision. The artifact further enhanced the images and within moments, the soldiers fully appeared in Envoy's vision. The alien metal catalogued the technology and adapted its own settings to account for it in the future. Any soldiers utilizing the same technology against Envoy would find their advantage of stealth nullified immediately.

"That's a nice trick, Gem. You'll have to tell me how you came up with it." Envoy immediately flew after an enemy. As she passed Sparrow, she blasted one of the two enemies he was sparring with, the man dropped.

\* \*

Sparrow still had one enemy, and he struggled to keep the stronger man from getting behind him. He began to lose the struggle when they were both suddenly hoisted from the ground. The man lost his grip and Sparrow struck the ground hard. As he rolled over, he looked up to see Fluxstone holding the invisible man high over her head.

"How dare you! How dare you attack us while we mourn our friends!" screamed Fluxstone.

From the look on her face, Sparrow feared she was going to rip the man in half. Instead, she flung him across the park.

*Crash!*
His invisibility died as he collided with a tree. He crumpled to the ground in a shower of leaves.
Energy blasts struck Fluxstone and she staggered forward a step before turning to face the direction of the attacks. Her enviro-suit was torn along her back, and there was a large blackened wound where the energy had stuck her. Her muscles rippled, and an instant later she charged forward and lashed out blindly. Her fists collided with an invisible target and it screamed as it was hurled backward. Screaming she charged off after Wavefront and Fenrir.
*Meta-humans,* cursed Sparrow as he rolled over to the body of an unconscious attacker, *I am way out of my league. Hell, even the norms have invisibility!*
He began rummaging through the man's clothing. An instant later, he pulled wires from inside the man's suit and the invisibly field faded. After searching the man, he moved on to another one. When he didn't find what he was looking for again, he moved on to yet another soldier and began his search.

\* \*

With Lady Gemini's tactical help and Wavefront's eyes, the enemy lost the advantage their invisibility gave them. Envoy and Wavefront blasted targets they could see, and guided by his keen sense of smell, Fenrir bounded unhindered from target to target.
Fluxstone waded in recklessly and swung blindly at spots where moments before energy blasts had originated to tear and char her skin. Her latest target was sent hurtling through the windshield of a car, and moments later she ripped the same car in half and flung parts of it around the battlefield.
Duo arrived and joined the fray. The two young heroes juggled targets between them before hurling them through windows and against buildings.
Slipstream responded to the battle like a machine. He displayed no emotion and moved from target to target with precision. Inside him, his emotions were in turmoil.
At full speed, Slipstream collided with a parked car. The car was flung backward to crush two soldiers moving around behind Fluxstone. Their invisibility was useless against his spatial awareness. Without

moving, he turned his head and blasted a third soldier. The soldier disappeared in the blast as the conflagration punched through the wall of a building and out the other side.

Paragon used more restraint than his teammates. He couldn't see his enemy but with direction from Gemini and his heightened senses, he put himself between the soldiers and Fluxstone's back as he avoided most of their attacks. His armor protected him from the few that got through.

As the air rippled with an energy blast, Paragon lashed out at the spot with the flat of his sword. The enemy crumpled under the strength of the blow. Stepping forward, Paragon grabbed the rear of a car and dragged it between him and the enemy. Using it as a shield, he prevented the soldiers from advancing around it.

\* \*

"The infantry is entering the park from the west," said Lady Gemini. "Two heavy tanks backed up by three Anti-Personnel Battle-bots! Two troop carriers and a dozen soldiers on the ground."

*Boom!*

The explosion rippled off Envoy's shield. Unharmed, she spun on the attackers. Across the park she saw the smoking barrel of a large tank and soldiers pouring from the back of the transports. One soldier dropped behind cover and pointed a large caliber weapon at her. An instant later a round bounced off her force field. The pavement thundered as large metal legs pounded it. Three soldier-driven battle-bots moved up to flank the troop carriers. The soldier contained within each bot lit up in Envoy's vision as her artifact automatically scanned the machines, and classified the soldiers as weaknesses. A list of weapons and armament for each battle-bot scrolled across her vision. Each bot contained more weapons and ammunition than both troop carriers combined.

A wave of shame passed through Envoy as she realized she had gotten caught up in the moment. With nearly twenty years as a soldier, it was the first time she had allowed the death of a fellow soldier to affect her so.

"Paragon, Slipstream, engage! No casualties! Equipment only! Shadow Spirit emergency evac now! Center on Sparrow!"

\* \*

"Damn!" cursed Sparrow as he felt the icy tip of a dagger sink into his back. He spun to find the attacker, but instead watched in shock as his shadow shifted and expanded. An instant later, Shadow Spirit stood over him. With eyes wide, Sparrow stared up at the cloaked man. After catching his breath he managed, "A warning would have been nice."

Taking his eyes from the silent man, Sparrow crawled to yet another target and began to search him. Shadow Spirit didn't respond, but stood guard over Sparrow as the battle raged around them. An instant later, a shadow reached out from under the Spirit's cloak and wrapped around an invisible target that had been only a few feet from Sparrow. The man screamed as he disappeared into the darkness beneath the cloak. Sparrow shuddered when the man's screams abruptly ended.

\* \*

*Boom!*

The air thundered as Slipstream blasted across the park. The tank's barrel exploded again and a shell whizzed by his head.

*Clang!*

Slipstream's metal body collided with the tank. The weaker metal of the tank peeled back and his momentum pushed it backward several feet. With little resistance, Slipstream ripped the battered turret from the top of the tank and swung it to strike a troop carrier. The soldiers spilled from the back of the overturning trucks. Without moving, he turned his head and energy from his eyes ripped across the park to collapse the street beneath several invisible attackers that were flanking Fluxstone.

Bullets bounced off Paragon's armor as he sailed over the soldiers. He knew the battle-bots were the greatest threat, but he also knew the invisible soldiers were in as much danger from them as he was. He hated man's modern weapons. They had no honor. They killed indiscriminately, even when in the hands of a child. They required little skill, and even less restraint.

Paragon flung his sword at the closest battle-bot as he dropped from the sky among the invisible soldiers. His grand wings flexed as he grabbed men and flung them from the battle zone. When the last soldier was clear, he turned to face the battle-bot. His sword had struck true. The bot was badly damaged and was unresponsive to the soldier controlling it.

*Thudda! Thudda! Thudda!*

Pain ripped through Paragon's shoulder and he was knocked over backwards by the force of the bullets. Blood poured from the holes in his armor, and his left arm was numb with pain. Rolling over, he saw a second battle-bot advancing on him. Inside the bot, he could see a soldier grinning.

"I forgive thee," Paragon mumbled.

In a flash, he rose from the ground and charged across the battlefield. Sunlight gleamed off his armor to blind the startled soldier. Paragon's sword was instantly in his hand and he brought the massive blade down on his metal target. The blade sliced through steel and wires to cleave the bot in two. The soldier's shoulder patch was sliced from his uniform, but his skin was left untouched.

\* \*

Sparrow found no identifying marks, no tattoos, and no personal information on the soldiers he searched, but he didn't relent. In the past he had faced similar soldiers, and he was counting on human weakness to find what he searched for. He hurried to another body. He paused when he realized it was the man Fluxstone had hurled across the park. The man lay crumpled against the tree. His invisibility field had failed, and he was dead.

Glancing around for Fluxstone, Sparrow briefly watched her as she continued her rampage through the invisible men. Turning back to the body of the man, Sparrow began to rummage through his pockets. He found what he was looking for. Along with a small angel charm, the man had a photo of a blond woman and two young kids. Regardless of how top secret a mission was, not all soldiers found it easy to leave their personal lives behind. Sparrow pocketed the items just as Duo glided over to him.

Kandi looked disappointed as she said, "Fights over. Envoy's ordered us all out of here."

Sparrow nodded. As he watched, the twins gently lifted Aegis into the air. A wave of panic hit him as he was also suddenly lifted from the ground. He felt weightless, helpless, and angry. No amount of struggling would free him from their mental grip. He bit his tongue to keep from screaming at the kids. With Shadow Spirit guiding them, they flew in the direction of the others.

\* \*

Fluxstone swung a wild blow that tore large chunks of stone from the corner of a building. The debris rained down on her latest two targets, silencing their screams. One of the men's invisibility suits short-circuited and he became visible. Fuming, Fluxstone snatched up a chunk of rock the size of a small car. Hoisting it over her head, she stepped forward to crush the unconscious man.

"Fluxstone! Stop!" screamed Envoy as she placed herself between Fluxstone and the helpless men. "This is not our way!"

Fluxstone hesitated for a moment. Her face was contorted with rage. Blood oozed from a wound on her forehead and she had numerous burn marks across her face and body.

"Aaaahhhhh!" Fluxstone screamed as she turned and hurled the large rock. It sailed through the air for several blocks and fragmented when it struck the street. Turning, Fluxstone began pacing and forced herself to take deep breaths.

Duo gently laid Aegis on the ground, and sat Sparrow down beside him.

"Gather," said Envoy as she closely watched Fluxstone.

A moment later, Paragon landed next to them. His armor was badly damaged and he still had blood flowing from several wounds. Envoy looked at him with concern. He shook his head to indicate he would be all right. Envoy didn't look away. It wasn't his physical wounds that she was worried about. She knew he could have healed them already if he wanted. It was the dark shadow across his eyes that worried her.

Fenrir had numerous burns and was in obvious pain. He snarled and grunted with each step.

Wavefront appeared unhurt. His force field had kept him protected. He couldn't take his eyes off the body of Aegis.

"Jack, are you okay?" asked Envoy.

Wavefront didn't respond. Envoy turned her attention across the battlefield to the only member of the team not present.

Both tanks and all three battle-bots were down. Most of the soldiers were scattered or fled. Slipstream stood over several frightened soldiers who held their hands up in surrender.

"Slipstream, let's go," said Envoy into her commlink

The hero gave no indication that he heard her words, but in the next instant he was standing next to her.

With her eyes on Aegis, Envoy said, "Spirit, take us home."

Sparrow turned to dive for cover, but before he could move, a coldness spread through his body and darkness closed in around him. The last thing he saw was the white sheet covering the body of Aegis.

# CHAPTER 12
## MEMORIAL

When the darkness cleared, Sparrow found himself standing in the pod bay.

*Damn*, he cursed. He shuddered from the lingering chill of the shadow-slide. Glancing around, he discovered the rest of the team had already recovered. Only Shadow Spirit still stood near him, and the man appeared to be smirking beneath his cowl.

*Meta-humans*, Sparrow cursed as he started across the room.

Brandon and several med-techs insisted on checking everyone returning from Paris. Sparrow waited patiently as a young nurse scanned him with a sidekick. Refusing to cooperate with the nurse would only bring Brandon over to conduct the scan. After only a moment, she smiled and gave him a wink of approval before moving onto Paragon. The winged knight smiled at her, and declined her assistance. His wounds were visibly healing.

Despite the large number of people in the room, it was subdued. Everyone spoke in whispers. Even the constant hum of the Citadel was unusually quiet.

As Diamond and Dreah entered the room, Sparrow adjusted his course to intercept them. A man in dark fatigues followed them. Sparrow recognized him and the patch on the shoulder of his black fatigues. Graham Bullock was the commander of TASC, Diamond's Tactical Armored Support Company, his private army.

Sparrow glanced at Dreah as everyone came together. The weariness in her eyes indicated she was ready to collapse, but she still walked with grace and poise.

As everyone gathered, Envoy said, "As you know sir, we recovered all four of our people. But the *Aegis* wasn't there."

Diamond nodded as he looked at the three bodies. Unmoving, Slipstream stood against a far wall. He didn't have a mark on him. Diamond considered asking Envoy's thoughts on the warrior, but decided against it. He had been working with Slipstream longer than any of them. He knew the man too well. Slipstream would not have opened up to Envoy. Turning the conversation, he asked, "Do you think the stealth team took the shield?"

"Unknown, but most likely," replied Envoy. "We were monitoring by satellite prior to our arrival. Perhaps Gemini can apply her trick to the file footage to track them. Their stealth was some of the best I've seen. When they moved, they had no fringe as is common with most invisibility. Without Gemini, I wouldn't have even been able to penetrate it. Besides us, there is only one place tech of that caliber could come from."

"Halo Corp," said Bullock. "Which means they were agents of the Adversary."

Bullock had a gruff deep voice that commanded the attention of everyone in a room when he spoke. Sparrow had encountered similar voices before. Soldiers could hear them even over the sounds of gunfire and cannon fire on any battlefield.

"Any leads on their actual affiliation?" asked Diamond.

Before Envoy could speak, Sparrow answered. "They weren't normal military or mercenary forces. If I had to guess I'd say they were street thugs, maybe low-level gangsters, with high-tech equipment. They were decoys. The real team was probably long gone by the time we got to the scene."

"What makes you say that?"

"Their tactics."

Everyone looked to Sparrow to continue.

"No experienced soldier is going to go into close combat with a meta-human if they can avoid it. That's the sort of thing overconfident amateurs do."

"Bullock?" Diamond turned to face the man in fatigues.

"I agree, sir. You've given TASC some top-notch equipment but we still don't close in with metas unless it's absolutely necessary."

Diamond sighed heavily.

"Any clues to help us locate the real team?"

Envoy glanced at Sparrow. "We didn't find anything, sir. Sorry."

Diamond looked concerned, but turned the conversation to Fluxstone. Lowering his voice he said, "How is she?"

As everyone watched, Fluxstone gently lifted the body of Aegis onto a gurney. As Duo pushed the gurney out of the room, she walked beside it.

"Bad shape. When she comes off her adrenaline high, those burns are going to put her down."

"Out of control," added Sparrow.

Paragon glanced in Sparrow's direction, but instead of scorn for Sparrow, there was only concern for Fluxstone on his face. Sparrow doubted the gentle warrior judged him as harshly as Fluxstone did.

"I'll go to her," said Dreah as she turned and left the room.

"Envoy, see to it everyone gets cleaned up. I also want to know the full status on Slipstream as-soon-as-possible. Debriefing in one hour. I've got to go answer a few phone calls. Perhaps one of them can answer some questions about the *Aegis*, and I'm sure the French want to know why we ripped up their troops." Diamond turned and started for the exit.

"They fired on us first, sir," said Envoy quickly. Diamond didn't slow his pace or look over his shoulder. "Damn," she mumbled as she turned away. Unconsciously, she rubbed her right arm.

\* \*

Sparrow peeled the top of the enviro-suit off and collapsed onto the bench. He rubbed his sore shoulder and looked at the bruise already forming. Age was not something he had considered before, and he briefly feared it was just another thing the Counselor had hidden from him. Maybe it was just one more reason why he had been tossed aside.

Grunting, he pulled off a boot and tossed it onto the floor. For a brief moment he wondered if someone else was going to clean up the room, or if there was something he was supposed to do with the suit. Then he questioned why he even cared.

Movement to his right pulled his attention away from the suit. Envoy rounded the corner. She leaned against the wall and studied him. Silence settled between them and Sparrow removed his other boot.

"Thanks," she said.

Sparrow looked at her and raised an eyebrow in question.

She smiled as she slid down the wall to sit on the floor across from him. "I know you didn't want to be out there. So, thanks. I failed to properly search those guys. You didn't."

Sparrow nodded his understanding. Envoy looked vulnerable for the first time since he had met her.

She leaned her head back against the wall and sighed. "I've been at this a long time. Alex trained me, first in the Army and then here as a meta-human. He was the best man I've ever known. I've given up everything, and everyone, to follow him. I don't know what I'm supposed to do now."

Sparrow didn't reply. He knew the last thing he should do was to try and counsel her on her emotional state. Silence settled over the room as Envoy waited for an answer. Sparrow didn't give one.

"You weren't the only one distracted out there," he said.

Envoy lowered her gaze. "Heather is a good person, you know. She has been hard on you. Probably because she has been at this a long time and has seen many people with checkered pasts fail."

"I won't defend my past to her or anyone else."

Envoy nodded in understanding. "You don't have too. Dreah has vouched for you. Alex didn't know why, but he accepted it and so do I. Heather will come around."

Preferring to keep the conversation on Fluxstone and not himself, Sparrow continued, "She was out of control. She could have gotten herself or one of us killed."

Envoy didn't respond, but the look in her eyes told him she knew he was right. She rose and started for the door.

"Finish it," said Sparrow just before she rounded the corner.

Envoy stopped and looked at him. "What?"

"You asked what you should do. You should finish it."

Envoy nodded to him and left the room.

\* \*

The conference room wasn't as full as it had been before the Paris excursion. Everyone present had a direct purpose for being there, and the smaller numbers allowed Diamond better control.

Fluxstone and Shadow Spirit were the only members of the rescue team not present. Fluxstone was with Aegis, and Shadow Spirit rarely had anything to do with mechanical or scientific things. He would not have offered any opinions even if he had been forced to attend. Clara, with eyes sparkling, did her best to keep track of the meeting. Maria sat with her legs pulled up onto the chair as she chewed on her hair once more. The leaders of the scientific expedition team, Allan and Mason, were present, but they spent most of their time in whispered argument over the data they had collected. Silent, Paragon leaned against a wall with his head bowed.

Meta-man had arrived at the citadel shortly after the team's return from Paris. He was a beacon in his gleaming metallic armor, but seemed relaxed and confident among the group. He spoke freely.

The man next to Meta-man was named Edmond, and he spoke to the American hero as if they were best friends. Edmond was thin and wore a white lab coat over a wrinkled white dress shirt. His tie hung loose and was stained in several spots. His pants and shoes were black. He wore dark framed glasses that he kept pushing back up his nose. They were thick and distorted his eyes. His hair was a dark brown and graying at the temples. It was uncombed and wild. He appeared nervous and didn't look anyone but Meta-man in the eye for more than a moment.

Carol Estingdale sat next to Diamond. She was dressed in an olive green loose fitting sweater and matching pants. She sat quietly with her glasses perched on the end of her nose.

Commander Bullock sat with his thick brow furrowed and his arms resting on the table in front of him. He sat forward in his chair and watched everyone with a critical eye.

"The international community is up in arms over your stunt in Paris," said Meta-man. "They think you may be responsible for this whole mess. The UN Security Council has ordered me to bring all of you in for questioning. I told them you would be hard to find, but I would look into it."

Bullock chuckled. "You should have just wished them good luck with that."

Diamond smirked. "Perhaps they should have listened to me when

I tried to warn them." Turning to Clara, he asked, "What is the status of the seeds?"

Clara leaned forward and replied, "We have spotters in place and all five are accounted for. Lekkas is proving difficult to keep track of, however. He has several enemies and stays out of sight. Thankfully, he is the only criminal on the list. The rest have very public lives."

Turning to Jonesy, Diamond asked, "What readings did we get from Paris?"

Jonesy sighed and glanced at Allan and Mason. "What we expected. A big fat nothing. Paris shows the same signs that all the other sites show but nothing new, and nothing we can trace. We need readings from the start to the finish of one of these things. Sorry, Mr. Diamond."

"What about the image of Facet and Glip-2 Sparrow discovered in the Paris footage? Is it reliable?" asked Diamond.

"The image is what it appears to be. I can't find any way to discredit it. It appears Glip-2 is in that shaft, and it does give doubt to the lost family tree. We may still have an undiscovered line and therefore an unknown target."

Glip-2 floated silently into the corner. "Don't worry Glip," said Wavefront, "You're still our mate, regardless of what Jonesy-boy thinks."

Diamond looked at Wavefront and then at the rest of the room, "Don't tell me Paris is a total wash, people. What about that team we encountered?"

"According to my contacts, they weren't connected to the French government," said Meta-man. "Everyone's denying association. Trying to sort through them all will be a political nightmare. It's a dead end."

"Gem was able to track them to a spot where an airship dropped them off," said Envoy. "It was a Halo Corp military craft. Unfortunately, satellite imaging only shows it came in from the west. All the local cameras were down at the time of arrival due to the pulse. We couldn't track its point of origin or get positive identification on it."

"The Adversary?" asked Meta-man.

"The Adversary," said Bullock.

"We believe the tech is his," said Diamond. "He has shown no interest in this so far, but who knows. The man has two faces and sometimes I don't think he even knows which one is showing."

"He is a crafty one," said Edmond.

"He won't deny the tech is his," said Envoy.

"No he won't," replied Diamond, "but he will deny any connections beyond selling it."

"I'll bet he can even produce a bill of sale for it too," added Envoy.

"Should we watch him?" asked Wavefront.

"We are always watching him," replied Bullock.

"Barring the answer just falls into our lap, we are out of leads to recover the *Aegis* then," said Envoy with a sad tone to her voice.

"Mr. Diamond," interrupted Carol, "It's important. We can't just let it disappear. The heritage in that shield is…"

"We won't, Carol. We will find it," reassured Diamond.

Switching the subject, Edmond asked, "What's the status on Slipstream? Why did he have a seizure during the event? And why did he attack Paragon?"

"Hurting," mumbled Maria.

Jonesy shook his head. "It's difficult to say. He didn't stand still long enough for Brandon to check him over. Not surprising. He hasn't spoken since then either, which is also not surprising. We think he experienced a flashback to his own event. Why he attacked Paragon is anybody's guess. I am more curious as to why he watched the cloud form. Given he is blind and his sonar's range would have been too short, he shouldn't have been able to even see it."

"Thoughts, anyone?" asked Diamond.

At first no one responded, but then Edmond offered up a suggestion. "He was dominated by the Psadan for a long time. That level of mental domination can leave a mind fractured. Given his metabolic system, I don't believe it was a simple seizure."

"*Psadan?*" asked Sparrow.

"The alien." The confused look on Edmond's face indicated he thought the answer was common knowledge. He glanced around the room nervously and pushed his glasses up his nose. The think lenses distorted his bright blue eyes.

"Remember my story, Sparrow," said Diamond. "Slipstream was in the cave when I found the alien, the Psadan. It tried to mentally dominate me. We believe Slipstream was under its mental control for forty years.

It was the first time Sparrow had heard a name given to the alien. He doubted it was a name pulled out of thin air. Diamond never did anything random. He knew the alien well enough to know it was a Psadan.

Sparrow glanced at Edmond. The glasses weren't used to just correct any vision problems. They were also used to hide the intelligence in his eyes. Sparrow wondered why.

"Can we trust him?" asked Jonesy.

Wavefront jumped to his feet, grabbed Jonesy by the shirt, and before anyone could stop him dragged the man over the table. "Listen up, bucko, never call a mate on the floor like that!" Envoy gripped Wavefront around the shoulder and whispered into his ear. He ignored her. "That man has saved the world a dozen times over, your butt included!" Wavefront glared into Jonesy's eyes while Jonesy avoided Wavefront's. Jonesy held his hands in the air innocently and waited.

After a moment, Envoy succeeded in pulling Wavefront free of the scientist, but Wavefront continued to glare at Jonesy. Envoy gently pushed Wavefront back into his seat, but remained standing over him instead of retaking her own seat.

Diamond glared at Wavefront. "Yes, he can be trusted. For now, we will avoid exposing him to an event."

Everyone sighed with relief and allowed a few moments to pass. They were all tense and tired. Allowing their anger to contribute to the meeting would accomplish nothing.

"What about the survivors?" asked Meta-man.

Reluctantly, Jonesy answered as he tried to avoid Wavefront's glare. "There are some. The actual numbers won't be known for weeks, but the preliminary reports indicate they were underground. The deeper underground the safer they were. The radius of the wave was only two miles, of course anyone outside that radius survived."

"Underground?" asked Envoy.

"So far reports indicate that at shallower depths, some people died and others lived. At deeper depths, they all lived. Extra thick shielding, such as that provided by bomb or emergency shelters, greatly improved the chances of survival."

"We may be able to use that," said Diamond. "Clara, acquire an underground safe house in each of the cities and do it fast. Riots are already breaking out, and as soon as word gets out that the survivors were underground, you can bet those who haven't fled the cities will be scrambling for a bunker."

"Yes, sir," said Clara.

The room fell into silence again as everyone reflected on the millions that had been killed by the incident. They were saddened by the fact that they had very little information to move forward on. Only Diamond sat without revealing his emotions. His eyes darted between all of them and he considered their current mental states, and their usefulness to him.

It was Envoy who finally broke the silence. "So we move on then. What is our next step?"

Without hesitation, Diamond answered. "We keep spotters on the seeds. We put a team on standby at all times. Jonesy set the satellites to watch for environmental anomalies. If one of those clouds appears again, we need to be on it. What's your gut feelings on the seeds?"

Jonesy hesitated as he nervously glanced around the room. "You mean as in most likely to pop, or whatever it is we are calling this?" Diamond nodded. "I don't have much to go on, sir. I've compared the data on all of them, but I can't be sure."

"Best guess," said Diamond.

Jonesy sighed. "Guess? You want me to guess? I don't know Mr. Diamond. If I were wrong, it would be on my head. I need more data..."

"Guess," insisted Diamond.

Jonesy hesitated and looked around the room. No one offered him help, even Edmond, who appeared to have the answer on the tip of his tongue. "Okay, best guess...Buenos Aries. Fuentes is the newest generation, barring Nazarov's unborn child. Of course, she is younger than Facet, and he went before her. Next to her, I'd go with Austin in Denver. That is the best I can do given the conflicting data."

Edmond nodded his agreement as he looked from Jonesy to Diamond.

Diamond turned to Clara, "Dispatch the *Exodus* to Buenos Aries. Place the *Gateway* on standby. If Butch is up to it, put him at the controls. What's the status of the *Portal*?"

"*Egress II*," interrupted Clara.

"What?" asked Diamond.

Realizing she had corrected him, Clara blushed and stumbled to recover. "Sorry, sir, I assumed you knew. We renamed her. The *Gateway*, we renamed the pod the *Egress II*. Butch requested it. Unless, of course, you object, sir."

"No. No objections. That's fine," replied Diamond, but his eyes lingered on Clara long enough to remind her that he expected to be informed of such changes long before they were made. "What's the status on the *Egress II*?"

Clara looked as if she wanted to sink beneath the table and lowered her gaze from Diamond's. "At least two weeks, sir."

Ignoring Clara's discomfort, Diamond continued. "Fine, as soon as she is ready, I want her sent to Denver. See if Butch can coax her along a little quicker."

"What about the targets, or seeds?" asked Sparrow.

"What do you mean?" replied Envoy.

"Millions of lives are at stake. Would it not be best to simply remove the targets?"

"Not going to happen!" said Meta-man. "I will not sanction murder. Especially when we have not ruled out all other options."

"I'm not hearing any other options," replied Sparrow.

Meta-man started to protest again, but Diamond raised his hand to silence him while also indicating that Jonesy should speak. "Jonesy," he said.

"We don't know what will happen. We may prevent the primary seeds from sparking off one of these events, but we also know that it doesn't take a primary seed. Slipstream is an example. He was not the center of his tree, but the event caused similar deaths. It was only a couple of hundred people; but it was in a rural area, so who knows. These people's parents, aunts, uncles, cousins – you name it – may become the targets if we eliminate the primary seeds. We have no way to track them all."

"The same problem exists if we reveal what we know to the governments," said Envoy.

Edmond pushed his glasses back up his nose as he replied, "Yes. They would disappear, by what means depends on the desperation of the government in question. Some might even seek genocide against entire bloodlines. It is barbaric, but it is not unheard of, or an unviable solution. It worked, as far as we can tell, for the Missing Man. Even without telling them about him, some governments may actually seek that solution."

Sparrow had read the brief on the Missing Man. Dyonis Harvie was one of the original settlers of Roanoke Colony. Sparrow's eyes darted to Meta-man. John Sampson, Jr., was also one of the original colony members. *Edmond?* Obviously, he and Meta-man had a long-standing relationship, maybe as far back as Roanoke. Sparrow made a mental note to check the roster for the name. He had already done so for Diamond, and most of those working closely with him. None of them had appeared on the roster.

As for genocide, Sparrow didn't have the problem with it Meta-man seemed to have. He had to admit it wasn't the best of options; but even with his emotions released, it seemed a better option than world destruction.

"Well that settles it then, this is on our shoulders," said Meta-man.

"Move them," said Maria.

Sparrow glanced at her. She hadn't moved. Her hair was still in her mouth and her blank stare revealed nothing.

"That's an idea," replied Edmond with a look of surprise on his face that quickly turned to embarrassment as he pushed his heavy glass up his nose once again.

"Explain," said Meta-man.

Quickly recovering, Edmond expounded on the idea. "We move them, or kidnap them, to a safe place. If they blossom, then no one dies. An isolated island, maybe."

Diamond shifted in his chair. "At this point that is a contingency plan. We are currently preparing an appropriate spot. Of course, we want to make sure the seeds are separated. We don't want one sparking off and killing the others."

"Or possibly worse, sparking the others," interjected Jonesy. His face soured. "We have no idea what that would cause."

"I don't like the sound of this," interrupted Meta-man.

Before an argument could break out, Diamond spoke, "It is only a contingency plan, for now. The details are still being worked out. With Paris, we had just over twelve minutes from the time the cloud started forming. If we have a team on site, that's plenty of time to make an emergency move if necessary. To do it however, we need to be prepared.

Envoy, make sure the Spirit doesn't leave the Citadel. We may want him without notice."

"Maverick may be able to help with that too," said Edmond.

"He is unreliable," said Meta-man, "among other things." A look of disgust passed over his face.

"Yes, but pay him enough and he becomes more reliable," Edmond countered. "As for the other things, sis can keep him under control. You know that. Besides, he is as experienced a teleporter as anyone can be. He could hit a dime on the surface of the moon."

"Contact him," Diamond said. "Offer whatever it takes."

Meta-man sighed and leaned back in his chair to rub his face with his hands.

"You going to be with us all the way on this, John?" asked Envoy.

Meta-man glanced at her, and then looked at Diamond. "Yes, I'm here until this is finished. I'm resigning from UNIT. Once they find out I'm working with you, I'm going to be as wanted as you are anyway."

"What?" asked Envoy.

Diamond shook his head. "Not so fast, Meta-man. Delay them as long as you can. Those contacts are valuable."

Meta-man looked around the room, and finally at Edmond who shook his head in agreement with Diamond and said, "Given the current crisis, I doubt they will just let you resign anyway, my friend. They won't be happy when they find out you are playing on this side of the fence without telling them, but at least we'll have all options open to us as long as you are on board. I would suggest you play along with the ruse of locating Mr. Diamond for them. We may even be able to take advantage of UNIT, and its resources through you. If nothing else, it gives us an overview of world politics and where the various governments stand on this whole affair. Right now, it appears they are focusing on Mr. Diamond, and we know that because of you. Without that info, Mr. Diamond could already be in international custody."

Meta-man nodded his head in agreement. "Okay," he said.

Again, Sparrow studied Edmond. Meta-man was the world's premier hero. He currently served the UN as the head of UNIT. He had served as a commander in numerous wars over the years. He was a man of prestige who was respected the world over; yet, he didn't hesitate to defer to Edmond. The two obviously had a long history. Meta-man was the leader, but Edmond was a source of wisdom behind that leadership.

Edmond had also referred to Dreah as *sis*, tying her even closer to the two of them. The man's glasses and demeanor were not everything there was to learn about him. It made him the least predictable, and thus the more dangerous.

Diamond turned to Envoy. "I'm pulling Heather from field duty, effective immediately. She is going to protest so expect some fallout." Envoy nodded her agreement.

"A memorial is planned for tomorrow morning at zero-nine-hundred in the garden." For just a moment, a look of sadness passed over Diamond. "I expect you all to be there. After the ceremony, the bodies will be turned over to the families. Aegis will be laid to rest in Arlington National Cemetery in three days. Stronghold is being returned to his hometown to be buried next to his parents. Incindiaro is being returned to his family in Mexico. If anyone wants to attend any of the official ceremonies, let's get their names to Clara, and she'll make it happen." Diamond met each of their eyes in silence as Clara made notes of his orders on her sidekick.

He then turned to Sparrow. "One last thing. Most of you have met him by now, for those of you that haven't, this is Sparrow. He has Omega clearance on all DSS matters. We are in the process of setting him up as a security consultant with full DSS credentials; but given the current state of things, it may take a few days before the background checks are completed and everything becomes official."

*Especially since we're not going to make Sparrow available for background checks until we've set him up with a new identity that won't send up red flags in every law enforcement database in the world*, thought Diamond to himself.

Taken by surprise by the introduction, all Sparrow could manage was a slight nod. He knew Diamond didn't need any official clearance or background checks. The statements had been meant to give Sparrow credibility to those that didn't already know his history. As usual, Diamond was controlling the information that was available.

As for any background check, Sparrow doubted he could even pass one. Before the Counselor, he would have passed even the tightest of security checks. Now even applying for a job as a janitor would alert certain major law enforcement organizations to his existence. Precautions had always been taken to conceal his identity, but there were branches of government that specialized in catching guys like him.

Any background check would alert them. Diamond wouldn't make any employment record, and any missions Sparrow was a part of would be carefully selected to always protect his identity. After all, he was already dead. A dead political assassin in the employ of Diamond Security Solutions would severely damage the organization's reputation.

"Welcome aboard, mate," said Wavefront as he slapped Sparrow on the shoulder. Meta-man extended his hand and vigorously shook Sparrow's. Clara's eyes sparkled at him, and Maria pulled herself out of her own world long enough to look at him and smile. The whole spectacle made Sparrow uneasy.

"Envoy, brief him on team capabilities," said Diamond. Envoy nodded. "Unless someone objects, that's it for now." No one objected. Diamond rose and quickly left the room with Bullock in tow.

Dreah had entered the room at some point during Sparrow's introduction. She smiled at him as the meeting broke up; but to Sparrow's disappointment, she went immediately to Meta-man and Edmond. She hugged each in turn and as they left, she walked between them holding their hands. The company of the two men brought a sparkle to her eyes.

\* \*

Dreah's hand rested against the transparent wall, and her eyes followed the man moving on the other side. "He can't see us, but I wish he could. We have no choice but to put him back where we found him. Samuel is trying to delay his return until after this crisis is over. He was lost to us for so long, I fear he will be lost again."

"Don't worry. We know who he is now, and we will keep an eye on him," replied Meta-man. Dreah looked at him and smiled as she slipped her arm around his waist and hugged him.

"Dyonis Harvie, I hardly remember him." Meta-man continued. "On the boat he skulked around everyone like a rat starved for cheese. I remember thinking he was creepy. After we landed, I got so busy with the settlement that I remember nothing more about him. It was so long ago. If I have encountered him since, I don't remember it either. How about you, Edmond?"

Edmond shrugged. "Of us all, you have the best memory of those events my friend. I barely remember the boat."

As the three friends watched, Harvie moved around a stack of books. When he was satisfied with the arraignment, he pulled a book from the center of another stack. He opened the book to a specific page and began reading it out loud. After reading a couple of pages, he replaced the book in the stack and repeated the process with a book from a different stack.

"He is very learned, there is no doubt in that," said Edmond. "Even now, he follows his subject from book to book, knowing exactly where to find it within each. To learn so much alone is remarkable. You say he can read from two texts at once?" Dreah nodded. "He is displaying traits similar to autism, and there are cases of savants performing similar feats. I bet he could teach me some things. You say he doesn't see us?" Dreah nodded again. "What does he see?"

"The room projects images of the library in his home, but the books are real." Dreah paused and studied Harvie with sad eyes. "For hours he gets lost in there, then when he gets ready for bed or for food or for something else he knows, he wakes up long enough to realize he isn't home. Panic sets in at that point. He had a few days where all he did was panic, and we had to sedate him."

"Mind scans?" asked Edmond.

"We have had some success, but his mind is like a jigsaw puzzle scattered across the floor, and we are putting it together blind."

Edmond looked at her and then at Harvie. "Fascinating," he mumbled. "Meta-powers?"

"We have discovered none other than his longevity."

Edmond frowned. "Come now, none?" he questioned. Dreah shook her head no. "Even his longevity seems flawed," Edmond mumbled to himself as he continued to study Harvie behind the wall of glass.

"At least we know who he is now," said Meta-man. "Samuel has asked us to contact William. I'll see if I can locate Jonas as well. Once we are all together, we will find a way to help him."

\* \*

Sparrow walked out of his bedroom and tossed his duffle bag onto the couch next to his scuba gear. Stopping, he stared at Glip-2. The globe had been hanging before the large bay window all morning, but he had failed to respond to Sparrow.

Shrugging, Sparrow moved into the kitchen. The toaster on the counter popped, and as he reached for his breakfast someone knocked on his door. Lying his breakfast aside, he moved to the door and opened it.

"Hi," said Kahori with a wide smile on her face. Without waiting for an invitation, she stepped past Sparrow and into the apartment.

Frowning, Sparrow shut the door and followed her.

Kahori stopped as she passed the kitchen. Looking at Glip-2 and then at Sparrow, she asked, "What's he doing here?"

As Sparrow buttered his toast, he replied, "I don't know. He was there when I got up this morning, and he hasn't moved since."

Kahori cocked her head as she studied him. "He's working."

"How do you know that?" asked Sparrow.

"His color. Oh, don't tell my you haven't figured that out yet. He's silver. When he's silver, he's working. Green usually means he's very relaxed, but he only displays it with close friends. Blue is his most common color, and it means he is calm but alert. And red..."

"Means he's agitated," finished Sparrow.

Kahori narrowed her eyes and glared at him. "Scoundrel. You were testing me. Is that any way to treat a friend?"

"I didn't know we were friends," replied Sparrow.

"Ha! You need all the friends you can get, cowboy. So you'd better be nice to me."

Sparrow smiled and took a bite of his toast. After a swallow of milk, he said, "Tell me about Maria."

"Maria? What about her?"

"She seems lost most of the time. It makes me wonder if this is the best place for her."

Kahori laughed. "Oh, don't worry about little poor Maria. It's just how her powers work. We go shopping sometimes. I guess she would be about my best friend around this place. Trust me, just get her around the girls and she can be a real motor mouth."

"So she wants to be here?"

Kahori's brow furrowed. "Sure she does. Trust me. That girl couldn't afford her wardrobe on any salary she'd earn anywhere else. It is creepy when she stares off into space, but trust me she isn't missing a thing. That's just how her mind works. She never forgets anything she hears or sees. Years later she can play anything back in her mind like a movie saved on a DVD. When she concentrates like that, she can read between-the-lines and understand people's deeper meaning. After meetings, she writes up reports with her interpretations of what people said, compared to what they meant. It is very hard to deceive her when she does it. I've tried to read a couple of her reports, but they are worse than a technical manual on the wiring of a space ship."

If Kahori was right, it would ease his concerns of Diamond using mind control to influence those around him. It still left manipulation, of which Diamond appeared to be a master. With money being one of the best ways to manipulate others, Diamond had plenty to work with.

Glancing around, Kahori asked, "So, where are you going?"

Innocently, Sparrow raised his eyebrows and around bites of his toast asked, "What makes you think I'm going anywhere?" Concerned, he kept an eye on Glip-2 to judge the globs reactions to Kahori's questioning.

"Well, there's the duffle bag on the couch, and I know you accessed the computer last night to look around the top side resort. You spent a little too much time focused on the boats that are docked in the bay. And lastly, you used video imaging to identify a woman on a crinkled photo, Katrina LaCone. I believe it matched up with a driver's license out of Missouri."

"Friends don't spy on friends," said Sparrow with a scowl. He glanced at Glip-2 again. The globe hadn't moved.

"True," Kahori replied, "but didn't you just say we weren't friends."

Sparrow grunted. He had actually been disappointed at how easy it had been to identify Katrina. He was used to a little more detective work. He was not surprised that someone had noticed, but he was grateful it hadn't been Glip-2. Changing the subject, he asked, "I would have thought you would be focused on the memorial service this morning."

Kahori frowned. "Yeah well, I don't like those type of things."

"Not going?" questioned Sparrow.

"No, I'm going at least one of me is."

Sparrow raised an eyebrow in question.

Kahori sighed. "Over the years I've learned that if I stay busy, I can dull certain feelings."

"Meaning?" replied Sparrow.

"Meaning, that if I split myself and find a bunch of things to do, and then come back together, it helps dull the pain. When the memories mix back together, I'm not so focused on stuff I don't like."

Sparrow nodded his understanding. He hadn't attended a funeral since his mother's. He was still unsure how he was going to react to the service, and he doubted anyone really wanted him there anyway. Unfortunately, he hadn't come up with a way to dodge it, and he wasn't ready to escape the Citadel yet.

"Eureka!" squawked a voice from the sidekick on the counter.

Jolted, Sparrow choked on his milk and nearly dropped his glass. Kahori laughed and turned to Glip-2 as Sparrow wiped milk from his chin.

"What's up, Glip?"

"I'm finished," came the voice from the sidekick, "and I've decided to take the rest of the day off. Tell your dad for me." His color shifted from silver to green.

Confused, Sparrow looked from the globe to the sidekick, then to Kahori, and then back to Glip-2.

Kahori laughed again. "He loves to do that. I bet you haven't heard him speak even once the whole time you've been here."

"No," replied Sparrow, "but..."

"But you've heard others talk as if they've spoken to me," said the voice from the sidekick. "Mwahahahahah! Got'cha. Brandon owes me twenty. He is such a sucker. You are the witness, Gem."

Kahori nodded and smiled as she pointed the index finger of both hands at the globe. "I've got your back big guy."

Sparrow didn't know whether to laugh, or punch the globe. He had never liked being the victim of a joke. He was pretty sure punching Kahori was a bad idea, but punching the globe seemed like a good outlet. Instead, he swallowed his pride and chose to play along with their little joke. "Hazing the new guy," he said.

The globe floated over to Kahori. She patted him like he was a favorite pet, and then Glip-2 floated over to the wall.

"Open-Says-Me!" exclaimed Glip-2 through the sidekick.

The image wall of the Austrian village split and rolled back to reveal a large hidden room. Other than having the appearance of glass and the feeling of being cold, the wall had been solid, as Dreah had said. The room before them had the same white walls and it had several matching counters and shelves.

"That's, *Open Sesame*. You nut," said Kahori.

"Want'a bet," countered Glip-2. "Try it and see if it works. I am the lock and the key sister!"

As Sparrow stepped into the room, Glip-2 followed. Sparrow glanced around the hidden space.

Glip-2's voice issued from the other room. "You seemed to like to tinker with things like security, and your little dart gun. I figured you needed space to do it."

Sparrow looked around at Kahori who snatched the sidekick off the counter and followed them into the room. Sparrow glanced at it and then at Glip-2.

"I don't have actual vocal cords. I need a medium to speak through. The Citadel's computers usually work fine, but a speaker, a radio, a stolen sidekick, all will do." Sparrow cocked his head at Glip-2 at the mention of the sidekick. "Mwaahahahaha! Yes, I know about the sidekick. You successfully blocked the signal for a while, but after you mapped my conduits, I searched for it until I found it. Kahori put me on to the idea."

The girl smiled and ducked away from Sparrow's playful swing.

"What? No furniture?" asked Sparrow looking around the room.

"I'm a doctor, Jim, not an interior decorator," joked Glip-2 in an overdramatic tone. "Mwahahahaha!"

\* \*

The memorial was set up in the Citadel garden. White chairs were laid out in rows upon the green clover. With the blue blossom tree as a background, a white podium with a large blue flower attached to its front stood before the chairs. White and blue ribbons were twisted together and ran along the sides of the chairs. A slight breeze ruffled them. The lighting of the garden was dimmed, and the pathway lights were lit up. It left the park in twilight to match the mood of everyone.

Issuing a soft mournful melody, the small memorial to Vox stood off to the side. It had been moved from its marble pedestal in the hallway outside the sherry room to a large wooden stand painted white to match the chairs. Its glass globe had been removed and the small metal device hung suspended in the air, spinning slowly. Standing in silent salute, the memorials to Gear and Floret flanked it.

Slightly higher and behind the three memorials was a larger white podium with a white front. It was decorated with the blue and white ribbon. Three new memorials sat on it, and a large blue flower appeared on the podium's face beneath each of the memorials.

The first contained the helmet of Aegis. It floated in silence inside the glass dome. The second one had a ball of fire suspend in midair that had no visible source. It burned brightly and never flickered. It flared brighter anytime anyone passed close to it. The last memorial contained a series of images that shifted and changed every few seconds. In each image, Stronghold held someone, who struggled to breathe, in a crushing bear hug. A small-overstuffed toy resembling the furred behemoth lay under the images. A picture of Stronghold and a young girl wearing a hospital gown lay under the doll. The young girl had passed away shortly after sewing the small doll for her favorite hero.

The three coffins were made of dark wood and had gold brackets. They rested on stands of black marble. Each hero lay upon white silk in a tailored Diamond Security Solutions formal uniform. The dark blue uniforms were trimmed in bright gold thread, and were adorned with vibrant patches. The chest of Aegis was decorated with the many ribbons and awards he had received over the years. Rose petals of flame yellow and fire red lay scattered around El Incindiaro. Stronghold lay in his coffin with all four of his hands folded across his chest. His upper set of hands held a picture of his parents. A small action figure of the giant was clasped in his lower hands. The American flag was draped across the coffins of Aegis and Stronghold. The Mexican flag adorned Incindiaro's.

The heroes who worked for Diamond were all dressed in ceremonial uniforms that matched those of the deceased. Many of them Sparrow had seen around the Citadel, but there were many he had never seen before. He struggled to try and remember them all so he could research their names and abilities later. Edmond and Meta-man were the only heroes not dressed in the DSS uniforms. Meta-man wore his patriotic metal armor, and Edmond was dressed in a business suit that he constantly pulled at as if it was a layer of dry skin that he desperately wanted to shed.

Sparrow stood at the back of the ceremony and avoided as many people as he could. He didn't feel sorrow over the deaths, but he was uncomfortable and feared having to explain his nervousness to anyone. Discussing his feelings or being caught expressing them made him feel vulnerable. Given his release from the Counselor, he was also unsure how he would react among the mass of mourners. His loss of control in the gym was still fresh in his mind.

Duo opened the ceremony by playing a challenging tune on a set of magnificent grand pianos. Kandi's notes were soft and caring while Brian's were powerful and adventurous. Together they conjured a melody around the mourners that spoke of tender hearts and bold spirits. By the time the twins were done, the listeners knew that both sides of the song needed to exist just as the heart and the spirit needed each other.

Diamond approached the podium as the last of the song's notes faded over the garden. When he spoke, he was calm and in control. His voice never wavered. There was no sign of the vulnerability he had briefly shown following the Paris incident.

"Heroes. There are as many ideas as to what a true hero is as there are heroes in this world. Each one grabs hold of his vision and pursues it in his own way. Some lose sight of that vision, they lose hope. The three men we are here today to honor never lost sight of their visions.

"Aegis followed the path of a hero as a soldier, putting responsibility before everything else. Incindiaro followed it as a man giving of himself to all of those in need, compassion his driving force. Stronghold followed it with a child's enthusiasm and with a temperament that made even the smallest child look beyond his monstrous appearance to see the hero within. To each one of them, a hero was a different thing; but in the end, their ideas came together to form the ultimate meaning of the word. Sacrifice.

"Aegis grew up under the legacy of his father and grandfather. Each of them used the *Aegis* to pursue their own paths. In his youth, Aegis turned away from that legacy and joined the Army. His intent was to become his own man, and not to be defined by their deeds. What he actually did was further his family's legacy down a path of honor and commitment.

"In the Army, Aegis gave tirelessly of himself and volunteered for the harshest of missions, all the while further molding himself into the man we all came to know. During those years, he sacrificed in ways most of use will never know. Physically, he battled adversaries that only a soldier can face. Spiritually, he struggled with a desire to understand why man commits such horrors against his fellow man. Emotionally, he learned to accept those horrors. He became the perfect soldier. But even the perfect soldier can overlook vital parts of himself.

"It was only after Aegis learned to push away from the military that he learned to embrace his other responsibilities. Despite what had been instilled in him by his absent father, Aegis learned to pursue the greatest gift any of us can ever receive, our families. I saw it in his eyes the very night tragedy took his wife, Lauren, and nearly his daughter, Alexis. He stood before the cameras with the *Aegis* in one hand, and Alexis in the other as fire consumed their home. He didn't know it that night, but he had come full circle, and learned to embrace his heritage. He was complete.

"His work here, as a friend and as a leader, built him up even further. We all came to rely on his wisdom. Thankfully, he showed he was the ultimate leader by instilling his wisdom in those under him. Even without him, we are able to carry on. Even if we didn't prepare for his passing, he did. His wisdom is still with us today, in each of you."

Diamond paused to give everyone a moment to reflect on Aegis, and then he continued.

"Even as a young man Incindiaro was filled with compassion. His youth taught him the evils of poverty. He pulled himself out of it, but he never turned his back on it. Instead of running away, he returned to it. He brought with him knowledge, and worked to end what he thought was the world's greatest sin. Through him, many young children avoided starvation.

"He never saw his greatest regret coming. What he thought was to be help for those he loved changed him. He was betrayed by his government, and turned into the fiery hero we knew. Many of those around him were killed; family, friends, and loved ones. It lit a fire within him that not even his death can extinguish.

"He worked to overcome those that had betrayed him, and he never lost hope. He found those responsible for the Tipis Street Nightmare. Many urged Incindiaro to put the incident behind him. They wanted him to cover up the corruption, and save his government from embarrassment. But he refused and brought it all to light. Incindiaro became an example to everyone faced with doing the right thing, even when pressure to do wrong comes from those closest to you.

"Some would argue that he never overcame that nightmare. Others would argue that it made him an even better man, that it gave his passion a different direction.

"No one can argue that few in this world have had the success that Incindiaro had in protecting the weak from those who betray their trust. His passion overturned corruption in the government of his own country, and in other governments around the world. It was even through this dedication that he brought down a conspiracy in this country that saved Stronghold from a horrible life as a servant to corrupt men.

"I have known many men over the years, but I have never known anyone with the level of commitment Incindiaro showed to his fellow man. Even though many of us have forgotten where we come from, Incindiaro embraced it. He used it to fuel his fire."

Again Diamond paused to allow everyone to reflect on his words and the hero they honored.

"Stronghold's passion for this job filled him with a youthful vigor that all of us secretly desire. Many of us experienced it as kids, but then we grew up. Stronghold always claimed that a wise man once said, *Some people grow up, and some just grow older.*

"As adults, many of us languish through life with regrets and unfulfilled desires. That youthful vigor traded for slavish devotion to work, and mounting bills and frustrations. Growing up causes us to forget how fun life can be. We listen to the demands of the world to forget the things we loved as kids, and to become mature adults. The world wants us to turn off the cartoons, and forget the joy they bring us. Discard the toys, and the imagination they inspire. It tells us that to be mature, we must give up the things in life that for many years brought us the most joy. In the end we get old and find ourselves envying those like Stronghold, those who didn't grow up, they just grew older.

"Incindiaro called the event that turned Matthew into the furry red behemoth that we all knew a tragedy. Stronghold did not. He embraced it, and found joy in it.

"I was there the day of the Hope Memorial Hospital tragedy. A man who had been lost even to himself set off a series of explosions across the city that left a path of destruction. When Stronghold arrived on scene, the media compared him to the monster that had caused the tragedy. His only response was a smile. Even as he raced into the hospital to rescue survivors, the media crucified him for his appearance. When the building collapsed, the media immediately blamed him.

"Nearly five hours later, it was an amazing sight to see the rubble finally shifted aside to reveal Stronghold and twelve small children, all alive. Stronghold held tons of building aloft as the kids used his furry body as a jungle gym. Unlike the adults, who had been tainted by the world's prejudice, those kids had seen through Stronghold's monstrous exterior to the youthful innocence inside him. He made twelve friends that day that he maintained contact with over the years. His actions turned the media around, and he became an instant celebrity. They followed the example of those kids and looked beyond his monstrous exterior to the man within. He never turned down an interview, and he did wonders to fight prejudice against himself, and other meta-humans who suffer from an altered appearance.

"Sacrifice. It is what all three of these vastly different men had in common. Each of them sacrificed in their own way to be a hero. They made the ultimate sacrifice together in Paris. They didn't know the tragedy was going to happen. But I have no doubt that even if they knew, they would have been there anyway. They understood what was needed from them. They all died knowing that; and now to be a hero like these three men, you too may be called on to make their sacrifice.

"We know this isn't over. Aegis, Incindiaro, and Stronghold only mark the beginning. Through commitment we will be able to get humanity through the greatest threat it has ever faced. Like Stronghold, we will have to endure the world's prejudice and misunderstanding, but in the end, enduring that will make the sacrifice all the more heroic."

When he finished speaking, Diamond turned and silently left the stage. As he descended the steps, Brian began playing the song, *Hero*. Kandi's voice filled the air in tune with her brother's music. Together, Duo's music filled the garden with a tight high melody that reflected the sacrifice of the three men. As Kandi entered the last course, Dreah moved onto the stage and waited patiently beside them to finish. Dreah hugged the Kandi and then Brian before moving to the podium.

Standing in silence and with tears flowing down her face, Dreah smiled and glanced at each of the three heroes before her before turning to the audience.

"Family," she said. "Most believe there are few things more

important than family. Many believe it commands blind devotion, that it forms inseparable bonds, and that it is thicker than water.

"I believe they are wrong. I believe such nonsense pushes people out of a family who should be embraced as part of it. I believe devotion should be replaced with an understanding that everyone is fallible. I believe bonds can be separated, but they can also be healed when both sides embrace the need for healing. I don't believe that we need blood to make us a family, or that we are made stronger by blood. I believe you are my family, and I believe every family has needs that those in it meet.

"Alex leads our family. He keeps us on the necessary path while giving us confidence and courage to become better than we are. He forces us to face our mistakes, and to take responsibility for them.

"Basilio is our conscience. He guides our compassion, and prevents us from forgetting that even the smallest life is important. He shows us that separated bonds can be healed.

"Matthew is our love. He shares it with us through warm hugs and heartfelt laughter. Through him we share ties with each other that has nothing to do with blood.

"My family is always with me, and it fulfills my needs every day. We are family. Everyone has a role in it, and nothing can change that."

When she finished speaking, Dreah went to each coffin and spent a quiet moment with each hero. When she got to Stronghold, she laid a picture gently into the coffin with him. In the photo, Stronghold held her tightly.

Envoy reluctantly took the stage after Dreah. She turned to face the audience with a look of deep sorrow on her face. She was nervous in front of the crowd, and when she started to speak she choked and had to stifle a fit of coughing. After several moments, she faced the audience again.

"I could spend all day telling you what each of these three men meant to me. I could spend a week telling you how incomplete I would be without them having been a part of my life." She paused as her voice cracked and she pushed back a tear. "I couldn't spend a moment telling you how much I'm going to miss them. I wouldn't know how to express it. As a soldier, I've faced the loss of many friends. I can tell you it doesn't get any easier."

She turned away from the audience to face Aegis. "Thank you,

Alex. You mentored me when others were ready to throw me away. If not for you, I would never have survived my first firefight. I will never be able to fill your shoes, and I pray I can be half the soldier you tried to make me."

She then turned to Incindiaro. "Thank you, Basilio, for being my friend. Thank you for giving me personal encouragement when I faltered. Thank you for forgiving me when I failed you and those around me. No one knows me like you did."

Envoy paused as she struggled to stifle her tears again. When she had composed herself, she continued. "Sorry, everyone." She wiped her face. "Matthew, your laughter will always echo in my head. No one ever made me feel more relaxed in tense situations. Thank you for sharing your joy with me."

Envoy didn't look at the audience as she left the stage.

As Wavefront took the stage, he took off his hat and laid it on the podium. After clearing his throat, he spoke. "I don't think I need to express how much I hate these things. I'd rather be dragged through a patch of cactus with nothing on but me underwear." He tried to smile, but his smile faltered as he looked down at Aegis. Wavefront cleared his throat and continued. "When I was asked to say a few words about Alex, I was lost. I didn't know what to say. Bloody hell, I still don't, and I doubt I could say it any better than has already been done if I did.

"As most of you know, I've been following Alex around for years now. Unlike Latisha, I've never been officially a part of anything. I wasn't recruited. I've just sort'a tagged along. I've never stopped much to consider it. I think maybe th'words spoken today have helped me to understand it though.

"I've never met anyone like Alex. For years, I've watched him move from cause to cause with each one bigger than th'one before. When he came here, I found myself shut out. No offense, Mr. Diamond. I understand, I really do. I never finished school, never held a job for more than two weeks, got no spouse, no kids, no nothing. But Alex, he, well, he stood up for me. As you can see, he must'a had some success because I'm here. I think that was it. That's why I've followed him. It's his loyalty. It's never faltered. It's never let anyone down, especially me. Coming from where I did, I'd never seen that before. Folks were scoundrels who thought of no one but themselves. Alex wasn't anything like that and through him, I saw a different world. A part of me may have always known this, but now I can see it.

"Alex," he said as he glanced toward the ceiling, "I've never much believed in Heaven, but if anyone deserves it, it's you. I hope you find rest, mate." As Wavefront finished, he quickly left the stage shaken and sobbing.

El Dragón Verde took the stage after Wavefront. He was from Mexico and currently worked with Meta-man as a member of UNIT. He had been chosen to speak for Incindiaro because of their long history together.

Dragón Verde wore a UNIT dress uniform with a dark blue jacket. It had the UN patch on the right shoulder and the Mexican flag on the left. Numerous awards adorned the left side of his chest, and he had a nametag on the right side. Pins marking his rank and country of origin were on each lapel of the jacket. He wore a white shirt under the jacket and a light blue ascot around his neck that was adorned with a large gold and blue United Nations pin. He wore a matching light blue beret that had the United Nations seal on it as well. His trousers were dark blue but had a matching light blue stripe down each leg. His shoes were black and shined brightly. Around his waist he wore a thick white belt that had a white holster with a flap covering the firearm. His skin was tanned and he had short black hair with streaks of gray. His face was scarred from a childhood filled with heavy acne. His eyes were dark and small.

Before speaking, he kneeled and bowed his head. Using his right hand, he touched his forehead, his heart, his left shoulder, and then his right shoulder. As he did so, he mumbled," En el nombre del Padre, del Hijo y del Espíritu Santo." Looking up at the three coffins, he said, "Amén." He stood and faced the crowd.

"Most of you don't know me personally, but I've known Incindiaro since he first came on the scene. We spent many of our early years working together. I tell you, he was a man of honor. He was a man deserving of the praise he has received here today.

"Like many in our home country, I was disappointed when he came to work here with Diamond Security Solutions. We saw it as him selling out, as him finally turning his back on the little man. Of course I didn't know all the details then, and like too many others, I was quick to judge him. I was proven wrong. He proved me wrong.

"Corruption in our government drove him to do what he did. But even separated from us, he continued to work for Mexico.

"Recently, El Incindiaro and I worked together. At first I was bitter at him, but by the end of the case, I knew that the man I'd once known was still there. I knew that he hadn't changed or turned his back on us. I knew that we had turned our back on him.

"Incindiaro wasn't wrong to come here. I don't know his reasons, or much understand what has led to today, but I know we were wrong to judge him so harshly. I promise you all, I promise him, that I will return home and I will defend his name. I will see to it that he gets the proper respect he deserves, and I will help restore his honor. Thank you."

A young girl named Jane took the stage next. She had very pale skin and a bright pink streak running through short black hair. She was dressed in a black tank top and dark baggy jeans. She had several piercings above each eye and along her lower lip. Her eye shadow was black and thick, and her bright red lipstick contrasted sharply with her skin. Her right shoulder was red and puffy from a fresh bright tattoo of Stronghold.

As she walked across the stage, she kept her head bowed and stared at the floor. When she reached the podium, she stood hunched over it so that her hair hid her face. When she spoke, her voice was soft and quiet. She never looked at the audience as she read from a piece of paper in front of her.

"What is a friend? Is it mutual affection? Is it a family faction? Is it an interaction? Is it reaction? Is it satisfaction? Is it an action?

"What does a friend mean to you? Is it a fundamental interaction? Is it an encouraged reaction? Is it consistent satisfaction? Is it a comforting action?

"How do you find a friend? Is it through experimental interaction? Is it through a chemical reaction? Is it through judgmental satisfaction? Is it through an intentional action?

"How do you treat a friend? Is it with psychological interaction? Is it with conditioned reaction? Is it with un-satisfaction? Is it with evasive action?

"How does your friend treat you? Is it with sacrificed interaction? Is it with loving reaction? Is it with unconditional satisfaction? Is it with forgiving action?

"How do you loose a friend? It is through psychological interaction.

It is through conditioned reaction. It is through un-satisfaction. It is through evasive action.

"How do you keep a friend? It is through sacrificed interaction. It is through loving reaction. It is through unconditional satisfaction. It is through forgiving action.

"How do you remember a friend? It is through influencing interaction. It is through suitable reaction. It is through joyful satisfaction. It is through intentional action.

"What is a friend? It is mutual affection. It is a family faction. It is an interaction. It is reaction. It is satisfaction. It is an action."

When Jane finished speaking, she quietly left the stage with her arms wrapped around her torso, and her head bowed. She didn't glance up as she passed Kahori.

Kahori stood in the center of the stage and cleared her throat, but when she opened her mouth, she choked on her sorrow. For several moments she stood in silence with tears rolling down her cheeks, and stared at her fallen family. Quietly, Dreah moved onto the stage and whispered softly to the young girl. Kahori shook her head no, and took Dreah's hand firmly in her own. After another moment, she cleared her throat and began to softly sing the song, *Amazing Grace*.

The lighting in the garden dimmed and small twinkling lights appeared in the glass ceiling. The small stars cast a deep twilight over the memorial as the lights of the garden paths faded completely away.

Kahori carried the first verse a'cappella. As she entered the first chorus, soft humming from the monument of Vox joined her. When she started into the second verse, soft music joined the humming. By the time she reached the third verse, background singers had joined her, and the somber melody carried across the entire garden.

\* \*

The ceremony lasted for over an hour, and it wasn't what Sparrow had expected. Given Diamond's flare and money, he had expected something flashier. Instead he had got something that was personal, reflected the individuality of each of the deceased, and impacted everyone present, including him. It presented a side of Diamond that Sparrow had begun to doubt existed.

As Kahori finished singing, someone stepped up next to Sparrow.

"I hate these things. I'm glad I missed it."

The man was dressed in a set of worn dirty black fatigues. A hood covered his face, and he wore a flack vest with several bullet holes in it. A sword hilt stuck up over his shoulder, and he had several knives tucked into his uniform. He had at least three large caliber sidearms and a shotgun. He looked like he had just walked off of a battlefield.

Without speaking, Sparrow turned away from the man and back to the ceremony. It was starting to break up. Dreah had one arm around Fluxstone and the other around Kahori. They were all three speaking with a blond teenage girl. Dreah looked even wearier than before, and for a moment Sparrow wished there was something he could do for her.

The man spoke again. "Don't worry about little sister. She's stronger than all of us."

"You read minds," said Sparrow without looking at the man. Sparrow heard him chuckle softly.

"No, friend, I hate mentalists. It's in your eyes. It's in everyone's eyes when they look at her." The man held out his hand. As Sparrow took it, he continued, "Good to meet you, Sparrow. Guess I'd better go say hi or she'll scold me for being rude." After shaking Sparrow's hand, the man started toward the crowd without introducing himself.

As the man walked toward Dreah, he suddenly disappeared and reappeared behind her. He attempted to startle her, but she simply turned to hug him as he reached for her. After a few moments, Dreah scolded him for the mask, and he removed it with a smile. Under the mask, he was a man of about thirty with sandy blond hair and a face full of stubble.

Sparrow turned and walked along the path away from the memorial. A part of him was glad he had stayed for it, and another part was glad it hadn't been longer.

\* \*

Sparrow sat in silence and watched the flowers blow in the breeze. Even though the sounds of the ceremony had broken up behind him, he had remained in the garden. It still brought him peace and allowed him to think without becoming overwhelmed by emotion.

Up until now, he had known what he was going to do. Paris and the funeral had complicated matters. Before them, he had put all his effort into escaping the Citadel, now he wasn't so sure it was what he wanted to do. For the first time in his life, Sparrow was faced with the dilemma of wanting to do the right thing, and with actually having the ability to make the choice.

Diamond had opened up to him, and he was now convinced Diamond hadn't manipulated his mind. Unlike the Counselor, Diamond had left him with free will. Still, he wasn't sure he was up to playing with meta-humans or even if he had the ability to do so.

Sparrow was pulled from his thoughts by a slight rustle behind him, and the scent of flowers.

"Hello Dreah," he said without turning.

Silently, Dreah sat down on the bench next to him. Several birds that had been following her landed in the trees around them and began to sing. Despite the sorrow in her eyes, she smiled when he looked at her. She reached out, laced her arm through his, and leaned into him. Together, they watched the birds.

"Tough morning," Sparrow said.

"Tough week," Dreah countered.

"But you knew it was coming."

Dreah sighed. "Yes, I knew. I knew the moment I saw you."

"How is that?"

"I'm a precog. Remember? I see things in my dreams. I had a dream the night you crashed here. I saw you standing among us, but I knew that someone else was missing. I couldn't identify whom. I wish I had more control over it, or could better interpret what I see. The dream is why I sent Glip-2 to guide you in. By the way, I did order him to safely guide you in. He blames the crash on your bad piloting skills."

Sparrow smiled. "And what do your dreams tell you now?"

"That you are going away for a while, but you will return."

"How can you be so sure?"

"You can never be sure when it comes to the future. It's always changing, especially with Samuel working so hard to do so. But it isn't precognition that tells me you will return. I'm pretty sure at least one of us has touched you deeply enough for you to find a reason to come back."

She laid her head on his shoulder and closed her eyes. The moments drifted into minutes and her breathing became steady. Sparrow suspected she had fallen asleep. He was disappointed when she spoke again.

"I'm sorry," she said softly.

"For what?" he asked.

"For everything. For what the Counselor did to you, and for what he took away from you. For you feeling trapped under Samuel's thumb. For the awkwardness you feel from my touch."

Even though her voice was a comfort, Sparrow felt an urge to shift away from her words. But he feared it would disturb her, so he resisted it. It was true that her touch, her very presence, made him nervous, but he had also grown to long for it when it wasn't there.

"The Counselor wasn't your doing. There is no need for you to feel sorry for that," he said.

"I can't help it. I care for those around me. I'm empathic too. Remember?"

Sparrow could feel her smile against his shoulder.

"I feel the pain of everyone, including you."

"That must be quite a burden."

"Years have taught me to live with it, although these last few days have been extremely difficult. Without your help, I don't know that I would have survived it."

"My help?" he asked.

She snuggled her head deeper into his shoulder and her body relaxed further. "Yes, you still push your emotions into hiding. I'm afraid it is something that you'll never unlearn. It leaves you empty, but strong, even if you don't feel it sometimes. Your strength in turn has helped me."

Strangely, Dreah pulling strength from him didn't bother him. At any other time, or in any other place, it would have been a violation. Now it made him a part of everything around him. At the funeral, she had spoken of how Aegis and the others fit into the family. To her, it was how he fit into it, even if he didn't see it. Sparrow allowed the conversation to fall away, and for the next hour Dreah slept peacefully.

# CHAPTER 13
# A PRIVATE MISSION

Sparrow entered Brandon's lab and found the young man vigorously working on the swinging mechanical arm. He was mumbling to himself, or talking with Sarah, as Sparrow snuck up behind him. Quietly, he reached out and poked the kid.

"Eeeeye!" screamed Brandon. The small instrument in his hand was flung across the room, and he jerked around to face his attacker. His eyes were wide with fright, and when he saw it was Sparrow, he collapsed against the table patting his chest with his right hand.

"Wow! You scared me!"

"Payback for the Glip-2 thing," gloated Sparrow.

Brandon grinned and stood up. His face turned red. "Yeah, sorry about that. Glip likes to pull that on the new people. I didn't think it would work on you though. It cost me twenty bucks."

Sparrow allowed Brandon his laugh and then got to the point. "Listen kid, I need a favor."

"Really?" asked Brandon. A smile spread across his face and his eyes brightened.

Sparrow forced back a smile. He hated to dupe the kid, but the less he knew about the plan, the less trouble he would be in with Diamond.

\* \*

An hour later, Sparrow slipped into the water of the airship bay. With his respirator in his mouth, he sank beneath the water's surface. The water was clear and the strange light of the Citadel lit it up as clearly as any of the hallways. Swimming under the catwalk, he made his way to the back of the cave where he found a set of large metal doors.

After his security clearance had been updated, Sparrow had immediately set to work exploring as many of the Citadel's systems as he could access. With years of experience exploiting weaknesses in security systems, it hadn't taken him long to plot a course out of the Citadel.

Before the *Egress* and the other pods, the team had used the large bay doors to come and go from the Citadel in the airships. The ships still functioned, but Sparrow didn't plan to use them. Opening the doors would force him to modify security records and leave a trail of his actions. His skills weren't good enough to avoid Glip-2 with such drastic changes, and he didn't want to leave any record in case he needed to escape the Citadel again in the future.

Sparrow had considered using the hidden door in the sherry room for his escape, but he still didn't know what was beyond it. It could have been freedom and it could have just as easily been only the first obstacle of many, so he had settled on the water bay instead.

Swimming deeper, Sparrow found two smaller doors near the bottom of the pool. Reaching into his belt, he pulled out Brandon's small sonic device. Glip-2 used panels throughout the citadel for maintenance and the small device was built to access those panels. Running the device along the wall, he searched for the panel the Citadel schematics indicated was there. After a couple of passes, he found the panel, and it popped open when the device released the magnetic field sealing it.

Pulling out his sidekick, Sparrow connected it directly to the interior circuits and checked the sensitivity of the water sensor. Satisfied, he disconnected the sidekick and closed the panel. Reaching into a bag at his side, he pulled out one of three thermos bottles and held it up next to the panel. When he opened it, its murky contents mixed with the water and after a moment the sensor inside the panel activated a series of pumps and the smaller doors beneath him opened. Fresh water began to flow into the bay as the contaminated water was sucked out.

Moving to the larger of the two doors, Sparrow took a deep breath and dropped his scuba gear. He pulled a small emergency air tank from his vest and placed it in his mouth. After testing it, he squeezed into the narrow intake tunnel. The outtake tunnel went through a cleaning system before dumping the water into the ocean. Besides allowing him a more direct route, the intake tunnel avoided the machinery.

As Sparrow swam against the flowing current, he struggled to breathe shallowly, and used a small pin light to guide him through the darkening tunnel.

* *

"What the hell do you mean he's gone?" demanded Diamond! "And why is my personal yacht missing?"

Clara looked like she was going to cry under the weight of his tantrum. "Sorry, sir, but Sparrow is not anywhere in the Citadel. He visited Brandon in his lab after the ceremony yesterday and then he retreated to his apartment. The records indicate he should still be there. He is not shown going through any of the checkpoints. But we know he has fooled the checkpoints before. As for the yacht, we suspect he stole it. A private jet was also taken from a private airport in Eureka last night, but no flight path was filed."

"The yacht has GPS," countered Diamond.

"Yes, Mr. Diamond. But it appears to have been disabled som..."

"Satellite tracking?" Diamond asked.

Clara looked exhausted and ready to faint. Slowly, she started to speak. "W-We..."

"Mr. Diamond, Sparrow chose his departure well," Bullock interrupted. "Early morning fog and scattered clouds concealed him from the satellites and the topside cameras. There were no thermal images either. I'd guess he floated off on the tides initially, or used a small skiff to nudge the larger boat from the harbor. He could have gone in any direction once free of the island. Given that we know he has fooled some of the Citadel's internal security measures before, it's not hard to believe that he was capable of disabling the boat's systems, as well as its hidden systems. His ingenuity is impressive."

Diamond wasn't going to be defeated. "How can he just disappear? Someone get Glip-2 in here now! He's been too lax with security lately! Where is Shadow Spirit? He is the only one to successfully teleport into and out of here uninvited. Let's find him and see if he was involved."

Diamond turned away from the others, and Clara used the moment of freedom to duck out of sight. He paced the catwalk and the loud banging of his shoes caused those below him to cringe. He ignored Kahori as she dodged his glare to duck into the Special Operations control room.

"Slow down, Samuel," said Dreah. "I cautioned you this could happen." She maintained her usual calm and didn't raise her voice. She was glad Sparrow had safely ducked out of the Citadel. He needed time to sort through all that had happened to him, and to assert his independence of Diamond. She was confident he would return.

Several years ago, Diamond had wanted to record everything that went on in the Citadel. The AI had the capacity to do that, and much more. However, Dreah had convinced him it would be a violation of privacy, and would cost him the loyalty of his people. In the end, he had set up checkpoints at the t-ports and at the entrances to certain sections.

Diamond turned on Dreah. "That doesn't give him permission. I didn't give him permission!"

"He will return," said Dreah.

"And how do you know that?"

"Trust."

Diamond froze and stared at her. He wasn't surprised she knew what words to use. She always did. Sparrow hadn't told her about their conversation, and there wasn't a need to. She knew him too well. As with all their arguments, she would win this one too.

Dreah's head lifted slightly. "Ebon is coming." An instant later her shadow shifted and expanded, and Shadow Spirit stepped from it.

"It's about time," said Diamond as he turned to face Shadow Spirit. "Spirit, find Sparrow. Bring him here."

The Spirit didn't respond, but his dark hood shifted as he nodded his head. For several moments everyone stood in silence and waited. Slowly the Spirit reached up and pulled his hood back to reveal his ebony face. He turned his gold eyes on Diamond. "I cannot see him."

"You have used him as an anchor before!" Diamond's anger was growing. "Why can't you see him now?"

"I am blocked. I cannot explain it."

It was all the explanation the Spirit would give, and it was all Diamond needed. He briefly met Dreah's eyes before starting his pace of the catwalk again. The glance was enough to let her know that he knew. Shortly after the Spirit's initial arrival in the Citadel, Diamond had demanded a way to block him out. Dreah had indicated it would be difficult. In the end, she had provided him with a charm that he now kept concealed in his wristwatch. It was not intended to keep the Spirit out of the Citadel, but it prevented the Spirit from targeting anyone who held it. It now appeared there were two such charms. Sparrow had some kind of hold on Dreah that Diamond couldn't explain. He glanced at her again but she had turned her attention away from him and to the people on the room floor. He had hoped to control Sparrow. He was beginning to think it was impossible.

"Sir," said Clara from the floor beneath him.

Samuel took a deep breath and turned to her, "What?"

"One of those bank account numbers you had us monitoring has been accessed."

"Finally, someone does something right," said Diamond as he moved to his console. Clara was right. One of Sparrow's hidden accounts had been accessed in New York City. His feeling of satisfaction faded when his screen flashed as another account was accessed, this one in Atlanta, Georgia. Diamond's brow furrowed as three more lights lit up along the east coast. All five accounts showed that Sparrow had accessed them within seconds of each other. His glare bored into Clara and she sought refuge. A door opening behind Diamond caused him to spin. Unaware of the tantrum he faced, Glip-2 glided into the room.

As Diamond opened his mouth to yell, his eyes fell on Dreah. "Trust," she whispered.

\* \*

"Damn!" Stabbed in the back, Sparrow spun searching for his enemy. Suddenly, pain flared in the center of this chest.

"Ow! Ow!" he yelped through clinched teeth. He struggled to keep from crying out.

The cold knife in the center of his back was gone, but the spot on his chest continued to burn. He patted his shirt and then jerked the cloth aside to reveal the pendant Dreah had given him. It glowed slightly and burned against his skin. He quickly pulled it out of his shirt. Beneath the pendant his flesh was red. He reached up and gently rubbed the burn until the pain subsided. The skin remained red but didn't appear to have permanent damage.

Shadow Spirit was obviously the cause of the initial discomfort. Sparrow had felt it in Paris just moments before the man had stepped out of his shadow. Even if he had considered the man, he would not have known how to stop the Spirit's abilities, but Dreah had. She had known he was planning to leave the Citadel, and that Shadow Spirit could track him. She had given him the charm to protect him.

A pang of guilt hit him when he thought of Dreah. He didn't want to disappoint her, but he knew he had to take care of himself. He pushed aside the guilt and turned his attention back to his surroundings.

Above him the sky was dark and the threat of rain forced him to pull his coat tighter around him. The street was damp and puddles dotted its surface. The day was dreary, reflecting the dark mood growing within him.

Tapping his old accounts had been a risky gambit intended to distract Diamond, and anyone else looking for him, like the Counselor. Unfortunately, the ruse had cost Sparrow most of the money. At twenty cents on the dollar, millions had been lost to the mob. Seeing the look on Diamond's face would have been worth every penny. Perhaps he should have warned Glip-2 so he could have captured it on video for later enjoyment. Sparrow reminded himself the money didn't matter. Diamond's resources were nearly limitless, and if he decided to return the *Aegis*, he would be able to tap them without concern. If he decided to sell the shield on the black market, he would be able to name his price and wouldn't need his accounts or Diamond's resources.

Either way, Sparrow was determined not to be a slave to Diamond, through mind control or through manipulation. Having the accounts pulled all at the same time told Diamond he knew they were being watched. It would convey the message that Sparrow was free, and intended to remain so.

Several minutes passed and no cars moved on the deserted street. It made Sparrow feel lonely. Forcing the feeling aside, he darted across the street and toward a narrow house on the other side.

Through the photo of the woman and kids, Sparrow had found the identity of the soldier in Paris. He couldn't help but marvel at how easy it had been, too easy in fact. He had to admit he liked Diamond's resources, but he also cautioned himself against getting to comfortable with them. He actually liked the challenge of the chase. Diamond's resources had stolen that.

People gave out too much information about themselves. They posted pictures and personal information online that they thought was harmless. In the hands of the right person, photos could be used to trace a person's life. Using credit cards online left the information vulnerable to anyone who knew how to get it. Pictures posted on line from cell phones and some digital cameras left the pictures electronically tagged with identifying information. In a few hours, a dedicated person could plot a person's complete life. In the past, Sparrow had stolen more than one person's identity to use as a cover. People made it easy. The Citadel's computers had made it too easy.

Todd and Katrina weren't married, but they had two kids, Isabelle and Jamie. He was a traveling salesman, and she was an unskilled laborer for a company that manufactured frozen TV dinners. They were in serious debt and barely making the bills. Todd was a former Marine with a less than honorable discharge. Sparrow hadn't bothered digging deeper into the cause of the discharge because he knew the man's employer didn't care. Even if his combat skills were only mediocre, they could still be exploited as a mercenary. His work as a salesman was a perfect cover for a mercenary that sold his skills cheap. Generally, mercenaries had little personal connections. Todd had been an exception and as a result, he had left Sparrow a trail to find the *Aegis*.

As rain began to fall, Sparrow turned up the collar of his jacket to keep it out, and reflected on the death of Todd. As a mercenary, Todd faced death all the time. Yet, it still bothered Sparrow, and he couldn't figure out why. Would Todd have actually killed him if Fluxstone hadn't interfered? Could he have stopped Fluxstone from killing Todd? Should he have even tried? These were questions Sparrow would have never considered before. Now it frustrated him that he didn't have the answers. It also bothered him to know that Todd and his men had been cast aside like table scraps to appease the dogs. Their employer wouldn't have come back for them no matter what the outcome of the battle had been. It created a disturbing parallel to his own situation.

Sparrow bounded up the steps to Katrina's home and rang the doorbell in one quick motion. As he waited, he hummed to himself. When Katrina answered the door, she left the chain attached for protection. Sparrow knew that behind the door the house was small and cluttered. He had searched it the night before, but had found no clues to help him locate the *Aegis*.

"Yes?" she said.

Sparrow smiled broadly. "Hello, My name is Blaine Braxton." He gave a slight wave. "Sorry to bother you this evening ma'am, but I'm with the University and we are canvassing the neighborhood in search of inexpensive apartments for rent by young college students. Would you or someone you know happen to have any?"

Katrina looked nervously at him, and then glanced around at the street before answering. She kept her eyes averted when she spoke. "No, sorry. I don't have any rooms. You will need to check with someone else."

"Sorry to have bothered you." Sparrow tipped his hat and backed down the steps. "Good evening ma'am."

"Sure, goodbye," said Katrina as she closed the door.

As Sparrow walked away from the house, he put a slight skip in his step, and ignored Katrina as she peeked at him from a window. He bounded up the steps to the next house and knocked heavily on the door. When the man answered, he declined to speak with Sparrow. Happily tipping his hat, Sparrow moved on to the next house. When he knew he was out of sight of Katrina's home, he glanced around to make sure no one else was watching him. When he was positive that it was safe, he dropped the act and darted down a narrow alley.

Circling around behind the homes, and away from prying eyes, he made his way back to his car that was parked three blocks away. Bugging Katrina's home had only rewarded him with the insufferable screaming of young kids, and the stress of an overburdened mother. Normally, he would have been patient and waited for some sign from her, even if it took days. But Sparrow knew Diamond was looking for him, and given his resources, he would zero in on Sparrow eventually. Sparrow had doubted his ruse would prompt Katrina into any action that would result in anything usable, but he had pursued it anyway. It was better than tying Katrina to a chair and beating the information out of her.

Once inside his car, he pulled out his sidekick and pulled up Katrina's phone line. The number was a public listing and the sidekick had hacked it in less time than it would have taken Sparrow to dial it. Her records had given him no leads, but now the sidekick revealed that

Katrina had made a call since he had knocked on her door. Pulling up a list of all the numbers dialed from her phone in the past year, he found that the number didn't appear on the list.

He placed his commlink into his ear and accessed the call while using the sidekick to trace the number.

"*Hello?*"

"*Chris? This is Katrina!*"

"*Yeah, Katrina. What do you want?*"

"*You told me to call you if anyone strange came by the house.*"

"*Yeah. So? What happened?*"

"*A tall guy just knocked on the door. He said he was from the University for some survey or something.*"

"*Did he ask about Todd?*"

"*No,*" Katrina's voice choked. "*Please, Chris, what's happened to Todd? Please? What did this guy want?*"

"*Calm down Katrina. It may have been a coincidence.*"

"*You told me you would tell me what happened to Todd...please Chris? The kids need their father...*"

"*Shut up Katrina! I said I'd tell you and I will. Just let me find out about this guy first.*"

The line went dead as Chris hung up on Katrina. The sidekick had already pulled up the address connected to the number and directions to it. Sparrow smiled and put the car in gear. As he pulled away from the curb, he admitted to himself that he liked having a sidekick. He was just glad it didn't wear a little yellow cape and green tights.

*Too easy*, he thought as he reached the end of the street and turned right.

\* \*

A light rain had started to fall by the time Sparrow found the address. The sun was setting and the streetlights were lit. Even though he expected the address to be a fake, he cased the building three times before approaching it. Light poured from several windows on the second floor.

After climbing the fire escape of the neighboring building, Sparrow stood silently in the rain and peered down into the alley between the two buildings. Even at the peak of health, the leap would be a challenge. With the injuries from the plane crash, it was down right dangerous. He shoved aside an image of a smirking Diamond approaching a hospital bed.

Tilting his head back and rubbing his left shoulder, he considered his options. The cold sting of the rain created rivulets down the side of his face that calmed him.

*It's not too late*, he told himself. *Just fade into the night and leave this to Diamond.* He knew he didn't need the shield to start over. It would be difficult, but he could do it. He would need it if he chose to return to the Citadel.

Images of the garden and Dreah sitting under her tree filled his mind, and he couldn't help but smile. The desire to see her again, and his fear of being alone, was proving to be stronger than his desire for escape.

A car pulling up in front of the building pulled him from his reflections. He opened his eyes to see a crying Katrina get out of the car and rush up the steps to the building. The faces of two small children were pressed up against the glass of the car's back window. Katrina pounded on the door for nearly two minutes before a man flung it open.

"Chris! Please," she begged. "I don't know what to do! I have no money! The kids need their father! Please, what happened to Todd?"

Chris reached out and took Katrina roughly by the arm as he pushed her back and stepped out onto the porch. He glanced around at the empty street and then at her car.

"Chris, please..."

*Slap!*

Chris struck Katrina across the face. She would have fallen down the steps if he hadn't held her by her arm. He jerked her around and grabbed her shoulders. Pulling her into his face he said, "I told you never to come here!" Without a warning he shoved her backwards, and Katrina flailed as she fell down the building's steps.

Lying on the sidewalk, Katrina cradled her arm. The pain of moving it caused her to whimper. "Please..." she begged. Blood flowed from a gash on her knee. The rain plastered her hair to her head and streaked mascara down her cheeks.

Chris pointed his finger at her and said, "Get out of here! I'll call you in three days, not before! If you return here, the kids will be missing their mother too!" Turning around he entered the building and slammed the door shut behind him.

Katrina lay on the sidewalk crying for several moments. Finally, she pulled herself up by the open car door. She was still sobbing when she pulled the car slowly away from the curb.

Sparrow felt pity for the woman and her children. The feeling unnerved him. It could prove to be a bigger master than the Counselor ever was, or than Diamond ever could be.

Backing up to the center of the roof, Sparrow stretched his shoulder and then charged the edge of the building. He flung himself across the alley and rolled with the landing on the other roof. The impact still jarred his side. He struggled to ignore the pain, but rose unsteadily to his feet. He breathed a heavy sigh, and removed a set of lock picks from his coat pocket. He quickly worked the lock, and by the time Katrina cleared the stoplight at the end of the street, he descended the stairs into the building.

Hearing voices, Sparrow paused as he neared the second floor. Cautiously, he moved down to the landing and drew his gun. The voices came from behind the only door with lights emanating from under it. The door was rickety and barely held upright by its hinges.

When he was sure no one was just inside the door, he gently turned the knob. It was locked. *Why bother*, he muttered to himself as he tucked his *Heckler & Koch* into his belt and removed his lock picks again. The lock turned easily, and he let the door swing inward on its own until it caught on a security chain.

Patiently, he waited and listened with his gun pointed into the door's crack. When no one approached, he peered inside. An opaque glass wall only a few feet inside the apartment blocked his view of the room. Shadows passing over it revealed men on the other side. Reaching through the crack, he slid the chain off the hook. Pulling a mask down over his face, he slipped inside.

Laughter from the men hid the creak of the door. With his back to the door, Sparrow replaced the chain, and with two quick strides he crossed the hall to place his back against the wall's wooden frame.

Glancing around, he found that he was in a small entryway. In the dark corner to his right, there was a large rack of coats. He quickly counted six. To his left there was a small waist high table. It was cluttered with several objects. There was a used ashtray, two sets of keys, numerous pieces of mail, and a small pile of change. On the shelf under the table sat a stack of books that included a phone book.

"...I told her to go away and I'd call her."

"Can you believe she actually came here?"

Listening closely, Sparrow estimated that there were at least five men in the room. Six if he went by the number of coats. The clank of a pool ball told him at least two of them would be armed. He took a few moments to judge each man's location and proximity to the others by the echo of their voices.

Sparrow inched toward the corner of the wall.

"I'm hungry," said one of the men. "I'm going to order something. Anybody else want anything?"

Sparrow froze. Glancing quickly around, he buried himself in the coats. He wouldn't escape close observation, but if the man was distracted, Sparrow would have a moment before being noticed.

Various answers followed the man around the corner. His attention was focused on the others and he never saw Sparrow slip out of the coats.

In one quick motion, Sparrow caught the taller man around his neck and kicked his leg out from under him. Surprised, the man dropped into Sparrow's arms, and Sparrow tightened his grip to cut off any cry for help. Sparrow pressed his gun tightly against the man's temple.

"With your fingers only, how many men?" Sparrow whispered.

The man gagged and pulled at Sparrow's arm, but with only one leg under him, he couldn't find enough balance to free himself. Sparrow tightened his grip on the man's throat, and bored the gun's silencer into his temple. The man grimaced from the pain, but couldn't cry out. After only a moment, he held up five fingers and then one finger.

Satisfied, Sparrow gently squeezed the trigger on the gun. When he felt the trigger set, it was like a gong went off in his head. He immediately released the pressure. He was breathing heavy, sweating, and confused. He had been about to kill the man, without so much as a second thought. *Damn*, he cursed to himself.

Looking around, he glared at the coats, but couldn't remember coming out of them to grab the man. He had done so solely on instinct. *Damn! I'm going to kill the Counselor.* Wiping sweat out of his eyes with his gun hand, he took a deep breath to steady himself.

He closed his eyes and tightened his grip around the man's neck. Within seconds the man stopped struggling, and Sparrow lowered his unconscious body to the floor. He then took a moment to calm himself and still his shaking hand.

"Hey jackass, you need help finding that phonebook?"

As the man rounded the corner, he was surprised to find Sparrow standing over the body of his friend. Before the man could react, Sparrow kicked him in the groin. A second kick sent him hurtling backward into the room.

*One.*

Committed, Sparrow rounded the corner. He kicked the man still clutching his groin in the head.

*Two*

*Thwith!*

Sparrow fired his weapon and a man's kneecap exploded.

*Three.*

Catapulting over a table, Sparrow kicked an overweight man struggling to rise from a couch back onto it. Landing on top of the man, Sparrow rolled to the right and pulled the larger man in front of him as a shield. Fearful of shooting his friend, a man pointing a gun at Sparrow hesitated.

*Thwith!*

Sparrow didn't and shot the man in the shoulder. The man tumbled over a chair behind him, and his gun skirted along the wall out of reach.

*Four.*

Sparrow hit the fat man across his throat with the butt of his gun. The man gagged and collapsed.

*Five.*

Spinning to face the pool table, Sparrow found two targets. His sudden appearance had startled them. Chris was still wearing his coat, and stood on the other side of the table with a pool cue in his hand. His partner was on the same side of the table as Sparrow.

As Sparrow approached the two men, the closest man recovered from his shock and swung his pool cue menacingly. Sparrow used his left arm to deflect the makeshift weapon while striking the man in the throat with his gun. He then dropped to the floor and swept the man's legs out from under him.

*Crack!*
The man's head struck the floor and he lay still.
*Six.*
Cautiously, Chris circled around the pool table with his eyes locked on Sparrow. Ready to swing, he held his weapon with both hands just behind his head.

"Now, listen here. I..."

*Thwith!*

Sparrow shot him in the leg. Chris crumbled to the floor clutching his injured limb.

*That's for hitting the woman in the street*, Sparrow said to himself.

Sparrow pulled a roll of duck tape out of his pocket and used it to bind and gag the men. He dragged them all into the main room and dumped them on the floor in front of the couch. He then made a pretense of searching the room. He dumped the couch and the tables between the men to hide them from each other's view.

Three of them bled from wounds, but they would live as long as he didn't take all day interrogating them. He had never intentionally left people alive before, and the mere thought of it unnerved him. It felt wrong. *This will take some getting used to*, he told himself.

"Recently, you were in Paris when you shouldn't have been." It wasn't a question. "I want to know why you were there." Reaching out, Sparrow ripped the tape off the mouth of the man he had shot in the kneecap. "Answer," he said.

The man clutched at his shattered kneecap with his bound hands. Blood flowed freely from between his fingers. "Screw you!" he screamed.

Without a word, Sparrow replaced the tape over the man's mouth, and then burrowed the silencer of his gun into the man's knee. The man screamed, but the tape muffled him. When Sparrow removed the gun from the man's knee, he collapsed sobbing. Sparrow stepped over to the man he had shot in the shoulder. The man had the most severe of the wounds. If the bleeding was allowed to continue, it would be fatal. The man already looked pale. Sparrow glanced around, and found that the man was hidden from view from the others by the couch.

Sparrow ripped the tape from the man's mouth. "Why were you in Paris?'

"H-how do you know about that?" he asked.

Sparrow slapped him across the head with his gun.

The man began to sob, "Man, pl-please, don't kill us."

Sparrow put the tape back over the man's mouth, and slapped him harder across the forehead with the gun. Stunned, the man fell out of sight. Standing up, Sparrow pointed his gun at the floor next to the man.

*Thwith!*

Fearing their friend was dead, the others cringed and turned away.

Sparrow stepped around the couch and looked at the remaining men. Each of them stared back at him with frightened eyes. They weren't professionals. Their actions were shameful; they were more like bullies on a playground than true soldiers.

He pointed his gun at the one he had initially kicked in the groin. "You?" he asked.

The man looked around at his friends. He couldn't see all of them but he could see the still legs of his friend sticking out from behind the couch. Looking back at Sparrow, he shook his head yes. Sparrow yanked the tape from his mouth.

He gasped for breath before speaking. "S-several days ago, we got a call. We're never told where we're going or why. Just before we got wherever it was we were headed, Paris got nuked. They turned us around and sent us there instead."

Sparrow doubted it would do any good, but he asked anyway. "Where was your pickup and drop off?"

"Here, in St. Louis."

*Damn,* thought Sparrow. "Where is it?" he asked.

"Where's what?" asked the man. Sparrow reared back to hit him. "Okay! Okay! Man, take it easy! We don't have it, if-if you mean the shield of that hero guy. They took it from us!"

"Who?" asked Sparrow.

"Man, we don't know. That's how this works. We don't know who they are and they don't know who we are."

Sparrow bet *they* did know who the men were. He looked at the man and considered his next question. "Who is your contact?"

"We...we don't know. We just get a call. We go. They pay...."

*Whack!*

Sparrow interrupted him with a slap from the gun. "You lie."

He placed the gun on the man's knee and started counting. "Three... two..."

"Wait!" the man screamed. Sparrow stopped counting. "Wait, please! You're right. A woman. She's called the Widow. She..."

Before the man could finish, Sparrow placed the tape back over his mouth.

"Money?" Sparrow asked another target without removing his tape.

The man glanced at a cabinet under the television. Once Sparrow was sure it wasn't booby trapped, he opened it. Inside he found a duffle bag resting on several bags of a white powdery substance. In disgust, Sparrow considered killing the men again. Thoughts of Diamond tracking him through their deaths gave him pause. Glancing back at the bag, he found it full of money.

Walking over to the men, he dumped a bag of the white powder over them, and then scattered the other bags around the room. As he moved toward the door, he grabbed the phone and dialed nine-one-one. Without waiting for someone to answer, he tossed it over his shoulder. It landed next to the men and Sparrow exited the apartment.

\* \*

Sparrow stood just inside Katrina's bedroom and watched her turn out the hallway light after peeking in on her sleeping kids. As she turned and walked slowly down the hallway toward him, she sobbed. She still favored her arm, and the fall down the steps had also left her with a limp.

Moving quickly away from the door, Sparrow took some of the money out of the satchel and stuffed it into his pockets. He dumped the rest onto her bed, and placed the picture and pendant he had taken from Todd's corpse on top of the pile. It wasn't much and it would never begin to replace a lost father, but it was better than what Katrina could currently give her kids.

By the time Katrina entered the room, Sparrow had left through an open window. A small part of him hoped Dreah would approve, if he ever saw her again.

\* \*

After driving to New York, Sparrow used old contacts to purchase a fake passport and took a flight to London, England. Several hours later he stood in the rain studying the sign over the *Old Maid* tavern. He found himself wishing he were dealing with meta-humans again. In all his years of working with the Counselor, he had never acted as a face man. His skills lay with carrying out the assignments, not with setting them up. Without the Counselor's network, he had no choice now but to deal with people directly.

The Widow had a solid reputation for fulfilling contracts, but many refused to deal with her directly. She was crude and people around her had a habit of getting killed, especially those she married. Unless he was careful, things were about to get messy. Sparrow had never had contact with her directly, but her name had come up one way or another in more than one of his missions.

Reaching down, Sparrow picked up the duffle bag and started for the door to the tavern. As he pushed on the door, he pulled his hat down low over his brow to hide his appearance from the entryway camera.

The tavern was dark with a narrow bar along the right wall. A row of tables ran down the center of the room with a series of booths along the left wall. Above the booths was a room-length mirror that did a poor job of making the room appear bigger than it was. Behind the bar, there was a door leading to a back room, and at the far end there was a set of stairs leading up. Sparrow's quarry sat at a table in the center of the room. There were two men sitting in the first of the three booths, and a barkeep behind the bar.

Unlucky Benny was the Widow's half-brother, and the only way to contact her directly. Sparrow had no idea why the Widow kept him around, except maybe for the blind loyalty that was brought on by being blood-kin. Dreah had spoke of its dangers at the funeral.

Benny sat at the table with a woman who looked half dead from a life lived on illicit drugs. She wore a loose tank top that did nothing to hide the needle marks on her arms. Scabs on her face made her difficult to look at. She leaned heavily on Benny.

He didn't look much better, but at least he looked only drunk and not high. Sparrow moved across the room and stood over their table while watching the barkeep in the mirror. It took Benny several seconds to notice him.

"What the bloody'ell do you want?" asked Benny.

Without speaking, Sparrow kicked Benny's chair out from under him.

*Crash!*

The chair shattered against a wall as Benny landed hard on the floor. His girlfriend collapsed on top of him. Before Benny could recover, Sparrow stepped onto his hand, and pulled a gun to point it in the direction of the barkeep.

"I advise against it," Sparrow said. The sound of the barkeep's shotgun being laid on the bar was his only response. The two people in the booth had their hands where Sparrow could see them, and they had sunk down in their seats for the limited protection the table offered.

"I'm looking for the Widow," said Sparrow. Benny ignored him as he struggled to pull his hand free from Sparrow's boot. Sparrow applied pressure and Benny screamed as his fingers cracked under the weight.

"If I have to actually ask, it will be painful," said Sparrow. He eased off the man's hand enough for him to catch his breath.

"Sh-she's upstairs you prick!" screamed Benny.

Sparrow took his foot off Benny's hand, and turned toward the stairs. He hadn't expected her to actually be at the bar. Suddenly longing for the solitude of a tall perch with a high-powered rifle overlooking the room, he began to doubt he was up to this task.

"Y-you can bet she knows you're here by now," said Benny. As he laughed, spittle sprayed the girl cowering next to him.

Without a word, Sparrow turned and started for the stairs.

Inching his way slowly up, Sparrow watched for any movement above him or below him. He doubted Benny was a threat, but he hadn't taken time to disarm the bar's other patrons. Along with the barkeep, they were still a threat.

On the second floor, Sparrow found a hallway that ran back in the direction of street. There were two doors on each side with a single door in the far end. Checking each door as he passed it, Sparrow found that the first two doors were locked. The third door on the left opened to reveal a small room with a single uncovered mattress resting on the floor. Trash littered the room and a rat scurried away from Sparrow.

The sound of a squeaking bed issued from the door at the end of the hall, and Sparrow turned to see movement along the crack at the floor. Keeping along the edge of the hall as much as possible, he checked the last door on the right and found it locked. The final door was unlocked, and when he turned the knob, it swung inward.

The Widow sat on the edge of a bed. She was only wearing a pair of black panties and a see through gown that was open down the front. She had a cigarette in her right hand, and a very large caliber handgun held haphazardly in her left hand. Light from a dozen candles flickered off its chrome barrel. Showing the bar below, a small television monitor sat on a dresser beside her. Benny was sitting at the table cradling his hand.

The Widow was pale and thin. She had black hair with highlights of white. Her fingernails and toenails were painted black. She had numerous body piercings, many in private places. A tattoo of a large white skull dominated her upper right shoulder just below her collarbone. Snakes crawled from the skull to slither around her torso and disappear behind her back. The tongue of a hideous demon caressed her small breasts. Both her arms were covered in sleeve tattoos that revealed gory wounds and broken bones. Insects crawled from the wounds. Monsters meant to torment a child's dreams decorated her legs.

Behind her the bed covers shifted. She blew smoke into the air and said over her shoulder, "Go back to sleep dear. Momma's got a little business to take care of." Deciding Sparrow wasn't going to shoot her, at least not right away, she rose and walked across the room to pour herself a drink. Turning around, she drank it all, and then sighed heavily. "So, are you going to use that gun, or do you have something else in mind?"

Sparrow held his position just outside the door. The right side of the room was hidden from his view, and despite what the widow had said, he doubted the individual under the covers was asleep.

"A few days ago you provided some men that were flown into Paris."

"What's that to you?"

"They took something that didn't belong to them."

"And?"

"And I want it."

The Widow walked back to the bed and sat down in a chair next to it. Sparrow wished she would display some modesty, but he knew he had interrupted her afternoon. She had not chosen the time or the place for their meeting.

"Sorry, big boy. I don't betray clients. You end up dead that way."

Sparrow tossed the duffle bag into the room.

"Twenty thousand, and all I want is a direction. Of course, it remains just between us."

The woman smiled. "I can think of other things that can be just between us. It's lots more fun, and sticking your nose into those places won't get it shot off."

Sparrow waited patiently.

After a moment, the Widow looked disappointed and glanced at the bag. Licking the piercings around her mouth, she leaned forward and rummaged through it. Leaning back and propping her feet on it, she said, "I don't have a name, just a direction." Picking up a piece of paper from the dresser beside her, she tossed it toward Sparrow. "Hong Kong," she said as the paper landed on the floor. "That little gun isn't going to be much good to you there. I'll sell you mine for another twenty g's."

Sparrow took his eyes off her just a moment to glance at the paper. On it was the image of a large letter *H* with a halo around the upper right portion of the letter. "Meta-humans," he cursed as he turned and left the room. He allowed the door to swing shut behind him. The Widow's laughter chased him down the hall.

\* \*

"Sparrow, are you sure you want to do this?" asked Lady Gemini. "Halo Corp is run by the Adversary, so it won't be easy. The team already suspects he may be involved. Maybe some backup would be best."

"We made a deal, Gem. No questions, and no one is to know about this."

Lady Gemini sighed. "Alright, lone wolf. I'll set it up. Your ticket to Hong Kong will be ready by the time you get to the airport. Will you be needing any other supplies?"

"No. I know where to get those once I'm in Hong Kong. I need you to pull up as much data as you can on Halo Corp holdings in and around the city. I'll need schematics of all the buildings. Also, run a check on flight plans for aircraft connected to the company and see what matches up with Paris."

"Roger," said Lady Gemini. She severed the communication and glanced over her shoulder to make sure no one had been spying on her. She could hear the others in the command center. Since she often used the special operations center to run scenarios for meta-human battles, her presence wasn't unusual. However, she also knew her dad was very upset over Sparrow's disappearance, and he often became unpredictable when he was that way.

It took her less than a minute to set up the plane ticket from Paris to Hong Kong under the name Sparrow had given her, and she smiled as schematics for various Halo Corp buildings filled her screen at the same time. She knew it was too easy so she dug deeper. What Sparrow was looking for would be buried. Nearly an hour later, she giggled with excitement when she found that she had been right.

* *

Dr. McCoy studied the image and scratched his head. The image of Facet trapped in the energy shaft with Glip-2 suspended over his head was life size and took up most of the wall. Jonesy had applied additional filters to it and cleaned it up. There was no doubt it was the globe in the image. Dr. McCoy shook his head in disbelief and turned back to Diamond.

"What do you think?" asked Diamond.

The doctor sat down before replying. "Quiet frankly, I'm shocked." Jonesy nodded his head in agreement, but the doctor ignored him. "We've known all along that Glip-2's energy signature was unique, but I would never have guessed anything along this line."

"If the image is correct, the energy has the ability to cause the meta-gene to mutate."

"With a direct application, that's correct," replied Dr. McCoy. "To think we've spent all this time experimenting with the meta-gene only to find the secret to unlocking it is wrapped up in that obnoxious little twerp." Again Jonesy nodded and again the doctor ignored him. "Are we still convinced he knew nothing about his?"

Diamond nodded. "I am."

"How do you want us to proceed, Mr. Diamond?" asked Jonesy.

"Quietly. Do either of you have any samples of his energy stored anywhere?"

"No," replied Dr. McCoy. "Frankly, I've always tried to avoid him."

Diamond looked at Jonesy.

"Yes, sir. I do. It isn't much, but it should be enough to run a few small tests."

"Good," said Diamond. "Turn it over to Dr. McCoy. I want to know if this can be used to our advantage. Keep the experiments small, Doctor. I don't want to cause an incident here in the Citadel. If initial tests prove positive, we will set up a facility for larger experiments. Jonesy, get with Glip-2 for additional samples." Jonesy frowned. "Once you have them, turn them over to Dr. McCoy. You've needed samples in the past so he won't be suspicious. Gentlemen, I don't want knowledge of this going beyond this room. Am I understood?"

"Understood, sir," replied Jonesy.

Dr. McCoy nodded his head in agreement. He was actually annoyed that Diamond felt he needed to request secrecy. Most of the work McCoy did in the Citadel was off the record. With these experiments possibly being the crowning achievement of his career, he had no intention of sharing them with anyone.

Diamond dismissed the two men and after they were gone, he sat in silence staring at the image on the wall. Dr. McCoy's recent success at forcing a meta-gene into dormancy had vast potential use for stripping meta-humans of their powers. The success was a first in meta-science. Now they could potentially activate the meta-genes of specific individuals. That wasn't a first for the science, but this was the first time the actual catalyst needed was known. If they could find a way of controlling the actual mutation, the potential would be limitless.

\* \*

Sparrow sat in the dingy apartment and studied the Halo Corp mega-building through a telescope. Beside him sat two large duffle bags of gear he had stolen from old contacts of the Counselor. To avoid being connected to the man, he had chosen not to purchase it through normal channels. The owners wouldn't report the theft to the police, and people in their line of work often had a lot of enemies itching to do just what he had done.

Looking to his sidekick, he thumbed through the list of possible targets Gemini had assembled for him. After three days, he had checked off all but two. The first was a small research facility located outside the city that specialized in development of military hardware. It was a logical choice. The top floors of the mega-structure in the heart of the city were the other possible target. Halo's construction of the building was widely known. Its ownership of the top four floors wasn't. That information that had been buried under two false companies and three legitimate ones. It was that section of the building he was concentrating on.

The mega-structure was Halo Corps crowning achievement. In cities like Hong Kong, space was a commodity and the structure took advantage of that. The base of the structure was built in the shape of a massive pyramid that took up several city blocks and rose more than one hundred stories above the streets. A tower rose out of the base and extended straight up for another forty floors. Inside the structure, people could live out their entire lives. Apartments ranged in size from one room to dozens of rooms and took up most of the structure. Special shafts of reflective material carried sunlight to the apartments in the center of the structure while the more expensive apartments around the outside were exposed to it directly. Open-air shopping malls that met a family's every need took up three or four floors at a time. Four five star restaurants with balconies open to the rest of the city were one of the many forms of entertainment that could be found. Businesses dominated the floors between the apartments. Corporations bought out entire floors of apartments and offered them as bonuses to employees who were employed within the colossal structure. Several sub-levels served as a massive parking structure.

It was logical that the *Aegis* would be in the military facility. It was known for its durability, and anyone who could mimic its properties and integrate them into armor stood to make a fortune. However, Sparrow was leaning toward the upper floors of the mega-structure. It offered seclusion and safety, and Halo Corp could easily dump the guilty company from its records and claim no knowledge of the shield. In addition, the tower structure had a helicopter pad that could have easily been used by the airship to drop off the shield. Last of all, but possibly most important, Gemini had run into several brick walls trying to access schematics for the floors. He was still without those schematics and he hadn't heard back from her for two days.

*Knock! Knock!*

Sparrow dove for cover behind a thin partition hiding one corner of the room. Pulling his pistol, he peered cautiously at the door to the apartment. With the room dark, he could see a shadow moving back and forth under the door.

*Knock! Knock!*

The knock was harder and more insistent. He began to inch his way around the edge of the room.

Once next to the door, Sparrow listened carefully. He could hear movement and the light under the door still flickered. Reaching up, he twisted a fiber-optic cable and peered into an eyepiece. What he saw stunned him.

Glancing at the balcony, he considered escaping by it. He dismissed the idea knowing that if he had been discovered, the balcony was being watched. Next to a window in the far wall sat a small black backpack. He started for it.

*Knock! Knock! Knock!*

The impatient knocks vibrated the door. Sparrow froze.

*Why would they still be knocking? Why not just burst in and capture me? Shadow Spirit could silently walk through the walls and take me without a fight. Slipstream could blast the apartment into the sea. Why let me know they have found me? Why give me a chance to flee?*

Curious, Sparrow stepped back to the door and used the eyepiece to scan the hallway again.

The lone figure grew impatient. When she raised a hand to knock again, Sparrow flung open the door and snatched Gemini out of the hall. Pressing her against the wall and covering her mouth with his hand, he slammed the door shut again. For several moments, he scanned the hallway through the eyepiece. It remained empty.

Gemini's eyes were wide with shock, and her body rigid with fear. After a tense moment, Sparrow stepped back. She reached up and removed an earpiece from each ear. Sparrow could hear loud music issuing from them.

"What the hell was that, dude?" she asked.

Sparrow ignored her question. "What are you doing here, Kahori?"

"People were getting suspicious of me hanging around the ops center. They kept telling me to go away and be a teenager; whatever that means."

Sparrow glared at her.

Gemini glanced around the small apartment and winched her nose in disgust. It was small and dirty. A couple of dingy lamps left most of the room in darkness. The walls were patched together with old cracked planks of wood. Bamboo mats hung over the windows. There was a small sleeping mat off to one side, and an old wood stove on the other. Her first thought was that it was used for heat, but the stains running down its side indicated other uses. Two sitting cushions sat in the center of the room. The television had a crack running down the center of its old dusty screen.

"One word, old man. Yuck! What a dump," Gemini grumbled. When she looked back to Sparrow, he was still glaring at her. She sighed heavily and held her palms up toward him in defense.

"Take it easy, old man." She shook her head in disbelief. "Look, I finally got those specs you wanted, and I couldn't just leave you hanging. So I set up a reason to be in Hong Kong and I came to deliver them." Sparrow's eyes narrowed. "Don't worry. *Evanescence* is playing in concert tonight, and I am meeting up with some local Internet friends. We go to concerts all the time. I got us all tickets, and I fly back out tomorrow morning. I've done it before. No one will suspect the real reason I'm here. In fact, everyone seemed to think it was a good idea for me to get away for a couple of days. Everyone there is so depressing right now anyway, and since Hong Kong isn't in the bull's eye, they figured it was safe."

Sparrow didn't soften his glare. If he abandoned the mission now, he wouldn't recover the shield. He couldn't return to the Citadel without it, and he couldn't sell it either. If he allowed Gemini to stay, he was opening himself up to discovery by Diamond, or worse, the Counselor.

"Gem, this is dangerous. You shouldn't be here."

"I know, but don't worry old man. I've taken precautions. I'm still at the hotel and preparing for the concert. I'm with friends, so everything will look normal." Gemini could see the question in his eyes. "Yes, I am a doppelganger, both of us are. But everyone back home thinks I'm the real me, otherwise this wouldn't have worked."

"I didn't know your doppelgangers could also split."

Gemini shook her head, "Normally no, but we can come together to ride along with each other for a short period of time. We are sort of one, but also two. It's complicated, and I don't understand it. It is way uncomfortable too because it kind of makes me feel bloated. Everyone knows my doppelgangers can't split, so by riding, I can fake a split and look like the original. No one knows about it, including dad. I use it as a way of sneaking out after curfew. I leave doppelgangers at home to split in front of someone, and make them think I'm really there. I'm meeting up with myself outside the concert hall in an hour. I'll rejoin, and no one will be the wiser."

Sparrow looked frustrated and turned back to the balcony. Kahori followed him across the room.

"You didn't leave me much choice you know. If you at least had your assigned sidekick, I could have sent you the data. Heck, if you even had a room with a phone, I could have called you. And by the way, what kind of person doesn't have a cell phone these days anyway?"

"One who doesn't want to be found," replied Sparrow.

"Yeah, well next time, don't hide so well from me. If I hadn't already known where to look, I'd never have found you."

"That's the idea. You know how to access the sidekick, why not now?"

"Because, you took it officially off the grid, and you don't run it all the time in case Glip-2 is searching for it. It is invisible to all but the main frame now, and like I said, I got run out of the command center. I missed our last contact window, so the only choice I had left was to bring you the information directly." The look on Sparrow's face told her she hadn't eased his worries.

"Don't worry," she said for the third time as she moved over to his sidekick and picked it up. After tapping a few buttons, she opened her small purse and pulled out a cell phone. Sitting the purse down, she held the phone next to Sparrow's sidekick and downloaded the information. As she walked away from the couch, her purse fell onto the floor. She glanced around at it, and then held the sidekick out to Sparrow. "Here," she said.

Sparrow took it and looked it over. It was a set of schematics on the mega-structure tower. He looked up at her as she scooped her purse up off the floor. She smiled at him.

"You owe me for those. You must pinky-swear to keep my secret about curfew, and my duplicates." She held up her left hand and extended her pinky. When he didn't immediately take it, she raised her eyebrows and said, "Between those and the concert tickets, this little jaunt has cost me most of my allowance. Professional hackers, and last minute front row seats to the concert of the year, aren't cheap you know."

"I thought you were a professional hacker."

Still holding her hand out to him and showing impatience, she continued, "Security, old man. That type of hacking would send up alerts, and I distinctly remember you saying that you didn't even want Glip to know what we were up to. He would have detected me pulling that kind of computing power from the mainframe."

She was smart. Sparrow had to admit that. She was better than many professionals he had worked with in the past. She had grown up around Diamond, and had access to pretty much anything she wanted or needed. In addition, she had worked alongside and learned from some of the most experienced soldiers and meta-humans on the planet. She knew how to do what needed to be done. Hesitantly, Sparrow hooked his pinky in hers. She beamed a smile at him.

Without another word, Gemini turned and started for the door. She checked the hall though the eyepiece, and slipped her earplugs back into her ears. She danced her way out into the hallway and shut the door behind herself.

As the door closed, Sparrow started to turn back toward the balcony, but something on the floor caught his eye. Bending down he picked up a small purple ribbon that had fallen out of her purse. He glanced from the ribbon back to the door. Placing it on a small table, he exited the apartment.

Sparrow shadowed Gemini across the city and to a restaurant outside a large concert hall. She nearly busted him following her twice. She was good.

After an hour, he watched her slip into a restroom after another doppelganger of herself. A few moments later only one of them emerged. It was only after he saw her enter the concert hall with a large group of teenage girls that he actually relaxed. It wasn't until the concert was over, and he had trailed her safely back to her hotel room, that he was satisfied she was safe enough for him to return to his mission.

# CHAPTER 14
# A DIFFERENT CITY ON THE EDGE

Jonesy hurried up the steps of the command center and into the conference room. Looking around, he found everyone staring at him. He was late, and Diamond wasn't bothering to hide his irritation over it. To make matters worse, he didn't have a valid excuse for being late. He had just allowed the time to get away from him.

Rounding the table, Jonesy sat down next to Edmond. The list of people attending the meeting was short. It meant Diamond had a specific agenda in mind, and that he intended knowledge of the meeting to remain in the room. It also meant Diamond wouldn't have much patience.

Besides himself and Diamond, only Meta-man, Edmond, Clara, Carol, Envoy, Maria, Bullock, and Glip-2 were present. He scowled at the list. Jonesy didn't understand why Diamond continued to trust the globe. He didn't, and he was not about to hide it. Clara was incompetent. Meta-man's moral code was only going to cause their mission to fail. Carol didn't have any business in the room at all. Maria was only a kid who didn't have any cares beyond her expensive clothes and boyfriends. Bullock was a brute, plain and simple. Even if he liked the man, Edmond was an outsider. Of them all, Jonesy only approved of Envoy. She was competent and understand what was at stake, but best of all, she followed orders.

Looking from Glip-2 to Diamond, Jonesy found that Diamond

was glaring at him and he realized the look of disgust on his face was being broadcast to the entire room. "Sorry, I was in the middle of something that I think you will all want to know about," he quickly lied. "It involved Glip-2." He knew Diamond wouldn't fall for it, but the rest of the room wouldn't know the difference. The readings were significant but before his tardiness, Jonesy hadn't considered them important enough to bring them up at the meeting. He picked up a sidekick and passed it to Edmond.

Displayed on the sidekick were a series of numbers that compared atmospheric conditions over Paris with those of a past experiment Jonesy had performed on the atmosphere over the Citadel. Edmond's eyes danced over the numbers and he memorized them instantly.

Diamond said, "Then let's get started with you. What do you have?"

Jonesy cleared his throat. "As you know, I've been analyzing the picture of Facet and Glip-2. Well, it got me to thinking. Several years ago, I was working on an experiment and I was getting some odd readings. It turned out Glip-2 was interfering with the experiment." Jonesy paused and glanced at the globe.

Diamond also glanced him; but unlike Jonesy, his face didn't betray what he was thinking.

"What?" asked Glip-2, feigning innocence. "It was just a joke, and Jonesy-boy needed a break anyway."

Without speaking, Diamond looked back around to Jonesy while a soft whistle issued from Jonesy's sidekick. Glip-2 floated away from the table into a corner of the room. The images displayed on the wall changed as he approached. Instead of the target cities, Glip-2 viewed images of several theme parks around the country.

"Its energy was giving me spikes in my readings that ruined everything. Since Glip-2 seems to be connected to this whole thing, I went back over my old research notes and compared the readings with the Paris incident. I found the same energy spikes in the atmospheric readings over Paris just before the clouds started forming. Since we weren't calibrated to record them, we didn't detect them, but I've recalibrated the satellites to specifically look for them over the target cities now. I'm hoping it will give us an early warning if those clouds start to form again."

"I suspect the readings will coincide with the initial physical changes in a seed," added Edmond. "I've reviewed the readings on Facet, and the energy spikes coincide with the rise in his core temperature."

Diamond nodded as he glanced over his shoulder at Glip-2. He knew Jonesy was faking his discovery. The results were real, of that he had no doubt, but he could tell Jonesy was only covering for his tardiness. Still, it meant that the incident in Paris wasn't a total loss after all. That was good news. As for Glip-2, it was just another example of how his growing personality was making it increasingly difficult to keep him under control. Diamond had no way to explain the globes fixation on Jonesy. Glip-2 was intent on making the man's life miserable.

"Good job, Jonesy." Envoy said.

"I mean, it won't be much, but maybe it will help," added Jonesy. Everyone nodded their understanding, including Diamond. To Jonesy it appeared his ruse had worked.

"Good," said Diamond. His eyes fell on Meta-man, and seeing no reason to delay, he pushed forward with his agenda. "I've called this meeting because I've made a decision on our next course of action. It's one some of you aren't going to like, but I feel it is necessary."

"We are going to move one of the seeds," said Edmond. Looking up from Jonesy's sidekick, his eyes briefly locked with Diamond's. Diamond simply nodded. "It makes sense, Mr. Diamond. It is the next logical step. John and I have talked it over, and we agree."

"Is that true, Meta-man?" asked Diamond.

Meta-man shifted uncomfortably in his seat and grimaced. "I agree that all the other choices are worse."

Diamond leaned back in his chair and looked around the room. No one else spoke. "Good," he said. "Now that we've gotten that out of the way, let's talk about the plan itself. Bullock?"

Bullock cleared his throat before filling the room with his rocky voice. "Our target is Austin, in Denver. We've chosen him because Jonesy and Edmond both agree that he is one of the top two most likely to mature next. This is a trial run, and if it's successful, we will move forward with the other targets. We skipped over Fuentes of Buenos Aries because we only have limited authorization to operate inside the Argentine Republic, and if we failed, they would bar us from the country. Of course, everyone here needs to understand that if we fail with Austin, we will further damage our reputation with the public and law enforcement here in the States. The Paris incident has already hurt us severely. As we are all aware, government sanctioning of DSS is rapidly disappearing. TASC has all but been grounded."

"You've worked hard to set up your operations and connections with the government, Mr. Diamond. Are you sure you want to do this?" asked Carol.

Without official sanctioning, Diamond Security Solutions would lose its ability to operate in the United States. DSS stood out among other meta-human security providers. Many of them had authorization to operate in the US, but most were restricted to limited geographic areas such as specific cities, and acted as special arms of the local police. In contrast, Diamond Security Solutions was one of only a handful of teams with national authorization in the US. It was also one of the few security providers that had been officially sanctioned by the United Nations. This allowed DSS to operate in UN member nations as long as UNIT, or operatives of the respective country, supervised the operation. DSS had more power than some federal law enforcement agencies. If that authorization were ever lost, Diamond's operatives could, and probably would, be arrested for simply using their powers in public.

Diamond replied, "Yes Carol, I'm sure. I don't see any other option. It may mean the destruction of DSS, but if we go to the governments, these people will disappear. If we go to the people, it will cause a panic and the rioting will tear apart these cities. I don't see any other option at this point. With that being said, anyone that wants to opt out of this may do so now."

"We aren't going to do this in the open are we?" asked Envoy.

"We will take precautions," replied Diamond. "However, we need to understand that we may need to abandon any carefully laid plan for necessity and safety."

"Meta-man, you have a lot to lose from this," said Envoy.

"We'll deal with it as we need to, Envoy. Like I said the other day, I'm here to stay."

Envoy was relieved by his answer.

"We have an island location where we will place Austin. Here," said Diamond as he drew everyone's attention to the video wall. A satellite image of a small island located in the Pacific filled the screen. "The island is on the edge of the Polynesians, but it should be secluded enough from any population centers if Austin becomes a threat."

Jonesy sat forward in his chair, "We have a small facility on the island that has been evacuated. Austin will have all the comforts we can provide, except communication with the outside world, of course. I will be taking a small research team to the island to monitor and record his condition."

"But we have no idea how long we will need to keep him there?" inquired Meta-man.

"No, we don't," said Jonesy. "For all we know, there won't be another incident for a hundred years."

"Is there no way of knowing?" asked Meta-man.

Jonesy didn't have an answer, and didn't want to admit it. As he struggled to find words, Edmond spoke up.

"At this point, no." Edmond pushed his glasses up his nose. "We plan to take advantage of this situation and learn from Austin."

"You mean experiment on him?" asked Meta-man.

"No," answered Edmond. "I mean we will take a few blood samples and give him a complete physical. Maybe it will give us something more concrete to help judge the others by."

Meta-man looked uncomfortable, but consented. "What's the plan?" he asked.

"Before we proceed with details, I think we need to include anyone who will be a part of this operation. Their input could be valuable." Turning to Envoy, Diamond continued, "This will be your show, Envoy. You will be field leader. Who would you like on your team?"

"Me?" asked Envoy. "Are you sure, sir? I assumed Meta-man would be replacing Aegis."

"No, Latisha," said Meta-man. I've already talked this over with Mr. Diamond. This is your show. You know your people better than I do, and Aegis trained you to replace him. I will gladly offer advice, but I doubt you will need it."

Envoy looked to Diamond but found him still waiting for her answer.

"Okay," she said, "if you are sure." Diamond nodded. "Since we want to stay off the radar, I would suggest a smaller team with as much firepower as possible." She sighed. "Given that we know Facet showed physical signs before the incident, I would suggest Dawn. She doesn't have much field experience, but she will be able to read Austin better than anyone. If anything starts to happen inside him, she'll know it."

"Agreed," said Diamond.

Interrupting the meeting, the door to the t-port opened. Dreah and Fluxstone entered. Fluxstone took a seat at the table, and Dreah sat on her couch behind Diamond with her feet tucked under her.

With her eyes on the table, Fluxstone said, "I know you think I should be resting, but I've been a part of this for a long time. I'm not going to just sit it out now." Lifting her eyes from the table she looked at Diamond. "I won't ask to be a member of the field team, but I'd still like to be a part."

Diamond considered her words, and then nodded his consent. "Go ahead, Envoy. Who else?"

"Paragon, of course, and I doubt we could get out of the Citadel without Wavefront."

"Are you sure you want him and not someone with more firepower, or more...stable?" asked Diamond.

"He is taking the loss hard," said Dreah.

"I'm sure," replied Envoy. "He's reliable when it comes down to it, and he has extensive field experience."

Edmond spoke up over his glasses, "Actually, I'm glad you chose him. I have a theory I'd like to discuss with him and Jonesy once this meeting is over. If it works, his special vision will come in handy."

Envoy nodded and Jonesy looked at Edmond with curiosity in his eyes. Picking up her sidekick, Envoy scrolled through a list of available personnel. She didn't need the list, but she went through the motions anyway. She stopped and glanced up at Meta-man. "Of course, I'd like Slipstream's power, but we can't subject him to this. John, you would make a more than an adequate substitution, if you'll have the position."

"Of course, Envoy. I'll gladly join you," replied Meta-man.

"I don't know what we have in mind with the actual extraction of Austin, but I think Maverick's teleporting ability would prove to be valuable. We have already called him in, right?" Envoy looked to Edmond and Meta-man.

"He's here and he'll help out," said Meta-man.

From the far end of the room Dreah said, "He understands the importance of this. He will cooperate. I can't guarantee he will play nice, however."

"Good enough," replied Envoy. "Let's also get Shadow Spirit. If Butch is up to it, we will put the twins on standby with him on the

*Egress.* I know we used Fenrir in Paris, but I'd like to keep him on reserve status as much as possible."

"I would agree with that," said Dreah. "His PMAD is getting worse. He is having more and more trouble shifting his shape back from full wolf form. He volunteered for Paris, and I'm sure he would volunteer for this mission, but I fear he would be lost to us completely."

Envoy glanced at her and then back to the sidekick, "Last of all, I'd like Gem to run operations. I know that it is a big step for her, but she thinks out of the box compared to some of the other operations techs. By discovering those invisible troops, she saved our bacon in Paris." Envoy looked to Diamond for agreement.

Without objecting, Diamond turned to Clara and said, "Okay, let's get those people up here and involved in this meeting."

Clara reached for a sidekick and immediately made the notifications.

"What's the word on Sparrow?" asked Envoy as everyone waited patiently.

Bullock scowled at her question.

Diamond's face didn't reveal the anger that still boiled in him. Sparrow's desertion had not only humiliated him, but it had also cost him a major asset in a time of desperate need. It was only because Dreah had continued to insist that Sparrow would return that he hadn't turned all his agents onto finding him. He had spent too many years working with Dreah to ignore her now. He would continue to trust in her on this, at least for now.

"None," Diamond said. "He has covered his tracks well."

"Do you think he'll go after the targets?" Envoy asked. "He didn't seem satisfied with our reasoning."

"No," replied Diamond.

"His absence is his method of soul searching," said Dreah.

"Yeah, well I just wish he would have told someone before disappearing. We still haven't even figured out how he got out of the Citadel," added Jonesy.

"There were no systems disrupted," said Glip-2 loudly through Jonesy's sidekick. Jonesy jumped and nearly dropped the device. He quickly turned down the volume. Ignoring Jonesy, Glip-2 continued. "The only thing I've had to address in the last few days is a malfunctioning sensor in the water bays and that is not uncommon. The systems down there have always had difficulty maintaining balance with the salt water because of having to integrate the Citadel's technology with the real world. The real stuff just can't keep up. Routine, routine, routine, oh the boredom of routine."

Edmond glanced up at Glip-2 and smiled.

Envoy's brow furrowed, and she ignored Glip-2's whining. She had come to know Sparrow's background. Fluxstone had shared it with her in hope of recruiting her to speak out against his presence. Her effort's had failed. Envoy trusted Aegis too much, and he trusted Dreah. Despite his past, if Dreah vouched for Sparrow, she would trust him. His past would make his usability limited in certain circumstances, but then again, even a one-armed soldier had uses. Besides, their conversation after Paris had left her with a positive impression of his abilities, and his motives.

While scratching her right arm, Envoy watched Gemini enter the conference room from the operations center. When their eyes met, Gemini quickly looked away and hurried to a seat at the end of the table.

"So no sign of Sparrow at all then?" Envoy said as she watched the young girl. Gemini's eyes shifted in her direction, and then darted away to avoid eye contact.

"Nope, none, nada, zilch, nothing," said Glip-2.

"Yeah, I just wonder," muttered Envoy. "Maybe he had help," she added just loud enough for Gemini to hear.

"Well, it wasn't me," innocently pleaded Glip-2 loud enough for everyone to hear.

Gemini refused to look at Envoy. Instead, she picked up a sidekick and studied the images on it. Envoy looked from her and back at the door the girl had entered. Envoy wondered just how long the girl had been standing outside the door listening to their conversation.

"Don't worry," said Dreah, drawing Envoy's gaze. "He will return." The two women's eyes met, and Envoy knew that Dreah believed he would.

Dawn entered the room and looked around nervously at everyone. She was rarely consulted in top-secret meetings and was unsure why she had been summoned to this one. Envoy always did her best to make the young woman feel welcome, but Dawn rarely felt comfortable around people, especially Diamond. She nervously found a seat in the corner where she would be out of sight of him.

When Butch entered, Gemini leaped up and ran over to hug him. Envoy followed the girl, and for the next couple of minutes everyone turned their attention to welcoming him back. Doctor McCoy had given him a clean bill of health despite the blood loss he had suffered. He seemed fit and happy to be back among friends. He laughed heartily, and even took a gibe at Jonesy over the car batteries.

Once everyone was present and seated, Diamond took over the meeting again. He used the first couple of minutes to rehash what had already been discussed, and he then asked if anyone wanted to opt out of the operation. When no one spoke up, Diamond led the discussion on how they were to proceed.

* *

As the meeting broke up, Diamond watched everyone rise to leave. He knew they each had different rituals to follow before departing on a dangerous mission. He knew them all better than they knew themselves.

Lady Gemini, Kahori, would do as much as she could to prepare. She would study maps of Denver and run scenarios to predict the most atrocious of outcomes. She would have a doppelganger up all night, and with their merging in the morning she would be as prepared as any of them could be.

Paragon would submerge himself in his classical music, and then he would pray for hours. He wouldn't pray for a successful outcome to the mission. He believed that was already decided and in the hands of God. No, he would pray for everyone's souls, and ask for a blessing of peace for them all.

Wavefront would normally spend his time irritating everyone else as much as possible. However, the death of Aegis had crushed the man's spirit. Given time he would recover, but it was a process he was fighting. Whether or not he would remain a part of the team was another matter. Diamond doubted he would, and he wasn't sure he would keep him around anyway. For now, he would forgo his usual pleasures and find solace in the bottom of a beer can.

Shadow Spirit would lock himself inside his chambers. Diamond had no idea what he did inside that room. Even when Diamond used astral projection to spy on him, Shadow Spirit always knew. He was still as much a mystery to Diamond as he was the first day he appeared in the Citadel uninvited. Diamond didn't doubt his loyalty. Dreah had vouched for it, and she had revealed his complete past. He never questioned orders either, and had given two years of loyal service as a testament to his pledge to serve. But Diamond preferred to know a man's motivations, to know what made him tick. He knew it for everyone under him, even Sparrow. Shadow Spirit wasn't human, and he wasn't motivated by anything Diamond could understand. He didn't want money. He didn't want fame. He didn't want to right the wrongful death of a loved one. He didn't want to fit in. He didn't want to confront evil. He didn't even seem to care about right or wrong. He simply served, and claimed he was where he was supposed to be. It was a motivation Diamond didn't understand, and if he didn't understand it, he couldn't control it.

Meta-man's public life made nearly everything about him common knowledge. He had spent as much time with Dreah and the Missing Man as he could since his arrival in the Citadel, and would most likely do so now. With his vast years of experience, he had learned long ago not to dwell on the past, or to worry about things yet to come. To do so would have crushed him long ago.

Maverick was the biggest unknown. Like Meta-man he was one of the Nine, and possessed centuries of experience. However, he was also a wild card and unpredictable. He thrived on chaos. If anyone hoped the plan would go wrong, it was him. To keep him occupied, he had been issued a late night mission to scout the island compound they were hoping to transfer Austin to as well as the layout of Denver.

Dawn didn't have any down time to consider the plan. Even as the meeting had wrapped up, the sun had set and she had switched places with Dusk. As for Dusk, she didn't care about the mission one way or the other, only Diamond's promise to continue searching for a way to separate the two kept her on board. The two were so completely opposite, it was hard to believe they shared the same body. Dawn was soft and shy. She had hid from him during the meeting, and not even questioned her part in the plan. Dusk was outspoken and loud. She had complained that it was Dawn getting to take part and not her. Unfortunately, she had also taken an instant liking to Maverick, which had prompted Diamond to send him on his mission. If he hadn't,

Dusk would have done her best to ensure Dawn was embarrassed come morning. It would have also left her tired. It would have been Dusk's way of taunting her sister for getting to be part of the mission, and it would have left Dawn too distracted.

Envoy would spend the night soaring among the stars. As one of the few meta-humans who actually possessed the ability of interstellar travel, she often took advantage of it. Diamond had considered grounding her in case an event kicked off while she was away, but had chosen not to. The solitude would allow her to work through the plan and find any flaws in it. She would most likely only get one or two hours of sleep, but she would be fully charged and ready to go in the morning.

For the most part, they were a good team. He had asked a lot from them over the years, and now he was asking for their lives. It was something he had no regret doing. Unfortunately, he was beginning to doubt they would succeed. Even without knowing fully what it was, he had worked for years building a powerful enough team to save the world from this disaster. His mistake had been to center too much of it on Aegis. Now he was dead, and the core team was falling apart. Of course, he had a contingency plan to solve that problem. It might call for permanently sacrificing Jane, and Aegis would not approve, but he would do what he had to do to win this war.

\* \*

Envoy stood next to the railing and allowed the wind to wash over her from the garden below. She had never been sentimental, but this was the very spot where Aegis had convinced her to join Diamond Security Solutions. At the time, she had been still trying to adjust to the fact that her arm was bonded with an alien artifact, and that she couldn't use her hand to so much as scratch her nose. She had hated life at that point. It was only after Aegis introduced her to a whole new world that she had found a reason to go on living.

She had loved him like a brother, and was ashamed that she hadn't taken the time to properly mourn him yet. By avoiding it, she felt like she was defiling his memory. She had spoken at the ceremony in the garden, and she had even taken the time to attend the burial at Arlington, but she still hadn't actually stopped to grieve. Even at the service, she had been doing what Alex had taught her to do, to plan their next move. Of course, at the time she had doubted that she would be placed in charge of it.

She worried that she would fail Alex. Sparrow had told her to finish it, but she doubted she could. She couldn't help but feel Diamond's trust in her was misplaced.

The artifact on her arm picked up the two people approaching her from behind. Even with her eyes closed, it had continued to track everyone on the level; but when the two moved toward her, it immediately targeted them, and scrolled information about them across her vision. Even with her eyes closed, they got no rest. If the two had been armed, the artifact would have already deployed counter measures. Envoy wondered if the artifact's responses were its own, or if it had adapted to her military bearing; always alert, always ready.

"Excuse me," said Dreah.

Envoy turned to Dreah. Q-Zone stood quietly behind her. *Great*, thought Envoy, *I am so not in the mood to deal with him.*

"Yes?" she replied.

"I'm sorry to bother you, Latisha. I'm sure you are planning for tomorrow, but Davin has something he would like to talk to you about."

Envoy looked from Dreah to Q-Zone. As he approached, Dreah turned and walked toward the common area and out of earshot.

"What is it, Q?" asked Envoy. She didn't bother to hide the irritation she was feeling.

"Listen," he said slowly, "I've been talking to some of the others, and I'd like to ask you why you didn't choose me for the mission tomorrow."

Envoy replied, "There were plenty of qualified people to choose from, and no one should be discussing a top secret mission with you."

"I know that, and please don't ask me who it was because I won't rat on them. But I do want to talk to you about it."

Envoy knew it was the twins. Q-Zone and Duo spent a lot of down time together. She suspected that time had even led Q-Zone to develop strong feelings for Kandi; of course he would deny them even to himself. Given Kandi's preference in partners, he would only be headed for heartbreak anyway. Given his womanizing past, he would probably deserve it. It was the thing Envoy disliked most about him, even more than his showboating. Since it wasn't her place to be the moral compass of everyone's life, she kept her opinion to herself.

She turned back to the shaft and leaned against the glass. She didn't bother asking herself what Aegis would do because his thoughts on the kid were well known. As she turned back to Q-Zone, he spoke up before she could say anything.

"Look, I know Aegis didn't think much of me, and God knows I've given him plenty of reason not to. I showboat and I'm not much of a team player, but I'd really like for you to give me a shot at this. This is real, Envoy. I mean, I've faced super villains before but it was just for the camera. This is real save-the-world stuff. I want to be a part of it. Aegis would just send me away without even hearing me out. But Dreah says it is your decision."

He was right. She wasn't Aegis. If she tried to make every decision based on what he would do, she would get someone killed. It wasn't how Aegis had taught her to be a leader, and it wasn't what he would have wanted her to do. He would expect her to go with her gut, to make her own choices. She had done so when she confided in Sparrow; and despite his disappearance, she was sure she had been right.

She turned back to the shaft and closed her eyes. The wind washed over her again. Aegis had loved to stand on the edge of the shaft. He claimed the wind relaxed him. The smells of the garden below cleared his mind and helped him make tough decisions. It didn't work for her.

Without turning to face him, Envoy said, "No one can deny your power, Q. But it takes much more than sheer power when you are out there. Your showboating may work for the paparazzi and your fans, but it didn't work for Aegis, and it won't work for me."

"Yes, ma'am," said Q-Zone. He bowed his head and slowly turned away. He started toward the common area.

Still without turning to him, Envoy continued, "You get one shot."

Q-Zone turned to face her. A grin spread across his face.

"If you mess it up, don't bother asking me for another one. I don't care how much Mr. Diamond pays you. Get with Duo, and tell them I sent you." She opened her eyes and turned to face him. "They can brief you, if there is anything they haven't already told you. We'll see how it goes."

"You won't regret this, Envoy," said Q-Zone. He turned and ran for the common area. "You'll see, you won't regret it!"

Envoy followed him around the shaft with her eyes. He kissed Dreah on the cheek and then ran off to find the twins. Dreah turned to Envoy and smiled.

*I guess I'm not Aegis*, she said to herself. *I wonder what Mr. Diamond and Meta-man will say now. They'll probably revoke my leadership position.*

Turning, she headed for a t-port as she accessed her sidekick through her arm. The shaft may have been enough for Aegis, but it wasn't enough for her. She needed to get out of the Citadel, but first she needed to see someone. After that, she could find some solace among the rings of Saturn.

Dealing with Kahori would be tricky. Like everyone, Envoy loved Gemini; but she hated the very idea of having to deal with the young girl's indiscretions. Until now, the duty had always fallen to Aegis or Fluxstone. Aegis was gone, and Fluxstone was emotionally compromised, that left her. Unfortunately, all she had to work with were her suspicions, and Gemini would know that. It would be tough because the girl was a master manipulator. After all, she had the best teacher. Nevertheless, the girl needed to be made aware of the consequences of her actions. There was already a divide in the team over Sparrow, and Gemini's involvement stood to widen that division. Secrets had a way of doing that. People kept them for their own gain or to protect others; but in the end, they always had the same effect. They caused hurt. Envoy didn't know exactly what was going on, but she feared Gemini knew more about Sparrow's disappearance than she was saying.

\* \*

"Status," asked Diamond from behind his command console.

"Status green," replied Lady Gemini from his right. She was excited that Envoy had requested her to run operations, and it showed in her voice. She felt disappointed about not being able to remain in contact with Sparrow, but she was also giddy over her position in the command center. Envoy had not been very happy with her.

"Green," said Jonesy from the left station. As usual, he was running several scientific simulations on his console at the same time.

"Green," said Curtis from the central console. Curtis was a man who always focused on the task before him like he was obsessed. Like Butch, he was one of the few in the Citadel that wasn't actually a meta-human. He didn't even carry the meta-gene, but he showed more determination and dedication than most. Diamond had nearly recruited him while he was still in the FBI academy. However, he had delayed the recruitment long enough to allow Curtis to become entrenched fully in the FBI and to have the opportunity to build a long list of contacts first. Now Curtis used those contacts to the fullest in support of Diamond's agenda.

Moving back and forth between the consoles, Clara didn't respond but she did give thumbs up and smiled at Diamond. Her eyes sparkled brightly in the dimly lit room.

Diamond taped his screen and pulled up Clara's latest log. Beside it he opened a report by Maria and scanned for her thoughts on Sparrow. There was still no sign of him, and it concerned Diamond. Dreah had continued to insist that he would return, and after analyzing the pros and cons, Maria agreed with her; but Diamond was beginning to doubt them both. He hated the thought of losing Sparrow. His skills were too useful. Perhaps the thing that bugged him the most was the loss of control. For years, he had dealt with people who possessed the power of gods, and he had stared down world leaders with their fingers on the atomic button; but now, somehow, a lone man had bested him and he couldn't explain how.

Forcing his thoughts away from Sparrow, he said, "Gemini, as soon as the team is in position, I want to know."

Gemini just smiled at her father's request. Of course it was unnecessary. She knew her job and she would do it right. A small portion of her even hoped something would go wrong so that she would have the opportunity to shine. Envoy's recommendation would go a long way to earning her a position on a field team.

After several minutes, Gemini's console lit up as all teams checked in. "Location of Austin is confirmed, and all teams are in place. Awaiting go status."

"The operation is a go, Lady Gemini," replied Diamond. Footsteps behind him caused him to turn to see Dreah enter the center. Without a word she moved across the catwalk and sat down on a cushion on the floor. It was rare she joined him in the command center, but it was comforting too. Her presence always told him he was doing the right thing.

"Alpha Team, you are a go for extraction. Good luck guys," said Lady Gemini over the commlink

\* \*

"You heard the lady, folks. Let's go," said Envoy to those gathered around her.

Together they waited for the doors of the *Egress* to cycle. After a few moments, Envoy began to wonder what was taking Butch so long since he had reportedly been in position for several minutes. She was about to radio him when the pod bay began spinning. The inner door to the *Egress* popped, and Butch appeared through it.

Butch bowed and said, "Welcome aboard, folks."

After everyone entered the pod, the doors cycled again. When the outer door opened, the team stepped out onto a helicopter pad on the roof of a downtown Denver high-rise. The sun would set in just over an hour and the sky was painted orange. Q-Zone waved to Envoy as the *Egress* lifted off the pad and rose skyward. If something went wrong with the extraction, the ship would be safely out of range.

"The capitol building is southeast of here," said Envoy as she pointed in the direction of the building. "Austin is engaged in a meeting to discuss his run for governor. It's late so the building will be empty, and the streets are starting to clear for the evening. Civilian contact will be minimal. You all know your parts, so let's do this right. Control, this is Envoy, status green."

"Roger," replied Lady Gemini.

Shadow Spirit cloaked them all with invisibility and then wrapped his shadows around them. As the cold emptiness of his dimensional slide took effect, the whole team was moved to a park adjacent to the capitol building.

As they arrived, a jogger shuddered and stepped away from a darkening shadow beneath a tree. He glared at it, but he was unable to see the team concealed within it. Shuddering, he jogged off, but he just couldn't help but glance over his shoulder twice before disappearing around a bend in the path.

Dawn looked to Envoy for confirmation, and Envoy nodded.

Dawn closed her eyes and reached out to place her hand on Maverick's back.

"That's it little lady, rub a little lower, lower, deeper baby. I like it hard."

Dawn frowned at his comment, and reached deep into his mind with hers. Slowly, she began to pull at his senses.

Dawn had taken an instant dislike to Maverick at yesterday's meeting; and after hearing how he had flirted with Dusk, she had been disgusted with them both. Her sister's chief motivation was to make life as miserable as she could. Their condition was well known to the members of DSS, and Diamond had put strict rules in place to protect them both. Dawn had no doubt that Maverick knew she shared her body with Dusk; yet, he had persisted in meeting up with Dusk afterward. Waking up the next morning next to him would have left Dawn feeling violated. Before DSS, she had come to know the feeling well. Thankfully, Diamond had found a way to keep the man away from her.

Maverick's peripheral vision blurred the deeper Dawn dug into his mind. The blur collapsed until it consumed his entire view. Sounds that reached him grew muffled, and soon fell into complete silence. Suddenly, his vision cleared and his ears popped. He could see every blade of grass on the ground, and hear the rustle of every leaf in the tree over him. He could count the threads crisscrossing his shirt simply from the feel of it against his flesh. He could hear the soft conversations of people all the way across the park.

Every living thing had an aura surrounding it. Even the metal artifact on Envoy's arm had an aura. One moment it matched Envoy's bright royal blue aura, and the next it was dark red. It made him curious, but he turned his attention away from it and to the rest of the world. Anything not living that had been recently touched by someone had the person's aura impressed upon it. The auras were different colors; some were dark while others were bright. Some moved and sparkled, while others were flat.

Dawn's aura was a white halo that twinkled with bursts of color. Its brightness blinded him. A muddy orange raced across his body like fire. He didn't know what it meant, but it made him smile. On a whim, he turned to look for Shadow Spirit. He scratched his head when he saw the man's aura was the blackest of all, and it lay against his skin like death. It crawled over the man with a life of its own. For the first time in a very long time, Maverick shuddered with fear.

Dawn could now hear what Maverick heard and see through his eyes. As she focused on him, she drifted slowly from the ground to float a few inches above the grassy park.

"That's kind of kinky, you know," said Maverick as he reached down and scratched his crotch.

Dawn cringed.

"Do you always see the world like this? I think it'd give me a headache. Can I turn it off?"

"Cut it, Maverick. Get moving. Don't forget that out there you won't be under the Spirit's invisibly."

"Roger that, leader lady," said Maverick as he looked at the Spirit again. "I don't need it anyway, and I don't think I want it anymore."

Maverick saluted Envoy and began falling over backward. Just before he hit the ground he disappeared, and instantly reappeared in a tree overlooking a large window of the capitol building.

Maverick sat perched in the tree for only a moment before spotting a safe spot inside the building. For a moment, he considered another destination. In his mind, he pictured a sunny beach he knew on the coast of New Zealand where the surf always rolled in off an ocean of deep blue. The sun would set in the distance, and he would relax under a swaying umbrella. It was so secluded he wouldn't even know when the world ended.

In a blink, his actions would tell Diamond and Meta-man that he didn't care about saving the world. He had already saved it numerous times before, and he doubted he would feel any better about it this time around.

The world didn't care either. It never had, and no matter what he or others like him did, it never would. It would just put itself right back on the brink of destruction again. The threat of annihilation never changed anything. The greedy continued to steal. The selfish continued to put their needs above others. The violent continued to kill those weaker than themselves. The hungry went unfed. The sick died while the ability to save them rested in the pockets of the rich.

Maverick often felt like pushing the reset button would be a good thing. Tucked away in their cities, the rich and powerful would die. The lowly and meek would inherit the earth. Money would be worthless, and power would shift.

"Maverick, what's the hold up?"

Envoy's voice broke his fantasy. *Screw you*, he thought. "Nothing," he said.

An instant later, he squatted behind a desk inside the building.

*I'd just miss all the fun on that damn beach anyway*, Maverick thought. If the city of Denver blew up without him, he would never forgive himself for missing it. He had never experienced the destruction of an entire city before. *It's going to be the biggest rush of my life.*

"So tell me cutie pie, is this as good for you as it is for me?" whispered Maverick. To his disappointment Dawn didn't respond.

Maverick teleported three more times. He paused when he discovered a tall red headed woman in one of the offices. He crouched silently behind a counter and watched her as she picked up her belongings to leave. Lingering longer than he needed to, he watched the sway of her hips as she left the room.

Finally he was left kneeling just outside the door to Austin's office. He could hear voices coming from inside. He couldn't see the men, but he found that if he stared at the wall hard enough, he could see each man's aura imposed on it. The men were seated and facing each other. Briefly, Maverick wondered what the colors of their auras meant. He liked that his aura was darker than theirs.

"So how about a date once this is all over?" he whispered. "I've met your darker side, and I must say, the three of us could have the time of your life. Have you ever seen the skyline of Tokyo while submerged in a steamy hot tub with a half empty bottle of *otsurui shōchū*? I'll even spring for the room."

Again, Dawn didn't respond.

Creeping up next to the door, Maverick scanned the room around him. Except for him, it was empty. Since it was already late in the day, the people who worked in the building had already gone home.

*Last chance*, he thought. *Just blink and enjoy the sun and sand.* He smiled and was just about to go through with the idea, when he suddenly thought of Dreah. She scowled disapprovingly. *Damn*, he cursed.

Dreah was the only person whose approval he actually sought. After the great fire of London, she had been so mad at him that she hadn't spoken to him for thirty years. It had been the longest thirty years of his life. He didn't love Dreah, and never fooled himself into thinking she could love him, but she did make him long for someone to love. Four hundred years was a long time to spend alone.

Maverick leaned down and slid a small mirror under the door. He could have teleported into the room blind, but without knowing the room's layout, his destination would have been a guess and possibly ruined his moment. He was looking forward to seeing the shock on their faces. If he appeared behind them, he wouldn't get to enjoy it.

"Last chance, sweetheart. I may just die here, you know. You wouldn't want me to suffer without knowing that I do it for you, would you?"

Dawn didn't respond.

The office was elaborate. Rich wood paneling lined the walls and there was a small fireplace on the right wall. Along the left, a large window stretched from floor to ceiling for nearly the whole length of the wall. It had a fantastic view of Denver's darkening skyline. A large bookshelf filled most of the wall behind Austin. A large painting of a prairie with roaming buffalo and a flock of birds dominated one wall. Austin sat behind the dark wood desk, and his guest sat in a chair across from him.

"If you are still listening, tell the bossy lady the target is present." Maverick retracted his mirror and folded it up before tucking it inside his vest. "I've run through the building. It's deserted. I'm a go for Austin in, three...two...one..."

An instant later Maverick appeared inside the room.

Austin was startled by Maverick's appearance and his voice caught in his throat. The man he was speaking with jerked back from the desk and dropped a glass he was holding. Perched on the desk between them, Maverick paused for a moment to allow the drama of the moment to engulf the two men. The looks on their faces had been worth it.

"Daddy's home," he mocked.

"Who the hell are you?" demanded Austin.

Maverick grinned at Austin, and then kicked the second man across his jaw. He was hurtled from his chair and sent sprawling across the floor. Spinning, Maverick pulled a large knife and squatted on the desk to face Austin.

"Who are you?" screamed Austin for a second time.

"Doesn't matter little man. Are you ready to ride the wind?" Maverick's grin deepened and his eyes sparkled with malevolence. "I promise to make it as uncomfortable as possible."

Maverick reached out for Austin, and the man's aura shifted. It went from flaring to boiling, the color darkened to black

Envoy suddenly screamed in his ear, "Abort! Maverick, abort..."

Austin's eyes darkened to match his aura, and his hand shot out to grab Maverick around the throat. Maverick grinned.

"That a boy," he said.

The rest of Envoy's message was lost as Maverick's senses reached across space and he jumped. Immediately, pain ripped through his abdomen. Maverick's scream was lost across the empty void between the office and his destination. The world went black.

\* \*

"Envoy stop him!" screamed Dawn to the others as she tried to pull back from Maverick. "Something's wrong!"

"Abort! Maverick, abort! I repeat abort!" screamed Envoy into her commlink. An instant later she was gone from the shadows under the tree and hanging over the capitol building.

Dawn felt a wave of horror as Austin's aura pulled and sucked at her. A wave of nausea passed over her as she spiraled down into the void surrounding him. When Maverick attempted to teleport, Austin's aura pulled on his power and swallowed it up instantly. Pain shot through Dawn's body. Instead of the tingle she had felt when Maverick had teleported earlier, she felt as if she were being pulled in two.

"Aaarghh!" screamed Dawn as she wrapped her arms around herself and collapsed.

Thunder rolled across the city, causing Envoy to cringe. Paragon flexed his wings, and he took to the air to chase after her. As he neared her, a glow spread from his sword. It flashed and he was instantly wearing his gleaming armor. His sword blazed with the fire of the setting sun. Meta-man cleared the distance almost as quickly as Envoy had. He dove toward the building. Wavefront briefly knelt over Dawn. Once he was satisfied that she was only unconscious, he ran after the others.

As he dodged a car, Wavefront yelled, "Dawn is down, but stable!"

"Roger," replied Lady Gemini.

"Ouch," moaned Maverick over the commlink. "Bad news, guys. I don't have Austin, and I feel like I left my intestines back in his office!"

"We have an Omega event!" screamed Jonesy over the commlink. "We have energy spikes over Denver. We have an Omega event!"

*Boom!*

The side of the building exploded outward. Envoy dodged the debris, and her force field protected her from the fireball. Meta-man also dodged the debris, but knowing his body would quickly adapt, he plunged headlong into the fireball. Paragon flexed his wings, and pulled back to avoid being singed.

A strong gale sprung up, chased across the city by more thunder. Darkness began to spread over the city as clouds appeared out of the clear evening. They twisted in on themselves in a fight for dominance. Churned up by the chaos, purple lightning flashed between them before being thrust downward to slice through the towering steel and glass structures of the city. Windows exploded and showered the citizens far below with shards of death. Traffic screeched to a halt as distracted drivers collided with whatever had the misfortune to be in their path. Lights flickered and died as power across the city was disrupted by the turmoil.

People fought the buffeting winds, and turned their eyes upward to gaze at the death forming over them. Panic instantly filled them. Mothers pulled frightened children to them, and their hearts sank with despair. Panic stricken, men turned to flee only to collide with others fleeing in the opposite direction.

\* \*

"Maverick, repeat extraction. I say again, repeat extraction," said Lady Gemini over the commlink.

As Meta-man landed, Austin turned to face him. His eyes were pools of total darkness. The sight caused Meta-man to hesitate. Austin raised his hand, flexed his fingers, and a wave of force rippled through the air to strike the hero.

*Whoosh!*

Meta-man's body instantly began to adjust to the attack, but he was pushed backward into a wall. He fought against the wave, and slowly stepped away from the wall as it collapsed from the force. Meta-man took another step toward Austin. Feeling like he was treading through water, he took another step, and then another. By the time he reached Austin, his body had fully adapted to the force and it was no more powerful to him than a slight breeze.

"We are not here to harm you! Stand down!" screamed Meta-man over the sound of the building ripping and shredding around him. Dark energy flaring from Austin's eyes was his only response.

*Wham!*

Paragon slammed into Austin. The force wave died as Austin was flung backward to crash into a wall.

Paragon flexed his wings, and pulled up to hover over Meta-man. The clouds pulled Paragon's eyes off Austin and the hero tilted his head back to peer through the shattered roof at them. He felt pity for the people of the city. Like them, he could feel the intense fear the clouds projected into the city. However, unlike the people of Denver decades of facing the vilest creatures Hell had to offer had made Paragon immune to fear. It failed to paralyze his muscles or muddle his mind. Looking back at Austin, he flexed his wings again and landed next to Meta-man.

\* \*

Envoy watched through the side of the shattered building. Her heart pounded against her chest and her breathing came in short gasps. Below her, people were fleeing in all directions as the winds worked to rip them from their feet and to hurl them to the ground.

*Crack!*

Envoy spun to see the crown of a massive tree ripped from its fractured trunk. The twisting mass of limbs hurtled toward a crowd of people taking shelter in the entrance of a building. The frightened people had no direction to flee in to avoid the crushing death bearing down on them.

*Skisss!*

Energy leaped from Envoy's extended arm. The tree was disintegrated, and only a few leaves reached the terrified people.

\* \*

Shadow Spirit reached out and pulled himself through Envoy's shadow. An instant later he was floating beneath her. He descended slowly into the building, ignoring the weight of the fear pressing down from above.

\* \*

As Wavefront neared the building, he glanced at the darkening sky overhead, and felt a wave of fear strike him. He staggered and immediately his eyes glowed as he shifted them across the visible and invisible spectrum. The clouds became a mass of colors as he tried to read their energy patterns.

"Guys, we got a problem! This thing is growing fast!"

\* \*

"It's growing faster than with Paris," said Edmond from the floor of the operations center. He turned toward the video wall and punched buttons on his sidekick. A satellite image of Denver showing hurricane like clouds swirling over the city appeared. Increasing wind speeds and dropping temperature readings scrolled across the bottom of the image. Calculations raced through his mind, and when he finished counting the final numbers on his fingers, he turned to face Diamond. "At this rate we have less than two minutes before the final event."

Diamond didn't voice his frustration over the prediction.

Jonesy struggled to gather all the data pouring in from the satellites and from Wavefront. Curtis tracked the local communications of the Denver police and rescue squads scrambling to respond to a disaster that was way beyond anything they could handle. Numbers of estimated dead spiked as he entered Edmond's calculations into the computer. Lady Gemini struggled to track the field team.

\* \*

Inside the building, the flickering lights caused deep shadows to dance menacingly. As Shadow Spirit floated down next to them, Paragon and Meta-man watched Austin climb out of the hole in the wall. Shadow Spirit's eyes glowed red, and the shadows of the room darkened further. When he extended his arm toward Austin, the man's shadow began to move independent of him. Red eyes appeared in the animated shadow and a fanged mouth silently screamed. With elongated claws, it reached up and pulled itself up Austin's legs. It wrapped around his torso and attempted to restrain him.

As Austin stepped toward the heroes, the floorboards where the shadow touched them buckled and splintered. He convulsed, and a flare erupted from his chest. As it streaked toward the heroes, it split into three separate flares.

As Meta-man dodged the first flare, Paragon swung his sword at the second. The flare was deflected, but singed the hero's face. Shadow Spirit's form blurred and became insubstantial just before the flare sliced through him. Pain seared him. He stifled a scream, but lost control of Austin's shadow. The shadow's red eyes faded and it slithered back to the floor at Austin's feet.

"We have flares," said Envoy as she dove for the building. Instantly, the flare that had passed through Shadow Spirit targeted her. Envoy dodged to the right and felt the heat of the flare on her leg when it deflected off her force field. Pouring more power into her protection, Envoy pulled up in front of Austin.

*Skisss!*

Energy rushed from Envoy's hand to engulf Austin. He staggered under the assault, but then stepped forward. Envoy doubled the energy output, but Austin simply held up his hand, and released an assault of his own that clashed violently with Envoy's. The furniture around them burst into flames as Envoy struggled to control the inferno flowing between the two.

*Swoosh!*

A flare struck Envoy from behind. Pain sliced through her back as the flare deflected off her force field. The distraction unleashed Austin's energy against her.

*Boom!*

Shattering what remained of the roof, Envoy hurtled from the building.

Having waited for an opening, Meta-man dodged and rolled toward Austin. A flare pressed down on him, but Meta-man sidestepped and allowed the flare to strike Austin.

Austin ignored the flare as it passed harmlessly through his body.

Meta-man didn't bother to curse his luck. Instead, he swung at Austin. Austin caught his hand, and with massive strength squeezed.

Meta-man's knuckles buckled and cracked. He grunted against the pain.

With his other hand, Austin grabbed Meta-man by the neck and squeezed. White spots danced across the hero's vision as his breathing and blood flow were cut off. His body began to adapt to the attack, but he felt himself growing weaker and dropped to his knees. As Austin's grip increased, Meta-man's grip grew weaker. Suddenly, a flare punched through Meta-man's shoulder. He screamed and lost his grip on Austin.

Paragon rolled to the side to avoid the flare when it erupted from Meta-man's back. Before he could recover to help the hero, a second flare streaked toward him.

Having recovered from the earlier attack, Shadow Spirit raised his hands again and Austin's shadow responded again. The red eyes appeared, and the shadow clawed at Austin's torso. It wrapped its elongated right arm around the man's neck and its legs around his torso. It extended its left arm out to a wall behind Austin and anchored itself to a large metal beam. The beam buckled, but held when Austin pulled against it.

A flare darted toward Shadow Spirit. He raised his arm toward it and conjured a solid wall of darkness between them. The flare struck the wall and the wall shattered. Chunks of dark matter were flung in every direction but faded to harmless shadow before striking anything. The pieces that struck Shadow Spirit were absorbed into this cloak. He dodged the flare.

Recovering, Shadow Spirit summoned a second wall of darkness. The wall was not solid and it sucked the heat from the room. Frost coated the floor where the wall touched it. Summoning the wall caused Shadow Spirit to shift some of his power away from Austin's shadow and it lost its grip on the metal girder. When the flare came around at Shadow Spirit, the wall blocked its path. The flare hissed and sputtered when it passed through the wall. Its momentum was visibly slowed by the wall's icy touch. Shadow Spirit lowered the wall's temperature further, and prepared for the flare's next pass.

"Maverick, attempt extraction again! We need a second extraction," commanded Lady Gemini.

"I'm working on it! Hold your panties," replied Maverick.

An instant later Maverick appeared next to Meta-man. Austin's black eyes turned on him as Maverick reached out to touch him. Maverick pictured his destination in his mind, but instead of jumping, he slammed head first into a brick wall. Stunned, Maverick staggered under the mental assault. Austin released Meta-man's arm and grabbed him around the throat.

Meta-man still struggled to break free, but found he was too weak. Even though his body had adjusted to the lack of oxygen and restricted blood flow, Austin's grip had drained his strength.

"Crap!" cursed Maverick. Austin tightened his grip and Maverick squirmed to break free. Choking, he gasped, "Screw you, buddy!" Pulling his sidearm, he shoved it in Austin's face.

*Blam! Blam! Blam!*

Maverick's sidearm echoed through the room as he worked to empty the magazine.

\* \*

Envoy reeled with dizziness. Stunned, she couldn't concentrate enough to fight against her momentum.

*Crash!*

The car buckled under the impact. Its windows shattered and glass pelted her before being swept up by the wind. Shaking the confusion from her head, Envoy fought through the pain in her back and pulled herself from the wreckage.

She was relieved to find the car had been empty, but was stung by pity when her eyes fell on the car next to her. Pressed against the car's backseat window was the face of a small child. Tears streamed down the little girl's cheeks, and her screams were lost to the howl of the wind. A large mailbox had smashed through the car's front window, crushing the girl's mother.

Looking around her, Envoy realized the little girl wasn't the only one in distress. There were numerous car accidents with obvious injuries. The fronts of several buildings were shattered and a fire raged on the second floor of one. The strong wind carried an elderly man along against his will. A young mother screamed as strong winds ripped her baby carriage from her hands to slam it against a tree. A dog strained against the leash that held it tied to a lamppost.

Envoy looked skyward and instantly wished she hadn't. As a dark vortex sank into the cloud, fear gripped her. Every moment of fright she had ever experienced rose up and overpowered her at that very moment. She staggered under the assault and gripped the car to keep from collapsing. Refusing to look up at the cloud again, she too several deep breaths. Feeling guilty, but knowing she was needed elsewhere, she leaped into the air and darted back toward the battle. Despite the horror below her, she kept her eyes locked on the ground, refusing to look up again.

\* \*

"Aaaiiiee!" Fluxstone's shout carried above the wind as she leaped into the building and struck Austin with enough force to fling him through several walls. The floor where she landed splintered and threatened to dump them all into the lower levels.

Freed from Austin's grip, Meta-man and Maverick collapsed to the floor. Fluxstone reached down and pulled Meta-man to his feet. Maverick waved her off and rubbed his sore throat.

Behind them, Paragon leaped after a flare, and it bounced off his sword. He stepped before a second flare and kept it from attacking the recovering heroes.

"I don't know where you came from but I'm glad you are here!" Meta-man's shoulder was still numb, but his body had already healed most of the damage. Rubbing the hand Austin had crushed, he felt the bones reset. Reaching out with his aura, he pulled on Fluxstone's enhanced density and felt his own weight and strength double.

Her heart set on revenge, Fluxstone charge off after Austin. The floor of the building cracked and buckled as Meta-man raced after her.

As Austin rose to his feet, Fluxstone brought both fists down on him, and he was slammed back to the floor. Meta-man immediately followed up her attack and crushed him through the floor. They plummeted into the lower level of the building. Fluxstone leaped through the hole to land on Austin.

Still rubbing his throat, Maverick tossed his useless gun over his shoulder. His voice cracked as he grumbled, "Showoffs."

\* \*

Paragon dodged a flare as Shadow Spirit threw a wall of darkness before it. The flare hissed as it passed through the cold shadow.

"They are slowed by my touch." Shadow Spirit hissed over the howl of the wind.

"Aye!" said Paragon as he swung his sword at a second flare. The flare bounced off the sword's metal blade. "Our enemy isn't mindless either! You need bait!"

Paragon leaped forward and charged the flare. He swung at it and then darted after it when it deflected off his blade. As he had hoped, a second flare dove for him. Shadow Spirit threw up a wall in front of it. The flare plunged into the darkness and hissed.

"Yyyyaaa!" screamed Paragon as he leaped after the flare. His sword cleaved it in two and it fizzled before disappearing altogether.

* *

Her muscles powered by her enhanced density, Fluxstone pounded Austin and he staggered backward with each blow.

"Die!" She screamed. Rage drove her forward, and her attacks were relentless. Even without the help of Meta-man, Austin would have been hard pressed to find an opening to counterattack. Together, the two heroes kept him on the defensive, but their attacks began to have less and less effect on him. Fluxstone could feel her density decreasing with each attack but images of Aegis lying dead drove her forward.

"Aargh!" she screamed as she struck Austin and pain lanced through her hand. She staggered backward clutching the hand to her.

Despite the warning, Meta-man pressed his own attack. He struck two more times before his arm jolted from a blow, and he felt the bones in it break.

"Damn!" he cursed.

Given a moment to recover, Austin lashed out at Meta-man. The blow sent him hurtling backward. Office furniture was scattered as the hero sailed across the room and through a wall. Austin followed up by swinging wildly at Fluxstone. She barely dodged the swing.

"Austin is leeching our strength from us!" shouted Meta-man into his commlink as he tore himself free from the wall. "He is leeching through contact!"

"Leech this!" snarled Fluxstone as she dropped her density far below normal and shoved her incorporeal fist into Austin's chest.

"Aaaarrggggghhhhh!" Austin screamed.

Fluxstone grabbed the back of his head with her free hand and shoved her hand even deeper into his torso. Her incorporeal hand tore at his internal organs, driving Austin to his knees.

\* \*

Envoy poured all her energy into her force field and projected it outward just in time to deflect a flare from Paragon's vulnerable back.

"Thanks!" screamed Paragon as he swung his sword at the second flare. He missed. "Fluxstone is here!"

Confused, Envoy spun to face the direction she had last seen Austin. The building was shredded and there was a large hole in the floor. "She's grounded!" Paragon didn't respond. "Control, did you copy last? Fluxstone is on scene!"

Suddenly, a flare darted away from the heroes and down the hole.

"I'm on it!" Envoy yelled as she flew after it.

Paragon turned on the final flare. Shadow Spirit floated over his shoulder ready to slow it with a wall of darkness. Together, light and darkness waited while their elusive enemy circled them.

\* \*

"Copy last, Envoy. She and Meta-man are engaged with Austin two floors beneath you." Lady Gemini had already hacked Fluxstone's commlink. Her bio-signs and video link were displayed on the monitor wall next to the others.

Lady Gemini's hands adjusted her monitor controls without her having to take her eyes off the imaging wall. When a face appeared in Dawn's camera, she reacted immediately. "Maverick, Dawn is facing civilian danger. Port her to safety immediately. Do not engage civilians. Wavefront, shift your stance ten yards to your right. That street lamp is interfering with the image."

"But I'll miss all the fun," complained Maverick. His camera image showed him taking pot shots at the final flare with his shotgun, while he also flung furniture at it.

"Now!" commanded Lady Gemini as she turned her attention to the fight with Austin. After a moment she allowed herself a quick glance at Dawn's video feed, and found that despite his complaint, Maverick was already kneeling over her. He held the civilians at gunpoint.

Glancing again at the combat with Austin, she said, "Fluxstone!

Meta-man! Alternate your attacks. Don't give him time to sap your strength."

\*   \*

Wavefront felt a pang of guilt as the throes of battle issued over the commlink. He knew his force field would be strong enough to protect the others, and he desperately wanted to help; but once they heard Edmond's idea, Envoy and Diamond had insisted that he follow through with it.

Reaching behind his ear, Wavefront taped a small electrode. He then punched several buttons on his sidekick and looked up at the sky again. He swallowed his fear as his eyes shifted across several spectrums of light to focus on the cloud mass. He had tried looking at the cloud without using his powers, but the fear the cloud generated had nearly driven him to his knees. Through his enhanced vision, he didn't see the cloud but instead saw an orchestra of colors swirling and cascading around a center that was so dark he could only describe it as a black hole. The fear emanated from that hole, but through his enhanced vision he could tolerate it.

*Crash!*

Wavefront took his eyes off the cloud and glanced behind him. A group of angry people faced him. Each of them had some kind of weapon and the leader held a bottle with a piece of flaming cloth sticking out of its neck. The wind dangerously whipped the fire around the man's exposed hand. One guy held the end of a broken bottle. He had struck Wavefront's shield with it.

"This is your fault!" screamed the mob's leader. "Your kind has brought this disaster on us!"

"Please, sir!" Wavefront screamed back over the howl of the wind. "We are trying to stop it! Please stand aside! Let us do our jobs!"

The man hurled the bottle in his hand against Wavefront's force field. It burst into a wave of fire that burned harmlessly against the energy field. The force of the wind quickly blew it out. "Sorry," muttered Wavefront as he turned his attention back to the readings on his sidekick. The man responded by snatching a large club from the man next to him and striking at Wavefront. The blow bounced harmlessly off the force field, Wavefront ignored him.

As the chaos surrounding him intensified, Wavefront concentrated on his work. Most of the people struggled to flee the terror of the cloud, but the crowded streets and wrecked cars prevented their escape. A few, like the man attacking him, lashed out with anger. They didn't understand what was happening, and people often responded to confusion with anger. They feared the death that was quickly approaching. Wavefront understood their anger. He understood their fear. He just wished there was something he could do about it.

Reaching behind his ear again, he tapped the electrode again. Through the electrode, his sidekick recorded the images as he saw them and projected them directly to the Citadel. The mob continued to harass him with hurled rocks and clubs of metal and wood.

\* \*

Austin struggled to pull back from Fluxstone's grip, but she held on as she twisted and gouged at him with her incorporeal fist. A tingle spread up her arm that quickly turned into a sting. When she pressed her arm deeper into his chest, the sting changed to pain. She could feel her intangibility being drained from her. Her arm was becoming corporeal again. She had never become solid inside a solid object before, but she feared it would be messy. Even though the pain continued to intensify, she refused to pull her arm back.

Her grip on Austin began to slip as his body began to shift into an insubstantial state. Using her own power against her, Austin began to escape her grasp. When his body was nearly insubstantial and Fluxstone was nearly solid again, he focused his dark eyes on her.

*Fwssh!*

Energy engulfed Fluxstone, incinerating her clothing and stripping the flesh from her body.

"Aaaiiieeeee!" she screamed.

\* \*

On the video wall, Fluxstone's vital signs spiked.

Gemini's voice cracked with fear. "Back off, Fluxstone! Meta-man, help her! Back off, Fluxstone!"

Fluxstone's monitor flat-lined as her camera feed died.

Diamond jumped from his seat and stared at the wall. His eyes bored into the spot with Fluxstone's bio-monitor. Below him, his team worked frantically, but he didn't see them. Behind him, Dreah held her breath, but he didn't acknowledge her. Meta-man's video feed continued to display the events unfolding, but he refused to look at it. Instead, he focused on Fluxstone's feed. His vision blurred.

The spot rippled.

Startled, Diamond stepped back. Glancing around, he found that no one else had noticed. Looking back at the wall, he found that it had returned to normal. Fluxstone's vital signs were still not registering and Meta-man's feed was normal.

A wave of nausea forced him into his seat. When Dreah placed her hand on his shoulder, he looked around at her. She looked worried, but she had not seen the ripple in the wall.

\* \*

"Envoy! Fluxstone and Meta-man need back up!" pleaded Gemini.

"On my way!" replied Envoy as she fired a blast at the retreating flare. It was quick, and it didn't bother to avoid obstacles in its path. It simple bored through them and maintained a straight path. Envoy soon gave up trying to avoid them as well.

As Envoy rounded a corner, she found the flare charging at her. She barely had time to increase her force field as it impacted with her. She was slammed through the wall and the roof collapsed on her as the flare sped off after Austin again. Struggling to her feet, Envoy resumed the chase.

\* \*

Even though Fluxstone had thrown her arm up to shield her face, the heat of the enemy's blasts tore at her flesh. Desperate, she plunged her density deeper, and the pain from the assault eased. When she could think clearly again, she swung wildly at Austin, but her fists passed harmlessly through his intangible face.

Meta-man swung at Austin as well, but like Fluxstone his fists passed harmlessly through the man. Stepping forward, he plunged his arms into the man's body. As he had hoped, Austin automatically began to leach his enhanced density.

Fluxstone could feel Austin growing solid again. She continued to force herself to become denser and denser. As she did so, Austin became denser as well. Meta-man pulled back, and then lashed out with an attack. Austin staggered under the blow and lost his grip on Fluxstone. She dropped to roll away.

As Fluxstone escaped, Austin turned his energy on Meta-man. Meta-man's metal uniform was melted by the assault, but he ignored the pain and lashed out at Austin. His blow staggered the man again. A third blow drove Austin to his knees. Digging down, Meta-man swung an uppercut to Austin's chin that flung the man backward. He plowed a furrow along the room's ceiling before plunging through the far wall and out of the building. Concrete and asphalt exploded where he slammed into the street.

Meta-man jumped through the hole after Austin.

Fluxstone rose slowly to follow him. Her charred right arm hung limply.

*Swhoosh!*

"Aeeiieee!" Fluxstone screamed as a flare pierced her shoulder. She dropped to her knees, and slowly raised her head to see it circle her. Exhausted, she was barely able to hold her head high as the flare dove for her.

\* \*

Envoy cursed when she realized she had lost sight of the flare. Guessing it was chasing after Austin, she followed the devastation left by the ongoing battle. As she rounded a corner, she saw the flare bearing down on Fluxstone.

"Fluxstone!" Envoy screamed.

\* \*

Fluxstone watched through tear strained eyes as death streaked toward her. "Alex," she whispered as the flare fell upon her.

*Boom!*

The flare exploded against Meta-man's chest and slammed him into Fluxstone.

\* \*

The energy readings spiked and Wavefront had to shield his eyes from the intensity. A shaft of light erupted violently from the center of the vortex to plunge toward the ground.

*Ka-Boom!*

Austin disappeared in the shaft of light. The shaft immediately began to spew off balls of fire that ignited everything they touched. They bounced harmlessly off Wavefront's shield as he maintained his position next to the shaft.

\* \*

Envoy's blood ran cold as she watched her two friends flung across the room. As she reached the fallen heroes, Wavefront screamed across the commlink.

"Clear out! We have final moments!"

Envoy shifted Meta-man's unconscious body. His armored uniform was shredded and his chest had a black gaping wound where the flare had hit him. He was breathing and his wounds appeared to be healing. Under him, Envoy found Fluxstone. Her uniform had been nearly incinerated, exposing her numerous severe injuries. She was barely conscious. Blood flowed from her mouth and ears. The right side of her face had been seared by Austin's attack, and her hair was burned down to the scalp. When Fluxstone tried to rise, the pain caused her to collapse again.

"Emergency evac," ordered Lady Gemini. "Emergency evac!"

Envoy glanced after Austin. She could not see him in the shaft of light, but the flare that had struck Meta-man was circling the shaft. The force of the shaft kicked up rock and concrete. Wavefront stood in the danger zone, and the flare bounced off his force shield several times before plunging into the shaft itself.

They only had seconds before the wave of death spread across Denver. Dread for the two million people of the city drowned Envoy, and she couldn't shake the image of the small child in the car's window.

"We have to go," screamed Envoy over the link. "Shadow Spirit! Paragon! Fluxstone and Meta-man are down! I need you here!"

Moments later, Paragon appeared through the hole in the ceiling. He swooped down to land next to them. Shadow Spirit pulled himself and Maverick from Envoy's shadow. Maverick held Dawn in his arms. Paragon shouldered the unconscious Meta-man, and Envoy helped Fluxstone to her feet. The larger woman grunted heavily from her wounds.

"Do we really have to go?" asked Maverick. "The ultimate ride is about to begin."

"Where are you, Wavefront?" asked Envoy as she did her best to avoid hitting Maverick. Wavefront had disappeared from her view of the shaft.

"On my way," he replied.

"Wavefront, your location hasn't changed. What is wrong?" asked Lady Gemini.

There was a brief pause.

"Get out, mates," he finally replied. "I've got to get these readings."

"No way," said Envoy to Shadow Spirit.

An instant later, darkness closed in around them and they teleported next to Wavefront. The crowd that had surrounded the hero had dispersed when the shaft began spewing flares. The heroes were held back from the shaft by the blazing energy, but Wavefront stood under it taking his readings.

*Rruummmble!*

The ground quaked, and the roar of the wind nearly drowned Envoy out.

"Out now!" she ordered. She could feel the heat of the energy shaft through her force field, and did her best to ignore the fear pressing down on her.

Wavefront looked at her, and then at the sky. Reluctantly, he shook his head in agreement. "Okay, go," he said as he stepped over to the group.

As Shadow Spirit spread his shadows over them, Wavefront suddenly darted away from the group.

"Da..."

"...aamn," screamed Envoy as she completed the slide. "Spirit, get him. Get him now!"

"His protections will prevent me," replied the Spirit. "If he is aware of my attempt, he can resist."

"Damn!" screamed Envoy again.

\* \*

Diamond watched the monitors as the team materialized in the pod bay. In Denver, Wavefront circled the shaft. His sidekick continued to transmit the images he was seeing.

"Get him out now!" ordered Diamond.

"Spirit, get him out!" shouted Lady Gemini. Her voice cracked with panic.

"Wavefront's force field will prevent the slide!" replied Envoy.

Everyone watched in horror as the shaft of light pulsed and Wavefront continued circling it.

Suddenly, Maverick materialized in the air over Wavefront and tackled the reluctant hero. The two men struggled as flares spewing forth from the shaft rained around them. The energy shaft pulsed, and the wave of death rolled across the city. The monitors and the two men's commlinks went dead.

\* \*

"Oooooyaaaa!" Maverick screamed as he dumped Wavefront onto the pod bay floor. "What a ride! Let's do it again!" Despite his glee, Maverick was pale and sweating.

Envoy ignored him and sprinted over to Wavefront. He was cold to the touch. Rolling him over, she found his eyes were sunken and his lips blue. She pulled him up from the floor and held him close.

"Jack! Jack, can you hear me?" she pleaded.

After a moment, Jack's vacant eyes found hers and he whispered, "I felt it...I felt what Alex felt." His eyes fluttered and he passed out.

Paragon knelt beside them, and Envoy hugged Wavefront too her. Through her tears, she managed, "You big dolt! Don't ever do that to me again." Memory of the frightened child haunted her.

A team of scientists struggled not to disturb them as they prepared to return to Denver.

# CHAPTER 15
# THE AEGIS

The story had been playing all night. Denver, Colorado was dead. Sparrow stood by the door to the balcony and read the words scrolling across the bottom of the TV screen, *U.S. City Destroyed in an Event Similar to Paris, France.*

The Chinese reporter relating the story was in better control of her emotions than the American reporter had been with the story of Paris. Sparrow's Chinese was rusty but he was able to successfully follow her. She was calm and her voice never wavered as she relayed estimates of the dead. As with Paris, there were no dying. Either the victims had survived or they hadn't.

*"...While the actual cause of the incident is still unknown, officials are speculating that it is similar to, if not related to, the events of Paris. The incident begins with dark clouds swirling over the city. Unconfirmed reports from survivors of Paris described the clouds as alive. The clouds form a hurricane like formation over the center of the destruction."* The view on the screen shifted to show pictures of dark clouds circling over Paris and Denver. Instead of an eye or empty pocket of air in the center of each formation, there was a funnel shaped swirl of air that extended high into the atmosphere above the clouds. The clouds remained dark despite the sun shinning on them. *"These images, taken from satellite feeds over both cities, show the cloud formations as nearly identical. There is dangerous lightning and high winds associated with the phenomena."*

The image on the screen shifted again to show one of the clouds close up. Bright flashes of purple lightning could be seen flashing throughout the dark mass. *"Citizens are cautioned to remain calm and seek shelter underground..."*

Sparrow clicked the remote, and the channel on the TV changed. The images of the clouds were replaced with an image of an angry mob. The mob carried large signs condemning the government and Diamond Security Solutions. They chanted angrily and one of the demonstrators smashed the windshield of a parked car with a traffic sign.

*"...Protests continue on the streets of every major US city. This group, known as Citizens Against Meta-Humans, is calling for the immediate arrest of all members of Diamond Security Solutions. DSS is an international security agency owned and run by Samuel Diamond of Diamond Enterprises. Numerous employees of the firm were reportedly in Paris during and after the event that destroyed that city. This video footage, found on a victim's cell phone after the incident clearly shows members of Diamond Security Solutions at ground zero during the Denver incident..."*

A video of Wavefront surrounded by an angry mob began to play. Fire exploded on his force field, but he ignored it and focused on the clouds above them.

Sparrow clicked the remote again and the image shifted to show a panel of men and women. The screen focused on the man at the center of the table. *Senator Charles Fitmore, (D) Iowa*, appeared beneath his image.

*"...Clearly these people have some knowledge of what is going on! I demand that they step forward..."*

"But Senator, many of these people have stellar reputations!" The image shifted briefly to show the woman who had spoke. *Cindy Kerns, Correspondent, New York Times*, appeared beneath her name. The image quickly shifted back to Senator Fitmore.

*"That is no excuse! Millions of people are dead! These people are criminals!"*

"Now see here Senator, I personally know some of these people..."

"I don't care! Tell that to the victim's families!" The Senator rose from his seat and poked his finger at the screen twice before turning it on Cindy. *"I swear to personally see these people brought down! I will not..."*

Sparrow clicked off the TV. Turning, he walked out onto the balcony. In the distance, the sun highlighted the Halo Corp megastructure. With his eyes he traced the structure from the top of the tower, down the sloped sides, and to the street far below. On the streets, the effects of the destruction of Denver could be seen.

Like many other cities, the people were fleeing, and the streets were in gridlock. Many had no idea where they were going. Others were moving to smaller communities, or to open parks and forests. Those that didn't flee sought shelter underground. They hid in old bomb shelters, basements, or underground parking garages; anywhere that put concrete between them and the surface.

Looting had robbed the stores of canned foods and bottled water. Since no one had any idea how long the danger would last, or even where it would strike next, they grabbed what they could to hold out as long as possible.

Worldwide panic affected every city. World leaders did their best to calm their citizens, but fanatics still fueled the flames. The world was tearing itself apart.

The smell of fire pulled Sparrow's gaze from the street to a pillar of smoke in the distance. Sirens were responding to the location.

Sparrow hated to admit it, but the Denver incident was good timing for him at least. When word reached Hong Kong, panic immediately closed every government office and private business. Rioting filled the streets. From where he stood, he could see that many of the lights in the Halo Corp building were dark. A day before most of them had burned brightly.

With Diamond Justice at the center of the news reports, the team's members were the focus of attention. Many government officials were calling for Diamond's arrest, and others were threatening to freeze his assets around the world. The only contact Diamond allowed them was through his lawyers. Members of DSS in many parts of the world were under house arrest and their activities under tight scrutiny.

Sparrow doubted the pressure on Diamond's holdings had him locked down. If what Diamond had told him in the sherry room was true, he had planned for this incident long ago. He would have anticipated much of the response. There would be money stashed in places others wouldn't even begin to consider. Shutting down Diamond's operations would only be superficial.

Diamond also had numerous undercover operatives, and there wasn't much anyone could do to stop someone capable of bench-pressing a city bus from leaving his home if he really wanted to. Many of the world's meta-humans were just too powerful for the local governments to control. For a very long time, many of them had relied on Diamond and his team to that for them.

A large part of Sparrow wondered what had happened in Denver, and if anyone had been lost in the disaster. A short message from Gemini had indicated a team was on the ground, but he hadn't heard anything since.

Gemini's message had also indicated that Envoy was on to them. Sparrow had known from the beginning that she would be difficult to manipulate. She watched everyone with a critical eye. Unlike Fluxstone, her eye wasn't blinded by prejudice.

As the sun finished setting, Sparrow spun and walked quickly across the room. He snatched a large duffle bag off the couch and headed for the door.

*By the end of tonight, Envoy won't matter*, he told himself as he slipped out of the small apartment and into the dark hall.

\* \*

When the train finished passing, Sparrow pulled his mask down over his face and slipped along the wall to a metal ladder set into the concrete. Slinging a large backpack across his back, he quickly scaled it. At the top, the grate was locked. Bypassing the lock was simple, and moments later he crawled through the mega-structure's sub-levels.

Following the electrical schematics for the building, Sparrow quickly located the control panel he wanted. After bypassing the lock, he attached a soft blue probe to the internal circuits. The probe had no visible circuits or wiring and resembled a simple blue suction cup. The color was the same as the liquid light in the doorframes of the Citadel. It was designed to allow the sidekick to access the computer from a distance.

Adjusting his sidekick, he synchronized it with the building's computers. He hacked the building's security and pulled up the cameras and alarms. As he expected, the system didn't grant him access to the Halo Corp floors in the tower. That would be a stand-alone system, and he would need to hack it when he reached those floors.

Closing the panel he started across the room. He didn't bother removing the blue probe from the system. The probe would self-destruct in twenty-four hours, or sooner if he sent a command to it from the sidekick, so he had no fear of it being discovered.

Scaling a ladder, Sparrow removed a grate at the top and entered a crawl space. After pulling his night vision goggles down over his eyes, he crawled through the dark until he reached a grate protecting the other end. He paused and waited for the counter on the sidekick. When it turned green, he kicked the grate open and pulled himself into an elevator shaft. He pushed the grate back into place, and stepped safely aside as the security camera swung around to the grate again.

Using the sidekick as a guide, Sparrow dodged and maneuvered around the security of the building. It took him several hours to make his way through the massive structure, but it wasn't difficult. The security was no more advanced than any expensive home system. With the aid of the sidekick, it was child's play.

He avoided the business areas of the building to keep from having to deal with their individual systems. He doubted they would have been anymore difficult but he wanted to leave as little trace of his presence as possible.

Sparrow took time to study the structure as he went. It was impressive. Offering a false sense of security against the disasters of Denver and Paris, the city within a city had everything a person could want or need. The structure was clean and in excellent repair. Mechanical problems were fixed quickly. Damaged walls or structures were replaced. The building looked like it had been opened yesterday, but Sparrow knew it had stood completed for nearly fifteen years now.

At one point he looked down on a large courtyard that was five stories tall. Surrounding a garden with exotic trees and free flying birds was a perimeter of shops and businesses like any would expect to find on any Hong Kong street. Only the lack of graffiti and litter set it apart.

Despite its isolation, the building hadn't escaped the chaos permeating the city outside. It wasn't racked with sounds of warring rioters, but instead sat silent as a tomb. Shops were closed and people were missing from the courtyards and businesses. There was no sign of the panic that plagued the streets of the city.

Despite its attractions, Sparrow didn't like it. The structure lacked the diversity of a true city. He liked the way architecture changed from block to block as the cultures that inhabited them influenced it. The people of the mega-structure seemed more like caged animals that had been pulled from their true environment and forced to live without the spirit of life. He also didn't like the idea of big brother always being just over his shoulder. To the inhabitants it was security; to him it was a prison.

\* \*

After several hours, Sparrow finally reached the upper floors of the pyramid and entered the Halo tower. As he expected, security was much tighter. The guard stations weren't deserted and the alarms were of a much higher quality. The security cameras actually focused on vital spots and even overlapped in some cases. He had to slow his pace to successfully navigate through the area. When he reached the base of the top four floors, the sidekick no longer held any information about the security, and he was forced to risk exposure to gain access to the information.

Fingering his gun, Sparrow felt the urge to dispatch the three guards at the station below him. Leaving someone at his back still bothered him. An image of Dreah forced his hand away from the gun, and he settled in to wait patiently. An hour passed before he got a chance to act.

Two of the guards left the station to perform routine rounds and one guard remained behind to monitor their progress on the cameras. As silently as he could, Sparrow lowered himself into the hallway from the air duct. Using the shadows, he made his way up behind the guard. Ducking behind a potted plant, he crouched and waited.

After several minutes, the guard hadn't moved from the desk, and Sparrow could see on the monitors that the other two were finishing up their rounds. Slowly he removed a small laser pen from his vest. He flicked it across a window overlooking the city several times before it caught the guard's attention.

The guard glanced at the monitors and then rose to walk over to the window. Sparrow quickly slipped out of hiding. He placed a sidekick probe behind the computer, and then ducked back behind the plant.

The guard stood by the window for only a moment looking for the source of the light. When he didn't spot one, he turned back toward the desk. He glanced around the room before scratching his head in confusion and sitting back down before the monitors. Quietly, Sparrow returned to the air ducts.

\* \*

Hacking the guard's computer was only slightly more difficult than hacking the previous systems. The computer attempted to dump a virus into his sidekick, but the small computer automatically dealt with it. It flashed him a simple warning and then began to hack the system a second time. It eventually pulled up the cameras and alarms for the area. Comparing the images with Gemini's schematics, he settled on a secured area on the top floor, and began his climb up through the tower.

\* \*

Diamond needed sleep but continued to deny it to himself. Even without him telling her, Dreah would know, but it couldn't be avoided. A task lay before him that he had been putting off. It would not be pleasant.

He stopped and rubbed his forehead as he picked up a glass and downed the alcohol in it. His head throbbed. He could feel the pressure of each thump behind his eyes.

The operations center was dark except for the light generated by the video wall. It held hundreds of shifting images from all over the world. The Citadel's AI recorded, evaluated, and cataloged each one. When an image met specific criteria Diamond had preprogrammed the computer to search for, the image expanded to fill the center of the wall where he could personally review it before the AI catalogued it further.

Each video predicted a future more bleak than the last. Chaos continued to grow around the world. Bankrupting many companies and even some governments, the fallout from Paris had crashed the stock markets. Denver had devastated those that had survived. Governments had tried to control the damage, but had failed. Riots were rampant in the streets. Whole cities burned. Villains of all kind released mayhem on helpless victims. Police and meta-human operatives were overwhelmed.

Diamond's personnel holdings were specifically targeted. Some had been shut down completely. Some of his people were even in police custody. One clash with the US Army had left both sides of the conflict reeling. Even now an office building in Berlin burned. Before they could be completely evacuated, a mob had dragged his employees into the streets. Four were confirmed dead and six more were missing. None of them had been meta-human.

Standing over his console, he stared at a blinking light. Reluctantly, he reached out and hit it. The video wall shifted and a new image appeared in the center of the wall. The image had been sitting along the bottom row for the past several hours. It was of a large conference room with a table containing the seal of the United States engraved into it. *Awaiting Uplink,* flashed in large red letters across the image. He considered hacking the feed to view what was happening on the other end, but decided against it. There was technology capable of tracking the signal back to him, and he didn't want to risk it until he knew their exact intent. Besides, he had a safer way.

He focused his attention on the image of the room and committed it to his memory. He then closed his eyes and saw the image burned before his eyelids. Due to the pounding of his headache, it took him longer than he liked, but he was soon able to astrally project himself into the secure room in the top-secret underground bunker.

Diamond stood in a heavy fog. It was suspended over everything and blocked his vision beyond a few feet. Muffled and incoherent voices issued from the murky haze. Turning, he allowed his senses to search for the source of the interference. He found the mind without much effort, and instantly he was standing over a young woman seated at a small desk at the back of the room. He focused on her, and she materialized out of the fog.

Diamond recognized her immediately from all the media attention surrounding her employer. He knew she was a meta-human from the Citadel files, and he had expected to find her here.

Jocelyn Kempt was a mentalist, and in charge of the President's psychic security. She was currently using her abilities to cloak the room in secrecy. She was attempting to keep someone from doing just what he was about to do. Clairvoyance wasn't an uncommon meta-power, and all the governments took extra effort to prevent it from being used to spy on meeting of importance and to protect state secrets.

Diamond reached out with his mind and touched Kempt's to study her power level. She was powerful, very powerful. He smirked as he noted her meta-human classification was wrong. She was easily an orange threat level, but she was officially rated yellow-two. He had no doubt that she would be successful at keeping almost anyone from reading the President's thoughts; anyone that is, except him.

Turning away from Kempt, Diamond stepped toward the center of the room, and brushed past Kempt's defenses with no more effort than a fish needed to swim through water. The fog immediately cleared, and the invisible astral form of Diamond stood silently over the back of the President of the United States. Kempt was left completely unaware of his presence.

President Gabriella Sanora sat at the table with seven of her preferred advisors. Diamond knew each one personally. As for President Sanora, he had known her for most of her life. His hand had been in her political carrier from the start, and she wasn't the first person he had supported financially and publicly in a bid for President. Despite how he personally felt about her, this time his primary motivation had been to remove the previous President from office. Sanora had been a long shot, and he had felt she was not qualified to run the country in times of crisis, but others had convinced her to run for president anyway. When things got tough, many of them withdrew their support and threw her to the wolves. Faced with only the two possibilities, Diamond stepped up. For once he chose what should have been the losing side. Some would say she owed him for that, but she would say she owed the people.

"...how horrible these disasters are." The President leaned forward and glanced around the table. "We cannot allow this to continue. Everyone is breathing down my neck to act. I know we've worked closely with Diamond and his people in the past, but I intend to demand that they come forward."

Across the table, Admiral Giles Roughead, Chief of Naval Operations, spoke up. "Madam President, Diamond Justice has worked closely with this Administration and previous administrations. I think we should hear him out first. Without them, more than one terrorist threat would have become a reality."

"The man is a terrorist."

Admiral Roughead glanced at Tani Poppendopalis and noted the look of anger growing on her face. Nevertheless, he didn't respond to her taunt. "I'm not saying that we shouldn't investigate this further, but I am cautioning you against making a rash judgment against a man who has supported this administration, and who commands the loyalty of some of the most powerful people on the planet."

"Rash judgment? Are you serious, Admiral? Millions are dead!" Tani looked like she was ready to burst. Her face was red and she nearly shook with rage. "And as for Diamond's people, some of them have ties to this administration, and other governments that goes beyond him. We can control them! And if we can't, we will arrest them!"

Tani was the Secretary of Meta-human Affairs. Despite her position, she had never been one of Diamond's biggest supporters. When Tani had first been nominated for her position, Diamond had opposed it, along with the entire meta-human community. She wasn't a meta-human, and her stiff support of harsh sanctions against meta-humans had been well known even before her nomination. If Tani had her way, meta-humans would be permanently segregated from the rest of the population, regardless of whether or not they had done anything to deserve it. Sanora had felt Tani would bring a fresh perspective to the position. At least that is what she had stated publicly. In truth, the appointment had been to placate Sanora's enemies. Sanora's presidency had been close, and had come with a price. Politics always did. Since Diamond had tried to block her appointment, Tani had taken it personally, and had chosen to make him her personal archenemy.

Roughead shook his head and did not raise his voice when he responded. "Secretary Poppendopalis, despite any ties you think they may have with this government or any other, they will support Diamond. Arresting those that won't cooperate will only anger the others. And God help us if we anger the wrong ones."

"I shouldn't have to remind anyone that the actions of Diamond Justice in Denver violated their sanctioning under the Greenbriar Protocols. And let us not forget that the constitutional concerns under the Twenty-Eight Amendment will lock up the courts for years to come. Yes, we have the authority to arrest Diamond and his people, regardless of where their loyalty lies." As Attorney General, Albert Rohm would be responsible for any legal matters coming out of the incidents. Legal challenges from the Paris incident had already landed on his desk. He would not hesitate to use DSS as a scapegoat. As he spoke, he looked around the room with his glowing red eyes, but as usual, very few people met his gaze. "The Cairo Accords dictate that he be brought before an international tribunal for investigation. They supersede the Greenbriar Protocols."

"Secretary Rohm that may be true, but..."

"Admiral, there is not much use in arguing this. I have already made my decision." At being cut off by the President, Admiral Roughead sat back in his chair, and relented the floor to her. "Diamond and his crew have to answer for Paris. There is no way around it. The best thing for them to do, for everyone involved, is to turn themselves in. All politics aside, the people of France deserve answers." Sanora bowed her head and sighed heavily. Raising her head again, she looked the Admiral in his eyes. "As for Denver, they attacked Mayor Austin in his office. No warning. No explanation. We *all* deserve explanation for that! Damn it, Samuel!" The President sighed heavily again, and as she rubbed her face with her hands, she added, "You sure have put us in a tough spot."

Diamond knew the President wasn't talking directly to him. She had no way of knowing he was in the room. Her comments had simply been a reflection her frustration, and of her waning loyalty to someone she had considered a friend for a very long time.

"I think Tani has it right in this case." The President briefly glanced at Tani before focusing again on the room as a whole. "Regardless of what their motivations are, or were, we simply cannot afford Samuel's form of *hard justice* in these matters. We have to bring him in, and we have to form some plan to do so when he refuses to cooperate."

Tani looked smug at President Sanora's use of the term *hard justice*. Attorney General Rohm and the vast majority of those around the table, nodded in agreement. Admiral Roughead bowed his head in defeat.

Diamond would have allowed himself a laugh at the use of the term *hard justice*, if it had come from Tani and not the President. Tani was well known for her use of the word as a mockery for the term Diamond Justice. Diamond even doubted she used it consciously now. It was a reflex since her outspoken agenda often centered on him and his organization. But the President had used the term.

Sanora was showing backbone she often lacked. Too often, she sought the middle road, and tried to placate both sides. *Good for her*, thought Diamond. She was not sitting on the fence in this situation; she was stepping up and taking command. Unfortunately, Diamond was on the receiving end, and apparently had only one ally in the room.

Roughead was a loyal friend, but he would follow orders when it came down to it, and judging by the mood in the room Diamond knew it would.

"Admiral," said the President, "Can we count on you in this?"

The Admiral looked insulted. "Of course, Madame President. My office is at your full disposal in this matter."

"Good, because I think this may call for the Andromeda Initiative."

Admiral Roughead looked immediately uneasy. He had a personal stake in the Andromeda Initiative, and had hoped the President wouldn't invoke it without at least speaking with Diamond first. "Of course, Madame President." After only a brief pause, he added, "How would you like to proceed?"

Even though he wasn't supposed to, Diamond knew what the top secret Andromeda Initiative was. It had been put in place by the previous President, mostly in opposition to the growing power of DSS, and was only known of by the President's inner circle. It didn't bode well for Diamond Justice, or for any meta-human.

Diamond considered pulling back from the room at that point, but decided to remain. So far, only Roughead had spoken out in his defense, and he wanted to know if any of the others would do so in front of the President. Patiently, Diamond circled the room as the discussion turned to implementation of the Andromeda Initiative.

An hour later, Diamond was back in his body. Sighing, he straightened his jacket and stepped into the center of the room. He tapped several buttons on his console and sent a signal through several satellites and through nearly a hundred different servers scattered around the globe. The tactic wouldn't prevent someone from tracking him, but it would give him several minutes before he had to worry about it. The Citadel's security measures and AI would easily expand that time to an hour. "Establish uplink," he said.

As he waited patiently for the President's computers to acknowledge the request, he contemplated countermeasures to the Andromeda Initiative. Having known of the plan for years, he had already developed several strategies, but he couldn't implement them without tipping his hand. Doing so would raise questions. He would have to wait until he knew the Initiative was in full motion, but that would be too late for some of his people. Given the complicated nature of the plan, he knew he had several days to safely consider his possibilities. He would be ready when, if, Andromeda was used.

When the uplink was finally established, he greeted President Sanora and then Admiral Roughead before turning to the others in the room. He greeted Tani last.

\* \*

Silently, Sparrow crawled beyond the latest guard station and lowered himself into an adjacent office. The guards were too close to the secured area. He couldn't leave them behind him without running the risk of exposure.

As he approached the guards from behind, he pulled the dart gun from his belt. It didn't have the weight of his pistol, and it felt uncomfortable in his hand. It also had only two shots. He would have to find an alternative once the mission was over.

*Thwith!*

As the dart struck the first guard, Sparrow grabbed the second guard in a chokehold. Surprised by the attack, both guards were rendered unconscious without offering resistance. Sparrow attached a probe to their computer, and used the security cameras to stalk the third guard.

*Thwith!*

As he came out of the restroom, Sparrow shot him with a dart.

By the time Sparrow returned to the guard desk, the sidekick had finished dumping a virus into the guard's computers to erase video of the incident, and prevented any further recording.

Sparrow retrieved his darts from the guards and loaded fresh ones into the gun. He tied the men up with computer cables from an office.

\* \*

Sparrow crouched in the hallway and studied the reinforced steel door before him. He didn't worry about bypassing the security keypad that barred it. It was the mystery of what lay beyond the door that gave him pause. He had no way of knowing who or what was there. Glancing above the door, he watched the small camera. His sidekick didn't show the camera, and he had no access to it.

Reviewing the schematics, he found the lab area touched the outer wall of the building along its backside. Unfortunately, he only had limited climbing gear, and the schematics indicated the glass could sustain small weapons fire before breaking. The door was his best option.

Backtracking down the hallway, Sparrow removed several motion sensitive grenades from his backpack and strategically placed them along the wall. He then broke into several offices until he found a lab coat and a baseball hat. Pulling his mask and night vision goggles off, he tucked them into his backpack. He reviewed his escape route, and then pulled out a couple of extra grenades and tucked them into his belt. Approaching the door, he turned his face away from the camera, and hid the sidekick as best as he could.

He quickly placed a probe on the keypad. He activated the hacker program and when the sidekick blinked, a green light above the door activated, and the door opened inward. Sparrow quickly stuffed the sidekick into a pocket, and gripped the dart gun with the same hand.

Stepping inside, Sparrow found himself in a narrow hallway with a desk just beyond a metal detector. A guard looked up from a magazine. Sparrow smiled and waved at him.

"May I help you?" asked the man in Chinese as he stood up and placed his hand on his weapon. "This area is restricted..."

*Thwith!*

Sparrow shot him with the dart gun. The man looked confused for a moment, before he collapsed behind the desk.

Sparrow avoided the metal detector by jumping over the counter. He yanked a cord from a computer and tied the guard's hands before stuffing a rag into this mouth.

Knowing the reinforced door would prevent a quick escape, Sparrow grabbed a clipboard off the desk and jammed it into a hinge. Then he pushed the door to. Except for the red light above it, the door looked secure from a distance.

Moving behind the counter again, Sparrow reviewed the area's security cameras. There was one large lab with several smaller labs surrounding it. The large lab was behind a glass wall, and in its center was a bright light shining from a window in the floor. The far wall of the lab overlooked the city. There were several offices and a break room down a side hallway. Inside the break room, a man sat in a chair with his feet propped on a table. He was reading from several papers in his hands. A second man moved behind the first, but due to the angle of the camera Sparrow couldn't see him. Satisfied the area had only two people in it, he dumped the virus into the computer to erase the security footage.

Through the lab's glass wall Sparrow could see numerous computer monitors flickering and various switches and glowing lights. The limited lighting they generated along with the bright light from the center of the floor allowed Sparrow's sensitive goggles to make out most of the room's detail.

Sparrow froze when he realized a man stood in the darkness just beyond the floor's blinding light. His eyes glowed a soft yellow, and he was staring directly at Sparrow. From the man's viewpoint, he had seen everything Sparrow had done since entering the area.

After a minute, the man hadn't moved. Curiosity inched into Sparrow, but he forced himself to remain patient. He didn't move for another full minute. Finally, he took a step to the right to allow himself a better view of the man.

What Sparrow had thought were blinking computers between him and the man was actually the man's open chest. There was a series of wires and small lights inside him, and he was connected to the computers around him with several cables. One monitor showed an image of his torso with various power readings. Above the image were the words, *Off-Line, Defense Systems Upgrading*. Another computer monitor showed an image of the *Aegis* suspended in a brightly lit room.

The man was a robot. *Android*, Sparrow corrected himself when he recognized it. Seraphim was a member of a super team out of New York City called Alpha-Wing. Typing the name into his sidekick, Sparrow brought up information about the android.

Seraphim was actually a series of military prototypes built by Halo Corp, and currently assigned to Alpha-Wing for field-testing. Their power levels were way beyond anything Sparrow wanted to deal with, and they were trying to integrate the defensive capabilities of the *Aegis* into its already impressive systems. Sparrow hoped the android's systems stayed off-line.

Sparrow considered his options. Never being one to count on luck, he moved down the hallway toward the break room. If the shield was in the lab as he suspected, taking out the two men in the break room would give him more time to obtain it.

As he approached the small room, Sparrow pulled his dart gun. One of the men laughed a lot, and his voice sounded like a sack of rocks grinding together. The second man was soft spoken, and he seemed uninterested in the gruffer man's conversation.

Sliding along the wall, Sparrow could see the soft-spoken man just inside the doorway. His back was to Sparrow. He had a visor-like device across his face. Sparrow recognized him. *Damn*, he cursed.

The man's name was Hagen, and he was the leader of Alpha-Wing. His visor was capable of emitting dangerous energy blasts and allowed him to see through walls. He also carried a wide array of various gadgets of his own design.

Sparrow raised his dart gun toward Hagen's back, but before he could fire the second man blocked his shot. The man was short and stocky with muscles bulging along his neck and shoulders. His clawed hands were large enough to encircle Sparrow's torso. His bare feet looked like they belonged on an ape, and not on a man. His name was Ogre; and like Hagen, he was a member of Alpha-Wing.

*Meta-humans*, cursed Sparrow as he quietly slid along the wall away from the room. He wasn't willing to take on two of New York's strongest meta-humans. He doubted his darts would have even penetrated Ogre's dense skin.

As Sparrow hurried back toward the lab, he tucked a motion sensitive grenade behind a potted plant. A few feet further down the hall, he placed a second grenade. They would give him fair warning if the two men decided to return to the lab.

Alpha-Wing was supposed to be the good guys. Having the stolen *Aegis* gave Sparrow doubt as to their true motives; but that was something for Diamond and his team to worry about. If Sparrow had his way, he would snatch the shield and be gone before they even knew he had been there.

With the sidekick, Sparrow easily bypassed the door to the lab. Once inside he erased all the access codes from the system. Then he propped another motion sensitive grenade against the door. He knew he was running out of time, but he wasn't about to get trapped inside the room. He confirmed the android was still off-line, and then went straight to a large window overlooking the city. He lined it with explosives.

Moving back to the android, he shielded his eyes against the glare and leaned over the window in the floor to peer into the room below. The *Aegis* was suspended in the center. There was a window along the far side, but nothing else of note.

Suddenly a mechanical arm came into view. It approached the *Aegis* and a laser on the arm's tip fired at the shield. The laser struck the shield in a blinding flash, but Sparrow's goggles easily compensated.

Glancing around the lab, Sparrow spotted a set of stairs descending into the area. Glancing at the android and then at the computers, Sparrow headed for the stairs.

At the bottom, Sparrow found a narrow control room with a series of computers beneath the long window. There was a single reinforced door leading into the chamber, but there was no obvious way to open it.

The computers indicated a series of tests were being run on the *Aegis*. The chamber was sealed until the tests were complete. Sparrow tried to shut down the tests, but the system flashed *Error* in response to his attempts. As he watched, a new test began and a thin laser struck the *Aegis*. It increased intensity until it reached a peak, and then it shut itself down. The shield glowed where the laser had touched it, but its integrity held.

Sparrow didn't like his options, but he knew his time was quickly deteriorating. He could continue to try to hack the computers and risk alerting security, or he could attempt to steal the shield during the twenty-second downtime between tests. Of course, blowing the window would alert the men in the break room. Sparrow glanced at his watch. He had already been in the room five minutes, and that was far too long. He made his decision, and slapped explosives along the edge of the window. He then raced back up the stairs to the window above the chamber.

Pulling his backpack off, Sparrow knelt over the glass. He pulled out a length of rope and laid it to the side. He then pulled his dart gun and exchanged one of the darts with his zip line. He stuffed it into his belt and pulled more explosives from his backpack.

As he applied them to the floor window, the computer monitor to his left brightened. In the reflection of the glass, Sparrow saw the two yellow eyes of Seraphim shift to red. The android turned its head in his direction.

"You are in an unauthorized area," said the android as it stepped down off its pedestal.

Sparrow jammed a detonator into the explosives, and rolled out of the android's reach. He leaped to his feet as the android's movements jerked equipment attached to it off the counters. With cables ripping free, the android swung at Sparrow.

The glancing blow caught Sparrow on his right shoulder. His foot caught on his backpack and spilled its contents as he hit the floor. Springing to his feet again, Sparrow ignored the sparks showering him from the exploding computer equipment.

*Boom!*

An explosion rocked the hallway outside the lab. The android paused and looked in the direction of the explosion.

*Boom!*

When the second explosion rocked the lab, Sparrow took advantage of the android's distraction and hurled a grenade at it.

*Kaboom!*

The explosion slammed the unsuspecting android into a counter.

Sparrow darted across the lab and dived behind a counter just as Hagen staggered into the hallway outside the lab. Hagen's clothing was torn, and he favored his left arm. A single glowing red dot darted across the visor's black faceplate. Sparrow moved around the counter to put as much of it between himself and Hagen as he could. He pulled a grenade from his belt.

From the hallway Hagen searched the room. Inside the lab Seraphim climbed to its feet. Hagen keyed his access code into the keypad, but the lab door did not open when he pulled on the handle. He quickly keyed in the code again, but the door still did not open.

*Come on, come on*, encouraged Sparrow as he glanced around for the android. It was moving in his direction.

Stepping back from the door, Hagen focused on it. The visor's dot suddenly grew brighter and larger.

*Fsist!*

Energy from the visor shattered the door. The door's destruction dislodged Sparrow's grenade.

*Kaboom!*

Hagen slammed into the wall across from the lab.

Sparrow leaped to his feet and flung his grenade at Seraphim. The android wrapped its metal wings around itself, and the grenade exploded harmlessly against the shell.

*Kaboom!*

Sparrow dove for the stairs and rolled down them as he pulled a compact *H&K USP* from a shoulder holster. The modified tactical pistol had far more punch than the dart gun.

Hagen lay stunned against the wall for a moment before brushing glass and debris from his armor. Climbing to his feet, he blasted the hallway lights to plunge the area into darkness. He then shifted his visor to thermal imaging and searched the room for Sparrow.

"Where is he?" growled Ogre as he joined his friend in the hall. Ogre had mutated. His features were more bestial, and he crawled around on his knuckles like an ape. His left eye was swollen and red. Bloody snot ran from his overlarge nose. His costume was torn, and his torso was covered with lacerations. He had caught the brunt of both blasts in the hallway and had taken a moment to recover.

Hagen glanced at Ogre and the android answered, "He dove down the stairs. He's after the shield."

"Careful," added Hagen, "he's set up booby traps."

"Most of my systems are still off-line," said Seraphim. "My reflexes are slowed. He has been able to take advantage of that."

Hagen nodded and shifted his vision. He looked through the floor and saw Sparrow in front of the computers. "He's accessing the computers."

Ogre bared his fangs and moved into the lab. "Graaaaa! Thief! I'm going to suck the marrow from your bones!" Grabbing a table, he hurled it across the lab, and then he leaped across the room to the top of the stairs. With Seraphim right behind him, he leaped again and landed at the bottom. Hagen took up a position at the top to prevent Sparrow's escape.

Sparrow was waiting patiently for Ogre to reach the bottom of the stairs.

The beast lumbered cautiously forward with the winged android crouching behind him on the stairs. Ogre glanced right, and then left before looking up at Sparrow and grinning.

"What? No more grenades?"

Sparrow gave him his gun instead.

*Blam! Blam! Blam!*

The bullets stung Ogre deeply. "Graaaaaaa!" he roared and charged forward.

Sparrow dropped under Ogre's grasp, and rolled under the computer console.

*Kaboom!*

The explosives lining the window exploded. Glass showered the room, and Ogre was flung against the opposite wall.

Rolling out from under the console, Sparrow leaped through the shattered window and into the testing chamber. Seraphim's steel grip dug into his shoulder and ripped his uniform, but Sparrow managed to twist free and avoid capture.

The light of the room was blinding, but Sparrow's goggles quickly compensated. He dodged the laser as it fired at the *Aegis*. Grabbing the swinging arm, Sparrow jerked it around at his pursuers.

*Zzzz!*

The laser sliced along the room's wall and cut deeply into Seraphim's delicate internal circuitry. Its eyes flickered and damaged systems began to shut down.

"Graaaaa!" snarled Ogre. He jerked the android out of the window, and Sparrow turned the laser on him. It sliced through his arm. "Graaaaww!" Fueled by the pain, Ogre ripped the computer console from the wall and hurled it at Sparrow.

*Crash!*

The computer ripped the laser from the swinging arm.

*Boom!*

*Thwith!*

Sparrow activated the explosives covering the hatch above him, and fired his zip line through the shattering window. As glass rained down, Ogre charged forward and Sparrow was jerked from the floor toward the ceiling. Sailing though the air, Sparrow grabbed the *Aegis*, and soared to freedom.

"*Nooo!*" snarled Ogre.

*Fsist!*

Hagen's blast sliced Sparrow's cable.

Sparrow flailed and tumbled back toward the hatch. The *Aegis* was flung aside, and he barely managed to grab the edge of the hole to keep from plummeting back into the test room.

*Fsist!*

Hagen's second blast struck Sparrow in his side as he rolled out of the hole.

"Graaaaa!" Ogre erupted from the hole. "Fight me!" He roared as he searched the dark room for Sparrow.

Any movement caused pain to shoot through Sparrow's side. His flack vest hadn't absorbed enough of Hagen's blast.

"He's behind the counter!" yelled Hagen. "I'll flush him toward you!"

They knew his location, and they were closing in. Sparrow was quickly regretting the mission. He could see Ogre's reflection in the surface of a broken computer, and he could feel the heat of Hagen's blasts ripping up the floor around him.

Sparrow shoved his dart gun into his belt, and pulled his *USP* and a flare grenade. Without hesitation, he rolled the grenade along the floor toward Ogre.

*Thumph!*

As it detonated, Sparrow leaped from his cover and dashed across the room. He kept as much cover between himself and Hagen as he could while firing wildly at Ogre.

*Blam! Blam! Blam!*

Sparrow's bullets bounced off Ogre's dense skin.

*Fsist! Fsist! Fsist! Fsist!*

Hagen chased Sparrow across the room with his energy blasts.

Sparrow scooped up the *Aegis* and dove behind another counter. Hagen stopped attacking, and Sparrow shoved his arm through the shield's strap to pull it across his back. He peered around the corner at the exit. Hagen blocked it. He glanced toward the window. Ogre blocked it.

"Where is he?" screamed Ogre. Tears streamed down his face and wiping his eyes didn't improve his vision.

"Straight in front of you!" screamed his teammate as he fired in Sparrow's direction.

*Fsist! Fsist!*

"Thief! Your flare didn't work on me!" Hagen blasted again and the counter rocked under the assault.

*Fsist! Fsist!*
*Thanks for the information*, thought Sparrow.

Ogre snarled and gnashed his pointed teeth at the air as he leaped upon the counter. "Scum, even if I can't see you, I can still smell you!"

"Ogre! Look out!" Hagen yelled.

Sparrow answered Ogre by firing his *USP* at the man's face.

*Blam! Blam! Blam!*

Again the bullets didn't penetrate Ogre's skin, but at the close range they stung like a swarm of angry hornets, and Ogre staggered backward off the counter.

Sparrow sprang to his feet and dashed for a new hiding spot.

*Fsist! Fsist! Fsist!*

A blast hit Sparrow in his right side, and the force hurled him across the room.

*Fsist! Fsist! Fsist!*

Hagen continued his barrage, and Sparrow curled up under the *Aegis* to prevent the blasts from hitting him. The searing pain in his side was making it hard to concentrate, and he was growing winded. He needed to move, but feared any shift would expose him to Hagen.

The assault abruptly stopped, but before Sparrow could react, he was grabbed roughly by the neck and hauled into the air. Holding Sparrow high off the floor with one hand, Seraphim glared into Sparrow's eyes with a demonic red glare. Pain paralyzed Sparrow's neck and shoulders. His vision blurred and spots danced before him. Out of the corner of his eye he could see Ogre moving quickly toward them.

Reaching into a breach in the android's head, Sparrow grabbed as many wires as he could and yanked. Sparks flew and the android's eyes flickered and died. Sparrow shoved a grenade into its chest, and twisted free of its weakened grip.

Ogre struck Sparrow and slammed him into a wall. The grenade in the android's chest exploded.

*Kaboom!*

Ogre staggered under the explosion, and the android was hurled backward with fire and smoke coming from its chest.

Ogre leaped after Sparrow and pounded the hero with both of his massive fists. Air was forced from Sparrow's lungs, and he barely managed to roll over enough to put the *Aegis* between Ogre and himself.

The shield absorbed the next round of impacts, and Sparrow struggled to catch his breath.

*Clang! Clang!*

Ogre reached down and yanked the shield. Pain exploded in Sparrow's shoulder as he was hauled into the air. Ogre swung the *Aegis* wildly, and Sparrow's arm slipped from the shield's strap. He was flung across the room.

Sparrow landed hard and slid into a counter. His shoulder burned and his side stung. He had lost his *USP* at some point, and he didn't have any grenades left. As rough hands grabbed him once again, his eyes fell on his spilled backpack. Frantically, he reached for it, and gripped a flash grenade as he was hauled into the air.

Holding Sparrow in a stony grip, Ogre raised him high above the floor. The monster held the shield in his other hand.

"Just hold him a moment!" yelled Hagen as he started across the room.

A monstrous grin spread across Ogre's hideous face, and his small beady eyes glinted with delight. "Out of tricks?" he snarled.

Through clenched teeth, Sparrow said, "No!"

He thrust the grenade toward Ogre, and allowed it to be batted aside by the shield. As the beast watched the grenade bounce off a wall, Sparrow yanked the dart gun from his waist, and shoved it into Ogre's right eye. Pressing down hard with both hands, he fired.

*Thwith!*

"Aaaarrggghhh!" Ogre screamed and jerked away from the pain. Blood and gore sprayed the room as Sparrow was flung across the room again. Ogre staggered backwards with his large hands pressed tightly against his face.

Sparrow rolled with the landing and immediately sought the *Aegis*.

"Damn you!" screamed Hagen as he fired at Sparrow.

*Fisst! Fisst! Fisst!*

Sparrow spotted the shield and leaped for it. He rolled and came up with the *Aegis* between him and his enemy. Hagen's blasts bounced harmlessly off it.

*Fisst! Fisst! Fisst!*
*Clang! Clang! Clang!*

"I hate meta-humans!" Sparrow yelled as he charged across the room at Hagen.

*Fisst! Fisst! Fisst!*

*Clang! Clang! Clang!*

The dangerous blasts deflected off the shield.

*Wham!*

Sparrow slammed the *Aegis* into Hagen and forced him back against the wall. Hagen didn't relent his attacks, but Sparrow shoved the *Aegis* hard against him, forcing him against the wall. When Hagen stopped firing to adjust his position, Sparrow reared back with the shield.

*Wham!*

And slammed it into the Hagen's face. Hagen staggered under the blow.

Sparrow raised the shield high above his head.

*Wham!*

Sparrow brought it down on Hagen a second time. The man's visor shattered under the impact, and Hagen collapsed against the wall.

Sparrow raised the shield again.

*Wham!*

Hagen's visor fell from his face. With anger flaring, Sparrow lifted the shield to strike again, but was stunned by the sight before him.

"Damn," Sparrow cursed as he staggered away from the man. Where Hagen's eyes should have been, the skin was smooth and unbroken. Blood flowed from a gash in his forehead. Sparrow shook his head in disgust at the eyeless man.

"Grrrroowwll!"

The deep low growl brought Sparrow around. "Seriously," he mumbled when he found himself facing off with Ogre again. "Meta-humans," he cursed.

The beast bared its fangs.

"Rrraaarraagggrr!"

Ogre had lost all sense of his humanity, and the animal within him was in complete control. He was a bloodthirsty dog that shuffled around like an oversized gorilla. He pounded his chest, and shook his massive head to spray blood and gore from his destroyed eye. The dart still protruded from his face. Spittle reached Sparrow at more than thirty feet away.

Nearly exhausted, Sparrow sighed and said, "Okay, then. Bring it on." He took a step away from Hagen.

Ogre charged.

Sparrow dodged Ogre's outstretched hands, and slammed the *Aegis* into his knee.

*Crack!*

Bones shattered.

*Crash!*

Ogre flew past Sparrow and slammed into the wall. It caved under the impact, and Ogre was buried up to his waist.

Sparrow rolled to his feet and fled for the reinforced door. Behind him, Ogre tore himself free of the wall. As Sparrow flung open the door, Ogre attempted to charge down the hall after him, but the monster's shattered knee collapsed under him.

"Rrraaarraagggrr!" Anger flared within the beast, and he struggled to pull himself up. Half dragging his leg behind him, Ogre gave chase.

Sparrow only got a few steps before Ogre slam into the door.

*Wham!*

A moment later, Ogre ripped the large metal door from its frame and hurled it down the hall after Sparrow.

*Crash!*

Sparrow dodged the door by diving around a corner. It sailed past him and through several walls.

Sparrow's pace was slowing, but he forced himself past the first of the grenades he had hidden along his escape route. His movement armed it, and when Ogre barreled blindly past, it exploded.

*Kaboom!*

Glancing over his shoulder, Sparrow saw that Ogre was down, but still moving in his direction. "Damn!" he cursed.

Instead of fleeing past the next grenade, he grabbed it from its hiding place, turned, and hurled it at Ogre. He ducked behind a corner before it exploded.

*Kaboom!*

He pulled his last grenade from its hiding place, and waited for Ogre to come around the corner after him.

When the beast didn't appear, Sparrow grew curious. He could still hear grunting and snorting, but it didn't appear to be drawing closer.

His patience shot and determined to finish the fight, Sparrow peered around the wall. Ogre lay where the last grenade had exploded. He still struggled to move, but his injuries were too severe, he didn't have the strength to rise. His leg was mangled and lay twisted beneath him. Sparrow eased around the corner to face him.

"Rrraaarraagggrr!" Ogre roared at the sight of his enemy and clawed at the floor. With the wood splintering and the carpet ripping free, he managed to drag his bulk toward Sparrow.

Like his mental state, Ogre's appearance had greatly deteriorated throughout the course of the battle. The angrier he had gotten, the more bestial he had become. Now, he didn't even look human. Sparrow pitied him.

Ignoring the defeated monster, Sparrow walked past Ogre and toward the lab. Each step sent a surge of pain through his body, and diminished his pity. Grunting, he tossed the grenade over his shoulder.

*Kaboom!*

The explosion silenced the beast.

Alarms were sounding all over the building, and despite the chaos of the city someone would be responding. Sparrow's injuries pained him, and he didn't want to deal with any more meta-humans. He was ready to go, but knew he had to complete the mission. Normally, he would have just grabbed the shield and fled, but this time he needed to cover his tracks.

Sparrow checked on Hagen and found him still unconscious. Satisfied, he moved into the lab.

The Seraphim android was sitting on the floor of the lab with its head twitching every couple of seconds. It repeated, "Rebooting," over and over again. It was heavy, but Sparrow managed to drag it over to the hole in the floor. He stuffed an incendiary charge into its chest, and then dumped it down the hole. He threw the computer equipment that had been attached to it down the hole as well. Last, he dumped the contents of his backpack down the hole.

Sparrow found his sidekick among the debris. Its blue screen was cracked, but he stuffed it into his empty backpack anyway. He also found several armor-like plates. They had been among the items Seraphim's movements had yanked off the counters. They were sturdy and strong, but extremely lightweight. They weren't made of metal or plastic, but he suspected they were connected to the experiments Alpha-Wing had been conducting on the *Aegis*. He stuffed them into his backpack.

In the break room, he found the papers Hagen had been reading and took them. As he passed Hagen on his way back to the lab, the man spoke.

"Who are you?"

Sparrow paused and looked at him. Hagen sat with his back against the wall. He had his visor in his lap. He had been trying to repair it, but had failed.

Sparrow considered several responses, but in the end he gave none. Silently, he turned and walked away.

Outside the lab window, Sparrow could see the flashing lights of emergency vehicles responding. A helicopter was approaching fast, but it was still several blocks away. Of more importance, an intensely bright light was descending on the tower from above. It likely concealed an airship of some kind. *Meta-humans,* he was out of time.

Picking up his backpack, he unzipped several side pockets. Pulling on several strong poles, he unfurled a small glider from within the backpack. He had designed the glider several years ago for a situation requiring a quick escape from a high altitude hit. It wouldn't work for long trips and couldn't carry much weight, but it would get him safely down to the ground several blocks away from the mega-structure. A parachute would not have gotten him as far.

Stepping behind a busted counter, Sparrow activated the incendiary charge stuffed in the android's chest. It exploded and coated everything he had thrown down the hole in a suppression resistant flammable gel. With flames shooting from the hole, he blew the charges lining the window.

*Boom!*

Strong winds blasted him as he climbed up onto the window seal. Looking out over Hong Kong, he took a moment to breathe deeply and enjoy the view.

Behind him, he heard the sound of running feet coming from the direction of the break room. Glancing over his shoulder, Sparrow saw several men round the corner to the lab. Flashlights lit up the area, and the man leading the pack immediately spotted Sparrow perched in the window. He was dressed in an Alpha-Wing uniform and wore opaque goggles. The man's image blurred as he moved across the room at superhuman speed.

*Meta-humans*, Sparrow cursed as he leaped from the window, barely avoiding the man's grip to sore safely out into the dark sky over Hong Kong.

Traxx stood in the window and watched his quarry disappear into the night.

\* \*

As Sparrow piloted the yacht into the bay, he took a moment to enjoy his view of the island. The sun was setting and the sky was clear. A gentle breeze ruffled the trees, and the lodge overlooking the bay sat dark and quiet. The place was deserted, but peaceful.

He had been away from the Citadel for just over two weeks, but it seemed like much longer. He wouldn't call it homesickness, but something about the place made him glad to be back. Then he saw them.

Bouncing on her toes impatiently, Gemini stood on the docks with Glip-2 hovering over her shoulder. The globe glowed bright green and pulsed rapidly. Dreah stood peacefully behind them.

He wouldn't call Glip-2 family, but his presence brought Sparrow a comfort he hadn't felt since he was a kid. Maybe friend was the way to think of him, but Sparrow hadn't had a friend in a very long time so he wasn't sure if that was right either. It was easy to see why everyone loved Gemini. He was going to have to guard himself to prevent her from worming her way into his life. As for Dreah, it was already too late to worry about getting too close. He understood why Brandon got tongue tied when speaking about her.

As the boat bumped against the dock, Gemini cheered and clapped. Dreah smiled. Sparrow quickly tied the boat to the dock. Swinging the *Aegis* onto his back, he stepped off the boat.

Gemini immediately threw her arms around him, and Glip-2 cheered from all the speakers on the dock in a chorus of unsynchronized voices. Dreah waited patiently, but hugged Sparrow at the first opportunity. When she stepped back, Gemini stepped forward again and put her arm around Sparrow's waist. It made Sparrow visibly uncomfortable. Recognizing his discomfort, Dreah took Gemini by the arm and pulled the young girl off Sparrow.

The four turned and started up the dock. Dreah laced one arm through Sparrow's and took Gemini's hand in her other hand.

Gemini suddenly stopped and turned around to look at the yacht Sparrow had piloted in. "Is that daddy's boat?" she asked.

Sparrow turned and looked from Gemini to the yacht. The *Vision Quest* was indeed Diamond's yacht. Sparrow had taken it the day he had fled the island. He had disconnected its transponder and most of the electrical equipment to keep it from being tracked, but other than that the yacht was just as he had found it. Sparrow's gaze ran the length of the beautiful vessel and he smiled. He had been surprised to still find it where he had hidden it upon his return.

Smiling at Gemini, Sparrow didn't answer but turned and started up the dock. "How did you know I was returning?" he asked.

"Duh," said Gemini as she sprinted to catch up. She took Dreah's hand again and pointed at the woman. "Precog. Remember? You're not very good at this are you?"

Dreah smiled. "I tried to keep it private for you, but I couldn't get topside without Glip-2 knowing. Security has been tighter since you left. And as for Kahori, she has been acting strangely ever since the news reported explosions in a Hong Kong high-rise. The city feared it was another event. She pestered me for information until I gave in."

Sparrow grinned and looked up at the resort. His eyes searched the shadows for anyone who might be watching.

"Don't worry about the resort," said Glip-2 from Gemini's pocket. "Mr. Diamond has shut it down, and the staff has been sent home. It was originally reserved for the wedding, but recent events have changed things..." His voice trailed off awkwardly.

None of them needed reminding of recent events. They walked on in silence.

\* \*

"Why did Dreah say she wanted to meet us here?" asked Fluxstone.

Diamond stared into the fire and shrugged. "Dreah often doesn't tell me any more than she tells anyone else." It was a source of frustration for him. Despite their long-standing relationship, Dreah still kept secrets from him.

Fluxstone grew frustrated. She had never liked the sherry room.

To her it was stuffy, and the antique furniture belonged in a museum. The room's darkness and deep cherry wood reminded her of a funeral home. The memorials to fallen DSS agents that stood just outside the door made it a funeral home. Memories of Alex assailed her and she sighed heavily.

Vexed, she threw up her arms and said, "Well, I've got things to do." She rose and started for the doors. "Maybe someone has found a lead on Kingsley while I've been sitting here."

Diamond didn't respond, but he turned to watch her go with a look of sadness in his eyes. Kahori was his goddaughter, but Heather was the closest thing he had to a real one. He had been looking forward to giving her away at the wedding, and now he longed for the ability to take away her pain. The fear he had felt at her near death in Denver still plagued him. He hadn't been able to bring himself to yell at her for her interference, and he still couldn't explain the ripple in the monitor wall.

The double doors opened as Fluxstone reached for them. Sparrow stood in the doorway with Dreah beside him. Gemini and Glip-2 stood behind them. Fluxstone froze at the sight of a large round object covered in cloth slung across Sparrow's back.

As Sparrow pulled the object off his back, the cloth slipped off to reveal the *Aegis*. As he held it out to Fluxstone, neither of them spoke. Slowly, Fluxstone reached out and gently touched its metal surface.

Diamond walked across the room to join them. A tear ran down Fluxstone's cheek. She still hadn't taken the shield, but stood silently tracing her finger along its curved edge. Diamond put his arm around her as Dreah took the shield from Sparrow, and put it gently into her hands.

Fluxstone collapsed to the floor hugging the *Aegis* to her chest. She began to sob, tears dripping from her eyes to slide down the shield's surface. Dreah and Gemini knelt beside her and hugged her close as Diamond and Sparrow retreated to the fireplace. Outside the room, the memorial of Vox filled the hallway with a mournful version of *Butterfield's Lullaby*.

Diamond poured two drinks and handed one to Sparrow. Despite their long-standing association, he still marveled at how accurate Dreah could be. Standing in silence and sipping their drinks, the two men watched the women.

Diamond was truly glad to have the *Aegis* back. Despite the importance it held for Fluxstone, it was a valuable tool. If he were forced to put his contingency plan into play, he would need it.

"Thank you," Diamond said.

Sparrow nearly dropped his drink. To cover up his startled surprise, he turned toward the fireplace. He had expected Diamond to lock him up upon his return. He had never even considered the possibility that he might receive a thank you. He doubted Diamond ever expressed gratitude, much less meant it.

"It was in a Halo Corp building in Hong Kong in the possession of members of Alpha-Wing. Specifically, I encountered Hagen, Ogre, and a Seraphim android. Traxx showed up at the end. He was probably disappointed to find he had missed the fight."

Diamond arched his brow at the mention of the super team. He was impressed that Sparrow had encountered three of its toughest members and survived. As for the Seraphim android, they were powerful enough to take on several of his operatives at once.

"They knew what it was, and to whom it belonged," added Sparrow. "They appeared to be trying to integrate some of its defenses into the android."

Diamond nodded. He wasn't surprised. Alpha-Wing was already connected to Halo Corp through the android. Whether they had been manipulated, or actually knew the true nature of the Adversary didn't matter. The Adversary had a way of corrupting good people, and then profiting from it. Why should Alpha-Wing be any different? They may have been ignorant of the Adversary's true nature but they were still guilty of associating with him. It was why Diamond had inserted his own spies into the team long ago. However, he had not heard anything from them concerning the *Aegis*. It was a matter he would have to look into further.

"Does this mean you've accepted my offer?" asked Diamond.

Sparrow downed his drink in one large gulp and turned on Diamond. Diamond turned to face him. As Sparrow sat his glass on the fireplace, he said, "I've spent most of my life dominated by the Counselor. I won't spend the rest of it dominated by you. I will make my own decisions, and I will come and go as I please. For now, I will work for you, but you will not dictate my actions. I will terminate our arrangement if I feel the need to do so. And, if I ever suspect that you've pulled a mind trick on me, I will kill you."

Diamond finished his drink while looking Sparrow in the eye. He looked away only long enough to pour himself another one. He didn't doubt Sparrow would follow up on his threat. Sparrow had left the Citadel without permission, and he had returned without warning. The *Aegis* had simply been an opportunity for him to demonstrate what he was capable of. If the shield's return kept Fluxstone off his back, so much the better; but Diamond knew its return had been intended to emphasize that Sparrow would not be controlled.

Diamond nodded. "My only requirement is that you leave your past behind you. You will not go seeking personal revenge. We will deal with the Counselor at some point in the future, together. But not right now."

Sparrow felt anger at Diamond's words, but quickly reined it in. "Agreed," he said. He turned and headed for the exit.

Dreah's hand brushed his leg as he exited the room.

# CHAPTER 16
# SLIPSTREAM

Even Slipstream's senses were blurred by his speed. Energy leaking from his eyes left a trail that stretched the length of the track. If there had been anything in his path, he would not have seen it in time to avoid it. Exhaustion wanted to end his flight, but he kept it at bay through willpower.

He had failed. Aegis was dead. Incindiaro was dead. Stronghold was dead. Paris was dead. Drowning in his own misery, he had even attacked Paragon. He had failed to be there for the others in Denver, and that city had died too. He had failed to face the only enemy that had ever eluded him, the enemy responsible for the death of his family. He had failed to face that which had made him into a monster.

Slipstream's anguished screams echoed off the walls, and he pushed himself on even harder. Exhaustion was forced from his legs. The ground beneath him groaned.

\* \*

As Sparrow exited the workroom the wall shut behind him, and the image of the Austrian mountains returned. Thoughts of a hot shower filled his mind.

*Knock! Knock!*

Reluctantly, he opened the door to his apartment.

Smiling, Dreah said, "Good morning."

"Morning," he said stepping aside for her to enter.
"Sorry, but this is not a social call. Samuel would like to see us."
"And he sent you to get me?"
"I volunteered."

Thoughts of a hot shower fading, Sparrow exited the apartment. As they walked, he matched Dreah's leisurely pace. After several minutes, she spoke.

"Thank you for returning the *Aegis*. It is special."

Sparrow glanced at her. She may have known he would return with it, but it was only after it was in his hands that he had actually made the decision to do so.

"You are welcome," he managed to say in response. He felt shame at having originally considered selling it. It would not have brought him near the satisfaction he now felt simply walking next to her.

Several steps later, Dreah spoke again. "You've had to make some tough decisions lately."

Sparrow glanced at her and she smiled at him, but the smile quickly faded and she cast her gaze at the floor.

"You face another decision."

"Oh?" inquired Sparrow.

Dreah kept her eyes on the floor. "I don't know when, or what the choice will be, but it will be the most difficult for you so far."

"Difficult? Why?" Sparrow asked.

Dreah stopped walking and turned to face him. He stopped, and she laid her hand against his cheek. Sparrow felt his face flush under the warm touch. The sounds of the breakfast crowd down the hall faded as he focused on her dark eyes.

She said softly, "Because you will sacrifice something that has come to mean a lot to you."

Sparrow waited for more, but it didn't come. Dreah had warned him that her visions were cryptic, but the look in her eyes told him there was more. She was keeping something from him. Before he could ask, Dreah removed her hand and the world jerked back into focus. Turning away, she started down the hall again.

"What does that mean?" Sparrow asked without following.

Already several feet away, Dreah paused. Partially turning to face him, she said, "I wish I knew." Looking away, she started down the hall again.

Sparrow fell in beside her. Despite his curiosity he did not press her for more, and a comfortable silence settled between them.

\* \*

As the t-port opened, Sparrow felt the floor shudder. It was the first time he had felt any movement from a port. He started to ask Dreah about it, but she either had not felt it, or had ignored it. Deciding it was just lack of sleep, he followed her.

Dreah moved through the conference room and into the command center to join Diamond and several others on the catwalk. Glip-2 floated along the edge of the monitor wall. Edmond and Jonesy moved among several technicians on the floor. As Sparrow approached, Fluxstone noticed his arrival, but didn't acknowledge him. TASC Commander Bullock nodded at him in greeting. Meta-man and Diamond were engaged in an argument, and everyone appeared to be waiting on them.

"It didn't work in Denver! I don't think we should try it again!" argued Meta-man.

Dreah reached out and took his hand. His face released some of its anger immediately.

Holding up his hand to silence Meta-man, Diamond said, "I agree! That is not the plan. What we will do is put a team on the ground in Buenos Aires. It will speed up response time. At the first sign of an event, we will be ready to act. The teleport didn't work, but my plan is to utilize a pod. We will physically move Fuentes as far from the city as possible."

Diamond seemed more confident than Sparrow had expected. Perhaps he was maintaining control better than Gemini thought.

Turning to Envoy, Diamond continued, "Envoy, keep everyone on rotating standby shifts, but plan for fast teams with enough power to move Fuentes physically."

As the conversation continued, Sparrow only half listened. It didn't seem to be anything he would be involved in. He had no plans to be on the ground during an event. Diamond would get to why he had been summoned once the issue was settled; so Sparrow used the opportunity to study the command center. It was the first time he had actually been in the room.

It was large and unlike any of the other rooms in the Citadel. An early mission with the Counselor had taken him into the space shuttle control center at Cape Canaveral during a mission launch, but even in a flurry of activity it paled in comparison to Diamond's room.

The room was darker than any other in the Citadel, and the walls were dull; but appeared to be made of the same material as the white walls. The displays on the monitor wall were crisp, sharp enough to appear live. The monitor wall had true depth. The images were three dimensional in a way that no other video monitor in the world could duplicate.

Originally, Sparrow had thought the sherry room represented Diamond; rich and arrogant. Now he felt the high-tech command center better represented the man; large, in control, and focused.

As Sparrow's eyes swept the room, they came to rest on a glass of water sitting at Diamond's station. The surface of the water rippled. Glancing around, he found no one was moving on the catwalk.

Reaching out, he gently placed his hand on the railing. A slight vibration ran through the metal. The Citadel always had a slight hum like a florescent light, and the brighter a room was the louder the sound; but along with the port ride here this was the first movement Sparrow had encountered.

He glanced around at the others and found Dreah watching him. He nodded his head in the direction of the glass. Without speaking, Dreah released Meta-man's hand and stepped over to the glass. Gently, she reached out and ran her finger around the rim. A moment later, she slowly dipped her finger into the water. She paused with her finger in the water and her eyes grew distant. A moment later, she turned back to Sparrow. Before she could speak, a shudder passed through the room. Everyone fell silent.

"What was that?" Dreah asked.

Sparrow shrugged. "An earthquake?"

Diamond immediately stepped over to the console. "We don't get seismic activity here." He adjusted several buttons and his display filled with a chart that showed increasing seismic activity all around the island. "Glip-2," he said, "explain these quakes."

Glip-2 floated over to the console, his pulse intensifying. If anyone else had asked him to explain the quakes, he would have given them an exaggerated explanation about tectonic plates, but he rarely showed his rebellious side with Diamond. After a moment, a larger graph filled the imaging wall. It covered up data Jonesy was working with and showed more activity than Diamond's smaller graph. It went back two days, and then expanded back two more. The activity had begun over forty-eight hours ago, and had steadily increased with time.

"We've been experiencing seismic activity for two days and no one noticed?" asked Diamond.

"Maybe they've found us," said Jonesy from the floor. He glanced at Edmond.

Edmond shrugged. "If you mean the government, that is unlikely. If you mean the Psadans, that is possible."

While Jonesy accessed security images of the island, Sparrow looked to Dreah. She stood in the center of the room, spinning in a circle, and staring at the floor.

"Nothing unusual," Jonesy said.

Jonesy had filled the wall with several graphs. They showed no indication of alien or government attack. The computer system's numerous Internet and outside connections were normal. All of the Citadel's doors were secure.

"No," said Dreah softly. "It's Slipstream." Everyone turned to her. She stopped spinning and looked up. "It's Slipstream. He's distressed."

"Since when does Slipstream's emotional state affect the Citadel?" asked Jonesy. "He's always distressed, and probably not even here. It's got to be a power disruption."

Diamond ignored Jonesy. "Where is he, Dreah?"

Abruptly, Dreah stood upright. She quickly turned and started for the exit. "He's in the track. Wolff. Heather. Latisha. Glip-2. With me. Contact Kahori and Lawrence. Have them meet us there."

"Why?" asked Jonesy.

"Just do it now!"

The harshness in Dreah's voice spurred Fluxstone and Envoy to follow her. Glip-2 beat them all out the door and to the t-port. Sparrow caught up just as the doors closed.

"He's been running since Denver," said Envoy.

"I know," replied Dreah.

They exited in a long straight hallway that had no side passages or doors. It had the usual stoic white walls, but the lights flickered. A strong wind blew through it.

By the time they reached the end of the hallway, Glip-2 was brighter than the lighting. The wind was strong enough to make each step difficult. The ground quaked beneath their feet.

"This is normal?" Sparrow yelled over the noise to Envoy.

Her eyes glowed slightly. "No!" screamed Envoy in reply. "Normally, Slipstream's aura controls his wake! Only when he releases control is there turbulence! My guess is he doesn't even know he's doing it! He uses the two-mile track to work off frustration, anger, whatever! He must be pretty troubled right now, because I've never known him to go for three days. According to the computers, he's broken mach eleven. He's running faster than he's ever been recorded!"

In the wall ahead of them was a round opening through which they could see the circular track. Slipstream's energy trail streaked through its center.

Her thin dress and hair whipping frantically around her, Dreah stood before the track and stretched out her hand. Bowing her head she extended her senses into the track. Suddenly her hair and dress fell still against her body. Six feet from her, everyone but Glip-2 still struggled to maintain their footing.

Gemini and Paragon arrived while everyone waited for Dreah. Butch was with them. The wind made it difficult for Paragon to restrain his wings. He was forced to pull them in tight against his body.

The minutes ticked slowly by. Finally, Dreah lowered her hand, and the wind blasted her backward into Sparrow's arms.

"Thank you!" she screamed over the noise as he helped her stand up. "I can't reach him! I need your help!" Everyone nodded and waited for her instructions. "Circle me and join hands! Glip-2, I need you in the center with me! Everyone think of Slipstream! Clear your minds of everything but him!"

Paragon took up a position near the exit where he could stretch his wings out behind him. It visibly pained him, but he didn't utter a complaint and held his hands out for the others to take.

Sparrow found himself with Fluxstone on his right and Paragon on his left. Fluxstone didn't even glance at him. Glip-2 floated in the center of the circle above Dreah. As everyone closed their eyes and concentrated, Glip-2's glow intensified.

Sparrow was unsure how to follow Dreah's instructions. He didn't know Slipstream. He knew the man's file, but he didn't know the man.

Their only meeting had been in the gym when Slipstream had punched the wall in retaliation to Sparrow knocking out Gemini. Sparrow peered around at everyone, but with heads bowed they didn't notice. Dreah opened her eyes and looked at him. Embarrassed, he lowered his gaze, and focused his attention on the floor. He turned his thoughts to the incident in the gym.

*No,* said Dreah in his head. *Don't concentrate on his anger. I'm exhausted, Wolff. I need your strength.*

Her voice startled him. It was loud and distinct. It was only the second time someone had spoken to him through telepathy. Diamond had done it during the dream-walk. Even though this was Dreah, it was only slightly less unsettling.

*Guard thoughts of yourself, Wolff.*

Sparrow quickly removed himself from his vision of Slipstream. His focus became Slipstream's expression of fatherly protection for Gemini.

The image grew clearer and clearer. Soon it was so clear, Sparrow felt as if the man actually stood before him. Sparrow's face was even reflected in the man's blue metallic skin.

Slipstream smiled. Startled Sparrow nearly lost hold of the image. When he regained control of it again, he found that it was no longer his face reflected back at him. It was Gemini, and she laughed and twirled before him. Slipstream smiled again.

Each of the memories generated by the others revealed another piece of the man's past. But it wasn't the facts that were important, it was how each of them felt about him that formed the correct picture of the man.

Paragon focused on Slipstream's heart beneath his impenetrable rigid armor, a heart as frail and in need of compassion as any other. It was a heart more powerful than his invulnerable metal shell. Envoy thought of Slipstream as a never tiring hero who cared more for the innocent bystander than he did for himself, a hero willing to sacrifice his own life for any of his friends. To Gemini, he was a big brother, never judgmental and always willing to listen. To Fluxstone, he was a mentor and teacher, always confident. Butch stood in awe of the man's power and force of presence. It wasn't fear or obsession, or even envy. It was respect and pride.

Slipstream's file made him a weapon. The memories of his friends made him a person.

* *

It took Dreah only a moment to summon her mental picture of Kevin. It had been several years since she had last used it, but she had allowed it to linger at the back of her mind in case it was ever needed. The others would pull from recent memories of their friend, but Dreah's image was of the man before the metal skin, a kindhearted father and husband. Once she had her image formed, she pulled on the memories of the others and joined them with hers.

Prepared, Dreah allowed her form to dissipate. As her outline blurred, her essence was pulled away on the wind. She quickly recognized the danger and pulled herself back together. Once she was whole again, she slowly let go of her form again. This time she maintained control, and when she was nearly to the point of full dispersal, she held her essence together and pushed forward. Like a ghost flowing on the wind, she glided from the circle and into the track.

The hostile emotions fused in the air crashed down upon her. Outside the track, they had been disturbing; but inside the track, they were like the full weight of the ocean crushing the life out of her. Fear filled her as the light around her faded. As she struggled to breath, she realized just how drained the last few days had left her. She feared she wouldn't have enough strength. Reaching out, she grabbed onto the group of gathered friends. Pulling on their strength, she pulled herself up from the darkness and forced her lungs to expand again. She feared her actions would dump some of Slipstream's powerful emotions on them, but by dispersing it among them, she was confident they could handle it.

As she swallowed the life sustaining air, the dizziness in her mind cleared. After several deep breaths she was able to think clearly again.

She cursed herself for not noticing Kevin's distress earlier. Her responsibilities had been great lately, but that did not excuse her for missing his need. His mind had been so fractured by the Psadan's dominance that it had originally taken her weeks just to get him to acknowledge the world around him. It took him years to build up the will to keep the Psadans at bay. She had believed it was as indestructible as his body, but she had been wrong. Distracted by the needs of the others, she had missed it shatter under a single assault.

Slowly, Dreah allowed herself to be pulled along with Slipstream as he passed through her insubstantial form again and again. Her spirit remained just outside the track while her mind merged with the track, and Slipstream.

\* \*

"Status," demanded Diamond.

*Rruummmble!*

As he responded, Jonesy glanced at the walls around him. The rumbling unnerved him and it showed in his voice. "S-status is worsening. Structural integrity of the mountain surrounding the Citadel is weakening."

*Damn*, cursed Diamond to himself. Glancing up from Jonesy's monitor station, he focused his attention on the section of the monitor wall that showed the events unfolding over half a mile beneath him.

Slipstream's track was connected to the Citadel, but it was also partially in real space, like the airship bay. A portion of the island's bedrock had been hollowed out to make room for it. If Slipstream's wake caused the foundation to crack, it would breech the Citadel's integrity, and open it up for invasion. Up till now, only Shadow Spirit had ever penetrated it, and Diamond wanted to keep it that way.

\* \*

...Kevin sighed heavily as he looked at his sleeping wife and their infant son snuggled up next to her. It was still several hours before dawn, and he hated that he had to rise so early; but the ride into town would take over an hour and he couldn't miss an opportunity for work.

It pained him to know they were on the verge of losing the farm Paula so loved. She had grown up on the place and it was special to her. Unfortunately, Kevin had proven he wasn't the farmer her father had been. A few bad decisions had pushed the farm into debt, and now they faced foreclosure.

Getting a job in town was the only way he knew to save it. It was ironic that today's opportunity came from the very bank that was threatening to foreclose on them. Thankfully, Kevin had been a smart kid, particularly with numbers, and he had more education than most of the people in their little community. Along with his father's input, he had a good chance of getting the job. If getting up early was the penalty, then he would gladly pay it.

Before leaving the house, Kevin peeked in on his two young girls. They both slept peacefully so he made his way out into the cool morning air. It took him several attempts to get the old truck started before he could begin the long drive into town...

*...Kaboom!*

The thunder created a low rumble deep in Kevin's chest. Leaning forward, he wiped fog from the window with his shirtsleeve. Glancing up, he found it was too dark to see the clouds overhead, but he could somehow feel them.

*Kaboom!*

When the lightning flashed again, he wished he hadn't been looking. The clouds were alive. They swirled with anger, and he feared the rumble in his chest was real.

The road was flooded, and the old pickup had difficulty plowing through the mud. Rain pounded the steel roof loud enough to hurt Kevin's ears. The humid night air didn't mix well with the cool rain, and it kept the windows fogged over. It was late and only getting later.

Kevin was already regretting his job at the bank. His new boss had not liked owing Kevin's father a favor, and he had not bothered to hide it. As a result, he had embarrassed Kevin at every opportunity. He had even rejected cost projections for an advertising campaign twice; and as a result, Kevin had stayed two hours after closing to rework them. He still hadn't figured out how it was his fault the campaign had failed when this had only been his first day on the job.

Sadly, he also knew that by the time he got home, and tended to the crops and livestock, he would be facing a twenty-hour day. With only four hours sleep, he would have to get up, and do it all over again tomorrow.

Leaning forward, Kevin wiped fog from the windshield again. As he sat back, the lights on the old truck flickered, forcing him to slow his pace. He was about two miles from home when the truck jerked, and its engine died. A moment later, the lights went out and plunged the cab into darkness.

"That's unfortunate," he mumbled.

Kevin sat quietly and watched the rain pound the windshield. The swirling clouds overhead left little hope that the storm would let up anytime soon. After a moment he got out of the truck. Pulling his jacket tight over his shoulders, he turned toward home as water and mud filled his shoes. Reluctantly, he glanced upward. It was an odd storm, and it frightened him.

*Kaboom!*

Shuddering, he placed his leather briefcase over his head and started for home.

Suddenly, a bright light illuminated the road around him. Stumbling to a stop, he turned and faced the light. At first, he thought he was looking at the truck's headlights, but then realized there was only one, and it was much brighter than the old pickup. The glare was blinding, and he had to shield his eyes against it.

"Hello," Kevin said. The silhouette of a man stood just beyond the light. Kevin took a step forward. To his right, a cow cried out loudly as it scrambled away from the road.

"Hello? Who's there?" he asked, but there was no answer. "I can see you! What do you want?"

The bright light pulsed, and the man stepped forward. He remained hidden by the darkness, but a wave of fear hit Kevin. The man took another step, and the fear paralyzed him.

*Kaboo-oo-mm!*

The sky lit up with a series of flashes, and the man was illuminated for the first time, only it wasn't a man.

Wet slick robes clung to the tall creature's thin frame. It had thin white hair that the rain had plastered to its round head. Its waxy skin was smooth and glistened under the glare of the light. Swallowing the light that struck them, large round black eyes dominated its face.

Kevin desperately wanted to scream out in terror, but he couldn't. He wanted to flee, but his limbs were frozen.

As the creature stepped up to him, it raised a skeletal thin finger and touched his forehead. The finger was like a hot poker, and the pain propelled Kevin from his paralysis. He stumbled backward and fell into the mud. As the creature leaned over him, Kevin rolled to his feet and fled.

The blinding light turned red and raced after him. It easily circled around to block the road ahead of him. Desperate to escape, Kevin turned and splashed through a ditch. The barbed wire fence protecting the field cut his hands as he struggled over it. The barbs snagged his pants causing him to stumble and fell. Climbing to his feet, he ignored the pain in his hands, and fled for home.

A vortex formed in the center of the clouds. Kevin could feel them pressing down on him, but he refused to look up...

*...Wham!*

Paula was jolted from her reading by Kevin bursting into the living room.

*Slam!*

The door slamming shut caused her to jump again. Collapsing against it, Kevin screamed, "Get my gun! Get my gun! There's someone outside!" Blood flowed from his nose to stain his white shirt.

Paula leaped to her feet and rushed out of the room. She was only gone a moment before the door shook violently. Kevin sobbed as fear clawed at him from the other side. He pressed tightly against the barrier and reached up to slam the safety latch into place.

Through the window the glow filled the room, and Kevin could see the shadow of the tall creature standing at the edge of the porch. At sight of the creature, pain splintered his mind, and he collapsed screaming.

"Eeeeyyyyyaaaaa!"

Paula returned to find her husband clawing at his head, and rolling around on the floor. When she glanced up, she saw a monstrous face looming in the window. She stared at it in horror. She was shaken from her shock by a drop of blood falling from her nose to strike the back of her hand. Looking down, she saw the dark liquid slide off her hand to strike the wood floor. She looked from her hand to the blood soaking the front of Kevin's shirt. She raised her hand to her nose, and peered in fright at the crimson fluid staining her fingertips.

"Mama! We're scared!" The little girl clung to her sister and they both huddled in the hallway.

"Get back baby," screamed Paula.

The pain in Kevin's head surged out through his body and he shook violently. His heart threatened to pound through his chest. An uncontrollable urge to open the door overwhelmed him. He fought desperately against it, but reached up toward the latch anyway. He desperately wanted to stop but couldn't. He pulled back the latch.

"Stop!" screamed Paula.

"I can't!" Tears rolled down his cheeks, and he started to pull the door open.

Paula raised the shotgun and fired.

*Boom!*

The front window of the house shattered, and the strange creature disappeared.

Freed from the monster's mental grip, Kevin slammed the door closed again. He locked it and crawled toward Paula. Rising from the floor, he took the gun from her. He flipped the action, and the shotgun broke open to eject the empty shell. He snatched a shell from Paula's trembling hand and shoved it into the gun. When the creature appeared in the window again, he slammed the shotgun closed and fired.

*Boom!*

The man fell out of sight again, and Kevin quickly reloaded. He immediately raised it, and even though he didn't have a target, he fired.

*Boom!*

"Get back!" he screamed as pushed Paula back toward the hallway. The kids wrapped around her legs. Kevin reloaded the gun again, and placed himself between the stranger and his family.

The red glow floated into the room through the shattered window. Kevin raised the gun and fired.

*Boom!*

The gun had no effect on the light, but it retaliated.

*Fwssh!*

A burst of energy from the globe struck Paula, and flung her backward into the wall. She crumpled to the floor.

"No!" screamed Kevin, scrambling after her.

There was a bright flash outside the house.

*Ka-boom!*

A beam of blinding energy punched through the roof of the house and engulfed Kevin before he could reach Paula. The two girls screamed as debris rained down from above. Extinguishing candles and the fireplace, rain poured in through the ceiling.

Kevin was in agony. Every muscle in his body convulsed, his bones broke under the strain. The light melted his eyes, and the air in his lungs caught fire.

The young girls shook their mother as the shaft of light engulfing Kevin pulsed and cast off flares of energy that sparked small fires around the room. A wave of energy suddenly burst outward from the shaft, and the house exploded...

...Pelted by rain, Kevin lay stunned in the wreckage. His skin burned and images of his wife's crumpled body haunted him.

Someone bent over him, and touched his shoulder. The touch sent pain searing through him. Images of the surrounding countryside burst upon his mind. Springing from the debris, Kevin knocked the man backward.

He was standing among the wreckage of his home. Without turning his head, he could see all around himself. Behind him, just over a mile away, stood the Jackson's house. The still bodies of his cattle lay scattered across the field between the homes. He could see each one, all at the same time. Everything had a strange vagueness about it. The trees lacked limbs. They were large sagging masses. Spread across the ground, the grass was a stiff carpet. There was no texture, no color, no light, no darkness, and no life.

Unafraid, the man-like creature stepped forward again, and anger burned within Kevin. The globe of light was actually solid, and he could feel it pulsing. Kevin's anger to built in intensity until he could feel the pressure of it against the inside of his skull.

The creature recognized the threat of Kevin's anger, and assaulted his mind again with its mental touch. Kevin fought back against the assault, and forced his head to turn toward the creature, but he couldn't raise a hand against it. It had killed his family, and with every fiber of his being, Kevin wanted to kill it.

The creature reached out and touched him. The touch burned, but its mental dominance kept him from crying out. As it ran its finger over Kevin's naked metallic torso, it left a glowing scar.

As if gloating, the creature finally gave Kevin enough freedom to throw his head back and scream.

"Eeeeyyyyyaaaaa!"

Energy burst from Kevin's eyes, reaching miles into the sky. The creature laughed at Kevin's anguish...

...Kevin raced across the land. The air flowed quietly around him. His vision stretched out far enough before him to allow him to avoid obstacles in his path. He flowed around the obstacles, or over them without slowing. He never touched the ground and it didn't feel like running, but his body went through the motions. It was too smooth, his breathing too steady, and he didn't feel the pull of fatigue on his legs. Sometimes the ground was fifty feet beneath him as he flowed over treetops, and at other times it was inches beneath him as he darted under a bridge. He didn't even think about avoiding the obstacles. It just came naturally to him. The whole thing gave him a strange satisfaction and an odd feeling of joy.

Even though he found he didn't mind the running, he still struggled against the creature's mental directions. It pained him that he couldn't stop himself from following them...

...The walls of the cave were smooth, but faded to rock further away. The glow pulsed nearby and the creature, hurt or stiff with age, moved around him. Kevin stood silently in the corner, his mind caught in a mental grip stronger than his own steel-like hands. Anger burned inside him, and his heart ached. Instead of tears, his eyes leaked energy. He desperately wanted to lash out at the creature, but couldn't even turn his head unless the creature allowed it...

...Kevin knew he was slipping away, and had stopped fighting it. He had no idea how long he had lived under the creature's control, and he no longer cared. He died that day with his family, but he hadn't gone into the afterlife; instead he had been trapped in a metal shell that wasn't his own.

The creature's dominance grew stronger each day, Kevin's resolve faded. Knowing the creature was dying gave him some peace. It remained strong mentally, but its body grew weaker each day. Soon it would die, and Kevin hoped he would die with it...

...Something was different. The pull on his mind was weaker, and somewhere nearby a man struggled to survive.

Something slammed into his chest, but he barely felt it. He only briefly wondered about it because painful memories assaulted his clearing mind. Little children cried. The house exploded. Charred bodies lay around him. Deep inside, he cried out and longed to return to the painless oblivion.

His finger twitched. His body desperately sought freedom even if his mind couldn't grasp it. Slowly the cave came into view, and he could see a man rolling around on the floor before him. Curled up, the creature lay along the far wall. Its body was a stiff dry husk, but its mind was still dangerous.

Samuel was dying as he had died.

The monster was responsible for his pain. It was responsible for their deaths, and it wouldn't let him die to be with them. It kept him alive to torture him with their memories over and over again. Its only purpose was to cause him pain. There was only one way to escape that pain, through death.

Kevin stared at the creature, and willed it to die. His wrath built in pressure against his eyes. It had been so long ago, and he had not been allowed to shed even a single tear for her. The pressure threatened to burst his skull.

*Fwssh!*

Energy blasted from his eyes and struck the monster. The dried husk shattered against the rocks.

As Samuel fled the cave, the creature died. Kevin waited for death to release him from his pain. It didn't come...

...He shouldn't have come. It had been too long. To him, the memories were yesterday. To the world it had been much longer.

The house before him wasn't his own. None of the houses surrounding it were his either. The wreckage was gone, and there was no sign that his family had ever existed. The creature had taken them away from him, and there was no way he could get them back.

"Hands up, mister!" cried the man behind him.

Standing beneath the large tree, Kevin ignored the lawman. It wasn't the tree that his daughter's swing had hung from. It was much younger than the old oak had been. His wife's childhood swing had also hung from that old tree. But like them, it was gone.

"You heard'em! Hands up, freak!"

He ignored the second man as well. Originally, there had been only one, but then two, and now six. All of them pointed guns at his back.

"You can't stay here! People here don't want you hanging around! You can leave now or we can arrest you!"

They were starting to irritate him. Through clenched teeth, he growled, "Go away!"

"Now, we don't want no trouble from your kind, friend! This is your last chance to clear the area!"

He hated them. He hated them for not understanding. He hated them for not even trying to.

As he turned to face the men, fear spread across their faces. His large black eyes never moved, but each of the men felt them boring into their souls. Frightened, the closest man to Kevin stumbled backward.

"What the he..." he stammered as he tripped and fell.

*Kapow!Ping!*

The bullet ricocheted off Kevin's chest and struck another one of the deputies. Kevin didn't feel the bullet that instantly killed the man.

Panicking, the others reacted and fired their own weapons. The rounds bounced off Kevin's metal body, creating a deadly hail of bullets for everyone but him. None of the bullets penetrated his dense skin, but each one stung him deeper than the men could ever know. To him the deputies were no different than the creature that had held him captive for so long. They didn't care about his loss.

"All I wanted was to say goodbye!" Kevin charged forward, faster than the men could react. He struck one, and the man's ribs shattered as he was slammed into a car.

*Crash!*

He grabbed a second man and hurled him more than sixty feet.

*Kapow!Ping! Kapow!Ping!*

Bullets continued to bounce off his dense metal skin. Another deputy fell to a ricochet.

*Screech!*

Kevin ripped apart a patrol car. The lawmen scrambled away from him.

"Eeeeyyyyyaaaaa" he screamed. Turning, he hurled the car engine.

*Boom!*

It blasted through the front of the house that now stood where his had...

...The days blurred together, and he spent his time on the island in solitude. Even the globe that had once kept him company had found a new friend in Samuel.

At first he had tried to run himself to death, but that had failed. He had slammed himself into the side of a mountain, but had survived that too. He had leaped from the top of the mountain, but had again survived. Standing on the ocean's surface, he had begged to be allowed to sink beneath its surface, but he hadn't sunk any faster than the world's continents. Death just wouldn't come for him. He was destined to spend eternity with his pain...

...As the woman approached him again, he tried to ignore her, but found it hard. Unlike Samuel and the other people on the island, she refused to stay away. Every day for several weeks, she had come to sit on the rocks next to him. The woman's hair was long and flowing. Her frame was thin and her dress clung to her. She was beautiful, and her very presence demanded his attention. She never spoke, but instead enjoyed the island's beauty, and his silent company. Small animals came with her. They flocked around her and sang to her. It was calming.

Like so many times before, they sat in silent peace. Then to his surprise she spoke.

"Hello, Kevin."

It was the first time he had heard his name spoken aloud in a very long time. He had nearly forgotten it. Slowly, he turned his head to face her...

..."Dreah, we need him out there!" yelled Samuel from behind them. He frantically adjusted a television monitor and typed at a keyboard.

Kevin couldn't see what was on the monitor. His sight didn't allow him to see what was on any monitor or printed page, but he could hear what was being said. Causing as much destruction as it could, a creature known as Holocaust was tearing through New York City. It was killing indiscriminately, and its radioactive body made confronting it difficult. No one knew where it came from or why. It appeared from time to time and raged for days before burning out. In less than fifteen minutes, it had generated a body count of nearly a thousand.

"Patience, Samuel," said Dreah.

"People are dying! We have to move! This is a perfect opportunity to reveal Slipstream to the world, and maybe get past his history!"

"Patience," replied Dreah. Turning her attention to him, she said, "We need you, Kevin. Those people need you. You are unique. You can stop this monster. If you don't, people will continue to die."

Without turning to face her, Slipstream focused his sonar on Dreah's face. He knew she was right. She was always right; and even if she had not been, he would have helped her anyway. He wasn't over the loss of his family, but she had taught him how to deal with it. His pain was still there, but tolerable; and he no longer wished for death. At first, he had feared she was trying to take them away from him, but in the end she had only helped him. Now, she wanted him to stop a monster, and he would.

Gripping her hand, he crinkled the small photo she held. Dreah said it was a photo of his family, and he believed her. He had no idea how she could have come by it, but if she said it was his family then it was. He gently took it from her, and turned to walk toward the rear of the aircraft. He tucked the photo into his trunks and waited for the door to open. The air rushed into the aircraft, flinging loose items about the cabin. Without hesitation, Slipstream stepped off the platform, and plummeted toward the ocean below.

Before he reached the ocean waves, Slipstream manipulated the gravity well around himself and his legs pumped on the air as if it were solid ground. He pushed outward with his gravity field as he plunged into the water. His aura forged a tunnel through the water, and he ran through a dark trench forty feet below the water's surface. Samuel had taught him how. He still hadn't learned to reach the ocean's bottom, but he no longer sought to do so either. He had learned that he didn't need to breathe anyway, so attempting to drown himself was pointless.

He rose to just above the water's surface, and allowed his aura to slip just enough to force the water into a plume that flared out behind him. He grinned when the water washed over the deck of a ship to drench the startled crew.

Bearing down, he pulled himself away from his amusement and dug deep within himself at the anger that he kept buried there. Using it, he increased his speed, and the world around him blurred. Within moments, Slipstream crossed a hundred miles of ocean, and quickly reached the southern end of New York City. He pulled his aura in tightly around himself to prevent his turbulence from causing damage, but barely slowed his speed as he sped past Ellis Island and into the streets of the city.

Still over a mile away, Holocaust became the focus of his vision. The monster was nearly ten feet tall. It was massive, with enough strength to topple mountains. Slipstream's vision barely registered the halo of fire surrounding its skull-like head. The monster held the broken body of a woman above its head. She screamed as the monster's touch incinerated her skin. The wedding dress she was wearing burst into flames. The ground beneath it was littered with the bodies of her friends.

Gritting his teeth, Slipstream extended his aura out ahead of him. The building between him and the monster warped, and Slipstream slipped through it. Anyone in his path felt a wave of nausea as Slipstream's wormhole bored through them. Space collapsed in around him when he exited out the other side.

*Boom!*

Slipstream's momentum carried them both across the street, and through the lower level of another building. Their indestructible bodies shredded the building's interior.

*Boom!*

Debris was flung for over a hundred yards in every direction when they exploded out the other side.

Slipstream was the first to recover. He stood silently over the monster and waited for it to rise to its feet. Holocaust glared at the hero. Casting its head back it roared with anger.

"Graaarrrraaahhh!"

When the monster's voice stopped echoing through the steel canyon around them, Slipstream said calmly, "Come beast, test my mettle. You will find yourself lacking."

"Graaarrrraaahhh!" Holocaust roared in protest. The flames around its head intensified. Stepping forward, it stomped the ground and hunched down. It opened its mouth to bellow again. Slipstream held his ground.

*Fwwooosh!*

Instead of the behemoth screaming, fiery energy erupted from its mouth and engulfed the hero. The torrent of destruction continued for several seconds, and the hero was lost in the blaze. When the beast had exhausted its energy, it stopped and stepped back. Its skeletal face didn't show its frustration over what waited for it.

Slipstream stood in a pool of molten asphalt. He glowed brightly, and along with the picture of his family, his trunks had been incinerated. He held up his hand. He could not see its glow, but he could feel it.

"Graaarrrraaa....!"

*Boom!*

Slipstream's attack cut off the beast's scream of frustration. The attack echoed through the city.

*Crash!*
Windows of the nearest buildings shattered, and Slipstream pressed his attack.

*Boom! Boom!*
The beast was stronger, but the hero was faster. Slipstream's blows rebounded throughout the city. Each one caused Holocaust to cast off a deadly burst of radiation that threatened the life of anyone nearby. Slipstream felt the burn himself, but ignored it. His metal skin glowed, and those watching had to shield their eyes from the glare of the radiation.

Years of pent-up anger and hatred had found an outlet. With each blow, Slipstream saw the face of his wife. With each blow, he expended years of pent-up anger over the deaths of his children.

Buildings shook, the ground cracked. Their blows hurled cars and other debris for blocks. Slipstream ignored it all while Holocaust was oblivious to it.

Holocaust was a beast that understood only death and destruction. It raged with a fire deep within itself that burned all reason from its mind. It didn't care who it hurt, and Slipstream was just as good a target as any other.

Despite its might, it wasn't long before Slipstream stood over the fallen beast. It lay in a pool of melted pavement, and its intense radiation marred the buildings surrounding it. People crept closer, and one reporter declared the battle over. Fear choked him when the monster's aura flared, and Holocaust rose to its feet.

Slipstream was glad to see the creature wasn't finished. It was the first time anything had lasted more than a few seconds against him. It was the first real challenge he had faced.

However, he wasn't blind to the destruction their battle was causing the city. The military and local heroes did their best to keep the area cleared of civilians, but if the battle continued, the radiation bursts would prove fatal to anyone within miles. Even if he cared little for his own life, Slipstream cared for the lives of the innocent.

*Boom!*
Before the beast could turn to face him, Slipstream burst forward at full speed and swept up the larger creature. Within moments, his powerful legs propelled them both out of the city.

Overcoming the momentum of Slipstream's speed, Holocaust

raised its massive arm and brought it down on the hero. The metal warrior shrugged off the blow, so the creature raised its arm again, and pounded with even more force. Slipstream stumbled, and let go of the beast.

*Crash!*

Uprooting and destroying trees, Holocaust tumbled through the forest.

Slipstream regained his footing, and raced after the beast. Before it could rise, he slammed his fists into its back.

*Boom!*

The forest burst into flames as radiation was cast off the monster.

The battle continued for hours, and destroyed several thousand acres of forestland before Slipstream finally stood over the burned out husk of the Holocaust. Slipstream felt a deep satisfaction from the victory...

*...Thudda!Thudda!Thudda!Thudda!Thudda!Thudda!*

The spray of bullets deflected from the surface of the *Aegis*. The group of teenaged girls screamed in panic as the hero wielding it protected them from certain death. Each round from the helicopter's mini-gun pounded the shield with enough force to knockdown an elephant. Aegis gritted his teeth, and pushed back with all his strength. Behind him, Fluxstone's dense body shielded the girls from any bullets that got past him.

*Clang!Clang!Clang!Clang!*

"We are pinned down!" yelled Fluxstone over the sound of pounding metal. "Slipstream, we could use your assistance!"

Slipstream burst from the interior of the ruined tank. It had taken him longer to deal with the pursuing artillery than he had anticipated, and now the group was under attack from the air. "On my way," he said softly.

*Boom!*

Slipstream blasted across the desert at full speed. The plight of his friends quickly came into view. He charged the helicopter, and with one great leap he cleared the remaining distance to it.

*Slam!*

The impact ripped the helicopter from the pilot's grip, and it twisted out of control. Slipstream's gravity aura automatically adjusted to compensate for the spinning g-forces. He ignored the screaming pilot and reached for the gunman. The man foolishly turned the mini-gun on the hero.

*Thudda! Thudda! Thudda! Thudda! Thudda!*

Bullets bounced off Slipstream's chest, and into the helicopter. The engine gagged on the metal fragments and fire erupted from the cabin. Grabbing the gunman, Slipstream hurled him from the plummeting craft. As the hero turned on the pilot, the aircraft slammed into the ground.

*Kaboom!*

A ball of fire erupted from the impact.

As Aegis stood up, Fluxstone moved to stand beside him. Together they watched Slipstream rise unharmed from the burning wreckage...

..."We need assistance!" screamed Envoy over the commlink. Sounds of battle followed her plea.

Butch responded, "Hold on, darlin! We will be on the ground in one!"

Fluxstone looked at Slipstream and smiled. He knew what she was thinking, but his face didn't reveal his feelings over it.

Fluxstone stepped over to the door and pulled it open. The sudden release in air pressure caused the airship to suddenly tilt violently.

"Dang it, Fluxstone!" cursed Butch.

Gripping the edge of the door, she turned to him, "Sorry old buddy, but you're a little to slow! See you on the ground!" She flung herself out the hatch.

Butch's curses chased Slipstream out of the ship after her.

As the two fell, Fluxstone flexed and angled into a steep dive. Her enhanced density increased the distance between them. Angling himself steeper, Slipstream plummeted after her.

*Thoom! Thoom!*

Two human torpedoes plunged through the earth and into the underground complex...

...Paragon flung the soldier to the ground, and dived on top of him.

*Kaboom! Boom! Kaboom!*

Explosions caused the air to come alive around the two. The ground where the soldier had been standing was left a deep crater.

Slipstream stepped between them and the cascade of death. Dirt blasted him, but he ignored it.

*Boom!*
The sound of Slipstream's charge drowned out the next round of explosions. The man controlling the powered battlesuit aimed the cannon at the newcomer, and fired.

*Kaboom!*
The shell exploded as it slammed into Slipstream's chest. The hero's gravitational aura pushed him through the shell's knock-back, and he never slowed his pace as he barreled out of the smoke.

*Skrack!*
Slipstream's first attack ripped the man's arm off along with the battlesuit's cannon...

...As everyone around him celebrated, Slipstream stood silently at the edge of the group. The bonfire blazed as the bottle of champagne was passed around. He allowed himself a smile when Gemini shoved an empty glass in his hand, and Wavefront tried to fill it. Drunk, the Aussie spilled more of it on the sandy beach than he got into the glass.

"There ya are, mate! For the toast!"

Staggering away, Wavefront grabbed Fluxstone around the waist and heaved her into the air. He collapsed under her as she increased her density. Wavefront spilled more of the alcohol, and everyone laughed. Fluxstone didn't hesitate to help him to his feet.

As Dreah entered the circle of friends, she raised her glass high. Everyone stopped to listen.

"My friends, we are here tonight to celebrate the engagement of two people dear to all of us. We love you both, and wish you the best. Samuel regrets that he can't be here tonight, but I promise, with this wedding he will spare no expense. You can trust me, I have his credit card!" Everyone laughed. "Cheers Heather! Cheers Alex!"

Gemini held her glass up to Slipstream. After a moment, he held his up to her.

*Tink!*

After tapping the glasses, Gemini drank along with everyone else.

Slipstream hesitated. He had stopped trying to eat or drink a long time ago. He didn't need to, and he loathed the metallic taste everything had now.

Gemini's smile spread across her face as she held her empty glass up to his full one. "What's the matter big guy, can't hold your alcohol?" Her smile burst into laugher when he threw back his glass, and swallowed its contents in one large gulp. Gemini took his hands, and danced around him as loud music filled the air...

...He could not see them, but he could feel them. The sky was alive, and it called out to him like that night so long ago. He desperately wanted to yell out to Aegis and the others, but the clouds had already taken a hold of him. They had gained a grip on his mind before he had even suspected the danger.

Desperately, he struggled against them. He had pushed that horror from his mind long ago. He would rather die than allow himself to succumb to them again. He pushed against the clouds, but they grew stronger. Despite his desperation, he lost the battle. His memories of loss and pain struck him with such force he was driven to the ground. It was as if he was experiencing the horror for the first time.

The sky opened up, and the energy shaft flashed down from it. Slipstream's body screamed out in pain. He felt every painful moment from his transformation. His body convulsed as his heart pounded against his chest, and his blood boiled.

His mind screamed for help, but no one could hear him. Just like his wife and children, his friends were going to die. He had been unable to defend his family, and now he was unable to defend the only people he had come to care for since...

...As the creature reached down and touched him, Slipstream reacted. Anger flared and he lashed out at the creature responsible for his family's death. It was sent hurtling through the wall.

They were all around him and mocking him. They thought he was helpless, but they were wrong. His mind was stronger than they knew, and he wouldn't give them time to re-assert their hold on him. Even now they thought he was in their grip, but he wasn't. The energy globe zipped over before him and pulsed rapidly, building in power. It suffered under the domination of the creature just like he did, but it would get no mercy from him.

*No!*

Something was different. He was in control and he wasn't supposed to be. Dreah had freed him from their control long ago. She had taught him to lock them out of his mind. He concentrated on her, and she freed him again.

Slipstream turned his head, and saw the energy being hovering over him was Envoy. Some distance away Paragon struggled to rise. Sorrow filled him as he realized what he had done to his friend. Almost instantly, he was across the park and kneeling over Paragon. Relief filled him when his friend smiled up at him.

"Sucker punch, huh? I don't remember teaching you that one."...

...Slipstream watched as Envoy hugged Wavefront to her. Even with all his power, he couldn't help. In turmoil, Slipstream turned and walked from the pod bay. He had never felt so helpless...

...Slipstream had no idea how long he had been running when he felt a soothing touch on his mind. He recognized it immediately. A part of him wanted to ignore it, but he let Dreah in anyway.

*Rruummmble!*

For the first time, Slipstream felt the tunnel rumbling around him.

*Hello, Kevin.*

Dreah wasn't alone. Slipstream could feel his friends with her.

*I'm sorry that I didn't recognize your distress, Kevin. Please forgive me.*

Dreah always used real names. To her, monikers were like masks. They hid the real person beneath a false persona. They had a way of making someone forget who they really were. Just by saying someone's real name, Dreah had a way of reminding them of who they were. Everyone was human. Everyone was subject to human frailties. Dreah didn't like masks because they allowed people to forget that.

*You have to forgive yourself, Kevin. Aegis' death was not your fault. It wasn't anyone's fault. Aegis does not hold it against you, and he does not want you to hold it against yourself.*

Slipstream knew Aegis didn't blame him. That wasn't the man's way. That didn't mean he didn't.

*You are not all powerful, Kevin. You are subject to the same failings as the rest of us. Your skin may be impenetrable, but your heart isn't. With your power even I sometimes forget that. Slipstream is often the only part of yourself you show us, but it isn't all of you. It's why you didn't come to me for help. You didn't even recognize you needed it. You kept your mask on, and when you came down here it took control of you. Together, we can work through it; together we will get through this. You need us, Kevin, and we need you.*

If he didn't allow her to help him, he would fail again and more people would die. The air around him whined as he slowed his pace...

\* \*

Instantly, it ended and Sparrow collapsed to his knees gasping for air. His skin tingled with power, his eyes burned with energy, and his muscles twitched with strength. He desperately wanted to hold onto it all, but it quickly fell from his grasp like water from his hand.

He wanted to plead, to beg, for an opportunity to touch the power again. With that much power, the things he could accomplish were unfathomable. The Counselor and Diamond would hold no more power over him than he held over an erupting volcano. He would be truly free.

A hand gently touched his shoulder. It pulled him from his longing and he glanced up to find Dreah smiling down at him.

"Thank you," she said. "I'm sorry that got dumped on you. I needed help, and pulled on the group for strength."

Gently, she helped him from the floor, he had to steady himself as a wave of dizziness swept over him. Embarrassment quickly followed. Glancing around, he found that the others were still recovering as well, and had not noticed.

Gemini shuddered as she recalled the deaths of the small children in the explosion. Fluxstone pushed her hair back, and took a deep breath. Memories of Aegis were visible on her face. Paragon bowed his head in prayer. Butch was breathing hard and sweating. Only Envoy seemed to have suffered no ill effects from the joining. She had already stepped forward to greet Slipstream as he stepped down from the track.

Slipstream's face didn't reveal what he was thinking, or feeling; but Sparrow knew it was shame. He would be embarrassed that his actions had endangered others. Sparrow knew Slipstream better than he had ever known anyone before. He had experienced Slipstream's past, his power, his dreams, his wishes, and his entire life in the short time they had been in the hallway. He could have guessed Slipstream's next move in a game of chess.

Still holding his hand, Dreah pulled him forward with the rest of the group to greet their friend.

# CHAPTER 17
# ROSTER CHANGES

Diamond laid the sidekick on the table, and looked up at Envoy. His mind ran through a thousand reasons why he shouldn't accept her recommendations. He suspected she already had answers for each one.

"How do you plan to deal with Slipstream?"

"Dreah actually requested that we use him. She feels he has to confront his demons to get past them. Since he survived the zone of death in Paris, I was already considering him. I've spoken with Jonesy and Edmond, and they have suggested a possible solution. They will use a mental inhibitor to limit the range of his spatial awareness to only a couple hundred yards. They believe the limited range will prevent him from experiencing the full effects of the clouds. I'll have Dawn monitor him throughout the mission. Besides, he insists on going, and I don't think we can stop him. We don't want him showing up in the middle of the mission and creating a bigger problem. I believe he will follow my orders."

"He has always been headstrong. Very well. Have them try the inhibitor, but have Dreah judge its effectiveness. It is no good if it prevents him from functioning all together, or if it doesn't keep him from seizing." Shifting the subject, he continued. "How will you deal with Heather?"

Envoy could see fatherly concern in his eyes. Very few people ever saw it. Silently, she cursed Fluxstone's stubbornness. She had already spoken to Fluxstone directly to prepare for his question.

"I know she is hurting, sir. But we both know that she is emotionally strong. She can handle the mission, and she proved as effective against Austin as Meta-man. With the strategy I've planned, she should remain effective with Fuentes. I have spoken with her about Paris and Denver. If she won't agree to follow my orders without question, I'll have the Spirit dump her back here in the Citadel, and then I'll have Glip-2 lock her down."

Diamond's business eyes shifted back into place. "Okay, Envoy. If this is the plan and the team you want, we'll go with it, but I do have one additional member."

"Who's that, sir?" Envoy asked.

"Sparrow."

"Sir, if I may? Why Sparrow? If this incident is anything like Denver, Fuentes will be at least a red-level threat. How can Sparrow cope with that?"

"Sparrow is resourceful, don't underestimate him. He has proven to be a keen observer, and his judgment isn't colored by his personal feelings."

Envoy nodded. "Very well, sir."

"Anything else?" Diamond asked.

"If you don't mind sir, I'd like to speak to the people on this list personally. If anyone declines the mission, I'll quietly replace them from a list of alternates." Envoy had selected the list carefully and doubted anyone would decline, but she wanted to give everyone an out if they needed one. The failure in Denver had shown her just how dangerous this mission would be, and everyone deserved the right to privately decide their fate.

"We'll meet for team briefing tomorrow at fifteen hundred," said Diamond.

"Thank you, sir." Envoy got up and headed for the door.

Diamond allowed himself a moment to relax as he watched her go. Perhaps he hadn't been wrong to rely on Aegis after all. He had prepared Envoy to replace him and she had stepped in and done just that. It didn't mean he would abandon his alternate plan, but now he could give the *Aegis* to Fluxstone to ease her suffering.

Envoy's plan was good. It was precise, and he could not have devised a better one. She had probably been working on it even before the Denver mission. She wouldn't approve of the real reason he wanted Sparrow on the team but he wasn't going to leave anything to chance. Sparrow would be his backup plan, and it would remain just between them.

\* \*

It was early and the hallways were empty. Except for the night staff, everyone was asleep and only the constant hum of the Citadel's walls and the echo of Fluxstone's boots filled the corridors.

Fluxstone was grateful for the solitude, and didn't envy the sleep of the others. Even before recent events she had never been one to sleep much. In fact, she hated sleep. Some of the most terrible things in her life had come at her out of the darkness while she slept. Her mom's boyfriend had been one that had driven her onto the streets at the age of twelve. To survive, she had done things in the dark while others slept, things that frightened her now, things she wasn't proud of, things she never spoke of with anyone. As a result, she knew what hid in the darkness, and that people should be afraid.

In her youth, only drugs and alcohol had dulled her fears and worries enough to allow her to sleep. Diamond had zero tolerance for drugs, and she chose to avoid the alcohol. Those days were behind her and she planned to never return to them. Now it was only exhaustion that granted her sleep. Even now it pulled at her, but she refused to give in. Like that child of so many years ago, she feared what sleep would bring.

She had witnessed it in others, even in Aegis. It had taken nearly ten years but Aegis had eventually gotten over the death of his first wife. Their daughter, Alexis, still blamed him for the evil that took Lauren and had done her best to keep Aegis from getting over it, but in the end he had. With time Lauren had faded from his memory, and the pain of her death had subsided. Their love had disappeared. When she first met Aegis, he still wore their wedding ring, but he often forgot he even had it on.

People liked to say that time healed all wounds. Fluxstone didn't believe it and didn't want hers healed. She even feared it. She didn't want her memory of Aegis erased. She didn't want their love replaced. She didn't want the future to come, and she knew that sleep would only bring it faster. By holding off sleep, she held off a future without Aegis. Time had never healed her childhood fears, and she didn't want it to heal her now.

She had never discussed her fears with anyone, not even Dreah. Dreah had tried, but Fluxstone just didn't feel the connection that everyone else felt with her. Except for Aegis, she had never felt a connection with anyone.

Sounds coming from the gym caused Fluxstone to pause. She hadn't expected anyone to be up. Silently, she crept forward and peered around the corner. Across the room, Gemini was sparring with Sparrow. Glip-2 was watching from the far side of the mat.

Judging from their moves, they were teaching each other. Sparrow was teaching the quick and deadly moves of an assassin who struck from behind and only once. Gemini was showing Sparrow how to control the pace of a match. In their earlier match, Gemini had used Sparrow's injuries and his recent work out to exhaust him. She had only lost because Sparrow had lost control.

For some reason, the others accepted Sparrow. It was most likely because Dreah vouched for him. To Fluxstone, he was one of those things that lurked in the darkness. He had even been trained to come at you from it. The Counselor's manipulations had only made him more dangerous.

Fluxstone gritted her teeth. She wanted to intervene. She wanted to send Gemini to her room and kick Sparrow through a wall, but memories of the shield's cold metal in her hands held her back. Its return had nearly broken her resolve.

Aegis had not backed her when Sparrow had first arrived in the Citadel, and now it was too late. Unless Sparrow screwed up, no one would back her now. She was even unsure of her initial assessment. Convincing others when she couldn't hold onto her own conviction would prove impossible.

Memories of Aegis flooded her mind and Fluxstone had to hold her breath to keep from sobbing. Wiping tears from her eyes, she turned and walked away.

\* \*

Sparrow gave Gemini a wave as he headed for a t-port. Their sparring match had lasted nearly two hours, and he was exhausted. She was good, but he could only learn so much from her. If he was going to play Diamond's game, he needed an experienced teacher.

Of course, the sparring with Kahori served another more important purpose. The information she had shared during the match was far more valuable than any of the reports he had read.

Everyone was taking the failure in Denver hard, especially Envoy. Sparrow didn't worry about her however. She was strong and would be ready for the next event when it came. Her leadership hadn't been questioned, and she had a soldier's resolve.

Fluxstone's interference in the Denver mission was a surprise, but Diamond's reactions weren't. He had been furious, even if he hadn't yelled at her in front of everyone. No one argued that Fluxstone had saved Meta-man and Maverick from death, but it caused concern for her mental state. She had deliberately jeopardized the mission and had appeared suicidal. Envoy was convinced Fluxstone would not have pulled out if she had not been too injured to protest.

Wavefront's actions had only been an extension of the depression he had been showing since his friend's death. He had been pulled from active duty until Dreah cleared him again. Sparrow wondered if she had seen a vision of the incident, and if Diamond would have sent Wavefront into battle if she had. Jonesy and his scientists were still analyzing the data he had collected. At this point, it was considered their biggest breakthrough yet. Jonesy was reporting that if a firecracker sized explosion of the energy appeared anywhere on the globe, he would spot it.

Gemini had led him to believe Diamond was losing control, but after directly witnessing him, Sparrow wasn't sure. It had been three days since Denver, and Diamond still hadn't made a decision on their next move. It was a sign of hesitation, and not something Sparrow expected from him. No matter how bleak things looked, they stood a chance of success with Diamond. No one else had the conviction to make the tough sacrifices, and no one had the insight that he had. Diamond was the drive that had gotten them this far, without him they would fail.

He knew Gemini had her own reason for the sparring match. Curiosity over the events in Hong Kong had been eating at her for days, and feeding her information was the only way to keep her in check. She had listened to his story with interest and excitement. He hadn't told her everything, but it had been enough to satisfy her.

Sparrow wasn't surprised by Envoy's interference in his working relationship with Gemini. It would force him to be more careful in the future, or avoid using the girl. If he put Gemini in danger, he wouldn't escape Envoy's wrath; and it was likely she would bring others with her. Currently, he had no plans to leave the Citadel or any special missions planed, so he decided to put off the issue until later.

Pausing just outside Brandon's lab, Sparrow listened for any indication the room was occupied. Satisfied it wasn't, he entered and made his way past the swinging arm to the table containing the broken sidekicks.

Rummaging through the pieces, he pocketed several parts before picking up a small compact model. He popped it open and found it mostly empty of parts. He left the lab with it.

\* \*

Sparrow bent the light lower and examined the sidekick through a magnifying lens. The larger sidekicks had more power, and they had more internal memory than the smaller units. Sparrow hoped to boost the smaller device with parts from his broken larger unit. It took several minutes, but he finally worked the larger piece into the compact model. He then picked up another piece and began to work it in as well. When the small part failed to fit, he sat back in frustration and stretched to stifle a yawn.

Glancing around, he admired the large room. Dreah had taken the liberty of furnishing it with tools and parts while he was away. She had never hesitated to believe he would return.

His eyes burned from lack of sleep, but instead of turning in he put down the sidekick and crossed the room. He stopped in front of a suit of military grade body armor. Reaching out, he picked up one of the stiff plates he had taken from Alpha-Wing's lab. Like the *Aegis*, the pieces absorbed energy and used that energy to strengthen their internal structure. He didn't fully understand the physics behind it, but his engineering talents had allowed him to design a plan to put them to good use.

Holding the plate in one hand, he reached out and began to pull and straighten a thick wire sticking out of the vest. As he worked, the wire began to glow red in his hand.

"Hello, Glip-2," he said without turning. "I know you have the run of the place, but you can still knock."

"No hands," said the globe as it glided up behind him. "What'cha doin'?" he asked as his color shifted from red to green. The wiring in Sparrow's hand mimicked the color change. "You're going to stand out in the dark with all those glowing wires."

Sparrow smiled. "Don't worry, they won't be seen when I'm done." He stuffed the armored plate into the vest, and when it touched the wire, it began to glow.

"Hum, lets see if I can figure out what you are doing. It looks like the wires are passing energy between the plates, probably to strengthen them. Am I right?"

"So you are a scientist too?"

"Me? Heck no," replied Glip-2. "I just have access to a whole lot of data. Sometimes I scan it for viruses and such, and pieces of it get stuck in my head like a bad song. I can access it anytime I need to put tab A into slot B, but that's about it. Except for the Citadel, I pretty much have trouble programming my VCR.

"You would be surprised by what some people write down." He paused as if waiting for Sparrow to ask what. When Sparrow didn't, he wasn't deterred. "Jonesy has a deep fear of spiders and," in a deep *Gomer Pyle* accent, he said, "surprise, surprise, surprise, he doesn't like me." He dropped the fake accent. "Clara has a crush on you, and Brandon thinks…"

"Stop," said Sparrow, holding his hand out toward Glip-2. "I don't think I want to know what Brandon thinks."

Glip-2 laughed as Sparrow went back to work on the vest.

"You know, if you had a power source, you could use those plates to create an inertial field. They would constantly generate defense that way. It would also open up potential uses beyond defense."

"What?" asked Sparrow as he turned to face Glip-2.

"Your vest. It uses energy to strengthen those plates. By the way, I don't have any record of them. Their properties are similar to the *Aegis*, but they don't exist in the Citadel records."

Sparrow glared at Glip-2.

Glip-2 took his silence as an indication he should explain. "If you had a power source, the plates would remain stronger all the time. You may even be able to generate a powerful inertial field to enhance strength and agility. I've accessed a file by Sarah from several years ago that might help you. It would power the field, and not rely on you being struck to power the plates."

Of all the people he had met since coming to the Citadel, Glip-2 was the most confusing. He couldn't help but think of the globe as a child who craved the acceptance of those around him, often going to extremes to garner it. Of course, he was also a child entrusted with the security of the world's most top-secret facility.

"Show me," said Sparrow as he held up his assigned sidekick.

\* \*

Sparrow entered the sherry room and found Diamond seated before the fireplace in one of the antique chairs. Without speaking, Sparrow took the seat across from him. He stifled a yawn as Diamond took a sip of his drink and sat the glass down.

"I expect by now that you know we are planning a mission to Buenos Aries. Yesterday, I asked to see you and the others to discuss options. Before we could begin, the issue with Slipstream interrupted us. Tomorrow afternoon, we will have that meeting, but I have already made the decision to go ahead with the mission, and Envoy has already formed a plan. I want you at the meeting because I have added you to her roster."

"You want me on the ground in Buenos Aries? Why? I'm not a meta-human, and the reports on Denver indicate I would have little effect on the situation."

"Precisely why I want you there. You pointed out a potential solution to our problem with the Paris incident, and I want you to test it."

Sparrow didn't like where the conversation was going. The last thing he wanted was to be at ground zero for an event, but Diamond had already turned his first excuse around to make it the very reason for him go. Wondering whether or not Diamond was reading his mind, Sparrow narrowed his eyes with suspicion.

"As you pointed out with Paris, the protective flares targeted the individuals with the highest threat potential. In Buenos Aires, I suspect that will be everybody but you. In fact, I'm counting on it. As long as you don't threaten the target directly, you should have free run of the scene. I want you to get as close to Fuentes as you can without directly threatening her."

"That shouldn't prove too difficult."

"Before you agree, there is another part of my plan you need to consider."

Intrigued, Sparrow waited patiently.

Diamond sighed, and took another swallow of his drink before continuing. "I want you to be my eyes and ears on the ground. Envoy and her team will do everything they can to contain the event, but I don't want any more surprises, and we can't have another failure. Maverick has never been a team player. Fluxstone refused to comply with my orders, and Wavefront damn near committed suicide. I cannot have any of them, or anyone else, jeopardizing this mission. I need you to help me make sure that doesn't happen. I want you to intervene if they do. I recognize you are not equipped to deal with meta-humans, but these should help." Leaning forward, Diamond flipped back a cloth on the table between them to reveal several items.

There were two compact sidearms that resembled the DSS blaster he had been issued for the Paris recovery. At a glance they would pass for any modern day firearm. However, Wolff knew that their housings were made of the same material as the Citadel walls. Instead of being white, they were steel-gray. They could also pass safely through most standard metal detectors. Each one had a small laser sight mounted under the barrel. Sparrow suspected the sights were infrared and therefore invisible to the naked eye, but not to his goggles.

Sparrow reached forward and picked up the third firearm. It was also compact for easy concealability, but it had its clip housing in front of the trigger instead of in the grip. Three clips lay on the table. The weapon was made of the same lightweight material as the twin guns, but it was a darker gray. The handgrip slid open to reveal a series of flashing lights and indicators. The infrared laser sight was built into the barrel.

"As you know, larger versions of the matching sidearms are common issue with Diamond Security Solutions. You are welcome to a standard issued weapon, but I figured you would prefer these compact models. They resemble standard handguns, but they are not.

"The DSS Disruptor in your hand is a weapon that I keep on hand for special occasions. It is not standard issue. I will have Glip-2 forward a brief on its operational capabilities to your sidekick. Just one shot from that weapon will slow down most meta-humans. The energy burst will disrupt his powers, temporarily. It will give you time to react. It is very expensive, and a very hard weapon to replace. Unfortunately, each clip is only good for a couple of shots."

Sparrow looked from the sidearm to the other items on the table. There was a large combat knife with a blade of light blue metal. It was the very knife he had used to defeat the leopard. He had no doubt it was also made of some special material.

Next to the knife there were two combat batons that resembled common police batons. They were black in color and each one had a rubber grip on one end and a blue metal band on the other. They weren't anything he would use on a regular basis, but knowing Diamond, they held a surprise for anyone struck by them.

Leaning forward, he sat the Disrupter back on the table and picked up one of several bullets. He turned the small item over in his hand and examined it. The high caliber round had a slight green tint and no cartridge. He had seen similar items before, and even used them. The round was fired from a gauss or rail gun. No cartridge meant lighter weight, and no mess left behind. A five-round box magazine sat next to the other rounds on the table.

Sparrow glanced up from the round to Diamond.

Diamond pointed across the room at a large case. "The caliber of the round is unique and is designed to fit the rifle in that case. The rifle's configuration is similar to a *DSR1* so you should be familiar enough with it. The rounds are powerful enough to punch through the defenses of most meta-humans. Some will be too strong, like Slipstream. I discourage you from even thinking that it will slow him down."

Sparrow glanced at the rifle case. Twirling the round in his hand, he considered Diamond's words carefully. They had a high degree of discretion, and of consequence if he failed. Sparrow doubted Envoy would approve. Diamond could not afford another failure, and he was going to extreme measures to prevent it.

Without speaking Sparrow made his decision. He rose and quickly placed the items in a small satchel sitting next to the table. He then picked up the rifle case and exited the room.

Diamond poured himself another drink.

\* \*

The conference room was crowded and people were forced to stand. Sparrow knew most of them, and from their files he recognized the two he hadn't personally met.

The first one was Cassius Aaronson, also called Samson. He was a member of the European branch of DSS. He was over six feet tall, and he had the bulging muscles of a flexing professional weightlifter. Like his Biblical namesake, he had long hair interwoven with leather braids. He was supernaturally strong and nearly invulnerable. He had a propensity for violence, and a reputation for being headstrong.

Rakesh Tripathi, also called Mecha, was also from the European branch. He was much smaller than Samson, but was far more dangerous. His powers not only broke the laws of physics, but openly defied them. His file described how they worked, but only a meta-scientist could hope to understand them. He had the ability to inhabit mechanical and electrical objects and to control their functions. He could inhabit a gun, and prevent its mechanical parts from moving. He could possess a car and drive it away. He could access and even alter the programming of a computer. The possibilities were nearly limitless in a technology driven world.

As Diamond stood up at the end of the table, the room fell silent. When he spoke, it was with confidence.

"Everyone needs to understand this mission is vital. If there is anyone here who cannot or will not follow orders, excuse yourself now. I will not tolerate another act of insubordination from anyone." The room remained silent and Diamond glared at everyone in turn. Most couldn't hold his stare and looked away. "Good, that is how it should be." Turning to Envoy, he said, "You have the floor."

As Diamond sat down, Envoy moved from behind him to stand before the video wall. The wall lit up with images of Buenos Aires and Elaina Fuentes.

"Our primary goal is to avoid sparking an event. We will only engage Fuentes if we have to. We are going to be on the ground in case we are needed. We do not have permission to operate in Argentina, so we are going to avoid contact with the authorities.

"Dawn is already on scene. She is the only one who has permission to be within fifty feet of Fuentes. She was dispatched two days ago and has been undercover in a group of reporters trailing Fuentes." Envoy turned to face Jonesy. "Jonesy?"

Jonesy looked annoyed as he glanced over the brim of his reading glasses. Sighing, he said, "So far Fuentes has not displayed any abnormal readings. She has not reacted to Dawn's presence at all." Jonesy arched his eyebrows at Envoy to indicate his briefing was finished.

Envoy looked to Edmond. "Anything to add, Edmond?"

Edmond sat forward in his chair, and pulled his thick glasses off his nose. Laying them on the table, he glanced around. His eyes reflected confidence, but he wrung his hands nervously as he spoke. "This situation is prime for an event. From years of research, we know that adrenaline is a key component in the development of meta-powers. Given the state of matters, it will be running high in Fuentes." Behind him, the wall shifted again to show a series of medical images and a spiraling DNA strand. A photo of Fuentes filled the center.

"Engaging Fuentes will accelerate the event. Judging from Paris, we should have several minutes from the time the cloud starts forming to the energy shaft. That time shortened to mere seconds in Denver. There is no solid metabolic reason for it. I suspect the reason lies in the Psadans. They are monitoring these events from somewhere. Everyone should keep their distance until the plan is ready to go. Once you start, you will only have seconds, and I cannot predict what meta-powers Fuentes may have. Likely, they will be similar to Austin. Wavefront's readings from Denver will allow me to predict the ring of energy to within two point five seconds, but be ready for anything."

"Huh! Are you sure about that, Quasimodo? You missed a similar prediction once. Remember?"

Edmond looked at Maverick. An old memory passed between them. It was one Maverick didn't appear to have gotten over. "That was different, William. I'm sure."

Maverick frowned, but didn't reply. Edmond grew silent and looked hurt. His left hand shook slightly as he picked up his glasses and hid his eyes behind them once more. Meta-man scowled at Maverick, but the antihero ignored him.

Envoy shifted her position to draw everyone's attention to her, and away from Edmond. She had no idea what Maverick had referred to but it had caused Edmond to clam up. Behind her, the video wall shifted again to reveal a large outdoor arena.

"In two days Fuentes is participating in a large outdoor concert. The apparent lack of the world's governments to control the current crisis is her newest cause. Originally, it was scheduled to be a small indoor concert but faced cancellation due to recent events. Fuentes held a press conference. We sent Dawn to that conference. Claiming government interference to her right of free speech, Fuentes denounced the governments and set herself up for a fight. Large amounts of money traded hands, and she is now pushing forward with the concert. The concert was moved to this larger, privately owned outdoor venue. Since Fuentes remains at the top of our list to mature next, we are going to be prepared and on the ground.

"Tensions between Fuentes and the local police will be high. There is the potential for this situation to go badly, even if there isn't an event. We are not there for any confrontation between her and the police. We will not reveal our presence if such occurs.

"Mr. Diamond will monitor the mission from operations. On the ground, I will be primary team leader, and Meta-man will be secondary. If an order, or an idea, or even an itch, doesn't come from one of us, it isn't to be carried out.

"Fluxstone, Slipstream, Meta-man, and Samson will deal directly with Fuentes." Envoy looked at each one as she spoke their name. "Each of you receives your enhanced strength through different meta-powers. It should slow down any leaching from Fuentes. Engage Fuentes in pairs, and if you feel your strength being drained, back off and let the other team take over. Continue switching out to retain your power.

"Paragon, Sparrow, and Mecha will be responsible for crowd control. If this thing goes bad, there will be panic.

"Butch, Duo, and Q-Zone will back up crowd control from the *Exodus*. Shadow Spirit and Maverick will be on standby for evac."

"What? Backup? You have got to be kidding?" Maverick crossed his arms over his chest and glared at Envoy.

Envoy wasn't about to be challenged. "Everyone has a part to play, Maverick. Your teleportation is key to our success. Shadow Spirit has more difficulty forcing someone to teleport. You can do so freely. Despite what happened in Denver, you are the best chance of success if Fuentes has to be moved. If things go badly, you will be vital to evac. If you are injured or killed, everyone is in danger."

"I'm over four hundred years old. I don't need to be mollycoddled."

Envoy started to respond but Meta-man interrupted. "Maverick, you will follow the plan. If you don't feel you can, step down. We will replace you. It is not open to debate."

Maverick glared at the hero a moment before looking to Diamond. Diamond met his gaze for only a moment before turning to Envoy. "Continue," he said.

Maverick still had his hands folded across his chest. Pushing back his chair, he propped his feet on the table. He creased his brow and tightened his jaw.

Deciding he was done speaking, Envoy continued. "Jonesy and Edmond will run science. Curtis will monitor local emergency response. Lady Gemini will run team operations. Clara will be on hand for any special assignments. Any questions?"

After a few moments of silence, Meta-man spoke up.

"This girl is a fool. She puts lives in danger just so she can perch on her soapbox. Is there nothing we can do to stop this event?"

"Her people haven't responded to money," answered Bullock. "People like Fuentes rarely do. The government can't seem to stop it."

"I figured some of you would not approve of death threats, so I skipped that option." Diamond hadn't singled anyone out, but everyone knew it was Meta-man who would have had the biggest issue with the tactic. "I have attempted direct contact with her, but so far there hasn't been a response. Records indicate she hasn't returned any outside calls since the press conference. This is not the ideal set up, but we will make the best of it. We will not fail."

"Paranoia often goes hand-in-hand with a personality like hers," said Dreah softly from her couch at the end of the room. "Until the event, she will avoid anyone she doesn't fully trust."

"It is irresponsible," said Meta-man. "The world is tearing itself apart, and this little girl is consumed with her ego."

Sitting straight backed, Dreah countered. "She sees it as her purpose in life, her responsibility. It is not unlike that which drives you to do this, John."

"I do not profit from it," Meta-man added.

"That would depend on how you look at it, big brother. I don't see you going hungry."

Meta-man didn't respond to Maverick's taunt, but it did spur Envoy to continue with the briefing.

"The ground team will engage Fuentes on my order only. We are not looking to get involved in a slugfest, but our goal will be to hold her until Butch can sit the *Exodus* down. We will then put Fuentes on the pod, and Butch will fly her as far as possible from civilization. Once we are safely away from the city, we will teleport out and leave Fuentes to her fate."

"That seems a little cold," said Gemini.

"Yes it does." There was sadness in Paragon's voice. *"Speak up for those who cannot speak for themselves, for the rights of all who are destitute."*

Envoy knew Paragon and Gemini were more hurt by the situation than anyone else in the room. Despite the sadness in his eyes, Paragon knew that there was no other way and he would accept the inevitable. Gemini was a different matter. Her love of people would drive her to seek alternatives. In the field, that drive would cause hesitation and get somebody hurt. Talking it out here and now was for the best. "We hope we will not have to follow through with it, but we all need to understand that if Fuentes matures over Buenos Aires, it will kill millions. Any hesitation in the field, and we fail. We need to be willing to trade her life for theirs."

Gemini was saddened by the prospect of the young girl's fate. "Can't we just...I don't know...pull it out of her?"

"No," replied Edmond immediately. When everyone turned to him, he looked embarrassed and wrung his hands before continuing. "We have to be able to get near her first. If we are perceived as a threat in any way, we trigger an event. You are talking about serious genetic manipulation once we do get near her. We can strip DNA from individuals, but we know that when we attempt such experiments with the meta-gene, we get unpredictable results. Everyone, including the subject, was killed in a Global Genetics Research lab just over a year ago when they attempted a similar procedure. Unfortunately, it was not the first such failure. I am exploring the option, but I am not ready to try it."

"Well, how about Dawn?" countered Gemini.

"Dawn will be at the scene, and she can slow or inhibit certain metabolic functions within someone. She will intervene if she can, but

I believe all she will be able to do is slow the process. Her powers have proved ineffective against Slipstream in the past, and we expect similar results with any of the seeds. There are other meta-power inhibitors, but again, we have to be close enough to use them." Edmond shrugged. "It is the best I can offer at this point."

Lady Gemini looked defeated. Edmond looked ashamed to have defeated her.

Envoy sighed heavily and shifted the subject. "Crowd control, you will be primarily responsible for keeping civilians out of the fray, and off the back of the containment team. If the flares come at you or the civilians, defend them as best as you can.

"If we do have to act and Fuentes does not show the same traits as Austin, Maverick will attempt to teleport her out."

"That's the spirit, girl! Ride the wind!" shouted Maverick. "We should jump straight to that."

Envoy glared at him. She was starting to dislike the man and now understood why Meta-man had hesitated on calling him in to help.

"If Maverick is incapacitated, Shadow Spirit will attempt it. Remember we are not there to spark an event, only to observe. We act if we have to. We believe our actions in Denver caused the event. We don't want to do that here. Does anyone have any questions?" Envoy looked around the room, and when no one spoke up she looked to Diamond.

Standing up, Diamond addressed the table again. "We cannot stay behind the curve, folks. Paris caught us by surprise. We made mistakes with Denver. Let's use this event to get ahead of this thing. Keep your eyes open. Watch for anything and report everything. The only way we are ever going to defeat this is by going to the source. Jonesy is convinced Wavefront got us most of the way there. I need you to get us the rest of the way. Don't lose hope. Do your jobs and we will beat this thing. No one else has to die." Standing tall, he buttoned his jacket. "Now, let's get started."

* *

Sparrow stood across the room from the armored vest and examined it. Like a SWAT vest, it was bulky. He had worn heavy gear during his military days, but while working for the Counselor he had learned to travel light; bulky armor usually didn't make his list of supplies.

Nevertheless, the armor was necessary. With Glip-2's files, he would be able to refine it down, but for now it would have to do. He didn't have time to complete it before Buenos Aries.

Pulling a DSS sidearm, Sparrow fired it at the armor. The weapon's energy ripped through the fabric, but it didn't punch through the plates beneath. Sparrow shot the vest several times, but each time the plates stopped the beam and left the mannequin unharmed.

Putting the weapon in its holster, he hung it next to the mannequin and picked up his wristband and dart gun. He moved over to the workbench, and spent the next several hours making adjustments.

\* \*

Impatient, Diamond paced the small room. Only Fluxstone or Gemini ever bothered him in his private chambers so he didn't worry about being disturbed. Whether or not the call came before the deadline wasn't what made him impatient. No, it wasn't the small details that bothered him; it was the whole cursed affair. Having spent his entire adult life preparing for the Psadans and their evolutionary manipulations, he was tired. He wanted it over with, and if it didn't end soon he feared he would end up like Harvie.

The parallels between their lives were disturbing. Obsession had pushed them both into struggles that had consumed most of their lives. Neither man had a personal life. Harvie had killed his entire family, and Diamond only had Gemini and Fluxstone; but with neither being his true daughters, their relationships were often strained.

Both men had spent most of their lives alone. Harvie had lived in seclusion for over a hundred years, and Dreah had been the closest Diamond had ever come to being in love. His obsession had driven a wedge between them.

Perhaps the most disturbing parallel was Harvie's insanity. It consumed Harvie's mind every day, and Diamond fought against his every day. If it weren't for the memories of the Psadan in his head, he wouldn't have even known about the danger facing them all. He didn't understand the vast majority of them, but they had guided him over the years anyway. The problem was that they were strong. It was a constant battle to keep them at bay, and he was growing tired. When he finally found himself unable to continue the fight, he would be driven insane.

He didn't curse his condition. That would have been a waste of time. There was no greater power cursing him, and his plight was no more burdensome than that of a man who faced terminal cancer and withered away slowly each day. It was infuriating, but it was simply his burden. Cursing his misfortunes would result in nothing. Only by meeting them head on did he have any hope of defeating them. He feared he didn't have enough strength to see things through to the end.

A call interrupted his thoughts, and unconsciously he breathed a sigh of relief. He hit the accept button and a dark-haired man filled the screen.

"Yes sir," said the man in a heavy Russian accent.

"Is everything in place?"

"Yes sir. Ve are ready and eagerly avaiting your orders."

The man didn't know who Diamond was, and the image Diamond projected to him was a fake; but Diamond knew him. The man's name was Anton Czajkowski, and his mercenary group was known as Black Sunday. Diamond had learned everything there was to know about them before establishing contact.

"You will await my orders. You will not engage without them. Am I understood?"

"Yes sir," the man replied. "I did not mean to imply othervise. For vhat you are paying, I vill sit and vait as long as you vish it."

"Good, see to it that you do."

Diamond ended the transmission. There was no need for them to discuss mission details. As long as the money held out, the man knew the assignment and he would complete it. Diamond would rather have relied on Envoy or Commander Bullock over the team of mercenaries. Envoy and Bullock did what they did out of a sense of duty, the mercenaries did what they did out of a sense of greed. When someone believed in a cause, they committed everything to it. Unfortunately, every member of the mercenary team lacked something Envoy and her team had. They lacked the meta-gene. As for TASC, this crisis had nearly stripped him of their use. He had Bullock and a couple of platoons in the Citadel as well as four in seclusion at various strategic points. The rest were under arrest around the world. He had no doubt Bullock was capable and would carry out the assignment without question. He simply wanted to continue to hold TASC in reserve.

If Black Sunday's mission were a success, TASC would complete the assignment. If they failed, they were expendable.

Sparrow's observations had made it abundantly clear that the seeds were capable of distinguishing between threats. Edmond believed this extended to distinguishing between human and meta-human. Jonesy argued that the one incident wasn't positive proof, but Diamond had made meta-humans his life's work. He understood more about their abilities than anyone. Edmond's observation was correct. It wasn't even a unique ability. Counting, Dawn, Dusk, and McCoy, he had seven such individuals in his employ.

Edmond had suggested that a seed's ability to detect a meta-human was part of its defenses. It meant the Psadans knew meta-humans posed a threat. It also meant the Psadans could deduce that Diamond and his team were a threat. Diamond wonder just how long he had before they interfered directly.

Using the mercenary team was risky, but they weren't directly connected to him. It was the best option at this point. The fallout from Denver had already doubled the cost of the traitor in Lekkas' private army. He couldn't continue to wait.

If everything went correctly, the mercenaries would isolate one of the seeds, and give him enough information to develop a reliable strategy for dealing with the others. The abduction wouldn't escape Clara's notice, and the fallout with Meta-man would be great, but success was more important than their relationships with him. In the end it wouldn't matter if Meta-man hated him, or even destroyed his empire, as long as the world was safe.

If the plan failed, his involvement would be hidden under a field of planted evidence. To Clara, and to the world, it would appear as if a turf war between mobs over prostitution rings was responsible.

The biggest loss would be the confusion to the meta-human family tree. It would be nearly impossible to identify the most likely target among the thousands of people in the family tree. It could potentially lead to the destruction of a major city. He didn't particularly want to lose Black Sunday either. They were discreet and efficient. Diamond could think of a dozen possible uses for them at any given moment. Replacing them would require effort.

Pouring himself another drink, Diamond sat down before a large fire and stared into its depths. The irony that he had surrounded himself with meta-humans in anticipation of this disaster only to find the solution in normal humans didn't escape him.

\* \*

Patiently waiting for the others to arrive, Sparrow adjusted the bulky vest. The armored plates gave it better defense than a normal vest, and Sparrow hoped he would be able reduce its size over time. It was uncomfortable and caused the hidden DSS Disruptor to poke him in the side. *Policie* was written on a patch across his back, and he wore a black police belt with a DSS sidearm and a pair of handcuffs. A large police band radio was attached to the front of the vest. The blue survival knife was secured in a leg pocket. He shifted the vest again and cursed.

"Problem?" asked Slipstream.

Sparrow glanced at the man before answering. Slipstream stood as still as any marble statue adorning any number of outdoor gardens around the world. He hadn't even turned his head to speak. Following the man's eyes, Sparrow suspected he was watching Envoy who was engaged in a conversation with Butch and Meta-man.

"I haven't worn a police vest in a very long time."

"I would have refused to wear it." Slipstream took a step toward the group.

Glancing at the hero's muscled chest, Sparrow grunted. "Yeah, well, tank shells bounce off of you. I'm not so lucky."

Slipstream didn't reply and started walking toward Envoy. Sparrow looked to see what had the man's attention.

Gemini had entered the room and was approaching Envoy. She was dressed in a black and purple padded uniform and carried a large high tech staff in her left hand. A belt around her waist had numerous pouches. Her hair was tied into a ponytail. She wore a large curved glass shield across her eyes that left the lower part of her face exposed. The glass was reflective on the outside, but when she turned her head, Sparrow could see that the underside was lit up like a computer monitor.

Following close behind was a second Gemini. She was dressed in a pair of loose fitting blue jeans and a purple oriental style top. She had soft purple slippers on her feet and carried a sidekick in her right hand. Her hair hung loose.

Envoy saw Gemini coming and stopped her conversation to face the girl. Taking in every detail, Envoy's eyes darted back and forth between the two girls. Sparrow picked up a large bag at his feet and joined Slipstream. The two waited within earshot of the group.

"Yes, Kahori?" Envoy asked.

"I want to come along."

Sighing heavily, Envoy raised her eyebrows and resisted the urge to roll her eyes.

"You know you are too young..."

"Kandi and Brian are only a year older than I am. Kandi was active when she was only thirteen, and Brian when he was seventeen. I'm ready, Envoy. I'm ready. Dad will approve it if you do."

"Girl," said Butch, "aren't you sharp today?"

Slipstream started to step forward, but Sparrow placed his hand on the man's chest, gently restraining him. Softly, he said, "She is ready, probably more ready than the rest of us." Slipstream held his distance.

Envoy shot Sparrow a hot glare. The artifact had picked up his words even if no one else had.

As everyone waited for Envoy, Sparrow studied the two girls. Gemini hadn't discussed it with him, but he knew everyone believed her doppelgangers were left-handed, while her original form was right-handed. He had no doubt the handedness of the doppelgangers was a farce. It was just another trick she used to confuse her real form with her duplicates. By not telling him about it, she had hoped to fool him with it as well. Despite the armored girl holding the staff in her left hand, he watched the girls closely for any sign as to which was the real Gemini.

Silently, Envoy considered the young girl's request. Her dark eyes looked for any trace of a trick by Gemini. Envoy knew her well enough to expect one. Finally, she glanced over at Fluxstone.

"You get no help from me. Aegis was right. At some point she is going to do this with or without us. With us, it is safer. I'm grateful it is your decision."

"Thanks," Envoy mumbled. Looking back to Gemini, she said, "This mission is extremely dangerous..."

"I know that," interrupted Gemini, "But truthfully, when are they not. If we wait for a safe mission, I'll be old and gray. I've studied your plan, and I know every detail of it. I'll remain onboard the *Exodus* with Butch. When Fuentes is transferred aboard, I'll be on the ground with Shadow Spirit. Envoy, I will follow your orders. I know if I screw this up, I'll never get another chance."

Envoy's heart sank as the girl's words defeated the only real defense she had. Looking into Gemini's eager eyes, she felt her age. In ten years, Gemini had used her doppelgangers to accumulate the knowledge and training of six life times. She was better trained than anyone else in the room. She knew every detail of their past missions, and next to Diamond, she knew more about meta-humans than anyone. Sparrow was right. She was ready, even if Envoy didn't want to admit it.

"Okay, little sister. If Mr. Diamond agrees, you may send one doppelganger. You will remain on board the *Exodus* until Fuentes is transferred aboard. Then you will stay within twenty feet of Shadow Spirit. Are we understood?"

"Yes ma'am," replied Gemini, barely able to contain her excitement.

Envoy and the armored Gemini stepped aside to contact Diamond.

Gemini stepped over to Sparrow and smiled up at him.

"Thanks," she said.

"For what?" he asked.

"I heard you, thanks."

"You may regret it."

"Oh no, I won't. I've been waiting for this my whole life."

"Follow orders and stay out of the way of the big boys."

"Scout's honor," she said as she backed away. Turning, she darted for the exit.

"She didn't wait to hear her father's response," said Slipstream.

Sparrow had no doubt Diamond cared for Gemini. He had been responsible for raising her from the age of ten, but he also hadn't spared any expense preparing her for this day. Diamond would agree to the plan.

Glancing at Slipstream, Sparrow added, "She's never been a scout either."

Slipstream grunted in response and the two men moved over to the pod doors to await the others.

\* \*

Without waiting for Diamond to give the order, Gemini smirked and tapped her controls. Plunging the room into command mode, the lights dimmed and the video wall shifted to make room for the team's bio-monitors. This was the largest field team Gemini had ever managed. It was going to be a challenge but with a doppelganger just thirty-feet away in the special ops center, and one on scene, she had backup. The three shared a special commlink that only they monitored. She could barely contain her excitement.

Diamond glanced around as the lights dimmed. He then turned to Lady Gemini. She ignored him, but he knew she was aware of him. Briefly, he felt a father's worry. Even though he had made the decision months ago, it had still been hard to deliver it to Envoy. Gemini was ready and would prove to be one of his best field agents. Still, he couldn't help but feel a sense of loss for his little Gem.

"Status?" Diamond asked.

"Green," replied Jonesy.

"Green," said Curtis.

"Green," said Lady Gemini.

"Green," replied Gemini's doppelganger from the special operations center.

Diamond's glanced in the direction of the small room, but he didn't comment. He wasn't surprised. Like him, Gemini was always prepared.

"Status green," said Butch from the *Exodus*.

"Green," said Envoy.

"Green," said Dawn. Her voice was nearly drowned out by the dozens of cheering fans surrounding her.

Standing up, Diamond opened his commlink and said, "Okay, people, no mistakes. We do not want to be responsible for an event today. Stay out of sight and keep a close eye on everyone and everything."

A video feed on the wall showed a throng of fans as they erupted into cheers in response to Elaina Fuentes walking out onto a platform overlooking them. The young woman waved energetically.

Everyone in the command center stopped to watch the scene. Jonesy duplicated the image and applied filters that altered the coloring and highlighted the woman's eyes and skin tone.

"There is no sign of the energy disruption over the city, and there is no unusual cloud activity. Subject's body temperature and adrenaline levels are slightly elevated but normal. Subject's eyes are not dilated."

Gemini looked over at him and frowned. "Jonesy, you are such an asshole. She is a person, you know. And she is only twenty-three. She probably wouldn't understand the danger even if we explained it to her. She is not *subject*. She has a name so use it. Treat her with respect or I'll come over there and show everybody just how big a nerd you really are..."

"Gemini!" Everyone turned to look at Diamond. "If you are to remain here, you will act professionally."

Gemini hesitated and then lowered her gaze. "Yes, sir." She turned her attention to the monitor in front of her and everyone else resumed working.

\* \*

Looking out at the gathering crowd, Envoy considered the plan. It was a good plan. It was a solid plan.

Focusing on Fuentes, the young woman was outlined with a soft red glow and data about her heart rate and blood pressure scrolled across Envoy's vision. A moment later, the artifact on Envoy's arm automatically highlighted Dawn, but as usual the artifact couldn't read her bio signs and registered her as an anomaly. Dawn was the only person Envoy knew that she couldn't scan. She suspected it had something to do with Dawn's natural ability to mimic the bio features of those around her.

Perched on a rooftop a block away from the arena, Envoy could see everyone was in place. She adjusted her vision to automatically track them. As long as they remained in visible range, she would be able to follow them without much concentration.

Only Sparrow moved among the crowd. He was disguised as a local cop and from time to time he disappeared from range. Concealed in the shadows by Shadow Spirit, the containment team and the crowd control team were off to the left of the stage. They were a mass of red in Envoy's vision, but only because she knew where they were. The Spirit could even keep them concealed from her when he chose to. The space they were in was way too small for a group their size, but somehow the Spirit held them safely there. When people passed through the shadowed area, they experienced a chill and often avoided it after that.

Envoy knew the team would grow restless, but it couldn't be helped. They needed to stay near Fuentes and since Diamond Security Solutions wasn't authorized to operate within Argentina, the small space was the best they could do.

She glanced up to confirm that the *Exodus* was suspended above them. It was a small dot in the distance. A normal eye would not have been able to see it at all.

After several minutes, Fuentes finished signing autographs and left the small stage. If the event stayed on schedule, it would begin within thirty minutes with a small local band. An hour later, Fuentes would take the stage. Envoy was already restless and knew she would only get more so as the afternoon wore on.

Fuentes took the stage on schedule and clouds began to cover the city, but they were puffy and white. No thunder rolled between them and Jonesy continued to report the weather activity for the area was normal.

The events of the last couple of weeks had whipped people into a frenzy, and the crowd had plenty of pent up energy. Like most of the world, Buenos Aires had suffered from rioting and looting, and everyone feared the end of the world had come. The concert was an excuse to cut loose.

It gave the local police plenty to do as fights broke out between those who had drank too much and those with something to prove, but it didn't give the team anything to do. Two hours into the concert, boredom began to take its toll on them and morale began to break down.

Envoy yawned as the latest round of radio checks gave Maverick an excuse to voice his frustrations.

"This is ridiculous. I've wasted an entire afternoon next to these head splitting speakers and I can't even understand what this bitch is saying. On top of that, it's too damn cold in this freak's shadow. We should leave these beans to their fate!"

"Shut up, you bigoted ass," snapped Butch. "Argentina is a region of immigrants from numerous European countries."

"Blah, blah, blah. Bite me, fly boy!"

"Cut the chatter!" interrupted Meta-man. "Mav, you have been told your attitude won't be tolerated. You are being well compensated for your time. Stifle it and bear it. Butch, ignore him. He's been this way his whole life."

"Let's stay alert, folks," said Envoy. "I understand everyone is getting restless, but let's not assume we are in the clear."

She doubted Meta-man's retort would keep Maverick in line for long but at least he was quiet for now. She suspected keeping the man in line was something Meta-man had been doing for a very long time. As for Butch, he rarely instigated such matters. He wouldn't hesitate to jump on Maverick's comments, but, unless they were about his motorcycle, Butch wouldn't go looking for a fight.

Envoy felt a headache coming on and grunted. Unfortunately, that was something the artifact had limited ability to deal with. It helped her wounds heal, but it usually ignored minor inconveniences caused her by either it or the environment. Reaching down, she opened a pouch on her belt and chewed the aspirin carried there. Always having them on hand was something Aegis had taught her.

\* \*

Sparrow stood aside as a crowd of teenagers passed. One of them glared at him and impolitely lifted his middle finger in salute. Sparrow retaliated with a menacing grin, and a wave of the automatic weapon strapped to his chest. The kid immediately disappeared into the crowd.

When Sparrow was between the stage and the fans, he took a moment to study Fuentes. She was not what he had expected. Instead of a rough nail biter with dark hair and black makeup, she was naturally pretty and energetic. She smiled a lot and had dark brown hair that was loose but not wild. Her large eyes were a light brown. Most striking about her appearance was her young appearance. He knew her age from the briefings, but her appearance still contrasted sharply with the image her reputation generated. When you rolled her reputation in with the threat she posed, it made him feel pity for her, and fear of her at the same time.

It wasn't her political influence that caused him his fear. With the pull of a trigger he could end that, and she would be forgotten in a week. One mission from the Counselor had more political influence than any statements the girl would ever make. The Counselor had once called Sparrow a Political Manager whose actions impacted nations for years. No, her politics were not a reason to fear her. It was the global threat she posed simply by being who she was, and the lack of control she had over it that was to be feared.

Fuentes made the nuclear threat of the cold war seem like fear of a firecracker. Denver and Paris had virtually shut down the global economy. The US was scrambling for emergency funds and Paris had plunged France into complete bankruptcy. The nation would take decades to recover. Europe was in chaos as it struggled to help one of its own, while facing the fear of further incidents.

People were fleeing major cities and screaming for the governments to protect them from an unknown enemy. The governments of weaker nations were failing and hunger was spreading like wildfire through the poorer countries. With everyone pointing fingers and no one trusting anyone, fighting between neighbors was common. No one, not even Edmond, knew how Fuentes would compound the problems. Fuentes was the end of the world, and Sparrow's finger itched to deal with her.

\* \*

"That's right people!" shouted Fuentes. "Our government has failed us! They have no idea what has caused the death of two of our sister cities. They will find that they are the cause!" She paused as the crowd cheered. "For years greedy politicians have been dumping our money into programs that create toxins and poisons and monsters that destroy our planet. They cover up their involvement and spend more of our money on false trials to find the truth!

"To this day they deny their connection to the Muskeg and to the innocent people it slaughtered! But we know it was all to create a bio-weapon for their wars. It has been proven. There is video evidence! They could not hide the truth then, they will not hide the truth now!" Cheering erupted again.

Over the last ten minutes, Fuentes had been working the crowd toward a riot. Her words were translated for the team over their commlinks, and everyone focused as much attention on her as they could spare. The stadium shook with the chanting of her fans and clashes with law enforcement were increasing. Thermal imaging showed that her body temperature was rising.

Dismissing Fuentes as a lunatic, Edmond focused his attention on his calculations. After all, he knew the Muskeg and Beatrice was as docile as a rabbit. The US government had created her, but she had not killed anyone. The psychos who had sought to control her were responsible for that. Sadly, he knew the complete truth would never be known and Beatrice would continue to be persecuted for it.

After several moments, he came to a conclusion and was about to announce it when Dawn's voice interrupted him.

"I'm growing concerned. Fuentes is really working herself up. Her heart rate and temperature are way up."

"I concur," said Edmond. "Her bio-levels are rising faster than they should. There is definitely activity here. If she continues at her current rate, I predict we will have an event in two minutes twenty-one seconds."

"Good, let's amp it up!" said Maverick.

"Look alive, people." Diamond was determined to keep everyone focused, and to prevent Fuentes from destroying Buenos Aires. "Remember, if this thing goes badly, focus on what is before you. Do not focus on the clouds above you."

"Sir," said Curtis. "Local police bands are heating up. They are growing concerned with the crowd and are making plans to shut down the event."

"We can't let that happen. It will be a serious adrenaline spike for her. It will push her over the edge."

Diamond looked at Edmond. "We have no influence over the locals. They shut us out."

Disappointed, Edmond went back to his numbers.

Fuentes was sweating heavily and wouldn't let the audience rest. The police were staging themselves at the exits and at key positions in anticipation of the riot everyone saw coming.

"Butch, drop your altitude in anticipation of a quick set down," said Gemini.

"Roger that," Butch replied. "Engaging stealth."

Diamond watched the monitors with anticipation. He feared being right, but had a longing for it as well. He knew how quickly things could go wrong, but he needed his theories tested in order to send Black Sunday into action. As for Buenos Aires, only DSS stood between it and death.

On the video wall, a counter ticked off Edmond's prediction and everyone sat on the edge of their seat. Envoy left her perch on the rooftop and circled over the arena. Those concealed in the shadows grew more impatient, and Sparrow watched from the front of the stage.

On the stage Fuentes was frantic and in the stands her fans were in a furor. As the countdown reached fifteen seconds, she picked up a bottle of water and threw it in the direction of several police officers. They responded by darting up the steps and onto the stage.

Suddenly, Jonesy's console lit up. "What the...," he mumbled as he looked down. He tapped a blinking light and a globe filled his screen. It expanded to reveal a map of Antarctica. There was a red flashing dot several hundred miles from the South Pole.

Edmond was confused. He frantically moved back and forth between his numbers and the monitor wall. "Something has changed. Her bio-signs have stopped rising."

"Wrong again, huh?" mocked Maverick over the radio.

"No, I'm not. Something has affected her bio-signs."

"No! Her system is spiking!" yelled Dawn as she raced up the stage steps. "It's happening!"

Edmond's timer on the monitor wall expired, and flashing red lights lit up the command center as a loud buzzing filled the air.

# CHAPTER 18
## DEATH OF A SEED

"Butch, on the ground now! Ground team clear him a spot! Move people, move!"

Envoy raced to the stage so fast it appeared to those watching that she materialized there. Shedding blinding light on the crowd, Envoy's glowing shield caused a hush to fall over the mass of people.

*Ka-bo-oo-om!*

Thunder rolled across the sky as Envoy locked eyes with Fuentes. Envoy saw a frightened plea for help that quickly vanished as the girl's eyes hardened, and turned black.

*Fwssh! Fwssh! Fwssh!*

Three flares erupted from Fuentes, and struck Envoy's shield. Envoy poured as much energy as she could into the blinding shield, and rocketed skyward with all three flares in pursuit.

Those people near the shadows concealing DSS fell back in fright as the shadows suddenly expanded to reveal the team. Meta-man arched over the heads of the people while Samson and Fluxstone shouldered their way through the crowd. A lone security guard grabbed at Samson, but the strongman easily shrugged off the feeble grip. Slipstream struggled to follow them, but staggered and swerved off to the side.

Mecha reached out and touched a power cable. His body faded from view as he entered the stadium's computer network.

Maverick instantly materialized at the front of the crowd, waving a shotgun at them. "Clear out, tatterheads! This place isn't safe anymore!"

A security guard reached for him, Maverick struck the man across the face with the butt of his gun. The man collapsed at his feet.

"I warned you it wasn't safe. Who's next?" Maverick stepped toward the crowd. It fell back from him.

Paragon unfurled his wings, and stepped before the crowd. "Please move back from the stage!" Despite his calm demeanor and commanding presence, the crowd's concern for Fuentes surged it forward.

*Fwsssssssshh!*

Steam gushing from the opening doors of the materializing *Exodus* less than ten feet above the crowd pushed it back again.

Gemini hung from the doorway with her staff in her hand. "¡Por favor, cada uno sigue siendo tranquilo!"

Duo flew from the ship and out over the crowd.

Shadow Spirit extended his hand and shadows leaking from under his cloak formed a wall between the stage and the crowd. It emanated a wave of cold that drove people further back.

Within moments Mecha had control of the network. He shut down the microphone on the stage and opened all the exit doors. Across the speaker system, he said, "This is a police emergency. Please, everyone exit in an orderly fashion!" To emphasize his words, exit signs began to flash in both Spanish and English. "¡Esto es una emergencia de la solícia! ¡Por favor, cada uno salida en una manera del ordenado!" he repeated.

\* \*

As the protection of the Spirit's shadows withdrew, Slipstream's mind rebelled. The clouds were more than just above him. They were all around him. They reached out to him and wrapped their evil talons around his mind. They were just too powerful, and bored through his defenses instantly.

The mental inhibitor shielded him from the full effects, but it didn't protect him. When movement around him had been small, he had been able to see through the effect. Now the inhibitor made the rushing crowd as confusing and chaotic as a colony of ants disturbed by a child's stick. The patterns had no purpose or reason. They left him drunk and dizzy. He could barely hold himself upright.

Slipstream prepared himself for the battle to come. The inhibitor made him useless to the others, and it was better to face one distraction than two. At least he was familiar with the clouds. He had faced it two previous times. Reaching up, he pulled the inhibitor from his head. The crowd disappeared as the clouds assaulted his mind. Pain and despair cascaded down on him.

\* \*

Meta-man could tell Slipstream was in trouble but he couldn't stop to help him. The stage cracked under the impact of his landing. Refusing to look up, he could feel the clouds growing above him.

"Slipstream is experiencing trouble," he said into his commlink. He stepped forward and held his hands up to Fuentes. "We don't want to hurt you! We want to help you!" He feared it was wasted effort, but he would not have forgiven himself if he had not at least tried.

*Fwssh!*

Meta-man dodged to the right to avoid the energy that erupted from Fuentes' eyes. As he came to his knees, the stage shook under Fluxstone's weight.

*Wham!*

Fluxstone slammed the *Aegis* into Fuentes.

Pulling on Fluxstone's power, Meta-man increased his own density, and doubled his strength. He charged into the fray.

\* \*

Envoy circled above the arena. She worked to stay out of reach of the three flares while also keeping them as far from Fuentes as she could. She did her best not to get too close to the clouds. As she dived between the flares, she shifted altitude and environmental data from her vision, and replaced it with the image from Meta-man's commlink. The image was partially distracting, but it worked better to keep her informed of what was happening than just the commlink.

As Envoy swung around in a wide loop, her artifact flashed a warning.

*Swhoosh!*

Envoy barely twisted out of the flares path. Glancing behind her, she found that two of the flares still pursued her. The third had anticipated her loop, and had maneuvered to block her. The artifact was having trouble tracking all three flares, but it was too late to change the plan now. She slowed her pace and allowed distance between her and the flares to close.

\* \*

The stage groaned under Fluxstone's weight, but she didn't let it distract her. She continued to enhance her density even as Meta-man lost his grip on Fuentes. Stepping forward, Fluxstone slammed the girl with the *Aegis*.

*Wham!*

The force of the blow snapped the girl's head back and knocked her prone.

"Fuentes leeches!" called Meta-man over his commlink. "Do not attempt teleport!" Taking a step back, he flexed his muscles and felt his strength returning. Before him, Fuentes was struggling to rise, but Fluxstone pressed her down with the *Aegis*. Glancing around, he said, "*Exodus*, are you in position?"

Samson circled Fluxstone and waited for an opening. When Fuentes began to push her way to her feet, he leaped forward and added his weight to the *Aegis*. Fuentes was forced back to the ground.

\* \*

"Roger that," replied Gemini to Meta-man's warning. "Fuentes leeches. Follow the plan people! Rotate attacks! The *Exodus* is descending. ETA to ground contact is five seconds. Shadow Spirit shift Dawn to Slipstream. He is down and needs assistance. Then give Envoy a breather. Maverick, stay on crowd control!"

Gemini quickly ran over the status of everyone as she gave directions. Envoy was putting out enough energy to boil an ocean. It kept the flares distracted, but it was taxing to her. Shifting Shadow Spirit to assist her would give her a moment to catch her breath. Getting Slipstream on his feet would be a big asset to the containment team. Paragon was doing his best to herd the civilians toward the exits, while Mecha lit up the pathways for them. Except for the team's, Mecha had also shut off all video feeds going out of the building. Maverick had resorted to shoving and pushing to get the people to move. Three people lay unconscious at his feet.

Only Sparrow was unaccounted for. He wasn't responding to her contacts, and his bio-signs were way too high. His camera jolted along with the fleeing crowd. Tapping a few buttons Gemini sent a message to her doppelgangers to search for him.

"Shifting local law enforcement to evacuation and perimeter control," said Curtis as a flick of his finger kicked the local dispatcher from the police band. His systems translated his voice into Spanish as he issued orders to the emergency responders. They reacted immediately to his instructions.

"By current calculations, we have one minute and twenty-nine seconds until full event!" Edmond shouted. His glasses had been discarded and he worked at a frantic pace.

"Meta-man, Butch is on the ground," reported Gemini. "Containment team, you are a go for extraction!"

As calmly as he could, Diamond tracked his team through the video feeds. He had done his best to put the right people in the right positions. Now it was up to them. Dreah's hand rested gently on his shoulder, and he reached up to squeeze it.

\* \*

Slipstream was crushed by the weight of the mountain of sorrow pressing down on him, but he refused to give in. As Dreah had instructed, he began to pull on memories of his family and friends. Each one was a part of him just like the clouds, but together, the memories were a greater part.

Each memory chipped away at the mountain, and pieces of it fell away. The burden lessening, he struggled to his knees. He pulled on more happy memories, but the clouds darkened and spiraled in on themselves to double their effort. Within moments the vortex would form. If he didn't break free before then, the clouds would crush him.

Concentrating harder, he pulled on a memory of Paula dressed in her wedding gown. The dress glowed brightly against the darkness. The effects of the clouds began to recede.

He smiled at Paula, but became confused by her dress expanding and flaring around her like a cape. A moment later the image shifted to that of Dawn standing over him with her hand on his shoulder. It was a memory from a battle nearly two years ago where the young girl had pulled an alien poison from his body. Now, she stood over him again, and the hand on his back wasn't just a memory. He had defeated the clouds just enough for her to succeed in reaching him mentally. Reaching up he took her hand, and allowed Dawn into his mind.

Dawn couldn't stop shaking. She could feel the fear the clouds were generating across the stadium, and it terrified her. It was even more dangerous to Slipstream, and she didn't want to see it as he saw it; however, she bit back her fear and pulled the burden fully onto herself. As it hit her, it crushed the air from her lungs. Struggling to breath, she frantically ripped at the collar of her shirt and collapsed to her knees.

His mind instantly cleared and Slipstream leaped to his feat. Throwing back his head he screamed up at the clouds.

"Eeeyyyyyyyyee!" Energy burst from his eyes to reach miles into the sky.

*Fwssh!*

The beam lit up the darkening arena as it sliced through the clouds. The clouds quickly collapsed back to fill the gap ripped by the energy beam.

Slipstream's feeling of rapture was instantly halted when he realized Dawn knelt next to him. Shaking and crying, blood dripped from her nose. He reached out to her, but she held her hand up to stop him.

"Go," Dawn choked between bouts of nausea and vomiting.

"But you..."

"I will...be fine. Go!"

The girl's empathic healing always took a toll on her, but this time the burden would not let up. It would continue to get stronger. Slipstream doubted she would survive it.

Reluctantly, he shifted his focus to the stage as he tilted his head back to look upward to the clouds. He could not see them, and thanks to Dawn, he could barely feel them. Leaving Dawn to battle his demons, he turned toward the action.

\* \*

Meta-man stepped forward and pulled Fuentes off Samson. The warrior fell to the stage, but quickly recovered enough to roll out of the way. Within a few moments, his strength would recover and he would rejoin the fight.

Time was running out, and they hadn't made any progress in getting Fuentes aboard the *Exodus*. When she swung at him, Meta-man caught her arm and jerked her off balance. As she stumbled, he grabbed her across her shoulders. He lifted her from the stage.

*Whoosh!*

A wave of force exploded outward from Fuentes. Meta-man's grip was ripped free, and he was flung from the stage. Fluxstone tumbled from the stage to nearly land on several security guards. Collapsing it, Samson slammed into a wall. It buried the hero along with several spectators. Fuentes fell to her knees.

Metal buckled and a large piece of scaffolding collapsed. Electrical wiring ripped free from equipment to create a shower of sparks that set flames to the curtains surrounding the stage.

*Boom!*

Slipstream's charge punched through the ripple of force, and he slammed into Fuentes. She spiraled from the stage and slammed into the back wall of the stage.

\* \*

Refusing to look up, Gemini stepped down from the *Exodus* and read a message scrolling across her visor's screen. When the wave of force from Fuentes struck her, it caused her to stagger. Her computer screen sputtered from the interference. She was more than fifty feet from Fuentes, and she had only felt a small portion of the woman's power, but it still unnerved her. Glancing at the woman, Gemini saw that Slipstream had already raced after her.

*Boom! Boom!*

Gemini cringed with each of the hero's blows. Their echo deafened her.

Quickly she turned her attention to her search for Sparrow. He was not where he was supposed to be. The image projected on her visor showed his commlink outside the stadium, but Gemini doubted he was with it.

A panicked man appeared before her, and reached for her.

*Whack!*

She slapped his hand aside with her staff. Glaring at the frightened man, she waved her finger at him. "No sea absurdo," she said calmly.

Rubbing his hand, the man looked at the staff, and then he turned and fled.

"Smarter than the average bear," mumbled Gemini. She turned back to her search.

Duo raced around the stadium to catch any falling rafters before they could crush anyone. On the *Exodus*, Butch ranted as he worked to readjust the systems the wave had disrupted. Across the stadium, Paragon menacingly waved his sword at several police officers that had foolishly decided to arrest him. It didn't take them long to abandon the idea, and to work with him to direct people out of the building. Shadow Spirit threw up a wall of darkness as a flare bore down on Envoy. It fizzled from the cold, and Envoy took a shot at it.

"So much for staying next to him," Gemini mumbled. Curiosity pulled her eyes upward. "No!" she said and forced herself to focus on the crowd.

\* \*

The scaffolding shuddered under Sparrow, but it held. Far below him, Slipstream struggled with Fuentes. As Sparrow watched, Fluxstone and Meta-man charged back into the battle, and all three heroes worked to restrain her.

Wishing he were anywhere else, Sparrow glanced up and witnessed the vortex sink into the cloud. The energy shaft was only moments away. The fear was overwhelming, and struggled to claim his mind. Closing his eyes, he focused his attention on the task at hand. Opening his eyes again, he looked back to the battle beneath him, and raised his rifle to his shoulder. He took aim at Fuentes, hoping his perch held out. The clouds lingered over him menacingly, but he focused and blocked them out.

\* \*

Samson pulled himself out from under the flaming debris. His muscles barely felt the weight as he lifted the steel girders high over his head to reveal the civilians that had been buried with him. Duo snatched them from under the collapsing wall.

"Aaarrgghh!" screamed Fuentes as she thrashed violently against the heroes. Her eyes flared.

*Fwssh! Fwssh! Fwssh! Fwssh!*

Her energy was flung in every direction.

The energy bounced off Slipstream's chest, and he used it to fuel his anger.

*Clang!*

Fluxstone blocked it with the *Aegis*.

Meta-man allowed himself to be struck, and after being struck twice, his body adjusted enough that the energy had no further affect on him.

Fuentes stopped struggling, and the air rippled around her.

*Fsssssss!*

Hundreds of small metal object rose from the ground. Fuentes' energy swirled around the stage, whipping the metal objects along with it. The debris pelted the heroes. The *Aegis* shielded Fluxstone. Meta-man mimicked Slipstream's powers, and his skin hardened and turned to blue sparkling metal. Slipstream ignored the swirling shards of death. Grabbing Fuentes around the waist, he lifted her off the ground and started for the *Exodus*.

*Fwoosh!*

Fuentes reacted with a wave of force that threatened to tear her from Slipstream's grip.

Leaping from the *Exodus*, Q-Zone reached out with his power to grip the energy surrounding the flying debris. He pulled the air out of time, and the motion of the pieces slowed. Fluxstone and Meta-man raced after Slipstream and Fuentes.

\* \*

"The event is accelerating! You have less than a minute to get Fuentes onboard the *Exodus*!" Edmond worked hard to keep up with his calculations, but each passing moment only accelerated the event.

"There are energy readings in the center of the vortex!" exclaimed Jonesy.

"Energy readings in the center of the vortex! Less than one minute remaining!" Gemini relayed the warnings to the team.

\* \*

Fuentes leached Slipstream's strength and powers from him. With each step he grew weaker, but he refused to release her. Where she touched him, his metal skin glowed brightly as it blistered and warped. He gritted his teeth and forced himself to focus through the pain.

When he reached the edge of the stage, the aura that always kept him from touching the ground collapsed, and he tripped on the edge of the stage. The two slammed into the floor. Still maintaining his grip on Fuentes, Slipstream struggled to his feet. For the first time in years, he found himself standing on the ground. The strange sensation of the stone floor against his bare feet caused him to hesitate, and his grip slipped.

Taking advantage of Slipstream's relaxed grip, Fuentes turned just enough to face him. When their matching black eyes met, she paused for a moment and stopped struggling. Then her face twisted with anger, and energy erupted from her eyes.

*Fwssh!*

Slipstream's upper torso disappeared in the inferno of energy.

*Wham!*

Fluxstone brought the *Aegis* down on Fuentes. The strength of the blow snapped the girl's head back. The energy stopped erupting from her eyes. Slipstream's face glowed red, and energy leaked from cracks around his eyes and mouth, but he still maintained his grip on Fuentes.

When Fuentes recovered from the blow, she again turned her gaze on Slipstream. Fluxstone struck her again.

*Wham!*

Meta-man wrapped his arms around Slipstream. He lifted the hero and his captive into the air and rushed toward the *Exodus*. Q-Zone stepped aside as they passed, and as Meta-man moved up the ramp, the ship's engines roared to life. Fluxstone and Samson leaped aboard after them.

Butch hit the accelerator and the ship launched into the air. The passengers were thrown to the floor. Fuentes continued her struggle against Slipstream's grip, and she reached out to touch the ship's floor. The *Exodus* careened to the right as she took control of the craft from Butch.

Meta-man grabbed the wall, cracking it under his strong grip. He maintained his hold on Slipstream, and prevented them all from tumbling out the open hatchway.

"Blasted piece of crap!" Butch screamed as he fought for control of the ship. "I knew we should have used the *Egress!*" Each time he issued a command to the ship, Fuentes countered it. Each time she issued a command, Butch countered it. The *Exodus* rocked back and forth from the conflict.

\* \*

*Skisss!*
As she shot at a flare, Envoy watched the *Exodus* swerve sharply to the right. The flare dodged her distracted shot, but came too close to Paragon.
*Fst!*
It sputtered and died as the winged warrior's sword sliced through it.
Floating on the air, Shadow Spirit reached out from under his cloak with a clawed shadowy hand. A second flare passed through the hand, but fizzled from the cold.
*Skisss!*
*Foom!*
Envoy's narrow blast of energy struck the flare, and it disappeared in an explosion.
Envoy's artifact flashed her a warning as it tracked the third flare streaking toward the approaching *Exodus*. Reacting, she shifted energy from her shield and into her speed. In a blink she cleared the distance to the ship, but wasn't quick enough to prevent the flare from punching through the pod.
*Swhoosh!*
"Aeyyyee!" screamed Butch from inside the ship. The *Exodus* tilted violently to the side again.
The flare emerged from the other side of the *Exodus*, and swung around for a second strike. Envoy threw herself before it and flung as much energy as she could at it.
*Skisss!*
*Swhoosh!*
The flare punched through her blast to strike her in the chest. Envoy was slammed into the side of the *Exodus*. Darkness claimed her as she plummeted toward the ground below.

\* \*

Butch pressed his hand against his abdomen, blood oozed from the burn. His vision blurred, and he fought against unconsciousness.

Fuentes had gained full control of the ship, and it wasn't responding to his commands.

"Going down!" he screamed through gasps for air.

"Evac, Maverick. Evac subject now!" shouted Meta-man. "Focus on Slipstream, not Fuentes!"

"About damn time!" Maverick responded. An instant later, he stood inside the airship. He caught himself on the ship's wall to keep from falling.

Meta-man still held onto the wall and Slipstream. Slipstream held his arms circled tightly around Fuentes. Fluxstone restrained the left arm of Fuentes, and the girl's right hand left glowing scars as she clawed at Slipstream's metal face.

Maverick took a deep breath and reached out to touch Slipstream. "I hope this is better than last time! Let's ride the wind, bitch!" In his mind, he pictured his destination and concentrated to pull all of them through space. Reality warped as Fuentes' natural defenses fought against the teleport. Maverick looked up and his eyes met Fluxstone's. "Shi...,"

The interior of the ship twisted and the space stretched outward, and then collapse into a single spot. An instant later it expanded violently.

*KABOOM!*

The side of the *Exodus* exploded outward and a wormhole formed between the ship and Maverick's intended destination. A fireball engulfed the interior of the ship. Fuentes and the heroes were sucked from the ship by the swirling chaos.

Fire from the *Exodus* spiraled through the wormhole and lit up the sky as it blasted through the upper floors of several high-rise buildings. The vortex shredded everything it touched. Debris and furniture were sucked up and carried along with it. Far out over the ocean, the horizon flashed and the wormhole collapsed. Flaming concrete, glass, and metal released from the wormhole rained destruction down upon the city. Flaming, Samson plummeted toward the ground several blocks from the stadium. The other heroes and Fuentes were nowhere to be seen.

"Brace yourselves!" yelled Butch as the *Exodus* spun out of control.

\* \*

Fire and smoke trailed behind the *Exodus* as it streaked toward the ground. Just as it was about to hit, the pod snapped back into the air as if it were attached to an invisible rope. Duo strained to hold the airship while also shielding themselves from flaming debris that rained down around them.

\* \*

"Maverick, status?"
Gemini worked frantically to get Maverick's video feed back online. It was down along with Slipstream's and Meta-man's. She had no way of knowing if the teleport had been successful.
"No change in energy readings over the city!" shouted Jonesy.
"Thirty seconds to energy shaft!" shouted Edmond.

\* \*

Gemini watched as the twins lowered the *Exodus* to the ground.
"I love this job!" said Q-Zone.
Glancing behind her, Gemini watched as Q-Zone lowered his hand from the *Exodus*. He smiled and winked at her as he focused all his attention on a large piece of scaffolding held suspended in the air. Shadow Spirit appeared over several young adults under the scaffolding. Wrapping them in his shadows, he teleported them out of the area.

Q-Zone turned his attention back to the *Exodus*. Extending his hand toward it again, the flames dancing across it began to slow and then to freeze in place.

Turning away from the others, Gemini continued her search for Sparrow. Moving among the burning wreckage she didn't find any sign of him, but she froze when she stumbled on Fuentes. The woman climbed to her feet. With one clawed hand she clutched Slipstream by his face, dragging him behind her like a rag doll. The metal warrior was conscious, but his prolonged contact with Fuentes had left him drained of strength. Gemini's blood ran cold when dirt and debris drifted slowly from the ground around her and Fuentes.

"Control, I have a visual on Fuentes! Teleport was unsuccessful! Slipstream is down!"

Mustering as much courage as she could, Gemini swung her staff at Fuentes.

*Crack!*

Gemini's hands jarred from the blow to the back of the girl's head. She took a step back and tried to shake the pain from them.

Fuentes was unhurt and turned to glare at her. She raised her hand slowly toward Lady Gemini.

"*Tawagoto*," mumbled Gemini.

*Whoosh!*

A wave of force struck her, hurling her backward.

*Crash!*

Gemini landed in a pile of broken speakers. Pain jolted her body and for a moment she fought panic as stars danced in her head. Through blurred vision, she saw someone moving over her. A rough hand clasped around her throat, and hauled her into the air. Pulling desperately at the vice-like grip, Gemini gasped for breath.

*Thwack!*

Fuentes jerked uncontrollably. Gemini landed back in the pile of speakers.

"Ow! Ow! That hurts," moaned Gemini as she rolled over and pressed her hand into her back where the corner of a speaker had jabbed her. Glancing up, she saw Sparrow kneeling on a piece of scaffolding high above her. He held a high-powered rifle aimed at Fuentes. Behind him the clouds groaned with anger.

*Thwack!*

Fuentes staggered again as Sparrow shot her with the rifle.

Gemini managed a smile, and she gave him thumbs up before rolling to her feet. Unsteady, she picked up her staff and rubbed her sore throat.

"Alright witch, sympathy time is over." Twirling the staff high above her head, Gemini danced around Fuentes. Another shot rang out.

*Thwack!*

As Fuentes recovered from the blow, Gemini followed up Sparrow's attack with a series of blows from her staff.

* *

As Fuentes jerked violently her grip on Slipstream slipped, dropping him to the ground.

His limbs refused to move, but quickly his vision sputtered back to life. Through pulses, he could see Gemini swinging her staff in wide arcs to strike Fuentes. The girl darted around Fuentes in a dance that kept her safe. He struggled to role over. His limbs still wouldn't respond and all he could do was lay there and watch.

In between Gemini's attacks, Fuentes jerked as if struck by an invisible force. It took Slipstream several moments, but finally he was able to focus enough to see Sparrow perched high overhead. Each time the barrel of his rifle shifted, Fuentes jerked. Together, they kept the woman distracted.

It wouldn't last. Even as Slipstream watched, Fuentes turned her attention to Sparrow.

*Fwssh!*

A beam of energy sliced across the sky to strike his perch. He rolled safely aside, but another attack by Fuentes would collapse the catwalk beneath him.

His arms stung with the burning sensation of blood returning to them, but his legs were still numb. Rolling over, Slipstream pulled himself along the ground until he was next to Fuentes. He clutched her leg, and began to pull his way up her body. His movements distracted her from Sparrow.

Glancing down at him, Fuentes' eyes lit up.

*Fwssh!*

A wave of energy engulfed the hero. Pain burned though him, but Slipstream continued to climb up Fuentes until he succeeded in pulling himself up out of the wave of death. Raising his arm high over his head, he struck her.

*Boom!*

The ground shook from the blow, and Gemini staggered backward from the force. Seeking to render Fuentes unconscious, Slipstream struck again.

*Boom!*

*Thwack!*

Sparrow fired in between each of Slipstream's blows, together they caused Fuentes to stagger.

"We need backup!" screamed Gemini as she swung her staff and struck Fuentes again.

"Roger that," replied Meta-man. "On our way."

Flying high over the stadium, he held Fluxstone with both hands suspended below him. As he approached the battle, she increased her density. By the time he was over the battle, he visibly strained to hold her.

"Clear out!" screamed Meta-man as he released Fluxstone. She plummeted toward the ground.

*Fathoom!*

Concrete exploded and the heroes ducked for cover. When the dust cleared, Fuentes lay unconscious, and Fluxstone kneeled next to her. Looking exhausted, Slipstream lay in the crater next to Fuentes.

Gemini breathed a sigh of relief, but Edmond quickly dashed her feeling of victory.

"Event! We have event!"

As if waiting for his cue, the shaft of light erupted from the center of the vortex.

*Ka-Boom!*

The force of the impact slammed everyone to the ground, and the shaft of light fully engulfed Fuentes and Slipstream. Rock was flung in every direction as the shaft bored into the earth.

Gemini slammed into the ground and her computer visor cracked from the impact and went dark. She ripped it from her face as she climbed to her feet. The sight of the energy shaft less than fifteen feet from her paralyzed her with fear. She could barely make out the forms of the two within it, but she swore she could hear them screaming over the roar.

*Rrrummmble!*

"We need emergency evac now!" screamed Fluxstone.

Raising the *Aegis* above her head, she stepped under the energy shaft. Protecting her, the shield deflected the energy; but the force of the shaft was so strong she was forced to lower her density further and use both arms to brace the shield. Energy deflecting from the shield incinerated everything it touched.

Shadow Spirit stepped from Gemini's shadow. When his cloak pulled back, Paragon and Samson materialized next to him.

*Meta-humans*, cursed Sparrow from his perch when the *Aegis* blocked his shot. Slinging his rifle across his shoulder, he fired a swing line from his right wristband. Even as the small spear embedded into his target, Sparrow stepped off the platform and plummeted toward the ground below. The line cushioned his impact and he rolled to his knees while bringing the rifle to his shoulder. The crosshairs of his scope settled on the silhouette that was Fuentes.

Meta-man dived under the *Aegis* and grabbed Slipstream. Meta-man's skin burst into flames and his metal uniform instantly melted. As his joints stiffened with pain, he pulled the metal warrior toward him. Meta-man's fingers sunk into the man's softened metal body, and they both collapsed when they were freed from the light. Slipstream glowed brightly. The ground burst into flame and stone melted where he touched it. Meta-man's arms were blackened and stiff. He couldn't even scream through the mind shattering pain.

Paragon leaped to Meta-man and grabbed the man's arms just beneath the burns. His hands glowed and he pushed healing energy into Meta-man.

The shaft began spewing off flares. Those heroes close to the shaft struggled to dodge the deadly barrage.

Alone under the shaft, Fluxstone tried to ignore the flares striking her. She screamed into her commlink, "I can't hold it! We need emergency evac…"

*Thwack! Fwoosh!*

The shaft of light disappeared in a flash and the sudden release of pressure flung Fluxstone to the ground.

Regret was instant. Sparrow had never felt it after a kill. It caused bile to form in his throat and he grew dizzy. His finger remained tight against the trigger, and he struggled to force the feeling aside. As he eased off the trigger, he lowered the rifle; revealing a two-foot wide silver globe suspended in the air just above Fuentes. Sparrow jerked his rifle up.

*Boom!*

Sparrow ducked to avoid the flash of energy. He recovered quickly and turned back toward the globe. It was gone. Lady Gemini held her staff pointed at the spot where it had been. The tip of the metal staff smoked. Her face was smeared with soot, and a single tear slid down her cheek.

"Sorry Glip," Gemini whispered.

Sparrow felt an immediate need to comfort her. He was relieved when Samson stepped up next to her. Taking the staff from her hands, the warrior put his arm around her.

\* \*

"Energy signature over the city dissipating! Cloud cover returning to normal!" Jonesy could barely control the excitement in his voice.

"They did it!" screamed Clara.

The command center erupted into cheering. Dreah hugged Diamond.

Diamond allowed Dreah her hug, and when she turned toward the others he turned his attention to his console. He tapped a few buttons, and then he paused to look up at everyone again. They were all still distracted. He tapped the command button that gave Black Sunday the go ahead with Lekkas.

# CHAPTER 19
## DECISIONS

Sparrow sat in the dirt and groaned. His left side hurt from his impact with the ground and smoke stung his eyes. He groaned louder when Gemini dropped to the ground in front of him. She was still shaken, but managed a smile.

"Hey, big guy."

"Hey," Sparrow muttered.

"Thanks for the assist."

"You're welcome."

Gemini grinned when she realized Sparrow was favoring his side. "Don't worry about that. Paragon can take away some of the pain in those old bones. He's with Butch right now. The poor guy took a nasty burn from one of the flares, and then he sort of crashed the *Exodus*. His luck has been really bad lately."

"I think I'll keep my pain. It reminds me I'm still alive."

Smiling, Gemini looked at Fuentes. She frowned. Fuentes sat crumpled in a large crater burned into the ground. Her leathery body was blackened and wrinkled. Red glowing cracks ran across her skin. Gemini could see the hole through the girl's left eye where Sparrow's bullet had passed. She felt sorry for the girl, and she wished the incident could have ended better.

"Gem, can you excuse us. Please?"

Gemini looked up to find Fluxstone standing over her. She glanced at Sparrow. Neither of them said anything.

Sparrow rubbed his side to hide his hand inching closer to the hidden disruptor. It wouldn't be what Diamond had in mind when he issued it, but at the moment Sparrow didn't care.

"Okay," Gemini said, shrugging. "But if you two kill each other, it's not my fault."

When the girl was out of earshot, Fluxstone sighed heavily.

"I don't think shooting Fuentes was the right thing to do. It could have been disastrous."

"The globe was the target, but I couldn't see clear enough. I took the shot I had."

Anger flared in Fluxstone. "But, what if..."

Sparrow leaped to his feet. "But what if what? What if it had made her whole damn family the target? What if it had caused us to lose the target completely? Well, I don't work with what if's! The globe was an unobtainable target! I took the shot I had! If nothing else, it stood to buy us more time. In case you failed to notice, we were out of it!"

At the sound of the shouting, everyone stopped what they were doing and turned in their direction. Sparrow ignored them. He had taken all he was going to from Fluxstone.

Fluxstone stepped forward. Anger boiled in her. On one hand, she saw his actions as unpredictable and dangerous. On the other hand, they had been out of time. Meta-man and Slipstream were down, and she was trapped under the shield. There was nothing anyone else could have done to save the city. She wanted to call his actions those of a dangerous man, one who had no business being there to begin with; but she knew differently. Sparrow didn't make impulsive decisions. He had thought out the shot long before the need to take it, and he had already known the possible consequences and benefits. He could have shot Fuentes in a vulnerable spot earlier, but he hadn't. He had waited until he had no other option.

"But you could have been wrong!" She finally managed to say through clenched teeth.

"Then we would be dead!" Sparrow growled back.

The two stared at each other. Both refused to look away.

"Heather," said Paragon as he approached. When Fluxstone didn't respond, he reached out and placed a gentle hand on her shoulder. Finally, she took her eyes off Sparrow and looked at him.

"What?" she demanded.

"The local authorities are demanding answers, and Envoy is still down. You know I can't heal her because of the artifact, and we either need to speak to these people or get out of here."

Fluxstone looked back to Sparrow and then to Paragon. Reluctantly, she nodded and turned toward several men who had gathered around the body of Fuentes. Several of them wore local law enforcement uniforms. Others were dressed as paramedics or firefighters. Two wore business suits. They all looked angry and impatient. One of them argued with a frustrated Samson. The hero's uniform had been burned from his body, and his hair was a tangled and singed mess, but he didn't appear to have any wounds.

Sparrow started to turn away, but Paragon gently stopped him.

"It is okay, friend. You did what you had to do, and she knows it."

"That doesn't make it any easier."

Sparrow turned and walked away. The kill hadn't been what he was used to. Killing the sparrow as a kid had caused him regret, and he had not liked it. Even as a kid, he knew a true hunter never felt regret over killing its prey, and if he felt regret over a simple bird, he could never become a soldier. He took steps to push it down and the Counselor had buried it. He wasn't sure he liked that it was back. It left him sick to his stomach.

\* \*

Everyone in the command center wanted to celebrate, but they were quickly pulled back to their stations. The destruction from the event had created a flurry of things that needed to be done, and the local authorities needed as much assistance with rescue efforts as they could get.

Jonesy tried to ignore the activity. He had quickly forgotten the victory and focused on the readings over Antarctica. Before informing anyone, he had to be sure they were correct. He ran his system through several tests, and then filtered the readings through four different programs before comparing the readings to those over Buenos Aires, Paris, and Denver.

The readings were not identical, but they were definitely from the same primary source. Over Antarctica a source of energy had briefly flared and then disappeared. It was gone now, but he was sure it had been there.

He transferred his data to his sidekick and then leaped up from his station. Heads turned to follow him as he hurried out of the room in search of Diamond.

\* \*

The shadow slide sent the usual chill down Sparrow's spine. As the room came into focus, he admitted to himself that he was glad to be back in the Citadel. The humming walls had a level of safety that he was getting used to. Inside them, he didn't have to constantly guard his back. Outside, he couldn't help but think the Counselor was around every corner.

At the moment all he wanted was a shower. His lungs burned from the smoke and his side ached. Unfortunately, he realized the shower would have to wait when he saw Diamond and Dreah enter the pod bay. The two moved quickly over to the returning party.

Diamond took Envoy's hand and energetically shook it. Envoy had partially recovered from her clash with the flares, but she still looked pale and she was weak. Diamond then turned to Fluxstone and Gemini, and he put his arms around both women. Dreah greeted everyone in turn, and she ended with holding Sparrow's hand in her right hand and Meta-man's in her left. With Paragon's help, Meta-man's arms had recovered from the burns.

"What you have all accomplished today is remarkable. Thank you all."

"Screw you," mumbled Maverick as he passed them headed for the exit. He held an ice pack against his head and walked with a stumble. Water dripped from him to puddle on the floor. Unlike the others, he had completed the teleport, and had to be fished out of the ocean. Everyone ignored him and he left the room.

"We did what you prepared us to do, sir," replied Envoy.

"Regardless, you saved millions of lives today, and you deserve all the praise I can give you. I set out on this journey a long time ago. Ever since then, I've been pulling you people into this with me, and today you showed me that it wasn't all wasted effort."

"Like Envoy said, it is what we do, sir," said Meta-man.

"I think what we all need is rest," said Paragon as he flexed his wings. His right one stung with pain, but he concealed a grimace. "Some of us need it more than others." He turned and watched Brandon wheel a gurney out of the room. Dawn lay on it shaking and curled into a ball. "She has suffered greatly."

"Agreed," said Diamond. "All of you should find some rest. We will debrief tomorrow. We will need to review exactly what happened. This event was stopped, but we need to know if it was because of the death of Fuentes or if it was because of the destruction of the globe."

At that moment, Jonesy hurried into the room waving a sidekick in the air.

"I've found them, sir. I've found the Psadans."

As Diamond took the sidekick and scanned the information, Envoy accessed it herself. After downloading the data and reading it quicker than any human eye could, she started for the exit. Moments later, she soared over the island and turned south.

\* \*

"Status," asked Diamond.

"Envoy is approaching Antarctica now sir."

"Status on the *Egress*?"

"Green, sir," replied Curtis. He stifled a yawn and pulled up a visual of the pod.

Butch was sweating and looked pale.

"You should be resting," said Dreah from behind Diamond. He turned to her, but realized she was speaking to Butch.

"I'm fine, mother. Paragon mostly fixed me up. Besides, I'm sure you want this little baby on site as quickly as possible. I won't be there as quickly as Envoy, but no one else would be either."

"Just get down there. We have a science team standing by." Diamond turned his attention away from the monitor and to his list of operatives. If they had indeed found the Psadans, he wanted to formulate a plan quickly. His feared they would increase their timetable upon discovery.

"You need rest too," said Dreah.

Without looking at her, Diamond replied, "I'll be fine."

"You'll be dead, or worse, if you don't get some rest."

"As soon as Envoy confirms our suspicions, I'll find some."

Dreah wasn't convinced.

"Promise," Diamond added. Even if he didn't want to, he knew there was no way around it. The Psadan in his head was pounding at him for freedom. If he didn't get rest soon, he wouldn't be able to continue holding it back.

Dreah moved aside to sit on her cushion. She was worried about Diamond, but she knew he wouldn't let her comfort him right now. He could see the end of his quest, and he would stop at nothing to reach it. A part of her couldn't blame him. Age was starting to slow him down and he had spent all his life working toward this moment. If he survived to see it, he would die happy.

\* \*

Below Envoy, the cold ocean gave way to ice. It stretched before her as far as she could see. Checking the coordinates, she pulled back on her speed and started her descent. Even in the cold air, she was sweating. Her injuries weren't severe, but her head throbbed from being slammed into the side of the *Exodus*. When combined with the lack of sleep from the last few days, she was feeling the toll.

"Control, status green."

"Roger that Envoy. Be safe."

As she neared the coordinates from Jonesy's data, a red dot appeared before her vision to mark the spot. It was suspended nearly a mile over the icy terrain. As she circled the area, the artifact tracked her destination. Slowing her speed further, she found nothing unusual. Descending to the ice, she found no sign of life or activity. The landscape was as dead and cold.

She used the artifact to scan for the energy signature. At first she found nothing but the frozen bodies of hundreds of penguins buried several feet beneath her. Judging from the scans, they had been there several hundred years. Scanning deeper, she found what she was looking for. It was faint and she had difficulty pinpointing it, but it was definitely there.

"There is something under the ice. The readings are similar to those of the Citadel. I believe we have found our target." Envoy rose gently into the air and started in the direction of the approaching *Egress*.

\* \*

Diamond knew everyone was tired, but he couldn't allow them rest now. They were too close to their goal and he needed a plan.

"We need ideas, people."

Displayed on the wall to his right was a team of scientists bundled in cold weather parkas. In the background the *Egress* rested in the snow.

"Mason has confirmed Envoy's initial readings. There is an energy source buried nearly a mile beneath the ice. It is nearly identical to that of the Citadel. You can bet it won't take long for them to know they've been discovered. We need to act now."

Everyone in the room sat quietly. Finally, Edmond sat forward. His glasses rested on the table in front of him.

"I think we have an advantage, actually. You have been manipulating their technology for years, Mr. Diamond. I think we should use that to our advantage."

Jonesy shook his head. "The problem is that the source is nearly impossible to pin point. It doesn't show up on thermal imaging, ground radar, topographic mapping, or x-ray. We can barely even locate it knowing where it is."

Edmond glanced at Jonesy and nodded as he continued. "Understood. But what we do know is that Glip-2 can manipulate it." Jonesy glanced at the silver globe hovering in the corner as Edmond continued. "I propose that all we need is the general zone, and Glip-2 will be able to manipulate the energy there just as he does here. Fuentes did it with the *Exodus*. All we have to do is create a connection for him to access it."

"How would we do that, Jonesy?" Diamond asked.

Jonesy sat in silence for a moment before answering. "We could set up a perimeter system of arrays that would enhance the signal, maybe. Glip-2 could then access it through the arrays." Jonesy didn't voice his opinion of Glip-2, but everyone saw the look of disgust on his face when he glanced at the globe.

"How do we make it happen?"

"Sarah," said Jonesy as he shrugged. "Except the globe, she has more success at manipulating the Citadel systems than anyone." Jonesy waved his hand in a dismissive gesture at Glip-2 as he finished.

Before Diamond could say anything, Clara picked up her sidekick and sent a priority message to Brandon. Her sidekick beeped in response almost immediately. "He's on his way."

Pressing forward, Diamond looked to Envoy. "Envoy, based on what they are suggesting here, we will need to divide our forces. One team will remain on the surface to protect the array system. We'll augment them with any TASC members we have here in the Citadel. A second team will confront the Psadans directly. I don't expect them to sit back and allow this. A third team will need to be on standby for an event over a target city."

Bullock spoke up. "Meta-man, how about UNIT? Will they stay out of this or will they demand in on the show?"

Everyone turned to Meta-man. After clearing his throat, he said. "I've been monitoring the news, and the event in Buenos Aires has helped your standing with some of the world's governments. Even though DSS wasn't sanctioned to operate there, our involvement has not been withheld from the media. Fluxstone did the right thing by remaining behind long enough to speak with the authorities. I actually suggest we call in UNIT for this, at least the core team. By including them, you stand a better chance of coming out on top."

Bullock laughed. "I don't recommend that. I doubt you will get that bunch to come together in time for this. Politicians, bah! Most of them would better serve their countries as door stops."

"I agree that the idea is sound," said Diamond. "Meta-man, if your standing has not been compromised by your involvement in Buenos Aires, I will leave contacting them up to you. We will need to discuss details of what information we will give them once we are done here."

Meta-man nodded his head in agreement as the conference room t-port opened and Brandon entered. The young man looked nervous and intimidated as he glanced around the room. Gemini and Maria both smiled at him, and it seemed to ease his worries.

"Yes, sir?" he stammered as he approached Diamond.

"Brandon, we need to talk to Sarah, please," said Diamond.

"Yes, sir." Brandon lowered his head and closed his eyes.

Sparrow glanced at Diamond and then at Brandon. He was confused. He had only given Brandon's file a cursory scan and had not noticed anything unusual. Brandon wasn't a meta-human. Sarah was his sister, but she was listed as dead. Sparrow had assumed Brandon's conversations with her were just his way of holding on to her memory. He cursed himself for not being more thorough.

After a few moments, Brandon raised his head and spoke. His voice hadn't changed, but he no longer stuttered or appeared intimidated. He stood taller and looked Diamond in the eye.

"Yes, Mr. Diamond? What can I do for you?"

Diamond nodded to Brandon, and then waved his hand toward Edmond and Jonesy. "Gentlemen, if you could, please explain the plan to Sarah." Both men got up and moved over to the video wall.

Curious, Sparrow watched the three men speaking in hushed tones.

"IMPACT can provide security for the team setting up the array system," said Meta-man.

"Agreed," said Envoy. "TASC could remain here in the Citadel as backup. I'll divide our forces between the three teams. With UNIT augmenting DSS, it shouldn't spread us too thin. In fact, given the power levels we dealt with in Fuentes, we will need all the help we can get. John, will UNIT follow our directions or the directions of their individual governments?"

"I am still chair of the team at this point. Power is not scheduled to rotate for another six months. However, given recent events, I would suggest we move quickly. It will take work, but I think I can get some of them to follow my lead."

"We will need you to solidify that power base then." Turning away from the table, Diamond addressed the three by the video wall. "Is the plan workable?"

All three turned to face him, and Brandon stepped forward. "Yes, sir. It is. We will get to work immediately. I estimate it will take me nearly six hours to draw up the plans, another two to have Glip-2 duplicate the systems for us."

Sparrow shuddered. He thought he had gotten to know Brandon better than anyone in the Citadel, but his current demeanor was disturbing. He continued to hold his head high and to speak with confidence. He had stopped mumbling to himself, and even continued to look Diamond in the eye. Up to this point the kid had almost wet himself every time Diamond entered a room. *Meta-humans*, he cursed. *You never know what you can expect.* Sparrow shifted his gaze to Diamond. The shift in personalities had not had any effect on him. Sparrow wondered what other secrets he was hiding.

"Good," said Diamond. Turning back to the table, he felt the weariness he saw in their eyes. "Okay, as much as I hate to do it, I'm calling for some down time." Turning to the video wall, he addressed Mason. "Mason, pull your crew back aboard the *Egress* and get out of there. We don't want to push the Psadans into any action."

"Yes, sir," replied Mason as he turned and ushered his crew back to the airship.

Addressing the table again, Diamond said, "Everyone go catch eight hours of rest. Dismissed."

Stifling a yawn, Sparrow stood up and headed for the exit. As he left the room, he felt someone watching him. Entering the t-port, he glanced back and saw Fluxstone was the only one left at the table. She watched him until the t-port doors closed.

* *

Meta-man stepped through the door and it closed behind him. He glanced nervously at the white walls around him, and wished the doors would cycle faster.

Several years had passed since Diamond had first offered him a position with DSS. It hadn't taken him long to learn that their ideals clashed too much for an ongoing working relationship. Of course that hadn't been the only reason he had turned down the offer. He hadn't wanted to work within the Citadel. Even though Diamond had added a human touch to the structure, it unnerved him.

The exposure to the shaft in Buenos Aires had reawakened old memories in him. He could still feel the burn of the light, and for the first time in a very long time he could picture Alis. She had been his only sane memory at the time and now she permeated his thoughts. He couldn't let go of the memories or the feelings, especially the moment of her death. The Citadel enflamed those memories and he expected to see one of the aliens around every corner.

When the doorway opened, Meta-man stepped out of the Citadel and into an office building in downtown New York. He passed through a large vault door, and turned to watch it close to seal away the Citadel doorway. Meta-man wondered if it was the only alternate exit to the Citadel. Physically the Citadel was all the way across the country off the coast of California, but the doorway granted instant access to New York City. The pods also contained instant doorways, but they could be moved anywhere in the world Diamond wanted. This opening was stationary and had most likely preceded the pods. It was rare that Diamond allowed anyone to use the exit, but Meta-man needed to be in place with UNIT when DSS was ready to go. Flying all the way across the country would have been an unnecessary delay. The doorways were the only technology Meta-man was aware of that allowed for near instant teleportation. Certain meta-humans could teleport, but technology had not been successful in mimicking the ability. Only Diamond and his Citadel could do it. It was too much power to be controlled by any one man.

Once on the roof, he leaped into the air and soared across the darkening skyline toward the United Nations Building. He was tired, but he had a long night ahead of him with the politics involved in activating UNIT. Under normal circumstances there would not have been a problem. He was still the commander. He could assemble and deploy field teams as he saw fit as long as he didn't violate the standing orders of the UN Security Council. The problem was that the current circumstances were anything but normal. Over the course of the last few days he had disobeyed direct orders from the Security Council, and he had openly collaborated with suspected terrorists in Denver and Buenos Aires. That collaboration had resulted in the destruction of Denver and the deaths of several million people.

*I'll be lucky if they don't arrest me on sight*, Meta-man mused as he began his descent towards the roof of the United Nations building.

\* \*

Sparrow's eyes burned with the need for sleep, but he refused to turn in. A large part of him hoped Diamond would not include him in the Antarctica mission, but the small part of him that did, kept him from sleeping. The adrenaline rush from the events in Buenos Aires had excited him. It had breathed a new life into him. Under the Counselor, even his excitement had been dulled. It was one emotion he was glad to have free.

At first the death of Fuentes had been difficult to deal with. It was the first time he had made a kill shot, and felt regret over it. The feelings had been so great at first that he had feared they would overwhelm him.

He had wanted to push them down into that deep hole that Dreah said he reserved for all his emotions, to lock it away. Fear of it leading him back to the Counselor had kept him from doing so. Instead he had chosen to deal with the feelings. It took him over two hours of wandering the garden's pathways to come to the same conclusion that had led him to make the shot to begin with. It had to be done. If he had not taken the shot, everyone would have died. Diamond and his people had already tried to find another way. He was responsible for taking the young girl's life, but it had been necessary.

After returning to his room, Sparrow had turned his attention to his armor. While he had been away, Glip-2 had made some changes to the design and he had spent the last hour examining them. According to the globe, he had been bored and his access of the files had not gone unnoticed by Sarah. After discovering his snooping, she had offered some advice for further modifications to thank Sparrow for the growing friendship between him and Brandon. Ironically, Sparrow knew his time with Brandon had been based on manipulation and not friendship, but it appeared everyone was benefiting in the end.

Over his shoulder he heard the doorbell to his apartment. Without rising, he said, "Enter." The door responded to his voice command and opened. Sparrow could hear a soft rustle and smell flowers.

"Hello," called Dreah.

"In here," Sparrow yelled back.

Dreah entered the workroom.

"You should be resting."

"You knew I wasn't or you wouldn't have stopped by."

Dreah smiled. "True." She moved up next to him and Sparrow felt her body brush against his. She reached out and took the pair of pliers from his hand, and he turned to look at her.

She stepped back, laid the pliers on the counter, and then pulled him to his feet. "Come," she said. "You are too tired, you will just make mistakes if you keep pushing yourself."

Reluctantly, Sparrow allowed Dreah to lead him out of the workroom. She sat down on the couch and the wall swung shut. The image of the Austrian mountains filled the wall.

"Night time," Dreah whispered and the skyline dimmed and darkened. Stars came out and a crescent moon reflected off the lake.

Reaching up, she took Sparrow's hand and pulled him down onto the couch next to her.

"Do you think this is appropriate?"

"Hush. I got over worrying about what is and is not appropriate a long time ago. Besides, what would be inappropriate about two friends enjoying each other's company under a beautiful moon? Now rest. You have a big day ahead of you."

"Has Diamond made final plans?"

Dreah didn't answer.

"You aren't going to discuss it with me right now are you?"

"No, I'm not."

"Have you learned more about your vision of me?"

Dreah breathed deeply before answering, "Sparrow, you are special. The choice will be tough for you, but you will make the right one. I've never met anyone like you before. Now sleep."

Sparrow didn't want to sleep. He still had too much to do. He was curious about Diamond's plans, and he still wanted to know what her vision was. Of course, he knew it was a waste of time to question her about any of it. She wouldn't answer.

When Sparrow finally drifted off to sleep, Dreah sat quietly and watched the stars move slowly across the sky.

\* \*

Envoy paced back and forth in front of the monitor wall as she listened to Jonesy lay out the plan for the array system. He was being more decisive than usual. Normally when lives were at stake, he was reluctant to commit to a course of action for fear of being blamed when things went wrong. Envoy wondered if it had anything to do with him working with Sarah again. His indecisiveness had played a part in her current condition.

As Diamond shifted in a chair near her, Envoy turned to look at him. As usual, Diamond's face didn't reveal what he was thinking but his eyes followed Jonesy closely. Diamond had been showing irritation with Jonesy lately. Perhaps that also played a part in Jonesy's current demeanor.

"We will have to position each antenna separately. They will then act as a focal point for Glip-2. Through them it should be able to target and access the Psadan energy."

As Jonesy stopped talking, Sarah, in the body of Brandon, walked between him and the table of observes. As she passed Jonesy, she scowled. Jonesy quickly looked away.

The cause of Jonesy's improved behavior may have been a mystery, but the cause of Sarah's bad behavior wasn't. Her hostile feelings toward him were showing. Of course, Envoy didn't blame her for holding a grudge against a man who had nearly killed her.

"The energy is identical to that of the Citadel tesseract, so Glip-2 will be able to manipulate it. The array system will act as a focal point for him to act through. Think of them as an access port on a computer. We plug them into the energy, and Glip-2 into them. Once he has access to the energy, he should be able to manipulate it as easily as the energy of the Citadel." Sarah paused a moment and looked directly at Diamond. "I don't know what plans you have Mr. Diamond, but if the field is even half the size of the Citadel, we could cause a massive release of energy."

"How massive," he asked.

"Mr. Diamond, the resulting explosion will crack the continent." Behind her, the video wall displayed an explosion beneath the Antarctic ice that resulted in large cracks running along the surface in all directions. The land mass split apart into numerous sections. "It will have global repercussions."

"How can we contain the energy release?" If Diamond was bothered by the possible destruction of the continent, his face didn't show it.

"I would recommend Glip-2 implode it. It will create a singularity that will still damage Antarctica, but it should keep the damage more centralized. Unfortunately, I don't know if Glip-2 can handle it. I doubt he has ever manipulated such a massive amount of energy before, but I have nothing else at this point to offer."

"Piece of cake, darling," said Glip-2 through speakers in the center of the conference room table. He floated up next to Sarah and when he was nearly touching her, he made a pretense of whispering to her through her sidekick. "How am I supposed to do that again?"

"You'll do fine, we have faith in you," said Sarah as she patted the globe.

Edmond leaned forward and spoke. "Glip-2 can absorb solar energy. Right?" He glanced at Sarah, and she nodded. "I suggest putting him in a low orbit, above any cloud cover, and have him absorb solar energy. He can then use that as a power boost. It will give him more control."

Sara nodded her head in agreement. "It would work, but we would want to time it as close as possible. Too much energy could pop him."

"*Boom!*" shouted Glip-2 through Jonesy's sidekick. Jonesy jumped. "No, wait! Are you serious?"

Sara placed her hand on the globe. "Don't worry." She said.

Ignoring Glip-2, Diamond addressed the room. "We move ahead with the plan. We will just have to monitor the energy absorption, and Glip-2 will have to do his best to control the collapse."

"Meta-man is making progress with the Security Council, and they should have a team ready to go within the next few hours. Envoy has already forwarded each of you your assignments. We will be dividing into three teams."

"I couldn't help but notice, I'm not on any of those teams." Gemini cocked her head to the side and stared defiantly at Diamond. She was the only one in the room who would have dared to use the tone that was in her voice. Judging from the look on Diamond's face, even she wasn't going to get away with it.

Looking her in the eye, Diamond said, "It's too dangerous, Kahori. You are not going."

Gemini quickly leaned forward over the table and pointed at Sparrow. "I've proved I'm ready! Ask Sparrow! He was there! He saw everything!"

Diamond didn't give Sparrow a chance to speak, or even look at him. "I said no, and we are not going to discuss it further."

Gemini sat with her mouth open in shock. Her eyes remained locked with Diamond's for several moments before she collapsed back into her chair. She scowled and folded her arms across her chest. Tears welled up in the corner of her eyes, but she refused to cry and swallowed them.

Diamond turned back to the table.

"Alpha team will be responsible for the array system. Sarah and Edmond will handle set up. TASC and IMPACT will supply protection and support. Lt. Reyes will command with Sparrow backing him up." Startled, Sparrow looked up at Diamond, but Diamond ignored him and went on with the briefing. "Beta team will be led by Envoy and augmented by UNIT. If the Psadans interfere with Alpha team, Beta will intervene to buy Alpha as much time as possible. Charlie team will remain here in the Citadel and await deployment as needed. Samson will lead that team.

"Unfortunately, there is a lot we still don't know at this point. We don't know the exact reason for the events. We don't know if the Psadans are actually present in Antarctica. We don't know if they even have control over these events. However, I don't believe the energy source is a coincidence, and Jonesy is convinced it is directly connected to the events themselves. We hope destroying it will prevent future ones."

Everyone but Gemini listened intently to Diamond. They followed his plan either through their sidekicks or on the video wall. Even Glip-2 remained silent. Everyone soaked in his confidence, and many began to sit taller with the weariness draining from their faces.

"The Psadans have kept largely out of matters over the last few days, but I don't expect them to allow us to attack their energy source. They may directly intervene with the arrays, or they may launch an event with one of the seeds. An event will push our timetable. We are counting on Beta team to prevent this."

"About the other seeds, Mr. Diamond...," Clara began to quickly shuffle through documents on several sidekicks.

Diamond held up his hand to silence her. "Not now Clara. I've already reviewed the information and we will discuss it in private after this meeting." He wasn't ready to discuss Lekkas openly. The man's abduction had been successful and he was currently hidden away. Diamond saw no need to complicate matters with Meta-man at this point.

"Very well, sir." Clara's voice trailed away in confusion as she shuffled through her documents.

Diamond pressed ahead. "We will try to coordinate deployment of both Antarctica teams. I would prefer to deploy Beta team before Alpha, but Meta-man cannot give me a specific timetable for his arrival. As soon as the system is ready, we will push forward." Diamond turned to Sarah, still in Brandon's body. "How long will you need to set up the arrays?"

Sarah tapped her sidekick and read the info there before answering. "It will only take a couple of minutes to calibrate each array. Edmond can place them while I calibrate them. We are using thirty arrays to cover the area so I would estimate about an hour."

"Envoy?" asked Diamond.

"With the depth of the ice, I'll need ten to fifteen minutes to reach the energy source. Given the power level we have witnessed so far, holding even two of them at bay will be extremely difficult, and we have no idea how many we are dealing with. I would recommend the team augment security for the arrays while I tunnel into the ice. If the Psadans intervene, we step it up and do what we have to do. If they don't, I'll hold up just before the energy signature."

"Good. Clara, contact the numerous research stations down there and warn them. Coordinate through Meta-man so the governments are involved. Maybe they can be convinced to clear out. Tell them we will assist with evacuations."

"Yes sir, Mr. Diamond." Clara made a note on one of her numerous sidekicks.

"Everyone else get suited up and ready. It's time we bring this thing to an end."

As Diamond ended the meeting, a flurry of activity broke out as everyone hurried to his or her assignments.

When Clara realized that Diamond was already headed out of the room, she quickly scooped up her gear and hurried after him.

Still pouting, Gemini remained in her seat. Maria spoke briefly with her, but when Gemini shook her head angrily, Maria left with the others. Sparrow waited patiently for the room to clear and then approached Gemini.

Without looking up, she spoke angrily to him. "Why didn't you back me up?"

"First off, I don't like being put on the spot like that. Second, challenging Diamond's decision in public would only have made him defensive. It would not have changed his mind."

Despite his irritation at being put on the spot, Sparrow remained calm and did not raise his voice. He had no idea how to deal with a teenager's temper tantrums, but he did know how to deal with Diamond. Yelling at Gemini would not have helped her.

"He can't keep me here. I'm going!"

"I won't stop you."

Surprised, Gemini looked up at him.

"That surprises you? Why? If I didn't think you were capable, I would never have allowed you to be involved in Hong Kong, and I wouldn't have supported you for Buenos Aires either."

"You going to tell daddy?" she asked sarcastically.

"No, but I suggest you do."

"Ha! Yeah, right! What makes you think that would go anywhere? He would just order Glip to lock me down in here."

"Show him the benefit of your going. Show him how you can help the team with your presence. Show him that you are as mature as you say you are. Defy him, and you'll lose the argument before you even begin it. He made his initial decision because you are his daughter, and not based on your skills. Remind him of just how much of his daughter you really are, and he just may change his mind."

Gemini sat in silence and Sparrow started for the door. Turning around, he added, "And tell him, I support you."

As he turned back for the exit, he was startled to find Fluxstone watching him from the edge of the doorway. *Damn*, he cursed at himself for having carelessly mentioned Hong Kong. He passed Fluxstone without acknowledging her.

Fluxstone stepped into the open and said to Gemini, "Tell him, I support you too." She then entered the t-port with Sparrow and they descended in awkward silence.

\* \*

Fluxstone sat alone on the floor of her apartment with her legs crossed beneath her, and the *Aegis* lying on a blanket before her. Diamond had briefly taken it from her upon its return and she was glad to have it back. At some point she knew she would lose it permanently. In his will, Aegis had left it to his daughter Alexis. That wasn't a surprise, and it was as it should be. Aegis had inherited it from his father, and passing the artifact onto Alexis was the right thing to do. Currently, Alexis wanted no part of the shield or the life it brought, and the will prevented her from possessing it until she was eighteen, which left it in Fluxstone's care. Maybe by the time she was forced to turn it over, she would be ready to part with it.

The shield's metal surface gleamed under the bright light of the room. Gently, Fluxstone reached out and traced her hand over its center. The dark rough interior was a testament to the shield's legacy.

It was all that remained of the original shield that had been carried by Aegis' father at the time of his death. Aegis and Diamond had forged it into the center of the shield before her. It was worn, dented, and scared.

Running her finger along the shield's edge she found it smooth and flawless, despite the countless battles Aegis had carried it through. Even her recent battle with Fuentes had failed to damage it. She would not have survived the battle without it.

Her life was like the center of the shield. Throughout most of it she had put forth a hard shell that recent events had dented and marred. Sadness welled up in her and she realized that unlike her, the *Aegis* had survived the death of Aegis.

*Zap!*

A spark shocked her finger, forcing her to jerk her hand back.

She sat in confusion and sucked on the injured finger. Aegis had tried to teach her how to pull the spark from the shield, but she had always failed to do it. Together they had joked that it must have been a hereditary trait of the shield. Aegis and his father could do it. Alexis could do it, while her mother could not. Aegis had assured her that their children would be able to do it.

Reaching out, she traced her finger around the edge again. When nothing happened, she repeated the process and got faster with each circle she made. She thought of Aegis, and after several times around the shield, she could feel the static building. When her fingers tingled, she threw out her hand.

*Kaboom!*

A bolt of lightning leaped from her fingers to shatter a mirror on the other side of the room.

Picking up the shield, she stood and faced the broken mirror. Placing the *Aegis* on her arm, she ran her finger along the edge again, pulling on the lightning.

*Kaboom!*

She shattered a potted plant with it.

*No,* she corrected herself. *It isn't a potted plant at all. Like my life, it is fake.*

Looking around the featureless room, she saw just how much it reflected her. From fake plants to pale walls, the room was cold and unfriendly. Again she compared herself to the shield. Like it, she was often hard and cold. Her continued mistreatment of Sparrow was just an example of how she often treated everybody; extreme but the same. It was not how Aegis had been, and it was not how he would have wanted her to be. Sadly she wondered how Aegis could have ever loved her.

*Kaboom!*

A bolt of lightning leaped across the room, exploding her pillow and coating the room in feathers.

*Kaboom! Kaboom!*

The excitement of bolt after bolt overcame her, and over the next several moments, she destroyed her apartment.

*Kaboom!*

A glass frame shattered and a picture of Alex burst into flame.

"Oh!" Embarrassed, Fluxstone glanced around the room to make sure she was still alone. When she looked back at the disappearing picture, she held her hands up and feigned innocence. "Sorry, Alex."

Turning back to the shield, she again ran her finger along its edge. This time she didn't pull at the lightning, but enjoyed the feel of the cold metal. Just beneath the metal surface she could feel the lightning. It was alive, and its touch excited her just like Aegis' touch had. As long as the shield was with her, he was with her.

Slinging the *Aegis* across her shoulder she started for the door. Flinging it open, she found Glip-2 floating there. His color was bright red.

"I detected elevated electrical discharges inside your apartment! Is there a problem?" His voice issued from a control panel next to the door.

"Nope," Fluxstone replied as she patted him and headed for a t-port.

As his color faded to green, Glip-2 floated into the room. "Holy bageeses!" he exclaimed through Fluxstone's sidekick. "I'm not cleaning up this mess!"

\* \*

Sitting with his back to the fireplace, Diamond scrolled through the documents on his sidekick. He ignored his father's disapproving glare from over his shoulder. Leading an army into battle against an alien race was not something Gaius would ever have approved of, or anything he would have thought Samuel capable of. Thankfully, Samuel had stopped caring about what his father thought a long time ago, and he had outgrown his father's expectations years before that.

Diamond knew he should have gone directly to the command center, but he had instead retreated to the seclusion of the sherry room after speaking with Clara. He had needed a moment to reflect on the approaching events and to make a decision on Lekkas.

As expected, Clara had discovered the kidnapping and the clues left by Black Sunday. Currently, Black Sunday, along with Lekkas, was aboard an old oil tanker somewhere in the middle of the Mediterranean Sea.

If killing Lekkas had been a viable solution, Diamond would have ordered it already. Many of those around him didn't think he would make such a decision, but he would; and he had. The first time had involved a fifteen-year-old kid who couldn't control his deadly powers. This time it involved a man who was already responsible for murder, robbery, and an uncountable number of other crimes. With the kid, the decision had been difficult, but with Lekkas it would be no more different than when a police officer faced a gunman threatening civilians. It was never the initial decision to kill that was difficult. It was the living with it afterward that destroyed some men.

But killing any of the targets wasn't an option. Holding him indefinitely wasn't either. Diamond could not see any other option but to delay the final decision for now. Antarctica would be over by the end of the day and either Lekkas would still be a threat or he wouldn't be. As for the others, they would have to wait until after the mission.

Tapping the sidekick he sent a message to Black Sunday. They wouldn't like having to hold up on the tanker for another two days, but the extra million he forwarded with the message would help keep them comfortable.

When the doors of the room opened softly, Samuel nearly missed them. Even the memorial to Vox had sat in silent respect to his seclusion since his arrival in the area.

Gemini stepped up to her father and stared at the floor as she waited quietly for him to finish reading.

"Yes, Gem?" Diamond asked when he finally looked up at her. He sat his drink down on a table next to him and laid the sidekick in his lap. Even though he knew why she had come, he resisted the fatherly urge to tell her no before she could state it.

She stared at the floor and bit her lower lip. The hesitation was unlike her.

"I'm sorry for my attitude in front of everyone."

Diamond barely contained his surprise. He had expected her to start by explaining why she thought he was wrong. Over the last few months, she had rarely spoken to him without starting and ending the conversation with an argument. Either Dreah was coaching her or she had grown up right under his nose and he had missed it.

"I know why you said no, and I understand. I really do. But I think it is the wrong decision. I understand the danger of this mission. I understand the danger of every mission. The hallway back there," she paused as she glanced over her shoulder and thumbed in the direction of the memorials, "is lined with my friends and family. It is lined with people I've known my whole life. They are people you put there."

She paused as she raised her eyes to his for the first time. Her eyes weren't dry, but she hadn't been openly crying either.

"I'm asking you to reconsider. I'm asking you to look at all the training I've put myself through. You have been preparing for this day for most of your life. I've been preparing for it for all of mine." She paused to collect her thoughts concerning Sparrow and Fluxstone, but when she started to speak again she thought better of it and bit her lip. She preferred to earn her place on the team herself, and not through them. Finally, she said, "That's all I have to say. Thanks for listening."

She turned and stated for the door. "Oh," she said, catching herself. Turning back around, she held out a sidekick. "I've run some scenarios of the mission with and without me. You may want to take a look at them."

She waited patiently for him to take the small device, but Diamond only sat quietly and looked at it. He didn't take it when he finally rose and put his arms around her. He hugged her closely and silently wished he had said no before giving her a chance to speak.

# CHAPTER 20
## ANTARCTICA

The Citadel was a flurry of activity over the next few hours as everyone raced to put Diamond's plan into action. The pod bays were filled with equipment and cold survival gear. Scientists checked and rechecked everything. Logs were used to track the equipment and to ensure everything got into the pile it was supposed to be in. Unfortunately, the hurried timetable didn't leave the team members time to go through their preferred pre-mission rituals.

After Lady Gemini had interrupted his quiet time, Diamond retreated to the command center where he watched over everything with a critical eye. His business face prevented anyone from bothering him with anything not related to the mission.

Envoy found herself reviewing the mission plans in her head while she worked and reworked the team rosters based on input from Metaman. He was still in New York and under the thumb of the UN Security Council. She longed for Aegis and the solitude of the rings of Saturn.

Paragon spent his time helping prepare equipment. He could be overheard mumbling prayers as he worked. His music player got lost somewhere among all the boxes and crates.

A newly invigorated Lady Gemini reviewed mission scenario after mission scenario in the special ops room. Her doppelgangers ran between everyone learning as much as possible about everyone's part in the mission. She even spent time with Jonesy until his constant negative comments about Glip-2 ran her off.

Even Wavefront got involved in the preparations. He was put in charge of monitoring the array system from the Citadel. The smell of his breath was enough to make anyone speaking with him tipsy, he hadn't shaved in days, and his clothes looked like he had been sleeping in them, but it was the first sign of life from him in days.

With the specs from Sarah, Sparrow finished his armored suit. It fit like a glove and allowed him the freedom of movement he wanted. The plates contoured to his body and the small energy source powered the inertial field as Glip-2 had predicted. It didn't make him a meta-human, but the suit enhanced his reflexes and nearly doubled his strength. It made him feel a little more like he belonged on Diamond's team.

Dreah spent most of her time in the garden and out of sight. Only Sparrow noticed, and he eventually went looking for her.

\* \*

As usual, just being in the garden brought Sparrow peace and the worries of the mission faded. Oblivious to the danger lying before the world, the animal life played as if it were any other day. As he expected, he found Dreah sitting alone under the garden's central tree. She looked up at him and smiled as he approached.

"Nice outfit," she said.

Sparrow made a pretense of modeling it for her as he spun in a circle.

"I don't know. Do you think the color fits me?"

"Black? Of course it does, dear." Sparrow smiled at her teasing. "Just don't forget it's the man underneath that is important."

Shrugging, he sat down on the grass next to her. The small sparrow speaking with Dreah flapped its wings in annoyance, and then it circled up into the tree above them. Dreah watched it go, and then she turned back to Sparrow.

"Ignore him," she said.

"I always do."

Friendly silence settled between them. It had once been an uneasy silence. Reluctantly, Sparrow broke it.

"I didn't mean to disturb you, but I noticed you weren't running around frantically like everyone else."

"I am not disturbed by your visit, and I had hoped you would come."

"You did?" Sparrow glanced at her curiously. "*Hoped* or *saw?*" Realizing his face was betraying his eagerness, he quickly glanced away. He was beginning to think he would never be able to play a successful game of poker again.

Dreah ignored his discomfort. "Hoped. I was wanting a moment alone with you."

"All you had to do was ask."

She smiled. "Well, my reason is a little selfish."

Sparrow laughed. "I've never seen anything about you to make me believe you are selfish."

"Oh, don't fool yourself, dear. I have all the failings and desires of any woman. And I've had a long time to perfect them."

"Fine, then. What is your selfish desire?"

Dreah lowered her head and studied a small tree blossom in her hand. She twirled it a moment, and then spoke. "I want you to survive today."

Sparrow was confused. "Can't you see the future to know whether I live or die?"

"I don't mean like that. I haven't had a vision to indicate that you will die today, but I have seen that something will hurt you. I've grown fond of you. I want you to come back as you are, but I fear you will not."

"You know our conversations would be easier if you would just tell me what you mean. I've never dealt with anyone who can see the future before. Does being cryptic always come with that power?"

Dreah reached up and laid her hand against his cheek. Looking him in the eye, she said, "And I've never dealt with anyone who filled me with the longing you do. I have no qualms of telling someone their future, Wolff. I don't believe it will damage anything. I believe the future can be changed and often should be. You will believe it too if you ever meet my brother, Jonas."

Sparrow had read the file on Jonas. Like the files on all the known members of the Nine, it was bare of any personal details, but it did detail his abilities enough to leave Sparrow hoping he never met the man. Meeting him usually meant something had already gone terribly wrong. Jonas had a special ability to time travel a day into the past.

His manipulations always left the present altered, and not always for the better.

"I have had no vision of you dying today, Wolff, but I have had visions of you not surviving. In my dreams, I see you become the man you used to be. That is what I mean by you not surviving."

Sparrow didn't like the thought of going back to the man he had once been. Pawn of someone else, cold-blooded killer, or loner; it didn't matter if she referred to all three or just one part of his old self. As for Dreah's visions, he knew everyone believed in them; but despite the wonders he had witnessed over the last few months, he still didn't have much belief. Due to lack of proof, he suffered from doubt.

"Does this have to do with the choice you said I will have to make?"

Dreah smiled and looked back to her blossom. "Don't fear the choice, Wolff. It will come, and you will make it. You have to. And before you ask, I will not tell you what the choice is."

"You just said you do not fear changing the future."

"That is not why I do not tell you."

As curious as he was, he knew she wasn't going to tell him. Sparrow looked into Dreah's dark eyes. "I have actually grown fond of who I am too. I do not wish to return to who I was either."

Dreah smiled, and their friendly silence settled between them again. Then, without warning, she leaned forward and kissed him.

The moment was over way too quickly for Sparrow. When Dreah pulled back, his lips tingled where she had touched them. Her eyes swallowed him. She smiled, and he smiled back.

Breaking the mood, Dreah stood up. "Samuel needs me, and you have work to do. I am sorry for distracting you." She turned and started along the path. Just before disappearing around a bend, she turned back to him and said, "Come back to us, Wolff. Come back to me."

\* \*

Like a love struck teenager who had just experienced his first kiss, Sparrow's head swam with confusion. He felt like he was walking on air, and weighed a ton, all at the same time. Already approaching the pod bay, he couldn't remember the walk there.

Sparrow had not spent much of his previous life dwelling on his feelings, and he had spent even less time trying to understand women.

Before the kiss he had not known how Dreah felt. Even now a part of him doubted he was reading her correctly. Dreah seemed to thrive on physical contact. She always held someone's hand, or had her arm around someone's waist, or stood with her hand resting on a shoulder. Thankfully, Dreah had made the kiss brief and then excused herself to allow him to consider his feelings. He hoped he was reading them correctly.

When he reached the pod bay, he paused and took several deep breaths to collect himself before entering.

* *

Diamond stood over the operations center, his mind racing through a thousand possible ways the mission could go wrong. Some of them had been contained in Lady Gemini's simulations, and others were born out of his growing paranoia of the Psadans. As if sensing it would soon be silenced forever, the voice inside his head was screaming at him. It shouted words of doubt and venomous hate. Only by focusing on the people around him could he hold the words back.

They were his people, all of them. He wasn't the one who had gotten them to this moment; it was they who had gotten him to it. The visions in his head had given him enough insight to guide them here, but it was their hard work, their dedication, and their caring that had gotten them here.

"What's the status over the target cities?"

Jonesy responded from his usual station. "All weather patterns are normal. No energy signatures."

"Keep a close watch on them, Jonesy. If we disturb the Psadans, we won't have much warning."

There were more people in the center than usual. Commander Bullock directly coordinated TASC. Jonesy had a whole team of scientists working with him to monitor the target cities. It would take three of them just to keep up with the calculations Edmond had monitored at the last event. Wavefront paced along the monitor wall, occasionally stopping to watch the video feeds of the team members and to adjust the controls for the best possible pictures. Clara moved back and forth and worked to keep everyone happy. Her eyes sparkled brightly in the dimly lit room, and she smiled as if she didn't have any fear of the upcoming events. Curtis monitored numerous news transmissions from around the world. Those that he thought were important, he forwarded to Diamond. Lady Gemini sat at her station and did her best to track every member of the two Antarctica teams. In the special ops room, one of her doppelgangers assisted her while also monitoring the standby team. Dreah sat on a cushion at the back of the room. She spoke quietly with Carol.

\*   \*

Sparrow picked up a large bag of tools Edmond was requesting in Antarctica and moved it to a stack next to the *Egress* pod doors. He marveled at how light the bag was. Without the suit, he would have barely been able to lift it.

"But the fruit of the Spirit is love, joy, peace, patience…patience…"

Sparrow turned to see who was speaking. Paragon was searching for something with his head buried inside one of the many boxes.

"Did you lose something?" Sparrow asked.

"Ha!" Paragon exclaimed as he stood up and pulled his music player out of the box. Turning to Sparrow, he said, "I have found it. Thank you for asking." Turning his attention back to the box, he rummaged around in it and pulled out a DSS parka. Holding it up, he examined it. Like Sparrow's, it was green with a DSS emblem on the shoulder, and it was much thinner than a typical cold weather parka. Sparrow hadn't actually used his yet, but given Diamond's resources he suspected it would be effective. Paragon's had obviously been designed with his wings in mind. It had large slits down the back. Grunting, he stuffed it back into the box without even trying it on.

"Don't you think you may need that?" asked Sparrow as he looked from the man's bare feet to his exposed chest. As usual all Paragon was wearing was a pair of loose fitting jeans, and the tattoo on his right shoulder.

Paragon stepped out from among the boxes and over to Sparrow. "Yes and no. It will be cold, but it won't fit under my armor. The armor doesn't adjust for thick clothing." He grinned as he added, "It isn't spandex."

Sparrow had no idea how the man's armor worked, but it did explain the lack of proper clothing.

Changing the subject, Paragon said, "You appear relaxed."

"Looks can be deceiving."

Paragon chuckled. "Not to me, my friend."

Surprisingly, Sparrow realized he was much calmer than he had felt since coming to the Citadel. He hadn't realized it before Paragon had mentioned it. His encounter with Dreah had left him unnerved, and he had thrown himself into his work to counter it. It had worked better than he had expected. Perhaps, he was starting to get a hold on his emotions.

Carrying a large box, Slipstream walked between them. "Excuse me," he mumbled.

The two men turned and watched him place the box near the pod doors.

"He has moved that box three times," said Sparrow.

"He is avoiding Antarctica, and yet he feels a drive to go there that crushes his soul. He stands on the edge of the ravine, but he can't find the strength to jump." Paragon didn't conceal the sorrow he felt for his friend. *"A man that studies revenge keeps his own wounds green, which otherwise would heal.* Only God will be able to protect them when he finds the strength to jump."

Footsteps interrupted the two men.

"Perhaps you should seek His help as well," mumbled Paragon. He quickly moved away toward the *Egress*. He picked up a bag of tools and entered the ship.

"What?" Confused, Sparrow spun to see what had frightened the man off. He came face to face with Fluxstone. Several tense moments passed between them. Finally, Sparrow said, "I have work to do. If there is something you need, I would appreciate you getting on with it."

Fluxstone's face softened as his voice drew her back into reality. She suddenly looked nervous. Glancing away and back to him several times before speaking, she said, "I'm sorry for the way I've treated you." Sparrow barely concealed his shock. "Losing Aegis has been difficult for me, but that is no excuse. I should have trusted him, and Dreah, more. I am sorry."

Sparrow was stunned. "Th-thanks," he stammered.

Fluxstone, briefly avoided his eyes, and then looked back at him. She nodded before turning away. Silently, Sparrow watched her go.

Moments later, carrying the same large box, Slipstream walked past Sparrow and said, "Take it and run, it'll never happen again. And if you keep staring at her like that, she'll come back and break your kneecaps."

Sparrow chuckled and tore his gaze from Fluxstone. At ease, he followed Slipstream across the bay.

\* \*

As the doors cycled, Sparrow pulled his parka tight around himself. When the icy cold hit him, it took his breath away. Reaching up, he pulled a pair of goggles down over his eyes and stepped out into the sunlight to join an army of men on the frozen surface of Antarctica. The scientists worked at a frantic pace, and TASC guarded their every move.

Slipstream moved past him still carrying the same large box and Sparrow felt a pang of envy. The man was practically naked, but the frozen cold had no effect on him whatsoever.

"Show off," grunted Sparrow loud enough for Slipstream to hear. Slipstream didn't reply as he sat the box down in front of Edmond and Lady Gemini. Lt. Carlos Reyes of TASC stood with them. As Sparrow joined them, he found Edmond explaining to Gemini how to set up the arrays. She smiled at Sparrow, and he paused a moment to listen as Glip-2 zipped past. Sparrow watched the globe as it circled and looped around everyone. He seemed to be enjoying his freedom from the Citadel, and he was making every effort to show it.

Sparrow was actually glad everyone knew their job. Despite his asking, he had not been given a clear reason for his appointment as second-in-command of Alpha team. Dreah and Diamond may have seen a leader in him, but he didn't. He had not even begun to get his life back in order, and he barely had his emotions under control.

"Alpha team and Beta team, UNIT is approaching by air," said Lady Gemini through the commlink.

"Copy," replied Reyes.

"Copy," replied Envoy.

After a few moments, they could all hear the roar of an engine rumbling across the frozen land. The group turned and scanned the sky for the source. A fast approaching airship hung low on the horizon. As it neared, others joined them to watch its final approach.

The airship was more conventional than Diamond's pods, and it was much larger. As it spiraled in its decent, the side of the ship came into view. Painted on it was the large blue and white flag of the United Nations. UNIT was printed in large letters under the flag. The ship's name, the *Phoenix*, was painted under the cockpit window on both sides of the airship's nose. There were large cannons on the port side, starboard side, nose, and on the spine of the ship. The thing looked like a warship descending into a battle zone.

Ice and snow were kicked up as the ship neared the icy surface. Slipstream stared unblinking into the stinging spray while everyone else turned away. As the ship touched the ground, the engines powered down, allowing the blowing snow and ice to settle. Envoy immediately started toward it. Reyes fell in stride next to her, and Sparrow followed. Gleaming in his metal armor, Paragon joined them. Everyone else stared silently at the massive ship until Edmond sent them scurrying back to their assignments.

As a large hatch opened on the side of the ship, Meta-man peered out of it and surveyed the crowd. The sun gleamed off his metal uniform and when he spotted Envoy, he started down the ramp before it could finish descending. Meta-man's uniform now had a brazen golden eagle on the chest and a UN patch on the right shoulder. The cold caused him to briefly shiver before his physiology adjusted to it.

The monstrously large man that followed Meta-man off the *Phoenix* was a tank on two legs known as Iron Bear. Most of his body had been replaced with metal parts that stuck out in all directions. His right arm was fully robotic, and twice the size of a normal man's torso. It ended in a metal claw that was capable of wrapping fully around a car's engine and crushing it. Several wires sank beneath the skin of his human left arm to connect the flesh to his metal parts. The arm and hand were supported by a metal brace. Iron Bear's torso was covered in a large metal plate. It was painted red and sported the two-headed golden eagle of the Russian Federation. The plate protected numerous wires and gears that ran throughout his body. They could be heard twirling and twisting with every movement he made. To support his massive weight, Iron Bear's robotic legs were large and bulky. They were not designed for running and caused the ground to tremble with each step he took. His head and shoulders sat atop the metal frame, but again there were numerous wires connecting the flesh to the metal. The right side of his head was metal, and his right eye had been replaced with a mechanical orb that twitched independently of his normal eye to take in every detail of the landing site. It paused and focused briefly on anything that could be a potential threat. In place of the man's right ear was an antenna. A large Gatling gun with rotating barrels stuck up over his left shoulder, and it was well known that his right arm concealed a rocket launcher.

Iron Bear's metal cannon clanged loudly against the side of the *Phoenix* as he stepped down onto the snow. He was UNIT's Russian representative, and when he saw Envoy his smile and booming laughter ran contrary to his harsh appearance. He made a beeline straight for her, and in hearty greeting he heaved her into the air with his human arm.

"It is good to see you my beautiful love!" bellowed Iron Bear as he hugged Envoy. She allowed the man his joy, even hugging him back.

The next man to step from the ship glanced around at everyone with suspicion, and he appeared uncomfortable in his thick unbuttoned overcoat. He was called Shishi, the Stone Lion of Fu, and he was the meta-representative for the People's Republic of China. Under his parka he wore a red uniform with a light brown image of his namesake emblazoned along the length of the left side. The right side of his chest held the five yellow stars of his country's flag. His parka and costume had the UN flag on the right shoulder.

Shishi was a meta-morph with the ability to transform his physical form into a giant lion. When in this form, his skin took on the hardness and durability of stone. It gave him tremendous strength and durability.

The newest of the meta-humans that represented the five permanent members of the UN Security Council, Shishi had a turbulent relationship with Meta-man and DSS. The source of the friction was an investigation conducted by DSS several years earlier.

A coalition of powerful Taiwanese businessmen hired DSS to find and stop the source of a new drug that was negatively impacting their workforce and threatening to destroy their businesses. The course of the investigation eventually led the team to a minor drug lord operating in China. Since international law required a national hero to accompany any foreign meta-humans during operations in any sovereign state, the Chinese government ordered Shishi, then the commander of the Chinese national team, to assign one of his team members to work with them. However, Shishi refused to work with or assign any of his team's best members to work with the mercenary agents of a decadent western capitalist investigating his fellow citizens. Instead, he assigned a minor member of the team, a healer named Ping, to work with them.

Within two weeks Diamond's team had uncovered a conspiracy by a group of high-ranking government and military officials to destabilize Taiwan's government and infrastructure as a part of a covert takeover of the island nation. The Chinese government denied any knowledge of the plot, and summarily executed all of the officials implicated in it. One of those executed was a man that Shishi had served with in the military prior to the manifestation of his powers. When Shishi objected to the execution and insisted upon the man's innocence an investigation was launched into Shishi's possible connection to the conspirators. Although Shishi was ultimately cleared of any wrongdoing the investigation came at an inopportune time. China's UNIT meta-representative was stepping down after more than two decades of distinguished service, and the government was in the middle of choosing a replacement. As the commander of China's national team, Shishi had been the obvious choice. However, the taint of having been investigated caused Shishi to be denied the post. Instead the Chinese government gave the position to Ping as a reward for his valiant service in helping to expose the conspiracy and bringing the perpetrators to justice.

Shishi was finally chosen as Ping's replacement several years later when Ping was accused of becoming too friendly with the meta-representatives of western nations, and for failing to represent the best interests of the People's Republic of China. When Shishi took up his post at UNIT, Meta-man's open association with DSS, the mercenary group that Shishi blamed for his friend's death, and his own political difficulties, made him appear tainted in the eyes of the new Chinese meta-representative. The two of them had been hostile towards each other ever since.

Shishi was now expected to replace Meta-man as team commander in a few months, and he had spent the last couple of weeks trying to hurry that transition along. He opposed the mission to Antarctica, but had not vetoed it after speaking with his superiors.

Madame Fantôme drew everyone's attention as she exited the ship. If one believed her story, Madame Fantôme encountered a derelict pirate ship when she was a young woman in her twenties. The pirates aboard that ship were ghosts, and their touch left her a ghost as well.

Now she possessed the ability to pass through solid objects, and much of the physical world had little effect on her. As for her touch, it was like the icy touch of death.

Due to Madame Fantôme's ghostly beauty, the story wasn't hard to believe. Her skin and hair were as white as the Antarctica snow. She wore a tight provocative outfit that matched her skin. Her low cut top was laced down the front, leaving nothing about her full bosom to the imagination. She wore tight pants that were slit down the outside. Laces ran along the slit. Her hair was long and played on the wind while her matching trench coat fluttered around her. The UN patch on her coat was white instead of blue. Her eyes were as brilliant as blue topaz, and she was unfazed by the cold. Her high heels didn't sink into the fresh snow when she walked upon it.

As she walked up to Paragon, she said in a heavy French accent, "I see zat you ver in Paris, handsome. Tsk, tsk," she added as she ran her finger down his cheek and along his jaw. Paragon flinched as a thin trail of frost formed where she touched him. "You 'ave been very bad. I vill 'ave to punish you. But don't vorry, naughty boy, you vill enjoy eet. If you do not, I vill enjoy eet for both of us."

Her brilliant blue eyes burned with anger and lust. She smirked and blew Paragon a kiss before she turned and sauntered off to join the rest of the UNIT field team. Paragon rubbed his face and flexed his jaw as the frost began to thaw.

*She must still be mad about what I did to those tanks*, he thought to himself as he turned to follow her across the ice.

Over her shoulder, Madame Fantôme said, "Si vous n'étiez pas bon aussi fichu dans le lit, je gèlerais vos boules et les alimenterais aux pingouins!"

Paragon was right. Madame Fantôme was France's meta-representative to UNIT, and like all of UNIT's meta-representatives, she was accountable to the government that appointed her. After the destruction of Paris what was left of that government had nearly recalled her after seeing her occasional paramour tear through a battalion of French tanks. Once politically well connected, Madame Fantôme had been forced to scramble to save her position. Most of her friends and what little was left of her family had died when Paris was destroyed. She had managed to save herself for the time being but her relationship with the French government was tenuous at best, and she owed favors to people she didn't like. Mad didn't even begin to describe her feelings toward Paragon.

A blast of cold air rolled across the camp and Dragón Verde shivered as he stepped down onto the ice. As usual, he wore a thin green serpent patterned uniform. Over it, he had a short parka that displayed the Mexico and UN flags. He didn't speak with anyone as he maneuvered through the many bodies to stand between Meta-man and Shishi, but his clear dark eyes noted everyone he passed and he nodded to those he knew. As he waited for the others, he began to shift from one foot to the other and to rub his hands together against the cold.

Mexico was not a permanent member of the Security Council, but Dragón Verde rarely missed the opportunity to go on a mission. He never failed to volunteer when the core five were involved. It was well known that Incindiaro had been offered the position before him but had rejected it over corruption in the Mexican government. Accusations of that corruption had followed Dragón Verde into the position. By staying active, he appeared to be beyond reproach and avoided those who felt he owed them favors.

Dragón Verde was a therianthropic chimera with a mixture of reptilian and human DNA. He was capable of suppressing his reptilian side to appear human, as he was doing now. However, this took effort and his primary form was that of a human-reptile hybrid. In that form, he possessed enhanced strength and was capable of great acrobatic skills. He could see in the dark as well as in daylight.

Rose rounded out UNIT's core five, and when she stepped off the *Phoenix*, her hair caught the sun and blazed as if on fire. It was full, wavy, and bright red. People swore that when Rose was in the sun, her hair opened up to catch the rays like a flower opening its petals to enjoy a new spring day.

Once getting past her hair, the woman's beauty left people stunned. It was enough to make any faerie tale princess jealous. Rose had skin that was tanned and a face that was flawless. She had high cheekbones, a soft pattern of freckles, full red lips, and bright green eyes. Her years as a hero had left her figure curvy with well-toned muscles. She was nearly six feet tall with long legs, and she walked with poise and confidence. Her costume sported a red top with a high collar. The front of her jacket wrapped across her chest and a row of gold buttons ran down the length of the jacket's left side. A red and white image of the

Tudor Rose of England dominated the upper right section. Like the others, the UN patch was on her right shoulder. Her pants were black and she wore a set of high-heeled black boots. She did not wear a coat against the cold, but she was surrounded by a soft red glow.

Only Meta-man had been a member of the team longer than Rose. She had served as team leader three times, and if it was ever left up to a vote, she would likely keep the post. When she overheard Madame Fantôme flirting with Paragon, she rolled her eyes and took up a position near Envoy.

Rose was one of the world's most powerful telepaths. She could read minds, control the actions of others, generate illusions in the minds of people, or assault their mind directly with psychic energy.

The last member of the Antarctica mission team was from Africa. Appearing as large as his namesake, Kilimanjaro was broad shouldered and seven feet tall. His muscles were well toned and added to his intimidating stature. His head was clean-shaven with a large African tattoo representing bravery dominating the right side. Humility was tattooed on the left side. He wore a brown uniform with black African tribal art along the sleeves and across the back. Around his neck was an African reed necklace with glass beads. Several matching bracelets were tied around both wrists. Each bracelet was a gift from the people of the many countries he had represented in the past. His pants were black and he wore sturdy boots and a large UN Parka.

The hero was capable of increasing his height to supernatural proportions. This enhanced his strength and durability while greatly increasing his mass. He could reach heights of nearly fifty feet.

Kilimanjaro first served UNIT as a representative of the United Republic of Tanzania. When Tanzania rotated off the Council, Kilimanjaro remained to represent the African nation of Benin. He continued his service by remaining the meta-human choice for many of Africa's central nations. This service was not due to a lack of qualified African meta-humans or corruption in the system, but due to the respect Kilimanjaro earned from all the people of Africa. As a hero for the continent, he not only crossed political barriers, but also language barriers by learning the many dialects of the people, racial barriers by uniting the people under common causes, cultural barriers by honoring the traditions of all Africa's tribes, and religious barriers by spreading care and joy regardless of the gods worshiped.

Kilimanjaro moved up to Slipstream and the two men shook hands as equals. The large man then turned to Glip-2, and the globe pulsed rapidly in response to his greeting.

The soldiers who served in IMPACT, UNIT's International Mechanized and Powered Armor Combat Troop, spread out to secure a tight perimeter around the *Phoenix* and the base camp. As soldiers stepped down from the ship, their armor shifted from UN blue to white to blend in with the snow.

IMPACT were the shock troops for UNIT. They were soldiers recruited from all over the world and trained to use powered battle armor. They carried the world's most high tech weaponry, and they received the most advanced training of any military unit. They were the elite of the elite. During deployments, while UNIT handled the meta-human threat, IMPACT handled everything else from perimeter security to the rescue of civilians to the filing of paperwork to the securing of prisoners. In the absence of UNIT, IMPACT stepped up and did the job.

Their powered battle armor made IMPACT appear to be soldiers from a sci-fi space epic. They wore full helmets with mirrored face shields that could be hermetically sealed against airborne toxins or pathogens. The helmet contained advanced communications equipment with direct satellite access. It had an advanced computer with scanning capabilities and the ability to track friendly and hostile targets across the face shield independent of the soldier. The armor's built in exoskeleton enhanced the soldier's speed and strength. The thick plates that covered their vital areas could withstand even the strongest firearms or energy attacks, and the special padding beneath absorbed even the strongest meta-human punch. The armor adapted to the climate to keep the soldier cool or warm as needed, and it shifted color to blend into the environment. It didn't provide full invisibility but its chameleon abilities were some of the best money could buy. Each man stored typical soldier's gear in a backpack made of the same plates as the armor and among the supplies was a capsule with two hours of breathable air. Among IMPACT's weapons was a high-powered energy rifle with an integrated grenade launcher. The weapon discharged energy pulses with more stopping power than the strongest firearms, and the grenade launcher had far greater range and accuracy than was typical. The battle gear was extremely expensive and a soldier had to endure two years of training to qualify to wear it. Each suit was custom built for the soldier it was assigned to.

Once Envoy convinced Iron Bear to put her down, she turned to Meta-man.

As they shook hands, Meta-man said, "We don't have a full team, but we are ready to assist."

"Even though we should not *assist* a decadent capitalist and his army of private mercenaries." Shishi growled.

"We're private security consultants." Envoy replied coldly.

"Yes, I'm aware of what you call yourselves," Shishi replied. "I'm also aware of what you've done. I am still not entirely convinced that you and your associates are as blameless as you make yourselves out to be."

"I've already told you…" Meta-man began impatiently.

"Yes!" Shishi said, angrily interrupting him. "Exactly! You have told us that they are not to blame. But your actions over the last several days have proven that you are not impartial when it comes to these people. You place these people above your duty to UNIT, and above the people you represent!"

Meta-man's face flushed red with barely controlled rage. "How dare you! I have never failed to represent the best interests of the American people!"

"Really?" Shishi countered. "Then your superiors in Washington knew what you were doing in Denver and Buenos Aires? You kept them *in the loop* the entire time you were lying to us and protecting *them*?" Shishi pointed towards Envoy.

Meta-man hesitated and Kilimanjaro took advantage of the brief silence to attempt to restore order.

"Be calm, friend Shishi. We already discussed these matters at length before we decided to come here. By helping Meta-man help these people, we help our own people."

Rose stepped up next to the giant man and Shishi looked at her.

"Kilimanjaro is right, Shishi. The situation may not be ideal, but we have to make the best of it."

"I did not say we should not take action. Just that we should not be taking orders from these people and that *he*," Shishi glared venomously at Meta-man, "is untrustworthy."

Having heard enough, Envoy stepped into Shishi's face.

"I don't need them to stand up for me, Shishi. I'm in command of this mission and I don't have time to stand here arguing with you. Get with the program or get lost!" Without waiting for Shishi to respond, Envoy turned and started across the ice. She had only gotten a few feet from the group when she heard Iron Bear's booming voice behind her.

"Latisha, wait!"

Envoy turned around and saw Iron Bear taking huge strides toward her. When he reached her, he put his human hand on her shoulder and spoke to her in a low voice that carried to everyone within twenty feet.

"I love you, Latisha, but Shishi is right. As members of UNIT our first duty is to the people we represent. If this is some kind of trick or trap, we will do whatever is necessary to stop you and protect them. Do you understand?"

Envoy looked at the UNIT members gathered around her. Her eyes lingered on Meta-man. Much of what they were saying was correct. Meta-man didn't trust Diamond, but he had trusted Aegis. The two had spent many hours side by side. Now he trusted in her to carry that torch. As for UNIT, they had responsibilities that trumped whatever personal relationships they had with her team. They would not hesitate to take out Diamond Justice if they felt it was necessary to protect the world from the threat it faced. She patted Iron Bear's hand.

"Yes, Pyotr. I understand." Envoy turned back to the group and forced a smile. "Your help is needed here. It is not an ideal situation, and the truth is we don't even know if what we are doing here is going to stop this thing. But I've lost friends and family to something I can't understand. And that scares me. So I am going to do everything I can to try and stop it. Battle between our two teams right now would do more harm than good, and we don't have time to debate leadership. I could use your help. So," Envoy's expression hardened into one of grim determination, "I *will* remain in charge of this mission. Stay and help us or get out of our way."

As Envoy turned away from Shishi, her eyes met Kilimanjaro's. His eyes held confidence in her. "Good to see you, Rafi."

"It is always a pleasure, Latisha," said Kilimanjaro.

She patted him on the shoulder as she passed. "And you too, Rose." She added.

Rose nodded in respond.

No one rejected Envoy's assertion of authority. They all silently fell in line to follow her toward the base camp. Sparrow found himself walking next to Iron Bear.

"Wonderful, isn't she," bellowed Bear as he slapped Sparrow across the back. The blow nearly sent Sparrow tumbling into the snow. "Oh, sorry about that. There is not much feeling in these old metal hands so sometimes I hit too hard! Of course, I also didn't realize you were so fragile."

Sparrow grinned. His armor had protected him from the unexpected blow. "I'm fine." Turning the conversation away from him, he said, "I have been impressed with Envoy in the short time I've known her. You two obviously know each other."

"Ha, of course we do my new comrade. Wait! You mean she hasn't mentioned me?" Iron Bear squinted his human eye and scratched his bald head with his human hand. As his face brightened again, he continued, "She saved my life once and we were married!"

Sparrow couldn't help but wonder if the wedding night was before or after the man obtained his metal parts.

"You can't prove that!" Envoy yelled from the front of the line. "Even the priest was too drunk to remember that night!"

"Govno! I forgot her ears were so good," whispered Iron Bear to Sparrow. Even while whispering, the man's voice carried across the ice. "That's why we don't live together, you know. My mouth and her ears are a bad combination." Trudging forward awkwardly in the snow, the man raced after Envoy. "But love, we both know it is true in our hearts!"

"We don't have time for this today, Bear."

The man wasn't fazed by Envoy's rebuke, and his deep voice echoed from the front of the line as he apologized to her.

"Sorry about Bear," said Rose as she took his place in line. "He has a good heart, and he would die for anyone here."

Sparrow marveled at her beauty. Rose was clearly one of the most beautiful people he had ever seen; but to him, her beauty paled when he compared it to Dreah seated beneath the tree in the garden.

"It's okay. He will be easier to tolerate than some of this doom and gloom bunch." The irony of his statement wasn't lost to him, but since Rose didn't know him, she missed it.

Rose grinned and held out her hand, "I'm Rose. I am pleased to meet you. I don't think we've met before."

Sparrow shook her hand. "Sparrow," he said.

"Hum, interesting code name. I'll bet there is a story behind that one."

Sparrow only smiled in response.

"Careful of zzat one, young bird," mocked Madame Fantôme. She walked next to Paragon and had her arm locked in his. Her hips swayed with each step and where she touched the winged warrior, ice coated his armor. "She is dangerous to zze man's heart." Madame Fantôme's flirtatious eyes danced between Sparrow and Rose.

"Ignore her," Rose whispered. "It's the easiest way, trust me."

Madame Fantôme winked in response and turned her attention back to Paragon.

\* \*

"Twenty-seven minutes," said Edmond.

Envoy looked to Sarah and she nodded her agreement. She turned to the group.

"Everyone knows their assignments. If you have any objections, it's too late to voice them." She turned to Reyes and Sparrow. "Keep a close watch on those arrays. If we are forced under the ice, give us time to get out before Glip-2 roasts the place. Glip-2?" The globe floated up next to her.

"Yeeees, love," he mocked through her sidekick.

She narrowed her eyes and pointed at him. "Never again. Now, get going and good luck. Don't blow yourself up. You owe me a beer."

"Piece of cake, looove." Before Envoy could slap him, he shot skyward.

Envoy tracked Glip-2 as he rocketed out of sight. He quickly faded from view, but in her vision, a red dot indicated his position. Next to the dot a series of numbers quickly climbed to indicate his height over the ice. The numbers slowed and stopped at just over ten miles up.

Envoy turned and nodded at Lt. Reyes. The young man nodded back and quickly turned away. Edmond and Sarah turned back to the arrays.

"Beta team, stay close. I'll prepare for a quick descent under the ice. Monitor your radios closely."

Moving away from the group, Envoy raised her arm and her eyes glowed slightly as she scanned the snow. After a moment, a dot began blinking before her vision. With a thought, she had her artifact recalculate the path to the energy source through the ice. The shaft's exact length and angle of descent filled her vision. Deciding she didn't want a steep descent at the base, she adjusted the image to allow for the shaft to level out before reaching the energy signature.

Flexing her fingers, she sent a wave into the ice that disintegrated it instantly, opening up a hole. Each wave of energy from her hand extended the hole deeper, and soon a shaft began to reach out toward the blinking dot. The sides of the shaft were slick and sloped at a steep angle that traced the path that only she could see.

Slipstream ignored the danger of Envoy's energy and stood on the edge of the dark hole. A moment later he stepped over the edge and glided down the slope. His muscles were tense and his fists were clenched. Envoy lifted off the ground and followed him. She didn't bother to tell him to get behind her. Iron Bear stumbled awkwardly on the slippery slope and peered down after her.

"Wait here, Bear," Envoy said, as she extended the shaft further and began to disappear into the darkness with Slipstream. "Protect the arrays. If we encounter trouble, we'll call."

Iron Bear looked worried, but he held his ground as the others gathered around the hole with him to wait.

\* \*

Deep under the ice, a thin hand slowed by age moved before an image hanging in the air, and the image shifted to meet the need of the Psadan controlling it. Usually dismissed as insignificant, the creatures crawling across the ice were swarming. He watched as the image shifted from one to another.

Finally the image settled on a group of them standing around a hole bored into the ice. The Psadan knew the purpose of that hole. The image focused on one of them garbed in a bright metal uniform and the Psadan felt a moment of recognition. Before he could understand where he had seen the human before, he dismissed him as insignificant. Alone he was nothing, but with the others he might pose a threat.

His lost brother had tried to warn them. He had tried to warn them that this race was different from the others. He had tried to warn them this race would fight back if they felt threatened. Foolishly, his concerns had been dismissed. He, along with their third, had felt humans were no more significant than any other race their kind had encountered over the eons. This race, along with all the others, would be used to further their own needs. If they perished as a result, the universe would never even notice.

When his brother's seeds had failed, fear that he had been diseased caused him to be cast out. His concerns had quickly been forgotten. Now realization that his brother may have been right caused the Psadan a moment of panic.

Turning, he pulled on the energy surrounding him and used it to move through the darkness. He felt worried. Immediately, two large glowing globes joined him.

He passed several shafts of light, but he ignored them and the creatures contained within them. At one point, they had been important, but others, better, had been found. The creatures unconsciously squirmed at his presence.

As he approached his brother and the two young, he pulled on the energy again and the image of the snow returned. The others watched closely as he showed the swarm descending upon them. Understanding passed between them all.

One of the young turned toward the globes, and his request for knowledge was answered. They weren't ready. They weren't mature enough. If there was interference now, they would never reach maturity. The young responded with anger at the thought of possible interference in his brother's birth. He was appalled by the thought. In response to his anger, three brightly glowing flares circled him. The energy surrounding the group condensed into a thick and soupy fog.

Stepping forward, the elder brother manipulated the energy again, and the image shifted away from the swarm to a large mass of pulsing energy behind them. To the swarm, the energy was a solid air ship. To the Psadans, it was no different than the energy they controlled to view the swarm. The image approached the ship and passed easily through the side. It stopped before an interior wall that was solid even to it. The blue apparatus in the center of the door spun. A human nearby jerked around when alarms sounded. Confused, he approached the door, but the image shifted away from him and passed through the door. Inside the Citadel, the image glided along glowing halls to an upper room where it stopped over the back of the swarm's leader.

Understanding passed between the two brothers and the young.

\* \*

The hair on the back of Dreah's neck tickled. Turning slowly, she reached out with her senses and searched for the source of her discomfort. She found it near the exit. Concentrating, she punched through the veil hiding it. An aura of energy snaked into the room and rose up over her. Without touching it, she could feel the alien minds controlling it.

"*Lumin!*" Dreah waved her hand in front of her as she said the ancient word of power. A burst of light briefly light lit up the room. Reaching out with her senses again, Dreah found the Psadan mind was gone and the energy snake was dispersing like the wake of a boat.

"Dreah?" asked Diamond from behind her. "Is there a problem?"

Turning slowly, Dreah found everyone in the room staring at her. "We had uninvited guests."

"I take it they ain't staying for dinner," said Wavefront.

"No," she said. Turning to Diamond she continued. "I suspect they will return, however. I suggest you send Samson and his team down to the pod bay."

Diamond knew instantly what Dreah was referring to. The plan officially called for Charlie team to be deployed to a city threatened by an event, but Diamond had a second reason for keeping them on reserve. If he could manipulate the energy of the Psadans then the Psadans could manipulate the energy of the Citadel. Dreah's guest had been the Psadans. They weren't going to sit on the sidelines.

Diamond quickly considered removing the pods from Antarctica. It was logical to conclude that the Psadans could manipulate them as easily as Glip-2 or Fuentes had. It was also logical to assume that they could directly enter the Citadel through them. Perhaps Dreah's guest had been just such an entry. Removing the pods from Antarctica would strand a lot of people on the surface. Sarah had already warned him what was going to happen to the continent once Glip-2 imploded the energy. The pods were the best way to get his people to safety.

That left the Citadel. Abandoning it would mean a severe loss of resources. But like any resource, it could be replaced; even if it had been his home for the last forty years.

Turning away from Dreah, he addressed the room. "Put the Citadel in a level one lockdown. Shut down all exterior exits except for Safe Harbor. Give me an evacuation of all non-essential personnel to that location. No one enters or leaves through any other exit without my direct authorization. That includes Alpha and Beta teams from Antarctica. Deploy Charlie team to the pod bay. Anything or anyone accessing the Citadel is to be considered a level red threat and engaged immediately." Diamond quickly tapped his screen and opened his commlink "Envoy, this is Diamond. We suspect direct interference by the Psadans. We are putting the Citadel in a level one lockdown."

"Roger," replied Envoy. "Meta-man, you read that?"

"Copy, Envoy. Beginning descent now."

Diamond's orders sent a flurry of activity through the room. Lady Gemini immediately reacted to put the Citadel in lockdown and to deploy Charlie team. Clara worked with Curtis to shut down the exterior exits, and to coordinate the evacuation. Jonesy adjusted a portion of the video wall to monitor all exterior exits and alert them to any activity.

"Excuse me please. I'll go see if I can help Samson." Turning, Dreah started for the exit.

"Do you sense something, Dreah?"

Dreah glanced back at Diamond. "Nothing you don't already know about. It's just that after the way the Psadans invaded this room, I fear Samson may need more than just physical help."

Diamond nodded in response.

\* \*

Iron Bear stumbled awkwardly on the slippery slope before his feet shifted and large spikes extended from them to sink into the ice. With his right arm, he reached out and grabbed the edge of the hole. His hand detached and he began to lower himself down by a cable with his hand acting as his anchor. His spiked feet kept him anchored against the wall.

As the others took turns following the metal behemoth into the hole, Meta-man was left standing over the darkness. He peered into it and his mind raced through distant memories. The darkness was familiar and the walls of the shaft reminded him too much of the Citadel. A feeling of foreboding washed over him.

Stepping up next to him, Maverick said, "About damn time." He stepped over the edge and slid after the others.

Meta-man glanced briefly around at those being left on the surface. He spotted Sparrow watching him. Meta-man waved and then quietly followed Maverick into the hole. He couldn't help but feel that something started a long time ago was about to come to a violent end.

\* \*

As the t-port doors closed, Dreah considered the problem. She had no doubt Samson and his team could defend the Citadel from any physical threat the Psadans posed. However, the invasion into the control room told her that the threat might not be physical. Psionic energy had been used to view them. It was likely any assault by the Psadans on the Citadel would also be psionic.

Reaching the central shaft, Dreah dived over the glass railing and her body dispersed. As a flock of small birds, she descended quickly to the garden below. The freshness of the garden greeted her, and she felt sorrow that it may not survive the day.

When she reached the bench she had shared with Sparrow, she fused back into her human form. A fit of chirping immediately reached her ears. Glancing up, she saw the little sparrow perched on a branch above her. He chirped loudly and twisted his wings in show.

She smiled at her friend. "Yes little one, I see your beautiful wings. You have shown them to me many times, and I am sorry that I don't have time to enjoy them today"

Dreah dropped to her knees before the bench, and a moment later it slid aside to reveal a hidden compartment underneath it. Reaching into it she withdrew several items. She started to rise, but hesitated. Leaning back into the hole again, she rummaged through the items until she found a slender curved dagger. She drew it out of the hole and pulled the silver blade out of the worn leather sheath. She studied it a moment before tucking it into her arm with the rest of the items.

As she rose from her knees, the bench moved back into place. Dreah turned and hurried toward the center of the garden. Behind her the sparrow chirped loudly in praise of itself.

Under the tree, Dreah placed the items on the grass. Sitting, she lit three candles and put them at three points around her. Picking up the dagger, she withdrew it from its sheath and tucked it inside her gown. She laid the sheath on the grass outside the candles. She flipped through a small book, and when she found the page she was looking for, she read the words aloud.

"Somes quod mens singulus. Somes quod mens singulus. Somes quod mens singulus."

When she was sure she had the words firmly in mind, she closed the book and picked up a small bell.

Looking at the great tree spread out above her, she whispered, "Help me, old mother."

She rang the bell three times. On the third strike, the sounds of the garden were shut out by the spell. The silence inside the candles was heavy and her breathing was as loud as an ocean wave crashing against a rocky shore. Her heartbeat sounded like a drum in her ears. Closing her eyes, she brought her breathing under control, slowing her heart rate. She began to chant the words of the spell aloud over and over again.

# CHAPTER 21
# SACRIFICE

Charlie team was in position in the pod bay, but Dreah hadn't arrived there yet. Her statements had led Diamond to believe she was going there when she left the control room. He had no doubt she was safe, but he was curious over her disappearance. After glancing around the command center to make sure everyone was distracted, he closed his eyes and pulled his senses inward. When the sounds of the room became distorted and slowed, he thrust himself out of his body.

Standing over the back of his chair, Diamond could see his body seated before him. Clara stood on the floor beneath him with her finger about to touch her sidekick. Wavefront was holding his floppy hat and poised to scratch his scalp. The Citadel glowed brightly where anyone touched it. The people and the objects in the room weren't frozen in time, but they didn't move at the speed of thought either. He thought of the garden and was instantly projected to it.

In astral space, the garden tree swayed and moved. Its blossoms glowed brightly. He found Dreah sitting beneath it inside three burning candles. As Dreah's spell took effect, her astral form rose gently out of her body. Her glowing white dress and dark hair floated gently on the air around her. A tendril of smoke anchored her astral form to her physical body. She would use it to find her body if it was moved during the spell.

As Diamond watched, Dreah turned slowly in a circle. A look of pain crossed her face and she stopped. A moment later she rose upward to disappear into the Citadel shaft.

An instant later Diamond was back in his body. Clara touched the screen of her sidekick and Wavefront scratched his scalp.

Diamond tapped the controls on his station and an image of Dreah sitting under the tree appeared on it. He quickly sent a message to Gemini, Wavefront, and Fenrir. Almost as quickly as she received the message, Gemini split and a doppelganger headed for the exit. Wavefront looked at his sidekick and then at Diamond. When Diamond didn't acknowledge him, he touched the video wall and shifted his workload to Jonesy and his team. He then hurried after Gemini. Jonesy grunted loudly when he noticed the new work added to his own.

Diamond knew Dreah hated projecting into astral space. If she had done so, it was because she suspected the Psadans would use some sort of psionic attack. By dealing with it directly, she left him free to run the operation.

"Status?" asked Diamond.

"Status green," reported Envoy. "We are approaching the source of the energy readings."

"Status green," responded Reyes.

"Green," said Samson.

"Green," said Gemini.

"Green," responded Jonesy. "There are no energy signatures over the target cities and cloud cover is normal."

"Greeeen!" Glip-2's voice echoed from several speakers in the room all at once. "I see stars!"

Jonesy grunted with disgust.

"What's the estimated time for completion of the array system?"

"Ten minutes," replied Edmond.

Sarah had already indicated there was no way to speed it up. She needed to program each array separately based on its positioning. Impatient, Diamond sat back in his chair and waited.

\* \*

The snow crunched under Sparrow's feet as Duo flew by overhead carrying another array. Slipping and nearly falling, Edmond hurried across the snow after them. Sparrow stopped at the closest array and found Brandon hunched over its control panel. He knew that Sarah was in control, but he couldn't help but think of her as Brandon. After all he had never even met her. Without looking up she spoke to him.

"You are not what I would expect in an assassin, Mr. Kingsley."

Startled by her words, Sparrow quickly glanced around to see if anyone had overheard her.

"Don't worry," she continued. "I've been keeping Mr. Diamond's secrets for a long time now. He didn't tell me, either. I figured it out."

"You are not what I would expect either..."

Sarah laughed. It unnerved Sparrow. He tried to imagine the woman in her file's picture standing before him, but it didn't help.

"How does this...work?"

"Are you asking about Brandon and me? Or the array system?"

"You and Brandon."

"I know it can be unsettling, but you will get used to it." Sparrow doubted that. "I'm a meta-human without a body. Your typical lab explosion caused by an idiot scientist working on an experiment only God should have been tampering with...Yes, yes, I'll tell him...Brandon says hi." Sarah continued to work while she waved a hand at Sparrow.

"When the smoke cleared, I was in the body of the idiot scientist. I really didn't want to be in there. There wasn't enough space in his head for his ego and me, and it didn't allow for any secrets between us. So, I grew to dislike him even more. Brandon felt it was his job to take care of his older sister, so when he volunteered I jumped for it. Besides, there weren't any other volunteers, and attempts to put me back into my original body had failed. We even tried several bodies that were as close to clinically dead as we could get without them being in the ground, but that failed too. A clone of my original body also failed.

"Brandon is usually in control, but as you can see, I am capable of driving the machine. I usually leave it up to him. After all, it is his body. Besides, as a woman, I'm still creeped out by using a urinal." Finishing with the array, she closed the front panel and started for the next one.

"So you can jump bodies?"

Sarah shook her head as she continued across the ice. "No. As long as the body is living, I can be pushed back and forth by Dawn, or I suspect by a powerful enough mentalist. I can't do it on my own."

"So the explosion changed you and Brandon."

"No. Just me, little brother is not a meta-human. Much to his disappointment, he doesn't even carry the gene. To clarify, we are stepsiblings."

"His strength with the pod doors was actually you?"

"All me. It is just one of the benefits of my presence."

Sparrow stopped to consider why Diamond had left nearly all of the information out of the files on Brandon and Sarah. Maybe the details were a trade off for the many secrets she claimed to keep for him, or maybe the lack of details was to conceal his own involvement. It was unlikely any of Diamond's scientists would be working on an experiment he didn't know about.

"I'd like to say thanks by the way." She pushed her goggles up onto her forehead and turned to face him.

"For what?" Sparrow asked.

"Little brother doesn't have a lot of friends, and you've been nice to him. I've told him he would have more friends if he would leave *Star Trek* out of the first hour of a conversation, but he doesn't usually listen. There is also his gambling problem, and the fact that he often talks to himself. It has become a problem even when I'm not talking back."

Sparrow considered the sacrifice Brandon had made for Sarah and it caused him a pang of guilt over his own sister.

"Brandon is an interesting guy."

"More so now I suspect...No, Brandon, I'm not asking him about the shot." Sarah turned and started for the next array again. "You can ask him yourself when we are not so busy."

Not wanting Brandon to press the question, Sparrow quickly pushed the subject in another direction. "Any idea how much longer it will be before the arrays are ready?" He already knew the answer, but he hoped it would keep him from having to discuss Fuentes.

Sarah was already working hard on the next one. "Edmond is placing the last one now." She glanced around and counted the number of arrays between her and Edmond. "I just have to program it and three more. I'd estimate a little more than seven minutes."

Sparrow stood by quietly and when she finished, she turned and started for the next array. To put some distance between them, he let her go. The thirty arrays were spread over an area roughly the size of a football field. The ice between them gleamed in the sun. A feeling of unease settled over him. Glancing around he looked for the source but didn't find anything. Shrugging, he glanced up at a bright star twinkling against a background of blue.

\* \*

Far below the ice, an image being viewed by the Psadan shifted from Sparrow to follow Sarah across the ice. Near him, his brother shifted a separate image to view the glowing energy mass sitting on the surface of the ice. The view passed through the side of the pod. Once inside, the Psadan found the way to the humans' leader closed. He pulled on the energy of the pod to punch through the door. He ignored the alarms that again alerted the human that something was wrong.

\* \*

*Twinkle, twinkle, little star, how I wonder what you are? Up above the world so high, like a diamond in the sky. Twinkle, twinkle, little star, how I wonder what you are! My kingdom, my kingdom for a voice!*

Gemini concealed a giggle as the message scrolled across her screen.

*And I wish I could see myself!*

Glip-2 was getting bored and it was starting to show. Gemini typed her response. *Don't worry, little buddy. I'll put a tape in the VCR to record it for you.*

*You would think with daddy-o's money he could afford DVR!* Glip-2 joked.

Tapping her screen, Gemini brought up an image from the *Egress*. It showed the sparkle that was Glip-2 high above the site. She forwarded the image to Glip-2 while she also checked the display of his energy readings. They were high but within Sarah's estimated parameters. As planned, he would be ready by the time the arrays were finished.

*I'm a star, Gem! How cool is that?*

\* \*

Water dripped from Envoy's brow. The thick ice prevented the energy she was using to create the tunnel from properly dissipating. The tunnel walls steamed and created a sauna out of the shaft, but it wasn't the cause of Envoy's sweating. Her life support easily compensated for the atmosphere around her. No, her sweat was from the unease she was feeling due to the large energy reading before her. During the descent, the energy source had grown in size until it was three times that of the Citadel. Now it pulsed rapidly just on the other side of a thin wall of ice.

The others could not see the energy, but tension had been growing with them since they had caught up with her and Slipstream. They had already shed their coats and Shishi had not spoken since they had left the surface. The man's open hostility had agitated Meta-man and further strained the relationship between them. Rose had taken up a position between them to ward off any open conflict.

Softly, Envoy said to the others, "The energy source is just ahead. There is only a thin wall of ice between it and us. The signature is massive."

"What can we expect from it?" asked Dragón Verde. His elongated face slightly slurred his words. During the descent he had shifted his shape and now he crawled along the ceiling of the tunnel in his hybrid form. His arms and legs were both long and lean. His fingers and toes were clawed and his feet sported a thumb-like appendage that aided him in climbing. A long tail balanced him as he leaped about. He no longer wore his parka and his skin was covered with green scales.

"Unknown. The Citadel is created out of the same type of energy, but we don't know how the Psadans use it."

Meta-man stepped up next to Envoy, "Do you think they know we are here?"

"It's too late to worry about that now." Turning her attention to her commlink she continued, "Control, this is Beta team. We are in position. Awaiting your orders. Be aware the energy source is three times expected parameters."

"Stand by, Envoy," replied Lady Gemini. "Less than three minutes to the completion of the arrays."

"Roger, Control. We are holding."

"Damn it," muttered Maverick.

Meta-man glanced at Maverick. "Easy, Mav. We'll wait." He looked around at the others. In the narrow tunnel they all looked uneasy and impatient. Movement ahead of him caused Meta-man to glance back around as Slipstream stepped up to the ice wall. He cocked his head to the side and stood there for several silent moments.

"I can feel them." Slipstream finally said. "They are there, and they know we are here."

"Well that's spooky," said Maverick. "Do you know where I left my keys too, tin man?"

* *

"Beta team has reached depth. They are standing by."

Gemini's message put Sparrow on edge. No one knew how the Psadans would react. Would they attack? Would they retreat? Would they set off an event?

Originally Beta team had been expected to wait on the surface, but the team had been deployed under the ice due to something occurring in the Citadel. It was being evacuated, but nothing else had changed about the plan.

*Kaboom!*

The ground beneath Sparrow's feet shook.

Spinning, he saw a large red globe hanging over a shattered array. A second globe rose up out of the ice and darted after Sarah. They both looked like Glip-2.

Racing after the globes, Sparrow shouted, "We have hostiles! They are after the arrays!" He drew his sidearm and fired at the globe, but it dodged the attack. He would not reach Sarah before the globes.

* *

"Alpha team has been engaged! Beta team you are a go!" said Lady Gemini over the commlink.

"No need to knock then," said Fluxstone. Stepping forward, she threw a bolt of lightning at the wall of ice.

*Kaboom!*

The blast echoed around Slipstream and ice showered him, but he never moved. When the smoke cleared, the party was standing before an opaque curtain of energy that shifted and moved. The curtain melted back when Slipstream touched it. As it peeled back, it revealed a large cavern with a ceiling made of complete darkness. In the distance, several shafts of light held up the oppressive ceiling, but they did nothing to illuminate the area around them. The air was dry, warm, and heavy. It clung to Slipstream's waist in a heavy fog that leaked into the shaft and made breathing difficult. The sounds of crunching ice beneath the party's feet became muffled.

*Swhoosh! Clang!*

Fluxstone reacted and blocked the flare with the *Aegis* before it could strike Slipstream. It circled around them and disappeared back into the darkness.

"Oh look, zzay blew us a kiss," said Madame Fantôme.

"Why does the flare not shine in the darkness?" asked Iron Bear.

No one answered him as the fog began to crackle and swirl to life around them. Flashes of light appeared randomly in it.

Gliding along the floor, two figures moved out of the darkness. They were dressed in long flowing robes that were flexible, but appeared to be made out of shiny stiff plastic. The robes fit snugly at the shoulders but flared out near the floor. Their thin arms were long and their fingers were gnarled like tree branches. Except for their large black eyes, their faces were human. Their thin hair was white.

Shishi glanced from the Psadan to Slipstream and noted the similarity of their eyes. Without taking his eyes off of the metal hero he spoke.

"When this is over, Meta-man, you and I are going to have a long talk about how you define *full disclosure*."

"Hush, Shishi!" Rose whispered. "This isn't the time or the place."

"Don't worry, Rose. I'm not looking to start a fight. I'm just wondering what other surprises our *friends* have in store for us."

Rose could not help but wonder the same thing as she glanced from Slipstream to the Psadans. Dragón Verde slithered away from the metal warrior. Madame Fantôme raised an eyebrow and smirked. Iron Bear either hadn't heard the comment or didn't care.

"Are you done criticizing us?" Fluxstone asked irritably.

"That depends. Are you done lying to us?" Shishi retorted.

"All of you give me a headache," grumbled Maverick.

"Enough!" Envoy said. "Meta-man, call it in."

"We have contact!" said Meta-man into his commlink. It crackled in response. "You are broken, Control. I repeat, we have contact with the Psadans!" The response was still garbled. "We may be on our own, people."

"I like it better that way." Maverick pulled a shotgun from over his shoulder.

"I don't," muttered Envoy. Hoping to find a way to punch

through it, she set her artifact to analyzing the static blocking their communications.

One of the Psadans cocked its head to the side and looked directly at Slipstream. Slipstream mimicked the motion. The Psadan sneered.

"No," replied Slipstream through clenched teeth. "We will not leave you in peace! You took peace from me a long time ago, and now I'm here for retribution!"

*Thoom!*

The dense fog muffled Slipstream's charge. He slammed into the alien and they disappeared into the darkness with Slipstream raining blows down upon it.

\* \*

Sarah spun at the explosion, and found Glip-2 bearing down on her.

"Aeeyyyeeee!" she screamed as she ducked the glowing red globe.

*Fwssh! Fwssh! Fwssh! Fwssh!*

The globe fired a barrage of energy blasts that kicked up snow and ice.

"Ugh!" Edmond staggered as he blocked the flares from striking Sarah.

After the globe passed, he pulled his parka from his mutated body and tossed it to the ground. The rest of his clothing was shredded. Edmond's upper body was twice the size of a normal man's. His shoulders were slumped and he had a large hump on his back that forced him to stand hunched over. His right arm bulged with muscled deformities, and his knuckles dragged the ground. His left arm was just as muscled, but slightly smaller and curled up tightly against his body. Both his hands were large enough to wrap around a man's skull. His deformed lower body was not overlarge like his upper body, but it was still twisted with deformities. His left foot was turned inward causing him to walk on its side. His skin was pale white and his gray hair was shaggy and matted. It ran from the top of his head down the center of his back. The right side of his face was swollen and blemished with warts and deep wrinkles. His right eye was completely white with a series of scars running through it. A large wart-like deformity overshadowed the eye. The left side of his face sagged. His yellow left eye bulged and was bloodshot. His nose was overlarge and flat. His cracked yellow teeth were crooked. There were several large burns across his upper right shoulder where the energy blasts had struck him instead of Sarah.

"Finish the arrays!" The words issuing from his deformed mouth were gruff and slurred as the left side of his face refused to move. Using his right arm as a brace, Edmond lumbered off after the red globe. He kept his left arm tight against his body. Despite his deformities, he was quick and the ground shook under his bulk.

Shaking with fright, Sarah glanced at Sparrow. He had halted his charge to watch the retreating back of the horrific monster that had once been Edmond.

*Rruummmble!*

The rumble of thunder sent a wave of fear through Sparrow. The sparkle of the ice dimmed as shadow passed over it.

\* \*

Diamond rose to his feet as the room burst into activity around him. Alpha team dodged two red globes as they sought to protect the array system. IMPACT and TASC attacked the globes with their energy rifles. Another array exploded as a third globe joined the battle. The globes were just as fast as Glip-2, and they were having no problem dodging the team.

"Status on Glip-2?" demanded Diamond.

"I knew it couldn't be trusted!" shouted Jonesy.

"It's not him, you boob!" countered Gemini. Images of all three of the red globes appeared on the imaging wall next to the star over Antarctica. Energy readings compared all four, and identified the star as Glip-2. Unknown flashed over the other three.

Grunting, Jonesy turned his attention back to his station.

"Control, we are under attack! The Citadel is breached!" A loud explosion cut Samson off.

The message caught Gemini by surprise and panic briefly filled her. She was barely tracking the chaos in Antarctica, and doubted she would be able to handle both battles. Without prompting, her doppelganger in the special ops room immediately took over monitoring the pod bay and worked to coordinate Samson's team. Freed from the responsibility of overseeing both battles, Gemini focused on Antarctica. "Alpha team has been engaged! The globes are not Glip-2! The hostiles are not Glip-2! Use appropriate force to protect the arrays!"

"Do we have contact with Beta team?" asked Diamond.

"Negative," said Gemini's doppelganger from the special ops room. "I'm detecting Envoy's signal, but it's not strong enough. I'm trying to get through the interference!"

"Cloud cover condensing over Antarctica!"

"What does that mea..."

*Rruummmble!*

Diamond stood in shocked silence. Slowly he turned searching for the source of the sound. The monitor wall flickered.

"Not again," moaned Clara.

\* \*

Searching for the Psadan, Dreah propelled herself through astral space as quickly as she could. She was nowhere near as accustomed to it as Samuel. Samuel would have been in the pod bay instantly. For her it was like swimming through water. The Citadel was unusually difficult. It tired her quickly and she was barely faster than a walk.

After several minutes, she neared the pod bay. The alien mind had grown stronger the closer she had gotten. The room was dark but bright pulses lit it up, and screams from Samson and his men reached her ears.

Pausing, Dreah extended her senses into the room. The energy in the air was thick and growing thicker. She recognized the horror guiding it. It constantly haunted Slipstream and Diamond. It was in the center of the room and was condensing the energy of the Citadel around itself. The energy pulsed and the Citadel shuddered. The lighting in the hallway went out. Taking a deep breath to steady her fear, Dreah pushed forward into the room.

Rifle flashes lit up the room enough for her to see Samson flung across the room and into a wall. TASC soldiers fired their energy weapons, but their attacks sliced harmlessly through the air to scar the Citadel walls. As she watched, the black wave of energy struck down one of the soldiers.

Beyond the soldiers, was a growing ball of black energy. Crackling bolts of black lightning flashed off of it. It was growing larger with each passing moment. The walls of the pod bay warped as they were being drawn in toward the energy. To Samson and his men, the ball of energy appeared as a deep shadow covering the center of he room.

Dreah could see a dark crack running along the edge of the door to the *Egress*. In real space, the crack was not large enough to be visible, but its effects were still felt. The air of the room, along with anything physical that wasn't tied down was being pulled through it. In astral space, the crack was much larger and the area around it was visibly warped. The space beyond it was an empty void. Dreah could feel the pull of it from across the room.

The soldiers could not see their enemy. It was psionic and not physical. It grabbed at the energy of the Citadel and condensed it into a form solid enough to strike at them. By the time they counterattacked, it had already dissipated and formed up somewhere else. Panic forced the soldiers to lash out blindly. It would be up to her to deal with it.

The aura of the Psadan was oppressive and dark. Its mind was the strongest she had ever encountered. She feared it was too strong to attack directly. Unlike it, she couldn't control the energy of the Citadel anyway so wrestling for control of it was useless. The only solution left for her was to sever the connection between the Psadan's mind and the Citadel energy.

Moving from the center of the room toward the *Egress* doors, she focused on the strand of mental energy. Before her, it began to glow like the thread that connected her to her own physical body. Her body shifted and mist flowed from her. The void beyond the door immediately captured some of her essence and sucked it away. The rest circled her on invisible winds and flowed outward toward the thread. As Dreah's mist neared the thread, it reared back on wings of smoke. An eagle formed at the head and silently screamed. An instant later, dozens of small misty birds burst from the eagle form and darted across the room to attack the cord with beaks and talons. They then swooped back around to flow through Dreah and reform for a second attack. The thread's resistance was great, but she pressed her attack. Dreah and her misty flock glowed brightly against the deepening blackness of the room.

A mental scream of anger flashed at her from the thread and the room's lights flickered back to life, but the thread didn't sever and the Psadan quickly recovered. The lights went out again and the Psadan retaliated with a wave of energy that slashed Dreah across her face. It was faster and stronger than she was. She refocused on the thread and doubled her efforts.

\* \*

Gemini knelt next to Dreah and desperately wanted to staunch the flow of blood running from the woman's cheek. Instead, she clasped her hands tightly together for fear of disrupting the spell. After a moment, she stood and picked up her staff. She felt helpless.

Fenrir slunk among the trees and bushes looking for any danger that could physically threaten Dreah. He knew little about what she was attempting to do, and he knew less about how to help her.

Wavefront knelt next to Dreah and extended his force field around her. He wiped blood from the corner of her mouth with his shirtsleeve.

\* \*

*Skisss!*

Envoy's energy blast didn't damage the Psadan, but it did distract the alien.

*Whoosh!*

A wave of force rippled outward from the Psadan at her. Her shield held under the attack, but she was slammed into the wall behind her.

"Envoy!" bellowed Iron Bear. His upper torso swiveled on his legs.

*Rrrrrrwwp!*

He raised his arm at the Psadan and fired a missile.

*Fwoosh! Kaboom!*

The fog condensed into a barrier before the Psadan, and Iron Bear's missile exploded harmlessly against it.

*Swhoosh! Clang!*

Fluxstone blocked a flare with the *Aegis* and dove at the Psadan's feet. Kicking out with her legs, she attempted to trip the alien. She missed her target's feet as they were floating just above the floor. She slammed the *Aegis* into the alien's leg to stop herself from spinning out of control on the icy floor.

Meta-man grappled the Psadan from behind and flung it to the floor.

*Wham!*

The impact cracked the ice. Meta-man immediately drove his fist into the creature's stomach.

Maverick materialized next to Meta-man. With his shotgun in the Psadan's face, and oblivious to any danger to Meta-man, he fired.

*Blam! Blam!*

"Honey, I'm home!" he screamed over the sounds of the exploding weapon.

*Blam! Blam!*

The blasts slammed the alien's head into the floor, but left no physical marks on the creature's face.

*Blam! Blam!*

When the gun ran out of ammunition, Maverick began to stomp the alien and beat it with the butt of the weapon.

"You alien piece of crap! I'm gonna pull your lungs out of your ass!" Maverick was deranged with anger and spittle sprayed from his mouth with each word.

*Swhoosh! Clang!*

Having recovered from her earlier blunder, Fluxstone blocked a flare that would have taken Maverick's head off. Spinning, she pulled on the shield's energy.

*Kaboom!*

Her bolt of lighting warded off a second flare bearing down on Meta-man. She quickly latched onto the feeling of euphoria the tingling brought her hand, and used it to fling a second bolt at the retreating flare.

*Kaboom!*

The second bolt struck the flare and it fizzled before disappearing back into the darkness.

\* \*

*Boom! Boom!*

Slipstream pounded the Psadan. It staggered under the assault. The hero's eyes blazed with the anger that powered his blows. Kilimanjaro and Madame Fantôme circled the raging battle looking for an opening.

Rose focused on the alien's mind, her eyes glowed.

*Wrwrwrwr!*

A dart of red mental energy raced from Rose across the room to strike the alien. The creature's defenses deflected the blow, and flung a backlash at Rose.

*Wrwrwssh!*

Rose staggered from the blow and collapsed to her knees. She struggled to see through blurred vision and to focus on the alien's mind again. After several moments, she shook off the attack.

*Wrwrwrwr!*

This time, Rose's attack was bolder and broader. It lit up the dark chamber in a bright red glow that struck the alien. The alien's mental scream echoed through her head as its black eyes flashed red. Its mental defenses had nearly collapsed under the assault. Prepared for the creature's backlash, Rose's own mental defenses turned it aside.

*Boom! Boom!*

Slipstream was intent on driving the alien's head through the floor. Screaming, he pounded the alien's face with both fists, while ignoring the mental attacks striking the creature.

*Swhoosh! Swhoosh!*

Two flares erupted out of the darkness and deflected off his back. The pain was intense and the flares left glowing red streaks, but he didn't relent in his assault.

The Psadan struggled for control beneath the tremendous assault. Its clawed hand flailed about blindly until it finally found Slipstream's leg. The alien's touch immediately pulled at the metal warrior's strength, weakening his blows. When Slipstream's strength slipped enough for the Psadan to focus through the blows, it unleashed a wave of telekinetic force.

*Whoosh!*

Slipstream was flung backward to disappear into the darkness covering the ceiling.

*Slam!*

Striking the ceiling, the hero fell to the floor where an avalanche of ice buried him.

Kilimanjaro immediately countered with a massive fist before the Psadan could rise.

*Slam!*

The cave's low ceiling had limited his height to only thirty feet, but he still possessed enough strength to prevent the alien from rising.

Beside him, Madame Fantôme sneered. "Bastard!" she cursed.

Flying forward, she thrust her hand forward and touched the alien's chest. Instantly, ice coated the creature. "Zat is for my family!" The Psadan tried to flinch away from her attack, but Kilimanjaro prevented it.

Shadow Spirit appeared next to Madame Fantôme. Darkness reached out from under his cloak to wrap around the Psadan. As the alien began to disappear under the enveloping restraints, Shadow Spirit smiled and reached out to pull on the darkness covering the ceiling to increase his power. The bands strengthened and began to crush the alien.

\* \*

In his stone lion form, Shishi circled the battle and kept his eyes on the pile of ice covering Slipstream. His movements barely disturbed the fog that kept him hidden from the aliens and the heroes.

No matter what Meta-man said, he didn't trust the metal warrior. He was obviously connected to the aliens. The eyes confirmed it. Diamond and his people may even have been the cause of the whole affair. He didn't trust Meta-man either. Diamond was a corrupting influence, and the fact that he had gotten to Meta-man was obvious. Shishi wasn't ready to turn his back on any of them.

As the ice covering Slipstream began to stir, Shishi crouched low and growled. He waited patiently for the betrayal he knew was coming.

*Swhoosh!*

A flare shot out of the darkness. His keen senses easily detected it, allowing Shishi to dodge it.

Paragon leaped out of the fog after the flare. His sword sliced through it, and it sputtered and died.

Slowly Paragon turned and glared at Shishi. Shishi growled at him. Paragon briefly glanced around to watch Slipstream climb out of the ice covering him before turning back to Shishi.

"Trust is a complicated matter, friend Shishi. It takes effort from all involved."

For a brief moment the two locked eyes, then Paragon turned his back on Shishi and moved off into the fog in search of another flare. He could feel fear growing in those on the surface, and he recognized the touch of the clouds on them. Unfortunately, he knew he could do no more about it than he could about Shishi's paranoia.

Shishi glared after the winged knight. He glanced at Slipstream again, and then he turned to the Psadan still battling his teammates. He still didn't trust the metal man, regardless of anything the knight could say. He would not be foolish enough to turn his back on Slipstream.

\* \*

Within moments, the three globes had destroyed five arrays. They descended quickly from above with an onslaught of energy blasts, and then they rocketed skyward to disappear into the clouds.

When the globes darted after an array, Q-Zone slowed them and Duo put themselves between them and the array. Using chunks of ice as shields the twins deflected as many shots as they could while TASC and IMPACT attacked the globes. Sparrow and Edmond did their best to assist the soldiers.

Gemini was scared. The growing clouds amplified her fear. Despite the fact that she had convinced her father she was ready, Gemini now doubted herself. The globes were fast and looked like Glip-2. Adrenaline and excitement had pushed her to strike out at the globe in Buenos Aires. Only after she had acted had she stopped to consider her actions. Now that she was focused, the globes reminded her too much of her friend. Only fear of new memorials outside the sherry room kept her from freezing up completely.

Glancing around, Gemini ensured that Sarah was still safe behind her, and then she turned her attention back to the sky just in time to see a globe bearing down on her.

*Fwssh! Fwssh! Fwssh!*

She dodged a series of blasts while firing her staff at it.

*Shshsh!*

The hasty blast missed the globe. The soldier beside Gemini took a direct hit and fell.

*Fwssh!*

As the globe shot past, a blast struck Gemini in the shoulder and spun her around violently.

\* \*

"Gemini, get communications on line with Envoy now. Shift TASC toward the southern arrays. They are too open. Clara, get a status on the evacuation. Jonesy, tell me what is going on with those clouds." Diamond kept his growing agitation out of his voice.

"The clouds have the same mass and energy readings as those over the target cities. They are forming an event over the arrays."

Diamond didn't like Jonesy's answer. However, the strategy was sound. If Slipstream was immune to the event, then it made sense that the Psadans were. Bringing down an event on the team would end the conflict. Diamond didn't have a clue how to stop it.

"Evacuations are thirty percent complete, Mr. Diamond!"

*Rruummmble!*

Diamond tried to ignore the rumbling. Each time it passed through the room it was stronger. He was relying on Dreah and Samson to deal with it. They would have to maintain their post at least until all evacuations were complete.

"Jonesy, see if..."

The command center plunged into darkness as the monitor wall went blank. The computer systems shut down.

\* \*

The Psadan struck Dreah again and the violent assault staggered her. Before she could recover, she was slammed into the door of the *Egress* by a second attack. The void captured her misty form and sucked at it. Fighting desperately against unconsciousness, Dreah barely blocked a third blow with a psi-shield. Exhausted and unable to concentrate, she collapsed to her knees. The mind of the Psadan backed off and focused on the energy of the Citadel again.

Dreah took the moment of freedom to regain some strength. She was slowing the Psadan down, but she was not stopping it. Although the alien recognized her as a threat, it saw her as little more than an annoyance. It focused on the Citadel, and only lashed out at her when she attacked it. Collapsing the energy from a distance required a lot of concentration, and every time she attacked it, the Psadan lost some control. Unfortunately, the alien regained it each time she backed off.

The rumble that passed through the room was muffled in astral space, but the walls of the room were visibly warped and cracked. The ceiling sagged and the floor buckled. The room was collapsing inward, and the rest of the Citadel was being pulled in with it.

Dreah recited a spell and her magic pulled from the tree in the garden. Her body filled with the tree's warm touch and she regained some of her strength.

Feeling better, Dreah reached inside her gown and fondled the hilt of the silver knife. Deciding against it, she pulled herself up and concentrated on her form again. Instead of attacking the thread with a flock of birds, this time she cut loose and small animals of numerous types flowed from her mist. She poured all her concentration into the attack and the animals grew larger and more solid.

The attack was violent and the Psadan's mental scream nearly burst Dreah's eardrums. She reacted quickly and struck again before it could recover. Again the Psadan screamed, but this time it quickly turned on Dreah and struck her. The mental slash ripped several of her animal forms in two. Dreah felt the attack deep in her stomach. She doubled over from the pain, and the alien's next attack drove her to the floor.

* *

In the garden Dreah's body convulsed violently. Blood flowed from her ears and nose. She gagged and coughed up blood.

"Can't you stop the bleeding?" screamed Gemini frantically.

"There are no visible wounds!" responded Wavefront.

Standing outside the force field, Fenrir said, "She's dying."

Wavefront didn't know what to say. He had plenty of experience patching up war wounds, but he had no idea how to deal with damage that was all in Dreah's mind. Hoping it would give him some clue as to what to do, he pulled out his sidekick and used it to scan her condition.

* *

Sparrow leaned over Sarah. The wound in her leg was ghastly. Hesitantly, he offered her a hand up. She shook with fright but managed to smile. It wasn't Brandon's smile and Sparrow suppressed a shudder. Sarah took his hand and Sparrow pulled her to her feet. She staggered over to the last array and began programming it.

"Make it quick! They seem intent on attacking you!"

Glancing around, Sparrow saw Gemini climbing to her feet. She had snow caked in her hair, and she favored her right shoulder. Her armor had absorbed most of the blow, leaving her pride hurt far more than her body. Sparrow grinned at her. She raised her right hand and extended her middle finger in salute to him for failing to help her up. Sparrow's chuckled.

A globe flared brightly and descended on them. Sparrow darted at it and fired his DSS sidearm.

*Zzap!*

It returned a series of quick shots and suddenly darted toward Sarah. Sparrow leaped toward her to protect her from the attack.

*Fwssh! Fwssh! Fwssh!*

"Yeeaa..." Sarah's scream was suddenly cut off, and the snow and ice became suspended in the air around her. The energy blast inched toward her, it wasn't going to miss.

The world around Sparrow also stretched and stopped. He was suspended in the air and his leap had slowed to a crawl, but his reactions were just as quick as ever. Sparrow twisted his body as the world slingshotted back into motion.

"...aaa!"

The blast glanced off Sparrow's armor instead of striking Sarah. When he hit the ground, he rolled and sprang to his feet, firing his weapon at the globe.

*Zzap!*

Again the world stretched as his shot raced toward the globe. Suspended in the time warp, the globe was slowed, but the sidearm blast wasn't. It struck true as the world snapped forward again. The globe sputtered and leaked energy as it circled out of range.

Q-Zone stood next to Sparrow. His eyes glowed bright blue and he held his hand extended toward the globe.

"Sarah, the array please!" Q-Zone said. He glanced at Sparrow. "Sorry dude, but they have learned to stay out of my range. It's made it hard for me to capture them." Sparrow grunted in response.

Slowly Sarah realized she was still alive, climbing to her feet and began working with the keyboard again. Q-Zone extended his other hand toward her, increasing her speed. Her fingers blurred as they darted across the keys.

*Meta-humans,* cursed Sparrow as he took up a position near the array. He held his stomach to keep from losing it. Next to him, Gemini giggled at his obvious discomfort.

\* \*

The Psadan grabbed Madame Fantôme's hand and pulled it away from his chest. A moment of panic filled her as she realized he was draining her intangibility. Pulling harder on her ice powers, she caused ice to spread up his arm to his shoulder. The ice cracked and shattered as the alien twisted her arm, breaking it.

"Eeyyyeee!" She screamed as the pain drove her to her knees. The Psadan maintained his grip on her arm.

Kilimanjaro grabbed at the alien to help, but sparks erupted in the dense fog around them. The giant hero was driven back as the sparks burned and charred his large body.

The Psadan continued to drain Madame Fantôme's powers, and her body became more solid, exposing her to the sparks. Her screams filled the cavern along with Kilimanjaro's.

Dragón Verde ducked to avoid an attacking flare, and then he leaped backward to arch over a second flare. When he landed, he leaped over the fog and kicked out with his foot to strike the hand holding Madame Fantôme. The alien didn't even flinch from the blow. Instead, with incredible speed it grabbled Dragón Verde with its other hand, and shoved Madame Fantôme's icy hand into his chest.

Dragón Verde tried to scream as Madame Fantôme's hand coated his heart with ice, but the effect was almost instant and his words froze in his lungs.

*Swhoosh!*

A flare burst through Dragón Verde's shoulder and neck. His body went limp and Madame Fantôme struggled to pull her hand from his chest as the Psadan dropped them both.

*Boom! Boom!*

Free from the ice, Slipstream ignored the cloud and struck the alien twice. His strength was back to full, allowing his blows to echo through the cavern. The Psadan staggered under the attack.

*Fwssh!*

Energy erupted from the alien's eyes to engulf the hero. Slipstream focused through the pain and braced against the torrent.

*Fwssh!*

Energy erupted from the hero's eyes. The conflicting energies from the two combatants lit up the cavern.

Envoy's heart sunk as she watched Dragón Verde die. She rushed forward and threw an energy shield to block a flare bearing down on the helpless Kilimanjaro.

*Swhoosh!*

It was deflected aside and she turned after it, tracking it back into the darkness. Even though she could no longer see it with the naked eye, it still appeared before her vision as a red dot circling them in the dark. The alien metal on her arm was quickly adapting to the Psadan's technology. She threw energy blasts after the flare.

*Skisss! Skisss!*

"Spirit, focus on the flares! Protect the others!"

Over the deafening sound of the battle a soft ping rang in Envoy's ear and data scrolled across her vision. The artifact had successfully punched through the static blocking communications with the Citadel.

"Control! This is Beta leader! We have contact with two Psadans! Green Dragon is down!" There was no response to her transmission.

* *

Shadow Spirit immediately obeyed Envoy's order, but in his own way. The darkness above him more than doubled the effect of his magic. Tendrils of shadow continued to restrain the alien while he turned and threw up a wall before a flare attacking Paragon. The winged hero used the momentary distraction to strike at the flare. It fizzled and died.

Rose abandoned her mental assaults against the Psadan. The creature possessed the strongest mind she had ever encountered, and she felt as ineffective against it as a three year old trying to stump Einstein; but years of experience had taught her to be effective in other ways.

Turning to the other fight, she screamed, "Meta-man, mimic its control over the fog!"

Not waiting for him to acknowledge her request, Rose reached out with her mind and touched his. Meta-man recognized her touch and allowed her past his defenses. A burst of mental power boosted Meta-man's clarity, and he reached out to mimic the Psadan's power.

Fluxstone stepped past Meta-man and lowered her density. She plunged her insubstantial fist into the Psadan and then slammed the *Aegis* into its forehead.

*Wham!*

Its head snapped back from the blow, and she struck it again.

*Wham!*

Shishi joined the attack and with his massive stone jaws he bit deeply into the alien's leg. The creature's psychic scream slammed into his mind.

*Thip!*

Iron Bear fired a large steel spike attached to a metal cable. It embedded into the alien's shoulder.

*Zzzap!*

A wave of electricity flowed down the rope and increased the alien's pain.

Even though the Psadan was staggered under the numerous attacks, it continued to drain the powers of those attacking it. It grew stronger and the heroes grew weaker. Reaching out with its mind, it thrust the pain it was feeling into the minds of the heroes. They collapsed as the attack sought to tear apart their skulls. Grabbing Iron Bear's cable, the Psadan sent a backlash of energy into the cyborg.

*ZZZAP!*

Sparks erupted throughout Iron Bear's body as wiring and internal parts fried.

The Psadan then reached out to the fog and pushed energy into it, but it didn't spark. Glancing up, he stared into Meta-man's glowing red eyes. The hero's jaw was set with concentration. Rose floated in the air over him with her eyes glowing red as well.

A brief wave of panic flooded the alien. It lashed out with a wave of telekinetic force that pushed the two heroes away from it, but its attack didn't diminish their control over the fog.

Shishi reared up on his hind legs and bit deeply into the Psadan's shoulder. Barely flinching, the alien reached over its shoulder and grabbed the stone lion, flinging him into the darkness. The Psadan turned back to Meta-man and Rose.

\* \*

As Sarah typed the last code into the array, her sidekick beeped loudly. Closing the panel, she reached for it. Just as she had predicted,

Glip-2 was at full power. She glanced around for Sparrow and found him next to Edmond. A globe swooped down on them.

Edmond slapped his chest with his left arm and scooped up a chunk of ice with his right hand to hurl it at the globe. As the globe dodged the ice, Sparrow fired at it. The blast struck the globe and it sputtered before veering uncontrollably toward the ground. Edmond took advantage of the moment and leaped at it. He landed a solid blow that drove it into the ground. Ice exploded around the impact, but the globe darted into the air again. Duo flung ice at it as it escaped.

Sarah raced across the ice. "The arrays are ready! Glip-2 is ready! Now is the time!"

A wave of relief spread through Sparrow.

"We've lost several arrays!" growled Edmond. "Will it still work?"

"I don't know!" Sarah shrugged. "But I do fear Glip-2's control will be diminished! We don't want to be here when it happens."

A wave of panic replaced Sparrow's relief. "Reyes! This is Sparrow! The arrays are ready!" There was no response to his transmission.

"Reyes, this is Sparrow. Arrays are ready! Do you copy?" Again there was no response.

Sparrow glanced around the battlefield, but he saw no sign of Reyes. The bodies of several soldiers lay scattered across the ice. Any one of them could have been the TASC lieutenant.

Meeting Edmond's eyes, Sparrow took the initiative, "Control, this is Alpha team. We are go!"

There was no response.

"Control! This is Alpha team! Do you copy?"

Again, there was no response.

Grunting, he turned to the others. "No contact with control!" He shifted to his commlink. "Beta leader, we are go on the surface! No contact with control! Do you copy?"

"Roger, I copy" replied Envoy. "Our comms are down as well. I recently cut through the interference, but received no response."

"Copy," said Sparrow. "We will dig in and hold our position. Notify us if contact is made."

"Copy," replied Envoy.

To those gathered around him, Sparrow said, "Protect the arrays. When the globes come at you defend against them, but do not chase after them."

\* \*

"The systems are completely unresponsive!" Jonesy couldn't see what he was doing, but he slammed his fist down on the dark monitor screen before him anyway. It sputtered back to life, but only for a moment before going dark again.

"Damn it, Jonesy! Get the systems back online!"

On the floor beneath him, Clara's eyes were the only things anyone could see in the dark room. "Sir, all the systems are down! Everything!"

Diamond struck his own console in anger. Thinking of Dreah, he closed his eyes and concentrated. The noise around him began to slow.

*Whack!*

Pain exploded in Diamond's head and white sparks burst across his vision as he was flung from his station to the catwalk. He struggled through his confusion and rolled over. A flicker of light from the video wall revealed the catwalk guardrail swaying over him.

*Whack!*

Pain shot up his leg where the rail had struck him. As the guardrail rose again for another strike, he clawed his way off the catwalk and plunged to the floor below.

\* \*

*Grrrinnd!*

The sound of rocks grinding against each other filled the darkness overheard; but it was so dark, even Fenrir's acute sight couldn't see what was happening.

*Crasssh!*

The sound of shattering glass drowned out the rumblings. On instinct Fenrir dodged to the side as the ceiling of the garden began raining down on him in chunks. Blind, he jerked left and right to avoid the large falling objects.

*Thoom!*

Wavefront's shield shuddered as it was struck from above. Gemini used her flashlight to illuminate the devastation raining down on them.

"Oh my," Gemini mumbled as large stones appeared out of the darkness.

*Thoom! Thoom!*
She screamed and ducked when they struck the force field.
Wavefront glanced around at the raining debris and shrugged. "Don't wor'y, Gem. The shield'el hold up the whole bloody mountain if need be. Jackson!" he yelled into the dark. "Over here!" There was no answer or sign of Fenrir in the darkness.
Gemini looked at Wavefront. She had seen his force shield hold under extreme stress. It had even held Slipstream at bay once. It would hold now and she knew it, but that didn't stop her from flinching every time a boulder struck it.
Ignoring the danger and turning his attention back to Dreah, Wavefront reached into his medical pack and pulled out an ammonia capsule. Breaking it, he waved it under Dreah's nose. "Bloody hell," he cursed when she didn't respond. "Can't anything be simple?" He reached into his bag and blindly fumbled round until his hand closed over a small injector.

\* \*

Fluxstone climbed to her feet and brought the *Aegis* up before her.
*Clang! Clang!*
The *Aegis* held against two of the flares, and as she turned her attention back to the Psadan, Paragon rushed past her after them. The alien appeared distracted with its battle of wills against Meta-man and Rose for control of the dangerous fog at everyone's feet.
*Wham!*
Fluxstone struck the Psadan with the shield. Its control over the fog vanished, and Meta-man sent it rolling over the alien. Sparks flared around it. Fluxstone avoided the fog as best as she could and swung again with the *Aegis*.
*Wham!*
The Psadan was flung backward out of the fog. Fluxstone charged after it, but the alien recovered too quickly. Fog rushed at her from behind the alien and wound up around her waist, lifting her from the floor. Before she could become intangible, energy erupted from the Psadan's eyes.
*Fwssh!*

"Aayyyiiii," Fluxstone screamed as the wave of searing energy seared the flesh from her body. The *Aegis* slipped from her hand.

*Clang!*

Clanging loudly against the rock hard floor, it rolled away to disappear in the darkness. The fog controlled by the Psadan hurled Fluxstone's limp body across the cavern.

"Fluxstone is down! Fluxstone is down!" Envoy screamed into her commlink. She was unsure if anyone would even receive the message.

Meta-man and Rose pushed their fog over the Psadan again and it recoiled at the sparks burning its body.

\* \*

"Fluxstone is...Fluxstone is down!"

Gemini took her eyes off the sky to look at Sparrow. "Should we do something?"

Sparrow didn't look at her, but kept his eyes on the sky.

"Beta Team will handle it."

Images of the hallway memorials flooded Gemini's mind. The sorrow she had felt at the funeral overwhelmed her. "But what if they can't? We aren't going to just sacrifice her are we?"

Sparrow bit his tongue to prevent the answer from leaping from his lips. He hadn't even considered the question but had nearly answered anyway. *Yes*, he told himself, but aloud he said, "Beta Team will deal with it! Envoy and Meta-man are there."

Gemini watched as several members of IMPACT drove off a globe with a barrage of shots. Two of their numbers fell before the globe retreated. Glancing around, Gemini could see the hole Envoy had made in the ice.

"I can't just leave her," she said.

Sparrow glanced at her and found her looking at the shaft. "We will wait here, Gem! Beta Team will deal with it!"

"But maybe I can help her!"

Sparrow glared at her.

"Incoming!" screamed a soldier.

Sparrow took his eyes off Gemini to scan for the globe. It was descending directly on them. Sparrow's muscles tensed and he prepared for the approaching attack. Suddenly, uneasiness filled him. Spinning, he saw one of Gemini's doppelgangers sprinting across the ice toward the hole.

"No!" screamed Sparrow.

*Fwssh! Fwssh! Fwssh! Fwssh!*

Distracted, Sparrow failed to dodge the attack. The energy blasts punched him in his side and slammed him to the ground. His armor absorbed most of the damage but his side still stung from the attack, and the delay gave Gemini's doppelganger a head start.

Pushing himself up, Sparrow struggled to breathe as he glared angrily at Gemini. She was obviously frightened and her eyes were wet with tears. Glancing around, he saw that several soldiers were attacking the globe that had struck him while Q-zone struggled to capture it in a time warp. He rose and darted across the ice in pursuit of Gemini's doppelganger.

"I can help her!" Gemini's pleas didn't stop him.

IMPACT soldiers fired at the globe as it circled the area. Suddenly, it altered course and chased after Sparrow and Gemini.

Sparrow's side burned, but he ignored the pain and quickly closed the distance between him and the doppelganger. He could feel the globe bearing down on him from behind. As he reached out for Gemini, a torrent of energy blasts rained down around him.

*Fwssh! Fwssh! Fwssh! Fwssh!*

Pain exploded across his back and slammed him to the ground. The doppelganger leaped for the hole, and disappeared over the edge amid the barrage of energy blasts.

Frantically, Sparrow pulled himself over the edge of the shaft to peer down into the darkness. Gemini was already out of sight.

"Damn!" His scream echoed into the darkness.

\* \*

Gemini quickly spiraled out of control. As her speed increased, the ice shredded her armor, and within moments it slashed at her flesh. Desperate, she tried to brace her staff against the wall to slow her speed, but it slipped on the slippery surface. She rammed the staff into the ice, but the impact nearly tore it from her hands.

Fighting against her growing panic, Gemini twisted the staff and a sharp blade projected from the end. Struggling not to drop it, she twirled the staff and then jammed the blade into the ice with both hands. The blade gouged at the ice and slowed her descent.

\* \*

Unsatisfied with the readings on his sidekick, Wavefront placed the injector against Dreah's neck. "I know you don't like these things, Dreah. Sorry." He injected a stream of nanites into her system.

As the small robots hit Dreah's blood, they immediately began sending detailed information about her condition to Wavefront's sidekick. He waited patiently while they imbedded themselves into her system. When they reached her mind, they confirmed his suspicions that the damage was cerebral. Some stress was causing her to hemorrhage. If it continued, she could suffer a full-blown aneurysm, the nanites would not be enough to save her.

Wavefront shrugged. "This won't hurt. Maybe." He punched several buttons on the sidekick and altered the nanite's programming. "Sorry about this, love."

Several of the nanites instantly attached themselves to Dreah's systems and began mimicking the properties of epinephrine.

\* \*

Dreah felt crushed beneath the Psadan's mind. She lay sprawled on the floor with it pressing down on her. Struggling to draw breath, she fought the darkness that was closing in on her. Behind her, the void sucked at her essence without restraint. With her concentration broken, she couldn't fight it or the Psadan.

Suddenly, a rush of energy forced her eyes open. She immediately recognized the burning sensation of drugs coursing through her system. The drugs wanted to return her to her body, but she resisted them. It would have saved her from the Psadan, but it would not have saved those she loved from it.

Dreah used her restored strength to push against the weight pressing down on her. As soon as she could breathe again, she took a deep breath and reached into the folds of her gown. Her hand closed over the hilt of the silver dagger. She withdrew it.

As if sensing Dreah had a spark of hope, the Psadan slammed her down again. The blow nearly caused her to drop the knife. Struggling against the pressing weight of the alien, Dreah clutched the blade tightly with both hands and whispered, *I love you.*

Turning over, she lashed out with the blade. The knife tore at Dreah's life force to power its magic and stab deep into the Psadan's mind thousands of miles away. The pain of her attack blinded Dreah, and the Citadel shook violently at the alien's pain. Barely conscious, Dreah struck again. The Psadan rushed to pull back, and Dreah clawed her way across the floor after it. Before it could retreat through the door and with darkness reaching out to claim her, Dreah struck a third time.

\* \*

In the garden, Wavefront watched closely for any sign that the nanites were working. Suddenly, Dreah jerked and gasped for air.

"Aaiiee!" Shocked, Wavefront jumped back.

Dreah stared at Wavefront, gasped and collapsed.

"Dreah!" Gemini screamed.

"Damn!" Wavefront turned to his sidekick, but stopped when he realized his hand was wet. Slowly, he pulled his right hand away from Dreah's stomach. It was soaked in blood.

# CHAPTER 22
# A HEAVY PRICE

*I love you.*

Sparrow felt the words and instantly a wave of dizziness overwhelmed him. His commlink yelled in his ear. Edmond stood over him trying to get his attention. Chaos raged across the icy landscape and an array exploded. Sparrow didn't see any of it. He didn't hear any of it. All he could hear were those three words, and all he could feel was a bone numbing dread that left him feeling that he had lost Dreah forever.

\* \*

Diamond's senses were jolted and he jerked to consciousness. A glowing pink faerie with the smell of ammonia fluttered over him. Carol smiled at him.

"Glad you're back with us, Mr. Diamond."

She smiled again and offered him a hand up. Diamond took her hand and allowed her to pull him to his feet. His head ached, and he had to take a deep breath to keep the room from spinning. His right leg throbbed and he couldn't put his full weight on it.

The command center lights were back on and the video wall was lit up, but the images on it were twisted and warped. Some of them were unreadable and they all flickered off and on. Battle still raged across the surface of Antarctica. The pod bay was dark and the evacuation holding room was empty. The room's ceiling sagged and one wall had a large bulge. The catwalk tilted heavily to one side and the guardrail was twisted. Blood dripped from one end. The wall between the command center and the meeting room had melted. Only half of it remained.

Several of the others in the room had injuries. Even Jonesy had a large cut on his forehead. He was near panic from the blood running down his face.

Gemini's screaming voice through the room. "Someone! Anyone! Help us! Dreah is down! She's bleeding! Someone, help us!"

Diamond spun and stared at a flickering image on the video wall. Dreah lay in a pool of spreading blood with Wavefront working frantically to staunch it. Crying frantically and rocking back and forth, Gemini kneeled in the grass holding Dreah's hand.

\* \*

Sparrow was nearly catatonic. Edmond had given up on trying to reach him. When Gemini's frantic words issued over the commlink, reality burst upon Sparrow and he leaped up. Nearly tripping over Q-Zone, Edmond fell back at the look of anger on Sparrow's face.

Diamond's voice quickly followed. "Alpha leader, are we go?"

Sparrow didn't answer. He looked around at those gathered and staggered under a wave of dizziness. He barely recognized them.

"Alpha leader respond!"

A hand rested on his shoulder and Sparrow looked around. It took him a moment ,but he finally recognized Edmond.

"You can't help Gem now. Mr. Diamond needs a response."

Shame washed over Sparrow. In his shock over Dreah, he had nearly forgotten about Gemini.

"Alpha team, respond now!" Diamond was getting impatient.

Edmond accessed his commlink. "Control, this is Alpha team, we are..."

"No!" screamed Sparrow. He wasn't going to lose Gemini too.

With everyone looking at him, he responded. "Control, this is Alpha leader. We are negative on ready status. We are not a go!"

"Alpha leader, you have an event forming on your location. Do you copy?"

Sparrow glanced up and found that he could no longer see Glip-2 because of the dark clouds. They weren't swirling angrily, but they were still ominous.

"We are not ready! Stand by control!" Sparrow didn't know how much time he had, but he wasn't about to abandon Gemini.

\* \*

*Damn*, cursed Envoy. Somehow Alpha team's status had changed and she doubted her team could hold the Psadans much longer. Dragón Verde was down. Fluxstone's status was unknown. Most of Iron Bear's systems were off-line. Kilimanjaro and Madame Fantôme had life threatening burns, and the *Aegis* was lost in the fog. "Sorry, Alex." She turned and flew in pursuit of a flare.

\* \*

Meta-man and Rose fought against the Psadan for control of the fog. So far they had held it off of the other heroes, but the alien had once again filled it with sparks and was now trying to push it onto them.

Iron Bear took advantage of the Psadan's distraction. "Got something for you!" he bellowed as the cannon on his shoulder whirled into motion, and then sparked and died. "Chush' sobach'ya!" he cursed. He slapped the weapon with his mechanical arm and it sparked again, but jumped back to life.

*Thudda!Thudda!Thudda!Thudda!Thudda!Thudda!*

A thousand rounds of ammunition lit up the darkness and drove the Psadan back to pin it against a wall.

Meta-man and Rose pushed a wave of fog over the alien, burning it with the energy sparks.

*Swhoosh!*

A flare darted out of the darkness and before Iron Bear could defend himself, it seared off his human arm.

Raising his stub, Iron Bear looked at it as his rounds continued to pound the Psadan. Instead of blood, clear liquid oozed from it. "*Govno*, I hate it when that happens."

\* \*

Kilimanjaro was forced to retreat from the battle between Slipstream and the Psadan. The fog had continued to burn him badly, and the energy the two combatants were throwing at each other ripped at the walls and collapsed the cavern around them.

As the giant watched, the Psadan managed to get the upper hand over Slipstream. Energy pouring from the alien's eyes washed over the hero. Despite the flood of death, Slipstream held his position and pushed back against the energy.

Desperate to help, Kilimanjaro pushed into the fog again. The fog reacted to his presence and condensed. Violent sparks nearly drove the giant to his knees. Despite the intense pain, he moved forward. The Psadan pointed his hand at Kilimanjaro, and the fog thickened further. It gripped at the hero's legs and restrained him. The sparks in it intensified. The giant fought hard against the burning restraints.

Slipstream took a step forward, and the Psadan doubled his effort. Taking another step, Slipstream closed the distance. With another step the metal hero was close enough to reach out and lock his steel grip around the alien's skull. Energy blazed across his chest as he squeezed and dug his thumbs deep into the monster's black eyes. The Psadan's energy continued to blaze from its eyes.

Kilimanjaro shielded his eyes from the glare.

\* \*

Its attempt to destroy the ants crawling across the surface was momentarily forgotten as the Psadan knelt over its brother's body. Both its brothers were gone now. It was alone with only the siblings, and they would soon abandon it. Perhaps its diseased brother had been right. This planet should have been bypassed for another one.

A red globe dropped from the cavern ceiling and changed from red to silver. It descended until it touched the body of its dead parent.

\* \*

An alarm sounded and lights flashed.

"What now?" moaned Jonesy.

"Glip-2 is reaching critical mass!" responded Gemini.

Looking at the video wall, Diamond saw that the area monitoring Glip-2's energy was too warped and distorted to read, but it flashed red. "Any way to slow him down?"

"Not from here," responded Jonesy.

"Can we pull him?"

"If we do, the energy he has absorbed will immediately begin to dissipate. He won't be able to hold on to it."

*Damn it*, cursed Diamond. *What is the delay?*

"What is the time to the event?"
"Unknown! Cloud cover has stopped building!"

\* \*

Gemini could see a glow at the bottom of the shaft. As she neared it, she dug her blade deeper into the ice and slowed her descent. When she reached the bottom, she leaped to her feet.

Deeper in the cave, she could see the battle. Several of her friends were injured; she resisted the urge to rush to their aid. Moving deeper into the chamber, she found the fog prevented her from searching for Fluxstone. It was thick and the battle had stirred it up.

A spark in the fog caught her attention and she turned toward it. The spark appeared again. Moving toward it, she found the fog got thicker and thicker the deeper she went into the cave. Just when she was about to give up the spark as a trick of the fog, she kicked something hidden by it. Reaching down into the darkness, her hands touched the cold metal surface of the *Aegis*. She lifted it out of the fog; it sparked in her hand. She studied the shield's surface and tears welled up in her eyes. Swallowing her sorrow, she glanced around. The shield had been with Fluxstone. She was likely somewhere near by.

Holding the *Aegis* in front of her with both hands, she fanned the fog with it. The fog was thick, but her efforts earned her glimpses of the floor.

\* \*

Sparrow was angry with Gemini, he was tired, his muscles ached, his head hurt, and he wanted nothing but to see Dreah. When another request to proceed came, he wanted to ignore it.

"Alpha leader, are we clear for go? Glip-2 has reached critical mass! Are we clear to go?"

"Negative! Negative! We are not clear for go!"

His response was curt, but he didn't care. He was angry and he was barely holding it in check.

"Glip-2 has reached critical! We need to go!"

"Do you need assistance?" Envoy sounded tired and her transmission ended with a loud explosion.

It was enough to make Sparrow want to scream. Why was he in charge? Why was any of this his problem? What had happened to

Dreah? Why had Gemini ignored him? He desperately wanted to leave it all behind and return to the ignorant bliss the Counselor's suppressed emotions gave him.

*Boom!*

The explosion demanded his attention and Sparrow slowly looked toward it. Again in monstrous form, Edmond hurled a chunk of ice at a globe attacking a stack of equipment. As it dodged his attack, it swung low over several soldiers. Their weapons created a salvo of death around the globe that battered it and caused it to drop low to the ground. Edmond grabbed up a piece of an array and leaped at the globe. The globe saw the threat and darted skyward. Edmond brought the metal club down on the globe and it exploded with the impact. Edmond was hurled into stacks of equipment.

Energy leaked from the side of the globe, but it wasn't destroyed. It flew to the center of the ice and descended into it. Edmond crawled his way out of the equipment just in time to see it disappear. Frustrated, he hurled a large crate at the spot where the globe had vanished.

\* \*

When Iron Bear's cannon ran out of ammo, it kept whirling. He smacked it, but it didn't stop spinning. Shrugging, he took several quick steps forward and slammed the Psadan with his mechanical arm.

*Wham!*

The metal of the arm buckled under the monster's defenses. Iron Bear ignored the damage and struck the alien again.

*Skisss! Skisss!*

Envoy swung around to the side and fired several shots at the Psadan. Sparrow had not responded to her offer of help, and she doubted he would. She had heard the transmission about Dreah, and she doubted Sparrow was taking the news well.

*Skisss! Skisss!*

Envoy poured as much energy as she could into several powerful blasts. The blasts deflected off the alien and hit the ceiling. Large chunks of ice rained down on it and Iron Bear. The Psadan crumpled under the avalanche and Bear struck it again.

*Wham!*

Meta-man expected to find the alien stunned, but as he reached for it, its hand shot up and grabbed his. The alien twisted and Meta-man was forced to his knees to keep his arm from breaking. His bones began adjusting to the pressure and the pain lessened. Rising over Meta-man, the alien took several bursts from Envoy and a blow from Iron Bear.

*Skisss! Wham! Skisss!*

Energy from the Psadan's eyes engulfed Meta-man.

*Fwssh!*

"Aaarrgghhh!" Meta-man's screams echoed across the cavern walls. His friends leaped forward to free him, but the Psadan deflected their attacks.

Reaching deep into Meta-man's mind, Rose found his systems already compensating for the assault; but the pain he was still feeling drove her to her knees. Fighting through it, she reached deeper into his mind and turned off the portion of his brain registering the pain.

Free from the pain, Meta-man climbed to his feet. With his right arm still trapped, he swung his left at the alien. The alien barely flinched under the blow. It flung Meta-man into the darkness.

\* \*

Meta-man slammed into the floor and rolled for several moments before he managed to stop his momentum. Immediately he started to rise, but froze when he realized he was at the base of a light shaft. Fear gripped him. Slowly he raised his head. The light was blinding, but he could see a body suspended inside it. He swallowed his fear and rose to his feet.

The shaft held a naked dark skinned man. His legs were pulled up under him. His thin arms were wrapped around his legs and his head was tucked into his chest.

Meta-man felt a pang of pity as memories of the light returned to him. He could not remember everything that occurred all those years ago, but he could remember the light. How it dulled his senses. How it took away his memory. How it stole his emotions. How it consumed his will. How he feared it.

Meta-man glanced around and saw that there were numerous shafts of light. Most of them were empty but many contained a still form suspended inside them. Turning back to the first shaft, he stared into its blinding interior. Slowly, he reached out and touched it...

...The jungle around him was alive with life. His people were hunter-gathers and they lived a simple content life. His mother was kind, his father was a great hunter, and his younger siblings looked up to him. He was happy, and then the devil clouds came. They preceded the demons.

Shivering from the fear, he stared up at the dark clouds. They invaded his mind and he wanted to run from them, but his limbs would not respond. Suddenly, a flash of blazing energy jolted him from his paralysis. The forest burned around him. Heat and smoke drove his people from the jungle and into the center of the village. The flashes and flames lit up the forest as the clouds overhead plunged the land into night.

He charged into the village and found his family lying next to their home. Their lifeless bodies sapped his strength, and he collapsed to his knees. The sky darkened further, the evil ate at his soul. He welcomed the death it promised.

Only the sight of one of the demons allowed him to conquer his despair. He grabbed a spear from his father's lifeless hand, hurling it at the monster. The spear bounced off its thick hide, and it turned to face him. Its dark eyes were even darker than the sky. They flared with dark light, and death streaked across the village, striking him. He was hurled backwards and collided with a tree.

Darkness reigned at the edge of his vision. His limbs were numb and wouldn't respond. Through tears, he watched as the demon knelt over him. With his mind growing as numb as his arms, he watched the demon reach out for him with a glowing hand. The demon smiled and then touched his forehead. Pain blasted through the numbness, and he screamed while the demon chuckled...

...Meta-man stumbled backward and fell, never taking his eyes off the man suspended in the light.

The light had unleashed the man's past upon Meta-man like a rabid dog. It gnashed and tore at his mind. Each bite threatened to take away who he was and leave him someone else. He could see every detail of the man's life. He could feel every hurt, every want, every desire, and every loss.

\* \*

Slipstream's skin glowed red where he touched the alien, but he refused to give up. Anger powered his muscles and determination prevented him from retreating. He squeezed the alien's skull and dug his fingers deeper into its eyes. In desperation, the Psadan clawed at Slipstream with its gnarled fingers, searing long glowing scars. Energy from the alien's eyes blazed from between the hero's fingers.

Kilimanjaro fought to ignore the burning cloud and struggled to pull the Psadan's hands away from Slipstream's face. Madame Fantôme floated just above the cloud, her touch coating the alien's side in ice.

The alien's skull cracked. Fighting frantically for freedom, it pulled at Slipstream's strength, but it found the hero resisted its power. With its eyes caving under the pressure, it lashed out with a mental assault.

The psychic wave drove Madame Fantôme back and caused Kilimanjaro's grip to fail, but Slipstream only screamed with rage as memories of his wife and children blocked the assault. Focusing on Slipstream's mental shield, the Psadan pulled at the memories and thrust them like daggers into Slipstream's mind. Each attack blinded him with pain, and doubled his anger.

Slipstream's muscles bulged and his armored shell cracked under the strain as he focused all of his hate and all of his anger on the murderer in his hands. His eyes blazed and his fingers sunk deep into the creature's eyes. The Psadan's screams shattered the ice walls and drove all the other heroes in the cavern to the ground. Slipstream screamed and slammed his hands together. The head of the alien exploded in a gush of gore and blinding energy. Lifeless, it collapsed at Slipstream's feet.

\* \*

On the surface of the frozen continent, the Psadan's mental scream jolted Sparrow from his anger. He forced his emotions aside and brought his breathing under control.

Across the ice from him, Q-Zone slowed a globe while the twins threw chunks of ice at it. They hit it, but it managed to escape and dart skyward again. Sparrow watched it disappear in the clouds near the spot where Glip-2 was supposed to be.

*Just don't forget it's the man underneath that is important.*

At the time he had been too consumed by Dreah's beauty to even hear the words. They came to him now as if she had just spoken them.

He glanced skyward again. A twinkle peaked through the clouds, and an idea struck him. Quickly, Sparrow sprinted across the ice toward the teenage heroes. He tried to ignore the commlink in his ear. Diamond was still demanding clearance. The energy was straining Glip-2 beyond his breaking point.

"Sorry, Sparrow. I thought we had him that time," said Kandi as he reached them. She was watching the sky for any sign of the globe. "I think it's the last one."

Sparrow shook his head. "Never mind that! Q, I need you to get up there. I need you to freeze Glip-2 in one of your time warps. I need you to keep him from going critical until you hear from me!"

"He can't fly," said Brian.

"I know. That's what the two of you are for. Get him up there so he can hold Glip-2 until we are ready. Can you do it?"

Q-Zone looked at Sparrow and then the twins while smirking. "Sure, I can. Just get me up there!"

Sparrow turned to the twins.

"We have never flown that high. The atmosphere is going to be too thin!" Brian said.

"Just get me as high as you can. I'll do the rest." Q-Zone's smile broadened. "Come on, it's me."

Brian looked to Kandi. She looked at Sparrow and knew instantly that he was serious. She looked up and then at Q-Zone. She shuddered at the thought of the cold they were about to face, and then rose into the air. Brian followed and together they gently lifted Q-Zone from the ground.

Q-Zone's eyes began to glow and the world around the three slowed and then stopped. Q-Zone smirked and all three of them blasted skyward.

The ground fell away as Q-Zone kept all three of them suspended out of time. They quickly approached the clouds and Q-Zone pushed his power to speed them up. The fear of the clouds peeked through his time warp, but before it could grab hold of them, the three heroes blasted through to the other side of the clouds. The blinding light of Glip-2 forced them to shield their eyes.

With the wind rushing past him, Q-Zone looked down at the twins. He envied their power of flight. Flying would be awesome. Of course, even without it he was about to earn the title of *World's Greatest Hero*. Perhaps after the celebration, he would learn to fly; that is, if he could find the time between the endorsement deals he was about to earn.

Brian gave Q-Zone a salute as the twins began to push him out ahead of them. Already ice was forming on their uniforms and breathing was becoming difficult. Brushing ice from the front of his coat, Q-Zone watched it tumble out of the time bubble and halt in its fall.

As their height above the ground increased and the distance between him and the twins increased, Q-Zone soon began to feel his powers stretched. He strained to keep the twins under his touch; knowing that if he dropped them, they would quickly freeze to death in the thin atmosphere. Duo fell out of sight and his head pounded under the strain.

Looking into the blinding light of Glip-2, Q-Zone began to reach out toward the globe. He pushed himself harder and strained to bridge the distance. His effort caused the pounding in his head to increase and his vision to blur, but slowly Glip-2 came into range. He smiled as the fire dancing around the globe slowed, and then froze as the flow of time was altered around it.

To Q-Zone and the twins the trip had taken nearly five minutes, but to the world it had taken only a couple of seconds. With the cloud cover far below him and a small sun frozen in time above him, Q-Zone felt like he truly was the world's greatest hero. Now he only had to stand the pain long enough to make the plan work.

\* \*

The twins and Q-Zone were gone. One second they had been hanging in the air next to Sparrow, and the next they had simply vanished. Turning his attention to another matter, he turned and charged across the ice.

\* \*

Gemini was confused as three signals on her board suddenly jumped to elevations that were miles above the earth's surface. Duo was holding at just over seven miles up and Q-Zone was at nine. The rising power readings of Glip-2 had slowed to a crawl.

"What's happening?" asked Diamond as he watched the monitor.

"Q-Zone, I think. He is holding Glip-2 suspended in a time warp. His power level hasn't stopped building, but it has slowed." Gemini was amazed, and a little jealous. "Glip shouldn't go critical as long as Q holds him."

"How about that suckers!" Q-Zone suddenly blared over the commlink. "How is that for the world's greatest hero?"

Diamond arched his eyebrows. Perhaps the kid was worth what he was being paid after all.

\* \*

Blood flowed from Gemini's nose and her head spun with dizziness. The mental scream had left her barely conscious. Slowly, she regained her feet. Gripping the edge of the *Aegis,* she staggered through the fog in search of Fluxstone.

\* \*

The elder alien stood. He had mourned enough. He too had heard the death cries of the young one. The dead were dead. Focusing on the air before him, he condensed it, and a spark of light appeared in the center. It grew brighter as the energy condensed tighter. Within moments it was blinding, but he stared into it unfazed. High overhead, clouds condensed and began to swirl into a vortex.

\* \*

Meta-man shook the effects of the mental scream from his head. "Envoy, we have civilians!"

"Roger! Control, this is Beta leader. We have civilians on site!"

Meta-man barely heard Envoy's response. He stepped up to another shaft of light and placed his hand on it...

...Life was harsh and his childhood had been filled with a violent father and a mother too weak to protect him. There were too many nights without sleep to count, and too many days without food to want to count. Fleeing that life, he found himself on the deck of a large ship with a dark flag flying overhead. He was as brutal as those around him. He took what he wanted and defended what he had with malicious hatred. When they came, they were just as brutal as he had been, and he believed it was God's punishment for his evil ways. God's angels rained fire down across the ship's deck as they waded through the frightened sailors claiming the souls of those they wanted, and sending the rest to eternal damnation...

...Meta-man staggered back from the shaft but didn't fall. He shook his head to clear it, and then he moved to a third shaft. He knew he was needed in the fight, but the victims in the shafts of light called to him. They begged for him to acknowledge them.

Inside the third shaft was a young woman with dark blond hair. Like the others, she was thin and pale. Holding his hand up to the shaft, he allowed her memories to flood his mind...

She had a good life. Her father and mother loved her and her siblings. There were many happy days as life rolled lazily by on the open hill where their small home rested. She worked with her mother to tend to the house and the farm animals while her father plowed the fields surrounding them.

Her happiness was wiped away when drought came and the fields shriveled up under the hot sun. Men came and threatened to throw her father in jail for debts he could not pay. The farm was lost, and they left that life on a boat. She thought she would never be happy again.

The many months at sea brought a new home along with new friends far away. It also brought a young boy who fancied her, and made her blush every time he looked at her. She could see the longing in his eyes and it excited her. She hid from the eyes of other men while allowing him to always see her. She actually became grateful for the events that had taken away her old home and forced this new one upon her. Without it, she would not have found him. But her new happiness ended all too quickly. A storm of evil came that took no pity on them.

She retreated into the small cabin along with the rest of the children to escape the storm. It was the most frightening thing she had ever experienced. Some of the children had been frozen with fright, and she had been forced to carry them to safety. Thinking they were safe, her father had barred the door behind them. Moments later, his screams had pierced the thin walls and she had desperately wanted to go to him, but the door to the cabin had opened and a hideous man strolled inside before she could move. His eyes were large and black. His white hair was thin and swayed on the wind. His clothes were stiff and clung to him. Behind him, a globe of light floated into the room and lit it up. The young girl looked for any sign of her father, but couldn't see past the light. The small children panicked and screamed at the sight of the man. She bit her tongue and prayed as she hugged a small girl closer.

Blocking the man's path, a small frightened boy lay on the floor. Irritated, the evil man raised his hand to strike the child.

Fright made her legs sluggish, but courage gave her the strength to dart between them. The man struck her instead of the boy. The force of the blow knocked her across the room and slammed her into the wall.

Her face burned where he had struck her, her shoulder ached where she had struck the wall, and her head spun with dizziness from both. Dazed, she rolled over to find the man leaning over her. Her scream was cut off when he gripped her around the throat and hauled her into the air. She gagged under the tight grip, but the man ignored her plight and dragged her across the room.

When the man neared the door, he snatched an infant from the arms of a young girl with his other hand. The girl clawed at the man to get the child back, but a flash of red from the globe of light struck her and flung her over a table. When she landed on the floor, blood flowed from a ghastly wound on her back.

The baby in the tall man's hands cried out, and the girl kicked at him. She was frightened, but she had found the will to fight. He ignored her attempts to hinder him and turned to the door. The door opened without him touching it.

Suddenly, her mother appeared in the opening and struck the monster with a piece of wood. The attack distracted the man, and the young girl managed to twist free of his grip. Rising quickly to her feet, she snatched the infant from his other hand and darted past her mother. The door slammed shut behind her as she stumbled out of the shack and out under the terrifying storm.

The young man of her dreams turned to face her as she raced toward him. His face was cut and bruised, and his bloody shirt was wet and torn.

"John!" she screamed as pain seared her back. Stumbling from the blow, she collided with him and shoved the baby into his arms. Together, they tumbled to the ground.

Her muscles refused to respond when John rolled over to look into her eyes. His eyes were wide with fright, and she wanted badly to reach out and touch him, but her arms would not respond. He screamed at her, but she couldn't hear what he was saying. The whole world had fallen into silence. She wanted desperately to tell him how much she loved him. A tear formed in the corner of her eye as she realized she would never get the opportunity to do so.

"Run, John, ru..." she managed to mumble.

John's face disappeared and the young girl stared in horror at the dark clouds above her. She prayed silently to God to protect her from them as she silently fell into them...

...Shocked, Meta-man jerked back from the shaft of light and fell backwards. His head spun and he struggled to remember where he was. He was seized by horror and his hands shook with fright.

Rose knelt next to him. "John! John, are you okay? John!"

Meta-man locked eyes with her and gripped the front of her shirt. "Alis! It's Alis! We have to help her!"

\* \*

As Envoy wrestled to clear her head, she glanced around to find the others struggling to their feet.

"We have a Psadan down!" She winced from the echo of her own words. Her head felt like it was splitting. The battle was nearly lost, and now Meta-man was reporting civilians on site.

She turned and found the Psadan kneeling over Shishi. As the fog swirled around the alien, it pressed its hand hard into the hero's chest.

*Sskraakle!*

Blinding energy erupted around its hand.

"Aaarrrghhh!" screamed Shishi as he struggled to escape the painful touch.

*Skiiisssss!*

Envoy fired a long blast of energy at the Psadan. It stopped attacking Shishi and turned to glare at her. Slowly it rose to its feet.

"Oh, darn," Envoy mumbled. She was exhausted, and barely staying on her feet.

*Fwssh!*

Slipstream's eye beams lit up the darkness. The Psadan was struck from behind and slammed into a wall.

Envoy breathed a sigh of relief and added her own energy to Slipstream's attack.

*Skiiissss!*

\* \*

Rose pulled Meta-man to his feet as explosions echoed through the cavern. His eyes never left Alis.

"We don't have time for this, John!"

In a fury, Meta-man turned on her. His anger quickly vanished when he saw understanding in her eyes. She didn't want to abandon them either. Glancing back to the lights, he nodded. He allowed her to turn him away, but painful memories forced him to turn back.

Looking at Rose, he said, "I can't leave them. Go. Help Envoy. Hold that bastard at bay. Give me just a minute, Rose. Please."

Rose knew his story, what little he remembered of it anyway. Like hers, it contained pain. It was pain that had haunted him his whole life. If he turned his back on the victims before them, he would never forgive himself. Rose nodded her understanding and left him to face the lights.

Without hesitation, Meta-man took a deep breath. Stepping forward, he shoved his hands into the shaft of light holding Alis.

Pain instantly flared throughout his whole body and every moment of his transformation flooded back to him. Four hundred years ago the pain had been too intense for him to even move. All he had managed to do was choke on his own bile when he tried to scream. Today, he swallowed his scream and forced himself deeper into the light. He wrapped his arms around Alis and hugged her to him. He then pulled her to safety.

The two collapsed to the floor with Meta-man cradling Alis tightly to him. It had only taken him a moment to pull her from the light, but like so long ago, it had seemed to last forever. Even now, the memories continued to wrack him with pain. His hands shock and his muscles twitched. He glanced at the numerous other shafts and rose unsteadily to his feet to confront them as well.

\* \*

Diamond did everything he could to control his anger, but he was finding it hard. The warped video wall was forcing him to work blind. Communications had to be run through Envoy, and he still had not heard anything further on Dreah. She had been moved to the infirmary, but no word had been received on her condition. He was out of ideas.

"Cloud cover increasing again!" shouted Jonesy.

*Damn*, cursed Diamond as Gemini relayed the message to the teams.

* *

Sparrow ignored yet another request for a status update and looked Gemini in the eyes. She had been avoiding him.

"Is this the real you?"

Gemini didn't answer and looked away.

"Sparrow! We need to go!" Diamond shouted angrily.

Sparrow pulled his commlink from his ear and grabbed Gemini by the shoulders to force her to face him. "Answer me!"

"Yes! This is the real me!"

His anger threatened to break through his resolve. Sparrow released her and took a step back to keep from striking her.

Gemini visibly shook and her voice wavered. "I couldn't just leave her! I had to help!"

"Has it been enough time?" he demanded.

Confused, Gemini mumbled, "What?"

"Has it been enough time? Has your doppelganger had enough time to reach Fluxstone?"

"I don't know!" Gemini screamed back. "I don't have a mental link or anything, and the comm isn't working."

"What happens if one of you doesn't make it?"

Gemini's eyes grew wide. Her mouth fell open and she stammered, "I...d-don't know. It's never happened before."

The look in her eyes made Sparrow wish he had not asked the question.

"There is feed...feedback from major injures. You saw what happened when you knocked out my doppelganger in the gym." Tears flowed down her cheeks.

"It will kill her," Sarah said softly.

Sparrow looked at Sarah, and she nodded to confirm her statement.

"Damn!" Sparrow held her eyes. "Are you sure?"

"Yes."

Sparrow stuffed the commlink into his ear. He accessed a secure channel and tapped into Envoy's signal. "Envoy, this is Sparrow!" There wasn't an answer. "Envoy, this is Sparrow! Do you copy?"

"Go ahead!" replied Envoy.

"Gemini is in the hole! She is not responding! Can you reach her?"

"Dammit, Sparrow! How did that happen?"

"We're beyond that, Envoy! Can you reach her?"

"I'll see what I can do! Stand by!"

Turning back to Gemini, Sparrow stared into her eyes. She had tears running down her face. Startling Sparrow, she stepped forward and put her arms around him. Hesitantly, he placed his hand on her back.

"I'm sorry," she whispered.

Turning to Edmond, Sparrow said, "Evac as many of the troops as you can. Get them aboard the pods or the *Phoenix* and get them out of here."

"The *Egress* is fried," said Butch as he stepped out of the pod. "She just isn't responding. The instruments are showing the inner door is open, but it doesn't appear to be open to me. If it was, we wouldn't be standing here. Alive, anyway."

Time was running out. "Fine," said Sparrow. "Continue to see what you can do, but hold it if you get it working. Edmond, use the other ships to get everyone else out of here. Brandon...Sorry. Sarah, go with them."

Edmond turned and limped off with Sarah following him. Edmond had several obvious injuries, but he appeared to be limping more than his injuries would dictate. Whatever the cause of his discomfort, he didn't complain and followed Sparrow's orders without question.

\* \*

Envoy knelt next to Iron Bear. Energy flowed from her into the man's metal body. Most of his parts had stopped working. After a few moments, several lights began blinking and some of his internal motors whirled to life. He slowly rose to his feet.

"Thanks, love," he mumbled.

Envoy only patted him on the shoulder. She knew it embarrassed him to need her help.

"Spirit, we have civilians to evac. Numbers are unknown. Zero in on Meta-man." Shadow Spirit didn't respond. He never did, but he would follow her orders. Turning, she assessed the ongoing battle.

Rose worked her way around the battle and assisted the others where she could. Even indirectly, her efforts were more useful than most of Maverick's attacks. He teleported into and out of the fight, dropping grenades, firing guns, whatever tricks he could muster, often without consideration for those around him. Slipstream, Shishi, and Kilimanjaro were keeping the Psadan busy. Madame Fantôme had retreated. Her burns were severe, and her broken arm left her barely conscious. Paragon had done what he could to diminish the woman's pain, now he focused on the remaining flares.

"Maverick, I need you!" Envoy hoped he wouldn't be too difficult. He didn't respond. "Maverick, get over here now!"

Suddenly, he appeared before her. Yanking his mask from his head, he stared her in the eyes. His eyes bulged and burned with anger. His left eye was blood shot and there was a large burn across it. Blood and spittle flowed from the corner of his mouth. One side of his scalp was burned nearly to the bone.

"What the hell do you want?"

Envoy felt a wave of nausea just looking at his injuries.

"Gemini," she managed to say. "She's down here. Find her and get her out."

Maverick glared at her. "Are you serious? You want me to babysit? Screw you, bitch!" He started to turn away, but Envoy grabbed his arm and spun him to face her. Anger flared in both of them. Iron Bear stepped closer.

Instead of screaming, Envoy closed her eyes and paused. She relaxed her jaw. When she opened her eyes again, Maverick was still standing in front of her. "Please, Mav. Help me find her."

Maverick's anger burned in his face and Envoy thought he was going to refuse. Instead, he took a step back and threw his mask at her. Glancing around at the darkness, he cursed loudly, "Dammit!" He disappeared.

\* \*

Meta-man staggered under the torment of the light shafts. His body showed no sign of injury, but every muscle in his body burned and spasmed. In addition to his own pain, he suffered under the pain of each of the victim's he had rescued. His meta-human powers did nothing to ease the pain. Each rescue took only moments, but the pain spanned four hundred years. Despite the torment, he was determined. He stepped in front of another shaft. His hands twitched as he raised them. He barely noticed Shadow Spirit stepping from his shadow.

"G...Get them out. Anywhere. I'll pull as many as I can before they nuke this place."

The Spirit placed a hand on his shoulder.

"No. You have done enough. Leave them to me. I shall pull them."

"I won't leave them to this!"

"Nor will I. You are needed elsewhere. I can manage this."

Meta-man glanced at the battle. He was needed. "Are you sure?" he asked.

The Spirit didn't answer. Shadows flowed from his cloak to claim the victims Meta-man had already rescued. They disappeared into the safety of his darkness. The Spirit then turned to a shaft of light and pulled his hood tight over his head. He passed silently through it. When he exited the other side, the figure that had been suspended in it was gone. Shadow Spirit's shoulders visibly slumped, but he moved on to the next victim anyway.

Meta-man reluctantly turned away and staggered across the floor toward the battle.

\* \*

Sparrow stood on the entry ramp of the *Egress*, watching the vortex in the swirling clouds overhead. They were only moments away from the event, and he was out of time. He sighed heavily and turned to face the others. Edmond held a sidekick in his hands, going over some data. Gemini chewed nervously on the nails of her left hand, and stared at the ground. Butch cursed loudly from inside the *Egress*.

At that moment, he hated who he had been. He hated who he had become. He hated the Psadans. He hated meta-humans. He hated Diamond. He hated Dreah. He hated the whole damn world.

"Butch, what's the status?" Sparrow called into the ship.

"Non-functional, boss. I can't get it to register the doors as closed."

"You're out of time. Let's move."

"We have a problem. According to my calculations, too many

arrays have been destroyed. Glip-2 won't be able to access the energy." Edmond glanced up from his sidekick to Sparrow.

Under Sparrow's glare, Edmond nervously reached up to push his glasses up his nose, but he then realized he wasn't wearing them.

"You didn't anticipate that?" asked Sparrow.

"Well, yes. We did. Or Jonesy did at least. We increased the number of arrays to compensate. But I still think too many have been lost."

Butch exited the *Egress*. The tension in the air puzzled him. "What? Did I miss something?"

"Any options?" Sparrow asked Edmond.

"Only one. Tell Glip-2 to target the ice based on the location of the arrays, but to forget accessing them and to punch a hole through the ice to the Psadans directly. He won't have the same level of control, and the devastation is going to be far worse. I calculate he has enough energy to punch the hole, and his experience manipulating the energy will be sufficient."

"Will it work?" demanded Sparrow.

"I calculate a twelve point two percent chance of success." Sparrow shook his head in disbelief. "It's higher than through the arrays," Edmond quickly added.

Butch looked around at everyone and then across the ice at the arrays. "You mean we are at ground zero?" He paused, but didn't receive an answer. "Shit!" He turned and fled across the ice. "Run little sister, run!" he called over his shoulder.

Edmond tapped several buttons on his sidekick, and he then turned back to Sparrow. "We should start running too."

"Go," responded Sparrow.

Edmond shifted into his monstrous form and started across the ice after Butch.

Sparrow glanced across the ice at the center of the arrays, and then in the direction of the fleeing men. He doubted any of them would escape.

Ice crystals lifted slowly off the ground around them. The hair on Sparrow's arm tingled as it rose up.

Looking skyward, he suppressed a shudder. Then he looked Gemini in the eye, and forced aside his feelings for her. She held his stare.

"Control, this is Alpha leader. We're ready. You are go."

A tear ran down Gemini's cheek.

\* \*

Silence gripped the room. No one moved. Everyone watched Diamond for the final order.

"Emergency evac!" he said into the commlink. "Alpha, Beta, get out of there! You have one minute until go!" Turning, he added, "Gemini, get Glip-2 online."

\* \*

Envoy felt a chill as the order finally came. Spinning, she searched frantically for Gemini and Fluxstone. In the dark, she saw neither; but she did see Maverick popping in and out as he searched for them.

"Beta team, evac now! Emergency evac Spirit!" Her words did nothing to slow the battle. "I said evac now! Spirit, civilians first, team second!"

\* \*

Kilimanjaro looked to Slipstream, "We need to go, my friend!"

Slipstream didn't slow his attacks and slammed his fists into the Psadan. Meta-man also ignored the order and struggled to hold the alien. Even as it pulled at his strength, he extended his aura to mimic Slipstream's powers and his skin turned to blue metal.

"We will cover your retreat!" Meta-man grabbed the Psadan by its arm and twisted. His enhanced strength forced the alien to its knees.

"We can all go!" Kilimanjaro did not want to leave them behind.

"Go! We will be right behind you!" Meta-man knew they needed to retreat, but he would not leave Slipstream alone.

Kilimanjaro started to protest, but nodded and turned toward the others.

\* \*

Shishi appeared out of the fog. He favored his front right paw and there were numerous cracks in his stone hide.

When Paragon arrived, he had the body of Dragón Verde. He had spent the majority of the battle holding the flares at bay and he had numerous burn marks across his armor and hands. He placed Dragón Verde on the ground and took up a defensive stance. He watched the darkness for any sign of the flares.

Rose stumbled out of the darkness and Madame Fantôme glided

along behind her. Rose had an open wound on her right hip that bled freely. The dark burns across Madame Fantôme's body contrasted sharply with her ghostly appearance.

Within moments, Envoy shuddered and the Spirit appeared among them. "Civilians are out," he mumbled to Envoy.

Envoy glanced at him. The man was sweating and breathing heavily. "Are you okay?" she asked.

Shadow Spirit nodded. "My magic is drained. I cannot promise I have enough power to get us all out safely."

"Gemini and Fluxstone? Do you think you can get us to them?"

Shadow Spirit raised his head so Envoy could see his eyes. They were entirely white, and blood leaked from the corners. "I cannot even sense them. The lights have blinded me, Latisha. I would not have been able to find you had I not known where you were. I am sorry."

"I'm sorry too, Ebon. Very well." Envoy turned to search the fog for the two women. Into her commlink, she said, "Maverick, what's your status?"

"Lost! This fog is too damn thick! I can't even find my own ass in it!"

Reluctantly, Envoy said, "Time's up, Mav. Get yourself and Metaman out. You have less than fifteen seconds. Thanks."

Turning to the others, she glanced at Paragon. She could see disappointment in his eyes. He wanted to charge off in search of the women, but he knew she would not give him permission to do so. "We will trust in Gemini," Envoy said. Paragon nodded. Turning to Shadow Spirit, she said, "Ebon, on my mark. Not before." Shadow Spirit's shadows began to creep over them.

Turning to the energy fog again, Envoy shifted all her energy into her senses. They punched through the fog and she scanned for any sign of life. She wasn't about to let anyone charge off into the fog, but she also wasn't going to leave anyone behind until she absolutely had no other choice.

\* \*

Sparrow and the others raced across the ice. He made sure not outpace Gemini. They weren't going to make it. Their only hope was that Glip-2 controlled the collapse. If he couldn't, nowhere within a hundred miles was going to be safe.

\* \*

Pain burned through Q-Zone's body. He felt like he was being torn in two. He had no idea how long he had been forced to hold onto Glip-2 and the twins. Relief filled him when the commlink finally crackled to life.

"We are clear for go! Q, get out of there!"

Q-Zone laughed through his pain and pictured the celebration waiting for him on the ground. He pulled back on his power.

Pain rippled through him and he nearly blacked out. He had pushed himself too far and could not control his power. Frantic, he pulled at it again, but it refused to respond and the pain threatened to render him unconscious again. Below him, he could feel his touch slipping from the twins. Fear gripped him and he fought for control, but he was not able to maintain his grip and they slipped away.

As his power slipped from the twins, it slammed into him and plunged him toward darkness. As he struggled to stay awake, his uncontrolled power spread out around him to engulf everything he could see. Frantic, he pulled at it, but it refused his control. The more he pulled, the more intense the pain. Finally, he managed to pull his power free of his surroundings. It slammed back into him and he lost his grip on Glip-2.

\* \*

Glip-2 bulged from the energy inside him. Each pulse threatened to burst him. He had long ago decided this just wasn't fun anymore. He felt a wave of relief when the clearance finally came.

He could clearly see the arrays below him, but the energy signature they were connected to was vague. Before he could access the arrays, a message from Edmond reached him. Edmond's calculations indicated too many of the arrays had been destroyed, fortunately he offered an alternative. Edmond wanted him to punch through the ice and access the energy directly. Edmond was convinced he had enough power to do so. Unfortunately, he would be on his own to make it work.

Struggling with doubt, Glip-2 sensed the *Egress* sitting near the sight. It automatically responded to his touch. The doors sealed and the systems reset themselves. Once he was fully connected with the Egress Glip-2 could now sense his friends fleeing on foot across the ice. Panic filled him.

His indecision grew as the *Egress* flashed a warning that the event being generated by the Psadan's was twenty seconds away. A preset message from Edmond accompanied the countdown.

*Do it, Glip-2. It has to be done. Do it now.*

Glip-2 had no choice. His heart tore in two as he issued commands to the *Egress* that sent it fleeing the area. Reluctantly, he released the solar energy stored inside him.

*BOOOM!*

The air around Glip-2 caught fire and moaned from the massive release of energy. Chunks of ice blasted into the air when the energy struck the surface of the continent. Antarctica quaked and split.

*RRUUMMMBLE!*

* *

*Damn, damn, damn,* cursed Maverick as he popped in and out of the fog. He had been given permission to clear out, not that he needed it, but he persisted in his search anyway. *Get out you idiot,* he told himself. *No one will even know if you searched. They will only know what you tell them.*

*Rruummmble!*

*Damn, damn, damn,* he cursed.

The cavern shook. A large chunk of ice fell from the ceiling and he barely dodged it by teleporting to safety. When he rematerialized, he was nearly thrown to the floor by the violent shaking. Teleporting again, he found himself near Slipstream and Meta-man. He had been meaning to go in the other direction. He was so turned round by the fog, he didn't known which way was up.

Meta-man and Slipstream still fought the Psadan. All three of them ignored the collapsing cavern.

A flare circled around them before diving toward Meta-man. Maverick teleported in front of it.

*Swhoosh!*

"Aaarrgghh!" The pain seared his back and Maverick collapsed to the floor. The pain was intense, but quickly subsided to numbness. "What the hell did I do that for? Damn!"

Glancing up, he saw the flare circling them. With the ceiling collapsing around them, Maverick reached out and touched Meta-man's leg. Barely able to roll over, he reached out for Slipstream's leg, but he could not reach the hero. Grunting, he jumped through space and pulled Meta-man along with him.

* *

Envoy searched the darkness as long as she could. When the ceiling began to collapse around her team, she said, "Get us out of here, Ebon."

Normally, she lost all sense of reality immediately when a shadow slide began, but this time the world around her faded slowly. In the distance, she saw Maverick take a hit from a flare, and then he and Meta-man were gone. In a rage, Slipstream battled alone against the Psadan as the area around them collapsed. She realized she had not even tried to pull him from the battle, and doubted she could have if she had.

* *

Gemini knelt next to Fluxstone with the cave collapsing around them. "Please be alive."

Plunging her hand into her med kit, she pulled out a small injector. She yanked the cap off with her teeth and with trembling hands she placed it next Fluxstone's vein. When she pressed the button, the injector sent a micro stream of chemicals into Fluxstone's system.

As the world quaked around her, Gemini rocked back and forth impatiently. "Wake up! Wake up, please!"

Fluxstone gasped for air and opened her eyes wide.

"Phase out! Phase out!" screamed Gemini.

As Fluxstone struggled to focus, the ground erupted around the two women and the ceiling collapsed.

* *

The ice groaned and splintered as Glip-2 struggled to control the energy boring a hole into the ground. When he reached the Psadan energy pocket, his energy violently clashed with it. The Psadan energy was like that of the Citadel, but it was also different. Where he and the Citadel had taken on life, this energy was void of it. This was what he had been. This was his existence before Diamond. He didn't like it.

Glip-2 pushed the energy pocket outward. The ice around it cracked and buckled. Then he forced it back in on itself and the ice around it collapsed. Tighter and tighter he compacted the energy. The Psadan struggled against him.

*K-A-B-OOOOO-M!*

The explosion sent chunks of ice flying miles into the sky. The vacuum created by the loss of the energy pocket brought the ice crashing down into a deep crater. Cracks split the ice for miles in every direction. The longest of them reached hundreds of miles to the ocean and salt water poured inland.

\* \*

Sparrow and the others struggled to flee with the ground shaking beneath them. When the energy pocket exploded, they were thrown to the ground and flung about helplessly. The ground split and collapsed around them.

Sparrow struggled to maintain his footing and to dodge snow and ice that rained down on them. He lost sight of Gemini.

\* \*

Sparrow was cold and his head hurt. His memories were foggy. It took him several moments, but when his head began to clear, he realized he was having difficulty breathing. Panic set in. Desperate, he struggled for freedom and at first his struggles were futile. Then slowly the cold surrounding him shifted. Light peeked in at him, and he scrambled for it.

Pushing himself up, Sparrow rose from the snow covering him. Around him, there were large blocks of ice and snow. In the distance, smoke rose from the wreckage of the *Egress*. Beyond it there was a large crater where the Psadan energy pocket had been.

"Kahori!"

Twisting, Sparrow searched for her. He spotted a small hand sticking out of the snow just a few yards from him, his heart sank. He scrambled over to it, and with a shaking hand he reached out and took Kahori's. He pulled her from the snow. He leaned forward and placed his ear next to her mouth to check her for breathing. Her chest was still.

"Damn you, Dreah!" Between sobs he hugged Kahori to him.

*..."I don't know when, or what the choice will be, but it will be the*

*most difficult for you so far...Because you will sacrifice something that has come to mean a lot to you...*

Placing Kahori on the ground, Sparrow leaned over her and began CPR. Around him the ground quaked and whole sections of ice collapsed into deep gorges.

# CHAPTER 23
# REFLECTIONS

From a balcony, Envoy watched Edmond examining Alis. Like the other survivors, she had little memory of her time in captivity, and her memory from before the arrival of the Psadans was sketchy. Otherwise, she was in good health.

Envoy glanced up as Meta-man entered the room and approached her. "They will be alright. At least physically."

Meta-man nodded. "It will be difficult for them. Edmond reports one of them has already attempted suicide."

Envoy nodded and pointed at Alis. "Have you spoken with her yet?"

"No. I am not the boy she knew. I do not know if she is ready to face that."

Turning to him, she said, "She's not ready for any of this. Don't wait too long, John. Even if you have changed, you are still a familiar face for her. They would all benefit from familiar faces."

Meta-man nodded, but didn't look at Envoy. He could not take his eyes off Alis. Before touching the shafts of light, she had only been a vague memory, a longing he couldn't explain. As if it had occurred yesterday, his memory was now fresh and vibrant, and Alis was the center of that memory.

"How are things for you?" asked Envoy.

He glanced at her and smiled. "Settling down. They are no longer trying to arrest me for not bringing in Mr. Diamond, but I still face charges from an international inquiry."

Envoy chuckled. "Call me if they try to arrest you."

He smiled again. "Regardless, I am being pressured to resign from UNIT. Shishi is not going to let this rest. It may do me some good. If I didn't fear Shishi being left unchecked, I wouldn't hesitate. You know anyone who would be interested in the position? You, perhaps?"

"Hell no," retorted Envoy without even looking at him.

Meta-man frowned. His offer had been serious, but she had not heard it that way. He didn't have the ability to actually name his successor, but he had been working to form a list of possible candidates for the position. Given his years of service to the US government, his word should still have some political clout with the President, despite recent events. It would ultimately be up to the President to name his replacement, but he hoped to prevent Shishi from gaining too much power. When Envoy had stood up to Shishi in Antarctica, she had confirmed that she had what it took. Given her experience as a soldier and as a meta-human operative, she had the necessary skills. Aegis had made sure she had the leadership qualities. Unfortunately, her answer had sounded final.

Disappointed, he nodded in the direction of Alis and said, "Maybe I'll spend some time helping them adjust to the world."

"You would be a good choice for that. Edmond wants to keep them here for a while. He plans to orientate them to the world before exposing them to it. This island is secluded and should do fine for a temporary home."

"Taking it slow is probably for the better."

After a moment, Envoy added, "You know you are always welcome to join us."

"And you know that Mr. Diamond and I don't see eye to eye enough for that. We got through this thing pretty well, but I wouldn't expect it to stay that way."

"True."

The two stood in silence for several moments and Meta-man watched Alis. As the young girl got up from the table, she glanced up at the balcony. Just before Edmond lead her from the room, she stopped and looked up at them again. Shyly, she raised her hand to wave. She then quietly left the room.

"I think she will be just fine," said Envoy smiling. "And I think she already recognizes you."

"She always was strong."

Without Alis and Edmond to watch, the two heroes stared across the room at the medical data Edmond had displayed on the wall. They were too far away to read it, but Envoy's artifact had already scanned it and now it scrolled across her vision. The flare in the final moments of the fight had caused severe damage to Maverick's spine. Paragon had healed most of it, but Maverick was still having difficulty walking. His long-term prognosis wasn't good. He healed quicker and better than a normal human, but he didn't have a healing factor. Not surprisingly, he was being a difficult patient.

Finally, Meta-man asked, "How is Mr. Diamond?"

Envoy sighed heavily before answering. "His legal woes are going to plague him for a while, but he has the best lawyers money can buy." It wasn't Diamond's legal concerns that worried her. Even though he hadn't taken any action to even defend himself against the charges and lawsuits that were being brought against him, Clara had taken up the challenge for him. What concerned Envoy was that Diamond appeared to be trying to drink himself to death. For the first time since she had known him, he was feeling regret. He had achieved his goal, but the cost had been too high.

"He is hurting like I've never seen him hurt before. He tore the command center apart after Gem collapsed. If I hadn't been able to locate Fluxstone's commlink we would have lost them both. Other than her renewed desire to tear Sparrow apart, Fluxstone will recover from her injuries. Thank God, Gem reached her in time…"

Envoy's hands became clammy and sweat beaded her forehead. She clung to the balcony's railing to steady herself. Meta-man placed his hand on her shoulder to comfort her.

After a moment, she continued. "Sorry. Sparrow began CPR, but…" Her voice trailed off again and she struggled to contain her sorrow.

"It is okay, Latisha." Meta-man removed his hand from her shoulder. "I'm aware that none of Gemini's doppelgangers escaped the psychic feedback."

A tear rolled down Envoy's face. All over the world Gemini's doppelgangers had dropped dead. Only the six in the Citadel had physically survived. Jonesy speculated that it was because the Citadel was sealed up, dampening the feedback. Envoy couldn't help but wish that none of them had lived. Thoughts of them were heart wrenching, and none of them were the girl Envoy knew.

One was completely catatonic. Unless sedated, another screamed day and night. Another tore at her own flesh with her fingernails and teeth. Naked and filthy, a fourth had written words of hate and malice all over her body, and now she refused to allow anyone within twenty feet of her. Yet another feared the dead she felt surrounded her. As for the last one, Envoy hadn't been able to bring herself to witness her horror.

"Edmond and Sarah were unable to help any of them. Edmond is bringing in a specialist. As for Gem, her body is in the infirmary. Mr. Diamond won't allow Brandon to...," Envoy choked on her sorrow. "Sorry. Mr. Diamond won't allow us to turn off the machines."

"If Sparrow had not called for Glip-2 to collapse the energy, we would all be dead, and the world would still be in danger." Meta-man knew his words wouldn't console her, at least not yet. Envoy would eventually accept Gemini's fate. She was a soldier, and Aegis had taught her to process loss and move on. There was always another war to be fought.

Envoy nodded. The price had been high, but Sparrow's choice had been the right one. She could not have made it.

Meta-man stifled his own sorrow over Gemini. The girl had touched him as much as anyone else. Hoping to divert Envoy's obvious pain, Meta-man steered the subject away from Gemini. "How are the twins?"

After a moment, Envoy was able to answer. "Good. They suffered from frostbite and hypothermia, but they are fine. Kandi passed out but Brian managed to get them down safely. Q-Zone doesn't appear to have been so lucky. Paragon searched for hours, but he couldn't find any sign of him." Envoy felt shame over Q-Zone. She had never liked him much, but his sacrifice was no less important than Gem's. Despite his rough start, in the end Q-Zone had proven to be a hero. "Sadly, I couldn't locate Slipstream either. He may have finally found something that could kill him."

The potential loss of Slipstream was a devastating blow to Diamond's operations. Diamond would not consider him dead until a body was recovered. It was a priority for Mason and his team, even over recovery of any alien bodies.

Meta-man straightened up and turned to face Envoy.

"You did good, Latisha. Aegis would be proud."

"Thanks, but I'm not so sure. Casualties were high." Aegis, Incindiaro, Stronghold, Q-Zone, and Dragón Verde were dead. Gemini was in medical, and only alive because of the machines. She had failed to find Slipstream. Iron Bear was in pieces in a lab in Moscow. Fluxstone would be out of commission for months. Diamond had shut himself off from everyone.

"There always is in war."

Envoy nodded. "But they seem to be getting harder to accept."

Meta-man and Envoy shook hands and he started for the exit. Looking back, he called over his shoulder, "Consider that offer, Latisha." He had decided to add her name to his list regardless of her initial response. Her political position wasn't any better than his, but he couldn't think of anyone he felt was more qualified.

Envoy's brow furrowed as she searched her memory for his offer. When it struck her that he had been serious about UNIT, he was gone.

An hour later, Envoy circled the moon and darted off into deep space to consider her future. She felt more relaxed than she had in weeks.

Back on earth, Meta-man introduced himself to Alis. He was happy to find the young girl filled with a spirit of enthusiasm. She recognized him immediately.

\* \*

In the command center, Jonesy tapped the monitor and scanned the readings scrolling across the screen. It was empty except for him, and he couldn't wait to finish his work so that he could get out of the room. It had sustained severe damage and the dried blood on the catwalk unnerved him. Even though repairs had begun on the rest of the Citadel, Diamond had refused to allow them to repair the room.

Jonesy looked up at the monitor wall and at the scientists. Behind them, the landscape of Antarctica was scarred with deep crevices. "Okay, Mason. Readings are normal. It looks like the ground is stable.

You guys should pull back to base camp now. We are ready to start phase two."

Mason saluted him from the video wall and then turned to move toward the crater's edge where several scientists waited for him.

Jonesy was glad things were over. There was no sign of the Psadan energy pocket beneath the surface of Antarctica. Mr. Diamond still wanted the bodies recovered, but Jonesy didn't care about that. He was not an undertaker or a biologist, and he had no interest in alien autopsies. He wasn't about to touch the blasted things. Besides, he didn't want to fight the international community for them either.

"Maybe things will finally settle down around here, and I can actually get some work done without having to babysit everyone." Picking up his sidekick, Jonesy started for the door.

Suddenly the lights flickered and went out, leaving the room in complete darkness.

Jonesy froze. "Dammit", he cursed. "Can't Glip-2 do anything right! Lights on!" Nothing happened. Grumbling, he reached out to find the steps, but stumbled and fell. "I hate him!" he grumbled.

A soft white glow slowly rose in intensity behind him. Nervously, Jonesy turned to face it. His eyes grew wide with fright as a Psadan stepped from the video wall and into the room. Its black eyes were pits of hate. It slowly raised its hand and pointed at him.

Panic stricken, Jonesy fled up the steps and out of the room.

Behind him the image of the Psadan froze and flickered. A moment later, Glip-2 floated out of the special operations room.

"Ha ha, ha ha," he laughed through Diamond's workstation. "I told you that would work. You owe me twenty buck-a-roos."

Grunting, Brandon reached into his pocket and withdrew the money.

\* \*

The sound of the ocean splashing against the ship's hull echoed through the steel room. His muscles ached and Yeorgi Lekkas had no idea how long he had suffered his captivity. Judging from his feedings, he suspected it had been several days. The men who held him had so far refused to answer his questions. He knew his enemies were numerous, but he doubted any of them would have kept him alive this long. They would have killed him already, or tortured him to get what they wanted.

*Thudda! Thudda! Thudda!*
*Kaboom!*

Gunfire shattered the sound of the ocean. Explosions and the screams of dying men quickly followed. In the dark room, Lekkas listened intently as the fighting drew nearer.

Lekkas grinned. *Finally*, he said to himself. *My people are coming for me. I know you not my enemy, but we shall soon know each other well.*

After only a few minutes, the metal door to the room was flung open and several people shuffled in. Lekkas heard the loud click of the room's lights being turned on. Grunts filled the air as something was thrown down in front of him. He could not see them, but several men surrounded him.

"Who's there?" Lekkas demanded.

There was no answer, and the room grew quiet. Lekkas began to fear that it was not his people who had come for him after all. Perhaps his enemies were fighting over him.

"Who is there?" He demanded.

His answer came in the sound of footsteps echoing on the metal floor of the ship. Slowly, they drew closer while the men surrounding him remained silent. The footsteps entered the room and approached. They stopped just before him.

"W-who are you? I have money! If you hurt me, my people will retaliate!"

"Ha, ha, ha!"

The cold steady laugh caused him to shudder.

"P-please..." The blindfold was yanked from his face. The sudden flood of light blinded him. It took him several minutes to clear his vision.

A single bright light directly above him lit up the man standing before him. The clean-shaven man wore a white business suit that gleamed under the light. Under his jacket, he wore a dark red shirt and a black tie. His hair was blond and neatly trimmed. On his back, he had a large pair of white wings.

Behind the man was a large dark man with glowing red eyes and a pair of metal wings on his back. To the right of the businessman stood a tall man with a large visor covering his eyes. His face had suffered numerous recent wounds. Skulking near the room's door was a man who shuffled around on all fours like an ape. Fresh blood dripped from his fangs and he panted like a dog. Just behind Lekkas was a tall Arab woman with solid white eyes.

"I do not fear your friends, Mr. Lekkas," said the Adversary. "Nor do I need your money. But it would appear we have a mutual enemy." While he spoke, the woman standing behind Lekkas leaned in and cut his bonds with a large knife. The Adversary reached into his jacket and pulled out a large caliber handgun. He held it out to Lekkas. "I would think you would want us to start here." The Adversary turned his head slightly toward three men who lay bound and gagged on the floor.

\* \*

From a small patch of grass high on the mountaintop Sparrow watched the orange glow of the setting sun reflect off the ocean waves. The wind gently blew puffy white clouds by overhead. He held a *Hacker-Pschorr* in his right hand, and he gently rubbed a small purple ribbon in his left. He took a long deep drink of the beer and sat it down on his right.

Sparrow had spent the last few days in solitude. After his debriefing, he had quickly packed a bag and retreated from the Citadel to a small cabin on the surface of the island. He had desperately wanted to be away from the Citadel, and everyone inside it. He would have retreated beyond the island, but the Counselor would have hunted him; and he wasn't ready to confront that demon yet. On the surface of the island, he avoided the others and escaped the Counselor. It wouldn't last forever, but it would work until he decided his next step. Unfortunately that was taking longer than he liked, and the longer it took, the harder it got.

Leaving the island meant a return to a life of violence and murder, but it also meant a life of solitude and loneliness. It was because of Gemini that he had moved beyond that. Because of the training and experience of his past, Diamond had seen him as an asset, another soldier for his army. Dreah had only seen his possible potential, who he could be; and that left him wondering if her love was based on that potential. Gemini hadn't looked at his past or his future. She had seen him as he was, and had chosen to be his friend. She had become his first real friend in a very long time.

Remaining on the island meant he would have to face the others every day. Never before had he worried about what others whispered about him behind his back. He had never known anyone long enough to consider such a thing to be important. Now, he would face it every time he looked someone in the eye. His retreat to the surface of the island had been as much to spare them from having to look at him as it had been for him to avoid their condemnation.

Even though the breeze blew in from the ocean in front of him, Sparrow smelled Dreah approaching behind him.

"You haven't come to see me in the infirmary. I was afraid you had left the island." Sparrow didn't respond or look at Dreah. Her playful smile faded.

Moving up beside him, she eased herself down onto the grass. She pressed her hand tight against her stomach and sighed heavily with the pain her movements caused. She was sweating and pale from the long climb up the mountain. As she settled in, her white gown spread out around her. She tucked her long hair behind her ears. A seagull flew by overhead. Before it could land, she waved it off.

Dreah glanced at Sparrow and started to speak. Thinking better of it, she bit her tongue. As the minutes passed, she tried several times, but each time she ended up unable to. As the sun disappeared over the horizon, she finally found the words.

"I know you hate me for not telling you that Kahori was the choice you would have to make. I don't blame you."

Each of her words stabbed Sparrow. He had wanted to hate her more than anything, but in the end he had found he couldn't. There was nothing she could do that would make him hate her. That realization only left him angry with himself because it meant he had succumbed to a new master. With the Counselor or Diamond, he had someone else to blame, or at least a target if need be. With emotion being the master, he was to blame.

"You would not have gone if you had known."

Sparrow had suspected her reasoning. Hearing her say it caused his anger to flare up. By not telling him, she had not even given him a choice, and that left him feeling manipulated.

"I know that makes you feel controlled, and maybe I was wrong. But you had to be there. They would have failed without you because Kahori would have still gone looking for Fluxstone. There would have been no one willing to make the call, and that would have doomed them all."

Sparrow was barely able to control his anger. He struggled to keep his hand from shaking and quickly grabbed for his beer. When his hand met empty air, his frustration increased. Looking down he found the beer was not on his right, but on his left. Gripping it so tightly that his knuckles turned white, he drained the liquid in it.

"You could have spoken with her," he said through clenched teeth. "You could have told me, and I could have spoken with her." Sparrow struggled to keep from yelling. He flung the empty beer bottle down the mountain.

"My visions concerned you, not her. I never saw the actual choice you would make, but the sorrow I saw in the visions led me to believe it was over Kahori. I tried to see her fate to be sure, but I couldn't. I am sorry."

"What happened to not being afraid to alter the future? Maybe I could have figured it out if you had told me."

"I do not fear altering the future. I fear altering the person. The wrong word or the wrong timing, and I alter someone in ways that can never be undone. I consider that every time I have a vision. People deserve to decide who they are. They deserve to make their own choices. My visions take that away from them.

"Samuel has relied on them for so long that it led him to send Kahori to Antarctica with the same justification that he sent you and all the others. She was a tool to be used. If I had held more back from him over the years, maybe he would have been more of a father to her and not allowed her to go. Of course, that would also have led to changes in her. She may not have been the girl we know and love."

"You mean loved."

"No, Wolff. I don't. Our love for Kahori is no less now than it was before Antarctica.

"As for you, I could not tell you because you needed to face that decision. You have come a long way, but your past still haunts you. You spent so long with your emotions suppressed that you struggle with them now. If I had told you what I suspected, I would have made the choice for you. You would not have gone. You would have avoided facing this. Now you are left to decide who you will be."

"Maybe I could have stopped her from going."

"No. You couldn't have." Dreah paused and shifted. The movement caused her to wince in pain. After catching her breath, she continued.

"I also confess, I faced my own desires with you, Wolff. It was unlike any choice I have ever had to make before. I wanted to tell you what you faced. I wanted to tell you what I suspected. I wanted to tell you to avoid it. I wanted you to stay here with me. I wanted you to be who I want you to be, not who you would choose to be. It may have been the wrong decision and I will always wonder. But I believed in you to make the right choice. Regardless of my desire, regardless of your anger with me, you had to be there. And I believe that Kahori had to be there as well." Dreah let the conversation drift into silence.

Sparrow believed her. She had never told him who to be or doubted who he was. Her visions of the future were real. He had seen enough evidence now to be convinced.

Dreah started to rise, but Wolff placed his hand on her shoulder. He was still angry, but he was also lonely.

"Stay, please."

Dreah smiled and eased back down. After a few moments, she reached out and took Sparrow's hand. Gemini's small purple ribbon was pressed into their palms. Together, they watched the last rays of the sun disappear and darkness settle over the island.

Under them deep beneath the mountain, a small sparrow sat on a swaying branch and watched the equipment puffing and whizzing as it pumped oxygen into Gemini.

\* \*

Mason and his men were relieved to finally be leaving Antarctica. When the ground trembled beneath their feet they feared the ice shelf would collapse beneath them. They froze in panic. Deep in the crater before them, a large chunk of ice was shifted aside by a shiny metal hand. A moment later, Slipstream pulled himself up out of his icy tomb.

The hero stood silently on the ice and enjoyed the warmth of the sun on his metal body. He could hear Butch and several others calling out to him from the pit's edge, but he ignored them.

It was over. He had suffered with his loss for so long that he didn't know what life would be like without it. His revenge had not brought him the peace he had hoped for, but at least it was done with. Memories of his wife and children no longer brought him pain.

*Boom!*

Ice and snow exploded as Slipstream burst from the crater at full speed. Within moments he cleared the continent's edge and raced across the ocean's surface with a plume of water behind him.

# Who's Who & What's What

## A

**Admiral Giles Roughead** – Admiral Roughead is currently the Chief of Naval Operations and a member of the Joint Chiefs of Staff. If he is a meta-human, he is not registered.

**the Adversary (Jonathon Michael Sykes)** – Publicly, Sykes owns and operates an international corporation know as Halo Corp. He is a known meta-human with bird-like wings sprouting from his back. He is known for his humanitarian efforts despite the manufacture of weapons of war by most of his holdings. As the Adversary, he is secretly in control of a vast underground criminal network.

**Aegis (Alexander "Alex" Diogenes)** – Aegis is a male meta-human with enhanced strength, durability, speed, and senses. He possesses the *Aegis*, a shield of immense defensive capabilities. He is the field leader of DSS.

**the Aegis** – The *Aegis* is a shield of mystical origin that can be traced back to the Olympian gods. The shield is virtually indestructible and is capable of generating an electrical field that the wielder can access for a variety of effects.

**Alexis Diogenes** – Alexis is the teenage daughter of Aegis. She carries the meta-gene but it is not active.

**Alpha-Wing** – A powerful meta-human group operating as law enforcement officers for the City of New York. They are one of the world's most popular hero teams. Members of the team include: Hagen, Ogre, Seraphim, Mindstorm, and Traxx.

**Andromeda Initiative** – The Andromeda Initiative is a top-secret government strategy to permanently eliminate meta-human threats set up by former President Schwartz. Knowledge of the program is limited to the highest echelons of the American Government.

**Anton Czajkowski** – Anton is the leader of the mercenary group Black Sunday. Anton is not a meta-human.

**Attorney General Albert Rohm** – Rohm is the current Attorney General under President Sanora. Rohm is a registered meta-human. Rohm's eyes glow red, but he has never demonstrated any other meta-ability.

# B

**Black Sunday** – Black Sunday is a mercenary group secretly employed by Diamond. They are not meta-humans, and they are not publicly connected with Diamond Enterprises or DSS.

**Blight** – The real name of the creature known as the Blight is lost to time. He/She/It appears as a deformed gaunt creature always cloaked in black rags. It carries an ancient katana that is green and black with diseased blood and filth. Even the slightest cut from the sword leaves the victim to suffer an extremely painful death. Paragon has sworn an oath to destroy the creature.

**Brandon** – Brandon is a male medical student with an above average IQ. He works for DSS as a medical assistant. After being accused of cheating and getting kicked out of medical school, his half-sister, Sarah, got him a job with DSS. He has a habit of arguing with himself. Brandon likes *Star Trek*, Dungeons and Dragons, and has a gambling problem (He loses).

**the Bronze Bull** – Only Dyonis Harvie knows the full nature and history of the Bronze Bull. The Bull is a large bronze statue of the Minotaur that Harvie is capable of animating for his defense. Whether the Bull is living or capable of independent thought is unknown.

**Butch** – Butch is the primary DSS pilot of the Citadel pods. He is a fun loving man who loves his pearl white *Harley Davidson Road King* motorcycle.

# C

**chimera** – An organism containing a mixture of genetically different tissues formed by processes such as fusion of early embryos, grafting, or mutation.

**Citadel** – The Citadel is a vast underground complex built from Psadan technology that is owned and operated by Samuel Diamond. It is located beneath a private island off the coast of Eureka, California.

**clairvoyance** – A meta-human ability to perceive things, palaces, or events beyond normal sensory contact.

**Cairo Accords** – The Cairo Accords is an agreement by the members of the United Nations requiring international cooperation when meta-human incidents cross national borders. It sets up an impartial tribunal to investigate the incident and then to bring formal charges before the International Criminal Court. The Accords arise out of an incident involving a meta-human villain known as Lord Pyrenees. At some point, he established a secret base under the Great Sphinx of Giza. A group of unsanctioned American and European meta-humans grouped loosely as the Meta-human Conglomerate discovered the base and an ensuing fight destroyed the Sphinx, and caused thousands of deaths across Giza and Cairo. Since the heroes were operating on foreign soil without authorization from the Egyptian government, an international incident was created. Members of the Conglomerate were some of the first individuals officially convicted of crimes by the International Criminal Court.

**Clara DeSimms** – Clara is a female meta-human with eyes that sparkle like diamonds under a bright light. Before her meta-gene became active, she was one of several dozen media relations specialist for Diamond Enterprises. After her genes activation, her sparkling eyes earned her great clout with the company and with Samuel Diamond personally.

**Commander Graham Bullock** – Bullock has been a soldier all his life. He is currently the leader of TASC, and he is a direct advisor of Samuel Diamond. Bullock is not a meta-human.

**the Counselor** – An unknown meta-human with vast psionic powers. He is capable of extensive mind control, and he runs an international terrorist organization specializing in assassination.

**Curtis Fox** – Curtis was recruited out of the FBI to work for DSS. Curtis is articulate, dedicated, and honest to a fault. He works primarily in the command center of the Citadel monitoring and assisting law enforcement agencies around the world during DSS deployments. Curtis is not a meta-human.

# D

**Dawn (Aurora Summers)** – Dawn is a female meta-human DSS field operative with empathic powers and the ability to manipulate, disrupt, or repair the various systems of the human body. She is a shy young girl who is easily embarrassed and prefers to use her powers to help others. Dawn shares reality with her identical twin sister, Dusk. Only one of them is ever physically present at any given time. Dawn is often embarrassed and ashamed of her sister's wild antics.

**Diamond Enterprises** – Diamond Enterprises is a multi-national conglomerate that was started by Gaius Coltar Diamond. When his son, Samuel Joseph Diamond, took control of the company its focus shifted to genetic research and medical facilities. Samuel uses the company to search for and monitor meta-humans around the world.

**Diamond Security Solutions (DSS, Diamond Justice, DJ)** – DSS is a private security firm with divisions in many parts of the world. DSS has limited arrest abilities in many of these countries, including the U.S. It has a meta-human branch (Diamond Justice) and a non meta-human branch (TASC). It is owned and operated by Samuel Diamond.

**Dr. Sabah Ashan** – Ashan is a female meta-human of Arab descent and one of the many doctors on staff for DSS.

**Dr. Dewey Charles McCoy** – Dr. D.C. McCoy is the primary doctor and geneticist for DSS. Dr. McCoy is a meta-human whose body has the ability to adapt to most environments through a process that requires him to absorb a special chemical containing animal DNA. (Dr. D.C. McCoy's name is an amalgam of several names; Charles Robert Darwin [evolutionary theorist], James Dewey Watson [co-discoverer of the structure of DNA], and a particular grumpy space faring doctor who shall remain nameless, or is it a particular furry blue mutant geneticist? Maybe it's both.)

**Dr. Dweomer [DWEE-oh-mer] (Carol Estingdale)** – Carol is a female meta-human who works directly for Samuel Diamond as an archeologist. Her powers often manifest in the form of physical "living" creations. Their forms unusually reflect mythical creatures such as faeries and unicorns. These manifestations carry out Carol's wishes willingly and independent of her.

**Dragón Verde [Green Dragon] (Jose Vaulk)** – El Dragón Verde is the Mexican representative for UNIT. Dragón Verde is a meta-human whose primary form is that of a reptile-human hybrid. In this form he has enhanced strength, reflexes, and senses.

**Dreah [Drā-ə]** – Dreah is an empathic female meta-human. She has limited precognitive abilities that manifests through her dreams. She also has the ability to disperse her body into multiple forms such as a flock of birds, a swarm of insects, or packs of small animals. She is able to cast a variety of magical spells and possesses numerous magical artifacts. Dreah is a personal friend of Samuel Diamond and has worked with him for years to help him achieve his goal. Charismatic and caring, Dreah is one of the Nine.

**Duo (Brian O'Connell and Kandace "Kandi" O'Connell)** – Brian and Kandi are young twin meta-human field agents for DSS. Brian is male and Kandi is female. They possess vast telekinetic ability that becomes more powerful the closer they are to each other. Unfortunately, their close proximity also creates a telekinetic storm that they must both work to control.

**Dusk (Kiera Summers)** – Dusk is a female meta-human DSS operative with empathic powers capable of manipulating, disrupting, or repairing the various bodily systems of others. Dusk is an outgoing rambunctious young girl who prefers to use her powers to inflict pain and cause discomfort in others. Dusk shares reality with her sister, Dawn. Only one of them is ever physically present in reality at any given time. Dusk hates Dawn and goes out of her way to embarrass her.

# E

**Edmond English** – Edmond is a male meta-human and a scientist who specializes in genetic research. He is one of the Nine and possesses the ability to transform into a grotesque and misshapen humanoid with superhuman strength and durability.

**Elizabeth Bachmeier [deceased]** – Elizabeth is the mother of Sparrow. She was of German descent and taught European history at Oxford University.

**Envoy (Latisha Anderson)** – Latisha is an African American female meta-human. She was a soldier in the US Army when her right arm was physically bonded with a piece of alien metal. Through the intelligent artifact, she is capable of controlling and projecting vast amounts of energy, and she can manipulate any mechanical or electrical machine. She serves as second-in-command for DSS under Aegis and as field commander when he is unable to.

**Éolienne (Windmachine)** – Éolienne is an android with the ability to control the weather. He was originally a mechanical assistant built by Dr. Girard Parnell. However, he eventually took on a personality, killed his creator, and incorporated the doctor's wind control technology into his systems.

**Euro-Block** – A high tech detention facility located in Germany and used to house powerful meta-human criminals.

# F

**Felix Kingsley [deceased]** – Felix is Sparrow's father. He was a renowned British historian who specialized in technological artifacts.

**Fenrir (Jackson Coy)** – Fenrir is a male African American meta-human operative of DSS. He possesses the ability to shape change into a human-wolf hybrid form. Fenrir is suffering from PMAD-A and recently lost the ability to return to his human shape. He has been placed on the injury reserve list.

**Fetch** – Fetch is a creature of unknown origin that possesses the ability to mimic the appearance of others. It posed as Carol Estingdale during an incident with the Sons of Mars to prevent DSS from locating the Dare Diary. The creature crumbled to dust when confronted by Diamond. Its current state or whereabouts are unknown.

**Floret (Rachel Fleur) [deceased]** – Floret is a deceased DSS field agent who possessed the ability to manipulate planet life. A memorial to Floret stands outside the sherry room in the Citadel.

**Fluxstone (Heather Stone)** – Fluxstone is a female meta-human who operates as the chief public relations officer for DSS. Fluxstone has the ability to increase her density, enhancing her strength and durability; or to decrease her density, allowing her to phase through solid objects.

**Freddie** – Freddie is a redheaded boyhood friend of Sparrow.

# G

**Gaius Coltar Diamond [deceased]** – Gaius Diamond founded Diamond Enterprises. He is the father of Samuel Joseph Diamond.

**Gear (Jordan Ironside) [deceased]** – Gear is a deceased DSS field agent with a genius level intellect who had the ability to construct and understand advanced technological devices. Gear suffered from facial deformities that led him to hide his face beneath a metal mask. A memorial to Gear holding his metal mask stands outside the sherry room in the Citadel.

**Glip-2 (Global Life-form Imitation Program, Generation 2)** – Glip-2 is a living spherical entity that serves as security officer and maintenance man for the Citadel. His color and the speed of an internal pulse designate his mood. Glip-2 is fun loving and enjoys playing pranks on people.

**Greenbriar Protocols** – The Greenbriar Protocols are a set of US federal laws established as a result of an interpretation of the twenty-eighth amendment by the Supreme Court. The accords are named after Chief Justice Paul Greenbriar, the Supreme Court judge who rendered the written interpretation of the court. The laws take into account the Meta-Human Threat Level assessment and are intended to govern the use of meta-human powers. The Protocols include requirement that all American meta-humans register with federal and local authorities, official sanctioning of meta-human operatives as agents of the government, a prohibition forbidding anyone under the age of eighteen from acting as a meta-human operative, and regulations governing information obtained during criminal investigations by meta-human mentalists through mind reading.

# H

**Hagen** – Hagen is the meta-human male leader of Alpha-Wing. He is blind but possesses a visor that allows him to "see" by various means and to project blasts of energy. Hagen has a genius level intelligence and uses it to construct and repair various technological devices such as his visor. He is of Scandinavian descent and taught ancient Norse mythology before his meta-gene became active.

**Holocaust** – Holocaust is a malevolent spirit that has inhabited several random individuals who possessed the meta-gene over the years. As Holocaust, the individual is driven mad and rages to destroy everything round it. The inhabited body eventually burns out and Holocaust disappears from the world for years at a time. Holocaust possesses extreme strength, durability, and stamina. It constantly generates an aura of radiation that is deadly to anyone within a hundred feet.

# I

**IMPACT (International Mechanized and Powered Armor Combat Troop)** – IMPACT is the non-meta-human division of the United Nations Armed Forces. It is composed of soldiers outfitted with powered battle armor that enhances their strength, speed, and endurance. They employ high tech weaponry. They are often deployed to provide tactical and logistical support to UNIT during operations, but they are also frequently given independent assignments. IMPACT takes its orders from the UN Security Council.

**El Incindiaro (Basilio Aguilar)** – El Incindiaro is a male meta-human with the ability to generate heat and fire. He is originally from Mexico and is currently a DSS field operative.

**Iron Bear (Pyotr Gorlovich)** – Iron Bear is the Russian Federation's representative to UNIT. Iron Bear is a cyborg with tremendous strength and a wide array of highly destructive weapons.

# J

**Jane Moeller (Crazy Jane)** – Jane is a female meta-human who possesses the ability to absorb the personalities, appearances, and meta-human powers of others. The personalities suppress her own identity until some outside force reinstates her. These personalities remain with her and she can later reinstate them over her own. She is on the inactive roster for DSS and is receiving extensive psychiatric treatment for depression and schizophrenia. Jane often expresses her inner depression through extremely bad poetry. Known alternate personalities include: Stronghold, Semex, and Joanna Moeller [mother]. Any other personas are classified.

**Jonesy** – Jonesy is a male human physicist who works for Diamond Enterprises. Jonesy has a genius level intelligence but lacks acceptable people skills. [According to www.urbandictionary.com: Jonesy - a name to replace the real name of someone who is prone to being an idiot and general idiocy; or an incredibly needed man.]

**Jonas (John "Jonas" Prat)** – Jonas is a male meta-human and one of the Nine. Jonas has the ability to *re-live* a day and alter the time stream.

**Jocelyn Kempt** – Jocelyn is a vital part of the security detail for the President of the United States. She is a mentalist meta-human who uses her abilities to protect the President from mind scans and mental attacks.

# K

**Kilimanjaro (Rafi Yeboah)** – Kilimanjaro is an African meta-human who has represented numerous African nations in UNIT. He possesses the ability to increase his size, mass, strength, and durability to superhuman levels. He is known for his bravery, wisdom, and patience.

## L

**Lady Cobalt (Helen Richards)** – Lady Cobalt is a female meta-human capable of projecting bursts of silvery-white energy. She served as a mentor for Kandi of Duo.

**Lady Gemini (Kahori Tokushima, Gemini, Gem)** – Gemini is a female Asian meta-human who possesses the ability to *split* off doppelganger versions of herself. These doppelgangers are capable of acting independently of her and share their experiences when they rejoin with the original.

**Lauren Diogenes [Deceased]** – Lauren is the first wife of Aegis. She was killed when a group of terrorists attempted to assassinate Aegis.

## M

**Madame Fantôme** – Madame Fantôme is a female meta-human with the ability to generate intense cold. Madame Fantôme's ghostly body is in a constant state of intangibility. It takes concentration on her part to become solid enough to interact with the physical world. Madame Fantôme is the French Republic's representative to UNIT.

**Mamertines (Mamertini – *sons of Mars*)** – A group of Italian mercenaries who played a major role in the First Punic War (264 to 241 BC).

**Maria Espinal** – Maria is a female Hispanic meta-human with the ability to *understand* or *absorb* the meaning of others, essentially reading between the lines. This ability allows her to see through deception, misrepresentations, and half-truths, or across language barriers. She is capable of reading material that was not written in her presence and on subjects she has no past knowledge of and then comprehending it as if she were the person who wrote it. Much of this understanding fades over time. She currently works directly for Samuel Diamond as a translator.

**Maverick (William Wythers, Mav)** – Maverick is a male meta-human with the ability to teleport over vast distances. He is familiar with nearly any kind of weapon, but prefers those that make lots of noise. He is one of the Nine.

**Mecha (Rakesh Tripathi)** – Mecha grew up on the streets of East India. He has the meta-human ability to possess mechanical and electrical objects, and then to control their functions. He works for the European branch of DSS.

**mentalist** – A meta-human who primarily possesses psionic powers.

**meta-gene** – The meta-gene is a mutated form of alien DNA that was implanted into specific humans by the Psadans. When a human with this gene is subjected to an outside catalyst, usually some form of high intensity energy or radiation, the gene causes mutations that result in powers or abilities.

**meta-human** – A human carrying the meta-gene in his DNA. The general public uses the term to refer to someone who has had their gene activated, however, the term officially applies to anyone who carries the gene.

**Meta-Human Conglomerate** – The Meta-Human Conglomerate is a group of meta-humans with American and European nationalities that represent the interests of some of the world's largest corporations. Their primary concern is protecting the assets of member companies, a job that often crosses international borders. An incident involving the team led to the formation of the Cairo Accords and convictions of some of its members for international crimes. Some of those individuals are still in prison and the team's activities have since been kept under strict scrutiny.

**Meta-Human Threat Level** – This is a Homeland Security Advisory System used to classify the potential threat of meta-humans. Meta-humans are required by law to register under this system. There are six levels of classification and the first five classifications are broken down into two ranks. The levels are: Green, Blue, Yellow, Orange, Red, and Indigo. The vast majority of the world's meta-humans are of green or blue rank. There are only a handful of known meta-humans of the red rank, and none of the indigo rank. This system also attempts to rate meta-human skills and intellectual capabilities based on IQ.

**Meta-man (John Sampson, Jr.)** – Meta-man is a male meta-human with the ability to fly. He possesses superhuman strength and durability, and he can mimic the meta-human powers of other nearby meta-humans, granting him great diversity. In addition, his body automatically adapts to the environment around him allowing him to survive unaided in extremely cold or hot climates, under high or low pressure, underwater, or even in deep space. His body's adaptation even heals him of life threatening wounds, but it is not immediate and it may take him several moments depending on how harsh the environment is. Meta-man is one of the Nine and the current leader of UNIT. He is the oldest known openly operating meta-human in the world.

**meta-morph** – Any meta-human who possesses the ability to alter or modify his physical form in any way.

**meta-powers** – Any ability or special condition that manifests in a meta-human as a result of their meta-gene activating.

**meta-science** – The study of the meta-gene and meta-humans. Branches of meta-science include, but are not limited to meta-biology, meta-genetics, and meta-psychology.

**meta-scientist** – A scientist who specializes in one or more branches of meta-science.

**Mindstorm** – Mindstorm is a female meta-human of Arab descent with the ability to blanket an area in a field of *static* that makes concentration extremely difficult and prevents the use of psionic powers.

**the Missing Man (Dyonis Harvie, Charles Stein)** – Harvie is a male meta-human and one of the Nine. He is a paranoid recluse with vast retention of written and viewed material. This ability seems to be more akin to a form of autism than to any meta-powers.

**Muskeg (Beatrice)** – The Muskeg is a female meta-human creature of conflicting origins. Beatrice was a US botanist working with the Canadian government to study arctic and boreal areas. Conflict with a local community resulted in Beatrice being transformed into an animalistic creature with a strong odor of an acidic poisonous bog.

# N

**Natalie Kingsley** – Natalie is the sister of Sparrow.

**Negus (Negus Negest** – *King of Kings*) – Even though he has never officially registered and his full capabilities are unknown, the Negus is considered the world's most powerful meta-human. The Negus currently rules over the area known as the Central African Empire. He has brought stability to the area and his rule is absolute. Despite the fact that violation of his orders is punished by death, he is well liked by his people. The Negus has demonstrated super strength, enhanced durability, energy projection, flight, teleportation, telepathy, clairvoyance, and the ability to survive in hostile environments (including deep space).

**the Nine** – The Nine are the first meta-humans. All other meta-humans are their direct descendants. They are each over 400 years old and often demonstrate vast powers. Known members of the Nine are: John Sampson, Jr. (Meta-man), Dreah, William Wythers (Maverick), Edmond English, John Pratt (Jonas), and Dyonis Harvie (the Missing Man).

# O

**Ogre** – Ogre is a meta-human member of Alpha-Wing. He appears as a stocky human with overlarge clawed hands and feet. When he becomes angry, he becomes more bestial in appearance and behavior. He possesses superhuman strength and enhanced senses.

# P

**Paragon (Lawrence Pentacle)** – Paragon is a male meta-human with large bird-like wings on his back that grant him the power of flight. Paragon possesses heightened strength and enhanced senses. He is capable of healing the injuries of others. Paragon possesses a mystical sword with the ability to teleport to his location or to allow him to teleport to its location. Paragon also possesses a suit of magical medieval armor that he can summon through the sword to protect him.

**Ping** – Ping is the former UNIT meta-human representative for the People's Republic of China. He possesses the ability to heal or mend the injuries of others. Ping appears to be a man of seventy to eighty years of age, but his ability to regenerate damage has greatly extended his life span. He is eagerly awaiting his two hundredth birthday.

**pod** (*Egress, Egress II, Portal, Exodus, Gateway*)– The pods are airships used by DSS to move around the globe. A pod remains connected to the Citadel through an extra-dimensional gate. People and objects are capable of instantly moving through the pod's gate to the Citadel.

**pod bay** – This is a room in the Citadel from which the various pods are accessed.

**President Gabriella Sanora** – President Sanora is of Hispanic descent and is in the second year of her first term as President. President Sanora is a conservative Republican in support of meta-human privacy rights. If President Sanora is a meta-human, she is not registered.

**President Jordan Schwartz** – Former President Schwartz served only one term. He was known for his outspoken agenda against meta-humans, and for his massive budget spending in support of his view. Samuel Diamond led a crusade to have him removed from office by supporting President Sanora. If President Schwartz is a meta-human, he is not registered.

**Progressive Meta-gene Activation Disorder (PMAD)** – A serious and currently incurable genetic disorder affecting one percent of the meta-human population. PMAD causes the meta-gene to remain in its activation phase and accelerates the development of meta-powers along the power scale, destroying the afflicted individual's control of their meta-powers as it does so. The specific manifestation depends on the meta-powers of the afflicted individual, but the disorder is most common amid multi-form meta-humans (PMAD-A), in which it first appears as increased difficulty in returning to their base form. This is followed by a complete inability to return to the base form and the loss of less frequently used alternate forms until the multi-form meta-human will only be able to assume their most frequently used alternate shape, eventually becoming trapped in it. This is accompanied by mental deterioration as the afflicted individual's personality is gradually replaced by the innate personality of their new form. This mental transformation frequently results in the afflicted individual going insane. In multi-form meta-humans with an animal as their primary alternate form this results in afflicted individual losing their intelligence and becoming feral. Frequent use of meta-powers by the afflicted accelerates the progression of the disorder. The cause of PMAD is currently unknown but the disorder is not contagious, and it is not believed to be hereditary. PMAD is sometimes referred to as Meta-Plague by anti-meta-human extremists.

**Psadan [Sā-dən]** – Psadans are a race of aliens that came to earth many years ago. Their manipulations of human DNA resulted in the meta-gene, and ultimately meta-humans.

# Q

**Q-Zone (Davin Stars, Quantum Zone, Q)** – Q-Zone is a male meta-human currently employed by DSS. He is capable of altering the flow of time around himself, others, or objects. Q-Zone is currently on reserve status due to his constant showboating and lack of teamwork.

# R

**Rose (Roselyn Jahr)** – Rose is the female meta-human representative of the United Kingdom to UNIT. She has bright red hair and possesses vast psionic abilities. Rose is highly respected for her leadership skills and wisdom. Rose takes her name from the glowing red aura that surrounds her when she uses her powers.

**Roanoke Colony** – Sir Walter Raleigh financed this early American colony in 1585 and again in 1587 on Roanoke Island off the coast of North Carolina. The first expedition disappeared and John White made a second attempt. Problems were encountered only a few months after arrival and John White returned to England for supplies. He didn't return to the colony for three years, and when he did, he found that all the colonists had disappeared. John

White's daughter, Eleanor Dare, gave birth to the first English child born in America, Virginia Dare, one month after their arrival in the new world. White left the colony for England only a few weeks after Virginia's birth. White's daughter and granddaughter disappeared along with the rest of the colonists.

# S

**sanctioned** – Official government approval or licensing for a meta-human to operate using his abilities.

**Semex** – Semex is a meta-human capable of generating dangerous and poisonous toxins within his own body and then expelling them through gaseous form or through skin-to-skin contact. He is currently wanted for several gruesome and violent deaths.

**Samson (Cassius Aaronson)** – Samson is a male meta-human of Israeli descent who possesses enhanced strength and durability. He works for a European branch of DSS.

**Samuel Joseph Diamond** – Diamond is the owner and leader of DSS and chairman of the board for Diamond Enterprises. He is not a registered meta-human, but he does display the ability to read minds and to project into astral space.

**Sarah (Sarah Rossi)** – Sara is a female meta-human and the older half-sister of Brandon. Sara is a scientist in the employ of Diamond Enterprises. Sarah's body was badly injured during a lab accident.

**Secretary Tani Poppendopalis** – Tani is currently the Secretary of Meta-human Affairs under President Sanora. She and Samuel Diamond often clash over their views of meta-human rights.

**Seraphim** – Seraphim are a series of robots designed by Halo Corp. They are capable of flight by means of mechanical wings, and they possess a wide arsenal of offensive and defensive weapons. They have great strength and durability. One model is currently being field tested as a member of Alpha-Wing.

**Shishi (Fai Tan, The Stone Lion of Fu)** – Shishi currently represents the People's Republic of China to UNIT. He personally dislikes Meta-man and strongly distrusts DSS and Samuel Diamond. He possesses the ability to transform into a large lion with rock-like qualities. He does not need to eat or breathe while in this form.

**sidekick** – A small handheld computer used by members of DSS that runs on alien technology and is connected with the Citadel computers.

**Slipstream (Kevin Clark)** – Slipstream is a male meta-human operative for DSS. His body is covered in blue alien metal, and he has superhuman strength and superhuman durability. He is physically blind and sees through a form of spatial awareness that functions similarly to sonar. He is capable of projecting energy from his eyes. He is considered one of the world's most powerful meta-humans. If there is a super-man, it is Slipstream.

**Sons of Mars (Mamertines)** – The Sons of Mars were a mercenary group hired by Dyonis Harvie to cover up his involvement with the lost diary of Eleanor Dare. The Sons clashed with DSS after they kidnapped Dr. Dweomer to prevent her investigation into the diary. At the time, members of the band included: Phobos, Deimos, Legionary, Hippolyta, Drakon, Brutus, Peacekeeper, Cycnus, Hardware, and General Martinus

**Sparrow (Wolff Kingsley, Blaine Braxton, Wayne Finger, Bruce Kane, Steve Marston, Clark Siegel, Kent Shuster)** – Sparrow operated as a professional assassin under the Counselor until he subconsciously began to resist the Counselor's influence. The Counselor attempted to kill Sparrow but failed. Shortly after fleeing the Counselor Sparrow was recruited by Samuel Diamond as an unofficial operative for DSS.

**Stronghold (Matthew West)** – Stronghold is a male meta-human with superhuman strength and durability. He has four massive arms and his body is covered in fine red fur.

# T

**TASC (Tactical Armor Support Company)** – TASC is a private military unit of Samuel Diamond. They wear protective armor and carry sophisticated weaponry. They are often deployed with the meta-humans of DSS, but they are just as often deployed separately anywhere they are required. They have their own rank structure that is separate from the meta-human branch of DSS.

**therianthropic** – The combining of an animal and a man.

**Traxx** – Traxx is a meta-human operative with Alpha-wing. He possesses the ability to move at super-sonic speeds.

**triquetra [trī'kwētrə]** – A symmetrical triangular ornament of three interlaced arcs used on metalwork and stone crosses.

**Twenty-Eighth Amendment to the US Constitution** – This amendment to the Constitution was ratified to guarantee American citizens protection from loss of life or property from meta-humans who operate within the borders of the US. Interpretation of the amendment led to the Greenbriar Protocols.

# U

**Unlucky Benny** – Benny is the brother of the Widow. He is a drug-addicted burnout who serves as a contact for his sister and the seedy underworld.

**UNIT (United Nations International Taskforce)** – UNIT is the meta-human branch of the United Nations Armed Forces. It is deployed for international incidents involving meta-humans and members of the UN. It is currently led by Meta-man, who takes his orders from the UN Security Council.

# V

**Vox (Vivian Cantante) [deceased]** – Vox is a deceased DSS field operative who possessed various sound and sonic based meta-powers. A memorial to Vox rests outside the sherry room of the citadel. The memorial is capable of emitting and mimicking a variety of sounds and musical notes, and it often does so of its on volition. Vox was killed by Blight's poisoned sword.

# W

**Wavefront (Jack Turley)** – Wavefront is an Australian male meta-human with enhanced senses. He is capable of hearing and seeing over greater distances, hearing sounds beyond normal human hearing, and of seeing through walls. He possesses a belt capable of generating force fields and small telekinetic bursts. Wavefront and Aegis are best friends.

**Widow** – The Widow is a female human who provides high paid mercenaries for nefarious or illegal assignments. She prefers anonymity for both the mercenary and the buyer.

**Winter Eagle (Shoshone Mike)** – Winter Eagle is a meta-human Native American Shoshone leader who was transformed into a shamanic spirit totem. He appears in the form of a large white eagle and possesses the ability to generate extreme cold. He is considered one of the world's greatest meta-human threats. An early agreement with the American government grants him limited immunity from prosecution as long as he is on his reservation.